CU00923081

THE off balance SERIES

VOLUME 2

LUCIA FRANCO

Edited by Nadine Winningham
Proofread by Amber Hodge
Cover Design by Okay Creations
Formatted by Champagne Book Design
Photography by Lindee Robinson
Cover Models Shelby Smith and Andrew Kruczynski

This is a work of fiction. Names, characters, businesses, places, events and incidents are either the products of the author's imagination or used in a fictitious manner. Any resemblance to actual persons, living or dead, or actual events is purely coincidental.

MORE NOVELS BY LUCIA FRANCO

The Off Balance series is a continuation series. The novels must be read in order to follow the story.

This story is purely fictional and does not reflect on real-life events.

Each novel in this five-part series follows a heavy May-December romance between a gymnast and a coach. If you consider this subject and any related content disturbing, then the Off Balance series is not for you.

Gymnastics is a hands-on sport that involves hours of close contact with a coach. My goal was to focus on the beauty of the sport in detail, show the emotional aspect of the dedication an athlete makes, and show how two people are able to cross forbidden boundaries and evolve together.

This story will push you, question you, and take you outside of your comfort zone.

The Off Balance series is intended only for readers 18 years of age and older. Reader discretion is advised.

—Lucia

GLOSSARY

All-Around A category of gymnastics that includes all the events. The all-around champion of an event earns the highest total score from all events combined.

Amanar A Yurchenko-style vault, meaning the gymnast performs a round-off onto the board, a back handspring onto the vault with a two-and-a-half twisting layout backflip.

Cast A push off the bar with hips and lifts the body to straighten the shoulders and finish in handstand.

Deduction Points taken off a gymnast's score for errors. Most deductions are pre-determined, such as a 0.5 deduction for a fall from an apparatus or a 0.1 deduction for stepping out of bounds on the floor exercise.

Dismount The last skill in a gymnastics routine. For most events the method used to get off the event apparatus.

Elite International Elite, the highest level of gymnastics.

Execution The performance of a routine. Form, style, and technique used to complete the skills constitute the level of execution of an exercise. Bent knees, poor toe point and an arched or loose held body position are all examples of poor execution.

Giant Performed on bars, a swing in which the body is fully extended and moving through a 360-degree rotation around the bar.

Full-In A full-twisting double back tuck, with the twist happening in the first backflip. It can be done in a tucked, piked, or layout position and is used in both men's and women's gymnastics.

Free Hip Circle Performed on the uneven bars or high bar, the body circles around the bar without the body touching the bar. There are both front hip circles and back hip circles.

Handspring Springing off the hands by putting the weight on the arms and using a strong push from the shoulders. Can be done either forward or backward, and is usually a connecting movement. This skill can be performed on floor, vault, and beam.

Heel Drive A termed used by coaches to inform the gymnasts they want them to drive their heels harder up and over on the front side of a handspring vault or front handspring on floor. Stronger heel drives create more rotation and potential for block and power.

Hecht Mount A mount where the gymnast jumps off a spring board while keeping their arms straight, pushes off the low bar, and catches the high bar.

Hop Full A giant to handstand. Once toes are above the bar, a full 360-degree turn in a handstand on the high bar.

Inverted Cross Performed by men on the rings. It is an upside down cross.

Iron Cross A strength move performed by men on the rings. The gymnast holds the rings straight out on either side of their body while holding themselves up. Arms are perpendicular to the body.

Jaeger Performed on bars, a gymnast swings from a front giant and lets go of the bar, completes a front flip and catches the bar again. Jaeger can be done in the straddle, pike, and layout position, and is occasionally performed in a tucked position.

Kip The most commonly used mount for bars, the gymnast glides forward, pulls their feet to the bar, then pushes up to front support, resting their hips on the bar.

L-Grip One hand is in the reverse grip position. This is an awkward grip and difficult to use.

Layout A stretched body position.

Layout Timers A drill that simulates the feel of a skill, or the set for a skill without out the risk of completing the skill.

Lines Straight, perfect lines of the body.

Overshoot, also known as Bail A transition from the high bar facing the low bar. The gymnast swings up and over the low bar with a half-turn to catch the low bar ending in a handstand.

Pike The body bent forward at the waist with the legs kept straight; an L position.

Pirouette Used in both gymnastics and dance to refer to a turn around the body's longitudinal axis. It is used to refer to a handstand turning moves on bars.

Rips In gymnastics, a rip occurs when a gymnast works so hard on the bars or rings that they tear off a flap of skin from their hand. The injury is like a blister that breaks open.

Release Leaving the bar to perform a skill before re-grasping it.

Relevé This is a dance term that is often used in gymnastics. In a relevé, the gymnast is standing on toes and has straight legs.

Reverse Grip A swing around the bar back-first with arms rotated inwards and hands facing upwards.

Round-off A turning movement, with a push-off on one leg, while swinging the legs upward in a fast cartwheel motion into a 90-degree turn where legs come together before landing on both feet. The lead-off to a number of skills used to perform on vault, beam, and floor.

Salto Flip or somersault, with the feet coming up over the head and the body rotating around the axis of the waist.

Sequence Two or more skills performed together, creating a different skill or activity.

Shaposhnikva A clear hip circle on the low bar then flying backward to the high bar.

Stalder Starts in handstand with the gymnast moving backward and circling the bar with legs straddled on either side of their arms or inside their arms.

Stick To land and remain standing without requiring a step. A proper stick position is with legs bent, shoulders above hips, arms forward.

Straddle Back An uneven bar transition done from a swing backwards on the high bar over low bar, while catching the low bar in a handstand.

Switch Ring Performed on floor and the balance beam. The gymnast jumps with both feet, lifting their legs into a 180-degree split with the back leg coming up to touch their head.

Tap Swing Performed on bars, an aggressive tap toward the ceiling in a swinging motion. This gives the gymnast the necessary momentum to swing around the bar to perform a giant or to go into a release move.

Toe On Swing around the bar with body piked so much the feet are on the bar.

Tour Jeté A dance leap where the dancer leaps on one foot, makes a full turn in the air, and lands on the other foot.

Tsavdaridou Performed on beam, a round-off back handspring with full twist to swing down.

Tuck The knees and hips are bent and drawn into the chest. The body is folded at the waist.

Twist The gymnast rotates around the body's longitudinal axis, defined by the spine. Performed on all apparatuses.

Yurchenko Round-off entry onto the board, back handspring onto the vaulting table and Salto off the vault table. The gymnast may twist on the way off.

twist

BOOK 4 IN THE OFF BALANCE SERIES

To my devoted and passionate readers…

Please forgive me.

I love you, and it's killing me.
—Anonymous

chapter 1

STAGE 4 KIDNEY DISEASE.

    There were five stages, and I was already at four. Like it was a *stage* of *cancer*.

Plus lupus.

My body ran cold and goose bumps broke out down my arms. The number four banged around inside my head, taunting me. I needed to start dialysis and get placed on a transplant list.

I knew better than to google anything, but I couldn't not. I needed to know what I was up against.

At first I started with the medications the doctors had prescribed. Antibiotics, steroids, blood pressure, and pain medication. Then curiosity got the best of me and I explored websites that led to other websites with normal to rare outcomes. Hours of researching how both diseases worked together consumed me. I read countless pages of life expectancy, threads on the side effects of treatments and both illnesses, threads on how my body could reject the transplant, chats on how difficult it would be to get pregnant and carry to full term, topics on how the disease escalated and ultimately had the power to take the life of a loved one.

The stress and anxiety of what could happen, and what most likely would, hammered through me at a pace I couldn't catch up to. I was sick to my stomach over everything. The truth was, I needed to start dialysis immediately, and I needed to find a match for a kidney transplant.

I stood in the kitchen of my condo staring at the row of medicine bottles with names I couldn't pronounce. Pills my life depended on.

My cell phone rang and I snatched it off the counter. Xavier's goofy face lit up the screen.

"Hey, big brother." I smiled, thankful for the distraction. "Long time no talk."

He groaned into the phone. "Yeah, I know I'm a flake, but I think of you all the time and it's the thought that counts, right?"

"Yeah, I guess so. To what do I owe this pleasure?"

"Dad called me." My smile disappeared and I grew quiet. "Ana?"

I hadn't heard that nickname in so long. "I'm here. What did he tell you?"

"Everything. I know everything. How are you handling it? Because I'll tell you what, it makes me sad and really fucking angry that you have to go through this," he said, his voice taking on an array of emotions. "If I could trade spots with you I would. I hate this for you."

I blinked, pushing back my emotions. I'd cried so much lately that I didn't want to start again, and I felt like I would from how sweet he was being.

I exhaled and reached into my refrigerator to pull out a carton of coconut water. I uncapped it and took a sip, eyeing the pill bottles with distain.

"Well, I'm currently standing in my kitchen with bottles of pills lined up and the warnings they print on the sides staring me in the face. May cause vomiting. Take with a meal. May be taken on an empty stomach. Take in the morning. May cause shakiness. Take as needed for pain. May cause drowsiness. Just about every symptom I have for lupus is the same listed for kidney disease. The headaches and hair loss, the pain in my chest, my drastic weight loss I attributed to training so hard. The brain fog and forgetfulness. Lupus has the power to kill people in their twenties due to a heart attack or a stroke, and often causes difficulty getting pregnant with half resulting in miscarriage. Kidney disease goes hand in hand with lupus. My immune system will attack my tissue, organs, and joints. Basically, I'm my own worst enemy."

I stopped when I realized I'd just repeated what I'd read online without taking a breath.

"I'm sorry," I said. "It's probably not what you wanted to hear."

"Don't apologize. And it's exactly what I wanted to hear. I just wasn't sure how to ask, you know?"

I swallowed. "Yeah, I guess."

"Are you scared?"

Fucking right I was. I didn't want to die. I had too much to experience first. And I wanted a family with two-point-five kids one day. And a dog. I wanted a dog, maybe two. Joy never let us have pets.

Kids.

Sadness consumed me. Kova and I had unprotected sex—a *lot*—and by some miracle, I hadn't gotten pregnant. Not that I wanted to right now. But the thought of not being able to ever have babies hit me hard with a force that took my breath away. I'd always wanted to be a mother someday. Dreamed of it.

Abortion…

Avery. God, my heart hurt, my chest feeling hollow for the way I shut her out. She'd gotten an abortion, and I treated her like shit.

"Ana? You still there?"

I shook away the melancholy. "No, I'm not scared."

Xavier chuckled and I did too. "I knew you'd say that. Always putting on a strong front. A Rossi gene that you're born with."

I let out a sigh. "Yeah, I am scared. Okay? It's a lot to take in, and it's really overwhelming reading all this crap online basically telling me how hard my life is going to be."

I walked over to the couch and plopped down. I leaned my head back and let out a tired sigh and stared at the ceiling, watching the fan move in a circular motion.

Xavier coughed. "It'll get easier in time." He paused. "Probably not what you wanted to hear. Probably don't believe it."

No, it wasn't. And I didn't.

I closed my eyes and drew in a lungful of air. I had to be up early for practice, against my doctor's better judgment. But I couldn't stop. Not after all I've ever dreamed of having was finally at the tips of my fingers. Gymnastics was the one thing I couldn't bear to have taken from my life. Gymnastics gave me life, it gave me freedom. I was nothing without it. I didn't know who I was outside of the sport, and having it erased completely from my life terrified me.

To be blunt, I don't see you making it into your twenties still competing and training at the rate that you are now. It's not impossible, just highly unlikely. My mind raced a mile a minute as Dr. Kozol's words added to the thoughts swirling around in my head, demanding to be heard.

My phone beeped and I pulled it away to look at the screen. *Dad's Cell.*

"Hey, Dad's calling me. I gotta take this."

"Oh, yeah it's cool, grab it. Just wanted to tell you I'm rooting for you. You're strong, Sis. You got this. I have an appointment to be tested to see if we're a match. Anything you need, even if it's just to talk or curse me out, hit me up. I'm your guy."

A sad giggle rolled off my lips. A tear slipped this time. "Thanks, Xavier. We'll talk later?"

"Later, little sis."

I clicked over.

"Hey, Dad."

"Sweetheart, why haven't I heard from you? I've been waiting all day."

"Because you already know," I responded quickly. Turns out he'd known before I did. He knew what I was walking into. "What else is there to talk about? You know everything."

Dad was silent for a moment. "You're upset with me."

"Yeah, a little. You should've told me. At least you could've prepared me. I've been in a state of shock ever since this afternoon."

"I wanted to, believe me, but I felt the doctors should be the ones to deliver the diagnosis so they could better explain." He paused, then said, "I was also worried you might panic and not show up."

I mused over his words. "I guess you have a point. I wouldn't have not shown up, but it would've been nice not to be blindsided either."

"I truly am sorry," he said, his voice full of regret. "Is that why I haven't heard from you?"

"Yes and no. I'm just all over the place right now with my thoughts, trying to figure out how I got to this point. Dad?" Emotion clogged my throat, making my voice sound shaky.

"Yes?"

Tears filled my eyes and I broke down faster than I could stop it. "I'm scared." The confession was a shattered whisper on my lips. My breathing deepened and I started crying. "I'm really scared. I don't want to die."

"Oh, sweetie." His voice broke, which only upset me further. "I'll be there first thing in the morning. Please don't cry. I promise everything will be okay."

"But that's the thing." I sniffled. "You don't know if it will be okay. No one knows. My life is in limbo now and it's terrifying. For the first time in my life, I'm seriously petrified of what's to come. I can taste the fear and it's suffocating me."

"Adrianna, I'll do everything in my power to help you." Dad drove his words home with absolution. I cried harder at the struggles I was facing. My future was now—and would forever be—an uphill battle. "You just have to be strong like you've always been. Keep pushing on. Don't let today affect tomorrow. Take your medicine and focus on gymnastics. I'll handle the rest. You will have everything you need. I can promise that."

"You're not going to tell me to give up the sport?"

"Sweetheart, I know how much it means to you, and I spoke in depth with Dr. Kozol. It's not unheard of for a pro athlete to still compete with illnesses like yours. It's rare, but not impossible. You'll have to work with him and his team. And you'll have to be completely open and honest about everything. No more pushing through the pain."

"I thought I was just overworked. It comes with the territory of training elite. I thought nothing of it."

I sniffled, trying to pull back my emotions. On top of everything, the pain

I had been feeling, the nausea and blood, Dr. Kozol informed me was due to a kidney infection. It was causing one of my kidneys to swell. My body was failing me, and failing me fast.

"How could I be this sick and not know it?"

"Adrianna, you can live a healthy, full life. Yes, there will be complications, but there are also precautions you can take to prevent them, or at the very least, slow them down."

I exhaled a heavy breath, then let it all out and told my dad what I'd read.

"Don't read any of that garbage on the internet. I should have every form of cancer known to man if it were true. In fact, I should be six feet under rotting away." He paused. "You know, if you decide you want to come home for a little while to take a break, you can do that."

I shook my head as if he could see me. "No, that would only put me behind and I'm too close to risk that. Thanks, though."

"I'm not sure you're aware, but with your Amex Black Card, you have a personal concierge on call twenty-four seven. They're paid to do whatever you want and get whatever you need—as long as it's within legal parameters, of course."

I was aware of that, but I'd never used the service before.

I wiped away my lingering tears with the back of my hand.

"You don't have to come tomorrow. I'll be okay."

"I'll be there," he insisted.

I softened. "It's okay, Dad. You'll be bored. I have back-to-back practice the next few days anyway, and then I leave for competition. I'll hardly have time to see you or talk to you."

"I'll be at your competition, then. If that's the only time I can see you, then I'll be there."

Damn it. The tears started up again. "Okay." My voice sounded so small.

"Sweetie," he murmured, "don't cry. We'll get through this together."

"I love you, Dad."

"Love you too."

I drew in a deep breath and attempted to shelve my emotions again. "Dad? Please, don't tell anyone else. Family is one thing, but no one else."

"Adrianna, your coaches need to know."

I sat up straight. "No."

"Adri—"

"Dad, *no*. I don't want them to know. They'd make me change my training schedule again. I've come too far for that."

Dad was quiet for a long minute. "They need to know you're starting dialysis."

I gasped, my jaw hung open. "No, I'm not. I'm not doing dialysis right now." Anger dried up my tears. "The trials are right around the corner, and the Olympics only last like two months from start to finish after that. I'll begin treatment once it's over."

His voice hardened. "Use your brain, Adrianna. You don't have the time to wait to start treatment. I've already made the appointment for you. You're going."

My nostrils flared. "Dad!"

"Adrianna." He said my name with frustration. "I will *not* lose you. You'll be at that appointment whether you want to or not. How are you going to enjoy being a gymnast if you're dead?"

I slammed my mouth shut, my teeth grinding together.

That was heartless.

"Dad, please." My voice was low, broken, and the stupid tears were back. "It's only a few months. I can handle a few more months. After everything I read online, if I start now, I won't be able to compete. I'll lose everything I've worked for because I won't have the strength to continue. I'll be even sicker. Please, I'm begging you to just give me more time."

"Sweetie, you simply don't have the time."

I swallowed hard and clenched my eyes shut. I hated that he was right.

"Please." I cried softly. "I'll do anything you want as soon as I know about the Olympics." We were both quiet for a long moment. "Please, Dad, please give me a little more time."

His voice was low, grim. "Adrianna, I just can't allow you to wait."

Tears were streaming down my cheeks. "Dad, a few more months won't hurt. I'll go to the doctor every week if you want me to instead of every three weeks just for a checkup. I'll bring a doctor to meets with me. Please don't take my gymnastics dream away from me. In a couple of months I'll have to say goodbye forever. Don't make me say it now, because that's what you'd be doing if I start dialysis."

I was crying uncontrollably. All I needed was a few more months and then I would give myself up to the diseases and do whatever my dad and my new team of doctors wanted me to do. Until then, this was all that I was asking for. I would be fine until then. I knew I would.

Dad let out a heavy breath while I held mine. "I don't think this is a good idea."

"If I feel like I've taken a turn for the worse, I'll call you and tell you. I'll go to the doctor. Anything, just don't make me start treatment now." I paused when I thought about when the Olympic Trials were. "I just need a few more months, that's all I'm asking for. It won't make that big of a deal if I take my medicine and go to my checkups. Plus, by then, I'll know if I made the team or not. Just give me a little more time."

"Adrianna, sweetheart…" I could tell he was caving. "So much can happen in two months."

"Nothing is going to happen. We wouldn't even be having this conversation if I hadn't gone to the doctor."

"But you did go and it changes everything. Your health is at risk." I heard the sound of ice clinking against a glass like he was taking a sip of his drink— drifted across the line. "I know what gymnastics means to you and I don't want to take it away, but as your parent, I'm responsible for your well-being."

"Dad, please, I'm begging you."

He groaned like he was torn. "If anything changes, or you need to talk, you better call me. I don't care if it's the middle of the night or if you already called fifteen times, just call me."

Hope surged through me. I sniffled. "Does this mean you'll let me wait to start treatment?"

He hesitated. I could tell he wasn't happy about this. "I don't like this idea, but I'd do anything for you, Adrianna. I hope you know that. You have a long road ahead of you. I just want to see you get well and keep you happy." I smiled sadly to myself. "Keep your head held high," he said, but he didn't seem too sure of himself.

My head was a messy configuration of emotions that I couldn't compartmentalize like I typically was able to. It was too much at once, but he was right. I needed to keep my head held high and focused. I'd gotten my way but needed a subject change before he changed his mind.

"Thank you! Thank you! Thank you, Dad!" He chuckled and it loosened the tightness in my chest. "So, um, not to change the subject, but I have a question about Mom."

"Your mother isn't—"

"No. I mean my real mom. Sophia."

Clearing his throat, he seemed caught off guard. "Oh? What did you want to know?"

I'd have to start asking family if they were open and willing to match test for me, otherwise I would end up on a long list of hopefuls and possibly never get a donor.

"How did you meet her?"

He let out a sound somewhere between a huff and a scoff. "Are you sure you want to have this conversation right now?"

"Why not? My life is already shit. What's one more thing?"

He sighed deeply into the phone. I imagined he was rubbing his forehead. "She was my assistant."

"Was she legal?"

"She'd just turned eighteen when she had you."

So, no, she wasn't. I'd had a weird feeling she was young after I'd met her, but I hadn't expected her to be *that* young.

"Did you love her?"

"Love…it's a tricky thing."

I laughed under my breath. Didn't I know that.

"Do you still talk to her?"

Silence stretched for such a long moment to the point I thought he hung up. Just as I was about to call his name, he spoke. "Yes, I do."

"How often?"

"Quite often, actually."

I rubbed the ache in my chest. Judgment and distrust blackened my vision as all the lies I'd been told over the years flashed through my head.

"How did she end up in your office that day when I came to see you? Before that when I asked about her, you told me you didn't talk to her."

"It's a long story, but I'll sum it up for you. After you were born, I foolishly thought we all could work out joint custody since it'd be in the best interest for you, but I should've known better." Dad's voice trailed away like he was deep in memory. "Sophia was young and poor with nowhere to live, and Joy used that against her to keep her out of your life. Sophia begged me not to take you from her…and I couldn't. It takes a selfish person to deny someone their child. So, I worked with her as much as I could and lied to Joy about it. My arrangement with Sophia went on for years until Joy hired a private investigator to keep tabs on me. Joy built a fictitious case against her, insisting she was mentally unstable."

My brows rose. This shit just got better and better. To our rich, little island, we were the picture-perfect family. Behind closed doors, we were all living double lives.

chapter 2

"**W**HAT?" I SAID. MY VOICE ELEVATED TO A SHOCKING LEVEL. "What was she trying to prove?"

"I tried to reason with Joy and asked her to put herself in Sophia's shoes and pretend it was Xavier. You know what she said?'I feel no pity for the whore you cheated on me with.' That's when I knew it would never be easy. In order for Joy to stop the harassment, I gave her the one thing I knew would placate her. Money. Reluctantly, I gifted Joy for her *selflessness*, but also to act like a mother to you. I thought everything would be okay, but it was far from that."

Gifted. "You mean you paid her off." I scoffed to myself at the sheer ignorance of it. "You paid off your own wife."

"Sophia fell into a terrible state of postpartum depression after you were born. It lasted a long time." Dad ignored my comment. "I felt guilty, like it was all my doing. When I stopped seeing her, she became irrational, highly unstable, and on top of her sister's death, she threatened to run off with you and disappear. I knew she loved you dearly, but I couldn't chance that. I told her if she wanted to seek mental health treatment that I'd pay for it, which I did. I gave her a fully furnished condo once she was out of the inpatient facility, and money to live on so she didn't have to worry. She tried to refuse both and fought me over it because she saw it as payment for you. I assured her it wasn't like that." Dad was quiet for a moment. "During this time, I became a total disaster. My business took a huge hit, I was drinking heavily, and I had a child with someone who wasn't my wife but I was madly in love with. I wanted a divorce. Joy knew that and used whatever she could to her advantage. She insisted I file for full custody so we could give you a healthy and stable home with your brother. She was so sincere…and I believed her. I just never expected Joy to exploit my affair or to use my child for her gain."

I frowned, feeling so low inside. What a bittersweet tragedy my birth caused.

It wasn't a happy occasion like the new life of a child should be. It was one full of misery and adultery. I was unwelcomed, and that only further solidified the isolation I fought deep inside throughout my childhood.

"Sophia and I started talking again once she was better." His voice was quiet.

"How long ago was that?"

"Oh, I'd say over ten years ago. At least."

My brows shot up. "What!" I yelled into the phone. "Over ten years ago? Is that why Joy is the way she is? I'm assuming she found out."

"She didn't find out until a couple of years ago actually. That's when things started to get really tense between us. She hired another private investigator."

"Sounds like she has them on standby."

"She does. It's her weapon of choice. She loves collecting evidence that would ruin someone." He took a sip of his drink again judging by the sound of the ice clinking against the glass. "Sophia and I, we've always had this connection that Joy could never break, no matter how hard she tried. I love Sophia and have loved her since the moment I met her. That will never change."

I grew quiet, feeling bad for my dad and Sophia. The longing in his voice for a love with my real mom curled around my heart like a wet piece of satin and saddened me. Joy may have been the only mother I've ever known, but now a lot of things that happened over the years made sense. She may be married to a multimillionaire and want for nothing, but she is still, and clearly will always be, the other woman. I'm sure that had to harden her heart.

Dad continued. "After living with Joy for so long and seeing her for who she really is, I needed to know what she was up to, so I hired a PI myself. I knew she wouldn't find much on me, other than being with Sophia."

"Did you find anything on her?" I clutched the phone in my hand, unblinking as I waited for his answer.

"I found out a plethora of things she was hiding, including offshore bank accounts."

"I can't believe I never knew any of this."

"You weren't supposed to know."

Fair enough. "I take it Joy won't bother being tested for me."

"She doesn't know about it yet."

I wasn't sure whether to be happy or sad about that.

"Maybe that's a good thing." I licked my dry lips. "I know I don't know her all that well, but do you think Sophia will be open to being tested?"

"It may not seem like it because you don't really know her, but Sophia will do anything for you. She's just a little sensitive right now after hearing about your illnesses. It brought back memories of her sister." He paused. "Sometimes when I look at you, all I see is Sophia," he admitted. "You guys could pass as sisters."

I choked back my emotion. Sophia once told me I looked like her sister. "Where does she live now?"

His voice dropped to a low, quiet tone after another long pause. "North. A few towns over."

My jaw took a dive, heart flailing into my stomach. My real mom lived a few towns over, and I never knew. I couldn't stop the questions from flying out of me.

"Does she ever ask about me?"

"All the time, sweetie. All the time."

I blinked long. "Does she still want to see me? Has she ever asked?" I held my shaky breath as I waited for his response, terrified of what he would say.

"She has asked about seeing you…" I could tell he was thinking carefully about his words before he spoke them. "I know Sophia would love to see you again one day, but I told her it would need to be up to you. She completely agreed."

I let out a long and heavy sigh, trying to wrap my mind around the last couple of days. From Kova saying I needed to start with my mother if I wanted answers, to being diagnosed with kidney disease and lupus, to effortlessly being able to talk to my dad about my real mom, I had so many questions left that I wasn't sure I'd ever get my thoughts in order to ask all of them.

"Does she have other children?"

"No. She didn't feel it was fair to bring other children into this world when she couldn't have you."

"Why didn't she fight to have me as I got older and she got better?"

"She didn't want to disrupt your life, so she stayed away thinking it was best for you. Looking back and realizing how Joy treated you, how I traveled a lot for work… You have to understand, Adrianna, I thought I was doing what was best for our family. I thought I was doing what was best for you. For that, I will forever be sorry."

Each word he spoke chipped away at my heart. He was filled with remorse, and I didn't want that for him. Up until Easter, I'd loved my life, even if I did feel like an outcast at times.

"Dad, don't dwell on it. I don't. I'm okay, and everything turned out just how it was supposed to. I've always been a firm believer that if something is meant to be, it will find its way. Things happen for a reason, and sometimes that reason makes no sense other than to just cause heartache and absolute destruction. Maybe this was how it was supposed to go."

"You are wise beyond your years, you know that?"

"Debatable." I laughed. "So, there's a reason why I was asking about her."

He chuckled. "Oh, really? I hadn't caught on."

I smiled sadly into the phone. "Does—" I didn't know what to call her. "Does Sophia have any other illnesses or diseases in her family history? Anything else I should be concerned with, aside from her sister having MCTD? I don't need any more surprises."

"Her father passed away from liver disease about ten years ago, and I think her mother is okay. I'd have to call Sophia and ask."

I perked up. "When do you think you'll do it?"

"I'll call her now. Once I talk to her, I'll get back to you."

Before we ended our conversation, we went over all my medications. Anything Dad wasn't sure about, he searched on the internet and we went over my symptoms, the importance of that specific medication, and which ones were crucial. He had me use Post-its to write down what they're used for and then stick them to the sides of the bottles. He knew I didn't want to use the pain medications, so those had different color sticky notes. It was much easier this way. The anxiousness that had filled my chest when I first got the prescriptions started to taper off. I was able to breathe again, but I was also too scatterbrained to handle it myself, too stressed and worried about everything I'd read, and where my future with this new diagnosis would lead.

My dad was there for me when I needed him the most, and for whatever reason, that made me emotional and tear up a bit.

"Dad? Remember, don't tell anyone. I don't want anyone to know except for our family, and well, Sophia since you have to talk to her. I have enough on my plate I have to deal with right now, and I don't want anyone to look at me any differently or feel bad or pity me." I paused. "I'd just rather not talk about it if I didn't have to."

"Sweetie, I'll do whatever you want, you know that, but we're all your family and we'll be there for you." Dad sighed when I yawned into the phone. "We'll talk tomorrow, sweetheart. Go get some rest. You've had a long day."

We ended the call and I curled up on my side, holding the phone close to my chest. My hands were shaking, and I had this void inside me that made me feel so cold. I needed someone to tell me it was going to be okay, to hold me tight and take this fear from my chest and make me promises they couldn't keep.

Instead, I was alone in a lavish condo on the beach with the world against me.

Reaching behind me, I pulled the throw blanket over my body and stared at nothing until I dozed off.

Pretending I was okay was easier than explaining why I wasn't.

chapter 3

I WANTED TO CALL AVERY AFTER I SPOKE TO DAD LAST NIGHT, BUT I didn't have it in me after the lengthy and somewhat emotional conversation I'd had with him.

I knew talking to her would expend any energy I had left, and I needed every little bit I could muster.

I'd been a shitty and pretty selfish best friend for a few months now and that wasn't fair of me. I knew it was wrong and I needed to rectify that. I just wasn't sure how.

At the next light, I picked up my cell phone and swiped it open to find my favorite contacts. I pressed down on a name I hadn't dialed in many months. It didn't even ring twice before I heard her voice.

"Adrianna?"

Her hopeful tone seared off another piece of my broken heart.

"Hey, Avery." My words came out thick. The phone trembled in my hand. Whether it was from the new steroids I was on, or from finally calling Avery, I wasn't sure. I only knew that I wasn't safe to drive like this. Thank goodness I was about to pull into World Cup.

"Aid…" She said my name again, this time backed with her own emotion.

We didn't speak a word to each other while we sat on the phone and cried together.

Then…

"If you ever press that fuck you button on me again—even once—I swear I'm going to beat your ass. I don't care how much stronger you are than me, I can still bite and pull hair with the best of them. I will totally punch you in the vag."

A giant smile spread across my face and I laughed. I wiped the tears away with the back of my hand.

"Oh man, I needed that more than you could imagine."

"Same here. I've missed you so much."

"Avery?"

"Yeah?" Her soft voice burst with optimism.

"I'm so, so sorry for the way I acted, and for the way I've been treating you. It was wrong of me… I'm so ashamed of my actions. I feel terrible."

And I truly was. I just hoped she could hear the honesty of my words through the phone. Remorse pierced my chest and I tried to rub away the tightness.

"No, *I* was wrong," she insisted.

I shook my head to clear my thoughts as I parked my truck. I didn't want her to feel wrong. She had no reason to.

"I should've been upfront about everything from the beginning, and I wasn't." Avery continued. "I hid how I felt about Xavier from the one person I never should have. If I could rewind history and do it over again, I would tell you in a heartbeat. Nothing is worth losing my best friend over. Nothing."

My shoulders sagged from the cracking of her voice. I hated that she felt that way.

"Just stop, Ave. It's okay. You did nothing wrong, and you could never lose me. This is all my doing. I was hurt, dealing with so much shit at one time, and I lashed out at the one person who has always been there for me. It wasn't fair to you. On top of everything, it was the beginning of gymnastics season and the perfect excuse to avoid the situation since my schedule was just go, go, go. I'm a shitty friend. I honestly don't even know why you didn't give up on me and say fuck you and throw in the towel."

"Ah, newsflash, idiot, you're my best friend. No matter what, I'd never do that. I just think we both were dealing with a lot of shit and didn't confide in each other like we'd always done in the past," she said. "I mean, how could we? You with your sexy-as-fuck coach, and me with…your brother. Two relationships that should've never ever happened did, and we couldn't even talk about it. Look at you and Fish Lips." She laughed, and I giggled at her old nickname for Kova. I hadn't heard it in so long. "It took you a hot minute to tell me about that whole thing, and I get that. Now imagine if you were in my shoes and you were secretly dating one of my dumbass brothers. You probably would've done the same thing I did knowing all I'd want to do is to steer you away from him. So, I get it. I understand now. We both were stupid and we both reacted wrongly."

"You're right," I said. I stared through the windshield watching some of the gymnasts practice. "So…are you still with him? With Xavier?" I held my breath and braced myself for her answer. I wasn't sure why.

"No. There will never be an Avery and Xavier again. You can believe that."

"But I saw on your Insta you were with him on the Fourth of July."

"Ohhh look at you stalking me."

I laughed again. "Hush. And here I was finally getting used to the idea that we could actually be family. Hopefully I still have the receipt for your wedding gift."

Avery grew quiet and it troubled me. "We don't need a stupid piece of paper to tell us we're family. But I promise we're not together. We tried to work through things, but, well, it's complicated. All we end up doing is arguing."

I softened at her words, though still concerned. "You're right. It would've been cool, though. What happened?"

"Honestly, Aid, I'm not trying to avoid the subject, but that's a conversation we need to have in person. Trust me on this. There's too much to explain, and some things are better said face-to-face. You'll understand why, and hopefully forgive me. It's not pretty. It's downright hurtful, and I may need my best friend to get through it. I'm not over it and I don't know when I will be. The story is long and sad and full of ugly tears. And, I just put my mascara on."

I smiled. Avery and her makeup. "Are you okay, though?"

She was quiet for a moment. I had my answer before she spoke.

"I'm okay now…at least as okay as I can be."

I knew Avery, and I knew she wasn't okay. I could hear in her voice she was still going through the motions.

"Let me check my calendar to see when I have a break in between meets. I can drive down. I want to see you. I need to talk to you too."

I had no time to spare in between meets but I was going to try and make it work, even if it meant driving both ways in one day. Avery Heron was my best friend, and she needed me.

"About what?"

My heart started to beat a little harder. I wanted to tell her about the doctor visits, but I couldn't find the words.

"I can take off on a Sunday. I'll drive down straight after practice Saturday afternoon, that way we'll have half that day and a full Sunday to hang out. I'll have to leave that night, though. Does that sound good?"

"Would it be easier if I came to you? I know you're busy with camps or some shit. What is it exactly that you do at camp, anyway? Am I going to hear a story similar to what happens at band camp, except some kinky girl-on-girl action?"

I laughed loudly. "Oh my God. Not even close! It's not like that. I can barely walk when it's over."

"Adrianna…" She drew my name out, then chuckled. "What kind of shit goes on down there? Leave it to Kova. He should write a book on sex positions and how to thoroughly fuck someone while doing gymnastics."

"Get your mind out of the gutter, Avery! Kova doesn't go to the camps with me, but he's had to literally carry me out of the airport because they're so brutal."

"Are you still fornicating with him?"

Fornicating. I rolled my eyes and smiled. God, it felt good to talk to her.

"It's a long story, one that's done better face-to-face as well."

"Understood. But are you?" she pushed.

"Not fornicating, but we did mess around a time or two. It was the first time since Easter, but nothing since then."

"Holy shit! That long! Why?"

Heat bloomed under my cheeks. "I'll fill you in once we see each other. Wait—how did you know about the training camps I was doing?"

"I've been following your achievements, dumbass."

My heart swelled. "On TV?"

I knew the big meets were televised and an internet search was just a few clicks away, but camp wouldn't come up unless the coaches were conducting interviews and mentioned one of us.

She stayed silent and then it hit me.

"Xavier," I said quietly.

"Aid. Please don't hang up or be mad at me, I just wanted to know how you were doing!" she shouted in one long breath.

"I'm not. I'm…just surprised."

"Let me put it this way—he hates me, and he'll never forgive me for what I did, but that doesn't stop me from asking how you are. A little nagging goes a long way." Avery was persistent, that's for sure.

I couldn't even begin to imagine what transpired between her and my brother, but I hope whatever it was, it was something that could be mended. Our families would forever be bound together by business. They had no choice but to be a part of each other's lives, whether they were amicable or not.

"I'm so proud of you, girl. You're really doing this," she said, her voice sounding heartfelt and genuine. I wished she was in front of me so I could hug her until she yelled at me to let go. "You know what? I'll just drive up and hang out for like a week or whatever. It's still summer and school doesn't start for a couple more weeks, and I don't have anything to do anyway. I'll go to practices with you, hang around, maybe trip Reagan and drop some Visine into her water, go shopping in between."

I laughed, my shoulders bouncing. "My practices are really long, Ave. I have extra ones added in, and I'm still doing therapy for my Achilles. I'd love for you to come, but I'll feel bad because you'll have nothing to do. If you don't mind being bored out of your mind, I'm game."

"Then it's settled!" she announced. A huge smile spread across my face and excitement fluttered in my stomach. I couldn't wait to see my best friend. "Wait. What is it you wanted to talk to me about?" she asked.

I glanced at the clock. I needed to get a move on or Kova was going to blow a gasket. "Listen, Ave, it's really good to hear your voice. I've missed it, but I have to go. I'll call you tonight and tell you. What I need to tell you, it's going to take time."

She was quiet for a moment, then her tone turned serious. "Are you okay?"

"No, I'm not," I admitted, my voice low.

"What's wrong? What happened?"

"I just… I went to the doctor recently for some checkups and discovered that I'm sick." I paused and exhaled a deep breath. "I'm really sick, Ave."

Tears filled my eyes. I didn't want to cry, especially while I was at practice, but Avery was the first person I was going to talk to about it outside of my family, and it was hitting me much harder than I thought.

"Sick with what, bestie?"

Bestie.

A tear slipped from the corner of my eye, the words lodged in my throat. I covered my mouth to hold back my silent cry.

"Aid?"

I drew in a lungful of air and let it out. "Yeah, I'm here."

"Sick with what?"

"I… I have kidney disease. Stage four kidney disease."

"What does that mean?"

"There are five stages, and it means my kidneys are failing at a crazy fast rate. The doctor said advanced kidney damage. I have to start dialysis soon, and eventually I'm going to need a transplant. I'm holding off on the dialysis right now, though, and started with medication that will hopefully suppress symptoms. My dad said he's going to talk with family to see who will offer to be tested, but if I don't match with any of them, I'll have to be put on a waiting list and basically pray for a miracle."

She was quiet again. I was trying to stay strong, but I could hear her soft cries in the distance and it only made it harder for me.

"Ave?"

"I'm here," she said, but I could barely hear her.

"I'm scared. I don't want to die."

Her cries came in a little stronger this time, and so did mine. I felt empty inside, terrified of the unknown, because no matter what I could do, my body was going to do whatever it wanted.

"Get your head in the game for practice. Let's talk more about this later. I love you, and I promise everything is going to be okay."

We said our goodbyes and I hung up the phone. Climbing out of my truck, I grabbed my duffle bag and made my way inside the gym to the locker room. Drawing in air through my nose, I took a couple of deep breaths to steady myself.

I felt awful for opening up to Avery when I'd shut her out for so long. But I needed her, and I needed her support to go through with this, especially if I was going to go the route I planned.

I quickly undressed out of my sweats, balled them up and stuck them in my bag. A slight pang shot up my leg, but I ignored it. I'd ice my calf and ankle once I got home. I had enough pain already to deal with and I hadn't even started practice yet.

chapter 4

"THERE IS NO GLORY IN PRACTICE. SPORTS REVEAL CHARACTER. Games, meets—they reveal your true character. What would it say about you?" Kova asked the girls. He walked past me to grab some mats. "The way you practice is the way you compete. Give me everything you got today, ladies. I want it all. Show me what you are made of. Prove to me that you deserve this."

"Someone's a little too happy today," Holly said quietly with a small smirk. "I'm kinda scared for what he has in store for us. There's too much pep in his step."

I laughed, totally agreeing with her.

Lifting my gaze, I observed the way Kova moved in a shirt I'd detest on any other guy. It was the crew neck kind where someone took a pair of scissors and cut the sleeves off with their eyes closed and made giant, jagged holes that drooped down to their hips. The only saving grace was the fact that Kova was shredded and his god-awful shirt showcased the part of his body I loved the most—the left side of his ribs, exposing the black Olympic ring tattoo that looked like it was floating every time he took a breath.

Damn this man. Damn his eyes. Damn his fucking body.

"He must be getting laid a lot right now," Reagan chimed in. I glanced over at her and felt instant aggravation over her words. She reached down to grab her toes. "He's totally giving Katja that D and boning her hard. He can give it to me any day." She snickered.

"What would give you that impression?" Holly asked, arms extended above her head as she stretched out her shoulders.

Reagan gave her a knowing look. "It's obvious. You'd have to be blind as a bat not to notice, Hols."

We'd already ran two miles and completed a thirty-minute warmup. We were seated in a straddle position on the floor and I was about to spark conversation with the girls when Kova came up behind me and grabbed my ankle, lifting it.

Kova's freshly clean scent enveloped me like an invisible trail. The citrus and cinnamon pulsed through my nose and invigorated me. I tried to lay forward, but he placed a hand around my ribs and stopped me. The warmth of his fingers spread through my ribs.

"What would it say about you?" Kova asked again. His body was so close to mine his heat radiated onto my back.

I glanced at Reagan, and a smile spread across my face. "I'm not sure what it would say about me, but I know what it would say about you as a coach."

"What is that?" he asked too proudly.

"You love to coach because it gives you the power to control everything and everyone. You like to dominate, like having the final say."

Holly and Reagan giggled. I pressed my lips together. I couldn't help but laugh myself.

Kova pulled my leg higher, closer to my side. I winced from the pull in my hamstring. "Relax. Breathe through your stomach, Adrianna, and focus," he said in my ear just for me. "Grab your ankle."

I wrapped a hand around my foot, struggling a bit. "Control equals glory for you. You like having the upper hand because that's how you win," I said.

"Ah, you think you know me so well." Kova shifted closer, giving Holly and Reagan a friendly smile. They blushed ten shades of red.

Kova kneeled to the side of me, his thick thigh pressed to my back. I was off balance and placed a hand in front of me to steady myself. With the pressure of his hand slowly sliding to my stomach, Kova forced me to sit up straighter. Shifting my hips, I pulled my shoulders back...and felt him, hot and long tapping gently on my back. If he had worn boxers then I might not have felt anything. But of course, Kova didn't own any, so I felt *all* of him.

I sucked in a breath and watched to see if my teammates would think anything of his hand movement. I knew they couldn't see his penis touching me so provocatively from behind. Not once in front of anyone else had he so boldly touched me like this.

Easing my leg down, I released a quiet breath as my muscles loosened. I stretched well on my own, but with Kova's helping hand it was always more intense. He had the ability to manipulate my body to the extreme, and I really did love to stretch like this. Kova shifted to the other side and mimicked his stance, pressing his body closer than before. This time he was plastered against me, and the girls didn't even bat an eye.

He wanted me to feel him, to show me his control ran deeper than just gymnastics.

"Do you trust me?" Kova asked, and repeated the words louder for Holly and Reagan. They nodded, while I hesitated for a minute. "If you do not trust me, then we have a problem. This control you speak of so sweetly is for your benefit."

If it were even possible, their faces were as red as a fire hydrant.

"Lots to work on today. Do not waste my time."

Kova moved over to work on both Holly and Reagan, but didn't get as close to them as he did me. All the while, our eyes stayed glued to each other's. The intensity he bled into me was the distraction I'd desperately needed. He always gave me what I needed. Even when I didn't know what I was missing, he was just there, silently encouraging me on. He was my biggest cheerleader. He believed in me. He saw my dream when no one else could.

He was my salvation.

And in moments like this, when I could feel his passion, I forgot every negative thing he'd done and said to me. I smiled and appreciated all that he'd actually done to get me where I am today, because I hadn't been so innocent and naïve either. He'd gone out of his way to give me what I've asked for when he didn't have to. Kova may be controlling, but I was demanding.

Two negatives make a positive. And that's what we were. Two flaws. But when put together, we were amplified in the most dazzling, inconceivable way imaginable.

"Did you not sleep last night?" Reagan asked a handful of minutes later as we stood near the vault. "You look terrible."

I kept my focus on the floor and stomped my feet in the container of chalk. "It was just one of those long nights." I finally looked at her. "I tossed and turned, you know. Couldn't sleep."

She observed me a little too closely. I knew my eyelids were swollen and my eyes glossy. Another symptom of kidney disease, I had learned, but after all the tears I'd shed last night, I assumed the puffiness was from that.

"Yeah. And after this next meet is when it gets real for you. You know, that is, if you qualify at this one to go overseas where the big dogs compete. Then it's the Olympic Trials for you, if you're lucky."

"I'm pretty confident," I said. My lips were a tight smile. "If I made it this far, there's a reason for that."

"Ladies!" Kova yelled, and we both looked in his direction. "Stop the gossip and let us go."

I stomped my feet in the powder again, smiling at the floor. "Kova and his lack of contractions," I said. "I swear, those three words are his favorite."

"I know," Reagan responded. "*Let us go,*" she mocked, and I chuckled. "Someone needs to tell him he sounds like a robot."

"I mentioned it to him once and suggested he take some classes. He said he wasn't doing his job if that was what I had on my mind."

Reagan glanced at me for a long moment, then burst out laughing. "That's such a Kova comment."

I smiled. "I know."

"You ladies want an extra hour of conditioning? Get your asses moving!"

"Go on," I said, my voice low, and got behind her.

We'd been practicing vault all morning and it was helping me keep my mind off yesterday. My focus had been solid and my training even better. Vault was one of two apparatuses I excelled at. It was my golden ticket.

Reagan landed and Kova gave her a few pointers, then he turned toward me and waved for me to go. I inhaled a deep breath then exhaled, and got in the zone.

Running toward the stationary object, I visualized what I needed to do, then I turned over my roundoff, backflipping onto the vault, and pushed off as hard as I could with my shoulders and hands. I soared through the air, euphoria bursting from me as I held on tight and twisted with force and drive.

I opened up and spotted the ground, then held my breath. With both feet together, I stuck my landing and fought not to hop.

I stuck it perfectly and smiled. Glancing over my shoulder, I looked for Kova. He stood parallel to the vault and stared at me, unblinking.

"Back in line."

My face fell. "What did I do wrong?"

"Nothing." He shrugged. "Absolutely nothing. That was flawless. Whatever you just did, you must do it every time. Wherever your mind was, go there again."

My heart began to bloom. I needed to hear that. Offering him a small smile in return, I nodded and jogged to the end of the white tape. When it was my turn again, I got right back into the frame of mind I'd been in just before and took off running.

"Incredible, Adrianna," Kova said, almost breathless and in awe. "A couple more and then we will move onto your second vault and practice that. I hope to see the same result for that one as well."

This time my smile was a little bigger. Hope burst inside of me and it was exactly what I needed after the night I'd had. He waved back in line, then signaled for Reagan. My second vault was a forward flip. It was much harder and took more energy out of me, but worth more points.

I could do it. I knew I could. I just had to keep my faith and my outlook positive.

I completed two good ones, but something happened on the third. Lethargy took over as I ran, and my vision danced with stars. As my hands met the leather horse, my sight turned blurry and pain shot through me.

Flipping forward onto the horse, I had too much momentum and panicked midflight. I lost control and stupidly focused on the throbbing pain in my back.

Kova noticed and swiftly reacted.

I descended like a block of weights, completely out of clean form. He reached out and tried to stop me from face-planting and belly flopping. Thankfully I caught my bearings just in the nick of time and tucked my arms and legs in as I flew out of the dismount and into a front roll.

I flopped open and stared at the roof of World Cup, out of breath and wheezing. Little silver spots danced in my vision. I closed my eyes and focused on breathing for a few seconds. My head was cloudy and dizzy. It took me a minute to regain myself.

"Are you okay? Does anything hurt?" Kova asked. When I didn't answer, he dropped to his knees and leaned over me with concern. I opened my eyes and locked onto his, but I wasn't looking at him. I didn't see him. It was more like I was looking right through him. Kova placed one hand on each side of my head and his brows bunched together. He knew better than to move me in case I'd seriously injured myself.

"Adrianna?" His voice rose with distress.

I wiggled my toes and fingers first, then I blinked a few times until I found my voice. "Yes." My response was a whisper on my lips. "I'm fine. I'm okay."

Kova released a breath and stood, offering me his hand. I slipped my palm into his and he held on. He didn't let go. He eyed me a little too long. My heart started to pound viciously against my ribs.

"Are you sure you are okay?" he asked again, his voice very low. "Do you need to take a break?"

My eyes shot around the gym nervously. A break? Since when was he okay with breaks? Maybe he *was* giving Katja the D like Reagan had said.

"I'm fine… I'm okay. I don't know what happened, but I'm fine," I responded, finally pulling my hand away. "I had a little too much power and I wasn't prepared, that's all. I'm just going to grab some water and I'll be back," I said.

Kova didn't respond. His gaze was on mine as he addressed the team. "Girls. Take a break. Meet me at bars in ten minutes."

I gave him the faintest smile, quietly showing him I was thankful. I knew he wouldn't miss it. Then I turned around and kept my eyes on the floor as I walked past Reagan like I was in my own world, despite her heavy gawking and ignored her silent will for me to look her way.

chapter 5

I WALKED BACK INTO THE GYM AND TOOK A DEEP BREATH, BRACING myself, nervous that Kova would ask questions.

I shook out my fingers and stumbled when our eyes locked, not expecting him to be there. In fact, he looked annoyed more than anything else.

Damn paranoia was already getting to me.

"Two miles. Now." He lowered his voice. "Running will help you regain your focus."

Nodding, I quickly returned to the locker room and changed into running clothes and put on my sneakers, then I headed outside. Despite my earlier run this morning, I didn't grunt about it. I needed to breathe. I needed to let go of all the shit on my mind. I was so irritated with myself for slipping up. Kova was right, though, I needed to regain my focus.

The diagnosis was still so fresh. I knew that was the sole reason for my mistake. The moment I'd felt an inch of fatigue, my mind shut down and I'd allowed the thoughts to take over. I couldn't afford to let that happen again. I could do better, I knew I could. I just had to push past the weariness and body aches like I had in the past and everything would be how it used to be.

I focused on my feet hitting the pavement, keeping my gaze ahead of me. I ran my best time—a seven-minute mile, twice. I was shaking and edgy by the time I was done, but the exercise was exactly what I needed.

Sweat dripping down my temples and my cheeks flushed, I walked back into World Cup with purpose. My heart beat hard, faster than usual. I had so much adrenaline pumping through me I was wired and ready to get back in the gym. Kova spotted me immediately and I smiled. There was something in his gaze that just felt like home. His forehead was creased, and I strode toward the locker room to wipe myself down and change.

"I said two miles."

I dug out some water from my bag. "I did do two miles."

"Not possible. You were gone for less than twenty minutes. You are usually running for at least thirty."

My back was still to him. Shrugging, I said, "I ran fast and regained my focus like you said."

"Get rid of that attitude you have. I will not put up with it."

I didn't have an attitude. *He* had an attitude. "Okay, *Coach*."

I wasn't going to argue with him.

Exhaling a long breath, I turned around to face him. He was studying me a little too intensely and it bothered me, but only because I didn't want him to dig. It wasn't that I didn't want him to ever know about my illness, I just didn't want him to know right now. Once everything was all said and done, and I'd achieved my goal, then I would tell him. Until then, I had to be careful not to slip up.

"So we are back to that again? *Coach?*" he asked me, eyes narrowing.

I took a gulp of water and nodded, trying not to be aware of how much that disturbed him. How sterile it was for us. I wasn't just Adrianna, and he wasn't just Coach. We were Ria and Kova, and we both knew that.

"That is too bad. We are not taking a step back."

Staying quiet, I placed my bottle back in my locker and grabbed my leotard and a fresh sports bra. I pulled off my tank top and balled it up and threw it into my bag. I hooked my thumbs into my shorts and leaned forward, about to pull them down when I realized Kova was still standing there.

I glanced over my shoulder. Our eyes met. The heat in his stare stunned me.

"What?" When he didn't respond, I said, "I'm trying to get changed. You can't be in here, *Coach*."

I smirked. His nostrils flared. I realized I liked to call him Coach when I was mad. This was how we roused each other. It was a game and I loved it, and I found I couldn't stop myself from doing it every single opportunity I was given. A perilous game that came with no winner or end in sight.

"What is going on with you today? Is something wrong?"

"Nothing is wrong with me. I'm just trying to get changed so I can return to practice."

Much to my surprise, Kova changed his tune. "When you are finished dressing, meet me by bars."

I nodded and quickly changed after he exited the locker room. Before I left, I checked my little white notecard Dad had wanted me to keep specifically in my gym bag. It had all the times I had to take medicine and which ones until I remembered them by heart. I read over it, then pushed my pill bag all the way to the back and locked up my locker.

Kova and I practiced hard together, him instructing me the whole way with any little tips of the trade he could offer. He barked out orders and I took them in silence like a good student. It was just like we'd done from the beginning and I craved that mentally. I'd completely forgotten about the dark cloud that hung over my head while I was in the zone.

"I think you are ready to move forward," he said, rubbing his hands together. The bold optimism in his eyes gave me the courage I was lacking today. There was no way he'd even consider this if he didn't think I'd thoroughly mastered the skill to move on to the next step—adding the full twist. This was huge for me right now.

Maybe I'd been too hard on myself.

"You feel like I'm ready to move on?"

He studied me. "I would never have you move on if I did not have complete confidence in you."

I smiled from ear to ear. If he felt I was ready, then I was ready.

"Okay…but will you spot me?" I asked, adjusting my grips. I needed him, wanted him there as cushion.

"Of course. I plan to be here until you are ready to do it on your own."

Stepping near the low bar, Kova moved to stand in front of me instead of behind me. I looked at him, a little trepidation riling me up. His eyes softened.

"It is only one more half turn. You can do this."

"I know I can, Coach. The first time is always the scariest, though."

One corner of his mouth turned up. "Adrianna, you do not have to keep calling me Coach. We both know I am much more than that."

I offered him the faintest smile, then pulled myself up onto the low bar before swinging to the high bar. A handstand and two full swings, I was letting go into the first layout, floating through the air into another straight body layout.

"Tight… Tight… Tight…" Kova said, his voice so close to me.

Right where I would twist, I pulled my arms to my chest, fists in snug balls and head tucked in, I cranked to the left and pulled a one-and-a-half twist. Spotting the ground, I drove my heels down, but my chest was too low and I felt my body leaning over.

Kova was there immediately. As a coach, he needed a sharp eye and quick reflexes. He needed to be a hero in that moment, and he was. His strong arm came out and coiled around my stomach to prevent me from falling farther. I took a step, and he pulled me back like it was nothing.

Breathing heavily, I grabbed his arm and dug my fingers into him. I was a little uneasy.

"Not too bad," he said, releasing me quickly. "There are a few things I could comment on, but seeing as it was your first time, I will refrain. Let us do it again."

Exhaling the anxiety, I chalked up, then I was back on the high bar. Another dismount, and Kova caught me again. I waited to be critiqued, but all he said was, "Again."

Gymnastics was all about repetition, repetition, repetition. Hours upon hours of the same thing over and over would seem daunting to most, but I loved it, because I still found it fun after all these years. Muscles needed to be trained to remember how to perform, and the only way to do that was to duplicate the exercise or skill hundreds and hundreds of times. It created a memory for the muscles and brain. And as much as I was hard on myself for not getting it right the first couple of times, I knew it was par for the course.

We were nonstop with no break in between. However, after two hours, a sudden sense of sheer exhaustion took hold of me just as I cast into a handstand on the high bar. I blinked a few times and breathed through my nose, gripping the bar as tight as I could.

"Squeeze," Kova ordered, drawing out the word. "Squeeze, Adrianna."

I tried so hard to fight it. My arms became weak and my elbows shook violently. I tightened my fingers around the bar and prayed I could hold on, but my heart was racing so fast and I felt winded.

Something wasn't right. And if I proceeded any further, I had a feeling it would be bad.

My hips dropped and I came down recklessly, slamming my pelvis onto the bar with an *oomph*. My arms bent and I let out a long grunt. I struggled to lock my elbows to pull myself up, but I just couldn't do it.

I released my hold, free falling to the floor.

And Kova watched me fall.

My knees crashed into the landing mat. Little specs of chalk floated in front of my vision. I closed my eyes, ashamed of how my body just gave out like that.

"What the hell was that!" Kova yelled. "Get back up! We are not done here!"

I got back up on the high bar, but lethargy was a pressure in my chest that consumed me. My hips rested on the bar. I couldn't lift myself into a handstand. I tried to swallow, but my mouth was dry. I blinked a few times trying to make the silver flashes of stars disappear. I didn't have the strength to hold myself up, and it scared me. My heart was pounding viciously. Had I always been this weak and I didn't know it, so I kept pushing until I could barely walk?

With his hands propped on his hips, Kova glared up at me. "Now, Adrianna. What are you waiting for?"

"Coach?" My quiet voice crackled with fear. I couldn't make eye contact.

He took a small step closer. "You have an hour of practice left, then conditioning. I was counting on you mastering this tonight so we could move on to the release skills tomorrow, and then connect it all for the meet coming up."

Letting Kova down—letting *myself* down—was the last thing I ever wanted to do, but there was no way I would be able to do any of that right now. Not with how I felt inside. There just wasn't. I simply didn't have the strength.

"Please…" My voice broke. "Please, help me down."

Without further question, Kova stepped right in front of my dangling legs and reached for my hips.

His gaze was painted with concern as he effortlessly lifted me and guided me down from the bar. Expelling a breath, I let go and wrapped my arms around his shoulders, but I couldn't tighten them. My head fell into the crook of his neck, and my toes tapped against his shins. I was so tired and felt like I could just fall asleep.

"Adrianna."

His voice was thick in my ear. He wrapped his strong arms around my back and held me to him. We were in a compromising position, but his warmth comforted me, and in this moment, I needed him.

"What is wrong? You are trembling."

chapter 6

"I DON'T KNOW WHAT HAPPENED. I GOT REALLY WEAK FOR A SECOND," I said, somewhere between the truth and a lie.

My forehead was pressed to his neck and I snuggled closer. I inhaled his cinnamon and citrusy tobacco scent and my body relaxed into his embrace. My eyes rolled shut.

"The only thing I do know is that I would've hurt myself if I continued. I need a break for a second, Kova. Please. I'm so sorry."

I hoped by using his name he'd hear my desperation.

His hand splayed across my lower back, and I sighed. "Ria," he said low enough so no one else would hear. "I have to put you down. There are too many eyes looking our way, we cannot be seen like this. *I* cannot be seen like this with anyone."

Pulling back, I shook my head and looked into his eyes. "Please, I can't stand. I feel like I'm going to faint."

It was the truth. I didn't have the energy to stand. I needed to go home, but I bit my tongue because I knew that wasn't an option.

With a frown, Kova curved an arm under my knees and brought me up higher, cradling me to him.

"Take me to the therapy room, please," I said, and he nodded.

When we got there, he gently laid me on one of the tables. I curled onto my side and allowed my eyes to close, lying there for a couple of minutes. The room was icy cold and my teeth were chattering. Kova stroked a gentle hand over the side of my face and pushed my stray hair back.

"I knew I was pushing you too hard." A string of what I presumed to be curse words in Russian flew from his lips. "I thought you could handle it."

Talk about a bolt to the chest to wake my ass up. "I can handle it. I've proved that already, haven't I?"

He cocked a brow, but his words were soft. "Then why did you have me bring you in here? It is clearly too much for you, Adrianna. I do not want to wear you down, but what happened out there? The way you were all over me could have raised quite a bit of questions. You know we cannot do that when people are here. Tell me what is going on."

"I almost fainted, Coach. I was *not* all over you."

Screw this. I pushed myself up to face him, my eyes blazing with anger. Kova's words filled me with resentment and I stared at him, letting him see just how I felt. How dare he. He made me feel guilty and I didn't like that one bit. Not when I'd proved myself time and time again. One mistake and it was suddenly the end of the world for me.

"*Nothing happened, Coach.* I just had a mental block and needed to stop for a second. I worked myself up, I guess. I didn't eat today either, and I got light-headed, but I'm fine now. Let's go. I'm ready to get back out there."

"No. Lie back down."

Christ, this man was infuriating. "I'm fine. Excuse me for not being perfect like you."

Kova released a long sigh and looked away. He scrubbed a hand down his face. "No...no. I am just being, how do you say it? A dick?"

"Wow. Is that your way of apologizing?" I asked, and he regarded me with jaded eyes. I was fighting internally to hold myself together. "You aren't the type to admit when you're wrong."

"Just know I do not approve of this. You need to be out there practicing, earning your spot on the Olympic team."

"What is it exactly that you don't approve of? What did I do that was so wrong?"

"Taking time off from practice? Leaving early? Arriving late? *Taking a little break because you had a mental block?* We were not finished for the day, and we have a lot of work ahead of us with so little time."

My jaw dropped. "That's funny. I recall you insisting I sleep in the bed that you share with your *wife* so I could relax. What about the time when you had me miss practice so I could recover from camp when I didn't want to? That's on you, not me. I could've handled it. Or how about the time when you wouldn't let me come back to practice until I went to the doctor to make sure everything was all right when I told you it was—which it was!" My voice rose with each sentence, and I could feel the vein in my throat straining from yelling back at him. "So it's okay for me to skip out on your terms, but not mine? I wasn't even asking to leave early, just to take a small break, which I never, ever ask for. How is this fair?"

I was getting so angry that I wanted to cry. "Answer? It's not. You're a walking double standard. It's okay when you say it's okay but not when anyone else does. You want everything on your terms so you can hang on to control. Your way or the highway, right?"

Kova's nostrils flared and he stepped closer. He was just a few inches from my face. Pointing a finger downward, he clenched his teeth as he said, "Lower your voice. What happens outside of these walls bears no weight on what happens inside. Inside World Cup, I push you, you take it, and we both win. Just like we have always done. I am doing my job, one you require from me because I am the *only one* who can give it to you."

A sarcastic laugh broke from my throat. I shook my head incredulously. "You're a piece of work, Konstantin Kournakova. You should be thanking your lucky stars Katja puts up with you."

His eyes glowed with newfound anger. The vascular veins in his arms twirled up toward an astoundingly handsome face. Even mad he was too good-looking for his own good.

"I will get your stuff and take you home," he said.

My jaw dropped. "I'm not leaving."

"You are. Go home and sleep. End of discussion," he bit out stiffly, enunciating each word.

"No."

Kova turned to walk away, but I reached out and grasped his wrist. "Then get Hayden. I want him to take me home." A low growl sounded in the back of his throat, and he twisted his wrist out of my hold. "I want Hayden."

"Very well."

Moments later, far away voices drifted closer and Hayden stormed into the room.

"Jesus, Aid. Are you okay?"

I cracked open an eye. "I'm okay. I'm just freezing. Is your practice over? Can you take me home, please? I forgot to eat today and I'm a little lightheaded." I wanted to add that Kova was being a dickhead and making me go home, but I didn't.

He glanced up at the clock on the wall. "I have an hour left, but I'm sure Kova will understand." He turned to look at him over his shoulder. "Won't you, Coach?"

Kova nodded but I shook my head hastily. "I can wait," I said. "I don't mind."

"It's no issue—"

"I'll wait for you," I insisted, my voice firm. I wasn't going to take away from his practice because of my actions. I should've just taken my chances and completed the dismount to avoid all this.

"Okay...let me get some clothes for you, though."

Hayden came back seconds later. I glanced at his hands, confused by where he'd found clothes. I'd rather freeze to death than wear Reagan's stuff.

"Here, let me help you."

"Where did you get that?" I asked, and raised my arms above my head.

"It's mine." He placed his T-shirt over me.

Thank God. I glanced down. It had a big, golden yellow M on it. *Michigan.*

I eased back onto the table and Hayden moved to stand by my feet.

"Kova, lift her hips for me so I can get these on her."

"I got it," I said firmly. Hayden handed me a pair of navy blue sweatpants. I slipped them on and felt warmer already.

"You don't have a jacket here, do you?" Hayden asked Kova.

"No."

He nodded. Not many people carried a sweater around in the middle of summer in Georgia.

"That's okay. She should be good for now." Hayden looked at me. "I won't be long."

"Thank you."

Once Hayden stepped out of the room, Kova looked at me with concern. "I think you should see a doctor."

He couldn't be serious. I was in this state because of him. Kind of. I laughed sarcastically, unable to control myself.

"I almost think you're a hypochondriac. Why do you keep wanting me to see a doctor?"

"Do not make me call your father," he gritted out. He wasn't impressed, but I didn't care.

"Go ahead and do whatever you want, you always do anyway," I said in surrender. "Just leave me alone. At least allow me the luxury of sitting in silence while I stare at the wall for the next hour."

"I do not approve of this."

"There's a shocker," I said full of mockery and turned my back to him. Minutes later, as hard as I tried to fight it, sleep consumed me.

"Aid…" I heard my name in the distance. "Aid… Wake up."

My eyelids were too heavy to lift. The voice sounded much closer, but I was too tired to care. I muttered something unintelligible, a leave-me-alone moan, and curled up tighter into a ball.

"Adrianna." I heard my name again, this time in an exotic tongue with a heavy roll to the R.

My eyes burned as I willed them to open. I exhaled a sleepy sigh. There were two different people near me. People I couldn't place who they were, but more importantly, where was I?

Disoriented, I cracked open my eyes to a blurry vision. I couldn't focus. I tried to sit up, but I didn't have the strength and collapsed back down, but not before strong arms caught me.

"Adrianna." This time my name was much clearer. I recognized the voice, but a familiar scent roused me.

"Hayden?" I yawned, and rubbed my eyes. They felt so swollen. "How long did I sleep for?"

"Maybe an hour? I'm not sure."

"That's it? Felt like so much longer."

"Yeah. Come on, let's get you home."

I sat up slowly with the help of Hayden, but my focus was on Kova. A fleeting shadow of regret cast in his eyes. I grimaced. Good. I hoped he felt like shit. It was too soon to forget the way he had spoken to me and how he'd made me feel. People often said no one could make a person feel inferior to anyone, but that was total bullshit. When your heart cared deeply for someone, it was impossible not to feel the weight of their words no matter how strong the front was.

Kova extended a hand out to help me, but I tugged my arm from his reach. My relationship with Kova was the same song and dance. One day I'd learn. Just not today, and probably not until I left World Cup for good.

"I need to grab my bag," I said, standing up. Jesus, I was so tired. I felt like I could sleep for a week straight. Yawning, I walked to the locker room and retrieved my bag. I couldn't leave without my medication.

Turning to Kova, I asked a bit detached, "Is it okay to leave my car here overnight?"

"Yes. That will be fine."

Hayden extended an open palm, waving his fingers at me. Placing my hand into his, he laced our fingers together and guided me out of World Cup to his car. Kova was hot on my tail, nearly stepping on my feet, but I played it off like I hadn't noticed. It didn't matter, though, because Hayden did.

"Why don't you just piss on her?" he yelled over the hood of his car, his blue eyes intense.

"Hayden, be nice," I said, stifling a giggle. I actually felt bad.

Hayden glanced over at me, his feelings shifting in his gaze. "Aid, I'm sorry, but I refuse to hold back where that man is concerned."

"Just doing my job and making sure the others do not get the wrong idea when they see you guys leaving together," Kova replied with a twist of his lips, unfazed by Hayden's comment.

"Whatever you need to tell yourself."

At that, Hayden got into his car and I followed, putting on my seat belt then leaning back against the seat. I glanced through the tinted window toward Kova.

I was drawn to his confidence and strength. I was addicted to the way he pushed me and challenged me. I could push past an injury and keep practicing. I could train for hours on the same skill without a single complaint. But this was something that caught me completely off guard and terrified me. It was like all muscle mass had disappeared and a fifty-ton boulder had been placed on my chest. I crumbled.

Pulling out of World Cup, I spoke once we were on the main road. "Thanks for taking me home, Hayden."

"You know I'd do anything for you," he said, and I smiled. I did know that. "Do you need me to stop anywhere? Get you anything?"

"No, I'm good. I just want to go home and crash. Can you pick me up for practice tomorrow?"

He nodded. At a red light, he angled his body my way. "Are you okay, though? You look pale, Aid."

"I'm just a little overworked and lacking sleep. I'll be fine."

"I'm worried about you. It's unlike you to leave practice early. Who's going to look after you when I'm gone?" He smiled sweetly.

"Ugh. Don't remind me that you're leaving," I whined. I was going to miss Hayden dearly when he left for college. "I can't believe you're leaving me here with Reagan." I stuck my index finger in my mouth and pretended to gag myself.

"You aren't going to be stuck with her for much longer. She'll be leaving for Louisiana around the same time."

"I totally forgot about that." Reagan had accepted a partial scholarship from the University of Louisiana.

About ten minutes later, Hayden pulled into my complex, right up to the front sliding glass doors to drop me off. "Thanks again for being there for me. I'll see you tomorrow."

"Anytime. Want me to come up?"

I shook my head but offered a gracious smile. I didn't want him getting the wrong idea. I'd rather buy a rope and hang myself before that ever happened again.

chapter 7

I HAD ONLY A HANDFUL OF COMPETITIONS LEFT THAT I NEEDED TO attend—and qualify for—in order to go to Worlds, which was an absolute must if I wanted to make the Olympic team, God willing.

World Championships were typically held out of the country and lasted for a week since there were so many qualifying rounds. There were other ways to qualify, but this was the most logical way and the least stressful.

Once I arrived at World Cup, I automatically ran two miles before changing into my leotard. I was thirsty and drank almost a whole bottle of water before I left the locker room. Yesterday was rough, but it was behind me. I was determined to make today better.

I smiled to myself and stepped inside the gym, embracing the chalky air and spirit around me. I was eager for practice to begin so I could take my mind off the reality of my life and what I was up against.

It was hard to wrap my mind around the fact that just as I was starting to come back from heartbreak, my body decided to betray me. This quietness that had taken over stuck to me like superglue. I didn't want it. I wanted it to leave, only, I didn't know how to make it go away. Instead, it grew with each passing second like an impending sense of doom. I felt different inside, alone, a little paranoid and completely isolated. I decided the more I practiced, and the more time I spent inside World Cup, that it would eventually go away. It had to.

I just wanted to be myself again. Only now I feared the way the cells in my body were destroying each other I would never reach my full potential as a gymnast, and that was devastating to me. Gymnastics was my life. I couldn't imagine not being able to do it.

I glanced around at everyone on the different events, looking for the one person who seemed to calm my worry without even knowing he did.

One look at Kova, and I could tell that he, too, looked like he hadn't slept all night. Dark circles lined his eyes and a thicker scruff dusted his chin. When he turned his head in my direction, I could see the anguish tormenting him. My heart clenched at the longing gaze in his eyes. He was staring back at me, asking for something he couldn't put into words. He didn't have to. I felt what he was saying, because I felt the same way.

I rubbed my eyes with the heels of my palms, then walked over to the balance beam where he stood.

"Adrianna, can we speak for a moment?" Kova asked.

Kova let his guard down for me to see and I studied him. There was no life in his eyes, no color at all. We were both numb. I was used to the empty feeling, but I didn't like seeing him like that. It bothered me immensely.

"Is it okay if we wait until after practice? I really just want to get to work."

He looked at me, brows bunched together, and gave one firm nod. Maybe he needed the release in the same manner I did that gymnastics gave me.

We practiced for hours on balance beam, breaking down my routine and working on connections, sequences, jumps, and leaps. Whatever Kova suggested, I did in silence, and I made sure I did it well. Each landing was soft, light and airy. Kova didn't commend me—it was rare he actually ever did—but I could tell I was practicing well because he didn't ridicule me either. He almost seemed pleased. There wasn't one balance check. I didn't fall, and I stuck the majority of my dismounts on soft mats. Even my turns were nearly on point, though not all, because turning on your toes was actually harder than doing backflips on the four-inch wide beam. Go figure, but it was true.

I knew now that pushing myself wasn't the brightest idea I'd ever had, but I didn't have any another options. I was backed against a wall. I didn't want kidney disease to be what stole gymnastics from me. If I never achieved my dream, it was going to be because of me, not because a disease stronger than me took it.

I hardly spoke until Kova finally cornered me when we rotated to vault.

"What is wrong with you today?" he asked, his voice low and laced with curiosity.

I shrugged one shoulder and averted my gaze. I watched my teammates. "Nothing. I'm fine."

Kova shifted on his feet. "Listen, if this is about yesterday—"

I glanced up. "It's not. I have a lot on my mind right now and I'm just focusing on the skill at hand. I'm sorry for my attitude."

He observed me for a long moment. Probably surprised I apologized for once. "If something is wrong, you would come to me, right?"

A mixture between a laugh and a huff escaped me before I could stop it. "Yeah, I'll run right over," I said full of sarcasm.

He stepped closer to me and angled his head down. My heart beat a little harder. Lowering his voice, he said, "I am serious, Adrianna."

"So am I, Coach."

Kova exhaled through his nose like he was defeated. "Let us get started on vault. You practiced well on beam today. I am very impressed."

I was a little caught off guard by his praise. A timid smile tugged on one corner of my mouth, and he returned it.

Little actions like that, they were what pierced my heart more than words. They brightened my day.

Vault practice was different. I went light on my dismounts. Kova placed a three-inch-thick landing mat on top of the foam pit so my heels wouldn't slam into the floor each time. I had a forward flipping vault and a backward flipping vault to practice.

"Two hours. One hour for each vault."

I nodded and chalked up, rubbing the dry, white powder on the bottoms of my feet and behind my knees. Stepping behind the white tape, I visualized my skill.

Clapping his hands, Kova crouched at the knees so he was parallel to the apparatus, and yelled, "Go!"

I loved when he turned coach mode on. It helped snap me into place.

And so it began. After the first hour, I was thirsty and needed to use the bathroom. My bladder was going to explode if I didn't relieve myself soon.

"Grab a drink. Ten-minute break."

"Thanks," I said and jogged to the locker room. I took a swig of water, then checked my notecard to see which medicines and vitamins I was due for. I was so happy my dad had suggested this idea.

Glancing over my shoulder to make sure I was alone, my hands trembled as I poured out the necessary pills. Quickly, I swallowed them back, pushed the bottles deep into my bag, and grabbed an all-natural protein bar. I peeled back the wrapper and took a small bite, then another, and another. I didn't have an appetite, but I forced myself to eat at least half. I didn't want to get lightheaded. Not after yesterday. I threw the rest away and brushed my hands together. It was really all I could stomach. Sticking to a low-calorie diet was easier these days when my mind was twisted with worry.

I grabbed an extra bottle of water to bring back with me into the gym. Sports drinks of any kind were not allowed inside, only water.

Right before I went back to train for the second half of the day, I stepped into the restroom. Pulling off a leotard during practice was like taking off soaked jeans. The struggle was real. I squatted to pee and hoped the burning sensation in my bladder left once I relieved myself, but the strangest thing was, while I had the urge to go, hardly anything came out. Guess I didn't have to go to the bathroom after all.

Washing my hands, I glanced at my reflection and frowned. I looked like a hot mess. There were flyaways everywhere. I tried to smooth them back with a little water and then tightened my ponytail. I had dark circles under my eyes and I was a little pale, but the good news was the rash I'd been sporting for the past two weeks had come down a lot. It was hardly noticeable now. That was a huge positive in my eyes because that meant the medications were working.

Kova eyed my water bottle when I stepped back into the gym. "That better be water." He nodded his chin toward it.

I gave him a droll stare. "No. It's vodka."

My lips twitched, so did his. "Do not start with me."

"Like I would ever do such a thing and talk back."

Kova didn't respond but I caught a shadow of humor in his eyes. A small smile tugged at my lips. I needed that.

Slinging my bag over my shoulder, I snatched my car keys from the bench and turned around to leave just as Kova stepped into the room looking as cool as a cucumber. Most everyone had left by now since it was so late in the day, so I wasn't surprised to see him in here with just me.

I drew in a breath. Our eyes locked. He had his hands in the pockets of his netted shorts as he leaned casually against the door frame. He wore a loose black sleeveless shirt and his hat faced backwards so the flat bill was in the back. He didn't have a line of worry on his face and he looked totally kissable.

Damn it. Don't go there.

My shoulders loosened. I was a little jittery inside, but his presence soothed me. I hated when he wore that hat because he looked so damn sexy in it. Black was his color.

It was also the color of his heart.

"How was ballet class?" he asked.

"It was actually great."

His forehead creased. "It was great," he mimicked.

No, I'd fucking hated every second of it and planned his demise in the process.

"Yeah! The new dance teacher was pretty awesome, and I liked that she had us do some kind of yoga stretching things at the end. That was cool. She said we're going to do it once a week."

Kova stared quietly. He wasn't buying it.

"Well," I said when he didn't say anything, "I'm gonna go. I'm beat. I'll see you tomorrow, Coach."

Walking toward Kova, I could smell the scent of his cologne before I reached him. He stopped me by placing his hand on the inside of my elbow. His thumb gently rubbed back and forth on the crease of my arm.

It was then that I noticed just how deep the lines under his eyes were. "What's up?"

Kova looked down and studied me. His eyes shifted, brows lowering. "Are you okay?"

I drew in a silent breath. "I'm fine, why?"

He leisurely shrugged one shoulder. "Just asking. When women say they are fine, it usually means they are lying, and I am fairly certain you said that you are fine a few times today."

He'd paid too close attention.

"I'm fantastic. How's that?" I retorted sarcastically with a massive smile that caused him to tug me closer until I was against him. I drew in a quiet gasp when our bodies touched. Without realizing it, I leaned into him and embraced his warmth.

I missed that. I missed him.

I missed us. What we used to be, what we had.

We didn't move, save for his thumb still running circles on my arm. I couldn't tear my eyes from his and went with what I was feeling in my heart. Leaning my cheek on his chest, I wrapped my arms around his back and closed my eyes. Kova didn't hesitate and that made my stupid heart even weaker for him. We melted into each other like this was where we belonged, where we needed to be. He hugged me tighter, then leaned down and inhaled deeply before kissing the top of my head. I squeezed him, releasing all the negativity in my life. I wanted him to come home with me, where I could just sit in his arms and forget about my issues.

Looking up at him, I felt the longing in his green eyes that I knew was reflected in mine and almost asked if he wanted to come over. I noticed the tight lines around his mouth and creases between his brows. But I didn't ask. Instead, all I could do was offer him a sad smile. He returned it, but I wished he hadn't, because that gave me the clarification I needed.

"I'll see you tomorrow," I whispered, then stepped away.

Kova reached for me, his hand dragging down my arm until he reached my wrist. He gave my hand a little squeeze.

The emotion swirling in his green gaze was overriding my common sense. I didn't want to leave, and I knew he didn't want me to either.

But Kova let go, and I finally walked away.

"Adrianna," he called right before I reached the lobby. I glanced over my shoulder. He was standing where I'd left him, looking so lonely that I almost ran back to him.

"Yes?" I finally said after a long moment.

His brooding eyes held me in place. My heart skipped a beat as I waited.

"Nothing. It is nothing. I wanted to talk to you, but we can pick it up another day. Go rest. I will see you tomorrow."

Without waiting a beat longer, I quickly walked out and climbed into my truck. If I didn't hurry up, I was going to turn around and run into his arms.

I had less than a week until my next big meet. I couldn't afford to break, but with everything on my mind lately, I felt like it was coming.

chapter 8

"**I** HAVE BEEN TRYING TO GET AHOLD OF YOU ALL DAY, ADRIANNA," MY father bellowed through the speaker.

I pulled the phone away from my ear. I'd missed a bunch of his calls this afternoon.

After I'd arrived home, I showered and then heated up something to eat so I could take my medicine with food. I'd skipped eating regular meals today since I didn't have much of an appetite. I'd only had half a protein bar and I gathered that could be the reason why I was so anxious and edgy. My hands couldn't stop shaking, my heart beat faster than normal, and I was a little nauseous.

"Couldn't you have sent a text at least? I was starting to worry. I almost called Konstantin."

I pressed the phone to my shoulder with my ear while I sat on a barstool. "I'm sorry, Dad. I was so busy with practice that I didn't have much time in between. I have a lot on my mind right now."

"I understand that, sweetheart, but we made a deal. I need to be able to reach you." He sighed, and I apologized again for worrying him. "I got your appointments scheduled for the day after tomorrow. Will that work for you?"

I swallowed a spoonful of bone broth. I loved this stuff since it was easy on my stomach. "Yes. I'll let Kova know tomorrow that I won't be in. Did you mention that if I need any tests done they'll have to be done the same day and to make arrangements for that?"

I hoped I hadn't come across as a diva, but desperate times called for desperate measures.

"Yes. Everything is taken care of."

My shoulders relaxed. "Perfect. Thank you so much for doing that for me. I was worried the receptionist would give me the go-around and make me come back for each issue if I'd called myself. I just don't have the time for that right now."

"It pays to know people in higher places. Anything for my daughter. I'll text you the info and times. Please keep me updated."

I smiled and thanked him again. After saying goodbye, I placed my phone down and forced myself to drink the rest of the broth. Between the acidic feeling high up in my stomach, and the awful metallic taste in my mouth, I knew eating was a must, even if I wasn't hungry. The broth usually helped settle that uneasy feeling.

I walked into the kitchen and reached into the refrigerator to pull out the carton of eggs, butter, bacon, shredded cheese, an onion, and some garlic. Then I grabbed an avocado and a lime I had in a bowl sitting on the counter. I had a feeling the medicines were messing with me and that I needed to create some kind of barrier to coat my stomach before I took them. The broth had helped a little, but I thought actually eating might do the trick.

I pulled out a plastic bag of whole wheat English muffins from the freezer. I hadn't had one in so long and decided I would make a breakfast sandwich for dinner, and an extra one for tomorrow morning.

I scrambled the eggs while standing barefoot in the kitchen, freezing from the icy tile under my feet. Goose bumps trickled down my arms. Quickly, I walked to my room and grabbed a sweater. I wasn't usually this cold and now I wondered if the chills had to do with some other underlying illness I may have now.

I was going to turn into a hypochondriac at this rate.

As the eggs cooked, I took out the necessary pills for the evening and placed them on the counter, then I took out the ones for the morning as well and placed them in a separate little bowl.

I was anxious about my appointment. With my Achilles injury, all I had to do was get out of bed the wrong way and I could pretty much snap it completely, but at least that was fixable. I had control of it, in a sense. But with the chronic illnesses I now faced, and all the family history I'd recently discovered, I had zero control over my body, and *that* terrified me. I wasn't in control of my thoughts anymore. They grabbed the reins and controlled me. Keeping my focus and emotions in place had been harder than I thought, and I was fighting blindly to take it back.

I wanted to call Avery and talk to her. I needed an outlet, and we'd always been each other's shoulder to lean on. No doubt she'd listen to me now—it was just who she was—but I still felt selfish for how I'd treated her when she'd wanted to come clean. I'd refused to allow her to and had shut her out for so long, yet here I was wanting to vent to her when I hadn't been there for her. She didn't deserve that. She didn't deserve to bear the burden of my thoughts and fears when I selfishly hadn't been there to hold hers.

I shook my head, disgusted with myself. I was a terrible person and regretted how I'd treated her. If I could go back and change how I'd behaved, I would.

Fifteen minutes later, I sat on a barstool with an egg and cheese sandwich piled high with bacon, slowly sautéed onions and garlic, and smashed avocado and lime. I took a bite and moaned. Thank goodness no one was around to hear the sounds coming out of me.

I took a few more bites, then I palmed my medicine and swallowed the handful of pills. I took another bite. And another. Halfway through I was full and wrapped what was left in foil.

I turned everything off and climbed into bed with my sweater still on. I was still too cold to take it off.

Exhaustion hit faster than I expected, my eyes heavy and trying to close. I yawned, pulling the blanket up to my chin and rolled onto my side. Now that I was sitting still for the first time today, my joints and muscles started to coil up and tighten. I swallowed, praying for sleep to take over so I didn't have to endure the pain I knew was about to hit any minute once my body had a chance to relax.

I bolted upright and ran to the bathroom in the dark. Before I could stop it, projectile vomit flew from my mouth and splattered on the floor just as I reached the toilet. Crashing to my knees, my hair fell around my face, shielding me in even more darkness. The putrid smell assaulted my senses as more bile climbed up the back of my throat. Blindly, I crawled to flip on the light switch. *Oh God.* My stomach twisted with knots as my body rejected more of what I'd eaten for dinner into the ceramic bowl.

I closed my eyes and tried not to breathe in the smell, knowing it would only make it worse. Little beads of sweat bubbled on my upper lip when more vomit came up. Leaning over, I grabbed the edge of the seat as I spewed, the tips of my hair falling inside the rim. My eyes widened. Tears were free falling from vomiting so hard and I panicked at how thoroughly grossed out I was at seeing my hair mixed in there.

After what felt like ten minutes of throwing up that ended with dry heaving, I was crouched on my knees holding my cramping stomach. Heat spread throughout my lower back and I winced in pain. Using the wall, I stood, wobbling on my knees and walked toward the shower. I pulled off my sweater, then grabbed my shirt and used it to wipe my mouth and face before discarding it to the floor along with the rest of my clothes.

I stepped under the spray and sighed from the heat of the scalding water when another surge of pain attacked my back. I cried out and braced myself, placing one hand to the tiles and the other on my back. I took deep breaths, panting heavily as I cursed everything I knew and prayed for the pain to stop.

Curled up in a ball, I was back in my bed with relentless shivering. I glanced at the clock and blinked. It was 3 a.m. Two more hours before the alarm would go off.

Tomorrow would be rough, but I'd endure it. I clenched my eyes shut. Tears seeped from the corners and I wept in silent agony as I fell asleep to the sound of my muffled cries and the throbbing pain beating on my back.

❦

"Coach?" I said, tapping lightly on his door. Kova was in the middle of paperwork or something. His hand was moving quickly over the paper he was scribbling on.

Kova glanced up and did a double take. He almost looked as bad as I felt, and for a brief moment, I wondered if he'd even gone home last night.

"Why are you here so early?"

"That's why I wanted to talk to you. Tomorrow I have an appointment to see my orthopedic doc. Now before you think—"

He looked down without letting me finish and started writing again. "I am already aware."

My stomach dropped and clenched. Kova's words were clipped with underlying aggravation. I hoped he wasn't upset with me.

"How'd you know?"

Such a stupid question when I already knew the answer.

"Your father."

"Oh, yeah. What did he say?"

He glanced up again, pinning me to the spot with a riled stare. I truly didn't think my dad would go against me like that, but now I wasn't so sure.

"You tell me, Adrianna. Is there something I should know?"

My jaw bobbed wordlessly. His brashness caught me off guard. "No, I just didn't want you to think I was trying to get out early or miss practice or anything, so I had my dad make sure everything was done in one day. That's why I came in early, so I could make up for time—obviously not the whole time because that wouldn't be possible—but as much as I can." I said the words so fast I didn't take a breath. His long, quiet stare provoked me. I propped my hands on my hips and said, "Well?"

"Well, what, Adrianna?" He enunciated each word with a bite.

I swallowed hard. "Is that okay with you?"

"Why would it not be? It would be unwise of me to say no. I may do questionable things at times, but I am not stupid enough to hinder your performance."

"But you're mad."

"No, I am not mad."

"You're mad at me?" I pressed, a little timid.

Kova was most definitely mad, I just didn't know why. His clipped tone was like little needles poking my skin.

His shoulders turned lax and his voice softened. "I could never be mad at you, Ria."

Ria. He only used Ria to get his point across.

I bobbed my head subtly and tried to fight the smile on my lips. I didn't want him to be mad at me. I wouldn't be able to handle that on top of everything else.

"Okay, well, I'm going to condition now."

I turned to leave when the sight of his sofa caught my eyes. I paused to stare at it, thinking about the night we'd spent tangled in each other's arms and the words Kova had said to me. Crazy how that felt like years ago when it had happened. My cheeks bloomed with heat remembering the positions we were in, how he'd added pressure to my throat at just the right time before I orgasmed…

"Is there something you *need?*" he asked, his voice taking on a huskier tone. I didn't miss the double meaning in his question.

I swallowed before replying. "No."

"I did not think so."

chapter 9

"**Y**OU LOOK TERRIBLE," KOVA SAID AN HOUR LATER.
I'd just finished conditioning and I was sweating profusely.
I shot a brief glance at my teammates, hoping they hadn't heard.
"Very…white," he added.

My nostrils flared, but I pretended his comment didn't bother me. Propping my hands on my hips, I shifted my gaze up to his.

"I think you mean pale. Sometimes your Russian gets the best of you," I said, and Holly chuckled.

Truth was, I was suffering inside. After I left his office, I climbed the rope ten times in pike position and did so many crunches I lost count, among other core workouts that left my muscles screaming in rebellion. That blooming pain in my lower back returned and it was all I could focus on for the last hour. It was growing stronger with each passing minute.

Kova didn't respond to me, but instead turned to the team. "Today we are doing jump conditioning, also known as plyos, which I am sure you know. It is used to increase speed strength. Your muscles will exert maximum force and you will thank me later for it."

Kova wore arrogance with pride. It worked for him.

"We are going to be doing quick switching of the feet, with bending and jumps. Lots of leg power here. Quick, quick, punch!"

Kova had us stand in a line on the floor with a folded mat that stood about ten inches tall in front of each of us. I jumped on and off, pin straight and as quickly as I could, making sure my body stayed tight.

"On and off the mat. You must jump way higher, quickly," Kova shouted. He was circling us like an animal eyeing its prey with his laser gaze trained on our feet. "Nice, extend those ankles and pop off. Off!"

I was afraid to extend too much in fear of worsening my injury.

"You can go a little lighter on your extension, Adrianna." I swear he'd read my mind. Strange. After a few minutes, he said, "Now do the same thing on one foot."

My thighs were on fire as we switched legs again and proceeded with the same technique. I looked at my teammates and we all wore the same pained expression.

"Okay. Enough. Get in line over here." He pointed to the white tape on the floor.

I stood with my hands on my hips and watched as Kova added two extra boxed mats that were waist high and chest high. I knew where he was going with this.

Kova instructed us to jump over the mats with our legs straight and tight together. Sounded simple enough, only it wasn't. Nothing that looked easy ever was, even if the floor had springs underneath and helped boost us.

One by one, we jumped over four spaced-out folded mats like we were little toothpicks bouncing around. As I neared the end, I dug deep and pulled my knees up to jump onto the taller boxed mat. Drawing in an audible breath, I shot up to reach the top of the last mat and crouched on it. *Finally!* Jumping down, I released a strenuous pant and got back in line, but not before I stole a quick glance at Kova to see if he'd caught how fatigued I was. His eyes were already on me.

"Extend, ladies. Reach and jump. Light and easy on your toes. This needs to be as clean as possible. If toddlers can do it at birthday parties, there is no reason you cannot."

I chuckled under my breath. World Cup hosted birthday parties like most gyms did. The youngest child he allowed for a party was four years old, and they weren't leaping over mats this high.

"Excellent, ladies. That is what I want to see."

We were all a little out of breath when we reached the sixth round. I looked at the clock and realized we had another two hours of this. I was already more winded than the rest of the girls.

A tickle in my dry throat caused me to cough. Covering my mouth, I fought back another cough as a choked, hoarse sound came from the back of my throat. Reagan watched me. Deep lines formed between her eyes like she was trying to figure something out, which only made me feel more insecure about my coughing fit. My stomach tightened as I fought a cough back again. I offered a smile like everything was okay and inhaled a deep breath and held it. Once I exhaled, I felt better.

"On the next set, squat and touch the floor with your hands on each jump. Like frog jumps over the mats."

Breathing through my nose, I watched Holly go first, then Reagan, then I went. I missed the last mat I had to jump on top of it, and tried again.

"Pull those knees up, Adrianna." My thighs were blazing hot and shaking. I almost kneed my mouth. "Good. Just like that," Kova added.

Since there were only a few of us, the sets went quickly, and each time it took longer and longer for me to catch my breath. I avoided Reagan's nosy eyes and looked ahead. Rubbing the side of my face into my bicep, I wiped away the sweat from my temples.

"Touch the floor, now jump! Again. Touch…touch…touch. Jump! That is it!"

I hopped over the mat to the next mat, overanalyzing over my reality. I was okay. I'd be okay.

Had I never worked out hard enough? I'd always used the extreme exhaustion I experienced as my motivation. Now that I knew about the kidney disease and lupus, it was my crutch, and I feared the possibility using it as an excuse to slow down. It would be so easy. But just like all those other times when I'd struggled, wrestling with my aching muscles and strength to keep going, I always got back up and pushed myself ten times harder.

I wondered if I was dealing with the repercussions of what I'd always done now.

Springing off the floor to the last box, I brought my knees up and crouched on top. I smiled a little to myself. It took a little more energy, but I did it.

My smile grew a little bigger. I just had to get my head clear, that's all I had to do. Then everything would be okay.

With the folded mats about seven feet across from each of us vertically, Kova said, "Large hop twice, front tuck onto mat, set. Turn around, hop off, front tuck. Let us go."

Taking a deep breath, I released it and got to work. Two hops and I was rotating forward into the air in a tight ball onto the mat. My feet punched the mat as I landed, and I stifled a low grunt in the back of my throat as pain shot up into my back. My body hardened, waiting for the pain to leave. When a gymnast performed a tumbling pass on the floor, the force of pressure was nine times greater than their weight. When doing conditioning skills like I was, the pressure was half that, but obviously enough to affect me.

I swallowed, almost afraid to land and exhaled through my nose, telling myself it would be okay. The thought of landing on my toes crossed my mind but I knew there was no way of getting it past Kova. He had eagle eyes and saw everything, which sometimes was a curse.

Blocking out the throbbing in my back, I traveled across the floor again, springing off my toes then front flipping to land flat on my feet. I held my breath and bared down, squeezing every muscle in my body. My abs were rock solid and burning from the stress of holding back the groaning pain.

On the next conditioning pass, this time, the pounding across my lower back intensified, and I clenched my eyes shut hard. My mouth fell open and I let out a gasp.

"I got this," I mumbled to myself.

There was no reason why I couldn't push past my thoughts or the pain and go on like I always had. I'd come this far not knowing I was sick. I had worked through the side effects the illnesses brought, on top of the Achilles injury, Kova's secret marriage, my torn friendship with Avery, my parents' impending divorce, and the discovery of my real mother. Even the sadistic camps I had endured. There was no reason not to continue just like I always had. If I got through all of that, I could get through anything. This was just another obstacle I had to overcome so I could move onto the next.

Only, it really wasn't. And that scared me. Because no matter how much I lied to myself, I still knew the truth and it messed with me.

I looked around. I needed to pull inspiration from my surroundings. I was grasping at straws, needing something, anything. My gaze skipped from each teammate until it landed on Kova.

I was already looking for him, but he always found me first. In this moment of self-doubt, with a sea of insecurities growing inside me with each breath I took, the pull was too strong to ignore. I could deny it all I wanted to, but the truth was, I needed Kova, and he knew that.

Chest rising and falling like there were resistance bands holding me back, every nerve in my body was reaching out for him to breathe life into me.

The pain taking over my body frightened me.

He could see that.

The gripping fear caged by my ribs consumed me.

He could see that too.

His eyes flickered with anguish and his body moved to take a step toward me, only for him to falter. Like it was in his nature to protect me.

My heart dropped.

I didn't want him to look at me like he had earlier. I didn't want him to think anything was wrong with me, because there wasn't. I was still the same old Adrianna, only now I came with a label.

No. Scratch that. I didn't want a label.

I didn't want to be known as *that sick girl*. Labels brought pity and sympathy and restraint from friends and loved ones. A label was a disappointment, and the thought of that was like a burning boulder in my gut. I couldn't bear it.

As much as I wanted to be wrapped in his arms, listening to his comforting words, I didn't want him to help me. I needed to do this for myself and prove that I could get past the mental block. I could do it, I knew I could.

"Stop daydreaming, Adrianna, and get your ass in gear."

I gave him a faux flat glare and playfully rolled my eyes. I knew he wasn't purposely trying to be a jerk. It was just his way of helping me, and I appreciated that.

Holly chuckled under her breath. Leaning into me, she whispered through a guiltless smile, "It's okay. We *all* daydream about him. Trust me."

I grinned. If she only knew.

I started up again. Each tuck I landed shot a new flame of pain up my back.

"Punch that ground, ladies. Stick that landing and make it tight," Kova said to all of us.

Another aching bolt shot through me the moment my feet hit the mat. I clenched my eyes shut for a split moment, forcing myself to block it out. And I went again.

"Quick! Quick! We want speed!"

"Yesss," he hissed happily. "Like that. Feet and knees together."

"A little cleaner, Reagan," he said. "You look like you are squatting to pee." Kova clapped obnoxiously. "We have five more rounds before we move on. Let us get it, girls!"

Bearing the pain, I bit the inside of my lip and completed the task. Five rounds felt like an eternity, but I smiled to myself, happy that I'd endured it.

We stood shoulder to shoulder waiting for our next assignment.

"Now we do handstand hops that we will add a back tuck to. What you are going to do is handstand onto the mat, whip your hips down and jump onto the floor, then onto the mat where you will jump backwards. When your feet hit the ground, whip them into another handstand. Let me show you."

Kova walked over to the mat and stood in front of it. He took his hat off and dropped it to the floor next to his feet. I rubbed my lower back with the heel of my hand trying to soothe the throbbing ache as I watched.

With his arms poised above his head, Kova flipped over into a handstand. His shirt fell down around his chest and revealed his toned, flat stomach with a peek of the rings tattoo. He snapped his hips down, feet pounding into the ground, then jumped right back onto the mat before jumping backwards into another handstand. At what I had to guess was two hundred and thirty pounds of solid muscle, the springs ricocheted loudly, and the vibration of the floor hit my feet. He did it twice, showing us exactly what we needed to do, and each time the fabric of his shirt bounced with him.

"Got it?" he asked us. We all nodded in unison. "Great. Get moving."

chapter 10

I STEPPED INTO A HANDSTAND AND KEPT MY PALMS FLAT ON THE MAT and my fingers spread wide.

I breathed in through my nose and whipped my hips down in a pike position.

"Snap your legs under faster, Adrianna."

I made sure to next time.

"Flatten those hips," Kova said to me. "Snap. Snap! Same for you, Holly."

I followed his instructions and pushed harder, shoving the increasing pain out of my mind. It only got worse with each hit into the floor. The more I did and the faster I went, the more lightheaded I became.

"Four more sets, then we are adding a back tuck."

I groaned inwardly. Adding a back tuck would make the skill more demanding on my body. It wasn't anything new to me. I'd done this set so many times I could do it in my sleep.

More importantly, I'd done this before I even knew I was sick. There was no reason why I couldn't do it now.

I bit down on my lip, angry that I'd let myself get so deep in my thoughts.

I snapped my hips down hard then popped right into a handstand. Repeat. I moved faster than I had before, driven by aggravation. I was so mad I could cry.

"Good, Adrianna. That is what I want to see. Holly, see if you can keep up with Adrianna. You too, Reagan. Make it a competition. Who could complete the last round the fastest—but safest?"

Once my last four sets were done, I stood with my hands on my hips in front of the mat out of breath while I waited on my teammates. Kova walked toward me.

"Nice job, Adrianna. Now add the tuck. Do it off the mat and set it," Kova said, and looked into my eyes.

I nodded, but my stomach plummeted to the ground. I hoped he didn't see my worries. Adding the tuck required additional force, which instantly said additional pain in my head. I had to whip harder and use more stomach muscles.

This should be fun.

On the first one, I saw stars. True, sparkly, silver stars floated in my vision. I knew seeing stars was a sign of dehydration. My mouth was dry, I just didn't think it was that bad. I slowed down on the second one to gain my stance correctly and glanced at the other girls. I rubbed my back again. They were moving so fast without pausing in between. Like little machines.

"What is wrong with you?" Kova asked me quietly in the middle of my handstand. I folded down and looked at him.

"What do you mean?" I asked, out of breath.

"For one, you keep rubbing your back."

"Oh." My jaw bobbed. "I think I just pulled a muscle or slept wrong or something." He gave me a pensive stare but I continued. "It's fine. I'm fine. Everything is fine. I plan to stop at the store after practice and get some of that Icy Hot stuff since I can't take Motrin. It should do the trick. I'm fine, though."

"You are *fine*," he said, his voice low, only for me to hear. And I knew what that meant.

I threw a smile at Kova, hoping he wouldn't say anything else.

"Come by my office before you leave today."

My smile faltered.

Fuck. My. Life. Damn it.

He knew. He had to know.

I nodded, then he turned to face all of us.

"I want twenty handstand tucks," he ordered. "Once you are finished with those, after you land the first back tuck"—he used his finger and drew an imaginary circle—"add one more back tuck, jump, jump to a handstand, whip down to the two tucks. I want twenty of these. Go."

Reagan and I glanced at each other. We both had the same thought: He was totally trying to kill us.

Or maybe just me. Maybe he knew I'd lied and the only way he could get revenge was through his lunatic training methods.

"Come on, girls! Get moving!" Kova yelled, clapping his hands loud enough to draw attention. "We have hours of work ahead of us! This is just a walk in the park for what I have planned."

Bringing my legs down, I snapped my hips and rebounded hard by punching my feet into the ground into a standing back tuck.

Searing heat reverberated across my back and I almost lost my footing. I gasped and palmed myself just below my ribs where it was nearly all-consuming and past the point of excruciating. I paused to arch my back, and inhaled through my nose. Bile tossed around in my stomach and I blinked rapidly a few times to get my head straight. I thought I was going to throw up. Eyes were on me, but not just any pair. I knew Kova was watching me without even looking at him. I could feel it.

I turned around and spotted him. He observed me again with his head tilted and stared deep in concentration. Kova was a perceptive man and that only raised my guard even more. The way his chin dipped lower and to the side caused a fluttering in my chest.

Pulling out my ponytail, I pretended I had to fix it. I shook out my chalky mop and flipped my head over to gather my hair, thankfully breaking the gaze. I stumbled for a second from dizziness, then I retied my thick locks into a messy ball. My shaky fingers sought the loose flyaways around the sides of my face and I brushed them back behind my ears.

"Kick those legs down hard, girls," Kova demanded.

I lifted my eyes to him and found his reflective gaze was still on me. Only this time, he was spinning his dumb wedding ring.

My back teeth ground together. That little act prompted a swift change to sweep through me. Like he was provoking me, trying to goad me to show him what I was capable of. I wasn't weak, and I needed to stop acting like every little thing affected me. Because it didn't.

I was annoyed with myself and said fuck everything. I let it all go, and began.

With each punch into the spring floor, I focused on the pain and told myself it wouldn't win.

With each backflip, I shoved the unbearable backache away.

Never in my life had I ever felt anything remotely like this.

I pushed harder, faster. My stomach was a sore mess and I could swear vertigo was on the horizon.

Still, I didn't stop. Not even when it felt like nails three inches thick were being hammered into my backside, I persevered.

I would not be held down. I refused.

I flipped and punched and hopped, chewing on the anger and spitting it out with each handstand tuck set I completed. I drove myself to move quicker, in spite of it all, while I whipped my hips and drove my feet into the ground, cursing the pulsating boulders that were attached to me. I resented myself for feeling this way, but I refused to allow my emotions to control my practice time anymore. I never had in the past, and I sure as hell wasn't going to start now.

Tears threatened to fill my eyes, and I thought I was for sure going to throw up from the sheer agony I was in. I wasn't sure how much more I could handle, but I wouldn't break without giving my all first.

Every second was pure torture, but I kept going…and going…and going. I wouldn't finish early. Not even when I added the extra back tuck and the fiery hot throb was all I could hear and feel and see.

Not today, kidneys. Not today.

Just maybe when I got home.

"Ah, Adrianna?"

Fuck. My hand was on the door ready to push it open. I was so close to leaving without having to talk to Kova.

All I wanted to do was go home and die.

"Yeah?" I said without turning around. I lowered my head and waited.

"I need to speak with you."

Shit.

I turned around to follow Kova, but he was already walking toward his office. Five minutes, I told myself. I would be in his office no more than five minutes, then I would leave.

He was seated on the front edge of his desk waiting for me when I stepped inside. Impassive, his face bore impatience. His arms were crossed in front of his chest, his beautiful biceps tight with irritation. I could feel his emotion without even touching him.

"Take a seat."

My eyes shifted between the chairs in front of him and the couch. I preferred not to sit on the couch for obvious reasons and salty memories, but I didn't want to sit in the chairs either. There would hardly be any breathing room between us.

So I sat on the sex couch.

I dropped my bag to the floor and plopped down very unladylike. I rested my head back on the cushion like I was at home and closed my eyes. I sighed as the little bit of energy I had floated away from me. It was my first time sitting for the day.

Yawning, I opened my eyes and looked at Kova. "What's up, Coach?"

"Rough workout?" One corner of his mouth tugged up.

"You could say that." My legs were so sore it took effort just to stand.

"So rough you forgot I wanted to speak to you, yes?"

I lowered my eyes. "I'm sorry. It won't happen again."

"What is on your mind?"

I looked up. His question was more intrusive than curious.

"Nothing. What do you mean?"

Kova stared at me. "Adrianna, I was not born yesterday, so do not take me for a fool. What is going on with you?"

Oh, God.

I sat up straighter. "Nothing is going on," I said. His jaw flexed but he remained silent. I tried to drive my answer home again, this time a little softer and more sincere. "Nothing is wrong with me, I just have a lot on my mind. That's all."

He pinched his bottom lip between his thumb and forefinger and turned his head to the side, then shook his head.

"*Chto-nepravil'no,*" he said under his breath. "*Chto-nepravil'no. Ya chuvstvuyu eto.*"

"What?"

"Something is not right. I can feel it." He paused. "You are lying to me."

I moved to stand. "Believe what you want, but that's the truth. Now if you'll excuse me, I need to leave."

"Sit down."

I didn't sit down. I toed the line. "I have a lot on my mind, okay? Think about when you were in my shoes and where your head was. How close you were to your damn goal and terrified that anything could go wrong at any given minute." I held my chest. "That's how I feel right now. We're so close to having it all. Don't tell me you were cool as a cucumber while under stress the entire time. You are not that perfect. No one is."

Kova's eyes widened and he stood.

"I almost ran to you today, Adrianna! In front of everyone!" he yelled. His voice echoed around the room and I reared back. "I saw the look on your face… in your eyes. I could feel it, feel you screaming for me to help you. Do you have any idea how hard it was for me to hold back? Any idea? What is going on with you and why will you not tell me?"

I glanced around in a panic. I was too ashamed to look him in the eyes.

"No one is here. Now, tell me what is wrong. Please. I cannot take it anymore."

chapter 11

MY CHEST ROSE AND FELL FAST. "NOTHING IS WRONG," I murmured. He leaned his head down toward mine. "You are lying to me." His voice was low and controlled. "You look sick, Adrianna. You are *pale*, you have dark circles under your eyes. Something is off. Give me your keys."

I scoffed. "We are not doing that again. And I could say the same for you, *Coach*. You look tired and have bags under your eyes. You haven't shaved in days and you're constantly lost in your thoughts. Most days you look absolutely miserable, but I don't push. I don't invade your personal space. I give you room to breathe."

"*I am miserable!* The only time I feel anything at all is when I am here, with you. And what I feel lately is detachment and sorrow. It is eating away at me." He shook his head. "You should push me, just like I push you. Outside these walls I feel numbness. I hate leaving here. You are the only light I have in my life, but right now, all I see is darkness in you and I do not like it."

My lips parted and my breathing deepened. He was getting too close to home and that terrified me. "Stop," I whispered. But he didn't. Kova stepped closer to me and I sucked in a breath. "Stop," I repeated.

"Sometimes we *need* people to push us, Adrianna. We want it. And I think you want me to push you. Just like I wish you would push me."

I shook my head and felt the tears climbing. He was right. I did want him to push me. I was unsteady, lost, scared. I needed someone to hold me.

I tried to step aside but Kova stopped me. "We were making progress, you and me. And then something changed in you and you woke up a different person."

"Yeah, I remembered you're married," I said defensively.

His vibrant green eyes darkened and his eyelids lowered to slits. Shifting on my feet, I deflected and glanced at the wall. That was a low blow. I didn't care that he was married. He knew that. His wedding band had never stopped me. It sure as hell had never stopped him either.

I turned and looked up at him. The turbulent look in his eyes pleaded with me to open up to him. "I'm sorry. My back hurts, okay? It's killing me and it's honestly the worst pain I've ever felt in my life. Since I can't take Motrin, I just have to deal with it. I thought that ointment shit would help it, so I was going to get it. That's all. Haven't you ever trained on a strained muscle? It's not that easy, you know."

Kova studied me. His eyes traced over my face, taking my features in. I stared back at him, hoping my words were enough to get him off me. It wasn't exactly a lie, but it wasn't the truth either. A pulled muscle didn't make someone this sick. It didn't cause persistent nausea or fever or dry mouth. A strained muscle didn't make me feel like I was actually dying. Or cause constant headaches. It wouldn't cause weakness everywhere.

"I know you are lying to me."

Letting go of my arm, he walked around his desk and opened one of the drawers. After shifting things around, he pulled out a tube of something and a box, then he was standing in front of me again.

I glanced down at the red, green, and white tube of ointment he was offering me. The box was the same thing, except they were in pad form.

"You just happen to have that in your desk?" I asked, my voice full of skepticism.

"Adrianna, I am a gymnastics coach. I am always prepared. I have a whole bunch of shit in that drawer. Take it."

I pursed my lips together and nodded my appreciation.

"Do you need me to apply it for you? I saw you grab your back a few times today. The gel may be hard for you to reach to rub in, but the medicated pads should be easy for you to apply. They just stick on."

"I think I can do it. Thanks, though."

I reached for the items, but he pulled them back. My eyes shot up.

"Let me do it for you, please. Let me help you."

There was nothing but genuine concern in his eyes. Sometimes I wish he wasn't so proactive about making sure I was okay.

A tired sigh rolled off my lips and I yawned. I just wanted to go home but I figured this might help get him off my case for a few days.

"I don't have anything to change into." Everything I had was damp with sweat from this morning's run. I refused to put that back on.

He shrugged like it wasn't an issue. "I will give you one of my shirts."

I frowned. "Do you happen to keep clothes here too?"

"Sometimes."

He was holding back. Now he wanted me to push. Whatever he wanted to say was on the tip of his tongue.

But I didn't…because I was scared to hear his answer.

"Will you let me help you?" he asked again.

I nodded. "Thank you," I said softly, and elation bloomed in his eyes.

"Let us go into the therapy room."

I glanced at his couch. "Can we just do it in here? That room is colder than an igloo."

He smiled, and I almost lost my breath. I hadn't seen Kova smile in what felt like ages and I missed it. I'd forgotten how much I loved seeing him like that.

"If you wish."

"I do."

He gestured with his hand. "Take a seat. Let me grab you a shirt."

I sat down and pulled at the straps of my leotard, sighing as I rolled the fabric down until it rested on my hips.

Kova glanced over his shoulder at me with a curious look on his face. His eyes dropped to my chest. I always wore a sports bra, so it was nothing he hadn't seen many times over.

"I love taking my leo off at the end of the day. It's like taking your bra off."

A chuckle rolled off his lips. "Well, I would not know how that feels, but I imagine good, yes?" He turned back to look through his things.

"It's sublime," I said. "The best feeling."

Kova pulled a duffle bag out of a drawer in his filing cabinet and ruffled through it. Without another word, he reached behind his head and cinched the fabric of his T-shirt in his hand and pulled it off. He shook his shirt out then handed it to me.

I looked away, but not before sneaking a peek of his abs. "Oh, no. I'm fine in my sports bra."

"Take it," he insisted.

"It's okay, really."

"Adrianna, take it." He waved the shirt in front of me.

I reached for it. "But what will you wear?" Slipping it over my head, I kept my arms under the shirt and removed my sports bra.

He shrugged like it was no big deal. "Nothing. I do not need a shirt."

Dropping my bra to the couch, I said, "But you can't go home without one."

He pulled back. His face twisted. "Why not? It is my home."

"Won't your wife say something?"

He gave me a dry, unamused look. I almost laughed at his expression. "Adrianna, please. You should know by now she will not say a damn word to me."

I always wondered why that was.

"She probably will not be home when I get home anyway."

He stared into my eyes, silently begging me to push. This was the second time he'd coaxed me to ask questions.

"How should we do this?" I ignored his unspoken request.

"Just turn around to face the couch and lean over. It will not take long. Just a few minutes."

Kova sat down behind me and lifted the back of the shirt. I gathered it in the front and held it just under my breastbone. Crossing my legs, I leaned into the couch and rested my head on the cushion in the corner of the couch.

"Point to your area of pain," he said, and I did. "Hmm. I thought it was much lower." His voice was full of concern.

"What do you mean?"

"Usually back pain is down here," he said, and dragged his finger just above my butt. "Not high up by your ribs."

"I probably didn't stretch out enough. I told you I could've slept wrong too. I'm just a little sore."

Kova didn't respond. I couldn't see what he was doing, but I could hear him rubbing the gel between his hands right before he applied it. His cool palms touched my back and he began massaging the peppermint scented stuff onto me.

I closed my eyes. I could fall asleep like this. The touch of his hands felt divine as he applied pressure to the sore points in my back.

"This feels amazing." I wasn't lying. It actually felt like it was starting to help. I'd feared the worst earlier, but maybe it truly was a pulled muscle or something.

"It should start to work pretty quickly. What did the pain feel like?"

"Just constant throbbing, but unlike anything I've ever felt before. I thought I was going to die when we were doing the tucks every time my feet hit the ground. It was taking my breath away and making me feel sick."

"You should have said something."

"It's nothing I can't handle."

After another minute or so, Kova pulled his hands away. "Okay. We are finished. This should work for a while. After you shower tonight, stick the pad where your back is hurting. It will be much easier than rubbing the gel on."

I protested. "No," I groaned, dragging the word out. I reached blindly behind me for Kova's hand. "That feels so good. Don't tell me it's over."

Kova chuckled and placed his hand in mine. My shoulders relaxed when his fingers wrapped around mine and I nestled further into his couch.

"It is. Unless you have any other areas of pain, you are free to go."

I should've gotten up and left. Instead, I placed his hand on my shoulder then tapped the top of his hand.

"Please, don't stop," I said, my face all but mushed into his couch. I smiled lazily. Kova laughed and obliged, but seconds later, his concern returned.

"You are all knotted up."

I grunted when he pushed on the curve of my shoulder. "I told you I slept wrong."

"If you want me to massage you, let us go into the therapy room where you can lay out. I have your table in there and I can give you a full massage. You need it."

"If I get up, I'm going home. I'm too tired for anything else. Plus, I'm really comfy right here. I like this couch." I made a little sound under my breath and wiggled for him to keep going.

Kova sighed. "I will never understand why I put up with your little demands the way I do," he said, but I could hear the smile and amusement in his voice, and that made me feel good.

"Because you love—"

chapter 12

I FROZE.

My eyes flew open.

Fuck.

Fuck.

Fuck!

How could I be so stupid!

His fingers tensed. A solemn pause. I could feel the tension and electricity in the air, and the deep pull of oxygen into his lungs like it was my own. Sixty seconds of dead silence passed. My heart was going five hundred miles an hour.

Trembling to the bone, I sat up and rolled his shirt down. "I have to go." My voice came out shaky, but I didn't care. "I have to go. I have to go. I need to go." I kept repeating.

I was definitely going to be sick now. I leaned on the side of the couch to push myself up, but I wasn't quick enough.

Kova grabbed my hips. "Wait."

My entire body shook. Goddamn it! I couldn't believe I'd said what I did. "No, I need to go."

I pulled away and slipped out of his grasp, but he grabbed me again and pulled me toward him.

"Adrianna, please, just wait."

The urgency in his voice did not go unnoticed. It was getting harder to breathe. My throat was closing up. How could I have been so stupid? Kova didn't love me. He didn't love anyone but himself.

"Why must you make me get rough with you?"

With one firm tug, he pulled back and I fell into his chest. A lungful of air gushed from me. Automatically I tried to spring forward and reach for the couch as leverage to pull myself away.

Embarrassment flooded me. I had to get out, but Kova refused and wrapped both his arms around me until I was securely in his lap. He enveloped me completely and brought his face to the curve of my neck.

My arms were stuck to my sides, my chest rising and falling fast. The warmth of his skin and the comfort of his body ignited my own. I struggled against his hold, but his thumbs began a soothing rub on my hip and shoulder while his fingers gripped me for dear life. The steady rhythm of Russian whispers against my ear calmed my rattled nerves.

"Kova…" My voice shook. "I didn't mean what I said. I didn't mean it."

"Ria." I squeezed my eyes shut.

"Please. I want to leave." And roll off a steep cliff and die.

But he surprised me. "Do you remember the first time I called you *malysh?*"

Flustered, my eyes bounced around the room. I swallowed as I thought back to that day shortly after I started training at World Cup.

"Yes." My answer came out in a broken whisper. "We were standing right outside your office in the hallway. You laid into me afterwards."

Kova tightened his embrace. "You had already begun to affect me." His breath tickled my skin. "I could not stop what I already felt for you and it fucked with my head every day, because every day my need for you grew. Calling you *malysh* felt so natural that it just slipped out. I was shocked and could not believe I'd said it, especially in public. I knew I had to fix it, even if you did not know the meaning, and what I said after came out harsher than I meant it to, but that was because I was so upset with myself for slipping."

"I'd always wondered why that happened, why you called me *malysh*, I mean."

"Truthfully," he said, "I could not believe it even came out of my mouth. I am always so controlled, meticulous with everything I do, but there has been something about you since day one that threw everything off balance for me. I am reckless when it comes to you. I do not think but instead move on feeling. I know when you need me, and I know when you are looking for me. Me and you… What you make me feel… What we have, it is maddening. Do not deny that it is not the same for you."

The same for me.

"You're one hundred percent right," I whispered, terrified to open up to him. Yet, the tension loosened from my limbs and I relaxed under his hold. I nestled into Kova's chest and brought my knees up, and he hugged me.

"So, *malysh*," he said, his voice thick with raw emotion. "You can see why I understand how that came out naturally for you, as it did for me. I want you to finish that sentence."

I turned my head to the side in shock and glanced up. Kova gave me a daring look. Our faces were so close. This man was certifiable. No chance in hell was I finishing my sentence.

"No."

"Finish it," he demanded. His heady stare pierced my heart.

I shook my head vehemently. "I can't."

"I will never understand why I put up with your little demands the way I do…" he repeated, initiating our conversation from just before.

I shook my head again. My heart raced so fast that every time I took a deep breath, Kova's forearm rose with my chest.

"Please don't," I said. My cheeks felt like they were swelling from the heat that had crept under my skin. If I said it, then it took us a step further. I wasn't sure if I could handle that.

"*Pozhaluysta*," he said, and for once, I knew the meaning. *Please.*

"Why?" I asked.

"For reasons I cannot explain." He waited a few seconds, then said, "Why do I put up with your little demands?"

The same reason I put up with his, and he knew it.

I licked my lips nervously and found the courage I needed to get the words out. "Because…" I stammered. "Because…you…love me."

Kova's eyes flashed with emotion that took my breath away. His lips parted just subtly.

"Again," he rasped. Now it was his turn to breathe deeply. We moved together.

"Because you love me," I said softly.

Kova leaned down and slowly bridged the distance between our lips. I held my breath as he grew closer, until he gave me the softest kiss imaginable.

He hovered above me, the tangible air thick with unspoken words that would never see the light of day. They'd stay between us. He panted as he pressed his lips against mine. Even the simplest action made the world fade away, allowing the true chemistry between us to grow even more. When it was just me and Kova and not the outside world to influence us, he put himself out there to show me who he was. Even if it was just a simple look, the embrace of his arms, an action that expressed his secrets, I *saw* him, and I *understood* him. Just like he understood me. Saying he loved me was the equivalent to *malysh* for him.

Kova broke the kiss but he didn't pull away. Damn his eyes and the way he looked at me. The smoldering heat split my heart open.

"I should go," I whispered.

"No, stay." He pressed his fingers down into me. "We do not have to talk anymore, but at least let me work those knots out for you. You will sleep better because of it."

God, the urgency in his voice and the look of dread in his eyes were hard for me to deny. I had to wonder if admitting his love for me was as intimidating for him as it was for me.

"Okay."

"*Spasibo*," he said. "Let me do it right. I will go grab the salve from the other room. Take the shirt off and lay on your stomach. I will be right back."

Kova released me and I stood up. I watched him leave his office, his gait marked with determination, his shoulders reminiscent of a tiger.

I did as he asked, then held his shirt to my chest, questioning myself as to why I was staying in the first place. Leaving would be the wisest decision.

Lying face down on his couch, I sighed at the softness and realized just how tired I really was. I folded my arms and pulled them up to my ribs. Kova was back in a few short minutes. He positioned himself behind me, squatting with one knee on each side without lowering his weight.

The moment his hands touched my shoulders, my eyes closed. A heavenly breath rolled off my lips from the blissful touch of his skilled fingers. He knew exactly how to target the tension and knead it away precisely.

"We should do these more often," he suggested.

"I'll make sure to pencil you in." I joked. "I hardly have time to shower, you know." The thought of finding time for a massage was tiring in itself.

"The life of an athlete."

"Tell me about it."

Kova dug deep and pressed hard and I moaned from the pressure. I loved it so much.

"There is a lot of tension. Let me know if I am hurting you."

"You're not. I like it harder…" I hummed in pleasure. "It feels good. Like when you press slow but deep, it feels the best."

Kova's hands paused, and it caught my attention. I felt the telltale signs of concealed laughter.

"What?" I asked, trying to peer over my shoulder.

He stifled a chuckle. "You say my Russian is showing, but sometimes you do not even realize what you say."

I thought about what I'd said, and how it could be taken any other way when it finally hit me. Fuuucccckkkk. Talk about delayed reaction. God, I was so stupid today.

"Oh, hell." I laughed, mortified. I covered my face. *I like it harder…it feels good.* "I wasn't thinking."

"Obviously. Anything that is innocently spoken to a man is never taken that way at first. Remember that."

"Believe me, I will now."

The quiet solitude of the room ensued, and I smiled to myself, happy that my plans for the night changed. I knew the moment I walked into my empty condo I would break down and cry myself to sleep. I'd felt it during practice and I almost looked forward to it. But now I felt lighter, more optimistic. My chest didn't hurt, and I could breathe a little easier. I didn't feel like crying anymore, and I was so happy about that. I hated crying.

I felt like Kova had worked out my issues without even knowing he did.

Days like this got to me. Days when Kova knew what I needed without me having to say anything. When he saw the underlying issue, could feel it trying to burst from me, and then took measures into his own hands to help me. There'd been countless times this had happened. When he saw what I needed when no one else had, and he gave it to me fully.

To live in this outrageous, intense and hectic world of elite gymnastics, everyone needed a lifeline. Someone they could hang on to when times were tough, when life felt all-consuming or the future seemed bleak, they could see the crash coming before anyone else and be there. We all had that one go-to person who we relied on when nothing made sense to anyone except them. Who accepted all our flaws and imperfections.

Kova was my lifeline whether I wanted to admit it or not. I didn't want to drown. I wanted to stay afloat, and he was my ultimate salvation. I clung to him.

He was controlling, but I was selfish. Had I ever once given him what he needed? Even once?

I didn't want to think about my answer.

I opened my eyes, tired and a little disoriented. Yawning, I glanced around the dim room trying to figure out where I was and why I was so stiff.

Across from me, Kova was asleep in his leather desk chair. His legs were spread wide with one leg straight and the other bent, his jaw was propped up on his fist, and still only in his netted shorts and nothing else. I watched him for a few moments, quietly taking him in. My gaze dipping to each feature of his handsome face when I noticed the tension knitted between his blackish brows. Unforgiving lines pulled at the corners of his eyes, his thick lashes laying in half moon crescents on his cheeks. Even while he slept, he had something on his mind.

Kova stirred, his eyes moving beneath his lids. He drew in a deep breath and exhaled. He must've felt me staring at him.

"Hey," I said. He gave me a lazy smile that was so damn hot. "I can't believe I fell asleep. You should've woken me up."

"You looked like you needed the rest. I did not want to wake you."

Early morning sleepy voice was sexy on Kova.

"But don't you need to go home?"

"Do not concern yourself with that. You looked like you were struggling yesterday with something. I wanted to be there for you, even if it was just for you to sleep."

I frowned, half grateful, half confused. What kind of wife was Katja for not tracking her husband down, let alone letting him sleep somewhere else? It made no sense to me.

"What time is it?" I asked.

Kova glanced at his wrist. I had the sudden urge to go to him and sit on his lap. I wanted to burrow myself into his warmth, feel our bare chests pressed together, and go back to sleep.

"It is almost five," he said.

Reaching above his head, he stretched his arms behind him. The Olympic rings tattoo I loved so much on his ribs contracted with each pull and shift of his fit body. He watched me watch him. I didn't think I'd ever grow tired of staring at him.

"How does your back feel?"

I thought about the agony I was in yesterday and if I felt the same this morning. I offered him a small smile. "It's okay. Not nearly as bad as before."

My bladder was about to burst as I sat up. "I need to get going... I have my appointment today that I can't be late for." I yawned again. "I can't believe how long I slept. I feel like I could sleep until tomorrow."

Kova nodded and stood, the cracking of his knees echoed throughout his office. He turned around and laced his fingers together behind his head and stretched once more. I lusted after his muscular back as it flexed with power, then I dropped my gaze to the two little dimples above his butt. Konstantin Kournakova was a walking, breathing Russian god. The urge to wrap myself around him was even stronger now, but I glanced away and slipped his shirt on.

"It's freezing in here. Aren't you cold?"

"No," he said through light laughter. "You do not know cold until you have been to Russia. It is bitter there."

A tired smile formed on my face. He was probably right. "Do you miss it?"

"Miss what?"

"Russia."

Looking into my eyes, he contemplated his answer. "Yes. I have not been back in a very long time. I would love to go back sometime in the near future, just not to live."

"Why not to live?" I asked, curious.

He rolled his bottom lip between his teeth before answering me. "There is nothing there for me anymore. Everything I want is right here."

My stomach sank to the floor, a sign to get moving.

Gymnastics. Katja. Me. Possibly in that order.

I felt like this was another one of those push questions, and I wasn't up for that, just like I hadn't been earlier. There were too many likelihoods and not enough energy left to handle them.

He must've sensed my indecision, because he continued.

"Let me rephrase. Everything I want is right here in this room."

All the air left my lungs. I blinked a few times then stood up with my duffle bag in hand. I shot a quick prayer up to God to slow down my pounding heart.

"I'll see you tomorrow. Thank you for everything," I said, and added a small smile to seal my words.

He nodded. "Hang on. Let me give you something."

My forehead furrowed in wonder as I watched Kova unlock his filing cabinet and reach all the way to the back behind all the folders.

My lips parted over what he produced.

"Read it later."

chapter 13

OUR NOTEBOOK.
     I'd forgotten all about it, but then it dawned on me. I walked over to him.

"Wait. Where did you get this? Last I remembered, I put it in my nightstand."

He relocked the cabinet and handed it to me. "I noticed it when I was at your place on my birthday. You did not seem too keen on giving it back to me any time soon, so I took it. I had some things I needed to get off of my chest."

I glanced down at the notebook, wondering what he'd written and when he'd done it. What he needed to get out.

"I don't even remember the last thing I wrote in this."

Kova grinned and his eyes flashed with amusement. "It was…colorful to say the least." His smile grew. "Go back and read it when you get a moment. I did not expect those words to come from your lips, that is for sure. Cannot say I did not deserve them either. I quite liked that side of you."

Oh man. My mind raced back to when I last had it in my possession and what the hell I wrote. I flipped the pages open but Kova stopped me.

He was right, I had to go. Nodding, I said, "I'll talk to you after my appointment?"

His head tilted to the side. Kova regarded me. I could hardly see the brilliant emerald color of his eyes. Finally, he nodded.

Clutching the spiral notebook to my chest, I readjusted the strap of my duffle bag, gripping it tight in my hand. I left his office and threw the bag and notebook in the back seat of my truck. I couldn't wait to see what he wrote.

Late into the afternoon, I sat on the patient table listening to the doctor go over my results from the ultrasound she'd just done on my Achilles.

By some miracle, and much to my surprise, I hadn't had any new tears, just the same micro-tears as before that were a little deeper, along with some inflammation. I couldn't believe it. I thought for sure I'd torn it.

"You seem shocked," the doctor said.

"That's because I am. I thought I'd torn something more, or worse. It was really bad. I could hardly walk. I was prepared to put up a fight."

"Well, you aren't far from tearing your Achilles completely. All that tightness and burning you feel is due to overuse, which is completely normal for an athlete of your stature given the sport you play. Once the season is over, I highly suggest we schedule surgery to repair the tears and give your injury the proper time to heal. I don't see you lasting another season with this. It's better to repair it while we can, which means less healing time if you tear it completely."

I sat staring unblinking at the doctor. After this season, after the Olympics, if I made it that far, I was supposed to start dialysis. Somehow I needed to fit college into the mix too. I could feel the blood draining from my face, feel the cold seeping into my bones at what my future held. I didn't like it.

The doctor regarded me. "Is everything okay?"

My jaw bobbed. "Ah, yeah, it's fine. I just recently discovered I'll need dialysis after the season too, and I was thinking about how I'm supposed to fit in a surgery on top of that now. Eventually I'm going to need a transplant down the line," I said. Lines formed between her eyes. "I have stage four kidney disease."

This time the doctor's brows rose to her hairline and her eyes widened. "You have stage four kidney disease, and you're still competing?" I nodded and she whistled under her breath. "I wouldn't worry yourself about how you'll be able to fit it all in. Given the declining state of your health, I'd meet with your team of doctors and devise a plan. It's manageable."

My shoulders sagged. Relief coursed through me and I smiled. "Thank you."

"If you're not on dialysis yet, are you on medication? Steroids?"

"Oh, yes. I take a lot of pills a day just to get through it."

I reached into my purse and pulled out the notecard listing my medications. I handed it to the doctor and her eyes scanned over it. Dad had said the doctor might ask what I was taking and to bring the paper instead of having to carry the bottles. It was a good idea.

"Do you have an infection? You're on a few antibiotics."

I nodded. "I have a kidney infection. A bad one I was told." I blinked when it hit me. My jaw fell open. "I'm so stupid! I've had terrible pain in my back to the point that I've been sick to my stomach. I completely forgot I have a kidney infection. I thought it was a side effect of the medications or lack of appetite

I've had." I shook my head to myself, feeling so dumb that I forgot about this. "I can't believe I forgot," I said out loud.

"It's natural for something to slip your mind given your situation, especially in your position. Don't beat yourself up over it. That being said, I would highly suggest you be in constant contact with your specialist and let the doctor know of the pain you're dealing with. If you're on medication, the infection should've started to clear up by now. Also, you can't take steroids a week before any platelet injection, should you need another, so we'll have to plan for that. You're on a few right now."

My teeth worried my bottom lip. I hadn't thought of that and now I felt even more stupid for not thinking about it beforehand. I just knew not to take the anti-inflammatory medications.

I was in over my head.

The doctor suggested I continue the blading sessions with Kova as needed, and the typical ice therapy I dreaded. She reminded me to stay away from Motrin, and I promised to make an appointment once the season was over should everything continue the way it was.

Easy-peasy.

Once I was back in my truck, I dialed up Dad to tell him about the pain in my kidneys and how bad it's been. I had promised him not to leave anything out. He called Dr. Kozol on another line while I waited. After three minutes, he came back and told me to go see him immediately.

An hour later I was sitting in front of the doctor. A kindness surrounded him that was very welcoming and made me feel at ease. I'd already given a urine sample, had blood drawn, and had a new ultrasound done on my kidneys right when I came in. The technician took photos and measured the size of my kidneys and heart. I watched the screen as she moved the wand around, trying to see anything but all I saw were black and white masses everywhere that ballooned and then shrunk. I had no idea what I was looking at.

Dr. Kozol reviewed the tests, then he got right to the point.

"Adrianna. Tell me what's been going on and don't leave a thing out."

I smiled and eyed the folder in his hand, then proceeded to tell him everything—how I've been feeling since I left his office a few weeks ago, how I threw up, how terrible my back has been, the headaches and chest pain, and the fatigue that made me feel like a ninety-year-old brittle woman. I told him I thought the medicine was giving me the shakes and I had nights when I slept like the dead and other nights where my eyes twitched from lack of sleep.

"I bet it's been a rough few weeks for you... A rough couple of months, hasn't it?"

I laughed lightly. "Yeah, you could say that."

"How are you handling everything?"

I shrugged. "Honestly, I don't talk about it. I just keep it to myself. It's easier that way."

His head angled to the side and he eyed me. "It's also very unhealthy to bottle your emotions in."

"I train close to fifty hours a week with tons of conditioning. It helps."

"Are you taking any other medications I'm not aware of? Any over-the-counter or prescriptions? Anti-inflammatory?"

I shook my head and explained I couldn't take them anymore due to my Achilles and the blading. He eyed my leg.

"You're almost eighteen and you're falling apart."

This time I let out a deep belly laugh. "Tell me about it," I said, and smiled.

Dr. Kozol placed the folder on the counter and then turned to wash his hands. "Right now, your immune system is weak, which means your body is a free-for-all. Not getting the proper rest your body needs will set you back, which it's clearly doing." He dried his hands off and pulled on a pair of latex gloves. "While there are preventative measures we can take to help reduce your flare ups and discomfort, ultimately, you'll need more intensive treatment. Your urine results show a slight increase in protein, but nothing I'm too concerned about yet." He pulled the stethoscope from around his neck and put the buds into his ears. "Take a deep breath." He moved the instrument. "Another," he said, listening to my chest. He pulled away and looked at me. "Lupus is a workaholic. It can cause headaches and weight loss, sometimes a low-grade fever. Joint pain. Pretty much what you're experiencing now. But coupled with the kidney disease, I need to be aware of everything you're dealing with at all times. Even if you think it's small, it could mean more to me. I wish you'd contacted me earlier about the kidney infection. The ultrasound shows small stones, which is why you're experiencing the pain you are." He listened to my back. "Take a deep breath... Another... Another." He leaned in, his brows bunching together. "Do it one more time for me." He paused. "Again?"

"Kidney stones?" I replied quietly.

"They're small and easily passable, but large enough to cause pain. Manageable, too, so nothing to worry about. Up your water intake and I'll give you something for the pain that will help break them down."

Dr. Kozol pulled away and placed the stethoscope around his neck.

"Is something wrong?" I asked.

"You mentioned chest pain, which I'm sure at one point you probably figured was from overexerting yourself at practice." Of course I had. I nodded.

"Lupus causes inflammation around your lungs, but right now, I can hear the faint sound of fluid grating around them."

My eyes widened. Kidney stones. More protein in my urine. Fluid in my lungs. This had to be a cruel joke. How many more shitty hands could I be dealt? Of course I'd get the highflyer of autoimmunes. That was just my life.

"I have pneumonia?"

"No. Sometimes fluid will build up between your lungs and your chest. It's called pleural effusion and typically goes away on its own."

I exhaled a heavy breath, feeling my heart picking up speed. I was panicking on the inside but trying to remain calm as Dr. Kozol continued to speak.

"It's not bad, but it's something we have to watch since I can hear it. We'll switch your medicine around and up your dose. At any time your chest hurts, you need to take a seat and breathe. You're pushing too hard, Adrianna. I'd order bed rest, but something tells me you wouldn't take the advice."

"Why do I feel a *but* coming?" I said.

Dr. Kozol's lips flattened. He eyed me carefully, and I took a deep breath.

"Your father said you'll start dialysis after this gymnastics season is over. I'm highly against that, as you know. A waiver had to be signed saying you're forgoing recommended medical treatment. There's too much risk involved, especially since we haven't been able to find a donor match yet."

I perked up. "A donor match? Wait a minute. Who was tested?" I didn't know anything about that.

Dr. Kozol picked up my file and scanned a few papers. He looked at me. "Your brother and biological mother. Neither one was a match. Your father is expected to be tested soon."

chapter 14

I LISTENED TO MY BODY—AND DOCTOR—AND TOOK ONE DAY OFF.
I'd called Kova after I left the doctor's office and told him the tears
were deeper but not completely torn. I'd also told him how my back was
still hurting and I wanted to rest it. Much to my surprise, he was quick to oblige.
He also said I only get one day and expected to see me first thing the following
morning. I laughed. Typical Kova, but I was cool with that.

Since I had stayed home, I took one of the pain pills before I fell asleep.
I woke up feeling so much better. It was like I had a brand new body and I
loved it. I slept nearly the entire day, only waking up to eat and take my medicine before falling asleep again. I'd been exhausted, not realizing how badly
my body needed the rest. It was a blessing in disguise, really, because it pre-
vented me from overthinking the fact that I'd yet to find a match for a kidney.

I also took the time to write in the notebook Kova and I shared. I'd
planned on rereading what I had written, along with Kova's responses, but decided I wouldn't. I didn't want to relive the past I held so much hostility for,
and since we were in a fairly good place, I didn't see the point in welcoming
those areas of negativity back into my life. All it would do is awaken old emotions I had put to rest. So I took the pages and bound them together tightly
with packaging tape. They'd have to be cut along the seams in order to be
read. Then I flipped to a new page and wrote him an honest note I'd give him
the next day.

*I wish I knew why I'm slowly giving you another chance and letting you back
in. All I know is this hatred was hardening my heart and would continue to take
up every last inch of space the longer I went on if I didn't let it go. I realized it's not
healthy, and I can't afford anything less right now.*

*I don't think you're a bad person. I just think you made questionable choices
with the intent of meaning well only for them to backfire on you. You're a double-edged sword.*

I just wish I knew why I want to be around you all the time.

I wish I could understand why I look for you when I'm alone.

I can't explain this feeling in my heart that only you give me. I probably sound so stupid and young, but I don't feel this for anyone.

Please, I'm asking you to not ever hurt me again. That brokenness I lived through was caused by you, and yet you're the one who's slowly placing the pieces back where they belong. I know you're trying, but so am I.

I walked into the café room the following day and went straight to the refrigerator for the plastic bag I'd brought with me this morning. My lunch was safe for my kidneys, and I had packed wheatgrass juice to drink to help break down the kidney stones.

I sat down and untied the plastic bag then grimaced when I looked inside. My red apple tumbled out and onto the floor as I shoved the bag away in annoyance. I dropped my head into my hands. I didn't have an appetite. I didn't want to eat. And I most definitely wasn't in the mood for this food.

I lifted my head and shivered, then remembered Kova had a hoodie in his office. I also realized this was the perfect time to place the notebook in his desk under the guise of getting his jacket.

My bare feet were ice cold against the tile as I stood and walked to grab the spiral bound book out of my duffle bag. I then made my way down the hall to Kova's office and pushed the door open. His scent permeated the room and I inhaled the dark cinnamon and citrusy tobacco smell. Sunshine flowed through the blinds as I walked around his desk. Bending down, I pulled open his bottom drawer and shoved the book under a bunch of files, making sure it was covered before closing the drawer.

I reached for the hoodie on the back of his chair and slipped it on, then left his office.

"What are you doing in my husband's office?"

"Oh!" I jumped and grabbed my chest. "Katja. I didn't see you there. You startled me. Hi."

She tilted her head and wore a superior expression on her face I pretended not to notice. Her eyes raked down my body then back up to mine. "And why are you wearing his jacket?" She scowled.

My chin bobbed, unprepared for her brash tone. I looked down. This definitely didn't look good, but it didn't look bad either. I tried to think of something quick to defuse her attitude. Kova's *jsah-hket*, as Katja had pronounced it, was nearly down to my knees and keeping me warm. I wasn't taking it off just because she stood in front of me.

"Ah, I was just—"

"I see you located my sweater, Adrianna. Good."

My eyes widened and locked with Katja's. She straightened, her back stiff as a board and shoulders pushed back.

I looked past her to see Kova striding toward us. I was stuck in my stance when I caught the go-with-it stare in his eyes.

"I did. Thank you," I responded softly, unsure where this was going. He stopped when he reached his wife's side and placed his hand on her lower back.

"Allo, Katja." He didn't smile.

She openly glared at him. "Konstantin. Why is she wearing your clothes?" she asked, flipping up her palm, fingers pointing toward me like little sharp knives.

I looked at him, waiting to hear his response myself.

"Adrianna was not feeling well and said she was cold. She was ill a few days ago, so I told her to grab my sweater and take a rest in the therapy room."

Interesting.

"Why not send her home if she is sick?" she asked. Her voice was high and pitchy, and flat out annoying. "She will contaminate everyone else, including you. And you know I cannot get sick right now."

I wasn't a walking disease, for fuck's sake.

Okay. Technically speaking I was, but they didn't know that. And I wasn't contagious.

Kova cocked his head to the side. His expression, the look in his eyes, it screamed common sense. I chewed back my smirk and eyed the floor. I knew that look and I almost felt bad for her.

"We have a very important week ahead of us, which I have mentioned to you. She has no time to rest."

I looked back up as Katja placed her hand over her heart. The glittering diamond was bigger than her knuckle. I wanted to bend that finger backwards.

"But what about me? About what we talked about?"

"What about you?" he retorted.

She glanced at me with bitterness in her steel gaze. My brows angled toward each other with deep creases.

"This is not what we agreed upon," Katja said, then looked at me again like she was trying to say something without saying it. Her gaze followed mine and she noticed I was back to staring at her enormous wedding ring and band.

I quickly glanced away, but it was too late. It wasn't even that nice. Just a dumb circle and thin band.

The air between all three of us thickened to an awkward silence. I was the third wheel. Hitching my thumb up, I took one step backward and said, "I'm going to go rest now…"

They both looked at me. I turned away. Katja's glare left me with an unsettling feeling and I didn't like it one bit.

"Ah, Adrianna?"

I stopped and looked over my shoulder. "Yes?"

"No more than an hour."

Damn it. "Yes, Coach."

I knew Kova was just trying to look out for me and I appreciated that, but Christ on a stick, I was going to die of hypothermia in the therapy room before kidney disease.

A little dramatic, but I really hated being cold. I despised it more than anything.

Curled up in a tight ball under Kova's *jsah-hket*, my teeth chattered while I counted down the seconds until my sentence was up. My toes were frozen solid and the only thing that gave me any kind of alleviation was the husky scent of Kova's smell imbedded into the fibers of his hoodie. I burrowed myself into his sweater.

I didn't last the full hour. Between the sterile room and the clipped Russian language that carried down the hall, I needed to get out of there and back into the gym.

I returned to the café to clean up what I'd left out on the table before making my way to the locker room. I took off Kova's sweater and folded it up, then placed it in my bag. There was no way I was knocking on his office door to return it now. Not since Kova and Katja had been going at it ever since they'd walked into his office. They seemed like they were at war with each other. At least that's what I'd gathered. Neither one was backing down. While Katja's voice rose and fell, Kova's stayed on the opposite spectrum.

I took a step to leave the locker room and hesitated at the sound of Kova's unrestrained voice. I held my breath and waited another beat longer until I thought the coast was clear.

I should've just hidden out.

A loud slap echoed down the hallway. I sucked in a breath and pressed my back to the wall, debating whether or not I should run for it. I assumed Kova had been slapped across the face. I didn't want to be there when it was all over.

Expelling a nervous breath, I made up my mind to run back into the gym when a shrill of Russian words sounded the same time the door flew open.

Jesus Christ, my heart. My back stiffened, feet rooted in place as Katja stormed out of the office. The door slammed into the wall behind her and bounced off. She halted to a standstill in her high heels when she saw me.

Our eyes locked. She looked downright murderous. My heart rate escalated to an unhealthy rate, pounding so viciously I could hear it in my ears. Her stunning, ethereal face contorted into a fury of abhorrence, twisting into something I never expected her to look like. She scowled down her nose at me before spewing something in Russian and marching off.

It all happened so fast.

I tried to replay the words in my head so I could look them up later, but my brain couldn't process them at the rate she had said them. Shed spoken too quickly. I don't think she even took a breath. It was like one giant run-on squeaky Russian sentence.

I watched in silence as she stormed out of the building. A muffled sound behind me drew my attention, and I glanced over my shoulder.

Kova stood stretching his jaw, cupping one side while he rubbed it. I caught sight of the red handprint on his skin.

Our eyes met and I was caught off guard by his reaction. He looked... sad, and it confused me. I felt pity looking at him when he didn't deserve pity.

Without thinking, I walked over to where he stood and gently dragged my knuckles down the side she'd slapped.

"I'm sorry," I said quietly.

His eyes softened. I thought he'd be angry that I heard and saw what I had, but he didn't appear that way at all.

Kova reached for my hand, his warm fingers pressing into my cold palm. My stomach dipped as he pulled me closer until we were just a few inches apart. He looked deep into my eyes.

For a moment we were suspended in time, forgetting where we were or that anyone could see us. I took note that this wasn't the first time this had happened. It'd been happening more so lately and neither one of us seemed to care. We were getting too comfortable and becoming reckless.

Kova brought my knuckles to his lips and gently kissed them. I swallowed hard, fighting to tear my gaze from his. My fingers curled around his before he dropped our hands.

"Trouble in paradise?" I asked, my tone good-natured.

And just like that, his shoulders relaxed and he fell into stride next to me.

"I probably deserved it," he said.

I nodded in agreement, and he chuckled.

Quietly, just for him to hear, I said, "I put the notebook in your desk under a bunch of green folders."

I looked up waiting for him to respond. Instead, he dipped his head once and I caught the faintest hint of a smile.

"Kova?" I said as we rounded the corner.

"Hmm…"

"Why'd you lie for me?"

Kova paused at the door to the gym and angled his body toward me. "Sometimes, Adrianna, we do things not for ourselves, but out of need for others."

chapter 15

WITH WIDE EYES, I LOOKED ALL AROUND ME.

There were photographers everywhere and not an empty seat in the house. Chaos and coaches. Gymnasts and anxiety.

Kova squatted in front of me, the black material of his dress pants stretched over his knees. I looked at his opened palm.

"Give it to me," he insisted under his breath. I handed him my sports tape. "What is wrong with you? Why are your hands shaking?"

I glanced at my fingers. I'd been tempted a few times now to skip the medicine, but after being on it for a few weeks, I was too scared of the repercussions I'd face if I did. I didn't want to mess with it, but the trembling had gotten so bad over the last week and it was starting to drive me nuts. My entire body felt like it was on edge, uncontrollable shaking down to the bone. I learned it was a side effect of the steroids and there was nothing I could do about it unless I called my doctor and asked for something else. I hadn't. Instead, I attempted to adapt to it and tried to regulate it the best I could, balancing myself by taking deep breaths, and flexing my hands and making sure I kept moving.

"Answer me," he demanded, his eyes shooting all around us.

"Nothing… I'm just nervous."

He paused before tearing off a strip of tape with his teeth. "Anything else?" he asked, lifting his eyes to look at me. Kova was acting strange.

"N-no," I said. "This is just a big meet and I'm honestly a ball of nerves, Coach. I'm nervous."

It wasn't a far stretch from the truth. I *was* nervous. The medications were kicking in and making me a little jittery on top of the meet stress. Unfortunately, they weren't helping with the fatigue. I was already drained. We'd traveled across the country for this one. The National Championships was a two-day meet where the best of the best gymnasts around the world competed, not to mention the Olympic team coaches were in attendance too. Next up if I got lucky was Worlds.

Kova's eyes softened. Maybe it was all in my head. He applied the tape then ripped off another piece. "I understand. Just remember you are here because of the work you put in. You proved that you are worth it, that you can handle the pressure. You are now considered a valuable piece to the Olympic team. You have what it takes and deserve to be here."

I gave him an appreciative smile. "You're just trying to make me feel better."

"Whatever it takes, Adrianna. But you should know by now that I do not speak bullshit."

I chuckled. "I do not speak bullshit," I said in a low faux Russian accent. The corner of his mouth curved up and a sense of ease rolled over me.

"How does that feel?" he asked.

I flexed my foot and moved it around. "Good."

"What about here?" he asked and placed a hand to my calf. "We have not done blading in some time."

"I haven't really needed it, but it feels good. Thanks."

Kova stood and held his hand out. I took it and readjusted my leotard, pulling it to cover my butt. I glanced around the stadium once more, trying to see if I could spot my dad.

"Do you want to know where he is?" Kova asked.

I glanced at him. "How did you know I was looking for him?"

"Wild guess."

I knew it was against the rules to see or talk to family before a meet, but something inside my heart was reaching for the kind of comfort only a parent could give. With everything I was going through, I'd been more emotional lately. Sometimes a girl just needed her dad.

I chewed my lip and nodded my head. Kova turned around and pointed. My eyes searched as quickly as my heart beat for the familiar face.

It didn't take long. He was already waving before my eyes landed on him. Our eyes met and happiness burst through me. I smiled from ear to ear, waving frantically. I hadn't seen my dad in months, but I felt like I'd grown closer to him despite the distance between us.

"Thank you," I said softly. "I'm surprised you let me say hi." It wasn't meant maliciously, but honestly, and he knew that.

He shrugged one shoulder. "I just want you to be mentally prepared for today and tomorrow, and if saying good day to your father is necessary for that, then sometimes rules are meant to be broken."

We broke the rules every chance we got.

"Good day?" I laughed, and smiled. "See? You need to work on your English. No one says that. You sound like you're from the Stone Age."

"I say it." He played back. "And I am not old."

I was still smiling. "You're insufferable. At thirty-four, you're kinda old."

One brow peaked. "Kind of old?"

"When you start growing grays, isn't that when you're considered old?"

His brows shot up to his hairline. "I have grays?" He patted his head.

I stifled a chuckle and tried not to smile. "I saw one the other day."

"One?" His eyes twinkled with amusement. "How close to my head were you to see one lone hair?"

I bit down on my lip and propped my hands on my hips. "I saw it, okay?"

"If I have gray hair, it is because of you, you know."

"Right," I said, drawing the word out through a smile from ear to ear. "You should start looking into dyes. After one, they start growing like weeds."

"Adrianna," he warned, and I burst out laughing at his tone. "You need to understand now that I will never dye my hair."

This was too much fun. "I can dye it for you."

"You will not."

"I'll get you to drink a lot of vodka one night. You won't be able to say no."

"I already feel like that with you," he admitted, this time seriously. "I find it harder and harder to say no to you."

A shy smile tugged at my lips that grew into a full blown one. My cheeks heated. I liked this easy back and forth with Kova.

"So that's a yes? Cool. I'll start researching dyes for men, and while I'm at it, I'll look for hair regrowth."

Propping his hands on his hips, he smirked. "Nice try, but I am telling you right now that it will never happen. I do not need to color my hair to look young. You make me feel young, and that is all that matters."

Kova reached out but quickly pulled back. Recognition dawned in his eyes. Sometimes when it was just us being normal and playing around, we tended to forget the outside world. I felt his pull, his playful need to wrap his arms around me and tug me to him. I needed that too. My emotions had been an array of sadness and fear, and something as little as this interaction gave me life and a reprieve from my thoughts. People usually took the big moments in life as what spoke volumes, but for me, it was the little things.

"Thanks," I said softly. I brushed back a few strands of loose hair behind my ear. "For this." He knew what I meant without having to say it.

Kova nodded, regarding me with a heartfelt look in his eyes. The way my pulse beat for him wasn't normal. The way he looked at me wasn't normal. And what I felt deep in my bones for him most definitely wasn't normal.

"Okay." He clapped his hands. "Chalk up and let us get going, yes?"

I turned to walk away, feeling so much lighter on my toes.

"Adrianna?"

I looked at him over my shoulder.

"It is nice to see you smile again. Oh, and when you get a private moment, check your duffle bag." He gave me a knowing look.

The notebook.

I could feel a flutter of the wing that had been clipped desperately trying to fly. Kova didn't know it, but he was breathing life back into me. Each day he helped me find my inner strength so I could grow strong enough to hold myself up again.

What scared me about that was I had a feeling he was going to be the only one who would help me get there.

This time I gave him a real smile that showed exactly what I felt in my heart. And I didn't give a shit if anyone saw.

"Okay," Kova said, rubbing my shoulders a few hours later. He bent down to look me in the eyes and said, "Two events down, two to go. You ready?"

I nodded. I was more than ready. I had this. After two rotations, I was in first place with just four-tenths of a point separating me from second. Anything could happen from here until the last event, but I had a good feeling about it. A really good feeling.

Those two events were my best ones—vault and bars. I stuck both dismounts and received almost maximum points for my routines.

"It is like gravity does not apply to you. You flowed more smoothly on bars than I have ever seen you do before and with height that made even my heart drop. Your lines could not have been more perfect. Let us do the same for beam."

The only event I was truly worried about was beam because of how jittery I already was. It was subtle, but enough to throw me off balance. My bones shook, muscles rattled, and I didn't like it. I couldn't feel it on the other events, but I had a feeling I would on beam.

Kova grabbed my hands in his. He glanced down. "You are still shaking," he said more to himself.

I tightened my fingers around his. "I'll be fine," I said. "Just nerves." The flash of a camera caught my eyes and I pulled my hands from his.

"Nerves are a good thing if you channel them properly. Focus and control."

I nodded and applied powder to my feet and hands, then to my inner thighs. I stood to the side, letting the judges know I was ready. When they gave me the green light, I saluted first then stepped onto the memory foam mat and walked up to the balance beam and faced it.

Exhaling a calm breath, my hands hovered over the four-inch piece of wood and shook a little. Clearing my mind of everything except this moment and what I was about to try and attain, I mellowed my soul and mounted the beam.

I finished eighty seconds later, both feet stuck together with a small hop that would cost me. But I felt good. Really, really good that as I walked off the podium, I went straight into Kova's arms.

We broke apart and walked toward my chair. I was breathing heavier than normal and my chest was a little tight. I rubbed the ache, thankful the pain in my back from the kidney infection had reduced to a dull throb.

"I wobbled on my turns."

"You still finished with an unparalleled amount of ease."

I glanced up at him. "I had two balance checks, *Coach*..."

"Everyone does," he said. "Just little things we will work on before Worlds." Worlds.

I nodded and took a few sips of water then dropped the bottle back into my bag. I stood up and adjusted the sleeves of my all black leotard that had an enormous amount of peridot rhinestones. It'd been my favorite to wear to date, and the colors were finally a good match for my auburn hair.

My knee bobbed.

"What's taking so long?" I said just for him to hear.

I took a deep breath again to regain my poise, hoping I would catch my breath too. Kova glanced at me, his brows bunched together, but I averted my gaze quickly and acted normal. I had a gut feeling the wobble would knock me down to second place. Or maybe the hop would. Or something they saw that I didn't feel. Maybe it was all three.

"Patience is a virtue."

I scoffed. "I hate that saying."

"Does not matter that you slipped up. You still had the highest amount of difficulty in your—"

I looked up to see what had interrupted him and followed his gaze. Chills wracked down my arms.

My score posted.

The only deduction I received had to be for the balance checks because my score wasn't far from the max. In fact, it was almost too good to be true for an event that was considered my weakest.

I stood in disbelief. Kova, on the other hand, was losing it.

He turned toward me and grabbed my shoulders. "You do not give yourself enough credit," he said, his voice much higher than usual. I gazed into his lively eyes. "Well, say something!"

"I... I'm speechless." I really was. "How the hell did I pull that off?"

Kova let out a loud good-natured laugh. "I knew you could do it! When you place your focus properly, you dig deep to do whatever it takes to get you there. I see it every time when you compete." He pulled me in for a bear hug. "I am so damn proud of you," he said then pulled back and grabbed my shoulders again and gave me a little shake.

A bashful smile splayed across my face. It wasn't over, but I could breathe a little easier knowing I only had floor left.

"Give yourself a pat on the back."

I literally patted my shoulder, and Kova smiled at me with more pride in his eyes than I'd ever seen before.

I was going to rock my floor routine.

chapter 16

"HOW DOES IT FEEL TO COME IN FIRST PLACE?" DAD ASKED, HIS voice full of cheer.

It'd been a couple of hours since we got back to the hotel room and the disbelief still hadn't worn off. Dad hadn't stopped smiling. Seeing my final score left me stunned with too many feelings to sift through. It was overwhelming in the greatest way. Today was my best meet to date, but it also required the most energy from me. Now my body was settling, and my muscles were crunching up into tight coils.

I couldn't believe I finished in first in prelims on the first day of nationals. On the airplane to the meet, I'd read a few articles that predicted I had a chance of finishing in the top three. The pros expected Sloan to take it because she was that good and finished in first place nine times out of ten. But I took it, while she fell to third.

I glanced at my dad, who was still smiling.

"I'm happy, but this is a really big meet. I still have another day, you know? I don't want to get ahead of myself, so I'm trying to remain calm and collected but prepare for the worst."

Today was surreal, but tomorrow was a new day with new possibilities. I could fall to third, and Sloan could take first. Anything was possible.

Dad's eyes glistened with pride. "My daughter is going to the Olympics." He took a sip from his crystal tumbler and grinned behind it.

I rolled my eyes and a little chuckle escaped me. "Don't get ahead of yourself. I'm not going to the Olympics just yet. There's still tomorrow, and then another competition after this. It really comes down to the committee and whether they think I can handle it or not."

"You're going all the way. I can feel it. Mark my words."

"I'm glad you can."

He tilted his head and a puzzled look crossed his face. "You don't?"

I glanced over his shoulder at the sheer curtains that hung from the ceiling to the floor in the penthouse suite of his hotel room. They reminded me of my current status: a foggy future that will be hard to wade through.

Anxiety filled my chest and a level of dejection settled in me. My life would forever have some sort of barrier to work through. Learning a new neck-breaking skill at practice didn't seem so terrifying anymore. Tomorrow seemed scary. Next week, next month, a year from now, it seemed impossible.

"I have hope."

"Okay." My dad placed his glass down and leveled a stare at me. "What's on your mind? You hardly ate dinner, and now you *have hope?* That's not you. Talk to me, sweetheart."

I squeezed my eyes tight, then I opened up about my insecurities.

"Today wore me out, both physically and mentally. I can barely keep my eyes open right now, and tomorrow is going to be even more exhausting. I ache *everywhere*," I said. "My bones actually hurt. It was hard today, Dad. Really hard. I was running on adrenaline and stubbornness but now I feel like I'm about to crash any second. I'm fighting it, honestly. Monday's practice will leave me crawling. Tuesday will be a fight to get out of bed. Wednesday will make me want to give up. It's been like this for months now and I never knew. I'm wondering when it'll all catch up to me—because it will. I selfishly ignored the signs for so long when I should've addressed them. Now they're stronger than me and pulling me down because I can't stop thinking about them. I pushed myself, which I can keep doing just like I've always done, but I'm worried I'm going to make everything worse and work against myself to the point that if I actually get hand-picked for the Olympic team I physically won't be able to make it."

He regarded me with sympathy. Softly, he said, "You mean the kidney disease and lupus? I never would've guessed it's even been on your mind. You hold yourself together so well."

I nodded faintly. One corner of my mouth tugged miserably to the side. Even when I was sleeping it was on my mind because I'd wake thinking about it. I couldn't escape the way it was suffocating me.

"Today made me realize just how big this battle is. I don't want to make myself any sicker," I said quietly. "But I'm terrified I will with the way I keep pushing my body. That's why I don't want to get my hopes up."

"Listen, I've done some research and spoke to a couple of people. While there hasn't been a whole lot of athletes who've gone to the Olympics with an autoimmune disease *and* kidney disease, there have been a few with one or the other. With the right attitude and team of doctors, it can be done. You have both. You just have to have faith. Think positive and remember it can always be worse. Yes, the signs were there, but anyone would've mistaken them for over-training. Don't beat yourself up over that. Try not to think about the things that can possibly hold you back, but look forward to this life you have and how lucky you are to have gotten this far when others haven't."

I finally looked at him. My emotions steadily climbed behind my eyes as I listened to his encouragement.

"There are so many more struggles now. So many more risks I'm taking that can hold me back. I'm worried I won't get there even if I have the aptitude. Like it's so close, but this fear, this voice in my head telling me it's hopeless and I won't make it because no matter how hard I fight I won't have the strength to keep going. It's so loud and always there. I hate it."

"You're the only one who thinks that way. You do have what it takes, you just can't see it yet because this is still very fresh for you, for us."

Harsh lines creased between my eyes. "What do you mean I'm the only one who thinks that way?"

Dad observed me for a long moment, unblinking. The silence grew thicker, dread curled its way into my stomach, one hefty bag of coal at a time.

No.

He wouldn't.

"Dad," I said, rattled. I sat up straighter. "Dad, you promised—"

He waved his hand through the air. "I just meant you're too deep in your head and reading too many what-ifs online. You put too much pressure on yourself and start thinking the worst. That's all."

"I had to read about the diseases so I could understand them."

I read all the good and the bad, even though it reduced me to ugly tears at times. Some of it was downright disheartening, but I couldn't live in denial. Being practical was smart. I needed to know. *I had to.* So I lost myself in article after article until I fell asleep most nights. It bothered me that he couldn't see it from my point of view and respect the fact I was studying up on it. I thought he, more than anyone, would want me to be informed.

His familiar eyes softened. "Your body is already used to this type of strenuous activity, sweetie, and has been for quite some time now. Nothing has changed except for up here," he said and tapped the side of his head.

I bit down on the inside of my lip and chewed it. I leaned back again as tears filled my eyes. "I'm not a mental case." My voice shook. "I'm just nervous."

"I never said you were. You're stressing yourself out when you have everything under control. Don't let yourself fall down a dark hole. It's not healthy."

A tear slid down my cheek. I wiped it away with the back of my hand.

"You have to keep your head up. Never look at the ground when you're walking. Your dreams, your views, your goals, all your aspirations, they'll come to a standstill because there's nothing to reach for when you're closed off. Instead, look forward with optimism and prospect. The path is wide open for you to take what you want." He paused like he was thinking about his next words. "Sweetheart, there's always going to be a mountain you'll want to move that'll make you question everything in you. You'll ask yourself how you can do it. That's how life works. And right now, you have it a little harder than others because you're surrounded by mountains with no view of the sky. Do me a favor."

I nodded, wiping more tears away and sniffled.

"Don't focus on the struggle of moving them because that's not what it's about it. It's about how much you put in when you decide it's your time. You can't move a mountain, and you certainly don't go around it. You climb that sucker and show yourself what you're capable of."

I burst into uncontrollable tears, my eyes heavy with strain and exhaustion.

Dad got off his chair and kneeled in front of me. He grabbed my hands and forced me to look at him. "Some days you're going to get knocked down. And you know what?"

"What?" I asked, my voice cracking. I attempted to sniffle back the tears but it didn't help.

"That's when you get back up and keep going to show yourself what you can do. I know it might sound impossible right now, but the battle will make it all worth it. One day you'll see."

He reached over to the table and plucked a few tissues from the box and handed them to me.

Between tearful breaths, I said, "I feel like I don't have the proper equipment to climb a jagged mountain in the dark."

I was surprised I came up with a good analogy to match his on the fly.

"You've always had it. You just lost your footing along the way. Look at it like you sprained your ankle."

I smiled through the tears. "Like little tears in my Achilles."

Dad pointed his index finger at me and gave me a look. I sniffled but my sad smile grew. "We get one life, Adrianna. You have to live it to the fullest and not let anything hold you back. I always thought I was until what happened at Easter. That day put things into perspective for me. I changed a lot after it, and very late into my life. I don't want you to have regrets and what-ifs plague you for the rest of *your* life. Be something now. And do it for you and no one else. Have no fear. Don't rest until you're about to drop."

I inhaled an audible breath, then exhaled the burden of the world I was carrying on my shoulders. A few more tears slipped down my cheeks. Talking to my dad was helping me cope with my thoughts. My chest didn't feel as constricted and I felt hopeful I could possibly take the reins of my life.

It wasn't that I didn't have the confidence, I did, but something shifted in me since I'd been diagnosed. I felt different. I felt like the world viewed me differently, like I was walking around with a stupid label. I felt like my time here had come to an end before I got to experience anything.

I lifted my eyes toward the ceiling and blinked a few times before responding. "My body is going to do what it wants whether I like it or not. On top of that, I've yet to find a match for a donor. That terrifies me and I think what stresses me out the most. What if I never find one?" My jaw trembled as I said it out loud for the first time. "I want it all so bad, Dad, so bad, and I don't want anything to hold me back. I'm scared knowing I have absolutely no control over that aspect of my life now. None. "

Dad glanced away, trying to hide his face falling, but I caught it. "That fear is normal for every single person in your shoes. Just don't let it scare you into a corner. Control isn't something I let go of so easily either. I'm a work in progress. It's probably a Rossi thing. Your brother is the same way. You'll get there. Just don't give up."

A smile spread across my face. Dad reached for me and pulled me into a hug. The comfort of his fatherly embrace eased my soul.

Maybe everything would be okay. Knowing that no amount of treatment could reverse the damage is what disturbed me daily. Knowing it could only grow worse from here on out is what taunted me.

I needed to find a way to accept that. I just hadn't figured out how yet.

"Am I making a huge mistake postponing the dialysis? Do you think I'm going to make myself sicker? Do you think I'll die sooner because of it?" My heart was frantic in my chest thinking I'd made a huge mistake.

My dad shook his head. "No, I don't think you're going to die because of it, don't ever say that. But you know where I stand on the issue. I'd rather you start treatment now, but after speaking in depth with your doctors, I understand that waiting a few months should be okay. That doesn't mean I don't think about it every day, because I do. I worry all the time, and if I thought for a second waiting would take you from me, then I would've put my foot down and pulled you immediately. You're going to have a lot of hurdles. I want you to have what you want while you can get it." Dad exhaled a heavy breath himself. "You've got this," he said, his voice thick with emotion. "You've got this, okay?"

I nodded and sniffled again as a knock sounded at the door.

"Who's that?"

Dad stood, his knees cracking. "I invited Konstantin and Katja for a drink."

Icy cold blasted through me at the mention of Katja. My heart sank. I hadn't even known she was here.

"Oh, that was nice of you."

His brows wrinkled. "Is that okay? You look pale."

I forced a smile. "Oh, of course it's okay. I just don't want anyone to see me crying and then ask why, you know? Once I get past the next few months with Worlds and the Trials, if I make it, then we'll tell people. Until then, no one. I'll get cleaned up while you let them in."

I quickly made my way to the bathroom and shut the door. Turning on the faucet, I didn't let it warm before I cupped the cold water and splashed it on my face. The last time I saw Katja, she'd given me dirty looks and mouthed off to me in Russian. I may not speak her language, but it didn't take a genius to see she clearly had an issue with me.

I frowned as I splashed more water on my face. I really didn't want to be in her presence right now. What would I even say with the three of them talking? Maybe I could excuse myself and go to bed early.

I patted my face with a towel, then leaned on the counter and stared at my reflection. I dabbed the puffy, dark circles under my eyes with my ring finger wishing I had some dumb cream my mom—Joy—insisted I use. My nose was red from crying, and my chapped lips were a little swollen too. I needed makeup…and about seventeen hours of sleep.

When I moved into the two-room suite earlier, I'd unpacked to prepare for tomorrow so I wasn't frantically looking for things at the last minute. Typically, gymnasts weren't allowed to stay with family during a meet, only afterward, but Dad had insisted I stay with him, stating Kova had approved it. I was secretly relived. Being the only gymnast at this meet from World Cup, I was glad to not be alone where I could stew on my thoughts.

I grabbed my Louis Vuitton makeup bag and applied just enough makeup until I looked halfway decent. I threw my hair up into a messy bun then glanced down at my attire. Yoga pants and an oversized sweater would have to do. I wasn't trying to impress anyone, anyway.

Expelling a heavy breath, I opened the door and smiled, preparing for an exhausting night.

chapter 17

KOVA WAS NOT HIS USUAL MEET SELF ON THE SECOND DAY, AND I
didn't like that one bit.

I fed off his energy. He gave me strength. Didn't he know that
by now? He was what I needed to thrive. I was nothing in this sport without
him. Nothing.

I had woken up feeling extremely emotional this morning. I hated when
this happened, when these deep feelings hit, or when the littlest thing made me
want to shed a bucket of tears. It wasn't often, but a few times a year I found
myself more sensitive than usual, like I was due for a good purge to cleanse myself. I could definitely use one now, considering all things.

Sometimes being a girl sucked.

But Kova was broody and moody and walking around with a perpetual
scowl since we got to the meet.

This wasn't him. He needed to get his shit together.

Last night after two hours of sitting in the same room with Dad, Kova,
and Katja, I excused myself and went to bed. I'd sat with them, but mostly kept
to myself reading a book on the chaise lounge. My eyes were on and off rolling
shut and I couldn't take another minute. When the hardcover fell on my face and
scared five years off my life, I knew I had to lay down or I wouldn't be fresh for
today. They'd understood and wished me a good night, except for Katja. It wasn't
like I'd participated in their conversation—I had no idea what they even talked
about—but last night I got the memo quite clear. Girls always knew when another girl didn't like them, and for whatever reason, Katja seriously disliked me.

I glanced at Kova and watched him. Creases lined his forehead as he shot
brief looks in my direction every few minutes. It made me wonder what he was
thinking about, if it was about me, because every time our eyes met, I got the
vibe his thoughts were of me.

That's it. I was going to ask him.

I sat on the floor with my duffle between my folded legs and rummaged through it for my tape and grips.

"Coach?" I said, and Kova looked at me. "Can you tape my wrists?"

He nodded without hesitation and squatted in front of me on one knee.

"Are you okay?" I asked only for his ears.

He nodded and wrapped the white tape around my wrist. "Yes. Why do you ask?"

"Because your mood is bothering me. You're not acting like you usually do when we're at meets together. I need the old Kova right now, more than ever."

He lifted his eyes but not his head. "What do you mean?"

"You're walking around like you're mad at the world. I don't like it. Did I do something wrong?"

"I am not mad."

"Then can you act a little more—"

"Adrianna, I am not mad. Okay? I just want today to be perfect for you. That is all."

I shut my mouth for a minute and watched as he wrapped my other wrist.

"Kova," I said, hoping he'd see I was serious. For the first time in a while, I was going to open up and tell him how I felt.

I dug deep for the bravado I needed to get my next few words out.

"I feed off your energy. *You* give me strength, and I need *you*. I feel like I'm nothing in this sport without you, but seeing you like this… It's messing with me. So, get whatever you have going on in your head straight and give me back my Coach Kova. Please." I paused, then added. "I need you, I need Coach Kova. I can't do this without him."

Ripping the last piece of tape with his teeth, he placed the roll back into my bag and stared at my hands. He picked up the cotton wristbands and slid one on to each wrist without a word. Tension rose in me like the building of a bass chorus.

I held my stomach in. My lungs felt constricted. I'd skipped all my medications this morning hoping the shaking would subside for the day, but my entire body trembled from head to toe. Kova noticed and took my hands in to his, comforting me.

He released a deep sigh and finally lifted his eyes to meet mine. A shadow of remorse cast in his gaze. Closing his eyes, he opened them to reveal his real emotion I was not privy to often. His steel green eyes pierced my heart and caused my lips to part.

"Did you read what I wrote you?"

I nodded and smiled timidly. I'd thought about talking to him about what he said, but I'd yet to bring it up.

Stop with the Coach bullshit.

I had laughed and turned the page, unprepared for his next entry.

When I saw you again after so many years had passed, I did not think you would become this important to me. I did not think you would be on my mind all the time, or that I would want so many things with you that I have never thought to have with anyone else. But you have, and now I cannot imagine you not here in my life. I will never hurt you again. You have my word. Hurting you inflicts pain upon me.

I'd tentatively turned the page again.

I have been thinking of calling you krasivaya instead of malysh. It suits you better.

I eyed him, and whispered, "I like *krasivaya.*"

If I didn't know Kova, or if I wasn't sitting so close to him, I would've missed the slight curl to the corners of his lips.

He shook his head, then looked down before meeting my gaze again. "I am so fucking proud of you and what you have become. I just want you to succeed. It is all that is on my mind. I promise. You have worked so hard to be here. I want today, the end result, to be everything you dreamed of. I apologize for making you feel any sort of way. I never meant to. I guess you can say I am stressed too."

My chest tightened. "Do you think yesterday was just pure luck and I can't place like that again?"

Kova pulled back, slighted by my words. "What? Why would you think that? Of course not. You know that."

I shrugged, then flinched when a photographer took a picture of us. The flash was nearly blinding and left stars dancing in my vision.

"I don't know. All I know is I don't like your energy right now. It's putting thoughts into my head and they're not good. I wasn't lying when I said I feed off you." I prepared to open up even more to him, show him I was being serious. "Some days when I'm really down and not feeling like myself, all I have to do is look for you and suddenly everything snaps back into place. I can't explain it, and I know this might sound cheesy, but you give me life. When I'm feeling weak and incapable or second-guessing myself, you breathe energy into me without even knowing it." I leaned forward and lowered my voice to almost a whisper. "But today, I don't see *my* Kova, the one who gives me strength. I see someone who is deep in his thoughts and confused and bitter."

His eyes glistened like my words were ones he longed to hear. Like they meant something to him. He was quiet for a moment.

"If I am being honest," he said lightly, his Adam's apple bobbing, "I had a very long night and did not sleep. There is nothing else on my mind but sleep, and you coming out on top. I promise, Ria. I just want the world to see what you are made of."

Ria. I knew the impact that nickname held.

One corner of my mouth tugged to the side. I felt a little shy now. "You and me both. My dad snores. Even with the door shut it's like a freight train coming through the room. At least you don't snore. I sleep like the dead when I'm with you."

My eyes widened, my cheeks blushing with embarrassment. Kova's head dropped and his back vibrated with silent laughter.

"You cannot say those things here, Adrianna." He looked up, his eyes flashing with amusement.

"I didn't mean to! It just came out." My voice was a high whisper.

"Come," he said, and stood with a grin. Kova placed his hand out and I took it. "Let us get going."

"Yes, let us." I mocked playfully.

He pulled me in for a side hug and glanced down. A real smile reached his eyes and his unspoken words poured out. I felt them. I saw them, and I let them comfort me.

"You only have floor left. You got this," Kova said bent over as he rubbed my upper arms.

I nodded frantically. My eyes lifted toward the scoreboard again but Kova stopped me.

"No. Only look into my eyes. Do not let the number throw you off. You hit bars, beam was rock solid, and vault is behind you. Now I want you to go out on floor and have fun out there. Be yourself and let your love for the sport shine."

I didn't have to look to know I was insanely close to dropping to second place, but I liked the reminder of knowing what I was up against. I was only 1.4 points away from slipping and I was a giant ball of nerves from it. The judges had been relentless today and stingy with the scores.

"Okay," I said.

I tightened my ponytail, then stepped onto the podium and made my way to the blue carpeted spring floor.

Within minutes I saluted the judges and took my position. The chime sounded before the music started, letting me know I was about to start.

A symphony of instruments echoed throughout the stadium and I knew all eyes were on me. Confidence radiated from me and I fell into pace with the music, knowing my personalized routine had to be in sync with the rhythm and beat or else I would face deductions. My routine was required to match the melody. The string of the violin shadowed the pounding keys of the piano, but it was the delicate harp that carried my heart as I floated across the floor from corner to corner in a series of dance skills and requirements.

With my first two tumbling passes completed, I stepped into the corner for my third pass. I brought my arms down and released a tight breath, then I started running. Halfway across the floor, I hurdled into a round-off, back hand-spring, double layout, and rebounded into a half-turn, wolf leap that we'd added into my routine for bonus points a few months ago. It was just one of the many revisions we'd made to my routine to up the difficulty. All my routines had been slightly modified for bonus skills, but the only way to receive the extra value was to execute it a specific way.

Only this time, I had so much power and momentum that I stepped out of bounds.

Fuck!

Recovering quickly, I sashayed across the floor, leaping and twisting along the way, flipping into handstands and practiced ballet skills until I reached the corner.

I've got this. Taking one last deep breath, I visualized my last tumbling pass and took off...

Only to step out of bounds. Again.

Oh God. That was twice now. I never, ever did it twice at a competition. Ever.

I finished my routine and saluted the judges, then immediately looked for Kova. He was already waiting for me near the stairs. I sprinted over to him with dread in my footsteps and unease in my throat.

"It is okay," he whispered as I stepped down and into his arms.

"I stepped out, twice!" My voice was hushed but heightened. I pulled back and we walked toward the chairs. There were cameras everywhere but I ignored them. "Who knows what other mistakes the judges caught. I knew it. I just knew yesterday was too good to be true. I just knew it."

Tears rose to my eyes but I pushed them back.

"Hey," he said, turning toward me. Catching my breath was a struggle. "Stay positive and take slow, deep breaths. There are still two more girls who need to compete, and from what I gather, they do not have the difficulty your routine does. Not even close."

I exhaled a deep breath. Blinking a few times, I stared at the scoreboard willing for my number to pop up. Without looking at Kova, I asked, "Did I step out with one foot or two?"

Inhale, exhale. I couldn't remember. Only that I knew for a fact I did on one. "Two."

My chin quivered. "Both times?" I held my breath.

"Yes," he replied, voice grim.

"Seriously?" I asked, unable to hide the horror in my voice.

I saw Kova nod from the corner of my eye. Fuck. I blinked rapidly. No tears would fall today. I refused. But that was 0.6 of a point right there.

I turned to face Kova. My eyes shifted between both of his trying to gage his thoughts, but then the crowd erupted, and not the way I'd hoped. Both of our heads turned in the direction of the scores.

My blood ran cold as I stared at the numbers in disbelief.

I was going to have a heart attack.

This was worse than hearing my diagnosis. By far, much worse. I could control stepping out…and yet I hadn't.

"How?" I asked, covering my mouth. "How?" This made no sense. There was no way my score could be that low.

I looked to Kova for an explanation, but he was already sprinting in the other direction.

chapter 18

I STOOD MOTIONLESS AND WATCHED AS MY COACH ADDRESSED THE judging panel with poise.

He was submitting an inquiry. He was entitled to since he was an accredited coach.

Meanwhile, I did the math in my head and added up the difficulty and bonus points. I knew I'd stepped out of bounds, but I didn't deserve to drop to third place. That was a lot to lose. Usually I was very in sync with my body and movement, and trying to figure out where I had made errors was proving to be difficult. I replayed my routine in my head.

My gut told me I hadn't made them. But the judges said I had. I frowned. I was scored on both execution and difficulty. Had my execution been that poor?

No, a voice inside my head said. There was no way. I may have been beyond drained when I stepped out onto the floor, and my joints felt swollen and inflamed, but I did not lack when I competed. Ever. I gave everything I had to offer, and then some. Every struggle I faced, every risk forgotten. I didn't hesitate. I sucked it up and expelled it out to perform.

Four minutes. Kova had four minutes to file the appeal to contest my score.

I watched the judges hand him a sheet of paper. He checked his watch. Dipping his chin, he turned and our eyes locked. He strode toward me, his long legs eating up the space between us. Kova was pissed.

"I need a pen," he said.

Quickly I shuffled through my duffle bag. I knew I had one because I'd stashed our notebook in there. I planned to write in it after the meet.

Handing the pen to him, he said, "Turn around and bend over."

I flattened my back and Kova immediately started writing. He spoke to himself in Russian, the pen hurriedly moving across my back. He had to answer the questions and then calculate my routine.

I turned my head to the side, and said, "The numbers don't add up, Kova."

"I know," he snapped, but I knew it wasn't meant to be mean. He pressed down too hard and the pen poked me through the paper. I didn't flinch but Kova cursed. "What number did you come up with?" I told him. "Right. I did as well." Relief swept through me for the simple fact that I knew it wasn't just me who felt the numbers didn't add up.

Kova finished and I turned around. He blindly handed me the pen as he read. I watched as his eyes scanned over what he'd written, his lips moving. He glanced up. Eyes narrowing in thought as he recalculated the numbers one last time just to be sure. He glanced at his watch. Time was of the essence, so I kept my mouth shut and didn't tell him to hurry up. He knew.

Reaching into his pocket, he pulled out a silver clip of hundred-dollar bills and walked toward the judges. He had to pay a steep fine to challenge my score to make sure I received credit for the skills I'd performed. If Kova proved to be correct, he'd get his money back. If he was wrong and the judges didn't feel they'd deducted unfairly, he'd lose his money.

Without a word, Kova returned to the judge's panel and handed them the paper and cash, then walked back to me.

I let out a tense breath. That was it. All he could do.

I chewed the inside of my lip, and the familiar metallic taste slid over my tongue. I chewed again. Cameras flashed and clicked frantically. Everyone was on their feet in anticipation to see what the outcome would be. The next gymnast couldn't compete until they were done with my score, so all eyes were on us.

Kova stood patiently next to me while we waited. If he was nervous, I'd never guess it. I folded my arms across my chest and he pulled me tight to his side. I leaned against him, trying to soak in his composure. The screen turned on and the judges leaned in to begin reviewing my routine, replaying it on the small television on their table that was only used during times like this to see if the correct points were awarded. It wasn't like football where every little thing was reviewed.

I broke apart from him and paced back and forth. I stared at the floor. I propped my hands on my hips. I looked up at the ceiling. I looked back at the judges. I cracked my knuckles. I looked at the score screen. I wiped my clammy palms on my leo. I looked at the screen.

Tension balled on the side of my neck.

Too much time had passed. Something wasn't right.

"What's taking so long?" I asked.

"I do not know," he said under his breath. Kova glanced at his watch then back at the judges. His eyes were fixated on them.

Just then, one of the judges stood. I drew in a lungful of air and held it as she quickly walked up the stairs to the technical committee. She was running out of time.

Chills pebbled down my arms as I anxiously waited, and waited, and waited.

"What does this mean?" I asked Kova. He would know more than me. When he didn't respond, I glanced over my shoulder at him and paled.

His face grim, defeat marked his handsome features. The only time I'd ever seen that look on him was when he'd lacerated my heart with the news of his secret marriage.

His look said it all.

His gaze never left the new group of judges. Time moved so slowly. My heart plummeted to my stomach and I looked back up the stairs. There were three people. Two shook their heads and one nodded.

Hope was a distant dream and my faith was slipping through my fingers... until the crowd erupted.

I spun around to face the screen and searched for my score. Shock ricocheted through me and my lips parted.

I was one-tenth of a point ahead, and back in first place. One-freaking-tenth.

This couldn't be real.

I reached blindly for Kova, but he was already reaching for me. He tugged me to him and wrapped an arm around my shoulders, hoisting me up. He gave me the biggest hug as cameras flashed around us. I squeezed him tight, holding back the tears.

He put me down. Kova, like all coaches when something profound like this happened, alternated between pressing a kiss to the top of my head and congratulating me.

"How?" I asked, my voice muffled against his chest.

Kova reared back with a smile bigger than I'd ever seen before. "The judges made a huge mistake. I knew they did and acted quickly. It looks like you got the difficulty points, and possibly some for execution."

My brows rose, my vision blurred. I sniffled through a smile. Only by the skin of my teeth was I in first place. It was too bad reviewing routines via television weren't permitted in general.

"Really?"

"Yes. You are only leading by a small fraction of a point now, but I have a feeling it is enough. You deserve to have those points you killed yourself for."

I went in for another hug, squeezing Kova in appreciation.

He rubbed my back. "Well done, Adrianna."

"Thank you, Kova," I whispered.

He looked at me with such an intense affection, like I was the only person in the room who mattered to him, and it filled my heart.

I gave Kova a smile only for him before I broke apart and turned to look for my dad in the stands. He was much closer today.

For the first time since I could remember, he had tears in his eyes as he waved frantically...with Katja next to him.

"I'm so proud of you. More than you could ever know," Dad said. "You amazed me today. I had so much pride watching you. I thought I was going to burst from it." He paused. "I regret not being at the other competitions, but that's going to change from here on out."

I smiled from ear to ear. "Thanks, Dad. You're here now and that's what matters."

We were in the airport, and I'd fallen asleep waiting for my plane to arrive. Dad wasn't flying back with me, but my plane was supposed to take off before his, so he'd stayed.

Sitting up higher, I winced from the stiffness in my joints. Everything hurt.

"You okay?" His voice conveyed concern.

I nodded. "I'm fine. Sometimes this happens once I finally sit down for the day. I swear I have the body of a ninety-year-old sometimes."

Dad chuckled. "I don't know about that. Where's your next meet?"

"I have to check with Kova. I can't remember where, but I think it's in a few weeks."

Thanks, kidney disease and lupus. Apparently brain fog was a gift from them.

With this meet, I'd victoriously secured a spot for Worlds since I'd placed first on both days and walked away with a few medals in the events for vault, floor, and bars. I'd just barely missed third place by a couple tenths for beam, but I was okay with that. I couldn't wait to get home to hang my medals on the wall. All of my medals held a special place in my heart, but these were more special. They were won after my diagnosis, and at my first big national competition. I really wanted to take them out of my bag and hold them right now, but I'd wait to do that in private when I got home. It was a little emotional for me, after all.

"I think it's in another country now that I think about it." I rubbed my head trying to remember which one. It was my first international meet—and another big one for me—I just couldn't remember where as there were a few meets that took place overseas.

Dad angled his head toward me. "Oh, yeah?" Then he looked in another direction.

I followed his gaze and masked my expression. Kova and Katja were walking toward us, both with drinks in their hands. Kova handed Dad a plastic cup of amber liquid and ice, and Katja extended her arm in my direction offering me a bottle of water. We three were on the same plane home. Hopefully in different sections.

"Thank you," I said, but she ignored it. I wasn't surprised. Katja had hardly looked in my direction. Normally it wouldn't bother me, but now it irked me. Her disdain was obvious.

Screw that. I was going to ask Kova when we got back.

"Adrianna tells me the next meet is in another country?" Dad said to Kova, stirring the ice with the little black straw.

I uncapped my water and looked the other way as they spoke, too tired and mentally drained to listen or participate. The icy water slid down my throat and I almost sighed. I drank half of it in one breath. No matter how much water I had to drink lately, I couldn't seem to quench my excessive thirst.

We had less than an hour before we had to board the plane. Bending down, I dug through my purse and pulled out our notebook. I rummaged for a pen then sat back and wrote.

I'm writing this while sitting right in front of your lovely, perfect wife. She hates me.

Don't tell me you don't notice the way she looks at me when I'm around. She acts like I'm a thorn in her side she wants to remove and throw away.

I'm not crazy.

I know when someone has it out for another person. She has it out for me. I can feel it in my bones.

What scares me is that I think she knows everything. She knows what we have between us. I didn't want to face the facts, but I think it's time I do. It's the only thing I can think of. The only reason why she acts the way she does toward me.

But my question is, why hasn't she done anything about it yet? Unless she has, and you just haven't told me.

I paused and looked up, thinking. My pen teetered between my fingers and my gaze shifted to Katja. She was staring at my lap, then lifted her eyes to mine. Placing my pen in the center of the notebook, I folded it shut and held it to me. This was the bluntest and riskiest I'd ever gotten with our thoughts, but I had to get them out or I was going to burst.

She continued to glare at me with hateful eyes and a stone-cold expression on her face. It amazed me how someone so beautiful could look so ugly. An evil kind of ugly. Her eyes dropped to my lap again, then she leaned over and whispered something in Kova's ear. He turned his head toward her while she kept her eyes on me. I couldn't see what his gaze expressed but he grabbed her hand and placed their laced fingers on his thigh with a small smile. His knee bobbed.

Fatigue washed over me. My eyes grew heavy and warm. God, I hated this feeling. Like a heavy blanket of iron was draped over me, and I suddenly got so tired that all I wanted to do was sleep. Usually I had to push through it, but this time I didn't.

I turned my head in the other direction and rejoiced when the attendant announced the plane was finally boarding shortly after. Shoving my notebook and water bottle into my purse, I slung it over my shoulder and said goodbye to my dad, then got in line. It was a five-hour flight and I knew the moment my head hit that scratchy pillow I was going to pass out hard.

What I hadn't foreseen was that my notebook would vanish by the time I'd arrived home.

chapter 19

L ATELY, I FELT LIKE GIVING UP.
Not because I didn't love gymnastics, but because my emotions caused by the reality of my life were too much to handle. My secrets were a burden. My very existence was a lie. I didn't know who I was anymore or what would become of my future. I was too lost in my head with no outlet to ease my soul. My skin crawled. I wasn't able to focus on one thing long enough except gymnastics, and when I was alone, my mind jumped from one topic to the next. I hated it.

I was so sick when I got home from the meet, but I wasn't going to let it hold me down. Exhaustion had taken over and my body cramped up. I had a small fever. Going to practice the next day was an absolute must and what anyone else would've done, so it's what I did too.

There was something about the powdery chalk and echoes of the apparatuses that helped calm my racing mind. For four days and four nights straight, I pushed myself and trained like a beast. No one questioned me. Madeline and Kova went along with it. To them, they probably assumed I was preparing for Worlds. And I was, but I was also just trying to keep my head above water the only way I knew how.

I kept telling myself that if I could do it before everything happened, then I could do it now. I ached more than ever, but I refused to rely on pain medicine at night. I knew it could have long-term effects and I wasn't going to go down the path of addiction.

Drained beyond comprehension, I kept to myself and didn't talk to anyone. There was success in silence, is what I told myself. Not even when I stayed later and only Kova was there. The walls of my life were slowly caving in, but being inside World Cup was the only way for me to breathe. I struggled to keep it together, yet this was the only way to remain whole. The only way I felt like me again, so I worked myself until I could barely stand.

But today… Today felt like more than I could handle. The pressure in my chest was mounting to capacity. I felt the break coming the moment I woke up, like a massive title wave forming in the distance, building up stronger and fiercer the closer it grew.

As I waited for my coffee to finish brewing, my phone dinged. Yawning, I opened the message from my dad and read it.

Dad Cell: Call me when you wake. It's important.

Frowning, I called him immediately. "Dad? Everything okay?"

"Sweetie. I didn't expect you to be up."

I glanced at the clock on my coffee pot and blinked. It was a quarter after four in the morning.

"I've been going into practice early, so I've been up at this time all week."

"Just like your father," he said proudly.

I was sure he only slept three hours a night at most just so he could work more.

He cleared his throat, then said, "Have you been watching the news?"

My brows bunched together. "No. Why? What's wrong?"

"A hurricane is headed your way. It's only a category two and nothing to worry about, but with the water still so warm and no land to slow it down, I want you to be prepared. A few early predictions say it could grow to a three. I want you to close the shutters even though the windows are double-paned. They should just slide shut easily. I'm going to have food and water delivered to your condo today just in case, along with flashlights and a radio."

"By who? Who has a key?"

"Thomas is already on the road and headed your way. He should be there in the next couple of hours. I figured you would be at practice, so I gave him a spare key."

My heart softened. "I'd love to see him."

"He'd love that too, sweetie, but I gave him strict instructions. I don't want him caught in traffic on the way back. You know how some people get when a hurricane nears, how the media hypes them up and creates chaos. I want him home and safe."

I laughed lightly. Being born and raised on the coast of Georgia, a Category 2 was nothing to blink about, but there were those who evacuated anyway.

"When is it supposed to make landfall?"

"The day after tomorrow, early morning and just slightly south of where you are. Turn the television on and watch. On your way to practice, fill up your gas tank just in case."

I smiled into the phone. "I know, Dad."

"Make sure all your medicine is filled and keep your phone charged."

I grabbed a mug and poured the coffee. "It already is."

"Wash any dirty clothes now. Don't open the fridge too much and turn the air down so it stays cool."

"Dad. It's just a two."

I was surprised he was worrying the way he was. He didn't typically worry until it crossed into a four.

"I know, but I'm not there to protect you this time. I just want to make sure you're okay. Anything could happen."

"Thank you," I said.

"I already spoke to Konstantin. He plans to close World Cup tomorrow as a precaution."

I froze midway of pouring the half and half. "What do you mean? It's only a two. Schools don't even close for that."

"He's playing it safe. I don't want you driving in that kind of rain anyway."

Oh God. A whole day alone, possibly more, to stew. My teeth dug into my bottom lip. I grew silent, wondering what I was going to do with my time. Maybe hang my medals and clean? I glanced around. I lived alone and I was rarely home. Who was I kidding? My condo was always clean. Maybe I should get a puzzle.

"Adrianna?" Dad said.

"Yeah?"

"Where'd you go?"

I thought swiftly. "I was thinking that I finally get a day off to rest. Thank you, hurricane!" I faked my enthusiasm.

He chuckled. "Just stay in the condo and don't make me worry. I have enough gray hair as it is."

"You can always dye it," I said, laughing to myself as I thought about how I'd said the same thing to Kova.

"Never in a million years. Listen, I gotta run. Call me and check in tomorrow."

"Thanks, Dad. Love you."

"Love you more, sweetie."

"Wait—" I paused. "Dad?"

"Yes?"

"I've been meaning to ask... Ah, have you gone and gotten tested yet?"

I tightened my grip on the phone. Testing could take weeks and I wanted to be prepared in case anything happened. He hadn't brought it up once to me and I figured I should.

"I actually began the process when you were diagnosed, I just didn't want to say anything until I knew for sure. The first blood test came back as a match." He paused, and my heart jumped so hard I had to clutch my chest. "But the following crossmatch tests ultimately showed we're incompatible and your body could reject the kidney." Dad's voice lowered. "I'm so sorry, sweetheart. I really thought it would happen. I was waiting to tell you after your gymnastics competitions. I didn't want it to mess with your head."

"Oh, okay," I said, my voice quiet. That's three people in my family with the highest possibility of being a match, and none of them were. I felt like the life had been sucked out of me once again.

"Don't lose hope. I've made some calls and am waiting to hear back from some people to see if they're willing to be tested. I didn't want to tell you yet until I had positive news to follow up with."

"It's okay," I said softly. "Back to square one again, I guess."

"It'll happen," Dad said. I could tell he was trying to pump encouraging words into me. "I know it will."

We said our goodbyes and I stood in my kitchen staring at nothing, wondering where I went from here, trying not to ask myself the one question I'd been avoiding since this shit started.

If I never found a match, would I die? Even with dialysis, would I die?

I knew the answer, though. Dialysis was not a way of life.

While sipping my coffee, I flipped through the weather app on my phone and read up on the impending storm. It was a good distraction to take my mind off what Dad had told me and to get my thoughts steered correctly. I really didn't want to stew on the fact I was back at square one again.

The storm was predicted to grow close to a category three. All the hurricane needed was a small shift and the eye would make landfall in Cape Coral. The feeder bands would last hours and do the most damage. However, I still wasn't too concerned. I had bigger pills to swallow.

I reached forward and picked up the medicine bottles. One by one, I poured out the necessary dose and took them, along with eating an apple. I'd been through countless hurricanes. I was in a secure cement building with shutters and having the proper necessities delivered.

What I did worry about was having no outlet to wear myself down to the bone the way practice allowed me to.

During all the research I'd done on lupus and kidney disease, many patients had reported their bodies aching more when there was a drastic change in the weather. I found it laughable someone would claim the weather affected their body, but then I thought about how I'd felt when I woke up this morning, and yesterday morning, and realized I had too felt it.

"Earth to Adrianna. You okay?" Madeline asked, eyeing me with concern.

"Yes," I answered, and yawned. "Why do you ask?"

Madeline took a bite of her banana and chewed slowly. I couldn't have those anymore, not unless I wanted to aggravate my kidneys.

"You're using the wall to hold you up. I thought you were about to fall asleep standing there."

"Oh." I smiled timidly, and shifted on my feet to stand straight. I'd been practicing with her all day. "I'm fine. Just taking a water break," I said, and gave the half full bottle a little shake. My throat was sore and my voice raspy when I answered.

"Alright… I'll meet you at vault. Don't keep me waiting too long. Use the bathroom, eat a protein bar, do what you gotta do, because we'll work for the next three hours or so straight."

"I won't," I said.

I perked up a little at the thought of getting worked to death. That meant no time to think about anything else.

Happy with my response, Madeline turned around. I watched her walk away, my gaze trailing her footsteps until she made an abrupt turn and my gaze latched onto Kova.

Rooted in place, I leaned back against the wall again and watched closely as Kova instructed the men's team. I hadn't trained with him today, or yesterday, and it felt strange. Foreign really, and I missed it more than I'd realized. I felt lost without him next to me.

A few days ago he'd paired me with Madeline to fine-tune skills she had a niche for, and we hadn't talked since. Not even when it was time to leave. All I got was a quick hello and goodbye. I'd hoped we would today, though. At least once before he closed World Cup for the storm. He was the only one I actually wanted to talk to, even if it was just for a few minutes. I'd take what I could get with him.

I couldn't take my eyes off him. He didn't know I was watching as his back was turned to me, but I stared. Even through the supportive way he coached the boys' team, I knew him well enough that I could sense something was on his mind. He appeared positive and reassuring, but then he turned around to pick up a thick landing mat, and I saw everything. I saw the dark circles under his eyes, the grim, firm line of his mouth. How the space between his brows was permanently creased with lines.

He looked much older than his thirty-four years.

Dragging the mat so it was centered beneath the rings, he dropped it with a loud smack and a cloud of chalk lifted around it. He scrubbed a hand down his scruffy jaw. His hair was a disheveled mess. The black hat he loved to wear was nowhere in sight. Kova looked as withdrawn as I felt.

He turned to the side and spoke to the men's team using his hands and giving examples of what he suggested they do.

I'd noticed he'd been at the gym longer than I had this week. He arrived before I did and left after. I frowned and drank the rest of my water. Had he even gone home?

Thunder cracked across the sky, the rumbling felt beneath my feet, and I jumped, grabbing my chest. I turned around and looked through the giant glass window at the thunderstorm rolling in. Large pellets of water came down hard and fast, the sound of the rain hitting the tin roof reminded me of a rainforest. It was oddly peaceful but then the sky darkened to a hazy gray and the world seemed to dim around me. My vision blurred and my lungs constricted. I loved the rain, but that impending feeling of doom curled through my chest again like it had early this morning. I was beginning to feel trapped inside myself. A tear leaked from the corner of my eye and I quickly wiped it away.

"Adrianna! Get moving!" Madeline shouted across the gym and clapped her hands obnoxiously. I looked at her, then shot a passing glance at Kova. I held my breath.

He was already watching me, which meant he saw me wipe the tear.

chapter 20

M Y PALMS BURNED LIKE HUNDREDS OF FIRE ANTS WERE CHEWING on my skin, and my inner thighs were chafed from the thick rope. I clenched my body, constricting every muscle I could to climb up and down the coarse rope. I'd alternated between crunches and rope climbing, utilizing every ounce of energy I had.

As my toes reached the floor, I let out a sigh of relief. I had thirty seconds until I was climbing back up. I was almost done with this round of conditioning I'd created for myself. The last thing I had to do was run, then I would be locked inside my condo for the next day or so. Hopefully sleeping the whole time.

"It is time for you to go home," Kova said, his voice flat. He was at the bottom of the rope waiting for me when I got down.

I glanced at him. His hands were propped on his hips and he wasn't smiling. Stern, he was trying to make a point, but I turned away and ignored him. I sat on the floor and laid on my back, then I placed my hands behind my head. Tightening my stomach, I pulled myself up to a sitting position.

One. Two. Three…

Kova dropped to his knees and held my feet down. "Adrianna."

"I'll go home when I'm ready," I said as I came up and faced him.

I was back down when he said, "I think you should go home now."

"No. I said I'll go home when I'm ready."

Kova hissed under his breath. "Adrianna—"

"I'll go home once I'm done. Okay?" I spat and focused on the ceiling.

"And when is that? When you cannot walk anymore?"

I ignored his cheap comment.

"Whenever I'm done. It's not like I'm in anyone's way. No one is even here. So what does it matter?" Everyone but Kova had left nearly two hours ago. "You don't need to be here anyway. I can handle myself."

His eyes bore into mine, one brow raised to a sharp point like he was holding back. "You are overdoing it, Adrianna."

That just irritated me. I was going to get plenty of rest for the whole damn day tomorrow and needed to exhaust myself enough so I could just sleep through it. Otherwise, I'd search things on the internet and feel bad about myself. I'd focus on the pain in my joints, and then they'd hurt even more. Pushing myself with extra conditioning until I could barely walk wasn't the brightest idea I'd ever had, but I was losing control of the situation and this was my way of grasping it and getting through. Especially after the conversation I'd had with my dad and the lack of donor match. I needed this more than ever. I needed to wear my thoughts out and shut my mind down. It's why I loved being at World Cup—it made me forget everything. I didn't want to be alone and stuck inside all day. God forbid the storm got any worse, then I would be stuck in there for days.

"Don't tell me what I need. I'm so sick of hearing what I need from everyone. Tell me, why did you push me off onto Madeline?"

"I did no such thing."

I sat up and faced him, hands still clasped behind my head. Sweat trickled down my temples. "Bullshit. You're lying to me."

"What is going on? Talk to me," he urged, his voice full of concern. "What is on your mind?"

Talk to me. I let out a haughty laugh and went back down. My heart was beating too hard while I tried to talk and work out at the same time.

"Tell me why you haven't spoken to me in days, *Coach*. Days. You barely even say hi, and now you want to talk?"

"Ah, *Coach*. You only use Coach when you are angry with me."

I wasn't really angry at him. I was just angry in general. He wasn't helping by telling me to leave.

"What happened between the meet and now for you to pretend I don't exist? I thought we were okay, for the most part anyway."

I hadn't deliberately sought anyone out, yet I wished he had at least tried to talk to me.

Then it hit me.

I'd gone many days ignoring him and now he was doing it to me. He'd only done it for less than a week and here I was turning into a cry baby over it.

"You're doing it on purpose, aren't you? Because I've been keeping you at arm's length since you married Katja, and you can't stand it anymore. This is your way of getting back at me."

"That is not true." Guilt laced his gentle tone and I felt myself breaking down, one stiff English word at a time. "Not true at all."

"So, I'm imagining it?"

"No. I mean, well…" He sounded remorseful and that was the opposite of what I wanted. "I felt like Madeline was better suited for what you needed. Is that why you are upset and forcing yourself to work out every day after practice now? Because you thought I was ignoring you? I would never do that to you. I am always here to talk if you need me."

I do need you, but I don't want to need you.

I sat up and breathed into his face, trying to catch my breath. My chest was so tight I fought back a flinch from the pain.

"I don't think anything. I know it. You're avoiding me."

Goddammit, I knew I was being irrational, only, I didn't know how to stop it.

Kova sat back on his heels and observed me. "I am not going to argue with you. Go home before the rain starts up and take time to rest. I will see you in a few days. Your attitude makes it clear you need the time off, and the *Coach* bullshit only solidifies it."

My eyes flared and I stood. Grabbing the rope, I fisted it and said, "I told you, I'll go home when I'm ready."

Gearing up, I held onto the rope above my head, but Kova grabbed my hips to stop me.

"No. You are finished," he said firmly and pulled me back. "You are going to kill yourself."

"I'm already dying anyway, so what does it matter?"

Kova's hands froze around my waist. I squeezed my eyes shut and dropped my head against the rope. Fuck! I couldn't believe that slipped out.

"What did you just say?" he whispered.

"Nothing. Just that everyone is dying the moment they're born. That's all I meant." I tried to wiggle out of his hold but had no luck. "Now let go of me so I can do my last round."

"I will do no such thing."

Blood simmering, I was fired up. Letting go of the rope, I spun around and slipped out of his hold. I glared up at Kova, expecting to see his anger, but I got the opposite.

"What's your damn issue? I'm just trying to stay focused and prepared for Worlds. Why are you holding me back?"

Kova stepped closer to me. "Do not put words into my mouth. I would never hold you back. I am concerned you are going to hurt yourself. Plus, with the storm coming, you need to prepare."

"I am prepared. This is my way of mentally preparing and dealing with shit."

His eyes lowered. "Every night this week I have held my breath watching you, trying to give you the space you so clearly need to deal with whatever it is you have going on in your head. But tonight, it stops. No more running yourself ragged."

I pursed my lips together. "Are you going to let me do my last one?"

"No chance in hell. I watched you enough tonight to know you are too weak to make it to the top. I thought you were going to fall the last time. That is why I came out here, to catch you if I had to."

Weak.

You are too weak.

Kova called me weak.

"You think I'm weak?" My voice trembled, and there was no concealing the hurt I felt. Calling me weak was by far the worst insult. It's what I'd been fearing, that I'd be too weak in the end to achieve anything. I'd rather him call me a bitch than weak.

Before I could stop it, tears filled my eyes as I replayed his words in my head. My jaw bobbed, my blood boiled with fury.

"Ria," he said softly, his brows angled with regret. Kova reached for me, but I stepped back. "I did not mean it like that. I just did not want you to hurt yourself."

I pushed my index finger into his chest, and whispered with a bite, "Fuck you, Coach."

I spun around and marched away from him. If I couldn't climb, then I'd go for my run.

"Come back here. Where are you going?"

Tears streamed down my cheeks as I threw the door open to the lobby. "To run," I shouted over my shoulder and rounded the corner. Kova was hot on my tail as I walked down the hallway. "You should know that by now since you've been here every night watching me like a freaking creeper."

"Like hell you are."

Oh, he was mad. Good. Now he knew how I felt.

I threw my locker open and reached for my workout shorts. I had a schedule and I needed to stick to it. I had to.

"You can't stop me. Why don't you go home and pick a fight with your wife and leave me alone."

I stepped into my shorts and pulled them up, then grabbed one shoe, but Kova stopped me. He spun me around and stepped up to me. I backed up until I was pressed against the locker. He pointed a finger at me. I had the urge to grab it and bend it backwards.

"Do not do this."

"Do what?" I yelled, my breathing heavy, eyes frantic. I shoved him away. I couldn't stop the tears from streaming down my flushed cheeks. My fingers trembled as I wiped them away with the back of my hand. "What am I doing that's so wrong?"

"You know exactly what you are doing. You had a long weekend, then you come in and train harder than usual by adding extra conditioning and hours to your schedule. You have a meet coming up."

"And? So? That's a bad thing?"

His eyes grew hard. "For you, yes."

Nostrils flaring, I said between clenched teeth, "Because you think I'm weak."

Kova stilled to stone. "Weak is the last thing I would ever call you."

"Then what is it?" I pleaded, my voice rising. "Why can't I finish like I've been doing?"

"Because I know you are sick and I cannot stomach to see what you are doing to yourself any longer!"

My lips parted in disbelief as air seized my lungs.

I stared at Kova, my jaw bobbing helplessly as I searched for words but came up short.

My mind had to be playing tricks on me.

I dug deeper, glaring at him, praying I hadn't heard those words.

The silence between us stiffened to a crashing sound, threatening me to an asphyxiating level.

"What?" I asked, breathless. I shook my head. There was no way.

Sympathy was in full effect and it made my heart crumble. He extended his hand, but I stepped out of his reach, as if I couldn't stand to be touched by him. Hurt showed in his eyes but I disregarded it.

"What did you say?"

"*I know,*" he said softly. And in my heart, I knew what he meant. "I know everything, and I cannot handle seeing you torture yourself knowing what I know any longer."

I kept shaking my head and inhaling deep and slow. "You know nothing. Nothing." My voice was a whisper.

"Ria, *krasivaya,* I have known since the beginning."

I could barely breathe. The cage around my heart fractured down the center and opened up, spilling out my heart. I turned around to wrench my bag from my locker. My other shoe fell to the floor and I didn't bother to pick it up.

Fuck running. Fuck everyone. Fuck this life I was dealt.

"No," I said more to myself. No, my dad wouldn't do that. He wouldn't lie to me, not after everything. *Everything*. "You're lying. You're just trying to manipulate me."

Tears fell fast and hard and I was unable to stop them. Just as I was about to swing the bag over my shoulder, Kova placed a hand to my upper arm.

His fingers, his truth, his compassion, it was all felt in his touch and said everything I didn't want to know.

I lost it. The touch was so simple and enough to shatter me completely.

The strap slipped from my hand and my bag dropped to the floor. Turning around, my teeth gnashed together as I pushed Kova's chest with every ounce of strength I had in me. He was rock solid and I felt like I was pushing a brick wall, but I persisted. He stumbled back and tried to reach for me, but I pushed him again.

"You know nothing!" I screamed through the burning tears. "Nothing! My dad wouldn't do that to me! He wouldn't lie to me like that!"

"Ria," he said sadly, only trying to soothe me, but it triggered me even more.

One word, three letters, and it said everything I needed to know.

I shoved Kova again and he stepped back. I pushed him harder until he was against the wall. I couldn't stop. I couldn't process anything he was saying. I couldn't hear.

"Stop it. Shut up! You know nothing!"

He gently cupped my arm, his compassion all too consuming. His touch told me the truth again, and I revolted against it. He let me hit him, slap him, shove him.

This was too much. I hated it. I was going to be sick. He didn't know. He was lying.

Kova was lying just like he always did, but then his next set of words shattered me completely, forever changing us.

"I know about the lupus and kidney disease."

chapter 21

I SNAPPED, AND TEARS FELL IN THICK STREAMS DOWN MY CHEEKS TO THE corners of my mouth.

They seeped into me, fueling me with fierce resentment and hurt unlike I'd ever felt before.

"No one was supposed to know!"

Kova grabbed my upper arms and I reacted quickly by swinging myself out of his hold. He grabbed me again and this time I slapped his chest. He flinched but tightened his hold.

"Let go of me," I screamed, my hand connecting with his chest. "Get away from me. Everyone is a liar. Everyone! I hate it so much. All everyone does is just lie. No one was supposed to know, including you!"

I yanked away, but Kova was too strong. He pulled me to his chest and I fell into him. I let myself cry for a moment, whimpering against him as he held me, my back vibrating with sorrow. I let out an exhausted cry, but I didn't back down and continued to fight him.

"Your father was worried. He meant no harm."

I drew in an audible breath and pulled away. "So you knew this whole time?"

Kova stared down his nose, his eyes low and sober. "I have."

I blinked rapidly trying to get the tears to stop so I could see clearly. "How? How could you have known for so long?"

"Your father called me," he said unsympathetically. "He said the doctor's office had called him with the lupus results and wanted to do further testing but you had not shown up. This was months and months ago. He was concerned and knew you were under pressure but did not want to panic you, so he asked me to convince you to go. He also asked that I not tell you I knew." His eyes roamed my face. Lowering his voice, he said, "I cannot handle seeing you like this any longer. I am worried about you, Adrianna. You are fading away and wearing yourself out, and I know why. You want to avoid the problem and act like nothing is serious, that it cannot control your life, but you cannot do that. It will only hurt you more in the long run. That is what my mother did, and I refuse to see you do that. You should have come to me."

My lips parted in realization. "When you told me I couldn't come back to practice until I went to the doctor... That time I stayed at your house... That's how long you've known?"

"Before that. Your father and I have been in close contact regarding your health. I learned when you came back from the training camp that it was a high possibility there was something wrong. I found out shortly after."

Hot tears silently poured out of me. This whole time I thought I'd been fighting against myself to prove I could handle my training schedule, when in fact Kova was just allowing everything because he felt sorry for me. His tolerance made total sense now, and it offended me. His way of handling my sickness was pitying me.

My eyes searched his. I wasn't sure what I was looking for, something other than sympathy. Was he sad that my chance of achieving my Olympic dream had lessened dramatically? Or that I had an incurable disease that could strip me as a person? Did it change how he viewed me as just Ria?

Or even worse. Did he label me now?

"I have always admired your tenacity, but this madness ends now."

He admired me.

"I...I..." I swallowed, trying to find my voice. "I need to leave."

I couldn't be held responsible for my actions at this point. Between the blind rage and numbness, his touch, the sound of his deep voice enveloping me, the energy was too powerful in me to break free.

Turning away, I blindly located my bag, looking but not really looking. I bent down and reached inside to feel for my keys. Grabbing them, I stood up and quickly walked toward the door in a daze.

"Adrianna," Kova said, clucking his tongue behind me. "Where are you going? You cannot drive in this condition."

"Go away."

I gripped my keys tightly. No way was he going to steal them from me this time, but Kova was quick on his feet and trailed me to my car.

As soon as I stepped outside, the rain pelted me in the face, soaking me instantly. I was chilled to the bone with aches. Kova muttered a string of words in Russian, and for once I didn't care what he'd said.

"Let me drive you home."

"Go home to your wife."

I reached for the handle, but Kova placed his hand on the door and stopped me. I blew out a frustrated breath through my nose and grinded my back teeth together.

"Stop this. Talk to me," he demanded, pressing his chest to my back.

"I'm sure she's waiting on you."

"She is not home."

A mocking laugh escaped me. "How convenient. No wonder you're acting like this. You have no reason to rush home or anyone to answer to right now, so you talk to me because you won't get caught."

God forbid, he, or anyone, ever put me and my wishes first.

He stepped to the side and angled his body toward mine. "No, you misunderstand. She is here in Cape Coral but staying with a friend who has a generator. She did not want to lose power and she was concerned for the puppy. She is five minutes from here."

"You got a puppy?" My voice was small and far away. I turned to look up at him. He confirmed it with one nod of his head. The thought saddened me. "Lovely. Next comes kids because that's what *everyone* does. They get a stupid dog first before they have a kid."

Kova's nostrils flared. He stared, breathing down my neck, not caring he was soaking wet from the rain. His silence solidified my statement and a little whimper left my lips. My jaw trembled with emotion that was suffocating me.

"Adrianna, please. Let me drive you home," he offered.

Thunder sounded in the distance. "I want to be alone."

Kova stood close enough that I could feel him without touching me.

For a split second, I wanted him to reach out and pull me into his arms even though I said no.

I wanted him to fight me and tell me everything was going to be okay, to let me cry on him until I passed out.

I wanted him to say he would always be there for me.

It was a ridiculous thought, considering all things.

I didn't like that he had gotten a puppy, or that he knew my secret. His life wasn't thrown off its axis like mine had been. His life wasn't going to change for the worst the way mine had. No, Kova was busy planning a future, while I was struggling to hold on to what was left of mine.

My breathing labored. An eerie calmness settled in me, a slow current of endorphins rising through my blood. I fought it. I didn't want to let go. I knew it wouldn't be good if I did. I knew every single thing I'd been holding in would come to the surface and I'd break. I needed to be able to control my emotions, but what I really wanted to do was scream and shout and lose it and just cry ugly loud tears to get it all out.

"Adrianna. Answer me."

I slammed my hand against the door and turned toward Kova. Chills slithered down my arms, the rainy breeze pressed on my skin like little knives. Through gritted teeth, I bit out, "You already know everything! What more do you want?" He remained silent, a pensive look crossed his face. "What, Kova? What do you want from me?"

"I know you have not told anyone, and that is not healthy. You have to talk about it, otherwise it will eat away at you and you will lose everything."

"I don't have anything else to lose," I said, looking him directly in the eyes.

A melancholy loss plagued his beautiful eyes, making me almost crumble into his palm. "I want to hear you tell me through your words and your voice. Let me be there for you."

My chest ached from the beating my heart was getting. I didn't want anyone to be there for me, to make me talk. They were there because they felt bad and no other reason. Not because they cared or wanted to hear me complain. No one wanted to hear complaints.

Tears mingled with the rain and I hiccupped. He was right. I needed to get it all out, but there was no way I could do that without crying, without freaking out. Without looking like a total crazy person. I'd held so much in to stay strong. I was already on the edge and that's not what I needed right now, especially during a hurricane that would keep me trapped in the condo for a whole day, maybe more.

Thunder rumbled across the darkening sky again, this time louder. The hair on the back of my neck rose. The clouds illuminated from the bolt of lightning I caught in the distance.

Kova placed an arm around my shoulders. "Come. Let me take you home."

Digging deep, I reached for resolute determination and exhaled through my nose. I'd talk when I was ready, not because people were talking behind my back and they felt bad so they had to coax it out of me.

Hauling my car door open, I climbed in. "No," was all I said, then quickly closed the door in his face and locked it. No way was I letting my guard down again.

I threw my duffle onto the passenger seat and wiped my eyes. Thunder roared and bellowed, frightening me. Kova immediately pulled on the handle but had no luck. I pressed the start button, then slowly reversed my truck with Kova walking next to me yelling and pounding on the tinted window.

I ignored Kova over the rumble and roar closing in on us. I strapped on my seat belt and headed for the main road, soaking wet and freezing as I leaned forward trying to see the color of the road lights. My cell phone rang and I reached blindly in the cup holder where I always kept it. Empty. Shit. After a quick glance down, I realized it was in my duffle bag.

Forgetting about it, I focused on the road and carefully drove home. Tears poured from my eyes. Misery consumed me but vengeance filled my blood. I could barely see the road between the rain and the blur of my anguish. My fingers tightened around the steering wheel until the skin on my knuckles stretched white. I was angry. Why did everyone have to hurt each other? So many lies meant to protect but ultimately caused the most heartache. It was horrible and sad and I wanted it all to stop.

Bright lights flashed in my rearview mirror. I sat up higher and shot a brief look over my shoulder at the black car with the dark-as-night tint in disbelief.

I drew in a small breath.

My cell phone rang again but I ignored it. I pressed on the accelerator, gunning it, driving faster, a little too fast for the rain. Red lights flashed ahead at the bridge and the barricades lowered as the draw bridge went up. I should've slowed down, but I pushed the gas pedal to the floor. My truck jolted and I flew over the bridge. A rush of fear steamrolled through my heart and I gripped the wheel tighter, praying I didn't hurt myself.

A quick glance in the rearview mirror showed Kova flying over the bridge behind me. I guess I shouldn't have expected anything less considering he drove a sports car.

Within minutes, I pulled into my condo complex and parked my truck with a little too much gusto. I sniffled and grabbed my keys but left everything else. I ran through the rain to the entrance and toward the elevator as Kova pulled into a handicap spot.

The elevator dinged and I stepped inside. I pressed the number for my floor and tapped the close button incessantly so the door would close faster.

"Adrianna!"

I glanced up with wide eyes to see Kova running toward me. Heart racing, I pressed the button harder and faster and chanted to myself, "Hurry up! Hurry up!"

I sighed in relief when the door finally closed in his face. Silent tears fell and I wiped them away as I leaned against the cold glass wall of the elevator.

The doors opened on my floor and Kova was standing in front of me. My heart dropped and I stumbled, wondering how the second elevator got here faster than mine did.

chapter 22

"**I** TOOK THE STAIRS," KOVA ANSWERED MY UNASKED QUESTION.
Of course he did.
We fell into step and walked side by side.

"Why are you even here?" I said.

"Because you are here."

"I want to be alone."

"I want to be with you."

I stuck my key into the lock and clenched my eyes shut. I tried not to feel his words or the gentle tone he used. Before I opened my door, I turned around and met his gaze.

"Listen, I know you're just trying to help me and be nice and all, but I'm not in the best of moods and can't be held responsible for my actions. You have no idea what I'm feeling inside right now. I'm hurt and upset and it's best if I'm left alone. So, please, go home," I pleaded with him.

"That is okay." He stepped closer, and the heat of his body made my heart skip a beat. "Take it out on me. Let me feel your rage. Give it all to me."

My jaw trembled. I didn't want him to be nice to me. Not right now.

"No," I whispered, and turned away to open the door.

"I know you are still angry with me and have been for a while now. I deserve it. I know what you are feeling has a lot to do with the secrets you hold inside. So, give me your worst. There is nothing you can do that I have not already felt anyway."

My breathing deepened, each breath lifting my emotions to the point of no return.

"You have no idea what you're talking about." I gritted my teeth. "I want to explode, okay? I want to punch things. I want to cry and scream and ask why me... *Why* me? What did I do to deserve this life? These odds? In the blink of an eye, my world changed overnight with things you have no idea about. I've been holding everything in for so long, on top of training and fighting against myself, and I just want to let go and do it alone. Why can't you understand that? Why can't anyone just let me be? Why does everyone have some sort of secret about me that just destroys my life?" I asked, my voice rising and tears climbing again. "Just go away, damn it."

A couple of hours ago I'd dreaded the thought of being isolated. Now that Kova was aware of my secret and had known about it for so long, I craved the seclusion. I felt weird inside. I didn't want him to see me any differently, but he already did.

He ran a hand down his face, then looked me directly in the eye. "I know about your mother. Frank told me what happened. I know everything, Adrianna."

All the air left my lungs again for the second time today. That was it. The tears fell again, harder, faster, and I couldn't stop them. I didn't want to. My head spun as my world spiraled away with one admission at a time.

"Why… Why did you not tell me?" Kova asked, the hurt in his voice did not go unnoticed. "You should have told me."

Prickles of resentment rolled down my arms. I bit the inside of my lip, trying to keep my composure, but knew there was very little to hold on to.

Any second I was going to burst. The dam was going to break and it was just going to come out.

"I should have told you? You have some nerve to tell me that after everything you've done. You know why I didn't tell you? Because it's none of your damn business, that's why. It has nothing to do with you! It doesn't affect your life."

He stepped closer and I pressed a hand to his chest. Inches from my face, he breathed down at me. "Like hell it does not. Everything you do has to do with me. Do you not see that by now?"

I scoffed and shoved at his chest but he didn't budge, and it only made me angrier.

"It's not, though. Not everything is about you. In fact, it has nothing to do with you! It's about me and my life, not yours. So, fuck off, Kova." I paused. "You know what? I'm done with this conversation. Done with you in my face. Done with the lies. Just done with all the bullshit. I wish I could just disappear."

I turned around and opened my door to slip inside. I tried to shut it but Kova was quick and pushed himself in. His cell phone rang and the tone set me off.

Kova answered the phone and I used it to my advantage by pushing him out the door. I shoved and pushed and dug my heels into the floor to get him out, but he was stronger.

He positioned the phone between his shoulder and ear and used both of his hands to subdue me. He kicked the door shut and grabbed me by my upper arms and backed me up while he spoke Russian into the phone. I fought him but it wasn't enough. He walked forward until I was against the breakfast bar where I usually ate. I could have yelled but I really didn't need any more of Katja's wrath. Thunder cracked outside and I yelped. I looked over my shoulder toward the sliding glass door. I'd forgotten to shut the hurricane shutters.

Face pulled tight and twisted with irritation, Kova shook his head for me to stay quiet while he spoke over Katja's high-pitched Russian. I cringed. Her voice was like nails on a chalkboard. They were speaking at the same time and over each other. I gathered they were fighting, but I couldn't be sure. I didn't really care.

My back hit the marble and Kova stepped up to me. I drew in a quiet breath, lips parting as his body was flushed against mine. I resented him for how I felt when he touched me. I resented my body. I resented us and everything we'd become.

I swallowed hard and licked my lips. I felt us click together, just like we always did.

Kova's Russian slowed to a whisper. He frowned at me, gazing at my tear-stained cheeks until his eyes moved to my lips while Katja continued to scream. I felt his sadness, his longing. I felt *him*, and I didn't want to. I wanted to stay numb to the world. Life was easier that way, but with Kova by my side, it was nearly impossible. He was my light, my life, my protector, even when I didn't want him to be.

Kova shook his head and mumbled something, which only set Katja off again. I leaned back, fighting us as he leaned in closer. My heart raced. Using the heel of my hand, I pushed at his jaw, angling his head back, hoping he'd back off. A vein strained along the length of his neck and the days old black stubble scraped my palm, but he fought me by holding my wrist down. Kova's body hardened, heating against mine, willing it to life.

This is what we did. What we were good at.

I whimpered, missing the strength of his body against mine, the way he'd make me forget everything when it was just us. Kova was so strong. He had no idea how much I drew from him for weeks until that dreadful day at the doctor's office. Since then, I hadn't been myself, and now that it was just me and him, I felt myself awakening again. I felt that pull, that strength I needed only he could give me. My emotions simmered at the surface and that scared me. I wanted to fight him, to unleash everything I had in me on him. And I wanted him to fight me back.

Breathing heavily, our chests mimicked each other's as he descended again. I pushed him away and turned my head, giving him my cheek. Russian words not meant for me danced across my skin as he kissed where the tears had fallen. I squeezed my eyes shut and it broke me inside how gentle he was being. He wanted to help, but I didn't want the nice guy Kova. I wanted him to fume and walk away.

Kova inhaled deeply and dragged his nose through my hair. He continued to pepper little kisses all over my cheek, nuzzling me. His hot breath tickled my neck and I let out a small cry, cursing myself for it. Goose bumps broke out over my skin and I trembled against him, hating the need to feel every inch of him.

Gripping the phone in one hand, Kova pulled back just an inch to peer down at me. His piercing eyes held me captive, and for a moment there were no barriers between us. It was just the two of us. He breathed life into me and I inhaled it deeply into my lungs.

There were a lot of things I didn't understand in this crazy world. But the most peculiar thing was that of me and Kova. He had no morals and I had no dignity. We willingly stripped each other of everything except us. When I needed to be alone, when I felt lost and empty, he forced himself into my life. Just like the few times when he actually admitted to needing me, I gave him every inch and then some without reason. I was positive I'd never understand this savage push and pull we fed off of, but then again, some things were not meant to be explained.

But that look. I knew that look. It was the look that made my heart skip a beat. Kova was going to kiss me, and the thought provoked something inside my heart. Even when I didn't want him here, when I was so angry at the world for the cards I'd been dealt, and even while he spoke to his wife on the phone, he was going to kiss me.

He had no principles, but it was obvious I didn't either.

I reached up and took his bottom lip between my teeth and jerked him to me. His body stiffened but that didn't stop him. Whatever he was in the middle of saying to Katja was enough to enrage her and allow me to force my way in for a brief second. But I didn't need to. Kova was quicker and kissed me hard, plunging his tongue into my mouth. His thick tongue stroked mine and wrapped me around him. I melted against him and opened up to draw his essence into me as my body roused with desire. My free hand tangled in the hair at his damp nape, and I latched on, tugging and pulling it between clenched fingers.

Kova pushed his mouth harder into mine, growling and devouring my lips with precision, and elicited a moan from me. Letting go of my wrist, his hand moved to my throat and my nipples tightened as he applied pressure. Sensation took over. I let out a loud and satisfied moan, forgetting why I didn't want him here. He kissed me again, this time long and deep and slow. My body rolled into his, into the rigid length that hung between his hips. Shifting my feet apart, I hiked a leg over his waist and grinded myself on his hard cock. Kova pressed his thumb down on the center of my throat and wetness seeped from me. I cried out, craving more, when I heard the shrill of his wife's voice from the other end of his phone.

Cold water washed over me.

I snapped and broke the kiss. Not because I was mad at myself for how I was acting—I was a little—but because Kova played right into it with me. It was sick we both got off on fucking around. Kova had never admitted to finding joy in cheating, but he never stopped either. Not even after he was married. I had to wonder if he liked the rush as much as I did. I shouldn't, but the truth was, I did. I loved it, and that made me a terrible person. Now that I thought about it, I was certain that was the reason for the hand I was dealt. The diseases were Karma's way of getting back at me. They had to be.

Tears blurred my vision again. I'd gotten what I deserved.

Reaching up, I yanked his cell phone from his hand and slammed it onto the marble counter next to us. I wanted to silence her voice and get him out of my condo. I couldn't take hearing her anymore. The screen shattered and the phone turned black. And thank fucking God she was gone.

"You are fucking crazy. You know that?"

"All woman are. Now get the hell off me and get out."

But he didn't. Kova stared where the phone had slid from my hand on the counter. His eyes hardened to deadly points, and his body stiffened. I followed his gaze...

To Hayden's shirt.

It was sitting in a giant decorative bowl on the counter. He'd left it at my house after we had sex but I'd yet to return it to him. I'd just forgotten.

I smiled to myself, knowing this was the fuel I needed to make him mad.

"Was that another thing I should have told you?" I asked sarcastically. "Because I did. You just didn't believe me."

chapter 23

KOVA WAS OFF ME LIKE MY BODY HAD COME ALIVE WITH FLAMES. I used his shock to quickly put distance between us.

There was no doubt the shirt was Hayden's, and Kova knew that. It had Michigan written across the chest; the college he was attending in the fall. The same college Kova helped him record a video to apply to the men's gymnastics team.

"Hayden came here," he said more to himself.

"Oh, he came all right." I wanted to hurt him the way he'd hurt me. I wanted to get it all out and not have any more secrets pressing on my chest.

Kova's eyes lit up as he glared at me. For a brief moment I stood frozen in place. Damn, his gaze was powerful. Dark and lethal, his eyes searched mine for the truth of my ambiguous words. I'd never seen him wear hatred this deep, or sorrow so profound like he was now.

As I looked him straight in the eye, a slow smile spread across my face from ear to ear.

"He came in my bed, in my shower, in my kitchen, in—"

I blinked and Kova was charging me, eating up the space I'd just put between us. My eyes widened with a little panic. I was nearly knocked over by the rage he emitted from across the room. I stepped back as fast as I could and hit a wall. Kova's hand flew out and grasped my neck. His thumb stroked over my pulse. I gasped and grabbed his wrist, trying to tug him off.

"You are lying." His eyes blazed so bright I was caught off guard by them. "Tell me the truth!"

My heart pounded so hard in my chest I thought I was going to have a heart attack. I knew he could feel it.

"Someone needed to take my mind off you, and Hayden did an amazing job at that."

"Did you fuck him?" His eyes were huge. I thought he was going to pop a blood vessel.

"Do you want me to spell it out for you? Better yet, I can describe his dick if you want me to. It's about five—"

A strangled sound erupted from Kova's throat. His face contorted like he was in agony. As he let go of my neck, he yelled out something in Russian. Kova picked up the delicate, sea-blue glass vase on the table next to us and slammed it down, shattering it into a million little pieces. I jumped and ran to the opposite side of the room, toward the sliding glass door, only to have him stalk me just as quickly, tracking me with his lethal glare. He was like a caged animal set free, ready to go in for the kill.

The tension between us simmered to a suffocating level.

Maybe now he knew how I'd felt when I'd found out he'd married Katja.

That dam I'd constructed to hold back the tears after the crippling and devastating moments that altered my life was cracking with each blink of my eyes. The flood of emotion in me was rising to a catastrophic level.

Could he feel it?

I felt it, and I couldn't stop it.

"Hurts, doesn't it?" I bit out with a sneer.

"Why would you do this to me? To us?" he said, sounding defeated.

I stopped moving.

My inner ticking time bomb just went off.

I. Fucking. Lost. It.

A maniacal laugh burst from my lungs. This time the tears didn't come because I was sad. No, they came because I felt rage pour out of me in ways I'd never experienced in my life. It inspired me and all I saw was blood.

Fingers trembling, I reached for the heavy candle next to me, and without thinking, I threw it, aiming for his head.

"How could I do this to us? Are you fucking kidding me?" I screamed, jaw quivering.

There was a pounding in my ears, and my chest burned with uncontrollable anger. The glass candle collided with the wall and broke. I would kill him. I would kill him for saying that.

"How dare you say such a thing to me. You're fucking married, Kova. That fucking ring on your finger is proof. You created this fucking mess," I said, moving my finger back and forth between us. "You broke me. You fucking broke us. How dare you try to turn this around on me. If it wasn't for the fact you got fucking married, none of this would even be happening!"

"I never cheated on you, though," he replied and then ducked when I threw another object at him. "Not like you think. I married her for you, not because I wanted to!"

Candles were missiles and I threw them one by one. I was determined to hit him. My breathing grew dense and thick with each intake of breath and all I wanted to do was inflict pain on him the way he had me. Why did my aim have to suck so bad?

I strode up to him with hate filling my veins. "Are you delusional? *You married her for me?*" He was breathing just as hard as I was. "That's what you're going with? No, you married her because it was a choice you made, then you came to me when you got married and fucked me on that couch." I pointed to my sofa, my voice cracking as I thought back to that night when I gave him every part of me. That night was the first and last time we ever made love, and it stayed with me ever since. "Another choice you made. How sick and demented are you to say you married another woman for me? How?"

"When did you fuck—" He scowled, the hurt prevalent in his eyes that I almost felt bad. He couldn't even say the word. Kova's eyes scanned the floor, he looked lost and tangled in his emotions. "I cannot believe you did this," he whispered, his accent thicker than usual.

My eyes widened at his ridiculousness. "When did I fuck Hayden? Is that what you're trying to ask me?"

He looked up. "Was it after the kidney disease? Or before?"

I broke inside.

"Don't say those words!" I yelled and offset his steps again with mine, crying so hard I could hardly catch my breath. Through blurry eyes, I grabbed the neck of the lamp and took a deep breath, struggling to hold on to the little sanity I had left. Kova's eyes dropped to my fisted hand then met my gaze.

"Was it after the lupus?"

"Stop it!" I cried. "Why are you doing this to me?"

Kova was pushing me, goading me, knowing I didn't want to talk about that. Anything but that. My face twisted with heartbreak and with all my might, I yanked the cord from the wall and swung my arm back to throw the lamp at him. An anguished cry left my throat as I hurled it through the air. I took off running to the kitchen, frantically looking for something to chuck at him if he uttered those words again. A wooden spoon would do, a glass, a pan, anything— my eyes landed on a knife.

I reached for the black handle when a heavy body flew into my back. Kova tackled me from behind. A gasp of air burst from my lungs as he spun me around.

"Get away from me—"

"Adrianna."

"Leave me alone. Why are you even here? Go home to your perfect house with your perfect wife and your perfect dog. Stop torturing me."

I shoved back at his chest with my free hand, trying to push him away, but he released all his weight and crushed himself to me. He was quick and pinned my hips to the counter with his strength. It was so easy for him. Air rushed from my lungs. Fuck. He was heavy. Given his height and frame, I estimated Kova to be around two hundred and thirty pounds of solid muscle.

My heart beat frantically against my ribs and hot tears blurred my vision. I thrashed against him, pushing at his neck with the palm of my hand to get him to move, but he only burrowed closer to me. He was such an asshole.

Kova yelled at me to stop, but I was too enraged and upset. He allowed this to happen.

"Aren't you ashamed of yourself?" I spat, trying to hit him. "Disgusted that you're married but here with me? What is she? Pregnant? Do you just unload your cum—yeah, I said cum, I use big girl words—in everyone and pray for the best? Do you have no integrity? No moral compass? How can you still fuck around with me while married to her?"

"Let me explain!"

"Let me explain," I mimicked in my best Russian accent. "You always need a reason to explain yourself, Kova."

I pinched his neck and his eyes blazed with fire. I dug my nails in deep hoping to draw blood. His skin broke under my fingernails, but he didn't flinch. Leaning in, I bit his arm and he grunted and yanked back. I moved my hips from side to side to show him my resistance but it only backfired. His cock hardened against me and I absolutely hated myself for reacting to it. The corner of his mouth pulled up into a smug grin. My arms broke out in goose bumps as a fire lit inside me.

It sickened me that I became hot against his dick. I was past the point of livid, but I needed to make him feel the weight of his words, I needed him to understand where I was coming from and how much he hurt me. He wasn't supposed to know about my secrets. I hated, hated, hated that he knew. Fighting him wasn't easy, especially when I was already so weak.

And yet I didn't stop, because the storm brewing inside me felt too good. The allure was too strong and it gave me a thrill to see him as hurt as I was. Provoking him only provoked me, which helped me breathe.

And that wasn't healthy for either of us.

"Once again, you've made me hate the sight of you. Here I was thinking you were my light helping me see past everything, but you really were just pulling my strings. You're a disgusting human being and I hate the things you make me feel. I'd rather be numb than live through what you've made me go through. I can't believe you would do this, come here and question me like you have some sort of right. And then to say how could I do this to you? The audacity. You are sick. This pulling me back and forth? I'm done with it. I'm done with you. Officially done with everything. I'm done with the medicine and the doctors and the needles. I want you out of my life and I never want you to touch me again. You're horrible!"

Kova let go of my wrist and surrendered. "Say what you need." He breathed heavily into me, almost as if he was struggling with me. "I know you do not mean any of it, but if it helps you, then take it out on me."

Gritting my teeth, I reared back, and with all my might, I slapped him across the face so hard his head snapped to the side and my palm stung from the connection.

An audible gasp escaped me. Tears filled my eyes over my cruel actions. The room grew jarringly quiet while it exploded with strain. Kova's entire body hardened to stone and I was nervous to see how he'd respond. I'd never hit another person before and I was surprised I did, but what shocked me the most was the lack of remorse I felt.

"You only ever give a shit about yourself. You're the most selfish man I've ever met."

The skin between his eyes crinkled together. "*Sumasshedshiy.*"

Seething, I slapped him again because I knew what he said couldn't have been good. His cock hardened to a rock as wetness seeped from me.

"Your ethics are fucked up." I raged, my breathing weighted with untamed emotion. "How can you tell lie after lie and never feel bad about it? You use me. You use me when Katja isn't around, then make me feel guilty for fucking Hayden like you have some claim on me."

Chest tight as a fist, I gasped trying to catch my breath. My eyes were huge as I stared at him, wired and ready for war. I didn't care that I sounded like a lunatic, because everything I said was the truth and we both knew it.

"Do not ever fucking hit me again," he said through clenched teeth.

Eyes wild, I grabbed his hair and yanked it back. His neck strained with a row of veins as he fought my pull. Our bodies pressed into each other's. Kova's cock was thick and full, like a weapon pushing against my own arousal. I was stunned by how big and hard he was, considering the way I was acting toward him.

But then it clicked.

chapter 24

ALL THE SCREAMING AND ARGUING I WAS DOING TO MAKE HIM SEE how I really felt was backfiring on me.

Kova was aroused, and oddly enough, I was too. My body flared with unshed desire that rocked me to my core, with emotion that I had buried. I was relentless, but I wouldn't cave.

"You've lost all control and you can't deal with it, so you're trying to use reverse psychology on me. It won't work."

"You do not know what you are talking about because you will not let me speak!"

"I don't want to hear your bullshit lies anymore! I can't believe you had the fucking nerve to say I did this to us." A mocking huff rolled off my lips.

Oh God. I couldn't take it. Why did he have to do this to me? I wanted him to feel the pain he had caused me. The lacerations of his actions and how they'd scarred me.

Whispering, I spoke slowly in a blind rage. He'd feel these words.

"You're nothing but a user and an abuser. I fucking hate you."

"You fucking hate me?" Kova yelled, his vibrant green eyes huge. Moving his hand to my hair, he grabbed a fist full of it and forced me to look at him.

Kova burned with a passion that made me question my statement. Did I hate him? Truly hate him?

I bobbed my head slowly, not holding back with a blanket stare.

"I never hated something more in my life," I repeated slowly.

Kova clenched my hair again and leaned down. I thought he was going to kiss me, so I swiped my hand between us. The tips of my fingers struck his nose and he flinched backwards.

"*Chyort poberi!!* I told you to stop fucking hitting me!"

He grabbed both my wrists and restrained them above my head to the cabinet.

"Fuck you, get off me!"

With his lips pressed to the shell of my ear, he spoke in his native tongue then translated it to English for me. "You could never fucking hate me." He was breathing harder, rougher, like he was struggling himself. "You cannot fucking hate me, because you love me. You. Love. Me."

I froze. My heart hitched into my throat, constricting with verity.

"What did you say?" I asked, my voice a whisper.

I angled my head toward him just in time for him to slant his mouth over mine. He devoured me with a savage kiss, a kiss I made him fight me for. I bit down and pulled his bottom lip between my teeth. Kova growled and delved his tongue around mine at the same time he rolled his hips into me. A groan vibrated deep in my throat. I softened, unable to not kiss him back.

"You love me," he demanded, pulling back. "Say it."

"I hate you."

He pressed his chest to mine, nearly suffocating me with his weight, and kissed my lips so viciously my heart ached for this untamed man who just so happened to be my coach.

Kova let go of my wrists. "You call me a liar, yet it is so easy for you to lie to my face. Tell me you love me."

I shook my head. "Never." I grit out. I'd never utter those words. I knew better.

"You have such a temper. Now tell me when you fucked Hayden."

My heart burned with fury and anger fueled tears filled my eyes. I was going to kill him.

Using every last ounce of power I had, I shoved at Kova's chest as hard as I could and turned around. My eyes landed on the black handle again.

Reaching for it, I grabbed it and took off, but I didn't get far. Kova grabbed my hair and yanked me back. I halted with a scream and he spun me around, pushing me onto the dinner table I never used. My feet couldn't reach the ground and I squirmed, trying to kick him. Kova stepped between my legs and locked me in. Without thinking, I lifted my arm with the knife but he grabbed my wrist to stop me. He wrestled me down until I was on my back.

"Tell me," he demanded, hovering over me. "I need to know."

"You're married." I paused, my eyes drifting over his irate features. "What difference does it make when I had sex with him? It doesn't. Just like my sickness has nothing to do with you."

His brows furrowed. "That is where you are wrong, Adrianna. Everything you do has to do with me."

I struggled in his hold, fighting against his power. I wanted to stab him, I wanted to hurt him. I wanted to make him bleed.

A devious smile spread across my face. My hand tightened around the base of the knife. I was going to make him feel the level of pain and destruction he had caused me.

"He came inside of me. All over me. And I loved it… I begged for it."

A tragic sound erupted from Kova's mouth that broke my heart. His hand shot out and clutched my throat. I strained against him. We both were breathing heavily and fighting the intoxicating desire streaming between us.

"You are a liar. You would never let him inside your body like that."

"I'm not a habitual liar like you. I let Hayden do whatever he wanted, however he wanted. Three glorious times," I said, drawing out the last three words with a sugary sweetness.

Kova released the hold on my wrist and lifted my leg. He turned me to the side and slapped my outer thigh painfully hard. I yelped, my hips jumping off the table.

"You want to know the best part?" I gave no fucks about hurting him, he deserved it.

"Adrianna," he warned. He looked so crazed, even his hands were trembling, but I knew I did too. Like we were both ready to kill each other. Kova wanted me to stop but I refused to this time. He was going to feel my wrath.

I continued, knowing this would set him off. His gaze dropped to my mouth. "He fucked me right where we're standing," I said, smacking the surface of the table. "Then he fucked me bare in the shower and I felt every incredible inch of him. He pulled my hair and bent me over until he was balls deep and then fucked me until I couldn't walk."

His face paled to a startling sheen of white. Frozen in place with only a deadly stare, I knew it would destroy him and I was glad it did. Only now would he be able to feel even an ounce of what he'd made me feel.

Without saying another word, Kova loosened his hand from my neck, but then he slammed his fist into the wood table three times insanely fast, right next to my head. I sat up and raised my arm with the knife held tight in my fist, and for a split second, I wondered if I could really stab him or not. That was how far Kova had pushed me.

Kova grabbed my wrist just as thunder struck outside. I could hear the rain pelting the balcony. Taking hold of my other hand, he placed them both behind my back and leaned into me. Our bodies flushed together in a bittersweet intimacy.

"Why? Why would you do this?" he growled and pressed his forehead to mine, then turned his head. His cheeks were red and he radiated with a heart-breaking emotion that I'd caused. Kova clenched his eyes shut and he pressed his lips to the side of my face, along my jaw, and down my neck, nipping and biting, sinking his teeth in and not caring. "Do you hate me that much you had to fuck someone else? Take it back," he pleaded, his hot breath trailed along the curve of my neck. "Tell me you are lying just to hurt me. Please, Adrianna, tell me you are making all of this up."

"Open your eyes and look into mine."

He did, and a sinful smile spread across my face, reaching my eyes. I pressed my chest into his and took joy in his revulsion.

"I had sex with Hayden," I said in a sultry voice purposely meant to taunt him. "I know it kills you to know another guy felt me come around his cock, just like it killed me to find out you married Katja. Even my diagnosis paled in comparison to that news. I don't think anything could equal that pain I felt. That's how much you destroyed me. Now you can feel what I've been feeling for months."

His eyes were a dark cavern of hatred. Lips a whisper above mine, he said, "I told you I would kill both of you."

"Do your worst. I'm already dead inside."

"You think you are the only one suffering? You think you are the only one dying inside?" His face was so close to mine. "Every day you have no idea what I am dealing with. Every day the darkness spreads to another piece of me. The numbness is unbearable. Now this with that little shit..." He shook his head and muttered in Russian. "The only time I ever feel anything is when I am near you, but now..." Kova trailed off and let go of my hands.

"I wanted him to make me forget you, what you feel like."

Cupping my jaw, Kova rubbed his face against the side of mine and laughed under his breath. I gripped the knife handle tighter as a chill rolled down my spine.

"And how did that work out for you, hmm?"

I didn't say anything.

"You know you will never be able to forget about me the same way I cannot stop thinking about you for even a fucking second of my miserable life. It is killing me."

"He replaced you."

Kova pulled back and eyed my hand with the steel blade. "You will never be able to replace me. Never. Just like I will never replace you."

I let out a strangled whimper at the truth of his words.

"Could you live without me? Because I cannot live without you, and that is the God's honest fucking truth."

I whimpered again, overcome with emotion.

"Let go of the knife, Adrianna," he pleaded, his voice so broken. I shook my head. "You cannot live without me, because I could not live without you."

"Let go of me."

"Why? So you can cut me?"

I nodded, breathing hard. I was worked up and running on adrenaline. "I want you to feel what you do to me. I want you to know what it feels like when I see you with Katja, when you called her and me both *malysh*, when you wear that fucking ring on your finger. Every time you've lied to me. I hate that you know my truth. I want you to feel it all and more."

"Just tell me why."

"Because I wanted to. Because I felt like it. Because I didn't want you to be the last thing my body felt. I wanted—no, I needed—Hayden to make me forget, and guess what, Kova? For a time, it fucking worked."

"But I have never intentionally hurt you, Adrianna. You did that to purposely hurt me. How can I hurt you like that when I love you so much?"

"Love?" I repeated, my jaw bobbing in horror.

Anger spewed through my veins. My eyes flicked back and forth between his. We both were breathing so hard the tension was stifling between us.

"You don't love me. You don't know what love is. You're incapable of love. What is wrong with you to say that to me? Why are you playing with my emotions like this?"

"Do not tell me I do not love you. I did not know love until I fucking met you! I love you! Everything I do is out of love for you."

My eyes bubbled with tears again. "Shut up! I'm so sick of all the lies. You don't marry one women, vow your love to her, then tell me you love me too!"

"Not once have I ever told Katja that I love her."

He was trying to give me a heart attack. "You're lying again!"

"I told her before we were married, but never since."

"You always lie! You married her because you love her."

"She knows about us, Adrianna! *I had to fucking marry her*," he gritted out angrily. "I had no fucking choice in the matter. She was going to the police, and your father. She knows *everything*. She has our notebook, and even hired an investigator that your bitch of a mother suggested," he said, and I gasped in shock. "Backed up against a wall with no option, I did what I had to. I was not going to let her ruin you. She had been pushing for marriage because her visa was up. She knew I did not want to marry her, and that she would be going back to Russia. We just happened to be the fuel she needed to light her flame. I have been trying to figure out a way to divorce her, but I have nothing to hold over her head yet, so I was counting my days and giving you the space you needed."

He was trembling, breathing so heavily.

"But now I am done giving you space."

chapter 25

"WHAT?" I ASKED BREATHLESSLY.

My mind raced through all the different scenarios. This was too much for me to process and just unreal.

"How? What?" I didn't even recognize my own voice. "So you were never going to marry her? And my... Joy...? Our notebook?"

"Do it," he demanded, pushing me. Kova's hand slid over the serrated edge of the knife and my heart rate kicked up to an abnormally excited level. "Cut me. If you want me to feel what you have been feeling, then cut me, but I promise you, *malysh*, a cut would never compare to the wound you just caused inside of me. You think you are the only one who is fucked up inside? Who is empty inside? You are wrong. Now you know what I have been going through. So put that knife to me and release me from the agony I deal with on a daily basis. Release both of us."

And I did. I didn't hesitate. Grinding my back teeth, I pressed the knife against his skin and sank it into his palm. I drew in a lungful of air. Kova's eyes widened for a moment in shock—he probably didn't expect me to actually do it, but I was so distraught over everything. The marriage. Joy. Sophia. Avery. The lupus and kidney disease. The lies and secrets. I didn't hold back.

Little by little all these life moments were annihilating who I was as a person that I couldn't take it anymore. It was too much, too intense for anyone. The worst was this feeling, this warped sense of love I had for Kova that made no sense. He was no good for me, we weren't any good for each other, but it didn't stop me from wanting him. I wanted to burn him to the ground, but I wanted him to take me with him. I wanted to hurt him with a passion I'd never felt before, but I wanted to hurt with him. He would let me, because maybe in the back of his convoluted mind, he really did love me, and I knew that. We both were guilty of having an unhealthy obsession of love for one another, but love was love, right?

Slowly, I pushed harder, drawing the knife down into his skin. Our eyes locked onto each other's, my tears finally drying.

Kova didn't flinch. He took the pain I gave him. To my shock, he wrapped his fingers around the steel and fisted it. He helped me cut him, pushing the blade into his palm. Warmth trickled over my hand, but I didn't stop. His lips parted and his eyes widened, and a euphoric rush of endorphins I wasn't expecting hit me. A little sigh rolled off my lips as a trail of dark red blood slid down his wrist and arm…when a thought hit me.

"Take your shirt off."

It wasn't a request, and he knew that. Reaching behind his head, Kova bunched the shirt and pulled it off with one hand, then dropped it to the floor. Warm blood seeped down the knife into my hand, into my palm, wetting the hold I had on the handle. A few drops hit my thigh.

A strange sensation took over that evoked feelings I'd never felt. Kova stepped between my legs again, igniting a darker edge of me. I welcomed it. My eyes lingered on the left side of his chest. I tried to block out the thoughts I had. Licking my lips, I dragged my teeth over my bottom lip and bit down. His tawny skin, too beautiful to mark yet I wanted to. Chest rising in falling, I didn't know where this urge came from to scar him, but it was compelling me to over his heart. To scar him the way he did me.

Tipping my head back with the tip of his finger, he looked deep into my eyes. "Every day when I look at myself in the mirror, this will be a reminder of the pain I caused you."

Chills danced down my arms. Kova was giving me the green light.

Our world came to a standstill. It was just us in this moment that only we controlled.

He grabbed my hand that held the knife and placed it to his chest. My chest rose and fell deep and slow. Eyes lingering for a moment, I hesitated as I took in his muscular shoulders and the honeyed curve of his neck, the vein trickling down. He was trying to steady his breathing like me.

I placed my palm to his chest and hesitated for a moment. Kova cupped my jaw, his blood coating my skin. I leaned into the slash on his palm, not understanding what was happening but for once not questioning it.

Instead, I let go and I felt him, this moment, us.

I felt his touch, the heat of his body, how his fingers threaded my hair. The way his lips danced seductively over mine, the desire building between us that we'd been fighting for so long. Little droplets of his blood fell to the top of my thigh. Tilting my head up, our gazes met and I held my breath. His green eyes were low and heavy, encased by thick, black lashes. Fingers grazing my cheeks, I sat up straighter.

"Do it. I want you to. I *need* you to." His voice was raw. "But just know the moment you put the knife down, I am going to fuck you senseless. Right here, on your table, and I will not hold back. I am going to spend hours inside your body to remind you of us. I have never in my life felt anything like this with anyone but you." He paused. "Tell me you feel it too, that it is not just me."

I nodded, admitting the truth. "I feel it…all the time."

Then, he kissed me.

Kova slanted his lips over mine and kissed me deep and hard, plunging his tongue into my mouth daringly slow and bruising at the same time. My body came alive, exploding with harbored cravings only he could satisfy. His tongue stroked mine, wrapping around it and rousing me the same way when he coached gymnastics. He was a ruthless kisser, one with unparalleled precision.

My hand vibrated from the rumbling in his chest, reminding me what I was supposed to do. Without another thought, I angled the knife and dragged the tip down, opening his flesh. The salty, metallic scent coated my nostrils and darkly curled through my stomach. Kova didn't flinch, he only kissed me harder, deeper, making me hotter than ever for him.

But I wasn't done.

Using my thumb to feel, I pressed into the bleeding, parted skin and felt for the top of the line I'd just made. I placed the blade right next to it and cut another angled line. Kova growled into my mouth and gripped my head in his palms. His erection pressed into my sex and I hooked my leg up to bring him closer. I wondered what it would be like for him to fuck me while I cut him. Wetness seeped from my pussy at the thought. His rich lips hadn't stopped, the thrilling silkiness of his tongue was overwhelming all my senses. Oh God. It was too erotic and my legs shook from the indulgence. I needed more. I needed to stop.

The wind howled outside as the storm grew closer. Locking my ankles around his back, I knew the next line would hurt and I wanted to trap him against me so he couldn't move. I pulled him closer and his erection pressed further into my pussy. I whimpered into his mouth. Reaching between us with my other hand, I stroked over his cock and felt his thickness. Kova growled again, then took his hand and guided mine into his shorts so I could feel his hot, thick flesh. I gripped him tight, feeling for my favorite vein.

"Kova," I whispered. My body was on another level of pleasure, like I was high even though I'd never done drugs in my life. "I need you." I found myself saying as I squeezed his dick.

"I know." He all but groaned out.

Feeling for the lines, my fingers smeared the blood and his tongue pene-trated deeper, teeth nibbling and tugging. A moan erupted in my throat, my le-otard wet with desire for him.

Turning my wrist, I pushed the knife into his chest one last time and made a horizontal line across the two I'd already created to form an A. I made sure I crossed over the open skin for further pain as I branded him. Kova's teeth sank into my swollen bottom lip. He thrusted his cock into my hand, releasing a wave of pleasure. I gasped a soft sigh and my body softened. I almost orgasmed from just this. I knew the last tear I made into his beautiful flesh hurt him. There was something exceedingly carnal when power was handed over and trust was given unconditionally. That's what he'd just done.

With one last caress around his kiss, Kova drew his tongue along the roof of my mouth and tugged my lip with him. Wetness seeped from me. Pulling back, our lips separated but he didn't go far. The heat of his breath drifted across my skin. The rain and wind had picked up outside while we'd created our own storm inside.

I opened my eyes and the first thing I looked for was the letter I carved into his skin. Fat, crimson droplets trickled down his chest, over his ribs. His cock was still hot in my hand, only now it was dripping with cum. My mouth watered at his tapered abdomen and the strong muscles beneath. He was a big man in pristine shape. Broad shoulders, a wide, thick waist. All I wanted to do was touch him.

My hand trembled slightly as I placed the knife on the table. I leaned in and dropped my forehead to his chest, and let out a gush of air. Kova's hand cupped the back of my neck, his other hand untied my ponytail. I touched the line of blood, spreading it over his obliques, the warmth stirring me. I lifted my head and looked at the mark I'd made. It wasn't small, about the size of the inside of my palm. One side of the letter was longer than the other. I'd done it blindly, but it didn't look bad either. There would be a scar for sure.

Something peculiar had taken over me. Something I'd never expected to do in a million years, or had ever considered doing until now.

Leaning in, I flatted my tongue and licked the blood, tracing the A and feeling the incisions I had just made. Kova's hand tightened behind me and his chest flexed as I tried to kiss the pain I had just inflicted away.

Slipping his hand under my hair, Kova twirled my locks around his palm then gripped my neck, angling my head back. His thumb pressed into the front of my neck and he tugged on my hair until our gazes met.

We'd been deprived for too long.

My lungs seized, desperate for air, and my lips parted against his. My expression mimicked his. The intoxicating stare in his eyes replaced the dark cavern of hatred, and I knew, that after tonight, after this moment, we would never, ever be the same.

"I am going to tear into you just like you did me," he said, his voice a rough whisper. And I was oddly excited.

Kova picked up the knife. He cut a tear into my leotard and sports bra, then into my shorts, and ripped everything off of me in the blink of an eye, along with his shorts. We were both naked and just as I thought he was going to slide into me, he picked me up and spun me around so I was lying face down.

"Put your knees on the table, *malysh*."

It was an awkward position at first, but my flexibility allowed me to lay on the table spread open with my hips pressing into the wood. My pussy and ass hung off the table, but I wasn't going to fall because Kova was right behind me stroking his cock.

Kova gripped my hips then plunged right into me in one long, hard stroke that took my breath away. My hand came up and slapped the table. The entire lower half of my body quivered in rebellion. I couldn't even take a breath before he was pulling out and surging into me so hard that I saw stars. He was warm and thick, and he let out a strangled moan like he was in utter heaven. His hand roamed circles on my ass as he rolled his hips into mine.

"Fuck! Damn it, Kova, hang on."

"This is not for you, Adrianna. This is for me. Now, take a deep breath and stay down."

He was relentless, driving into me rough and hard and fast. His heavy sack tapped my clit, teasing me each time he surged into my pussy.

"Did Hayden fuck you like this?"

Oh, he was angry. I liked angry Kova.

My eyes were closed as I focused on how good he felt. "No, he fucked me better."

Kova's hand reached up to grip the back of my neck while the other pressed down on my lower back so I couldn't move. I gasped, drawing in a long moan as he squeezed me so tight that I was going to have a bruise. I was at his mercy and I found it utterly intoxicating.

"I am going to make you regret ever fucking that little boy." I giggled softly and that only excited him further. "Arch your back," he said, and he took me deeper. The giggles subsided and soft moans rolled off my lips as pleasure took control of my body. Kova didn't hold back and took me hard, painfully hard, but I was okay with that. I wanted it this way.

Fisting my hair, he yanked me upright and the wood dug into my knees.

He wrapped an arm around my waist so I couldn't move, then placed his other hand around my neck and pulled me to his chest. My heartrate kicked up a notch.

"Did he squeeze you like this?" he said through clenched teeth near my ear. My pussy tightened around his cock, loving this angry side of him. "Go ahead and lie to me," he urged me on. "I already know the truth."

"Yes," I said breathlessly. He squeezed me so tight I could barely swallow. "I couldn't walk after."

Oh God. The sounds Kova made only heightened my pleasure. I liked hearing him like this and I began riding his cock.

"Did he make you bleed with his cock the way I do?"

My eyes opened and I glanced down. There were droplets of blood on the table and the top of my pussy was smeared with blood. Kova fucking tore me.

He chuckled in my ear when I noticed. "I can make you bleed too."

Kova held me immobile and increased his thrusts. I leaned against his chest and within seconds, I was coming on his cock with his hand around my throat. I reached up and had him choke me tighter. This angle was too good and I couldn't hold on any longer. My hips whipped back and forth as I rode his dick.

"Go ahead and lie to me again, tell me you came on his cock as hard as you just did mine," he said through clenched teeth, then he was unloading his hot cum inside of me, rolling his hips hard and slow into me like a crashing wave. He moaned in my ear and I wanted to tell him to keep making the sounds because they were so erotic and by far one of the sexiest sounds I'd ever heard in my life.

"I came all night with him." I taunted, out of breath.

"Fucking liar," he responded, then forced my head to the side so he could plunge his tongue into my mouth and kiss me good. "You better not ever fuck him again, or anyone else for that matter. You are mine and your pussy is mine."

I didn't argue with that. It was the truth and I knew it in my heart. He had ruined me in the best way possible.

Loosening his hold on my neck, Kova pulled out and turned me around. My legs felt like Jell-O. "Put your arms around me," he said, his voice scraping over me. Guttural.

I nodded. Kova picked me up, his hands under the back of my thighs as he carried me to my room. Our gazes never wavered, not even as he gently placed me on the bed and climbed onto the mattress. I scooted back until we were in the center and laid down. The softness against my back cooled me down as I opened my body to him. He hovered above me and placed his weight on his elbows, his heavy, wet length rested against my inner thigh. We looked at each other for a moment in silence as the whirlwind storm outside thrashed against the side of the building and my windows.

Reaching behind him, Kova grabbed the blanket and pulled it over him to encase us in a cozy tunnel. He reared his hips back and reached between us to grip his length. My gaze dropped to his lips in anticipation.

"Eyes on me, Adrianna. Now let me show you how much I love you," he said, his voice raspy.

Everything stopped.

Something inside my heart mended the tattered seams back together at the mention of those words again and the way he said them, like his life depended on them.

Nodding quietly, I widened my legs, knowing he was positioning himself. Heart racing, there was no foreplay was needed. His pleasure was still dripping out of me. Kova leaned down and whispered against my lips, his Russian like silk wrapping around my body. We both were ready and on the edge of something inconceivable to even understand.

Sliding his hands over my wrists, he laced his fingers through mine as he eased his way in. Our lips parted against each other's the same way our palms met. We both drew in an echo of breath at the feelings of our bodies uniting together again. Pure euphoria tangled us into a cluster of loops and ties. Kova's eyes darkened to a depth that sent chills down my spine and opened my heart to him.

We kept our eyes open as he slowly inched his way in, reaching a deeper intimacy. He pushed past every tender inch of my pussy, slowly, making sure we felt the other until he couldn't go any further. The pressure of him inside of me increased to an intoxicating level of bliss.

Our bodies locked together and we both inhaled. My heart pounded at our held breaths.

This was mind blowing.

This was how we were always meant to be.

One. Together. Whole.

chapter 26

HEAT FLOWED BETWEEN US, KOVA IGNITING ME IN WAYS I COULDN'T explain.

The weight of his body on mine, and the way he looked at me, was enough to make me remember where my home was, with him. It wasn't his length that tugged on every nerve in my body, it did, but his gaze was what held me immobile.

I released a breath of relief knowing this was how it should be when two people made love.

My thighs quivered, and I trembled beneath him as I readjusted to his size. Kova gazed into my eyes like he was lost inside of me. This was one of those rare moments where he was exposing himself, where he wanted me to look into his eyes and see what he felt. Because we both knew what he felt was wrong, and it pained him to say he loved me. When it came to Kova and our situation, it was all about touch, about actions when we were alone and in our own world, about looking deeper and feeling our emotions.

"Sometimes words are empty," he said. "Let me show you how I really feel about you."

Dragging his teeth over his bottom lip, Kova brushed his nose over mine, his mouth dancing seductively over my lips but never completely closing the distance. He looked down, then reared his hips back and created a desperate ache between my legs nice and slow, his gaze never flickering away from mine. A breathless rush of air escaped me and my back arched as he slid all the way in again. My fingers tightened around his, knuckles digging into his as he held them cushioned to the bed. Nipples pressing into his chest, Kova pulled out all the way to the tip and lingered. Without saying a word, I begged him with my eyes for more. He dropped a kiss to my lips, then he was sliding back in.

It was all too much to handle after not having him inside of me for so long. A sigh escaped my lips and I clenched around him. I sighed again and his jaw flexed in gratification. Pleasure blossomed as his sensual thrusts created a maelstrom within us. I hitched up my leg to hook around his back, trying to push him in faster, dying for more, but he stopped me.

He shook his head. "Let me take you slow this time, let me feel you," he said, and I nodded, licking my lips. "I have missed your body as much as I have missed you."

He was an earthquake shattering me with his passion.

Kova thrust in deep and my back arched, a pleasure-filled moan rolled off my lips. He decorated my jaw with rough kisses. His teeth nipping my skin only heightened the pleasure as he thrust into me with a sweet slowness that almost killed me. Sweat beaded on his chest, small drops of blood dripped from his wound, and I welcomed all of it onto me. It was raw and gritty and dirty, and I loved that he loved it with me. That we thought nothing of it. We accepted each other's lusts and fed our dark desires without question. He knew what I liked, and he gave it to me. Just like I did with him.

"Straighten your legs." Kova extended my arms above my head, his hands still in mine, and I looked at him in confusion. "Trust me, *malysh*."

So I did.

My body was stretched out beneath his, my nipples pressed to his chest. He made me feel so sexy like this, like I was all he'd ever need with the way he held me and looked at me.

With one of his knees on the side of my hip and the other leg straight next to mine, the pressure grew unbearably intoxicating as he plunged into my pussy with a degree of shameless finesse. The drag and pull of wetness echoed around us and it only added to the moment.

"Fuck me," he groaned from the tightness.

The pressure was building. It was so good and so addicting that I reached forward with my mouth and devoured him. I was so completely restrained and in a daze from the chemistry of our bodies fusing together that something unleashed inside my heart.

Kova kissed me back with the same ferocity. My toes curled as he pulled out then pushed back in with an unrestrained smoothness about him. My hips bucked and I whimpered as the pleasure reached new heights.

"I'm so close, Kova, please..." I begged, my heart racing.

The way my hips pushed forward and how my legs were closed brought the sweetest friction to my clit when he thrust in. My inner thighs shook, I couldn't wait any longer.

"So, let go."

"What about you?"

He laughed next to my ear. "Adrianna, I am only getting started. I told you, I am going to spend hours inside your body," he said, and pushed in until he hit my clit. "You are going to have to beg me to stop, and even then, I still might keep going."

My lips parted and he kissed me.

"Relax for me, *malysh*, and make love with me."

I nodded, my mind and body opening up completely to him.

"Think about what I am doing to you, how I feel in your tight, little pussy, and know that no one will ever make you feel the way I do."

He was right.

"Kiss me," I whispered, and he did.

Kova's body made love to mine, his lips matching the tenacity of his hips, so nice and slow until I was quivering and on the verge of release.

"Oh, just like that," I moaned, my eyes closing.

"Look at me. I want to see your face when you come around my cock."

That was all it took. I opened my eyes and searched for his, my orgasm taking complete hold of me while my body rippled with pleasure. I gasped, taking little breaths of air as euphoria took hold of my body. My hands squeezed his, and he returned the gesture. I was coming so hard I was on the verge of tears.

"Yes, like that, Adrianna. Just…like…that…" He drew out like he was proud and rocked into me. "I wish you could see your face when you come. How your eyes get glossy, feel how your pussy pulsates around my cock. You squeeze me so fucking hard I just want to tear into you harder."

My thighs were sticky with my pleasure, but I didn't care. Kova loved it, and so did I.

"Do it. Give me everything and don't hold back," I said.

Desire subsided and Kova loosened his grip on my hands and sat back on his knees to straddle me, still nestled deep inside. Breathless, I didn't move and stared at my ceiling in a state of astonishment. How could sex be this good? I was dazed and confused by how something like this could be felt. It wasn't normal. It couldn't be.

Palms skimming my stomach to my breasts, Kova cupped and tugged on my nipples. A zing shot to my core and I drew in a breath. I glanced at him and my eyes immediately dropped to the A on his chest. The blood had stopped and I could see the swollen outline of the letter. His eyes followed my gaze. The corners of his mouth curved into a sexy-as-fuck smile and he pinched my nipples harder as he looked at the mark—*my* mark—that would scar him forever. His cock jumped inside me and I exhaled from the tenderness.

Looking down at me, Kova's eyes were glittering with depraved thoughts, and it sent a shiver down to my toes. I bit the side of my lip and awareness sparked through him.

"You were wet when you cut into me. It made you feel good."

I nodded subtly. It was partially true. There were things that made me curious, I just never spoke about them because I thought it made me weird.

"I was also so over everything that I wanted to inflict pain on you because I wanted you to feel the pain that's consumed me for months. What I felt inside was because of you, and I wanted you to experience it. I wanted you to feel it more. But then the kidney diagnosis happened, and I feel like I'm constantly being lied to for my protection. I feel like I have to have this tight hold on my emotions for everybody else's sake and I just fucking snapped. Cutting into you felt like I was releasing all this pent-up emotion, like I was hitting this crazy high and it was all coming out of me. No one to fight me, no one to control me. No more lies. I was in control for once, and I was free of this fucking burden that couldn't hold me down anymore." I licked my lips. "I'm ashamed I used you like that. I'm so sorry."

"You wanted to keep going," he stated, thrusting into me.

I mused over his statement. "I don't know. Kind of. The feeling inside my chest scared me a little. I don't think you would've stopped me if I wanted to keep going."

Kova reached between my sex and felt for the sensitive little ball of nerves. Separating my swollen lips, he caressed my clit.

"No, not yet," I said through a sigh and softened.

I was trapped under him with his hard cock still inside me. The sheer pleasure felt so good the way he rubbed my clit that my hips took on a slow roll. My teeth dug into my bottom lip.

"Do not tell me to stop," he said. "I told you, all night." Kova glanced down and pulled my lips open to expose my clit. "You are correct, though. I would not have stopped you. If you needed to mark my entire body, I would have let you because I understand what you were feeling, you forget I also felt strongly too. Every day it was getting worse for me, but then you pressed the blade into me, and I knew it was something we both needed. I felt like I could breathe. We were both letting everything go and starting brand new."

Kova was exactly right. I had felt like I was being born again. All my sins were washed away with his blood, and my knife was freeing his demons.

"I am yours, however you want me," he said. Something wild entered his eyes as he watched himself pump little thrusts into me. "Always and forever."

I could watch him do this all day, the way he looked at my pussy, how he reached forward and gripped my hips fiercely and drove in harder. His head rolled back in pleasure and Kova seemed lost to the sensations taking over. He was growing closer. I could see the thick vein in his neck trailing down and over his collarbone.

"I love seeing you like this," I admitted. My voice was so husky, but I wanted to compliment him the way he did me. He needed it too. "So free and open to me when you're yourself. I could stare at your body for hours, feel your hands on me for days. I've never felt anything like this but with you."

"Oh, Ria…" he ground out, "it is taking more restraint than I ever knew I had to not relentlessly fuck you again. I love watching you fall apart under me."

Licking my lips, I said softly, "I'm yours. Take me however you want."

Kova didn't hesitate. Gripping my hips, his fingers dug into me, nails scoring my skin as he drove his cock in and out with skill. Thrusting sinfully hard three more times, he was coming. He held me so resolutely and shoved his way in so fucking deep that I felt a little tearing again, but I didn't tell him to stop. His warm cum leaked from me down my ass. It made me feel good, sexy and wanted, to see him aroused from me.

Chest blushing from ecstasy, he looked at me, and said, "I am sorry. I should not have finished inside of you, but I do not know what happens to me. With you, I do not think clearly. I am consumed with *us*. This obsession takes over and I lose control and make stupid decisions. Only with you, Ria. Only with you do you make me do and wish for things I should never." He panted like he was trying to catch his breath. "I will be better about that. No more after this. I will buy us condoms."

"It's okay. I do too." I swallowed hard. "I like when you come inside of me," I said honestly.

Tears instantly climbed the back of my eyes and I sniffled. I didn't want to cry, not after what we'd just shared but I couldn't stop it from happening either. Kova was worried about pregnancy. While I appreciated that, it also hurt because after what I'd discovered, having children one day seemed like another dream that I might not ever reach.

"Ria? What is wrong? Am I hurting you?" Kova pulled out and wrapped me in his arms, nestling me to his chest. We laid face to face on our sides with the blanket around us. Intimate. Like we'd done it every night of our lives.

"No, not at all."

He frowned, and a tear slipped from the corner of my eye from the reality of my situation.

I looked into his eyes and my jaw trembled. "It will be incredibly difficult to get pregnant with my illnesses. I think it's why I never did before. All those times we had sex, and when I took the Plan B, sometimes I took it late. Thank God I didn't get pregnant, but I should have." I paused and sadness cast in his eyes. "So you coming inside me doesn't worry me at all. Of course I'll get Plan B tomorrow just to be safe, but I'm not concerned like I used to be."

chapter 27

HIS BROWS BUNCHED TOGETHER. "I DO NOT UNDERSTAND. WHAT do you mean?"

"I mean because I have both lupus and kidney disease. I'm stage four, Kova. Both mess with fertility, so it'll be a struggle to get pregnant. Everything I've read and learned so far tells me that, and it makes sense now, given our history." I glanced at his neck, my fingers moving over the plump vein and pressing on it softly. "I think I've been sick for a while, years, only I just didn't know it, so both illnesses went untreated and caused irreversible damage. That's what happens and what I've been reading about. Think about it. Why did I not get pregnant? Not that I wanted to—I would've had an abortion—but I should have. We never used condoms—"

Kova cut me off.

"You know what I think?" he asked soothingly. "I think things happen for a reason, the way they are meant to. Just because you did not get pregnant does not mean you never will. Maybe there is a bigger plan for you and that is why."

"A bigger plan... Like, God? I'm not sure I believe in God. Especially not after everything that's happened."

His frown deepened. "You would have had an abortion?" he said gently but seemed upset over it.

"Yes," I said without hesitating. I frowned. At least I thought I would. Now I wasn't sure. "Why do you seem bothered by that? I thought you would be relieved."

Kova rolled me onto my back and leaned over me. He kissed my tears away and brushed back the hair that was matted to my face.

"Do you want me to be honest?"

I nodded, and Kova sighed then exhaled.

"Do I want you to get pregnant and have a kid? That is a firm fuck no. A child would ruin our lives right now. However, I would never tell you to get an abortion. Yet hearing you say that you would have for some reason does not sit well with me. I know it does not make sense. It is your life and your choice. Your body is your body and I would never tell you what to do with it." Pressing a quick kiss to my lips, Kova continued. "Listen to me. You took those pills at the correct time, Ria. I made sure of it. That is why you did not get pregnant, not because of your illnesses. Did it worry me in the past that there was a chance you could get pregnant? Yes. I have never been so reckless with anyone in my life. I have used protection, so it did panic me a bit, especially given our situation and ages. But I do believe you will have a child one day, Ria. It would be a crime if you did not pass along all the amazing qualities you have."

My jaw trembled and before I could stop them, lone tears slid down my temples. I hoped one day that would happen.

"One day at a time," he said, and I nodded.

Cupping the side of my face, Kova leaned down and kissed me softly, taking it slow and spilling his passion into me. This was the last thing I'd expected to happen, and yet I wasn't mad at myself for caving after I'd sworn up and down I never would again. Had it been two months ago, it would've been a different story. But things changed. Maybe it was time I let go and accept what he said was the truth, that he had no choice in the marriage. I'd like to think Kova had more power in such a situation, but there were so many questions I wanted to ask before I jumped to any conclusions.

Pushing into him, I rolled Kova onto his back and straddled his hips. I sat up and without asking, I looked into his eyes and reached between us for his length and positioned him at my entrance. I sank down until my clit rested on his mound. Kova seemed pleased as our bodies infused together, a rush of heat flowed through me as I felt him swell. I didn't understand all these feelings hitting me other than I felt good for once and I didn't want it to end. Tonight, I would just let go and feel.

My teeth sank into my bottom lip and I moaned knowing it wouldn't be long. Hands skimming my thighs to my hips, Kova helped guide me. My hips rotated back, forcing my clit to drag back and forth over his pubic hair. Little sounds escaped me and I fell forward, bracing myself on his stomach to hold myself up. It already felt too good and I hadn't even shifted to slide up and down, I was just taking his length and indulging myself on him. I attempted to wait for Kova, but it was a struggle while I fell deeper into the decadence. Something that felt this intense was easily addicting.

"Am I hurting you?" I asked.

Kova let out a sexy chuckle. "Impossible," he said, then helped me reach the point of no return. He hardly pulled out, just little thrusts, as I rocked harder on him. "Let go on me," he said.

I shook my head, eyes closed as I tried to fight the orgasm off. "I want you to come with me."

"Do not worry about me. I am far from done with you."

Opening my eyes, I glanced down and took Kova's body in. The firm planks of abs, his pillowed pecs and dark nipples, and the A I'd carved into him was enough to make me see fireworks. I stared at the letter and released myself on him, teeth biting into my lip as I squeezed his shaft and came so hard it took my breath away.

My body weak, Kova sat up and cupped the back of my neck. I breathed into him, finally feeling like I'd been sated. Like a huge boulder had been lifted from my shoulders and I could find a moment of absolution.

He pressed his lips to my forehead, and said, "You know I can feel your pussy contracting around my cock?"

I blushed. "Really?"

He nodded, and I said, "That's kind of embarrassing."

"Why? I love knowing I can make you feel so good. It makes me even hotter for you. I have also noticed that you need to come at least twice each time."

"I do?" I hadn't realized.

Kova nodded.

Before I could say anything, he had me up and turned around so I was on my knees with my back to his chest. His arm was wrapped around my waist to hold me up, keeping us both on our knees as he reached between us and grabbed his shaft to position it at my entrance.

"Ease down," he said, kissing my neck as I took him again.

I tensed at the sensitivity, not sure I was built for more sex right now. I was already so tender as it was, but his kisses were luscious enough to make me soften to him. My head rolled to the side and a light moan vibrated in my chest as Kova thrust into me from behind like this was his talent. I quivered at the heightened ecstasy from this angle. God, he was good at this. Thighs pressed to the back of mine, we rode the same ride of rapture together in perfect harmony. The pleasure was already too much with the way his hands roamed my naked body like he couldn't stop touching me.

"Ohh," I sighed, bearing down on him.

He turned my face to his and stared at my mouth. "These lips"—he licked the top and tugged it into his mouth—"are mine."

I drew in a little gasp. Wetness seeped down my inner thigh at his seductive tone.

"This pussy," he said, pulling all the way out, "is mine," then he reared back in. Kova was so deep at this angle.

His hand found my throat and a little spark of anticipation swelled through me. Something cold touched my skin but it was quickly replaced with the hunger of Kova's words.

"Did he kiss you the way I do? Did he make you crazy and eager enough to make you come from just a kiss the way I can?" He kissed me the way he was making love to me.

Kova's tongue was everywhere in my mouth, stroking and tugging, working me up until I was pushing my hips back into his, meeting him thrust for thrust, whimpering into him to take me harder.

"Did he?" Kova asked again, and pushed all the way in until he was seated as deep as he could go.

I shuddered around him, feeling stretched to the max and almost afraid to move. His hand tightened around my neck and a shot of fire burst through me. I wasn't going to last much longer. His width was painful, but then again with Kova, pain and pleasure went hand in hand, and I welcomed it with open arms.

Lips puffy, I broke the kiss and shook my head. "I've only ever felt like this with you."

"Did he fuck you the way I do? Did you beg for more? Did you come for him the way you do for me? Did you fall apart in his arms the way you do mine?"

I didn't have to say it for him to know the truth. He knew I only burned for him.

"No," I said breathlessly. Looking into his eyes, I told him the truth. "I couldn't come every time. And when I finally did, I had to think about you. It was the only way I could finish, imagining you were fucking me. You have ruined me for all other men."

Kova's eyes flashed wildly. His hips pumped eagerly into me faster, crueler, demanding, like he was climbing into me. Air lodged in my throat, but I didn't panic. Not when I'd experienced this in the past with him and knew what was coming. It excited me.

Kova dropped his head to my neck. His hands were in my hair. Hot thick breaths tickled my damp, heated flesh. He grunted, the delicious vibration in his chest caused chills on my back with each thrust. I felt every inch of his thick cock down to the vein I loved to touch.

This wasn't just sex. This was making love. A deep, heart-tugging, animalistic form of lovemaking that no one would understand but us. I realized I didn't want anyone to understand us. Only we mattered.

Kova held me firmly in place and I found it insanely erotic. I knew he loved the fight, so I purposely struggled against him. The strength in him, the way his hips moved against mine, I wanted to grab him and hold him close and show him how much he meant to me too.

"That is where you are wrong. There will never be another man, Adrianna. Never," Kova stated, then sank his teeth into the curve of my neck.

Ecstasy shot through me, and I let out a long moan. Bliss exploded throughout my wanton body and ignited my veins with a pleasure only he knew how to give me. My pussy throbbed and my clit ached for his tongue. I wasn't going to last much longer. My eyes rolled shut and I moaned long and loud while he licked my heated flesh. Back arching wildly, I ached for him to bring me release already. I was close to yelling out the L word, but I refrained.

"You know why that is?" he asked, his voice heavy with desire. He turned my head again to look at him. Before I could answer, he did. "Because you are mine and will always be mine." Kova surged in deeper and I whimpered because it was the truth. I was forever his. "Just like I will always be yours," he added, then kissed me without remorse or guilt, like he worshiped the ground I walked on.

His hips rolled into me like a wave crashing, hitting so deep I gasped each time. My orgasm was climbing, and his cock twitched. We were reaching the pinnacle of ecstasy.

I'd never understood what lovemaking was until now.

As his hand tightened around my neck, I blindly found his other one and brought it to my clit. I helped him stroke myself and sighed breathlessly from the lust. Kova's body hardened and I took satisfaction in that. Reaching a little farther, I wrapped my thumb and forefinger around his girth at the base and helped guide his cock back and forth into me. Our pleasure covered my hand and I squeezed harder from the slippery mess we'd created. Kova bit down on my neck and chills scored my skin. He liked it, I loved it.

"Are you mine? Really mine?" I asked out of nowhere. If I was his, it was only fair he was mine.

"I have been yours since the day you walked into World Cup, *malysh*. The moment I saw you, I knew that was it and that I would have you one day."

He didn't need to say more. I knew why things had gone the route they had. Only this time, I actually believed him.

chapter 28

MY THIGHS SHOOK.
I reached behind me and fisted his hair, pulling on the strands as I brought his free hand to rest on my mound.

"Feel that?" I pushed his hand down as he thrust his cock inside me. He growled against my jaw. He felt what I felt and it was hot as hell. "That's your cock fucking me. In and out, you can feel yourself taking me and how deep you are.

He shook his head. "This is not me fucking you, this is me making love to you, because, *Ya lyublyu tebya, malysh. Ya lyublyu tebya.*"

My lips parted and my breathing labored at his candor, but I couldn't say it back, even though my heart ached to.

I knew better.

"Come with me, *malysh*," he said, and I nodded. I was beyond ready. "Let me show you just how good it can be." Then he kissed me roughly, biting my lips, and I gave it right back, meeting his needs.

I placed my palm over our joined bodies to feel us orgasm together. I wanted to feel his cum leak from me, to know he felt just as good as I did. My lips, swollen and plump, were spread wide. There was something sexy about our bodies and how they moved and stretched to fit our carnal needs. Kova's fingers sped up on my tender clit, and the hold he had around my neck tightened to an asphyxiating level but I didn't fight it. I couldn't. Not when I was drowning in the pleasure he gave me.

Hips thrusting harder and faster, my nails scored his cock as our bodies trembled on the edge of desire. We were both there, and we both let go.

Kova released inside me, his cock pulsating as his warm semen filled me, seeping out the sides. He coated my fingers and my pussy softened around him to soak up what he gave me. His body shook behind me and a gratified smile tipped the corners of my mouth as I bit down on his lip. I loved knowing he felt what I did. I quickly followed, coming on him. Reaching farther, I grabbed his sack and squeezed. The hand on my throat tightened to the point I couldn't breathe, but the pleasure was so intense that I didn't care. I wanted more, and more, and more, and to never come down from this high.

Little silver stars danced in my vision as the orgasm wracked through my body. My heart beat so hard and fast and an exhausted blissful sigh rolled off my lips. An out-of-body sensation prickled down my arms that ended with my toes curling in need. Kova was right. I didn't come apart in Hayden's arms the way I did his.

Kova was showing me who he was and what he had to give. His hips hadn't stopped moving, and I was too high on this intense thirst for more to realize the smoky black clouds crawling across my vision was partially from the sensuality and depraved passion only Kova could deliver, and from the grip he had on my throat.

I released a sigh just as the darkness closed in, and felt the plush softness of my bed against my back.

Opening my eyes, I took a deep breath and blinked a few times. I looked around. I was a little foggy, my head disoriented. Kova was leaning over me, his head propped on his palm and a sensual smile on his lips. His hand was between my legs, gently, softly, stroking me through his cum. This man never got tired.

"Did I fall asleep?" I asked. My throat was raw.

"Sometimes when the pleasure is so extreme, people will pass out. You passed out."

My brows rose. That couldn't be safe. "For how long?"

"Not very long. Just a few minutes or so."

"And so you took it upon yourself to touch me like that?" I joked.

His eyes flickered with wickedness. "I like the idea of my cum deep inside you," he said and gave me a little kiss as he inserted two orgasm-soaked fingers slowly into my sore pussy. The wet suction echoed in the confinement of my room. "It makes me utterly fucking hot for you."

My back bowed, lifting my breasts into the air. "No more, Kova," I said, breaking the kiss. "I'm too sore and I'm tired."

He shook his head. "I want to touch you."

I couldn't deny him. "Fine, but I'm going to sleep." I laughed and rolled into his chest with a smile.

I felt a million times lighter, like I was normal again. His fingers stroked me, teased me, but never penetrated again. A simmer of heat kindled in me as I fell asleep. I caught myself rolling over onto his hand and grinding down when a little pinch nipped at my skin, just hard enough to send me over the edge again and into oblivion.

I'd only slept for a few hours before I was rousing to the scent of spices wafting through my condo. I sat up and got out of bed to quickly grab a shirt and slip it on. I shivered as the material draped over me, a chill setting in my bones when I realized I'd forgotten to take my medication earlier. Shit.

I rubbed my eyes with the heel of my hand feeling so exhausted but less stressed at the same time. I knew Kova was the reason for that, but I didn't know if it was because we'd succumbed to our secrets, or the sex. Or both. I didn't feel a wedge between us anymore. I didn't feel like I was a foreign object trying to find its place in the world. There was still a lot to talk about, but the pent-up anger sitting on my chest wasn't there anymore.

The wind howled outside as I left my room, and I jumped from the sound of a bang on my wall. My patio furniture was sliding around. I should've brought it inside but it was too late for that now. Not with the hurricane on us the way it was.

I stepped into the living room and stopped short when I spotted Kova standing at the stove. His back was to me and he was in nothing but the shorts he'd had on earlier. They sat extremely low on his hips, revealing the two little dimples above his ass. They were so sexy. My hands ached to be on him, to touch him. I stared in a daze, my eyes traveling higher, dancing across his bare back while I took in every muscle as he cooked. I was salivating, and not from the delicious smell emanating from the kitchen.

Kova lifted a glass of water to his lips and I took note of the beautiful, sinewy curvature of his arms. I had no idea what he was cooking, and I didn't care. I just wanted to bite him.

I drew in a breath and he turned at the sound. Our eyes met and my lips parted. I'd forgotten about his Olympic ring tattoo inked in black lengthwise along his ribs. I loved it so much but it was only noticeable when he lifted his arm or moved it to the side. Like a little secret only privy to those who were fortunate enough to see it. I was drawn to it like a goddamn magnet.

I questioned if there would ever be a time when my stomach wouldn't flutter or my feelings wouldn't rush to the surface when he was around. I wasn't sure what one would call it, but the energy when he was near was exhilarating. I craved him, and I think he craved me too.

My feet carried me to him. I glanced at the stove and briefly wondered where this variety of food had come from when I remembered Alfred had dropped it off. It smelled divine and looked restaurant quality.

Kova placed his glass down on the marble countertop then lowered the heat and looked back at me. A lazy, happy smile formed on his face and it made me feel good. He seemed free from the restraints of his world. Uninhibited, like me. I stood before him, my head coming just below his honey-colored pecs. Kova was larger than life in my eyes, and I was so small in comparison to him.

Going on basic necessity, I reached out to touch his stomach. I needed to feel him again. Just to feel and nothing more. My fingers pressed his taut skin. His abs dipped while my nails feathered across the little fine hair. My other hand came up to touch his hip, my thumb creating a continual swirl on the incredibly delectable oblique V that accentuated his physique. I liked when he let me touch him. His gaze darkened and his eyes lowered. Earlier I'd surrendered to exactly what I promised myself would never happen again, but now, now I was a different person with different desires, cravings, and temptations. Different limitations.

It was all there, ready to shatter the surface again. Taking one last step closer, my knuckles brushed his ribs to trace over the ink. Kova sucked in a breath. His ribs contracted from my delicate touch.

"Why do you like it so much?" he asked.

I subtly shook my head, unsure of myself. I didn't have a reason why I was drawn to it.

"Maybe one day you will have one."

My eyes lit up at the possibility but were quickly doused at a thought. I wasn't sure now I'd ever get a tattoo, or make it as far as he had, but I liked the idea of having one similar to his.

"I might never get the opportunity you had." I sketched all five circles with my nail, then, without thinking, I pressed my lips to his tattoo.

"Ria," he whispered. His stomach flexed beneath my kiss. "What are you doing?"

I shrugged. "Your body is so beautiful. I can never get enough of it."

I acted purely on wild, untamed desire. Both my palms moved slowly up his chest, and when my hands danced over his nipples, he moved fast and gripped the back of my head, fisting my hair and twisting it around his hand. He yanked me so I was flushed against his hard body. We both gasped, then exhaled. This felt so right. I was shocked my body wanted him again so soon. His fingers sensually massaged the back of my head and I reveled in it. Kova's nostrils flared, his jaw ticked, and I stared at his lips with a sudden need to suck on them. Desire swirled in Kova's gaze and I blinked, melting into this enigmatic man I should stay far away from.

"You should know none of what happened between us was any of my intention when I came here today."

Then he smashed his mouth to mine. Kova's tongue slid along the seam of my lips and I opened just enough for him to thrust inside.

chapter 29

I ROSE UP ON MY TIPTOES AND WRAPPED MY ARMS AROUND HIS BROAD shoulders.

We kissed like starved animals, ravaging each other as if we were each other's last meal.

We consumed each other to an unhealthy degree, taking as much as possible.

He gripped my sore body, so mean, so rough, and lifted me up. My heart was beating so wildly for him that I almost told him I loved him. I slid along him, my legs automatically wounding around his waist as our tongues twirled erotically against each other's in a forbidden dance of life and death. Kova's hand cupped the crest of my ass and hip almost cruelly. I was beginning to think he was unaware of his strength and briefly wondered if I had marks on my neck, but his fingers slid dangerously close to my sex and every thought I had vanished.

It only took seconds for me to drip with desire from Kova's kiss, which wasn't surprising. The man's mouth was a gift.

"God, I have missed you," he said between kisses. "I thought you were going to wake up with regret and hate me," he said. My heart pounded viciously against my ribs and I felt bad he feared that. I needed to tell him. "I thought you were going to throw me out. I thought we were not going to be able to talk. I definitely did not expect this."

A tiny smile pulled at my face. I shook my head. "Quite the opposite. I feel alive again, thanks to you."

Kova slammed me into the refrigerator. His body rolled into mine and I felt his erection straining against his shorts. He tugged on my hair and I squeaked. I rocked my hips into his, silently begging for more. The budding bloom of an orgasm began to glow. I locked my ankles and squeezed so he was perfectly aligned with my pussy and rubbed myself on him.

I whimpered, a frenzied covet reverberating in my chest. I was wholly addicted to him and the sexuality he brought out in me. How amazing it was. There were no words for what he made me feel, only that I wanted it all the time.

"More," I begged breathlessly.

Kova growled, and I fucking loved the sound of it. The tips of his fingers teased my sex, prodding the seam, but I couldn't take it any longer. Reaching down, I moved his hand to where I wanted it and almost came.

"No. I think you should take a break," he said.

I shook my head. "I want you. I need you, Kova, so bad. You make me forget my reality, and I needed that more than anything."

He pulled back and grinned so sexy I wanted to jump him. "You just want my cock," he said. "Is that all I'm good for, Adrianna?"

Leaning forward, I bit his lip and tugged it into my mouth. I smiled and met his gaze. "I love your cock," I admitted, then sighed into him when his tongue met mine, but he swiftly moved his hand away.

With my back bowed and shoulders pressed to the refrigerator, my hips came off the cold appliance to get more of his cock. I moved his hand back to where I wanted it and he growled again, this time not liking my assertiveness because he pulled his hand away quickly.

He wanted to play like that. Fine, I could too.

I reached between us to palm his dick through his shorts, rubbing it to build friction, making sure to show attention to his sack too.

Kova exhaled a heavy breath and moaned, pressing his forehead to mine. "I love this untamed side of you." Then he bit my lip, tugging on it with his teeth.

I yelped and wetness seeped from my pussy. I slapped his bare back so he'd let up, but he didn't. Kova jerked on my lips, much harder this time, crueler than I'd expected. I felt a sharp pinch and gripped his cock, squeezing his swollen head in return. I was too delirious with pleasure and pain and undulated into him again. He grunted in satisfaction and slapped the door next to me. Kova thrust his hips harshly against my pelvis and shoved his tongue back into my mouth where I tasted blood. My blood. He'd bitten me to the point of bleeding.

I pulled back and he cupped my jaw with both his hands. Hair matted my face. I looked into his eyes and knew his glossiness mirrored mine.

"I made you bleed," he whispered, his gaze trained on my mouth. His hoarse tone was somewhat animalistic and it made my heart race. I felt a trickle of something slide down my jaw. "I made you bleed," he said again, as if needing to hear his own voice.

"It's only fair since I cut you."

"I love that you marked me. It took every ounce of self-control I had not to tear your clothes off and have you do it while I fucked you."

I gasped at the enticing thought.

"You want that," he stated. "You want to feel the knife press into my skin while you come on my cock."

My lips parted, cheeks flushing with embarrassment. I couldn't answer that honestly.

Kova flattened his tongue and pressed it to my chin, dragging it up where the drip was and licked it clean before kissing me deeply. I kissed him back with the same intensity, tasting the rich blood on my tongue. I was thoroughly spellbound by it and allowed him to lick my mouth all around, lapping at it before kissing me again.

"Kova." I panted. "Jesus…"

"I know," he said, reading my thoughts, knowing I wasn't asking for sex.

Reaching for his shorts, I tried to push them down. His pubic hair tickled my fingers, exciting me, but Kova pulled back and locked eyes with me.

"No," he said, stopping me.

"Yes."

"*Malysh*, no. You need rest."

I smirked and held still for a moment, but pushed the elastic waistband down farther. Per usual, Kova wasn't wearing boxers. His eyes glazed and his lips parted in pure erotic bliss. I smiled lazily. The back of my fingers grazed his cock and I slipped my hand inside his shorts, pushing them down his hips. I cupped his firm, round ass and pulled him to me. His skin was so soft and smooth and full of muscle.

"I just want to feel you," I begged softly. I stroked Kova, feeling the veins twirl down his length. "You know I love this the most," I said, and pressed on the vein.

His face was a mixture of confusion and smugness. I wanted to feel the flatness of his abs as my hands slid down to cup his balls, the thickness of his thighs as I held on to them. I loved Kova's body. Maybe not *him* at times, but his body, I could admit to loving that.

Kova shuddered as I caressed his length. He kissed me, softly, slowly, tenderly. As I brought my hand up, wetness hit my wrist. I glanced down at the swollen purple crown pressed against my pussy and saw a pearly white drop of liquid. Using my thumb and index finger, I rubbed it over his head, then an idea hit me. He moaned, guttural and hot, loving the attention I was focusing on his cock. His head rolled back and I pinched the tip. He sighed and clenched his jaw, releasing a breath. I pinched again and saw the vein in his neck pulse.

"Why do you do this to me?" he bit out. "Fuck."

My thighs trembled around his hips as he muttered something in Russian against my mouth, then he slowed his kissing.

"Let me down," I said against his mouth. Kova looked at me in confusion. "Let me down and turn off the stove."

His eyes widened. He'd forgotten he'd left it on, but I hadn't. As he lowered me to the floor, he reached over and switched the stove off. Still sandwiched between him and the refrigerator, I got on my knees and looked up at him. My body might have been sore, but my knees were okay, and I could—wanted—to give this to him.

His cock stood erect and thick against his toned stomach. Grabbing his hips, I gently slid his shorts down to his ankles. Kova was a sight at this angle, a beautiful virile sight. A man who made me ache for things I couldn't name or explain, something riskier that provoked an intensity between pain and pleasure. Much like gymnastics.

"What are you doing?" I asked as he pulled away. "Let me do this for you."

"No." He moved to pull away again, but I dug my nails into his thighs.

"I want to. Let me give this to you."

Before he could protest again, I took him into my mouth and wrapped my tongue around his length. I tasted myself on him and sucked hard. At least, I tried to. His body became lax. He brought his arms up and rested them against the refrigerator, laying his head on his forearms. Kova shuddered, releasing a moan so primal and unhindered I couldn't help but wonder what he had bottled up inside for that kind of relief to break free.

Taking him as deep as I could, which was only halfway or else I would've gagged, I suctioned my lips around him as much as possible and glanced up. His strength was more pronounced at this angle, and I could see every powerful, pliable curve and arc of muscle in his magnificent body. But his face was twisted in a blend of gratification and shame. The very two words that defined our illicit relationship.

Using my hand, I wrapped my fingers around the base and slid them up and down in sync with my mouth. Something told me he liked a tight squeeze, so I tightened my hold, digging my nails into his shaft. He drew in a breath when my tongue twirled around his heat and stroked it up and down.

"Ria...more."

"Tell me what to do. I don't know what I'm doing." I dug my nails in more and reached for his balls, mimicking the motion.

Kova let out a sexy growl and I smiled around his thick erection, knowing I was doing it right.

"Just like that," he whispered.

His hand came down and cupped the back of my head, pushing me into his painstakingly slow rocking pelvis. Kova groaned deep and low as he grew in my mouth, and a slight saltiness coated my tongue. His movement, high from pleasure, made me needy and hot for him.

"Suck harder."

The sucking was getting a little harder on my jaw and cheeks, but when I did what he asked, Kova released another moan and it made it worth the ache. The sounds escaping his lips were so incredibly erotic and I wanted to hear him do it again.

"Scrape your teeth *gently* down my cock and flatten your tongue." He slowly rocked into my mouth again. "Oh fuck… *Malysh*, what… Do not… Oh God." He drew the last word out with a slow roll of his hips. He couldn't formulate words and I basked in the glory that I was making him feel good.

His fingers gripped my hair and knotted it into a twist as he held my face pressed to his hips for a few seconds. I jerked my head to the side and flinched from the hair pulling and accidently bit down. I thought he'd be mad that I hurt him, but I tasted another gush of liquid on my tongue that told me he'd actually liked it.

I swallowed. Kova was a freak.

"Move your hands," he ordered.

"Where do I put them?" I asked with him still in my mouth. It came out garbled, but he knew what I'd asked.

Kova grabbed my wrists and wrapped them around until I was cupping his ass. Kova's dick was long. There was no way I could take his entire length into my mouth and not gag. The kind of vulnerability that came with this position worried me, but I let go and gave this to him.

Shifting his feet, he stepped closer and placed both hands on my jaw to hold my face. There wasn't much space left between me and the kitchen appliance pressed to my back, so I wasn't sure where he thought he was going.

"Relax your throat, *malysh*."

chapter 30

Unsure of what that meant, I glanced up and met Kova's eyes. He saw my confusion and repeated what he'd said, then slid further into my mouth. My brows furrowed and my tongue automatically blocked him from proceeding. There was no room left for him to go deeper.

"See?" he said. "Loosen your shoulders."

Kova reached down and tenderly massaged my throat with his fingers. A shot of pleasure went straight to my pussy and my eyes rolled shut. I was ready to jump his bones. Puzzled wasn't a strong enough word to describe why I liked this so much—his hands on my neck coaxing me to learn a sexual act—but I did. A lot.

"Breathe through your nose and flatten your tongue so I can get to your throat."

I moved to pull away to compose myself a little better, but he pushed me back and kept me there. Clearing my mind, I focused on his words and did as he asked.

"Yes… Just like that, Adrianna. Just…like…that…" He slowly pushed in more, hitting the back of my throat.

I gagged and choked, my eyes filling with tears. He pulled away and I quickly inhaled before he was back at it again, my eyes watering now. His cocked tapped the inside of my throat with each thrust and guide of his hips, his hands threaded in my hair and massaged my neck at the same time.

"I want to feel the back of your throat. I need to get deeper…" He groaned. "Oh, the thoughts you give me, my girl, the things I want to do to you…"

That was the most bizarre thing I'd ever heard. Why the hell would he want to touch the back of my throat? I had no desire to ever touch the back of *his* throat.

"Have you ever swallowed?"

I shook my head no, and his eyes darkened. I hadn't. I'd never given a real blow job before.

I pulled back and quickly said, "I told you I didn't know what I was doing."

His mouth tugged into one of the sexiest grins I'd ever seen on him. Then he began a deep and hard roll with his hips, driving into my mouth so artfully.

"I am almost there… Oh, fuck. Just remember to breathe through your nose and loosen up, it will all slide down and you can swallow."

Okay. Sounded easy enough.

But it wasn't. Not even close.

Kova's cock slid over my tongue and past my throat into my neck. My fucking neck! The sounds that came out of him were not normal. They were carnal and sensuous and deeply hot. Something warm slid down my throat and his hand massaged the outside of my neck. I moved to pull back as panic set in me from the large obstruction in my esophagus, but my head hit the stainless steel refrigerator. My eyes watered profusely. It was like he knew my next move because he found my wrists and held them behind him. My nails scored his ass cheeks as he pushed farther into my mouth.

I was going to die from giving head. My family would be shamed for all eternity.

"Oh yes, take it all, take it all." He came…a lot.

His cock pulsated and stiffened. I wasn't prepared for the thickness of his semen or how awfully salty it was, but it filled my mouth, and if I didn't do as he said and gulp it back, I was going to throw up. I could bite down, but he'd probably like it.

I had to make a decision fast.

"Swallow it, Ria. Swallow every fucking drop."

My fingers dug into the seam of his cheeks, and it was in that moment I decided to do something no straight man would ever want. At least, I didn't think they'd want.

My throat contracted and I closed my eyes as I drank him down. It wasn't easy but I focused and managed so I could give him what he wanted. And I wanted to. I needed him to have this.

Kova yelled out in ecstasy while my fingers skimmed his round ass toward forbidden territory. Just when I thought he'd pull away, he did the opposite and trembled against me as I poked and prodded the puckered little hole with one finger. His butt cheeks clenched together, and I pushed deeper.

He fucking loved it.

Kova loved it so much, he let go of my wrists and cupped my jaw and the back of my head as he finished coming in my mouth. He shoved himself down and even though tears ran down my face, I kept sucking until I swallowed every single drop. He was sexy as fuck when he moaned.

"Never better," he slurred in a trance, and I pushed my finger in one last time. "Oh, fuck…I have never come so hard in my life."

He withdrew from my mouth before I could swallow the last drop and it dripped down my chin. Kova lifted me up. My legs automatically wound around his hips as he smashed his mouth to mine, not caring that I hadn't swallowed the last little bit of his cum, and he kissed me hard. I wrapped my arms around his neck and kissed him back with the same intensity. So much so my heart throbbed for this beast of a man who could be so cruel and passionate at the same time. Something forfeited inside me, something I was holding back. Something more than liking him, more than lusting after him.

His hand found the back of my hair and his tongue delved into my mouth, consuming me, not giving a fuck he that was tasting himself as he kissed the shit out of me. We pulled back at the same time, panting heavily into each other. His eyes exposed a collection of feelings, twisting my stomach with the impulse to listen.

There was that L word again.

I offered him a tender smile. He wiped my chin with his thumb and I grabbed it to suck it clean.

"Who are you?" he asked in sheer wonderment.

I laughed and shook my head, then slid down his body to stand.

Kova kissed my lips. He pulled his shorts up, but not all the way. I had a partial view of the width of his cock peeking out. I licked my lips. He was too sexy for his own good.

"I like this look on you," I said and rubbed his light mound of hair. With each passing moment I spent with Kova, I found I had a little less modesty.

He brushed my hand away, veiling a grin. "Now that we have worked up an appetite, let me finish cooking for us." He smirked, then slapped my ass as I walked away.

Before I sat down, I walked to where all my medicine bottles were lined up. I studied them, hating that I had to take so many pills and that I had to do so for the rest of my life. I wasn't sure what would happen since I'd missed a dose—hopefully nothing too extreme. I wasn't sure how much more I could handle.

"Don't watch me," I said quietly when I felt the weight of his gaze on me.

I uncapped a bottle and poured out two capsules.

Kova handed me his water glass, stirring the food on the stove with his other hand.

"Want to talk about it?"

I downed the first two capsules without looking at him, then I opened the next bottle.

"Not yet."

"I will take it. That is better than a no."

I stared straight ahead, trying to figure out a way to avoid this conversation. I took the next set of pills.

"You already know everything, Kova."

"But I did not hear it come from you."

I turned toward him, frustration simmering below the surface. Kova turned off the stove and looked my way.

"Why do you need to hear it from me?" I asked. "To hear that I'm scared? That I don't know when I'll be stage five and that terrifies me? I'm fragile right now, okay, Kova? Not talking about it is the only way I can deal with it."

Kova's voice softened. "I am asking so I can feel what you are feeling. So I can get inside your head and see where you are, what I can do to help you. I told you, we are a team. I exhale, you inhale. I want to hear from your lips what is going on in your head so I can get on the same level as you and understand. You do not have to do it alone."

My jaw trembled. I hadn't expected that or the compassion in his eyes or for it to wrap around my heart. It moved me to observe him with a little more kindness. He was trying, just like I was.

"Do you want to talk about Joy, your wife, and the way they blackmailed you into marriage?"

"I know it seems that way, but yes, I do want to talk about it. I am not ready to discuss the fact that both the women in our lives are dirty little serpents, but I do want you to know why I married Katja and that it was not something I wanted."

"But at one time you did. One time you wanted to marry her and planned to," I retorted, then cringed, wondering when I would let that go.

"Yes, I did. I even bought the ring for when the time was right."

My burning heart dropped into my stomach and I sighed, looking away. "I hadn't known that. I shouldn't have said anything, I'm sorry."

"Do not be sorry. I really want us to be open with each other," he said, and I narrowed my eyes at him. He chuckled. "I am a work in progress, but I promise I am trying. I just want to focus on you right now."

I chewed the inside of my lip in contemplation and finally nodded. "I feel like I'm taking another huge risk for you, Kova. One hand is saying trust you, the other is saying run far away. Please, do *not* lie to me ever again. I honestly don't know if I could handle it if you do."

Regret weathered him. "I am eternally sorry for what happened and the way I handled things. I did and said a lot of things I didn't mean. It was not right and I am not making excuses for my actions, but I was backed up against a wall. Once you know everything, then you will understand. At least, I hope you will."

Turning back toward the bottles lined up against the wall on the counter, I stared at them, hoping they would give me a sign or an answer to the questions in my head and the feelings in my heart that I tried to ignore.

Reaching for the third bottle, I uncapped it and dumped the pills into my hand, then threw them back and swallowed them. Only four more bottles to go. At this point, I didn't have much left to lose.

chapter 31

KOVA PLACED THE LARGE PASTA BOWL I DIDN'T EVEN KNOW I HAD ON the counter.

I glanced inside as he twirled the food around then spooned it into two bowls and placed one in front of me. My eyes widened. Grilled chicken and asparagus in an Alfredo sauce. The steamy delicious aroma filled the air and my stomach growled. I hadn't had this kind of meal in ages.

"Wow. I didn't know you could cook like this." I laughed.

Kova sat next to me. "I actually love to cook. Last time I did, you did not eat."

I definitely didn't know that about him.

"Thank you," I said.

My heart shifted, like a small piece that had broken was glued back in place. Kova was a good guy. Despite his outlandish ways, he had a good heart. Albeit a tarnished one, but nothing that couldn't be cleaned and wiped anew.

"I know we do not have a normal"—he looked at me in search of the right word, but typical Kova and his lack of English mixed it up—"relationship, but I am always here for you. And I do not mean that on a coach/gymnast level. I hope you know by now I sincerely more than care about you."

That was the thing. He had been there for me, and much more as of late. I didn't loathe it, but I didn't love it either. I needed to find a way to come to terms with it.

"Just please, don't baby me. I know you were probably careful with me since you found everything out, but don't be. In order for me to be the best, I have to train hard, and part of that is you treating me like any other person training under you. Otherwise it will mess with me."

He stared at me for a long moment and rubbed the back of his neck. I thought he was going to disagree, but he surprised me.

"I will promise to go hard on you the same way I used to, if you promise to tell me when you are not feeling well. It can be as simple as a headache, but I need to know. Deal?"

I lit up. "Deal."

Kova put his hand out to shake on it, but instead, I threw my arms around his shoulders and sealed the deal with a hug.

Twirling the pasta on my fork, I took a bite and the flavor exploded in my mouth.

"Oh, my God! This is amazing!" I said, then twirled more onto my fork.

Appreciation spread throughout his face. This was restaurant quality. I should've known better. Anything Kova sets out to do, he does well.

An easy calmness settled in the air while we ate. Rain drenched my patio and hit the sliding glass door, but there was something rather peaceful about this moment. There wasn't an awkward second between us and I loved that. Kova had seconds, but I was too full after the rather large portion he'd given me.

Once we were finished, Kova took our bowls to the sink. I watched as he cleaned up my kitchen and thanked him again.

"I can't remember the last time I ate something so delicious or was this full. I probably won't need to eat again until tomorrow."

He chuckled, and I loved how light and airy it sounded. Relaxed. It was surreal how this moment felt completely normal, like there was no huge age gap between us, no rules, no one to offer their two cents to us or look at us in disgust. Like we'd done this a million times. I wondered if this was what it was like to be in a full relationship with him.

"Oh, God," I said suddenly, clutching myself as cramps rocked my abdomen. My stomach quivered, little bubbles swaying and popping inside me.

"What is wrong, *malysh?*" he asked, turning off the sink and drying his hands with a cloth. He eyed me with concern.

I shook my head. Hunching over, a cramp tore through my stomach and bile climbed up my throat. Heat curled through me raking its claws across my lower abdomen. Kova came over to help me up, but I couldn't stand. My legs trembled, and I felt weaker than I'd been in years. My hand gripped the table for leverage just as Kova was there to catch me.

"My stomach. It hurts so bad. I need the bathroom. Now," I insisted, chewing my lip raw. Anything to not focus on the shredding of my stomach.

I tried to take a few steps, but my legs were of no use. My knees buckled and I almost fell to the floor in a heap, but Kova was quick and scooped me up, cradling me to his chest.

"I have you," he said, his lips pressed to my forehead.

I covered my mouth, and muttered, "Hurry, Kova. I'm gonna be sick." I felt the food I'd just eaten coming up and prayed it stayed down, trying desperately to not vomit all over him.

Kova flipped on the lights and then let go of my legs, keeping a hold on my chest to help me stand. My sluggish body slid down his tall frame.

The sight of the toilet triggered me. I gagged and covered my mouth, fighting the vomit, but it was of no use. My stomach clenched and cramped. I ran from Kova's hold and lunged for the toilet. My knees slammed down to the tile floor with a loud whack and I bent over. The pain didn't register in my head. I was just in time to expel everything I'd eaten. My fingers curled around the ledge and the smell of the water coated my nostrils. Everything came up.

Tears slid down my cheeks as every conceivable disgusting sound spewed from my lips. Embarrassment burned my cheeks. I wanted to die. This was not how I'd pictured tonight going.

Though I was pretty sure my stomach was empty, I couldn't stop hurling. My hair stuck to my face and snot dripped from my nose. I tried to shove at Kova's bare chest but I got nowhere. He wasn't budging.

"Go away," I choked out. I didn't want him to see me like this.

"Let me help you," he said sympathetically.

Thankfully, Kova did what he was good at and ignored my pleas.

He pulled my hair back, making sure to get the strands that were stuck to my damp face. Some of the tips had dipped into the vomit and I was instantly hot all over. Kova flushed the toilet, and a little mist hit my face. My teeth gnashed together as I tried to fight throwing up again, but it didn't help. Eyes clenched shut, I leaned deeper into the bowl, unavoidably inhaling the rancid water as my body trembled violently. The back of my neck burned. Little pebbles of moisture beaded my tepid skin as I broke out in a sweat. Slowly, I opened my eyes only to realize it was a huge mistake because I vomited one more time.

Kova held my hair back with one hand and rubbed my back with his other. He flushed the toilet, then handed me a washcloth. I wiped my face, gagging.

When I was positive there was nothing left in my stomach, I shut the lid and folded my arms over it to rest my head. I couldn't get up. Everything felt swollen—my eyes, my lips, my body, my feet. I felt like I had a fever. I was uncomfortably bloated and a little pulse thrummed under every square inch of my skin. I felt so incredibly weak down to my bones. I just wanted to crawl into bed and hibernate under the covers. Kova took the wash cloth from my hand and gently dabbed and wiped the side of my face and neck as I stared at the wall in a daze.

"Thank you," came out in a broken whisper. My throat burned. "There's nothing worse on this planet than throwing up in front of someone. I'm sorry."

"Nonsense. It is normal and does not bother me. But I think you may have spewed your pills."

My eyes fluttered. "I feel disgusting." I licked my parched lips and I became nauseated all over again. As if he read my mind, Kova stood and turned on the shower.

"I think you look beautiful as always."

I almost laughed.

Using every ounce of willpower left in me, I held onto the wall and used my thighs to stand. Despite all the muscle in my body, I was useless. A few steps and I was in front of the shower reaching to feel the warmth. The heat engulfed my face and I sighed in content, feeling a little better. I loved steaming hot showers.

Drained with barely any energy to stand, I looked at myself in the mirror right as I reached to pull my shirt off and caught sight of my face. Christ on a stick. Mascara streaked my face like a badly designed maze. My full lips were abnormally swollen and red, and my eyes were puffy and bloodshot.

Exhaling a sigh, I tugged on the seam of my shirt and attempted to pull it over my head, but I was too faint and didn't have the strength. Kova walked back in just in time to see my struggle and took over. I didn't object. He gently pulled the shirt off, then dropped it to the floor.

Steam filled the bathroom. I glanced down. My stomach was caved in, hollowed, with a steep slope toward my ghastly protruding hips. I knew I'd lost a ton of weight due to the illnesses, but it was something I'd learned to ignore.

A hiss flew from his lips with a subtle shake of his head. "Ria," Kova whispered in disbelief, the back of his hand grazing down my pelvis. "I did not notice before."

He was concerned at the sight, and quite frankly, I was too now that I finally let myself look in the mirror.

"I'm fine. Just help me, please," I said, reaching out for him.

"You are too small," he said more under his breath than to me. I pursed my lips together. I hated to hear the pity that was conveyed in his voice. "I do not like this, Ria. You are wearing yourself down too much."

"Kova, please," I said, shutting him down.

He wasn't wrong, but I didn't want to hear it. I knew I was wearing myself down too much, but I told myself this was what I wanted and what I needed to do. I didn't want to be treated any differently, especially not now. My dream had become an addiction, and I'd willingly done anything and everything to achieve that high, now more than ever. I may have destroyed myself in the process, but I wasn't going to stop. I was too close to the pinnacle of victory. There would be no change come tomorrow.

I stepped under the waterfall spray and closed my eyes. The heated water felt heavenly as it prickled down my skin. There was just something about a scorching hot shower that I loved. Squeezing a dollop of shampoo into my hand, I began washing my hair, but was suddenly overcome with fatigue. There was a rumbling in my stomach and the bubbles were popping again. I wasn't sure why was so sick, or why I felt the way I did now. It was a probably a culmination of things and I knew moving forward I'd have to make sure I was more careful about myself. My arms fell to my sides and I exhaled in a huff. I just wanted to go to sleep.

The glass door slid open and I looked over my shoulder. My heart soared as Kova stepped under the water until his chest was pressed to my back. I was so grateful.

He wrapped his arms around my shoulders, and I leaned back and took in a moment of harmony. He dropped a light kiss to the top of my head. Kova brought a sense of security that I soaked up each time and never questioned. A peace in me that I just rolled with that no one else ever gave me.

The water around our feet ran pink from the dried blood. I'd forgotten we both had it on us. We rinsed and lathered each other, and I made sure to be gentle around the A while I cleaned him. Kova washed me in the most affectionate way possible. He took care of me like he was devoted to me…and I let him. Because it felt right. Because it didn't occur to me to not let him. Because within these walls, it felt normal for us to be and feel what was natural between us, regardless of age.

chapter 32

COACH OR NOT, KOVA WAS THE ONLY PERSON WHO GAVE ME THIS soothing comfort, making me feel like everything was going to be okay. I needed his strength right now. I didn't care that he had a wife or that there was a hurricane outside. Maybe that made me selfish, but when it came to Kova, my heart beat only for him. My accomplishments were for him just as much as they were for me.

God, I hated being so emotional. Everything was rising to the surface and I couldn't stop it.

Stepping out of the shower, Kova handed me a towel and said, "Dry your hair and wrap it up. I will take care of the rest."

He studied me, his eyes roaming over my face. I shot a fleeting glance in the mirror. I looked like death.

I put my hand up. "I know... I look like the ghost of Lucifer."

The corner of his eyes crinkled and Kova laughed. "I am pretty sure that is impossible," he said, hanging the towel up. "You could never resemble the devil. How do you feel?"

"Much better actually. I'm so tired, but I don't feel as sick anymore." I bit my lip. "I'm so sorry about that. I don't know what happened. I think I just need to rest a little."

I followed Kova out of the bathroom, my gaze on his perfectly round butt and the two little dimples above it as he walked toward my bed. I was infatuated with his body and could stare at it for hours.

The power flickered and my heart stopped for a second.

"Shit. The storm," I said.

"Where is your lighter?" Kova asked.

I pointed to my nightstand. He opened the drawer and shifted things around. He pulled out a tube and I drew in a mortified breath. Not the lighter he was searching for. He held it up and looked at me with one brow arched.

Shit. I'd forgotten I'd thrown my lube in there for the times when it was just me and myself.

I reached for it but Kova pulled away. "Stop embarrassing me and put that away."

He grinned and I wanted to junk punch him for it. One by one, he lit every candle around my room just in time for the power to go out completely.

"Good thing we showered when we did." He joked. Handing me the lighter, he said, "But something tells me you do not mind being dirty."

I hid a smile and dropped it back into the drawer. Thank goodness he couldn't see the blush that crept up my cheeks.

"Get in the center of the bed and lie down," Kova ordered.

Once I did, Kova climbed on and lifted each ankle so my knees were bent, my body open to him. I watched him with unfazed curiosity. Little by little he stole my modesty and turned me into a vixen with loose morals.

He took my towel, and starting at my neck, he patted me dry, moving down each arm and breast. Kova was hard as a rock, his erection straining and the tip a deep purple, but he didn't try anything, knowing I wasn't feeling well. He made his way to my stomach and thighs, down my legs. Dropping the towel to the floor, he sat between my legs and pushed my knees apart. I widened them further for him until I was completely exposed.

"Kova, what are you doing," I whispered, lust filling my tone.

"You will sleep soundly after this. Let me give you what you want. You need this."

I nodded, hoping he was right. I couldn't remember the last time I'd slept well.

Kova dipped a finger inside of me and curled it. My thighs quivered, and I clenched around him. He slipped another in. This wasn't what I'd expected, but I didn't protest. His rough thumb circled my throbbing clit and I bit down on my bottom lip. My hips rolled toward him in a slow, sensual wave, feeling the touch of him in the most delicious way.

Our eyes met. Neither one of us said a word. He continued to pleasure me slowly, in and out, in and out. Aside from the rain outside, our heavy breathing and the sensual suctioning were the only sounds in the room. It was erotic. Lips parted and knees leisurely widened on their own. I was too aroused to remember I wasn't feeling well.

It wasn't long until Kova's tongue found my center and licked me to the point of orgasm, only to pull back. I yelled out his name, begging for him to let me finish, but he told me to wait. I wanted so badly to hold his head down and smash his face between my legs. Kova was a bittersweet tease. I needed that pressure, that force, and all he did was hold it above my head and dangle it in front of me. His tongue caressed my sensitive clit while his fingers slid in and out, and just when I thought he was done, his teeth gently scraped over my swollen pussy lips…

And sank into the tender skin.

I yelled out and arched my back, twisting my body into him and clutching the sheets in my fists. He ignored me and bit my other side. A rush of desire seeped from me. I moaned, confused by how much I liked this. My eyes rolled to the back of my head and I was suddenly on cloud nine, floating in a beautiful bliss, high as my hips undulated in sweet desire and sexual frustration.

"You are very much like me in many ways, Ria." I looked at him, his face suctioned to my pussy. Deep down, I knew in many ways it was true. "You like a bite of pain with your sex, and I like to give it."

"How do I know I like it?" I asked hardly recognizing my voice.

Kova didn't reply, instead showing me by giving me one long stroke of his tongue, followed by a tight suck to my clit. I moaned in ecstasy, drowning in him.

"I know everything about you, *malysh*. I can tell by the way your body reacts. If you were not aroused this much by it, you would not be this wet."

With his eyes locked on mine, this time he bit my inner thigh, but then kissed it right after. I watched his tongue slip through his lips. Legs widening, I angled my pussy toward his face and rolled my hips up, praying he'd go back to it harder. His teeth tugged on my skin and desire leaked out of me.

"Oh, oh, oh," I moaned, my legs scissoring the sides of this face. "Kova… I can't hold on much longer." I was utterly aching to the point of pain for him and for release.

I leaned up and looked at the marks he'd made. I watched against the flickering candlelight as he flattened his tongue and licked the little crimson pearls. It pooled to new droplets and he licked again. But I couldn't formulate words because his thumb rubbed my throbbing clit in fast circles and I was too turned on watching him drink me in.

Without moving his head, Kova lifted his eyes to mine. He exhaled through his nose and the heated breath cascaded across my pussy. He was a wicked man. The corners of his delicious mouth curved up just slightly into a crooked grin before his head descended. The tip of his nose danced over my mound. My stomach swirled, this time in a good way, as he parted his lips and his teeth sank into my clit.

"I cannot get enough of you," he said, his voice hoarse.

A string of unexplainable sensations shot through me. My toes curled and I clenched around his pumping fingers on the edge of something amazing.

I didn't scream or yell out. I couldn't. I panted, gasping for air. Kova rendered me breathless, certain he punctured the skin thoroughly by the way he pulled on my flush, his tongue sucking at the same time.

"Oh, Kova…" I whimpered, unable to tear my eyes from what he was doing. My nipples hardened to hard points. "I'm about to go… I need to…"

"Not yet," he said around my flesh.

He pulled his fingers out and licked them clean, then sat up on his knees. His cock was erect and bare, the tip purple as it strained between us.

He slid his hands under my lower back and lifted my hips, massaging them. Looking directly into my eyes, he said, "I made love to you last time, but this time, I need to fuck you until you remember who loves you."

I sighed under my breath, my heart clenching. I needed him just as much.

"Say it. Tell me, Adrianna."

"Kova." His name was a whisper on my lips.

In one swift motion, he slid all the way in. We both moaned in unison, our bodies fused together in the most deliciously illicit way. My thighs quivered to adjust to his size and there was a pinch from being stretched, but I loved it and reached for him.

Kova leaned over, his lips pressed to my neck, his breath hot. "Fuck, I do not know how I am going to do this." He pulled out then thrust back in hard and fast, my hips arched taking him deeper. "Be married to her but only want you."

No female in the world ever wanted to be the other woman. I never wanted to, never really thought about it until now, but when you're faced with losing in the situation like I was, you have a change of mind and heart and take whatever you can get.

"Then don't give me up," was all I could say. The thought of losing him physically hurt me. I was willing to be the other girl. "Don't leave me."

"I do not think I can," he said between thrusts. "I love being inside you. I love everything about you. I cannot keep going on like this without you by my side."

Kova pulled out and I cried in protest. "What are you doing?"

Naturally, he ignored me. Kova got off the bed and stood at the end of it. He grabbed my ankle and yanked me to the edge and flipped me over. He clutched both hips and hitched me up.

"Face on the bed. Arch your back."

I did as he said and turned my head to watch him. Breathing heavily, I thought he was going to slide back in, but I should've known better.

Pulling my butt cheeks apart, he bent over and dragged his flat tongue from the tip of my clit all the way up to my little puckered hole. I reached out and fisted the sheets, sighing as he circled the entrance.

"What is it with you and my ass?" I could barely say the words.

"One day you will beg me to take this ass."

"Never," I whispered as he devoured my pussy, his finger trying to penetrate the little hole. My eyes rolled shut in blissful agony. Why did it feel so much better at this angle? "I want to sit on your face," I admitted.

"Let me fuck you first, then you can," he said, then thrust in so hard and fast I wasn't expecting it.

This time I screamed. I shot up, but Kova pushed me down, making sure I took every inch of him at this angle. He rocked into me, forcing my hips into a roll and clutching my butt cheeks. He had a mean grip on my hips as he thrust so ruthlessly. His hips pounded my ass, slamming into me with brutal force, pulling me to him while he thrust into me at the same time. His cock hit deep and hard, penetrating without reserve. My bed slid across the floor from how hard he was driving into me. I clenched up and he pressed a hand to my back again forcing me to stay down.

"Ah, ah, ah." I moaned somewhere between pain and pleasure.

My stomach clenched, feeling a little more pain than usual, kind of hoping he would be done already. I wasn't sure I would be able to come like this myself. He was so deep inside of me that it hurt at this angle.

"Take it. Take all of me, please. Just take me as I am," he begged, then thrust faster than he ever had and came inside of me. "Let me have you like this." He grabbed my hips, helping me take his full length all the way. "Oh, Ria... Fuck..."

The pleasure was almost too much. I watched over my shoulder, fixated on him as his head rolled back and his sexy muscles flexed then contracted. He smashed into me hard, pumping, then holding me still as he orgasmed. He scooped an arm under my waist and held me tight, his other hand squeezing the back of my neck, his cock throbbing with virility and warmth as his seed spread through me. His damp chest was pressed to my back as he grunted and groaned and drove into me with the power of a hundred men.

Okay. Maybe I was exaggerating a little bit, but that's what it felt like.

"Do not move," he said, breathing heavily.

My thighs quivered relentlessly as he pulled out. I continued to watch over my shoulder, but Kova was engrossed with my sex.

"Push it out," he said, his voice hoarse.

I shook my head but gave it to him anyway. A little plop sounded, and I shifted to look between my legs. Kova's cum dripped out of me without even having to try.

"Do it. Push my cum out and let me watch it drip down your pussy and over your clit."

"You're such a dirty man," I said, then brazenly did exactly what he'd demanded.

The thick gooeyness did exactly what he said it would do, only it didn't drop onto the bed. Two of his fingers caught it and pushed it back into my aching pussy. My hips reared back and I moaned, riding his fingers, still needing the release. Kova's eyes glistened like he was in a trance while he shoved his cum back into me.

"Kova," I said in almost a whine. "This isn't fair."

In the blink of an eye, he was on his back with his head near my headboard. "Give me that pussy. Sit on my face, *malysh*, and do not hold back."

I was a little shy, but I didn't hesitate as I crawled up his body until I was up on my knees with my hands on the headboard. I looked between us. My nipples were hard and rosy, and he was staring right at them. We'd never done this before, and I was suddenly a little embarrassed. Kova sensed it and pulled me down to his mouth.

It was all over after that.

"Oh, fuck," I said, drawing out the word.

My hips took over of their own accord. I grinded on his face, hoping I wasn't hurting him but not really caring if I was. The pleasure felt too good and I didn't want it to stop. I guess he liked it because he pulled me harder to him. I rubbed myself on him, his stubble heightening the desire while I rolled my hips over him.

"Just like that," I said breathlessly. "This might be my favorite position."

Then, he stuck two fingers in me and bit down on my clit. His free hand pinched my nipple until I saw stars.

I. Was. Done.

My orgasm hit hard, exploding through my body. It prickled my skin and throttled me to high after high. A scream of ecstasy tore from my chest as I fucked his mouth with my pussy. I reached between us and fisted his hair to pull his head as tight as I could to my sex as I grinded down and came all over his mouth. Kova took me just like I took him. My thighs quivered and squeezed his face. I was probably hurting him. Hopefully he could breathe.

My heart slowing, the orgasm faded and I released my hold on his hair, hoping I didn't pull any out. God, that was amazing. Kova had me on my back in one breath hovering above me. He brushed my hair back. His mouth wet with my pleasure and his eyes a crazy intense kind of lust flaring with emotion.

"I fucking love you," he growled, then crashed his lips to mine.

I loved him, too.

chapter 33

"ADRIANNA... ADRIANNA."

I was sprawled out on my stomach with my head burrowed beneath a pillow. There was a chill in my bones but I felt so hot at the same time. A hand rubbed circles on my back as I slowly stirred awake. My eyes burned like I hadn't slept very long, but the deep slumber I was coming out of said otherwise.

"Adrianna." His thick Russian accent was a whisper that seemed so far away.

"Hmm...?"

I moved the pillow off my head and brushed my hair from my face, trying to look toward the sound of his voice. I opened my eyes but they felt like they were on fire. My entire body felt like it was swelling with heat. I attempted to sit up, but my elbows gave out. I felt horrible. Lethargic and dead tired. If I didn't know any better, I'd say I was having a flare up.

Rolling onto my back, I rubbed my forehead and a soft sigh escaped off my lips.

"I'm so lightheaded." The room spun and my head felt like an inflated balloon. "What time is it?"

Kova sat down on the edge of the mattress and looked down. It was still dark, but the light from the bathroom illuminated parts of the room.

"It is almost six in the morning. I need to get to the gym."

I frowned. "What about the hurricane?"

"It has passed us and luckily did not turn into a cat four. Your power is back on."

I nodded and tried to sit up again, but Kova didn't allow it.

"No, I have practice. I need to go. I have to be there." I struggled against him, but he was so much stronger and insisted I lay down. I wasn't sure how I'd do at practice feeling the way I did, but I needed to be there.

"Absolutely not. I want you to stay in bed. You have a fever and you look awfully pale. You need rest, Ria," he urged.

Last night I vomited, and now I felt like I had the flu. My body was completely worn down and I felt sluggish. I blinked my dry eyes rapidly. Fear consumed me.

"Kova?" My voice cracked, my throat tight and in need of water. "What's wrong with me?"

Was I having a flare up again?

He leaned down and kissed my forehead. Immediately I wrapped my arms around his neck and squeezed him. He pulled me to sit on his lap and I burrowed my face in his neck as he comforted me. I was still naked, but it didn't bother either one of us.

"Nothing is wrong with you, Adrianna. You are just extremely exhausted and need uninterrupted, deep sleep. You have a fever and your cheeks are red."

I nodded. "But I can't miss practice and you promised not to treat me any differently."

He pulled back and gave me a warm smile. "I was selfish and had you many times last night. You barely slept." He looked so pleased. "And"—he held up a finger—"I told you I would not treat you differently so long as you were feeling okay. You cannot push your body or your body will completely shut down. Missing practice will be out of our hands. Stay here and sleep. Hopefully that rash will go away. I will see you tonight."

Hope filled my chest. "You're coming back?"

He nodded.

"Take my keys so you can let yourself back in. What about Katja?"

Kova gave me a look that said don't go there. So I didn't. It was on the tip of my tongue to ask if he could bring me my medicine bottles and a glass of water, but when he kissed the top of my head and whispered, "*Ty ma-yo sak-ro-vee-sche,*" it wasn't long until I was drifting off to sleep, forgetting about my pills.

It was déjà vu all over again. Kova trying to rouse me. His hand on my back, his voice far away.

I sat up, swiping my hair from my face. I was certain I hadn't moved in hours.

"God… What time is it?" I asked, looking around in confusion. My eyes were swollen, my body aching even more.

Kova tilted his head, and his eyes narrowed. "Have you been sleeping all day?"

"I don't know?" I responded softly.

"It is eight o'clock…at night."

My brows shot up and my jaw dropped. "You're kidding me. I slept for fourteen hours straight?"

Kova reached out and pressed the back of his knuckles to my forehead. His palm cupped my jaw in concern. "Are you okay? You still feel warm."

"Yeah, I'm fine. At least I think I'm fine. Apparently, I was much more tired than I thought I was… Wow."

"Your body must have needed rest more than we both thought."

I agreed and moved to the edge of the bed, dropping my legs over the side to sit next to him. I needed to find some clothes.

"I don't think I moved at all after you left."

I was sure I could sleep another ten hours. I clenched my eyes shut then opened them, still feeling so tired.

"How do you feel?" he asked.

"Honestly? I hated that I missed practice, but I feel much better." I paused, my lips forming a thin, flat line. I didn't want to speak my next set of words, but he needed to hear them. "Thanks for making me skip today. You were right, I needed it badly. If you hadn't insisted, I would've been there and who knows what would've happened."

He shrugged shamelessly. "Good thing the gym is closed tomorrow, because I do expect you at the gym bright and early Monday morning."

My heart bloomed with happiness. He was sensitive yet stern. I kind of loved it.

"I'll be there with bells on."

"Coach knows best."

A chuckle escaped me. I laid back down and cuddled under the blanket. "Don't go getting cocky on me, *Coach*." I paused, somberness overtaking me. "Can you stay?"

Kova looked at me for a long moment like he was contemplating his answer, then nodded.

"Can you do me a favor? Can you get my medicine bottles and a glass of water for me?"

"Of course."

Kova came back and placed a glass on my nightstand then lined up the bottles so I could read the labels. "Your father called me."

I froze, panic heaving through me. I sat up. "What'd you say?"

"He was concerned about you and said your phone was off. I told him I would check on you and let him know."

"Shit. My phone is in the car. I forgot all about it." He must've been so worried he couldn't get ahold of me, especially during the hurricane.

Kova opened a can of ginger ale and placed it next to the water, then he reached into his bag and revealed a sleeve of crackers. One by one I poured the pills into a pile on the comforter. A groan vibrated in the back of my throat. I hated having to take so many a day.

"Do you have your phone? I'll call him now."

He grimaced. "You broke it."

My brows shot up, remorse staining my cheeks. "I did?"

"When you slammed it down, you cracked the screen. It still works, but be careful not to touch the glass. I do not want you cutting yourself."

"I'm sorry," I said, my voice low. I did get a little heated when he was talking to his wife on the phone.

One side of his mouth tugged up. He reached into his pocket and pulled the phone out. "It is okay. Nothing that cannot be replaced." He handed it to me.

I dialed my dad.

"Konstantin?"

"No, it's me, Dad."

"Adrianna? Are you okay? Of all times you don't answer, and during a hurricane?" he roared. I clenched my eyes shut, shame filling me that I'd worried him so badly.

"I'm so sorry, Dad. My phone died and I've just been so tired and sick that I came home and went right to sleep. I think I was having a bad flare up... I don't know. I didn't mean to make you panic."

His voice morphed from angry and panic stricken to distressed and concerned. "Sick? What's wrong?"

Kova stepped out of the room to give us privacy. I opened up to my dad about how I'd been feeling lately and what's been going on, and how I forgot to take my medicine. I even went as far as to say that I'd been working myself to the bone just to take my mind off the diseases.

"Sweetie, you can't be so hard on yourself. If you need someone to talk to, I can find you the best therapist on that side of the coast."

I contemplated it for a moment and glanced down at the pile of pills I hadn't swallowed yet. "It might not be a bad idea, but let me see if I can work on it first."

My front door closed and Kova walked back into my room. Holding his phone to the side, I asked him, "Where did you go?"

"To your car to get your phone." He held it up, waving it toward me. I smiled and mouthed thank you.

"What happened?" Dad asked. I relayed the events of last night, only telling him about Kova helping me during my vomit session and not the other fifty times we had sex. "He's such a good man. I don't know what I'd do without him being there for you. He's helped ease all my apprehensions I had about you going there in the first place."

I glanced at Kova. My stomach churned…

"Now that I know you're okay, put Konstantin back on the phone, please. I have something I want to ask him. Oh! And take your medicine now, young lady."

A sad smile tugged at the corner of my mouth. "Sorry to worry you, Dad. Love you."

I handed the phone back to Kova and he stepped out of the room.

Scooping up the assortment of pills into my palm, I stared at them with utter disdain. Taking Motrin was one thing, but these? I hated them with a passion I never knew one could have for medicine.

Reaching for the glass of water, I exhaled and then threw all of them back at once. Some of them were small, and some the size of horse tranquilizers. Of course that messed with my head. They lodged in my throat and I panicked for a split second, then I closed my eyes and forced them back. I drank half the contents of the glass.

Kova strode back in. He placed his hands on his hips and looked down at me. "I brought chicken noodle soup for you. I want you to eat it."

I grimaced. I knew I should eat, I just didn't want to. "I really don't want to eat after what happened yesterday. Can I just eat these crackers?"

"I really think you need to eat, Ria, even if you just sip it. How about we talk while you eat?"

I chewed the inside of my lip. Tempting, but I had a better idea.

"We as in you?" I suggested, hopeful.

"Fine. If that is what it takes, then yes."

I beamed up at him, happy he was making a compromise. I shifted the blankets off me and tried to stand, but Kova stopped me. I glanced up at him in confusion.

"What are you doing? I'm going to get the soup."

"Stay here. I will get it for you."

"I don't want to be babied, Kova. I can get it."

Kova's lowered his eyes like I'd insulted him. "I am not babying you, Adrianna. I just…" He paused. "Do you not know by now that I care for you deeply? This is for your own good. Please, let me take care of you," he pleaded.

I got the vibe he truly wanted to wait on me. I conceded and agreed, and his entire face lit up.

"Wait—What did my dad say?"

He shook his head, his eyes filled with pure shock and excitement. "You will never guess."

I tilted my head to the side. "What do you mean?"

"He asked if I could stay the night to watch over you. I almost told him I already was."

My jaw dropped. "You're kidding me."

"I wish I was."

My gaze wandered away, shame eating away at the lining in my stomach. I was going to give myself an ulcer at this rate. I placed the half-eaten cracker on my nightstand and then brushed away the imaginary crumbs on my blanket.

"Kova?" I asked softly, now picking lint.

"Yes?"

"What do you think would happen if my dad found out about us? We know Joy knows, and why she hasn't told my dad is beyond me. I feel like she's holding onto the information for some reason, I just don't know why. Katja is aware and knows everything. But my dad? He thinks you're staying here as a favor to watch over me, because you're his friend…"

My voice trailed off and the guilt I'd felt before multiplied by ten.

chapter 34

"IHONESTLY DO NOT HAVE AN ANSWER FOR YOU."
Kova sat on the edge of my bed. His face was drawn, and he appeared as horrible as I felt. "I wish I did, but I do not. Even if I was not Frank's friend, I do not believe it would go over well."

"How would you feel if the roles were reversed?"

His eyes sharpened. "If I ever have a daughter, she will be on lockdown until she is thirty-five. No cell phone. No television. No friends." Kova raised a pointed brow, then said, "No friends who like to—how do you say—smush other friends."

A sad smile tugged at my lips and I laughed. "Did you just say smush?"

"I did. I am not too old to not know what that word means, and do not tell me a boy can fuck like a man at seventeen. They only just discovered their cock."

I smiled bigger. "You're terrible."

Kova shrugged without care. "I am who I am."

Reality faced me again. Guilt was chewing me up. "This is so wrong, Kova. I feel bad for my dad. I never realize how wrong it is until it's looking me in the face."

Kova sighed deeply. "Believe me. Every day when I look at you, when I think about us and the things I want, it will never be right. But here, Ria," he said and placed his hand over his heart, "I do not care what is right or wrong. All I care about is you. So if I have to sneak behind your father's back, then so be it."

"And you're okay with that?"

"What other choice do I have? Give you up? Never. I have tried and it did not work. Could you cut ties with me completely?"

I looked into his eyes. I knew the answer without having to say it. He did too.

Our love and pain were entwined, curling around us whenever we breathed the same air. We were stuck in a cycle. A painful, endless cycle that had no light at the end of the tunnel.

We were going to destroy so many relationships, but hopefully not ruin our own in the process.

I tossed and turned all night.

Glancing at the clock, annoyance steamrolled through me. It had only been a few hours since I'd fallen back to sleep. So not really all night, but it sure felt like it. I turned on my side and watched Kova sleeping in the dark. The only light streamed in from the blinds. His arms were folded behind his head, the carved vascularity of his biceps accentuated at this angle. Kova was a brawny man, physically beautiful with immense strength and a surprising softness to him.

His naked chest expanded and contracted with each pull of air. I reached out, wanting so badly to touch him, to trace the tattoo on his ribs. But I didn't. I rolled over back onto my other side and closed my eyes, praying for sleep. After I'd had a large mug of soup, I curled up next to Kova with the intention of talking, but my eyes drifted shut before I could stop them and I fell back asleep, only to wake up every few hours or so.

"What are you thinking about," he asked softly, spooning me. Kova wrapped an arm around my waist and fitted me to him like a puzzle piece. His body was so warm and inviting. I sank back into him and sighed. My butt burrowed into his hips and I pulled up the covers over us.

My fingers laced his and I pulled them to my chest. "I didn't mean to wake you."

Kova kissed the back of my neck and asked me again as he cupped his legs to the back of mine. "What are you thinking about?"

"Nothing. Everything. I have a hard time staying asleep some nights. I'm so physically tired I can barely move, but my mind doesn't stop."

"Do you take anything to help you sleep?"

I shook my head. "No. I figured with all the other medications I take it wasn't a good idea to add more to the mix."

"Tell me something that is on your mind."

I picked a simple topic to start with. The darkness made it easy to expose myself without reservations.

"Remember my best friend, Avery, who you met when she came to watch me at practice? She's coming to visit me soon and I'm nervous about it. I've been friends with her since we were babies. Our fathers are business partners, our families live next door to each other. We tell each other everything, but she kept a huge secret and lied to me." I paused and thought about how Kova had done the same thing to me. I tried to not let that harden my heart again. "I've been so hurt over it. She was sleeping with my brother for well over a year and kept it from me. She got pregnant and had an abortion. I found out by accident, and I can't help but wonder if she ever planned to tell me."

Kova whistled. "What were her reasons for keeping it from you?"

"I don't know. She really didn't have a good one other than she thought I'd be mad. And I was. I was fuming. This was at the same time I found out other shit that just completely destroyed me. And then to hear she got pregnant? I kind of blew up on her. She cried hysterically, saying she needed me more than ever, that she was hurting in ways I couldn't fathom, but I just left her there." I shook my head. "I shouldn't have left her."

"If she told you from the beginning she was interested in your brother, would you still have objected to it?"

I pondered his question. "I probably would've tried to sway her from being with him."

"Why is that?"

"Because Xavier is a player. He's a one and done kind of guy. He doesn't care about girls, or feelings, or emotions. He cares about himself and money. How much he can drink in one night. Nothing else. I love Avery, and I wouldn't want her to be another notch on his bedpost, and I probably would've tried everything in my power to make sure that didn't happen."

"So, you would've objected regardless of what she wanted," he stated.

I chewed my lip. I hadn't thought of it like that, and putting it that way made me feel kind of bad.

"I guess so." I sighed. "God. That makes me such a shitty friend."

"Have you spoken to her?"

"I've only recently finally decided to talk to her and it almost broke me inside when I heard her voice. I felt so bad to hear how happy she was to talk to me and apologize. Before that, she'd called me numerous times, but I never picked up. I never responded to her texts."

Kova snuggled closer and sandwiched his leg between mine. The warmth of his body triggered me to fall deeper into him and absorb what he was giving me.

He kissed the back of my neck. "When did this happen?"

"Right before I found out you were married."

Kova groaned in the back of his throat. "We both did a number on you, yes?"

I ignored that because he knew he did.

"Does that make me a bad person that I shut her out? She never would've done that to me."

"No, you are young. It is normal to react that way. You were hurting so you reacted out of emotion, but I think you should talk to her. Explain where you are coming from and listen to her. Just listen. Do not shame her for her choices. No one is perfect."

I laughed lightly. "I know. I just don't even know how I'm going to start the conversation. I miss her so much. I miss her sarcastic humor, her laugh, the sound of her voice. I miss talking bullshit with her. I miss my friend. It's going to be that awkward silence and all because I'm an idiot and lashed out. I'm such a fool."

"You are not a fool. It will only be awkward if you make it awkward. If you guys are as close as you claim, the hardest part is the actual part where you admit you are sorry and apologize for your behavior the way she did to you. After that, it will go back to how it always was. Just have a little faith."

Slipping my hand from Kova's, I turned around so we were chest to chest and flung my leg over his hip. He nestled his thick thigh against my sex until our bodies were completely joined together. I released a sigh, wondering how I could ever live without him. Kova settled the anxieties in my heart and calmed my soul when it was just us. In moments like this, I wish it was always just us. We were in an extremely intimate position. Personal. The kind where two people held a link to salvation.

My hand searched for his and I laced our fingers together, bringing them to rest between our chests. I could fall asleep like this. There was a comfort and security I found in his touch that warmed me. I had to wonder if I did the same for him too.

The obscurity of my room made it difficult to see beyond the bed, but at this closeness our faces came into view. Kova's eyes glowed with vulnerability. In the darkness he was defenseless, but he still found a way to hold on to me.

"Now you tell me something," I said.

"Are you just going to skip over the lupus and kidney disease?"

I was quiet. "I was kind of hoping you'd forget. My dad told you everything anyway."

"I want to hear it come from your lips."

Exhaling a deep sigh, I gave Kova what he wanted.

"What do you want me to tell you? That I'm scared? That I want to live a long life and I'm terrified I won't? Because I am. I don't want to acknowledge how sick I am, so I do stupid things to keep my mind busy, like extra conditioning. I hate taking all that medication and sometimes I choke on it. I want to have a family one day but my chances are slim. I want to travel, I want to see the world. Right now I want to go to the Olympics. I'm so close but I'm scared something will happen and prevent me from making it all the way. That I'll get too sick. I don't want people to look at me with pity and feel bad, or look at me any differently. Will my kidney disease progress to the point I have to go on dialysis sooner than expected? Will I get so sick and worn out from it that I won't be able to do gymnastics any longer? When will I finally need a transplant? Can I even go to college or am I too sick? What happens if no one is a match? Because right now, no one is and the thought of never finding one terrifies me more than anything. Am I killing myself, literally killing myself for not starting dialysis now? What if the lupus causes me to have a flare up during a meet and I get so deep inside my head I become a basket case and ruin everything?" My voice shook and tears filled my eyes.

"I'm trying to stay positive, but my hope is slipping. Every day my window of optimism shuts a little more. The anxiety and fear is smothering me and all I do is cry about it. I'm too young to feel like this, but I don't know how not to think about it." Then, I went into a spew about all the medications and doctor visits and blood work and tests I have to do and how often. I let it all out without holding a thing back.

And it felt good. Really good.

Kova held me tighter. Dipping his chin, he lifted my face until our lips were just a breath apart. "If you were not scared then I would be worried. Yes, I knew all these things, but I needed to hear them from *you*. I needed to hear your voice speak them. Thank you for finally telling me." Kova paused and kissed the top of my hand. "I want to be that person for you, Ria. I want you to come to me, to talk to me whenever you are scared or worried. We both know I have not been great at that, but I have been working on it, which you have known. Our toxic moments are over, yes?"

I nodded.

"Good. We need to be there for each other at all times."

"I don't like talking about it though, because then it makes it real." I sniffled. "I don't want to make it real. I just want it all to go away."

Kova kissed my forehead. "Do not let lupus define you. Do not let kidney disease beat you. That is not what you are about. You are a fighter and why I love you so fucking much. Instead, look at it differently. Do not let it drown you. Let the diseases inspire you. Make them give you the life you have always wanted to live."

My voice hitched. "How do I do that? I don't know how. I feel so lost, so scared."

"You just live. You live like every day is your last. You live, and you let those who want to live with you, live too. Do not shut the world out because you are hurting. You are going to miss everything that is beautiful about this chaotic thing we call life. You have a reason to fight now more than ever."

A tear slipped from the corner of my eye and rolled down my temple.

"And you have me. You will *always* have me." Kova pressed a hard kiss to my lips. "Let me live with you."

I squeezed my eyes shut while Kova held me closer. His last words nearly broke my heart because they were honest to God so real and I felt them in every fiber of my body. Little whimpers left my vulnerable lips. I was petrified about my future. My heart burned with resentment for all the things I may never be able to do. But Kova's soothing words, the way his heart coated them with tenderness, meant more than saying I love you.

He was right. I needed to live, and let those who wanted to, live with me.

"I told you I love you, Adrianna. I have only ever truly loved you."

"You're only saying these things because I'm sick."

"Make no mistake, I have loved you since I saw you." He stared reflectively at me. "But when life flashes before your eyes, you take all the risks you can. I do not want you to second-guess me anymore. I want you to know how I feel." He licked his lips. "This is us, Ria. There is no going back after this. Only forward."

Nodding my head, I kissed him hard. I wasn't sure how this was going to work, but I wanted to do exactly what Kova had said.

I would live like every day was my last day. I *wanted* to live.

And I wanted to do that with Kova.

chapter 35

KOVA HADN'T BEEN AT PRACTICE ONCE I RETURNED AFTER THE hurricane had passed.

It hurt my heart a little and I actually wondered if it had something to do with what we shared at my condo. About how he let me cut him and how he'd said he loved me, how he wanted to live with me. I tried not to focus on it too much, but when he didn't come in the following day, or the day after that, I really started to question everything. He'd been absent three full days, which again, was something completely unlike him. The last time he had done this he'd gotten married. My gut told me there wasn't a drastic reason this time, but I started to worry and contemplated texting him. I controlled myself, even though it was a struggle. I didn't want his absence to affect me, but he'd told me to live.

How could I live when he wasn't here to live with me?

Maybe he'd lost faith in me. Maybe what he'd said in my room a few days ago wasn't true. I'd shown more than just a moment of weakness. I'd let down my guard completely and welcomed him back in.

After practice I decided to take a drive by his house once the sun set to see if his car was there. I should've gone home to catch up on sleep I desperately wanted, but I knew my mind wouldn't rest not knowing.

Total stalker mode activated.

Much to my satisfaction, his car was parked in the driveway, but so was Katja's and a couple others I didn't recognize. Not that I would. The lights in his home were on and I could see shadows walking back and forth through the sheer drapes. If he didn't show up at the gym tomorrow, then I'd send him a text tomorrow night.

Thankfully, Kova did show up the following day, but he wasn't himself. He seemed restrained. His shoulders were rolled tight and his eyes were haunted. My heart felt lighter just from the sight of him. I smiled, but it vanished as he strode into his office without so much as a glance my way.

A knot formed in the pit of my stomach.

I inhaled, then exhaled. I had to let it go. I had a job to do, but the nagging feeling in my gut wouldn't go away now.

God. This sucked.

Madeline worked diligently with me for most of the day. Kova hardly looked in my direction. Usually when I looked for him, he was either already looking at me or would look because he felt me looking for him. But today he didn't acknowledge my presence. Not once. I didn't even feel the weight of his stare on me like usual. It was as if I didn't exist, and that hurt my heart so much.

Thankfully Avery would be here this week. I could vent to her and she could tell me what to do, and tell me if I was acting crazy or not.

When it came time to rotate to bars, Madeline said, "Great work today. You've shown so much improvement. It's like you're not the same person who arrived meek and afraid of her shadow on beam. All that hard work has paid off." She finished with a big smile. "Go over to bars. Don't keep Coach Kova waiting on you."

I nodded and smiled. During my day of doubt and questioning, I needed her praise more than I'd realized. "Thanks, Coach."

Taking a deep breath, I walked over to the uneven bars. I knew we were going to pick up where we left off with perfecting my dismount, but I also knew we had to start with the new release moves today too in order to stay on schedule.

"Hey," I said, walking right up to him.

Kova stood with his body angled away and his hands on his hips as he stared off into space. I glanced in his direction to see what he was staring at, but nothing caught my eye.

"How are you feeling?" he asked, still looking away.

"Much better…thanks for asking."

He nodded, his brows drawn together. "Let us get started."

"Kova…" I carefully and slowly drew out his name. "Are you okay? Is there something wrong? Did I do something wrong?"

He finally looked at me and his shoulders relaxed. Kova blinked rapidly a few times and the intense air surrounding him dissipated within seconds. He took a breath and I inhaled. Kova regarded me with a look of compassion that eased my doubts, then leaned in toward my face only to stop. He pulled back and I stared wide-eyed up at him.

His lips pursed together and he covered his mouth, smiling behind his hand. He'd been planning to kiss me as if it were normal for him to. I loved he had the instinctive urge to, just not here.

He cleared his throat. "Everything is fine. We do not have much time today with how much we need to accomplish, so let us get a move on. Wait—"

"Yes?"

"Are you feeling okay? Like really okay?"

One corner of my mouth pulled to the side. "I'm okay."

Kova nodded then walked over to the side to stand next to the bars. He retrieved his cell phone from his pocket and scrolled. I guess he'd gotten the screen fixed while he was away from the gym.

Chalking up, I watched him, his face scrunched up like he was reading something that bothered him. I picked up a small block of chalk and broke it, then sprayed water on my grips before applying more powder. Kova's fingers quickly moved over the screen and I knew I couldn't hold back. It still bugged me not knowing why he hadn't been at the gym.

Tightening the Velcro, I asked, "Where've you been?"

"Home."

I bobbed my head, knowing that was all I was going to get. I clapped my hands, then wiped the chalk on my thighs.

"Sorry I asked."

The next three hours of practice felt like the longest hours of my life. He kept his promise and worked me on bars the way he always had and not like he pitied me and needed to make sure I was okay every ten seconds. I was relieved and took every direction he gave, but it was his attitude that got under my skin. He seemed bothered, even though I was doing everything right.

Kova may not have been barking out orders, but he grilled me with every opportunity that arose. His eagle eyes didn't miss a beat, and there was an indignation to his words that poked at my already sensitive nature. Kova barely touched me. He purposely stayed away from me and instructed me from behind the wires of the bars, yet I'd seen him earlier in the day work with other gymnasts at close range. There were times when I needed his guidance, his hands on me to show me how my body needed to be positioned, but he didn't budge. My frustration grew.

His engines were revved and poised for an argument, I could feel it. There was a storm brewing in Kova's eyes, I just wasn't sure if it had to do with me or not. I wanted to crawl under his skin and flush out what the issue was going on in his head. I wanted to give in, but I knew the only person who would suffer would be me. And that was upsetting for me because for some ridiculous reason I had no answer for, I wanted to help him like he had helped me.

At one point, I flat out yelled, "I don't understand! Show me how to do it!"

Still, he stayed back.

Even when tears coated my eyes from my inability to master a skill the way I wanted to, he stayed back. He saw my struggle. He was aware of how frustrated I had become. The distress in his torn eyes was clear, and so I resented him for making me open up. All I could think about was how dumb I was. How he could tell me he wanted to live with me only to put a ten-foot wall between us.

The clock struck seven and I clocked out mentally. Quickly, I gathered my things and rushed out to my locker, passing Reagan and Holly as they left. We said our goodbyes. The gym was nearly empty save for a few parents in the lobby. I needed to get home.

Stuffing my clothes and shoes into my duffle, I felt him before I even saw him.

"I'm sorry I let you down," I said through a broken, fragile voice. "I'm sorry I ever said anything to you." And I was. I wished I had never opened up now.

"Adrianna."

I didn't answer him. He called my name again.

Shaking my head, I ignored him. This wasn't fair. He didn't get to talk to me only on his terms.

I slammed my locker shut and turned around ready for a fight, only the Kova I saw wasn't the Kova I was expecting. I softened a bit, but I left my aggravated expression firmly in place to show him I wasn't accepting his cute little smile like he was finally happy to see me.

Kova stepped into the room and walked right up to me. He grabbed my elbows and tried to loosen me up. I spoke before he could.

"You don't get to tell me you love me one second and then the next second act like you don't give a shit about me. That's not fair, Kova." I paused, feeling myself get totally emotional over this. "You said you wanted to live with me," I whispered. "I took that to heart."

"I know, and I apologize. It had nothing to do with you. I promise."

I frowned, unprepared for that or for the absolute sorrow in his green eyes.

"Will you give me a few minutes for the rest of the people to leave so we can talk?"

His head tilted to the side and he gave me a lazy smile that was impossible to refuse. I nodded. I didn't want to stay mad at him, not after what we had shared in those few days, and I wanted to know what had happened.

"Wait in my office."

I nodded again. Kova glanced over his shoulder, then quickly dropped a kiss to the top of my head. Turning around, he strode out of the locker room only to stop at the threshold. He paused with his hand on the ledge of the doorframe and looked over his shoulder at me.

His gaze dropped to the floor for a moment then met mine. "Just… Just know you did not let me down. I have some issues with Katja right now and that is on my mind nonstop. Not you." Then he was gone.

I tugged my duffle bag onto my shoulder and left the locker room, heading for his office with a little smile on my face. I felt a smidge better.

Opening the door, I reared back in complete surprise. Blood drained from my cheeks.

"Oh. Hey, Katja."

chapter 36

S HE KNOWS. REMEMBER, SHE KNOWS, I TOLD MYSELF.
And she had my damn notebook.

"Adrianna," she said, rolling the R. She was seated in Kova's chair behind his desk, slowly swiveling side to side like she reigned supreme. "How is it you do?"

I plastered on an innocent smile and played it off. "I'm great. Just looking for my coach. I thought he was in here. I couldn't remember if we had a blading session tonight."

Eyes narrowing, she angled her head to the side. I had no reason not to like Katja. She'd been nothing but kind to me up to now, yet she was his wife and that was enough to make me hate her.

"But did you not have one just two nights ago?"

My brows bunched together. "Two nights ago?"

"Yes, Konstantin said he was here treating you."

Between her honeyed voice and devious grin, something told me she already knew the truth.

"Oh, yes," I said, covering for him. "I was here, we just didn't finish because it hurt too much. I asked if we could pick up another night."

The grin vanished from her flawless face and her eyes dropped. Katja had played me.

"Is that so?" she asked, and I nodded. "Because two nights ago Konstantin was not even in town. In fact, we just got back yesterday afternoon."

I nearly choked as I tried to swallow with a dry throat. Katja stared me down. The pounding rate of my heart was like a loud drum in my ears. I wasn't sure how I could get out of this one. I needed to remain calm and think of a casual response without muddling up the situation even more.

"Two nights ago? Oh, I thought you said a few nights ago. Or maybe it was last week. I can't remember. The practice hours are long and the days tend to blend together. The brain fog is real with lupus," I added with an airy smile, playing it off. I was a little upset with myself over using that as an excuse. "I never thought it was until recently."

"Ah, yes. Konstantin did tell me about your death sentence a couple of months ago."

I sucked in a quiet gasp and pulled back, hurt that anyone could stoop to such a cruel level. I adjusted the strap on my shoulder and held it a little tighter.

"I don't have a death sentence. I'm fine."

"Well, you will never get better now, will you? Just continue to deteriorate." Her sugary words prickled my skin. She spoke like a know-it-all. "And you will never know if tomorrow you will take a turn for the worse, or three years from now, yes? One day the medicine will not help."

Sadness crept into me like black grease. The small smile I wore slid into a frown. I stared at her, stunned by how she could attack anyone in such a horrible manner. I knew I deserved it a little bit—I was sleeping with her husband after all—but she'd stooped to a level that was off limits regardless. What she'd said was what I had feared the most and what I was trying to work through.

Katja was as heartless as Joy. For a fleeting moment I wondered if Kova knew how mean she really was. Tears threatened to well in my eyes and I swallowed what little saliva I had left. The tightness in my chest was holding me down and I needed to get out. Her words were harsh. She knew that, which was apparent by the satisfied smile on her face and the glistening satisfaction in her eyes.

My jaw quivered, and I knew if I spoke my voice would shake. Instead, I just bobbed my head and flattened my lips, exhaling through my nose. I glanced around his office, my eyes scanning the floor. The awkwardness reached a claustrophobic state and I needed to get out. I'd talk to Kova later, he'd understand. There was no way I could outswim a shark who was chasing the scent of blood. And that's what she was.

There was nothing left for me to say. I knew in my gut she'd come back ten times harder if I did. I couldn't handle that. Not when she went for the jugular.

Turning on my heels, I walked toward the door. Her snicker crawled over my delicate state, but I ignored it, reaching for the knob as the door flew open and Kova walked in.

I froze, anger replacing my heartache. Here he was in all his glory knowing his wife was in here. He'd sent me into the lion's den. I was strong, but I wasn't that strong. We all had our limits.

Troubled eyes scanned my face until he looked over my shoulder. His gaze lowered to slits and the glare he gave Katja said everything.

He had no idea she was here. And he sure as hell wasn't happy to see her.

I glanced at the floor. "I'll see you tomorrow," I said quietly.

I tried to step around him, but he put his hand on the crest of my elbow. "Wait."

My heart dropped. Kova was touching me in front of Katja.

I looked up at him and he dropped his hand. He was trying to convey something through his eyes, and even though I didn't want to listen because I was upset, I gave him a subtle nod.

Stay.

He had no plausible reason for me to stay here instead of his wife. I turned around and crossed my arms in front of my chest. Chewing the inside of my lip, I averted my gaze to the floor. This was uncomfortable.

"Katja." Kova said her name so differently than I did. "When did you get here?"

"A little while ago. I came in through the back entrance."

He placed his hands on his hips. Resentment flowed from him, circling around us.

"Is there something wrong? Are you okay?"

"Everything is just fantastic, my love. I missed you."

She stood and walked around his desk to stand in front of him. I could smell the perfume I once commented on only to learn it was her body wash Kova had shipped from Russia. It really did smell incredibly alluring, and I hated that she wore it.

"Why are you here?"

"Is that any way to greet your wife?"

Her seductive tone didn't go unnoticed. Katja leaned in to kiss Kova, but he stopped her. She pulled back and gave him an icy glare. *Hell hath no fury like a woman scorned.* I couldn't stop staring at the heavy mascara that made her eyelashes resemble tarantula legs.

"I am busy with work and trying to finish up. Can this wait? Go home and I will see you there," he said firmly.

"If you are only doing a blading session, then I will wait for you. It will not take long," she said, a suggestive smile reaching her eyes. "I have a surprise for you that you are going to be so happy about. *We* are going to be happy. I wanted to give it to you here since this place is your second love."

"I'm… I'm gonna go," I said quietly.

"No," Kova barked with his eyes still on Katja, then switched to his native tongue.

Heat flushed through me and I clenched my eyes shut trying to swallow back the knot that was stuck in my throat. This wasn't good. The back of my neck was clammy from the embarrassment I felt being in this office. The tips of my fingers tingled and my palms were damp. I hated when they switched to Russian. Not because I was nosy—I most definitely was—but because it was uncomfortable and made me feel like they were speaking about me. Their voices were growing louder. I stood there feeling like the third wheel that I was.

I stepped backwards, thinking they wouldn't notice my departure, but I was wrong.

Kova reached behind him and latched on to me. My wide eyes dropped to his vice grip on my forearm. I held my breath and stood stone still.

Shit. Shit. Shit.

My heart was going to explode from my chest. I might as well just shoot myself to end the misery.

The intense argument reduced to an alarming silence. I looked at them. Katja scowled at Kova's hand on my arm before moving her focus up to my face. Her beautiful, crystal blue eyes were sharper than a knife and aiming for me. I had a feeling if she could choke me out right now, she would.

But then, then she stunned me.

Katja straightened her back and inhaled, collecting herself. I frowned, watching as she tugged the hem of her shirt straight down, then brushed a few loose platinum blonde strands of hair behind her ears adorned with massive diamond studs I'm sure Kova bought her.

She reached into her purse and pulled out a white envelope. She shoved it against his chest. Kova placed his fingers over hers, his brows bunched together as he glanced down then took it from her. Katja said something in Russian, then stalked out of his office, seemingly trying to remain dignified.

Kova frowned as he unfolded the sealed envelope and looked at it. There was a printed return address at the top, but the rest was left blank. He flipped it over between his fingers, looked at the back, then threw it onto his desk without a care. He dragged both his hands down his face, and for a split second I felt bad for the exhaustion he exposed when he dropped his hands.

"I should go, Kova. We can talk tomorrow."

"No," he said, his tone defeated, "please do not go yet."

I shifted on my feet. "But do you think it's a good idea that your wife, who knows about us, left instead of me? I'm worried she may do something stupid."

He shook his head. "Trust me. There is nothing else she can do that would be any worse than what she has already done."

Dropping his hips to the edge of his desk, Kova dragged his weary eyes up and down the length of my body. A small, needy smile curved on one side of his mouth. Reaching forward, he tugged the strap of my duffle bag toward him, pulling me with it. He removed it from my shoulder so it fell to the floor, then he grabbed my hips and pulled me between his spread thighs.

Kova wrapped his arms around me like I was his lifeline, sighing like he was finally home. I leaned into his chest and allowed him to soak up whatever he needed from me. He inhaled deep and held on to me like he was afraid to let go. His fingers pressed into me and I could feel in his touch, the way he leaned harder into me, the way his heart pounded against his chest, that he was sinking into a dark hole.

This was us. Everything that was wrong and everything that was right. It was like this subliminal feeling that couldn't be explained. When one of us needed the other, we were there. It could only be felt. We did what we had to do without question, because he loved me, and even though I never told him, I loved him too.

"I needed this," he said very quietly, breaking the silence.

"Needed what?"

"You. I just needed to hold you. I have missed you these few days. I never realized how much I do not like to go a day without seeing you."

Don't do it. Don't do it. Don't do it.

"Kova?" I said hesitantly, staring at his chest. "Where were you?"

"Dealing with Kat."

I lifted my gaze and waited for him to elaborate. Kova held a pensive stare as he looked at me like he was considering his words. He waited a good couple of minutes, then gave my hand a little squeeze and kissed my knuckles, leaving his lips pressed there for a moment.

"I suspect Katja is lying to me about something. She is not herself and has been too distant. I am not complaining that she is, but something is off, and I do not know what. It is bothering me. She used to fight me at night to be home, now she seems relieved when I have to stay in the gym, which I find peculiar given what she knows about us. I have a feeling she is trying to plan something big. I just do not know what it is yet."

chapter 37

A DEFLATED LAUGH ESCAPED ME.

He couldn't be serious. The thought provoked me with a pull of jealousy so deep it startled me. I wasn't typically a jealous girl, but I was glad his wife was refusing him. Jealously meant I was fragile, and I didn't like to think of myself like that. The last word I'd use to describe myself was envious. But when it came to Kova, that was a different story. I didn't want to share him. He was mine, just like I was his.

Still, I couldn't let it go.

I scoffed. "Wait a minute. You are *not* telling me you try to touch her, to have sex with her, and she isn't having it, are you?"

"I am trying to placate her so she does not go to the police, Adrianna." He sounded offended. "I have to use *my* body to protect *us.* I am disgusted, but that is the truth."

I ground my teeth so hard I heard the enamel crushing. Every time we took one step forward, we always took ten steps back. Always.

"Do you have any idea what would happen if we got out?" he continued. "There is a possibility we both would be at fault... I could go to jail and you could not attend the Olympics." He paused solemnly. I tensed. "Actually, I do not see the committee letting us pass due to the eye of the public. They would claim your health or injury before casting negative light on the committee or gymnastics."

The committee would never allow it.

Breathe in, breathe out.

I hadn't even thought about that.

Kova was right. They wouldn't brush this under the rug. He'd be stripped and shoved behind bars, and I would be forced to retire due to an "injury," and that was that.

"I hadn't even thought of that," I whispered. I was scared now.

Was it crazy of me to tell him to keep placating her? Because if that was going to be what it took, then he should do whatever he needed to. I just didn't want to hear *how* he did it.

"She is arranging something. I just cannot figure out what it is."

"So what's your plan in the meantime? Fuck her into oblivion to silence her and then dig around when she's sleeping?" I stepped back and threw my hands up in the air. I was instantly angry again. "Why are men so stupid?"

Kova stood. Much to my surprise, he didn't jump down my throat. He remained calm. "I have to play her game for us to come out on top until I can find out what she is up to, then I can use it against her."

I exhaled a heavy sigh. This was so messed up. "For how long, Kova? How long do you have to play her game and pretend you love her?"

"For however long it takes until we are both in the clear."

My jaw dropped. "So that's where you were the last few days? Placating your wife when you were supposed to be coaching me? Listen, I'm all for you trying to make her happy for the time being since she's clearly a loose cannon, I just think I shouldn't hear about it anymore."

His face paled. The last thing I wanted to do was hurt him, but it physically hurt me to hear things like this even if I said I wanted to. I was not as strong as I thought I was, I guess.

"I had to be the doting husband and put her first to let her think she still had control over me. If I am going to play her game, I have to play it a few steps ahead of her."

Breathing heavily, I could feel tears climbing, but I forced them down. I pointed to my chest. "I tell you about my stupid disease and open up about the most heartbreaking moments of my life, and you respond with this stuff?" My voice broke. "You have to be kidding me. Why do you hate me? Do you get off on hurting me?"

Kova's face fell. He reached for me and I stepped back. His hand dropped helplessly to his side. "Do not do this, Adrianna, please. I am begging you. It is not like that, I swear on my life and everything I have to give it is not like that. I am just trying to talk to you and tell you what really has happened."

I exhaled a heavy breath trying to take control of the situation. "You're right. I did ask for this, and you're just telling me the truth. It doesn't mean I have to like it though." I paused, my jaw wobbling. "It just really hurts, Kova. Okay? I didn't mean to overreact. I'm sorry."

"Do you think I liked hearing that you had sex with Hayden multiple times? Or when you talk about your future that clearly does not involve me? We have to be able to talk about everything, is that not what you always say to me? Sometimes it sickens me to hear the things you say, but I try to not hold on to them and keep moving. We both do things we do not like right now, but think about it—if it were just me and you, would we do any of this crazy stupid shit we do? No."

He shook his head, his eyes so full of anguish it gripped my heart. He was right. I swallowed, surprised by how civil he was acting and not being defensive, and here I was letting my emotions get to me.

Softly, I said, "It's hardly the same thing and you know it."

He put his hands up and surrendered. "You are right. It is not. But I would never sleep with Kat, and you would have not been with Hayden. We would never have talked about this shit, and we would never fight because we are good together without any of that, and you know it is the truth. It would just be us and that would be it, but we are both stuck in situations we cannot get out of just yet, and probably not for a while. So we do what we have to and will continue doing it and talking shit out, whether we like it or not, because I never want there to be a secret between us again."

My heart pounded harder. "What do you mean?"

" Even if I divorced Katja tomorrow, we would still have to hide our relationship. I do not think the people around us would take lightly to it."

He was right again and here I was basically acting my age. That embarrassed me. I grimaced, wishing I thought ahead before I spoke. Here we were, just two people trying to find a way to each other only for real life—people and the law—to get in the way.

I looked at Kova, really looked at him. His eyes bore into mine like he was pleading with me to see his reasons, to agree with him that they made sense. I hated to admit they did. I was about to turn eighteen. What happened to us after that? Would I go to college? Would announce our relationship then? Would we have a long-distance relationship?

I shook my head and let go of the resentment I held and tried to focus on the now and not worry about the future.

"I'm sorry," I said again, my voice dropping. This was so hard.

"I am sorry too."

"This isn't normal," I stated softly. "I wish we didn't have to deal with this."

"As do I."

I'd give him that.

Propping my hands on my hips, I faked an attitude to lighten the dreary mood.

"You're needy and controlling and overbearing every day, but sometimes you're right and I don't like adding that to the mix. Your head gets big."

His eyes lit up. "I am always right."

I puckered my lips together to mask my smile. Kova reached for me again as he sat back on his desk. I stood between his legs and looked at him, then wrapped my arms around his shoulders.

"I like you," I said playfully.

"I love you," he said seriously.

Kova kissed my forehead and glided his palms up my thighs and over my butt. He scooped me up and I spread my knees to straddle him. I snuggled up closer to him, unable to ever get close enough, and basked in that feeling.

"Listen to me," he said, hardly moving his lips. "Only we matter to each other and that is that. Right now, things are not how we may want them, but I hope one day they will be. Until then…" He leaned in and dropped a kiss to my lips. "I want you, all of you. We are good together, Ria. I cannot help being addicted to you. We both feed each other what we desire, and that is what makes us *us*. Fuck what everyone else thinks. I know I am demanding and controlling, but I think you like that. Just how I like when you confront me and argue, going from sweet and innocent to angry and fired up and just want to fight in three seconds flat. I will always want you, Adrianna, always. I wake up in the morning thinking about you. I go to bed thinking about you. When I am buying groceries I am thinking about you. I make coffee, I think about you. I drink vodka, I think about you. I stroke my cock thinking about you. You are always on my mind because I only ever want you."

I shied away. "Kova…" I said, slightly embarrassed. My head dropped to his collarbone. "Why do you always have to find a way to be crude?"

"I am who I am. Now give me a kiss."

No thought needed, I kissed him with everything I had to give. We lost ourselves in the sensual tangle of our lips. Time stood still as our hearts beat against one another. There was no judgment, it was just us falling deeper and deeper in the seclusion of his office. If one paid attention, a kiss revealed truth, and his told me everything I worried he didn't feel but actually did. I wondered if he knew I felt the same way for him.

Kova cupped the back of my head and kissed me like he hadn't kissed me in months. Like I was his world and no matter what I would always be. His length hardened beneath me and I automatically circled my hips. I wound my arms tighter around his neck and nestled closer, returning that same affection, showing him just what he meant to me.

"Tell me what else is on your mind," I said, breaking the kiss. It was so natural for us to lose ourselves in the moment.

He kissed me one last time. "I am sorry for bringing her up. I never should have."

"No," I said, stopping him.

He was truly apologetic and making the effort I had asked of him. It wasn't fair of me to ridicule him for that. My heart beat faster for this man I never should've had the chance to be with. He'd been putting in the time these last couple of months and I had to not only show I respected that, but that I saw it too.

"I could tell something was on your mind when I asked you. I need to be asking you hard questions like this, and I shouldn't get upset when your response isn't the one I want to hear."

"I do not deserve you," he said.

I chuckled. I'd never heard anyone say that before. "I don't think it's about deserving someone. Does anyone deserve anyone? I think it's more about finding someone who understands you and accepts all your flaws but also helps you work through them. It's so easy to shut the door and keep walking, but it takes strength to hold it open, to see what that person is going to walk in with, and if it's worth it or not. The risk has to be greater than the chance, and I think you're worth it, Kova."

Kova's Adam's apple bobbed. His green eyes were rich with affection as they pierced the center of my chest. I held my breath from his deep stare.

"*Bog, ya chertovski lyublyu tebya.*"

I waited on him to translate. When he didn't, I tilted my head to the side and smiled softly. "Tell me."

He shook his head. "You will not believe me, just like you never do every other time."

Ah. I knew. "It's that stupid word love again, isn't it?"

His eyes darkened like he was offended. "I do not find it stupid when I say it to you."

My heart bloomed even more for him. "Fair enough."

"God, I fucking love you. I really do."

chapter 38

I BLUSHED, SLIGHTLY EMBARRASSED.

I'd thought he was going to say something mushy, but I wasn't expecting that.

"You're cute," I said.

Kova's head fell back and he barked out a laugh. "One day I hope you can find a way to love me the way I love you and actually say it."

I swallowed. He didn't know I already loved him, but something in my heart told me not to tell him just yet.

"What else? Tell me what happened with Katja."

Kova groaned. "I do not want to talk about it when I am hard for you. Talking about her is going to make my dick soft."

At that, I swiveled my hips down on him and smirked. "Tell me," I said, drawing out the words.

"Adrianna, I do not want to talk about my wife when all I can think about is sliding into your pussy right now."

"You know, I'm never ready for when you say that word."

"Pussy?" he repeated with a peaked brow, and I nodded. Kova smirked. "Let me bang you real quick. Then you can ask all the questions you want. I promise to answer them."

This time it was my turn to bark out a laugh. Bang sounded so foreign on his lips. "Did you just say bang?"

"Well I figured if pussy bothers you, bang might be a better word. I am too old to use smush sesh. Do not ask me to say that. I heard some boys saying it. I can say bang, but smush is where I draw the line. I said it once before but I cannot say it again. Unless you just want me to fuck you."

His eyes were alive with amusement. I couldn't hold back the giggles in my throat and burst out laughing.

"I can't even deal with how funny that is coming from you. It sounds so weird."

Rising up on my knees, I palmed his face and pressed my lips to his. Kova wrapped his arms around my lower back. I leaned into him and forced him to lay back on his desk. I hovered above him and kissed him again, my hand sliding down his stomach, over his rock-hard abs to cup his thick shaft over his sweat pants. I squeezed his cock and he twitched in my hand. Kova groaned, his back arched, and damn it all to hell, it was all so sexy the way the light from the moon shone between the shadows of the blinds over him.

There was something seductive and risky about us in his office like this— the thrill of getting caught loomed over me—and I fed off it. *We* fed off it.

"Adrianna," he moaned out my name. He gripped my hips roughly through the struggle of my hold on him.

I pressed my lips to his. "Tell me what happened and we can smush." I laughed. I could hardly say the word myself.

Kova chuckled darkly. His face lit up and it did stupid things to my heart. He looked so carefree and happy and I wanted to see more of that.

"You are so fucking not normal," he joked.

"You're right, but this is our normal, remember, and it's what I want. I like to ask about her when you tell me not to." Even though no sane person would ever ask about the other partner the way I did, I relished in reminding him he was still here with me. It was so wrong and for reasons I couldn't explain, I loved it. "So tell me about your wife while we bang."

He gripped my wrist to stop me. "You get off on it."

"Is that a bad thing?"

Kova loosened his grip on my wrist, flipped his hand over and cupped me over my shorts. My lips parted with a breath and I almost fell on him.

"Jesus Christ, you are wet. You do like it."

I nodded silently. A zing of desire shot down my back. I wish I understood why I loved the devious aspect of it all. And because he was still with me—mind, body, and soul—and not her.

Reaching into his sweats, I felt for his warm, swollen cock. I stroked him from tip to base, twisting my wrist around his length. I didn't bother hiding the moan in the back of my throat.

"You know, I have wanted to fuck you on my desk. Never did I think you would have me on my back like this."

A slow smile slid across my face. "I actually like being on top, so this is better for me."

"Whatever you want, however you want, just take it from me," Kova responded.

I shrugged off my zippered jacket and dropped it to the floor so all I was left in was a sports bra and tank top. Kova helped me remove my shorts and panties. In one swift move, he inserted two fingers into me. I sighed at the pressure and sank down on them, allowing the little bites of bliss to stream through me.

I rose up a little and placed one hand on his chest to slide up and down his fingers while I held onto his erection with the other. His thumb hit my clit at just the right spot and I let out a rushed breath.

"She is rarely home," he started. "Neither am I due to work, but I do not leave Georgia as often as she does."

The brittle sound of his voice tugged at my heart.

"Keep going," I said, and rose up to position his tip at my entrance. I was already hot and ready for him.

Before I could gently slide down, Kova thrust his hips up and slammed into me. He groaned, and I felt it deep inside me.

I slapped his chest. "You are such a bastard sometimes," I gritted out. "That fucking hurt, Kova."

"You make me this way."

"Sometimes I think you're too big for me," I moaned.

"I wish you could see what I see like this," he said barely above a whisper, like he was mesmerized.

I glanced down and angled myself so I could see, but I couldn't.

"Stop deflecting."

"It is hard to focus when all I see is your pussy squeezing my cock."

I chuckled. "Kova..." I warned, my voice coming out raspy.

His head fell back and hit the desk. "You are the biggest pain and tease in my life. Fine," he said, swallowing hard, and I started to slowly ride him.

"She added a passcode to her phone. She has never had one before. She is cold, and I swear she has an attitude all the time. Her change in demeanor and secrecy raises too much curiosity in me. I know I should not question her, but with what she knows, anything is possible."

"So you're worried she's sneaking around behind your back."

"I used to be one step ahead of her and now I am not. She does not get to force me into marriage and then spread herself around and demand shit from me while holding you over my head."

I rode him harder, hating his words but taking them anyway. He breathed heavier each time I sank down and that only riled me up. I would never admit it to him, but I liked that she was behaving this way. She had blackmailed him, and while Kova was finally seeing her true colors, he'd only grow more distant with her. Our age difference may dangle between us, but our connection ran deep and the numbers were long forgotten when it was just us. Our conversations came naturally, and I didn't think anything truly did for him and Katja anymore. After what he'd told me about how they grew up together, I came to the conclusion they were convenient and just got comfortable. She may have found a way to hold on to him right now, but it wouldn't be forever. At least, I hoped not.

I took ease with my next set of words. I didn't want him to be offended by them, but it aggravated me that he was so concerned with her.

"Do you think it's a little hypocritical of you to be upset that she's lying about something when your cock is inside my pussy right now? That you're in bed with your gymnast any chance you get?"

Kova moaned, his back arching again. He looked at me with sensual eyes and a tight jaw through a sexy-as-hell smirk. I pushed up his shirt to look at his toned body.

"That is exactly why I try not to ever question her," he said, thrusting into me. "It *is* hypocritical of me. I try to not raise my voice because I am no better. I am a terrible human being. A terrible husband." He thrust hard again and grabbed my hips to hold me down so he could piston into me.

I inhaled and held my breath, my thighs quivered around his hips. I felt like I was stretched to the max and it hurt, like little tears were ripping in my tender flesh. Kova pulled back and I let out a gush of air.

"I thought since I brought her to the United States in the first place I should give her free reign to do as she pleases. I set her up nicely. There was a time when I wanted to make her happy, but she changed, and I saw a side of her that disgusted me. Then, I saw you."

Wanted. Kova said it in past tense. They were both going in different directions and playing the game with each other now.

"Did this start when I came to World Cup?"

My heart raced in anticipation. An orgasm was climbing but I wasn't ready to let go just yet. Once I had Kova in me, I always wanted more. I never wanted to stop feeling him or this intense pleasure he brought to the table each time. Kova was an addiction and he knew how to take me higher than anyone and anything. I was spellbound as I watched his hips roll into mine so slowly and sensually that I lost my train of thought for a moment. He was so fucking sexy with the way his body moved. I sighed a breath, feeling good, and allowed myself to just sink down into him. I was floating on a cloud, my entire body tingling and on the edge of desire.

"God, you feel so good," I said, biting my lip. "When?"

"It started before you came here," he said. His forehead scrunched together, almost as if it'd just dawned on him. Kova looked at our joined bodies again. "I would say about six months or so before that. You had nothing to do with it, but you did not help the situation either. It just showed me things I wanted more, things I was missing."

"Maybe she feels the same way about you and it's why she's acting the way she is. Have you tried speaking to her about it?"

"Adrianna?"

"Yeah?" I said breathlessly.

"Can we not talk about her anymore? I just want to watch my cock slide into your little pussy."

chapter 39

MY EYES ROLLED SHUT AND A SHOT OF BLISS WENT DOWN MY BACK. "I did say something to her." He answered my last question. "I am a very confrontational man if you have not noticed. She denies there is anything wrong." Kova was fixated on our bodies.

He carefully took my lips in his fingers and spread them. My jaw fell open and my head rolled back. I almost stopped moving from the passion of it. He pinched my clit and angled his hips so I hit his mound when I slid down.

Kova was good. Too fucking good.

"Oh, *malysh*, if you could see this…" His voice was rough like gravel and goose bumps danced down my arms. "Put your hands behind you on my legs and lean back."

I did as he said and almost orgasmed right then. I rolled my bottom lip between my teeth, trying to hold back. It was too much, too good every time at even the slightest angle.

I wanted his honesty, I wanted him to open up to me, and he had. The oddest feeling surged through me while we had sex. Like we both were free. I wasn't hurt. If anything, something reassuring settled in my stomach I couldn't name. Most people would refute the idea of a cheater talking to the other woman about his wife in this manner.

But we weren't most people. And I didn't consider myself the other woman. And, truth be told, we wallowed in the suspense of it.

It was sick. But I honestly didn't care. Kova told me it was okay to feel the way I did, and so I believed him.

"There is something else…" Kova gritted out, still staring at our joined bodies. "You are not going to like it."

Immediate panic ignited within me and I rode him faster and harder. I wanted to hear what he had to say, but I was too close to the edge of desire. I wasn't sure if I could handle it and changed the subject.

"Do you have a mirror?"

He looked at me like I had spoken Russian. I almost laughed.

"Why the hell would I have a mirror? And why do you need one now? I am about to come inside of you and you want to look at yourself?"

This time I smirked. "Close. I want to see what you see, how you see our bodies."

His eyes lit up and a shadow of hearty desire cast through them. Kova liked that I wanted to see too, and that excited me.

I thought quickly about what I could use so I could see before we finished. We both were close to the end. Spotting his cell phone on the desk, I reached for it and asked for his passcode. Funny how he didn't like that Katja had one even though he did. I unlocked his phone, then went for the camera icon and clicked on video. I angled the camera screen so it got our bodies and not my face.

Kova's cock slid effortlessly into my plump pussy, my lips suctioning around him with my tender clit showing. He stretched me wide and I wasn't sure how I fit him. He spread my lips again so I could see what he saw and my mouth parted, a breath rolling off my lips. I could see every fold and crease as his wet, rigid length pushed in and out. I caught a view of that sex vein I liked to play with and positioned the camera to get it on tape. I let out a sigh and moaned while I watched it disappear into my pussy. This was highly arousing and way more than I anticipated.

The sounds of sex infused with heavy breathing. Our panting and watching us on the camera is what got to me. Oh, God. It was all too much. I leaned back on one arm to get a better view and his cock pulsed inside me. My eyes locked with his. He was there, and so was I.

I glanced down. His cock looked massive from this angle. I couldn't tear my eyes from the screen. Now I knew what he meant and why he liked to watch us.

A few more voluptuous rolls of his hips, and Kova gripped my thigh, digging his fingers into my flesh. He moaned long and deep. I pulled back just enough to watch his thickness pulse as he came inside me. The veins on his stomach that led to his groin strained. Kova gripped me harder, his decadence streaming into me as he let go. I let out a long sigh as his nails scored my thigh. I tightened my grip around his phone and we watched together as he filled me to the point where his cum oozed out of the sides, coating my pussy, my thighs, and his mound.

My lips parted in wonder. I was fixated on our pleasure. His orgasm had come out of me in the past, but I never actually saw it happen until now, and I found it insanely erotic to see. His cock twitched. My teeth dug into my bottom lip and I shuddered above him. Kova was still hard, and I was still beyond turned on by this.

Turning the camera off, I placed the phone face down and reached for him. I fisted the center of his shirt and pulled, forcing him to sit up. Kova's arms wound around my back as he slammed his mouth over mine. I kissed him deeply, only to have him return my hunger with more passion as I rocked into him.

"Tell me you love me. Say it," he demanded, his voice a husky whisper.

"I hate you."

Kova thrust into me without reservation and held himself deep inside. I groaned, biting down and pulling on his lip with my teeth. I wouldn't say the words he wanted to hear because then he'd have every part of me, and I needed to reserve something for myself.

He pressed his chest to mine, nearly suffocating me with his strength, and kissed my lips so fiercely my heart ached for this untamed man. I couldn't control the sounds erupting from my throat as he devoured me with a savage kiss, a kiss I made him fight me for.

Kova's nose nestled into the curve of my neck. He held me tighter and ran his hands up and down my body. I could feel him smiling against me and that made me happy.

"I know you are not done, and neither am I."

A throaty sigh escaped me. "You're right."

"You always need at least two rounds."

"You know, it's a good thing we don't live together. All we'd be doing is having sex."

Kova chuckled, his hot breath tickled my collarbone, and I shivered.

"And that is a bad thing?"

"What were you going to say that I wasn't going to like?"

"She wants a baby."

The silence was a thunderous beating of my heart. It was all around me. His words were a whisper and enough to reduce me to a speechless state. His cock was still hard and hot inside of me, and I wasn't sure how to feel about such a thing.

No, I knew how to feel, I knew exactly what I was feeling, and I was trying, trying so damn hard to be rational and listen. But this...

There was no way, and he knew that.

Kova bit down on my neck and held me immobile. I tried to pull away but he latched on firmer. First the puppy, now a baby. I knew it. I fucking knew that was coming. My gut said it was but I'd pushed it away and ignored it.

She wants a baby.

Chest tight from the four words that nearly broke me inside, I was struck with bone-deep hurt. A baby. Him being blackmailed made me think he was going to go through with it.

Kova let go of my neck and stood, holding me in his arms. He probably knew I was going to try and pull away. He walked to his office door and pressed my back to it. He adjusted us so we were still joined, then he pulled out and my back bowed when he glided me down his shaft until I couldn't go any further.

"Adrianna," he said, his voice filled with distress. "Look at me. Look into my eyes and listen to me, really listen to me." When I did, his face was blurry. "She has been asking me for a while. I told her it will never happen, just like I have each time she has asked."

I raked my nails harder down his arms, leaving red trails that made me feel good to see. I hoped it hurt. "You really know how to make me a fiend for you and then hate you." Kova held my hips down and drove into me without remorse. "When you fuck your wife, do you come inside her the way you do me?" I couldn't hold back. The images in my head of him screwing Katja were too strong and elicited a rage so deep I felt it creeping through my blood. "Does she let you lick her the way you do me? And I mean *all* parts of me? Does she know how nasty you can be?"

I couldn't say the words, but he knew exactly what I was talking about. He knew I liked those nasty sides of him, but did she?

"Does it leak out of her, and do you watch it? Do you bite her hard enough to make her bleed and then lick it up?"

Oh God. My heart could only handle so much.

"Adrianna…" He groaned, thrusting deep enough to make sure he caressed my clit.

My eyes rolled shut and I melted in his hold. I locked my ankles around his back and his mouth tickled my neck. His sweat pants were still on, only partially pulled down.

"Just shut the fuck up and stop talking," he said.

I struggled in his hold, trying to push him away. He was harder than ever, and the sad part was that I was so wet he was sliding in without resistance.

"You do, don't you," I said, grabbing his hair and pulling it. Such a girl thing to do, but I needed *something*. "You just unload your dick whenever you please. A drop and run kind of thing."

"No," he said below a whisper, and for a second, I thought he sounded hurt. But then I realized who I was talking about and that he didn't get hurt very often.

Grabbing my wrists, he stretched them above my head and pinned them to the door. His cock jerked inside of me and hit just the right spot. A delicious spot. My chest pushed out and I exhaled a breath. He knew the game he was playing, and I was ready to fight. But then he looked at me and his gaze surprisingly upset me, because he actually appeared hurt. I frowned.

I was seething and yet he was still thrusting into me. "I bet you fuck her bare because the perfect amazing Kova can't be bothered with condoms."

He drew in a long breath. "Never. I wear a condom every time."

A dark laugh escaped my throat. "Yeah, right. You actually think I believe you?"

"I bought them when I bought your Plan B."

Oh, he didn't. He did not just say that.

I resisted in his hold, struggling. My thighs squeezed around his hips, and I clenched his length. Kova's pupils dilated and he surged into me. We both held our breaths, our mouths open and mimicking each other's ecstasy. It made me want to taunt him just so I could feel that divine rush through me.

"This weekend? That's when you started?" I all about screamed my response.

What a joke. This fucked-up conversation was putting me through the ringer of emotions.

"No, it was the first time I bought your Plan B, you foolish girl."

My nostrils flared and I held back my emotions. I swallowed hard, almost believing him.

"Let go of me."

"Never. Have you not realized by now I can never let you go?"

chapter 40

I GASPED AND CLENCHED MY THIGHS AROUND HIM.
Our hips smashed into each other and I allowed myself to bask in the warmth of the paradise our fused bodies were deeply in. A slow roll of my pelvis at just the right angle, and it was an overwhelming sensation for both of us. I sighed, not caring for a moment. It felt too good. *We* felt too good. Kova shuddered against me, feeling us. We both were close to the peak again and I softened around him.

Lacing our fingers together, his voice was a mixture of pain and fact. "I fuck her from behind so I do not have to look at her."

Kova surged into me, taking me like the animal that he was. I gasped, then released a breathless sigh veiled by rage with the news he'd just dropped on me. My skin prickled with heat, both ready for a fight and the pleasure that was about to tear through me.

"You would screw your wife like that because you're a beast."

"You have never been more wrong," he insisted. "I do it because I only want to see your face when I fuck. I put her face down and do not let her touch me. I even turn out the lights. The amount of vodka I drink is borderline dangerous, but it is what I do to get it over with. She does not get my cock hard. Only you ever get this part of me now. I swear it. If you never believe anything, believe this."

My jaw trembled. "You're going to give her babies, aren't you?" Giving Katja children would bound her to him forever.

He shook his head vehemently and drove into me. "No. Never," he whispered. "She will never get kids from me."

"I don't believe you. You'll do anything she wants right now."

"I have my limits, Adrianna."

"Sometimes you fuck me from behind."

His eyes dropped and he smirked. "That is only so I can look at your ass and spread your cheeks while I do. Do you have any idea how sexy you are from that angle? I told you your ass will be mine one day."

His raspy words coated every inch of my heated skin, almost making me wish he would take it now. I was too embarrassed to admit I liked when he touched me there.

As if he read my mind, his large palm slid to cup my ass. My lips parted in anticipation and I took a deep breath, tensing up when one of his fingers found my tiny, little hole and pressed on it. I drew in a blissful sigh, chest pushing out, and undulated on him.

"Kova," I said, swallowing hard, wondering if what I was about to ask was a waste of breath. "Please, don't hurt me anymore."

"Never again, my love. Never again."

The way he kissed me left me with no choice but to believe him. He released my arms and I wrapped them around his shoulders. My tongue delved around his and the movement of our bodies were one and the same.

It was scary how we couldn't get enough of each other.

Kova lifted me and took us to the couch. He pulled out and sat down, then turned me around so my back was to him and I straddled his lap.

"Reach forward so you are on your hands and knees."

I did as he asked, feeling very exposed. Grabbing my hips, Kova shoved me down harder and I released a gasping breath. This was a new angle for me, and by far the best one yet. I glanced over my shoulder as Kova brought his fingers to his mouth, then penetrated my tight hole.

"This is what I love to see," he said, spreading my cheeks. His eyes were fixated on our sex and my ass. I clenched up, and he whispered, "Relax for me, *malysh*." The tender ring of nerves he penetrated burned, and he said again, "*Malysh*, relax for me."

He demanded, I listened.

I nodded and did as he asked, rubbing my clit over his full sack. His finger slipped in my hole and I tried to breathe calmly.

"Fucking hell. You know I can feel my cock sliding in and out of your pussy like this." He all but moaned.

Kova's sexy, husky words took me to another level. The sensations flowing through me were all too much and I couldn't stop wiggling on him or rearing back, absolutely loving the ecstasy of both the pain and pleasure from both sides. My thighs quivered and my toes flexed and curled from the stimulation of his skilled fingers and dirty mouth.

"I want you to stop having sex with your wife." The words spilled from my lips.

"You know that is not possible," he responded and thrust so hard into me I lost my breath.

My lungs ached for air. Kova pushed deep and held me down. I became insatiable for this orgasm and started grinding myself on him.

"You can."

A whimper escaped my lips as I tried to shift because I was pretty sure he tore me again.

"Ria, I have to play the game, but I will make a deal with you."

I hesitated. Another instant that most definitely wasn't normal relationship talk, and yet it was ours. I couldn't think straight when an orgasm was about to shatter me, but I nodded anyway.

"She will never get my cock the way you do. I will never look at her face when I fuck her."

Kova groaned, and I got the feeling he wasn't finished. His fingers picked up the pace and so did his hips. He was close, just like I was.

"Kova…" I dug my teeth into my bottom lip. "I can't hold off any longer, and there is nothing you can say that will make it okay for you to be with me and your wife at the same time."

His seductive chuckle challenged my words. "I will never fuck her raw, and I will never, ever come inside her again. The last thing we need is for you to get pregnant, but the thought of my cum inside your pussy makes me so fucking hard it is painful."

My clit throbbed and I felt his dick swell inside me, enlarging to a thickness that said he was telling the truth. We both let out a guttural moan, our flesh slippery with lust and illicit desires.

"Ria…" he said, his finger still carefully working my ass. I actually found myself rearing back for more. "Do that thing with your pussy where you squeeze my cock." I thought about what he said and I tried it. "Yes…" he moaned, thrusting so slow and hard I knew I wasn't going to be able to walk. The tip of his cock hit deep. I ground my pussy on him and squeezed again. "Just…like…that…" Kova whimpered, and it was by far the sexiest sound he'd ever made. I wanted to make him do it over and over. "Harder," he begged, and I squeezed as tight as I could.

"She never gets your cum," I said. "Only I do." His hips picked up speed and for once I felt like I was in control. "Not even in her mouth will you come," I said, shocked by my own words. "Only mine."

"You cannot talk to me like that." He sounded like he was suffering.

"I don't even want you to come in your condom when you fuck her. You can use your hand or rip that condom off and come on top of her, but never inside of her."

His breathing deepened, and it excited me. "Keep talking to me like that."

"Want to know a secret?" I asked, pushing back so my ass was nearly in his face. "I love when you come inside my pussy. I love how wrong it is, that it should never happen. I get wet thinking about how you're my coach and I'm your gymnast and I can feel your dick pulsing inside. It's so fucking risky, and even though you have a wife, you're still here with *me*, coming in *me*, and I love that."

His body trembled and I made a mental note that Kova loved dirty talk.

"Do you hear me? You only ever come inside my pussy," I said, breathing heavily. "My young, little pussy that you broke and took for yourself." I was about to orgasm any second. How I'd held on this long was beyond me.

"You like that your coach is fucking you?" he asked, almost surprised by his question.

I moaned. "I think about it when I touch myself."

"You... You touch yourself? Fuck..."

"All the time," I admitted.

"With what?" he asked, breathless.

"My fingers, but you want to know another secret?" He nodded. "I just bought my first vibrator and I came on it three times in a row thinking it was your cock."

It was a lie. I hadn't bought anything, but it felt like something he'd want to hear.

Kova's rhythm slowed down. His breathing was rough and ragged as he pulled his finger out, but then he poked at my entrance again with two fingers this time.

"I want to fuck you until you cannot walk. Pound you so hard you are too bruised to sit down for a week."

A gasp rolled off my lips. My eyes widened and I tensed, then remembered him telling me to relax. I tried but my heart was hammering in my chest. I knew he wouldn't hurt me but it still made me a little apprehensive. Heart racing, my ass felt like it was on fire but not enough to ruin what we had between us. My thighs weakened and I could barely hold myself up anymore from the onslaught of pleasure taking over my body. Kova noticed and sat up so I could lean back against him.

"I... I can't hold on any longer. I need to come," I said, then turned my head around to kiss him. "But I will only come if you come with me."

"I will do whatever you want, anything, if you tell me you love me."

"No," I said, my voice below a whisper. "Why are you asking me this right now?"

His hips surged into me faster. A routine of perfect harmony enough to seduce me to a wild mess of passion.

"Tell me," he begged and I almost caved, but I stood strong and shook my head. "I want to hear you say you love me like I love you."

"No," I said again. He wouldn't get that from me.

"Tell me," he begged, placing his hand on my throat. "Please, so I know I am not the only crazy one."

"Oh God, it's right there," I said and reared back so I was riding his cock at the same time. My heart was fluttering and once again he took me to a new level I knew I would crave again after this.

"Tell me," he said one last time, and I partially gave him what he wanted to hear.

"I love the way we make love."

That was all he was getting.

Kova reached between us and pinched my clit so hard I screamed as he drove into me from behind. He used his strength to shove me down on his dick as loud moans purred from my throat. The pleasure was too much and I closed my eyes and let myself fall. Silver stars danced behind my eyelids as he tightened his grip. My breathing took on a sound of its own, and my body rode his wave until the pleasure subsided and we slowed down.

Our heavy breathing was the only sound in the room. Kova pulled his cock out with a little pop and leaned back against the arm rest of the couch, taking me with him. I glanced down between us, his length semi-hard and glossy with our abandoned cravings. A thin white line oozed from his tip and stuck to my inner thigh. His hand flattened against my entrance and I looked over my shoulder at him quizzically.

"Squeeze. I can feel my cum trying to leak out of you." He covered my tender vagina with his hand to hold it in. He was so filthy, but I loved that about him. "Leave it where it belongs." I nodded, trying to catch my breath, feeling it trying to pour out of me.

Turning over, I got up to face him and sank down on his lap. Kova grabbed my face and kissed me passionately and tenderly, something I'd noticed he did each time after we had sex. This was his way of showing me affection, I thought. He pulled back and I smiled. We both looked between us. His penis hung over his elastic waistband looking completely used, and I could see my clit as his cum leaked out of me onto his shaft. My teeth dug into my bottom lip as I moved my pussy over his length, rubbing his thick white pleasure on his cock. I lifted my eyes to study Kova. He was watching us intently.

I leaned forward to push his head back so I could press my lips to his neck, I slid my tender pussy over him. Kova growled and I felt it against my lips.

"Go ahead and come on me like this, Ria, I know you want to."

And I did. I rubbed our desires all over him until I was trying to squeeze his dick with my pussy lips and came again.

"God," I said breathless once I was done. I sat up feeling a little lightheaded. My eyes were wide with surprise. "I don't know what comes over me when I'm with you. I feel like I turn into another person and all I can focus on is sex."

Kova grinned then kissed me hard. He stuffed his penis back into his pants and then dropped to his knees. Grabbing my hips, he placed a soft kiss to my mound and lifted one leg and placed it over his shoulder. I watched, curious to see what he was going to do when his bottom teeth gradually danced over my clit. I shuddered, a current of euphoria slaying through me. My fingers threaded his tousled locks and I raised my hips, rocking into his face while he teased me some more. If he wanted to give me more, fine by me. Kova flattened his tongue and pressed it against my sex and I almost came again. It was raw and dirty, but truth be told, I loved that he was tasting us.

"I love your pussy," he said like he was on cloud nine.

I felt a thick, slippery gooeyness trail down my ass onto the couch. I looked down and watched two of Kova's fingers wipe it up then push it back into me. He stroked the tender walls of my pussy with a softness that didn't quite match his rough exterior, massaging his semen into me. Kova's carnal desires resonated within me. I understood where he was coming from because I was just like him.

Kova looked up at me. Our eyes connected and something in my heart shifted into place. Each day he was mending what he broke inside of me. His vulnerability was back, defenses were down, and I saw the love he had for me. Not from the orgasms he gave, but from the way his distressed eyes stared into mine, the way his face contorted with agony and yearning. He dropped his forehead to my stomach and his shoulders bunched tight. He expelled a breath and then wrapped his arms around my waist and held me, releasing whatever pent-up emotion he had.

And I took it. I took all of it all, feeling the weight of his body and absorbing it deep into my bones. It was strange how I felt him more through touch than his words. I understood him. But sometimes when he looked at me, and how his body sank into mine, how he trembled beneath the surface, it was the only answer I needed.

Moving to my knees, I embraced this man who was so tormented by his feelings and actions. I wanted to tell him I loved him. I had too much empathy for him, and I didn't know how to close that gate to make it stop from happening, because the reality was, I'd unlocked the door and held it open for him to begin with.

"Promise me," I said softly. He nodded.

Kova was right. This wasn't normal, but it was our normal...and I was okay with that.

chapter 41

KOVA MOLDED BACK INTO HIS OLD SELF WITH EACH PASSING DAY, AND within weeks I was greeted daily with his cocky brashness I'd come to know and love.

I never realized how much my mental health relied on his coaching and what we accomplished in the gym, because despite the fatigue and bone aches, I was doing better than ever. I took all my medicine, I didn't miss my scheduled blood work, and I actually slept. I was even eating a little better. I hadn't gained weight, but I felt alive and I knew it was because I had rekindled my relationship with Kova.

I still didn't have a donor match. That was one thing he couldn't do for me.

We were both trying so hard to find the right medium to make things work. Inside the gym, we picked up where we left off and practiced my routines for hours each day, breaking down the skills and practicing to perfection. Wash, rinse, repeat. We were completely civil to one another and back to business. I ate up his words. My first, huge international meet was coming up, then one more competition a couple of weeks after that where the selection for the Olympic team took place.

This was it. The moments I'd been waiting for were finally here.

As the day drew to an end and practice was just about over, I caught a flutter of neon pink in the corner of my eye. I glanced over at a face I hadn't seen in many long months. Bright blue globes for eyes, a giant smile from ear to ear that I felt down to my soul, and platinum blonde hair and pinks tips she'd dyed.

Avery Heron. My best friend. Was at World Cup.

Excitement I hadn't felt in ages whooshed through me. My face lit up and I bounced on my toes eagerly. I wanted to run to her, throw my arms around her neck, but I couldn't just leave in the middle of practice, not even to take a break—I needed permission.

I searched for Kova, and he saw my silent plea. He nodded his head with a kind smile. I ran. Maybe opening up about Avery to him had been a blessing in disguise.

Within seconds I was in the lobby throwing myself into my best friend's open arms. She caught me and I wrapped my legs around her like I was a damn spider monkey. She stumbled back but luckily for both of us regained her footing.

"Adrianna!" she squealed in my ear. I almost cried hearing her voice in person. "Oh my God, you're squeezing me to death. Let go." She feigned a choking sound.

I chuckled as she released me. Our hands joined together and we stood inches from each other.

"I can't believe you're here! I figured not for a few more days!" I said.

"I wanted to surprise you, so I came early!"

I was so happy, tears filled my eyes. I hugged her again and squeezed. "You don't know how much I've missed you. How long are you here for?"

"For however long I want to be. I don't have a schedule."

"I'm so excited!" I nodded with a stupid grin on my face.

The door chimed and in walked the definition of a perfect woman. Katja.

She looked directly at me and I mused to myself that I didn't even know her last name. Not that it mattered anymore since she was now a Kournakova.

"Adrianna."

Her Russian accent was thicker than Kova's. She looked at Avery with questionable eyes, raking a bitter glance down her body. I swallowed nervously, thinking about how the last time I saw her Kova had kicked her out of his office for me.

"Hi, Katja," I said quietly just to be nice.

"Does Konstantin know you are out here?"

An odd question, and I decided not to answer her. She didn't need to know he gave me permission.

Katja made a little sound under her breath and squinted toward the windows that led to the gym. I looked at Avery, who wore the same baffled expression as I did. We both shrugged at the same time and laughed.

"You're so tan," I said to her. "Just like Ba—"

She pointed her index finger at me and raised one brow. "Don't you dare say Barbie, bitch. You know I hate that fucking shit."

I laughed as she scolded me. But she did. She was a life-like version of Barbie but with deep sun-kissed skin I envied. Aside from my Italian roots that blessed me with a Mediterranean tone, I was pale in comparison to her, and now I would always be because of the reaction the sun caused in conjunction with lupus.

"Fine. You look like Paris Hilton."

Her face scrunched up. "Ewww. A walking disease?"

I laughed. "Taylor Swift?"

Her eyes sparkled. "Much better."

"I have to finish up. I have about two hours left. Do you want to wait or go straight to my condo?"

"I'll wait. I don't mind."

"Sweet. I was hoping you'd say that." I smiled from ear to ear. "Ah! I'm so happy you're here!"

I opened the door that led to the gym, and for the second time today, something caught my attention. But it wasn't a color this time. It was Katja's hushed words drifting through the air, and I frowned. Her giddiness caused me to stall with my hand on the knob.

I fought with myself. I didn't want to turn around to see what she was doing, but I did anyway. I learned from Kova that everything she did had a motive, so her presence at World Cup meant something. I watched Katja hold her stomach as she spoke to a parent from one of the teams and I caught the faint purr of broken English that nipped my mended heart. I saw smiles and I swear I heard blessings of some sort.

"Hey," Avery said softly. Her brows were bunched together as she glanced over my shoulder. "Ignore that dirty gnat and whatever you heard. I have a feeling not everything is what it seems with her."

A sad chuckle rolled from my lips. "Did you just say gnat?"

One side of her mouth pulled to the side. She shrugged her shoulder. "Yeah, I heard it in a new rap song and I loved it. So everyone I find annoying is a gnat."

"Which is everyone since you hate the world."

"Except for you." Her smiled reached her ears. "Finish up and we'll talk later. It seems we both need to have a long girl talk."

I walked back into the gym trying to forget what I saw. I wanted so bad to ask him why she was here, but I couldn't bring myself to. He knew where I stood and how I felt. I wouldn't stoop to that level and lose respect for myself completely.

Inhale the chalk, exhale the bullshit.

For the next two hours, I pretended like I didn't have a care in the world except for gymnastics.

Kova didn't speak to me except when he was coaching, but then again, I didn't expect anything else since his scheming wife was here to watch her husband.

"Adrianna?" Kova said low, and only for me.

I pulled back the Velcro from my grips to loosen the straps. "Yes?" I said without looking up. Taking off my grips felt as good as taking off my sports bra at the end of the day.

"Look at me."

Hesitant, I raised my eyes. Kova rubbed the back of his neck, his face twisting in distress.

"Do not go there. I know what you think you heard, but it is not true."

I swallowed hard, praying what he said was the truth.

"I told you she wants one, not that she has one."

My stomach tightened, stunned that he was risking such a conversation in public.

Kova muttered under his breath in Russian. "I am asking you to please believe me. Please."

chapter 42

"HE WANTS YOU TO BELIEVE HIM?" SHE RETORTED, HER VOICE surprised. "Did you tell him to go fucking kick rocks?"

I gave Avery a knowing look. "You know I didn't."

She sighed. "Sometimes I wish you would grow a spine and tell him to eat shit, then walk away." Avery's eyes widened and she looked a little worried and tried to retract her words. "Not to say that you don't have a spine, ah, I just that I wish you wouldn't let him walk all over you."

We were sitting on my bed having a powwow while we drank freshly squeezed lemonade Avery had made. We'd been talking for hours and it felt so good. It was the long-awaited girl talk we should've had a long time ago.

I left no stone unturned. I told her every single thing that had happened with Kova, leaving nothing out. I opened up about Joy, and Avery cursed her to seven different hells. She'd never liked Joy. I told her about my real mom and how I met her, the illness in her family and how it was genetic. Avery encouraged me to meet with her again one day when I was ready. I was honest and told her I was afraid of dying young.

She listened to me. She cried with me. She didn't judge, didn't criticize my choices. She was the ideal best friend who just sat and heard me. Sometimes just listening can be more powerful than anything.

I sighed in understanding. "I know what you mean, it's just hard. I guess I want to give him the benefit of the doubt since we don't have a normal relationship."

"But is it that? A relationship?" She posed her question carefully.

I picked at the imaginary lint on my comforter. "I honestly don't know what to call it." And I didn't.

"Maybe it doesn't need a label. Sometimes that can ruin a good thing," she offered.

I smiled at her, appreciating her effort. "Yeah, I guess so." I paused. "Does it make me stupid? Be honest."

"It doesn't make you stupid. Love makes people do things they wouldn't typically do, but it doesn't make you, or anyone, stupid. Maybe in that moment it was right and that's really all that matters." She eyed me with a challenge. "And don't even deny you love him. It's obvious you do."

I chuckled sadly. "To you? Or to everyone?"

"I mean, I didn't see you look at him with hearts in your eyes today. I'm sure you're careful not to in public, but when you talk about him, you get this cheesy ass dreamy look in your eyes that embarrasses the shit out of me, but yeah, I can see it. I also know you, so you're asking the wrong chick."

"I'm scared he's going to hurt me again," I said quietly. "I don't want to be hurt again, Ave. I don't think I have the heart for it."

"Aid?"

I looked up.

"He's done a lot to hurt you, there's no denying that. Call me crazy, I can't even believe I'm going to side with Fish Lips, but I don't think all of it was intentional. Your situation isn't a usual one, and you both did things you wouldn't normally do. Do I think you should tread lightly? Fuck yeah, I do, for more reasons than one. Love is risky, and even though they say love shouldn't hurt, it always does because no one has a perfect love. It's all trial and error. If you allow yourself to love someone, you're giving them power over you. To me, that hurts. I don't want anyone to have any kind of power over me ever again. Yes, there are a ton of reasons why you should walk away and let it go, but can you think of at least one reason that makes you want to stay and chance it?"

I nodded immediately. I didn't hesitate.

"What is it?" she asked, her eyes soft.

"It sounds so stupid—"

"No, it doesn't. If it makes sense to you, then that's all that matters."

"He encourages me. I want to be a better person, a better gymnast, because of him. I can feel his energy and I love it. It gives me life. He's made me strong, even at my weakest point when I shut the world out, I could look for him and he would always just be right there. He doesn't even have to say anything, Avery, it's just like he knows, and I'm suddenly okay. Like a peace settles within me. I'm sure what I'm saying doesn't make sense. I know he does things backwards all the time, says all the wrong things, and he doesn't always make sense in that moment, but eventually, it does." I paused and shook my head. Nothing I said out loud made sense. "You know what he said to me when I felt hopeless? When I was terrified and sinking into a deep depression? That I should use my sickness as inspiration, that I should live for it instead of allowing it to kill me." My voice dropped. "He said he wanted to live with me."

I glanced up and Avery had tears in her eyes.

"You should marry that stupid Russian."

I burst out laughing. "Too late. He's already got a ring on his finger. Not that I could marry him now anyway."

"It won't last, Aid. Trust me, it won't. Not after everything you told me about the blackmail, Cuntja, the way—"

"Cuntja?" I asked, finding a comical flare to the sound of it.

"Yeah, Katja and cunt. Cuntja," she said like it was obvious.

A burst of laughter erupted from me and I giggled hysterically.

"Oh my god! That's the best!" I said between fits of laughter. It was the perfect name to describe his wife. Sobering up, I asked, "Do you think it's fair, though? I mean, she's probably the way she is because of me."

"You said Kova told you the issues between them started before you got here, so no. She's just a bitch because she was born with it in her blood, and because Joy also gave her the ammo to be a vindictive bitch at that."

I nodded, agreeing with her. Still, I was sure I didn't help their situation.

Avery continued. "What I was saying was, the way he is with you when it's just you guys is not the same guy you see out in the public. And who cares? What matters is how he is with you. He has to deflect right now and be a dick. I think it probably bothers him that he's banging a gymnast who is still a teen. At least, I hope it would." She laughed nervously. "Think about it. If it were you, like if you were in Kova's shoes, what would you do? Right now is the wrong time, yes, and some days he needs an attitude adjustment, but one day everything will be right in the world, and it will be for you guys too."

I smiled appreciatively at her. I loved my best friend. She sorted out my muddled thoughts.

"You never knew about any of this? About the lupus and kidneys? Xavier never told you?"

She shook her head and looked down with a sad expression on her face. I was genuinely surprised.

"No." Her voice was low. "I honestly never knew."

"Wow. I figured he would have."

"We haven't done much talking since everything happened..." she said quietly, like it hurt it to utter those words.

"But I saw you guys together on Instagram on the Fourth of July."

She shook her head and looked down. The sadness on her face told me everything I needed to know.

"It's not like that. I promise. We tried to hang out, but he can't get over what I did."

"You mean the abortion?"

She nodded silently. "It's not what you think… I didn't have an abortion."

chapter 43

"WHAT? WHAT ARE YOU TALKING ABOUT?"

Avery exhaled a large breath and eyed her glass of lemonade. A few seconds ago she'd been my rock, giving me inspiring words. Now she seemed broken inside, her face paling. Her thumb rimmed the lip of the glass as she blinked, like she was lost in her thoughts.

"Are you sure you want to hear this?" she asked me, her voice low. "It's not all rainbows and butterflies, and you have to make me a promise to never tell your brother, no matter what I tell you."

I reached for her hand and her fingers wrapped around mine. I didn't say anything. I didn't need to. She knew I'd never do that. We both positioned ourselves against my headboard and sat back.

"There's a lot you don't know about your brother," she said quietly.

Didn't surprise me. Most siblings were like that.

"Tell me when you started to date him."

She looked at me with guarded eyes. "We never dated. We were together but we never dated officially."

"I kind of gathered that. I just don't know how you guys made it work when he was in school."

"He came home on the weekends a lot to see me and then we hid out in the guest house together or went to parties. Or I'd go visit him. It wasn't hard to sneak around, honestly, and no one thought anything of it because my brothers were there too. I just looked like the little sister that tagged along, you know?"

I nodded. Made sense. Anything was possible with enough courage.

Avery released a breath like she just let the weight of her world go.

"Don't hold back from me, okay? No more."

She glanced in my direction and smiled softly.

"It sucks because I still want him, even after everything. He's a different person when it's just me and him. Kind of like with you and Kova, I guess." She paused to swallow, then chewed on her bottom lip like she was nervous to tell me. "We started up about two years ago. We teased each other like siblings do, but then something somehow morphed into something else and we became more. He was like a best friend with benefits in a way. Once we started hooking up, we fell hard for each other. I loved him... I think I still love him."

My brows shot up. "I can't believe I never knew. How did I not I see it? I feel like everything is so obvious now, but at the time... Like New Year's... I should've seen it."

"You wouldn't have. No one would have. Our parents were never around. You were doing gymnastics morning, noon, and night, and we were good at hiding it. It was so easy."

I nodded my head back and forth. She had a point. Sneaking around is easy when you want something bad enough.

"The parties, though...that's where all of our issues stem from. There's so much drugs and aggression and testosterone at them. At the time, we didn't think anything of it. We were living our best life, but hindsight is a bitch. We'd drink and smoke some weed, then go back to his house and smush like rabbits. But it wasn't just like any hookup. It was way more for both of us. I can't explain it, like it just was, and he knew that."

Avery exhaled another big breath like it was hard for her to get into the nitty-gritty of the story. I felt bad.

"If it's too hard to talk about, we don't have to," I said gently.

She shook her head. "No, I need to tell you everything."

Scooting closer to her, I rested my head on her shoulder, hoping to give her the courage to keep going. "Go on."

She waited a long moment.

"So I'm not sure if you know, but Xavier's into fighting. Like MMA shit, but it's underground. He's good at it too, undefeated...or at least he was." Her voice trailed off like she was saddened by the memory. "Xavier said I was his lucky charm and he had me in his corner at every fight. He didn't lose a match, until we stopped being together. He hasn't won since."

"I had a feeling he was into something reckless, but I didn't know it was that." I thought back to one of the times I went home and he had some cuts and bruises on his face and how he had played it off. I just assumed he was being an idiot with his friends and left it alone. "How cliché of him. Rich punk into underground fighting." I rolled my eyes.

"He makes money, girl. Good money. Well, he did."

I shook my head, puzzled. "Why, though? He doesn't need it."

She shrugged one shoulder. "Because he's good at it and can. Why does anyone do stupid things like that? It was a rush to watch him, and he'd tell me that's what it was like for him too when he was fighting. He was high all the time, so I'm sure the adrenaline and coke were making him feel twenty feet tall."

"He was doing cocaine?" I asked, my voice low, as if someone might hear me. Cocaine and fighting couldn't be a good combination on the heart. Dread began to cultivate in my stomach like black smoke and I started to fear the worst possible scenario.

"Oh, he was doing more than that. Coke, Ex, Oxy, Vicodin, Xanax, anything he could get his hands on, however he could take it, he did. Snorting, shooting, chewing pills, he did it all. He'd get so high he didn't want to come down, so he'd move on to something stronger."

I was going to be sick. Instant worry for my dumb ass brother and his recklessness struck me when something else dawned on me. I lifted my head up and turned toward Avery.

"You were doing drugs with him, weren't you?"

She looked away. Embarrassment flushed her cheeks and she nodded.

My lips turned downward. "Ave, is he still doing this?"

"To an extent, yes." She struggled to admit. "It's one of the reasons I walked away. Every minute of every day, he was high and gearing up for a fight."

I frowned. I couldn't believe I didn't see any of this. "I'm so confused."

"We broke up and got back together so many times. Like we weren't together, but we were. When I walked away the last time, he said he was done playing with me. I was hurt and thought he was lying, but I said fine by me and gave him the finger. When he talked shit to me, I gave it back ten times harder. Xavier shut me out, and man, is he good at it. But that's what we did, you know? We fought then apologized and then went back to being how we were. I figured that's what would happen, but then we didn't talk for over a month until I saw him again."

"What did he say when he found out you were pregnant?"

"He was not what I expected at all. I thought he was going to flip the fuck out, but he was oddly excited about it."

My brows shot up. "What? That doesn't make any sense."

"Yeah, I know. It was weird. He was beaming like a fool and touching my stomach any chance he got. Here I was crying and panicking inside because, hello, I was only seventeen and pregnant. *Teen Mom*, here I come. But Xavier was jumping up and down and kissing me and hugging me nonstop. I'd never seen him so happy, Aid. I remember this feeling of relief, like okay, one down, ten more to go and then everything would be okay. My love for him developed into something more during that time. I also remember thinking we would actually get to be family like we always talked about."

I shook my head, unsure what to feel anymore. Xavier's reaction about the pregnancy was odd and it messed with my mind. They both were so young and shouldn't want a baby, yet he did.

"That doesn't make any sense," I told her. "He wasn't thinking clearly. No one wants a baby at that age. It had to be the drugs. Had to be." I paused, deciding to tell her what I was thinking. "Unless he really loved you...?"

Her shoulders dropped. "I don't know anymore. Honestly. I think maybe he did love me and we both didn't know it, but he sure as shit doesn't now. Not after what I did," she said, her voice cracking a little. "All I could think about was your ratchet mother—well, Joy—and how my parents were going to react to the news. Telling Xavier made my hands shake and my heart pound. Our parents? My stomach cramped and I was a sweaty mess. I mean, I'm in high school. I can't have a baby. But I was. I was gonna have a kid."

I rested my head back against the wood and put myself in her shoes. I couldn't imagine having a child at our age, let alone going through such heavy emotions with no one to lean on. We both had dealt with situations where we'd needed each other's support during a critical time, and we hadn't had it. I had to deal with the fact that Joy wasn't my mom, Kova secretly got married, and a stupid sickness was wearing me down. Meanwhile, my bestie was pregnant by my brother and had an abortion—only she hadn't.

God, I wished we both had had the strength to talk to each other. I couldn't help but wonder if we'd had each other to lean on if she would be here holding a baby now. But the past is the past and now that we were talking it through, I was going to make sure this never happened again. I couldn't reverse time, but I could try and prevent the same mistake from happening twice.

I lowered my eyes, regret spilling through me. I was the definition of a shit friend. Absorbed in gymnastics and Kova, Avery had to deal with this on her own. I'd make it up to her, though. Somehow, some way, I would.

"Keep going," I said softly. I knew there was more.

Avery took a sip of her lemonade. "I wasn't worried about needing financial support. I knew eventually our families would come together and our child wouldn't want for anything, but I was scared. God, I was so scared, and I had to tell our parents. I had to tell you. That was the worst part. I was more afraid to tell you than our parents. I didn't want you to hate me or to never talk to me again. I went back and forth about how to say something, but I could never find the courage to. I didn't want to lose you and I was so scared I would." Her voice shook. Avery pulled her knees up and wrapped her arms around them. "Not only was I hooking up with my best friend's brother, I gotten knocked up by him too." Avery burst into tears, and I knew why. She did lose me for a little while.

And it was my fault.

chapter 44

I REACHED OVER AND TOOK HER GLASS AND PLACED IT ON MY NIGHTSTAND, along with mine, then I wrapped my arm around her shoulder and pulled her into a hug.

She hugged me back and cried softly while my heart broke for her and us. I couldn't imagine having to tell her something like that, and it made sense now why she hadn't. Opening up to her about Kova was a hard pill to swallow. But if I had to tell her I'd gotten pregnant by one of her brothers, I don't think it would've gone over well either. I probably would've done the same thing she had.

"I'm so sorry for the way I acted," I said honestly. "I wish I would've known. I wish I would've been there for you. I wish I would've given you the opportunity to explain. I wish I wasn't such a bitch toward you."

Avery hugged me back tighter. "It's not your fault. I was such a mess and so were you. I couldn't talk about it when I needed to. I kept to myself and ran through all these different scenarios in my head, thinking they had positive outcomes, but they really didn't. I was lying to myself and I knew I was."

Pulling back, I made her look at me. Her usually stunning blue eyes were bloodshot and screaming with shame. I wanted to take that from her so she never felt it again.

"Before you say anything else, let's make a pact. From here on out, we promise to never hold back, no matter how scared we are to tell each other something, okay? I never want to go through this again with you, because the truth is, we need each other."

She nodded and sniffled. "Never again."

"Never."

"There's more." She sounded scared, but I nodded anyway, and she began to tell me about the life of Xavier I never knew he had.

"Xavier was doing all these underground fights, and he was killing it. Right before each fight, he'd kiss me in front of everyone and tell me I was his, and afterward we would celebrate at a party with drinks and whatever we were in the mood for. I did them with him, I wanted to. He never left my side, couldn't take his hands off me, and if any other guy spoke to me, he got possessive and totally alpha. At first I loved it. I thought it was hot, you know? We were glued to each other and I know you don't want to hear this, but we had the best sex when we were like that after a fight. He had so much adrenaline in him." She smiled sadly. "Well, one night he was banged up pretty badly and almost lost a fight. The guy he fought knew about your brother's winning streak and prepared for Xavier's left hook. He was determined to take your brother out."

Chills zipped down my spine, a sense of fear curling in my stomach. I had a feeling this was going to be bad. Underground fighting was probably one of the dumbest things I'd ever heard of.

"Xavier was so hyped up from the fight and the drugs, that right before he almost went down, he looked at me one last time and gave me a naughty ass grin. It was so fucking sexy, Aid. God, I can remember it like it was yesterday. Anyway, this guy thought he would antagonize Xavier by using me."

"Oh shit. What did he do?"

"Oh shit is fucking right." Avery shook her head like she was there again living it. "He told Xavier he was going to fuck me raw after he won." She paused, and shuddered. "I thought Xavier was going to kill him. I really thought he was gonna go to jail for murder."

I'd never seen my brother enraged except during Easter when he'd pushed our dad up against the wall. This was all news to me.

"Even though blood dripped from one corner of his lip, and his eyes were swollen and already bruising, Xavier went to town on the guy. I don't know where his energy came from. He was hyped and beat the shit out of him *bad*. I mean, like, he pulverized him to the point it took a few people to pull Xavier off him. It was horrible. The guy was barely moving. He laid on the floor in a pool of blood with teeth missing. Xavier spit on him, said some shit, and then turned toward me. I thought he was gonna give me a celebratory kiss like he usually did, but he was angry, and it scared me. There was a blank look in his eyes."

I sat in utter silence listening to this side of Xavier I never knew existed. The thought of him like this scared me. Reckless and wild was one thing, but this was asking for a death wish. Hearing him take so many drugs and fight? That was a deadly combination. Someone needed to talk some sense into him. I wanted to do that, but I didn't want to betray Avery's trust either. Sighing inwardly, I didn't know what to say. I couldn't give advice because it was already said and done, so all I could do was listen.

"At the party afterward, he barely said two words to me but wouldn't let me leave his side either. He was strung out, but I sat on his lap like I always did while he drank whatever was handed to him. He wouldn't let me ice his face or help put anything on it to reduce the swelling. I tried to kiss him, tried to have sex with him like we usually did after a win, but nothing worked. All he would let me do was hold his hand. His fingers shook after he laced them through mine and his grip was so strong, almost like he was afraid I was going to leave. We did lines of coke together, probably shared an eightball that night, but then he took it further and took a Xanax and popped some Ex. I didn't, though, not even when he begged me to roll with him. I didn't like mixing uppers with downers because that's like asking for a death wish. But he did. I remember having this weird feeling in my stomach that night. He wasn't acting like himself, he'd had so much to drink, taking shot after shot of tequila. I begged him to stop but he wouldn't listen and got angrier by the second. He was like a ticking time bomb. Still, I stayed by his side." Avery's voice drew quiet and she lowered her gaze. Tears filled her eyes. "Around three in the morning, he fucking overdosed," she whispered. Her shoulders shook and she started to cry again.

I drew in an audible breath and my stomach dropped. Cupping my mouth, I stared, unblinking as I replayed the words in my head, not sure I'd heard her right.

"What? He overdosed?" I whispered, my jaw trembling. I blinked a few times trying to put everything together. My vision blurred imagining my brother like this.

Clenching her eyes shut, she nodded her head and wiped the tears from her cheeks. "We had to use Narcan to bring him back."

I frowned, brows deepening. "You just happened to carry that?"

She sniffled and took a deep breath before exhaling slowly. She could hardly look me in the eyes.

"No, one of the guys he was chilling with had it, but after that happened I carried it because I had to use it on him again another time. During the time I was with him, he overdosed a total of three times." She let out a sob that broke my heart. Now I was terrified for my brother. "Every night Xavier pushed the envelope. He turned into a completely different person, so mean when he was fucked up. I knew he wouldn't lay a hand on me, but his rage was a side of him that scared me. He became so volatile."

Red-hot fear sliced through me. "Avery," I whispered. My heart thundered in my chest at the thought of losing my brother. I wasn't supposed to say anything to him, but this was a matter of life and death and I wasn't going to risk it.

"We have to do something about this. Is he still like that?"

She shook her head. "From what I hear, all he does is drink now and take Xanax. Still a dangerous combo but better than what he was doing. I tried to help him at first, but he wasn't having it. That's when our fighting got bad. He was spiraling out of control and I couldn't stop him. He wouldn't let me. The first time I walked out on him was when he OD'd the second time. I thought it'd wake him up. But the third time it happened was the last straw. He didn't even give himself time to recover from the overdose when he was back at it again. Being that I was pregnant by that point, I was sober, so I saw just how far gone he was. I know I was just as bad at first—I don't claim to be a saint—but he was toeing the line to see how far he could go every night. I told him if he didn't get help I was leaving for good. He was so mad that night. We literally screamed at the top of our lungs at each other. He told me he'd take care of his kid, but he was done playing with me because all bitches are the fucking same and only good for one thing. I didn't believe it because it's what we did, you know, but I guess he was serious. For weeks he shut me out and wouldn't see me, wouldn't talk to me. Unfollowed me on all social media sites and blocked me. It was horrible. I was pregnant and so alone. I'd heard he was hooking up with new girls every night but then losing every fight too. When I finally did get to see him, it was at a charity event. He was with a girl your mom had set him up with." Avery's face scrunched up and she looked absolutely sick. "God, it killed me to see him like that. Xavier was all over her. He'd look at me then kiss her. It killed me inside. There I was wearing his favorite dress hoping to sway him, pregnant with his child that I was still hiding pretty well, and he was loving up on someone else."

"Ave," I said. I had a bad feeling about this. "Don't tell me you had an abortion because of that."

She looked away. "Yes and no... The cramping started that night, only I didn't realize they were cramps. I just thought my belly was stretching. The next day I went to the pool house to try and talk some sense into him. I could barely walk to my car, let alone drive to your house and walk to the pool house. The pain was unbearable, but I missed him so fucking much and wanted to fix things. I was willing to do anything, only when I opened the door, I found him tangled in the sheets totally naked with the same chick. Seeing him like that sucked the air from my lungs. It was the proof I needed to truly be done with him. I thought I was going to be sick and I held my stomach and leaned on the doorframe. Xavier got up when he saw me and walked over to me. He told me to get the fuck out. The weird thing was I could see his pain when he was yelling at me, I could feel it, how much it hurt to look at me because I knew he still wanted me just like I did him. His eyes were bloodshot, his hands shook, he had bruises everywhere. It was like he let himself get beat up. He gave me a little shove on my shoulder, but it wasn't bad or anything. I begged him to come back to me. I let myself cry in front of him. I told him my stomach was hurting but he brushed it off saying I was using the pregnancy as a way to keep him."

Avery took a deep breath and lowered her voice. "I didn't know stress could cause a miscarriage, but that's what happened. I never had an abortion, Aid. I had a fucking miscarriage. I lied to Xavier. I lied to everyone."

"How far along were you by then?"

"I was about five months when I had the miscarriage. You'd never know it, though. I hardly showed and hid it well."

Avery let go and her tears really started to fall. I reached over and pulled her into a bear hug. She softly cried on my shoulder, shaking. I cried with her over the loss of everything at once. She held me tight as she sobbed, her tears coming in fast and hard. My heart broke as she relived this moment I was sure she wanted to forget for the rest of her life. This whole time she was living a lie with no outlet. I knew that feeling and how it could consume someone, how the pressure mounted into something more, how you're stuck with these depressing thoughts.

But this was different. She had carried a life inside of her. Her child.

A child she lost.

And I had missed out on being an aunt.

chapter 45

"**I** DON'T KNOW WHAT TO SAY, AVE. I'M SO, SO SORRY. GOD, I'M SO sorry," I said again through my tears.

My issues felt so small in comparison to hers. Now I knew why she wanted to tell me in person. This wasn't a conversation to have over the phone.

Avery sniffled and drew in a deep breath. Pulling back, she used her shirt to wipe her eyes.

"I asked him to feel my belly that day because our son was kicking. I wasn't far along enough to feel kicks all the time, but they did start. Small ones, but I felt them. I thought if he wouldn't talk to me, then at least that could work. I remember feeling a sliver of hope, like my heart was going to pop out of my chest because he stopped yelling at me and looked down at my belly. His eyes changed, his demeanor changed, and I saw the old Xavier for a split second. Even though he claimed he didn't want me, he wanted our baby. His hand reached out only to pull back just as quickly. His wall slid back into place and he kicked me out, slamming the door shut. I cried for him to take me back. I didn't make it far inside your house when I fell to the floor in pain. Joy found me."

My entire body tensed over Joy being the one to find her. Then all at once everything clicked into place, and my mind flashed back to Easter when shit had hit the fan. Joy had said she'd cleaned up their mess and helped with Avery's miscarriage like she was proud of it. I clenched the back of my teeth while I tried not to relive that day.

"What happened next?" I asked, dreading to know exactly how Joy had helped.

"She took me to a private clinic," Avery said, her low drawl a hint deeper.

"Did she know it was a miscarriage?"

Avery hesitated. "She did. She said it would be better if I said I had an abortion. She knew about Xavier's partying and said he wouldn't take it as hard, so I did. Call me crazy but I agreed with her. I never knew when his next high was going to kill him and I didn't want him to take any of the blame at all, so I agreed and lied to him."

My jaw dropped and a splinter of heat zipped down my spine. "You're kidding me. Did she encourage it? I swear, Avery, I will kill her."

God. I was starting to seriously hate that woman.

Avery sobered up a little. "No, not really. I mean the doctor said I was in the early stages of having a miscarriage and that's when Joy suggested I just do the procedure to get it over with to move it along faster." She sat quietly for a moment. Her jaw quivered. "So I did. I killed my baby. I didn't know stress would do it. I didn't know how easy it was to miscarry," she stated, breathing heavily. "I didn't know anything," she cried out. "Now I'll never get to hold him, and Xavier will never get to call him Rocky."

"Rocky?"

She shrugged one shoulder dejectedly. "He joked that he was going to name him Rocky."

We were both quiet for a little while, letting everything sink in. I held my best friend's hand, trying to breathe spirit into her. It physically hurt me to see her like this and I wanted to take away her pain as much as I could. I wasn't naïve. I knew she'd never forget something like this, but if I could help make her a little happy, then I wanted to.

"Why not just tell him the truth?"

"I'd rather him hate me than think he caused the miscarriage and hate himself. If we were together and never fought, then I'd be sitting here with a baby with you. I don't blame him for anything, but I knew he'd blame himself. He went on a bender and pushed the partying the furthest I'd seen yet."

Avery burst out with more tears. "I'm so sorry," she sobbed. I told her to stop and to just to get it out. She shouldn't be apologizing. This was what I was here for.

"If he knew he was the source of the miscarriage, it scares me to think what he'd do."

"I bet he lost it when you told him." Not only was I sad for my bestie, but for my brother too. Just when I thought my problems were bad, there was always someone who had it worse.

Avery raised her head, eyes as wide as the moon. "It was the first time I ever saw him cry. He trashed the pool house, put holes in the wall with his fists and head, got wrecked every night for weeks. Joy had to hire people to redo the whole thing. I thought he was going to overdose again, and for good this time. Thank God he didn't."

"So what happened with the Fourth of July?"

She licked her lips and glanced down. "I wasn't sure when I got pregnant, and my period was irregular, so I was given two due dates. The doctors said that only time would tell as the fetus grew." She paused. "July fourth was in the middle of my due dates. I got pregnant sometime in October, but I didn't know until December."

"Wait a minute. You were pregnant on New Year's Eve and drinking?"

She shook her head. "I didn't actually drink. I pretended to sip it and when no one was looking, Xavier took it."

"I can't believe I didn't know." I was in shock.

"No one knew. We hid it well and I hardly showed. Once I had a small bump, I switched to more Boho style clothing."

"Okay, keep going."

"Before the Instagram post, we hadn't spoken to each other since the day I told him about the abortion, so when he asked to see me, I ran. It was the fourth." Avery grew quiet and I feared more heartache was coming from her. "We tried to be together on that day, but we barely lasted through the fireworks. I hurt too much. Xavier told me he would always look at me as the mother who'd killed his child. He wasn't mean about it, just hurting like I was. I don't blame him for saying it." Her eyes lowered to the bed. "He looked horrible, Aid. So bad. He unblocked me from social media after that day. Of course I'm always stalking him. While he looks happy, I know the look in his eyes is anything but that."

This time, it was my turn to cry. I couldn't stop the tears from pouring out of me and I cried so deeply for them and what they would never have again.

I wiped my eyes with the back of my hands. "I never would've guessed any of this happened. I didn't expect it at all. I don't know what to say to help you. I feel useless."

She regarded me with love. Avery shook her head. "There's nothing you need to say. Just telling you is all I need."

"What happens after this? Like with you guys?"

She glanced away with longing in her eyes. "Nothing. We go on like it never happened, I guess." She waited a long minute before she spoke again. "We'll never be the same."

My heart broke for the both of them. "You don't think telling him the truth would be better?"

She shook her head rapidly. "No. It won't do anything to bring the baby back, and honestly, the damage is already done. Like I said, I'd rather him hate me than think he had anything to do with the miscarriage. It's better that way."

After talking and shedding more tears, we ate popcorn and watched *Cruel Intentions.*

Avery and I agreed that coming clean to each other was cathartic. We were way past overdue for it and promised each other again to never let it happen.

She said she wasn't going to contact Xavier again, even though I wished she would. I encouraged it, but after she told me she was going to cut my hair in my sleep if I didn't stop, I shut up. My hair loss had increased the last few months, so I needed all I had left.

I felt awful knowing how bad both Avery and Xavier were hurting, but more importantly longing for each other. And as much as I initially hated the idea of them together, from what I gathered, it seemed like they really were into each other. Crazy to think of them like that, but I had no room to talk anymore.

Hello, Kova.

Thinking of Kova…shit. I realized I forgot to tell him I had an appointment tomorrow.

"Hand me my phone, Ave. I forgot to tell Kova I have blood work tomorrow."

Avery paused our favorite movie before grabbing my cell phone off the nightstand and handing it to me.

"Thanks. I forgot all about my appointment. You don't have to come…it'll be boring. I have practice after, so if you wanna shop or sightsee or something, you can."

"You're so wrapped up in gymnastics that you forgot what tomorrow is."

I quickly shot a text to Kova then frowned at her. "What's tomorrow?"

Her eyes widened. "Your birthday, dummy."

I paused and stared at her. Holy shit.

"Oh, my God. How did I forget?"

Tomorrow I would turn eighteen. I'd been so wrapped up in my life and focused that I'd forgotten my own birthday.

"Why do you think I'm here?" she asked with a smile on her face.

It felt good to see her smile after our long-winded conversation. I couldn't take all the credit for it, though. She was a bit obsessed with Ryan Phillipe and swore one day she was going to move to Hollywood and marry him.

"Since I missed it last year, I came to celebrate your big day. I have an awesome surprise planned for you that no one will ever be able to top."

I continued to stare, dumbfounded. "I can't believe I forgot!"

"We'll just blame it on the lupus."

For once I could laugh about being sick.

"So I'm coming with you tomorrow to your doctor's and then I'm taking you out."

My happiness faded a little. The thought, though it sounded like loads of fun, was short-lived.

"I can't. I have practice after."

Avery shook her head, her blonde locks swaying across her face. "You don't," she said proudly, and popped a piece of popcorn into her mouth. "I cleared it with Kova. You're mine for the entire day."

Brows scrunched together. "What? How?"

She looked extremely proud as she wiggled her shoulders from side to side. "I have my ways."

I felt a smile tug at the corner of my mouth. My lips twitched. "For real?" I chuckled.

"Yes! I have the whole day planned. I've been looking forward to this, you have no idea. You're going to love it! Just trust me on this one, okay?"

I threw my arms around her shoulders and squeezed her as tight as I could. "I haven't taken a day just to hang out in ages; I usually just sleep on my day off. You're seriously the bestest friend ever!"

"I know I am." She joked, pretending to flip her hair even though it's tied up. "Now let me get back to my future ex-husband."

Then she said her next set of words so quickly I don't think she took a breath.

"Oh, you'll have to be at practice at six the following morning and take an extra ballet class, but don't worry, it'll be worth it."

chapter 46

"**D**O YOU WANT THE GOOD NEWS OR THE BAD NEWS?" Dr. Kozol asked me.

I gave him a bland stare.

"I don't know, Doc, how much worse can it possibly get? I'm basically on my last leg."

"At least you haven't lost your sense of humor." Avery snickered next to me, and I grinned at her.

Dr. Kozol flipped open my file, his merry expression not going unnoticed. It was good to see my doctor had a sense of humor too. It helped me a little, mentally.

I'd already given blood and had done the usual physical. Now we were sitting in his office with the door shut reviewing my treatment plan and making sure the medicine was helping maintain my symptoms. I'd gotten to the point I knew this was par for the course every time I came in.

"The bad news is, while I'm going to send out your urine sample along with your blood work, your protein is still rising. Not by much, but enough to have me concerned. Have you been sticking to your new diet plan?"

"Yes, I have."

"That's good. And your medications? How are they working out for you?"

I hesitated. There were some side effects I'd gone through, but overall, they weren't too bad. I really didn't want to test out new medications.

"It took some time to adjust to them, but now I think they're okay. Like if I don't eat with two of them, I get really sick to the point of vomiting. I learned to follow the rules on the side of the bottle. I don't take any of the pain medications, though. I try my best to push through it. For the most part, the meds seem to be working, I guess."

He nodded and scribbled a few things down. "It's really all trial and error, as no two patients are the same," he said, reviewing my patient chart. Dr. Kozol paused to level a stare at me. "And none of them usually forgo treatment either."

Grimacing, I flattened my lips. I knew the risks I was taking, and I also knew if I didn't take them that I would regret it. Under normal circumstances I wouldn't have prolonged dialysis. I would've gone to the hospital for further testing like he originally suggested. It was just hard to grasp that after coming so far I would stop everything now. A few more months wouldn't kill me. Hopefully.

"I'm not forgoing treatment, per say, I'm just delaying it."

Dr. Kozol studied me, his pen wavering back and forth between his thumb and index finger. "You do know time is of the essence, right?"

I nodded. "I do. Trust me, it's on my mind all the time. What about my lungs? Last time I was here you said there were sounds you didn't like." I couldn't remember his exact words, just that he was concerned about them. "You heard liquid I think, right?"

He nodded. "They're better. I can still hear it, but it's definitely improved."

My face lit up. "At least I have one good thing going for myself, right?"

Dr. Kozol offered me a kind smile. "You're a week late to see me, you know. When I spoke with your father and we went over your new plan, I expected you to keep to the promise."

I averted my gaze and crossed one leg over the other. He was right. I was supposed to come in last week but never made it. I had pushed it back. He probably thought I didn't care or take my illness seriously, but that wasn't the case.

Sitting up a little straighter, I looked my doctor directly in the eye.

"I know the last thing you want to hear is an apology, but I really am sorry. It won't happen again. I promise. Last week…" My voice trailed off as I debated telling him the truth. "I've just been deep in my emotions, struggling since everything happened. I only just started telling people. I know it's not an excuse and I'm not trying to make it one, I'm just telling you why I wasn't here. It's a lot to handle and it scares me. I know I need to start dialysis, and the fact I'm not is on my mind all the time. I'm honestly just trying to not let the illnesses get the best of me." I paused, swallowing. "Sometimes they do. I'm slowly accepting it, even though I don't want to."

His face softened with empathy. "Understandable, but Adrianna, I hope you're aware of the risk you're taking. I don't like reminding you how sick you are every time I see you, but…"

I smile. "I know, I know. It's not a matter of if I will die, but when."

Morbid, but it was the truth.

"I'll let it slide this one time, but please don't do it again." Dr. Kozol glanced down at my file and started writing again. "Alright, when the blood work comes back, if anything is amiss, I'll let you know. Are you ready for the good news?"

I nodded vehemently. I couldn't imagine what it was.

Dr. Kozol exhaled a deep breath. "I'm happy to tell you we've found a kidney match."

I froze.

I couldn't move.

I didn't breathe.

"What?" I said, my voice a little raspy. "What did you say?"

Avery reached out to grab my hand, offering me support. My fingers were cold, her palm hot to the touch and she gave me a little squeeze. I glanced over and met her gaze. My smile was weak, but I tried to show her I was thankful she was here with me.

I blinked so many times trying to hold back my tears while her eyes glittered with profound happiness and love.

My breathing grew dense. "How? Who? When…" I had so many questions running through my mind. I couldn't think straight.

I was scared this was a dream and I was going to wake up to the nightmare I'd been stuck living inside of for the last couple of months. I prayed it wasn't a sick joke.

"You found a match," I said, and he nodded. "But who? My dad told me he, my brother, and biological mom were not matches. Did he find a distant cousin or aunt or something?" I wasn't going to get my hopes up that Joy was tested, but crazier things had happened.

"We have a match, Adrianna," he said again gently. "In fact, she's sitting right next to you."

Tears blurred my vision and my body broke out in a cold sweat. Wide-eyed, I turned to look at my best friend.

"What?"

I could barely get the word out without my voice shaking. My heart was racing. Before I could stop them, a few tears slipped down my cheek. I knew I wasn't the only person in the world looking for a kidney and the chances of finding someone to donate were slim. That's why my doctor was so adamant that I start treatment. My faith in finding a match had been a bit shaken, but I'd held out hope. But this…my mind wasn't processing everything.

"Avery?" I said, my voice shaking.

Her eyes were glossy with tears, and she was biting into her bottom lip. Her jaw trembled and I could see the truth in her gaze.

"It's true. We're a match."

My head shook at the sound of her raspy voice. A tear slipped out from her crystal-blue eyes and she quickly wiped it away.

"We really are a match." Avery sniffled.

Heart pounding viciously against my ribs, I was in complete shock. "I don't understand. How?"

"When you told me about everything, I went to your dad the next day and said I was willing to be tested." Her head angled to the side. "Frank then went to my dad and they talked about it. Eventually they reached out to him," she said, pointing to Dr. Kozol. "After a couple of days, they both gave me the green light and I got tested. I'm not big on praying, but I prayed like crazy and pretty much swore to every god there was that I'd do anything just to be your match." She stopped to regain herself. "I figured there wasn't a better time to tell you this than on your birthday."

I blinked a few times, making sure I'd heard everything correctly. Avery Heron, my best friend, was going to give me one of her kidneys.

When I didn't say anything, she chuckled. "We were all in shock, trust me."

An airy laugh rolled off my lips. "It's just… I don't know what to say, what to think. Are you sure you want to do this?"

"You're my best friend. I'd do anything for you. When you're ready, my kidney is your kidney. No more kidney failure for you. Not on my watch."

We both giggled over her cheesy lines, smiling at each other. I stared at her in utter awe that she would do this for me. We weren't talking about borrowing a shirt or a pair of earrings—she was giving me an organ that she could never take back.

I let out a huff and wiped away the fresh tears that clouded my vision.

"I don't know what to say other than thank you, Avery." Emotion clogged my throat again. "Thank you."

She squeezed my hand again. "Kidney besties for life."

chapter 47

AFTER SPENDING ANOTHER HOUR AT THE DOCTOR'S OFFICE GOING over the finer details and plans, we returned to my condo and shed more tears before calling our families.

I still couldn't believe it. I was going to get a kidney. Not right now, but eventually.

We sat on the couch drinking hot chocolate Avery had made from scratch. My cheeks ached from being unable to stop smiling, and I'd been crying on and off. Being an organ donor was a selfless act and took a huge heart on someone's part. I was extremely close to having renal failure, and Avery was willingly giving me a part of herself to help me live a longer life. She was changing the ending of my story by offering me the ultimate gift, something I could never, ever repay her for.

"I'm forever indebted to you, you know," I said quietly. Shit. Tears filled my eyes again.

She wrinkled her nose at me. "It's a good thing I know where you live."

"No takebacks." I joked. I licked my lips and drew in a deep breath.

Avery gave me a droll stare. "Like I'd ever do that. Oh! I have something for you," she said and jumped up from the couch. She placed her hot chocolate down on the coffee table, then ran to my room. A minute later, she was back and handing me a gift bag.

From the corner of my eye, I caught the glittery design on her shirt. I stared at what looked like lima beans. She must've chanced when she went to grab my gift. I frowned as I read the words and finally recognized the images. My jaw dropped and my eyes widened with laughter.

"Oh my God. I just realized what's on your shirt!" I said.

Two kidneys with the words underneath, "We're a match! Who wouldn't want a piece of this?"

I laughed out loud. "Where did you find that?"

"I got connections." She nodded her chin toward the gift bag she handed me. "Open it, but don't read the inside of the card right now. I got a little fucking mushy and I'm so embarrassed. Just read the front." My eyes drifted down as I opened the card.

I heard urine need of a kidney. Want mine?

"Oh man." I laughed.

"I know. I had a blast picking stuff out for you."

I placed the card back in the envelope and placed it to the side. "You didn't need to give me anything, you know. You're giving me a freaking organ."

"Yeah, but I wanted to."

I smiled, feeling grateful.

"This is for when surgery is over," Avery said as I pulled out the first gift wrapped in tissue paper. "You have to wear it."

"Promise," I said without even looking at it.

I unfolded the shirt and read the bold block letters. STRAIGHT OUTTA TRANSPLANT SURGERY. It had two little kidneys next to the wording.

I let out a belly laugh, and grinned from ear to ear. This was the first time in months I felt like I could breathe again, like there was a light at the end of the tunnel, and I owed it to my bestie. It was surreal.

"I love it! Leave it to you to find a shirt like this."

I reached into the bag again and pulled out another tissue wrapped gift. I held up the green shirt, the color associated with kidney disease, and read the white lettering. KIDNEY THIEF.

Avery poked her head around the side. She beamed with happiness. I loved that I could see her like this again but felt bad that it was only from being a match. But that was Avery. Always going above and beyond to make someone else happy.

As I pulled out yet another shirt, she said, "And this one is for now. There's two. One for you and one for me."

KIDNEY BESTIES FOR LIFE.

My lips parted. "This is what you said to me at the doctor's office today."

"I know. You didn't catch on to anything," she joked.

I couldn't laugh, though, not when I was crying again. My head fell into my hands and I burst into tears at her thoughtfulness. Avery reached over and pulled me into a hug, holding me tight as I cried softly on her shoulder.

"I love you, girl," she said, sniffling. "I know we had our first—*and last*—most epic fight ever, but that doesn't change a thing between us. I would do anything for you, like I know you would for me."

Damn it all to hell, she wasn't helping, but she was right. If the roles were reversed, I would do whatever I could to help her.

"Thank you, Avery," I said, pulling back. "Two words just don't seem adequate enough for what you're giving me."

"Stop," she said and wiped away the tear underneath her lash line. "If I didn't want to do this, then I wouldn't have been tested." She grabbed my hands in hers and scooted closer. "I want to do this for you, okay? I don't want you to feel like you have to say thank you all the time or that you have to try and find something to give me in return. That's not what this is about. I love you and I want to help you."

I nodded and dug my teeth into my bottom lip as I struggled to fight the tears. One day I would repay her, I just wasn't sure how yet. I'd find a way, though.

Reaching into the bag, Avery handed me something a little heavier. "This is the last one."

I unwrapped a mug and turned it around.

I got 99 problems but my new kidney ain't one.

"Oh, my God." I laughed again. "You really went to town with the kidney stuff." I smiled again, loving each gift so much. I had no idea where she'd found any of it, but it was so thoughtful and funny, and I'd cherish it forever. "I can't wait to use it."

She shrugged like it wasn't a big deal. But it was. It was a very big deal.

"Figured it was better to try and turn it into something fun rather than depressing. This is a good thing and we shouldn't be crying or sad about it." She handed me one of the matching shirts. "Put it on."

As I pulled the shirt over my head, there was a knock on the door.

"Are you expecting someone?" Avery turned to me.

I shook my head. "No."

I walked to the door and opened it.

"Kova," I said, a little surprised. "Hey. What are you doing here?"

His eyes softened. "Ria, may I come in?"

"Is that Kova?" Avery yelled, and ran up behind me. Placing her hands on my shoulders, she leaned over me. "Hey, handsome. You're looking mighty fine."

Kova shot an uneasy glance at me. My cheeks flushed and I mouthed sorry. While Avery knew everything about Kova and me, Kova didn't know that. I imagined he was panicking inside.

"Come in," I said.

He ran his hand through his hair and I shut the door. He seemed anxious.

"I will not stay long. I just wanted to bring you this," Kova said, then lifted his hand to reveal an iconic teal-colored gift bag.

"Oh-em-gee," Avery drawled, rubbing her hands together impatiently. We both looked at her, and she looked back at us. "Ah, I can step out to give you guys some time," she said, then turned and walked to my room. I heard her plop down on my bed.

"Don't worry," I said when I noticed the unease written on his face. "Avery is like a vault. I swear on my life she'll never say anything to anyone about us. I promise."

"Does she know…?"

I nodded. I wouldn't lie. "She does."

He expelled a deep breath. "If you say so, then I believe you. I will not take too much of your time since you do not see her often. I just wanted to bring you a birthday gift."

My eyes widened as he handed me the bag. "You knew it was my birthday?"

"Yes, of course."

"Really?"

Kova nodded and my heart beat a little faster for him. I wasn't one to broadcast my birthday, so the fact he knew without having to tell him moved me inside when my family forgot half the time. Stupid, I know, but I guess it's the little things in life.

"You didn't have to get me anything."

Kova stepped closer to me and I could smell his cologne. His tantalizing scent swirled deliciously around my head. He brushed a few strands of hair behind my ear and cupped my jaw. Tipping my chin back, he gazed into my eyes something fierce.

"You mean the world to me, Ria. I wanted to give you something special to show you that." He leaned in and his lips brushed the shell of my ear. "I really want to kiss you, but I will not with your friend here."

Turning my face toward his, I tenderly kissed his cheek without a sound.

"Thank you for stopping by," I whispered.

As he turned his face, I pressed my lips to his and snuck him a quick kiss. Kova swiftly grabbed the back of my head and pressed his lips harder to mine, inhaling through his nose like he was breathing me in.

"Please," he said against my mouth, "open your gift."

Pulling back, my cheeks heated as I grinned up at him. He moved to stand behind me and watched as I removed the square box from the bag. I placed the bag on the counter, then pulled the white satin bow loose. Kova played with my hair, moving it to the side to drape over my shoulder. I leaned back against him, falling into the heat of his body as he wrapped his arms around my stomach. My heartbeat rocketed but everything shifted into place in his arms. Inside the velvet box was a soft rose gold bracelet. It was double chained with an infinity symbol.

Lips parting, I removed it from the box and placed it in my palm. I drew in a gasp. My finger grazed over the thin chain to the charm in the center. Kova didn't say anything without thinking it through. He was terrible at exposing his feelings. But when he actually did both, they meant something, and something told me he'd put thought into this specific gift. I knew the meaning behind an infinity symbol. All I could do was focus on the delicate piece of jewelry and feel the tears well in my eyes. Damn it, I cried so much these days.

"It's so beautiful," I said under my breath. I lifted it to him. "Put it on me, please?"

Kova clasped it under my wrist. He laced his fingers through mine and lifted our joined hands to his mouth to press a kiss to mine. The outside world had no idea how sweet he could actually be.

"There is one more thing."

My brows angled toward each other. I didn't realize there was another box in the bag. Letting go of his hand, I reached inside and pulled it out, then opened it.

I stared unblinking at the dainty matching necklace. It was stunning and delicate and so damn pretty.

"Kova, you gave me too much. This is…it's beautiful. Thank you so, so much."

"There is no such thing as too much when it comes to you."

chapter 48

HIS WORDS TICKLED MY NECK.

I was very close to telling him I loved him.

Kova placed the necklace around my neck. Turning around, I grabbed his jaw and pulled it to mine. Inhaling, I kissed him. Kova's strong arms wound around my back. He lifted me up and placed me on the counter and stepped between my legs, kissing me back with the same intensity. I loved when he did that. I loved when he gave back ten times harder. Like we were proving who loved each other more.

"I love you, Ria," he admitted only for me to hear.

I licked my lips. "Ever since my secret came out and we talked about it, you tell me you love me all the time."

"Life is too precious. We take it for granted. I realized that when I found out how sick you were. I told you I do not want to hold back from you anymore. I want you to know how I feel all the time."

I smiled softly at him. "Thank you," I whispered. My fingers twirled the hair around his neck as we stared at each other.

"Can I come out now?" Avery yelled from my bedroom.

My smile widened, and Kova and I started laughing together.

"I love seeing you laugh," I told him. Then I angled my head and yelled, "Yes!" to Avery.

Avery showed no shame and came bouncing out of my bedroom.

"Show me the goods."

Shaking my head, I lifted my wrist and picked up the necklace to show her. She came up next to us and Kova scooted a little closer to me.

"Oh, you did good, Coach," she said as she examined the jewelry, then turned to Kova. "Do you have a brother?"

I chuckled and Kova side-eyed me in confusion. Avery was a whole lot of personality to handle if you didn't know her.

She patted his arm. "I'm just playing. I don't do brothers anymore," she said, then walked into the kitchen to grab a bottle of water.

My cheeks flamed, but God, did I love my best friend.

"So I have heard," Kova responded.

My gaze snapped back to him and I took note of his face. My lips twitched. He wrapped an arm around me again, laughter highlighting his eyes.

"You told him!" she yelled at me, lifting her arm. Her gaze was accusatory but I knew she wasn't truly mad.

My jaw bobbed. "Sorry?"

"You're lucky it's your birthday and you're my bestie." She took a sip of water. "It's cool. I'm over it."

Kova let go of me and stepped back. He looked from me to Avery. I followed his gaze, trying to figure out what he was looking at.

"Why are you two wearing the same shirt? Is that a bestie thing?"

I burst out laughing over him saying bestie. It sounded like he'd eaten something sour.

Then he read the words. And he looked back and forth between us again.

"You didn't hear?" Avery said.

"Did not hear what?" Kova's eyes snapped up to mine.

"Tell him, Aid."

I bit into my lip as he stared at me. His chest rose higher and faster, and I swear I could feel his heart pumping. Kova watched me, waiting, looking hopeful.

"Ria?" he asked slowly.

I averted my gaze and hopped down from the counter.

"Well…" I began, and walked over to Avery. "I haven't really had a chance to tell you and honestly, I wasn't sure how I would." I wrapped my arm around the back of her neck and tugged her to me. She hugged me back, dropping her head to my shoulder and hooking her arms around my waist. I could see from the corner of my eye she was smiling softly at Kova.

"This birthday has been the best birthday of my life. Not only did you surprise me with a meaningful gift, but Avery, well, she…"

Shoot. Emotion hit me faster than I could stop it from happening. Tears filled my eyes and my jaw trembled. Trying to say I had a kidney match proved to be harder than I thought.

Avery lifted her head off my shoulder and looked at me. A tear slipped out of my eye and down my cheek. I still couldn't believe what she was going to do for me.

"For Adrianna's birthday, I surprised her too." She looked toward Kova. "I'm her match. Well, we already knew that." She joked with a playful roll of her eyes. "I'm a kidney match. When the time comes, because I know she's stubborn and won't do it now, I'll be giving her a kidney. I got these shirts for us since we're kidney besties for life now."

I watched Kova's face shift through a handful of emotions. The color in his cheeks drained and he stood stone still, like he was in shock and didn't know what to say. His Adam's apple bobbed. Lifting his hand, he ran it over his mouth and looked at the floor. Then, he walked toward us and surprised us both.

I thought he was going to pull me into his arms, but he didn't. Instead, he pulled Avery into his arms and hugged her.

My jaw dropped and my eyes widened as I watched his face twist into a blend of heartache and relief. Squinting, I caught the subtle shaking in his arms.

Avery looked to me for guidance. All I could do was shrug my shoulders because other than when we were alone, or he was with Katja, I never saw Kova show an ounce of emotion, let alone touch anyone. Right now, he was pouring himself into her.

Eyes twinkling, Avery went with it. She wrapped her arms around Kova's back and ran her flat palms ever so slowly up and down from his shoulders to his hips. Her eyes floated shut and she smiled from ear to ear.

"My, Kova, what a strong back you have," she said.

I laughed.

Kova pulled back, his lips twitching. "Thank you, Avery," he said. His voice was hoarse.

He turned and looked at me, almost making my heart stop. Raw love and affection filled his eyes. I knew he loved me, he told me often, but this time it was different. His love rendered me speechless. This was a side of Kova he never exposed to the outside world, for obvious reasons, yet he was allowing Avery to see it. It made me fall for him even harder.

"From the bottom of my heart, thank you, Avery," he said again, blowing out a heavy breath. He was struggling with the news the same way I had. "I cannot imagine my life without Adrianna."

We both stared at him in astonishment. Kova followed up with a few things in Russian, though I didn't ask him what they meant. Something in my gut told me to just give him a minute.

Avery recovered and pretended to dust her shoulders off. "Now that I made it so you guys can fornicate for the rest of your lives, show me her mark." Kova looked confused. I didn't know what she was talking about until she said, "Adrianna told me about the A, and I want to see it. Take your shirt off."

I covered my mouth. "Ave," I said, trying not to laugh. She was so unpredictable.

She looked at me like it wasn't a crazy request. "What? It's the least he can do for me. I want to see it. I think it's so sexy and sweet." Avery had a wistful look on her face that made me laugh even harder.

"No," he said, shutting her down.

Her jaw plummeted to the floor. She looked at Kova like she was offended. "What? Why not?"

"No."

"Okay. Fine. Don't take your shirt off, just lift it so I can see."

Kova turned to me for help. All I could do was offer him an apologetic look.

"No."

"What?" She huffed and looked at me. "Help a sister out."

"Just one peek?" I asked him, hesitantly.

He shook his head. "That is for Ria and I only."

"Aww, that's so adorable." Avery leaned into me and cupped her mouth next to my ear while looking at Kova. "Get a picture while he's sleeping," she whispered loudly for him to hear. "Don't be afraid to take a few and send them to me. I promise not to tell anyone."

Shaking his head, Kova's sexy smile curled around my heart. I shot a glance at Avery, and I could see she felt his charisma too by the way she watched him with a twinkle in her eyes. I wanted to kiss those lips again but I held back.

Walking up to me, Kova pulled me against his body. "*Ya lyubuyu tebya navsegda,*" he said, then kissed the top of my head. "I must go. Happy birthday, *malysh.*"

"Just one look," Avery pushed as Kova walked toward the door and opened it.

"It will never happen. I am just as stubborn as Ria. Ask her." Kova paused right as he was about to leave and looked over his shoulder at me. "I expect to see you bright and early tomorrow."

I nodded and he left. Turning to Avery, she looked like she was going to liquefy into a pile on the floor. I chuckled. She was finally starting to see what I saw.

"I hope you marry that stupid Russian one day," she said dreamily.

chapter 49

"SHIT," I WHISPERED UNDER MY BREATH.

I blinked, hoping the pink tinted toilet water was something I was imagining.

It wasn't.

Ever since I'd started training at the rate I was over a year ago, my period had been inconsistent. Sometimes I got it in four weeks, other times almost seven weeks would go by with no sign of it. Sometimes I had heavy periods, other times I would spot for three days. My body underwent a tremendous amount of strain, which caused it to mess with my cycle. With everything going on lately, it slipped my mind, so I hadn't been thinking about it.

I closed my eyes and took a deep breath. This would happen to me. Not only did I wake up with a raging headache and my stomach tossing around from nerves, I was in Scotland preparing to compete at an international competition, and now I needed tampons.

Quickly, I pulled down my leotard and wrapped a towel around my body. I opened the door and stepped into the room I shared with Holly. Reagan declined the meet due to not having the funds for it, so it was just us this time around.

"Holly?"

She looked at me from where she sat on her bed texting on her cell phone.

"Do you happen to have any tampons with you? I just got my period and I don't have anything."

She gawked and immediately stood. "You don't bring them as backup? I always just leave them in my suitcase."

"I wasn't thinking, I guess."

Holly handed me a bunch of tampons and I looked at them in horror. "What size is this?"

"Ultra. My flow is always really bad and heavy. Sorry, I don't have anything else."

"No worries. I'm just grateful you have them. Thanks," I said.

I went back into the bathroom and took care of business. I hated having my period during a gymnastics meet. I was always afraid it would show somehow. Luckily my leotard was a hunter green with encrusted hot pink Swarovski crystals. If I did leak, it wouldn't show.

"Girl, you always should have them on you," Holly said when I emerged from the bathroom dressed and ready to go.

I offered her a smile and nodded, then walked over to my suitcase to pull out my scarf and coat. My nerves were a little wired, but overall, I felt confident. After this meet, there was one more in Italy, the Olympic Trials, and then the team would be selected.

"I usually do but I don't know what I was thinking to not bring them. I guess I just have a lot on my mind. That's all." I would never forget after this, that was for sure.

She eyed me curiously. "Yeah, Hayden's mentioned you've had it rough lately. I know he's been worried."

I hesitated for split moment, then wrapped the headscarf over my ears. There were so many things he could've told her.

"What do you mean?"

She brushed it off and zipped her coat up. "Nothing we can't talk about tonight if you want." She smiled but it wasn't enough to smooth out my feathers. "It's not bad or anything, he's just been worried about you for a while. We both were."

I stared at her, wondering which direction this conversation would go in when she pointed to my makeup bag. I turned and found I hadn't zipped it closed, and the tops of my medicine bottles were showing.

"You don't need to explain anything to me, I just hope you're okay," she said gently.

Shit. I'd been good at hiding my illnesses for the most part, but with my head focused on my routines and the two-day meet we were at, I'd left the bottles out in the open. Taking the medicine had become second nature to me these days, and I'd been coming to terms with it. Kind of.

Holly walked over and hugged me. "I know we haven't known each other all that long, but I'm always here for you. I love you like a sister."

I smiled and thanked her. "Those are prescriptions from my doctors. I have an autoimmune disease and I have no choice but to take them. I'm fine, Holly. Honestly. I'm better than I've been actually, but we can exchange war stories tonight if you want to."

That was all I was giving her. I wouldn't add I that had kidney disease, or that I'd ultimately need a transplant. I wouldn't add I that was better because of Kova and the words he'd said to me.

I want to live with you.

But it was the first time I had spoken positive about my future, and surprisingly, it made me feel good.

Rubbing my shoulders, Kova looked down at me. I was freezing, and he was trying to help keep my joints warm before I stepped onto the podium for my first routine. I was a little jealous that he was wearing a thick turtle neck. Combined with his business slacks, Kova looked fine as hell dressed in all black. The color accented his alluring green eyes perfectly.

I shivered and rubbed the side of my head. The headache I woke up with hadn't subsided.

"You are ready," he stated.

Tight-lipped, I nodded as my eyes skirted around trying to take in everything at once. I chewed the inside of my lip. Nerves and a nauseous stomach were a terrible combo. Not only were the best athletes in the world here, but there were sports agents, news stations to televise the competition, college coaches trying to recruit gymnasts, and the Olympic committee too.

"Hey. Look at me," Kova said, and my eyes snapped to his. "Focus on me. Do not look anywhere else and do not watch the other gymnasts. Keep your head in the game."

He tipped his head down and his eyes bore deeper into mine. He was quiet for a moment, helping me find my ground, giving me comfort. I released a breath I hadn't realized I was holding.

"You got this. You have never been more prepared than this moment, yes?" he said, and I bobbed my head. "Remember why you are here, think about how you got here. You did it because of your perseverance when the world was against you and because of your hard work and determination. You got this, Adrianna. Do not let that voice in your head get to you."

"I'm working on it."

He leaned in and lowered his voice. "Two of your routines have the most points in difficulty than all the girls here. That is huge. It already puts you one step ahead. Even with everything you have been up against these last six months, you kept going when everyone else would have folded. You got this. Just get your head right. Think only about your routine, and smile. Have fun out there. You earned this."

He had a point. Even if the other competitors were able to maximize all their points, I could still take the lead in vault and bars—taking the World

Champion titles. The only way that wouldn't happen would be for me to make a mistake. But I wouldn't. I'd worked too hard for this to let anyone take it from me. Especially now. Floor was my favorite and my routine always got the crowd and judges on their feet, so to speak. And beam, well, that was a whole other story, but I wasn't worried.

As usual, Kova was right.

"Adrianna?" he said, and I glanced into his eyes. "It is you against yourself. Some people thrive under pressure while others concede. You flourish more than anyone I have ever seen. And I am not saying that to fill your head with empty words just to encourage you or give you a little pep talk. It is how I truly feel and what I see. It is the truth. Remember, let *it* inspire you to live *your* dream. You came to win. Nothing else."

Exhaling a ragged breath, the tension in my neck loosened. I knew the "it" he was referring to was the kidney disease. He was trying to be as discrete as he could because he knew I didn't want anyone to know about it. My face softened. I knew Kova meant what he said, he wouldn't waste his breath on useless words. He was honest to a fault and I guess I liked that about him.

"Thanks," I said quietly. He was always right.

"Now go chalk up. I am sure you could use more."

I forced back a smile and walked over to the chalk bowl. I plunged my hands into the powder and it puffed up in a cloud in front of me. I could taste it in my mouth.

"I'm so nervous," I said to Holly, who was standing next to me. "Why am I so freaking nervous? Maybe I should've eaten something before I left. My stomach is in knots and I'm overanalyzing."

She chuckled. "Ah, because you have a lot more riding at the moment than I do? I'm just hoping I can gain the attention of a college coach. You want the freaking Olympic coaches to notice you."

"You haven't heard back from Alabama yet?"

"No, but it's still early. I'm just stressed and wished I had applied to other schools as a backup now.

Holly placed her hand over mine and took it in hers. I looked at her and she frowned.

"It's the medicine," I whispered. "Sometimes it gives me the shakes and makes me jittery."

"Nerves are good. They're what keep us going, make us feel alive. If you didn't have nerves, then you kind of lose the fun of the sport. Am I right?"

My heart pumped the adrenaline through my veins at a high speed, like a build up to the climax of a movie. I could feel it coming and I couldn't wait to feel the beat drop only to replay it over and over again.

"Yeah, you're right. It's just, gymnastics is so unpredictable, you know? And there are so many incredible gymnasts here and we all pretty much want the same thing. We're all fighting for a chance to prove ourselves."

I sighed, my shoulders heavy with the weight of the world.

Before Holly could respond, the bell rang over the intercom. A signal to let us know the meet was about to start. I brushed the excess chalk from my hands and wiped it on my thighs.

Go time.

Looking for my coach one last time, our eyes locked for a brief moment. With his hands propped on his hips, I felt like he was giving me the courage I needed to be brave.

Putting one foot in front of the other, I walked up the stairs.

chapter 50

"WHAT IS WRONG?" KOVA ASKED, SQUATTING IN FRONT OF ME. I was sitting on the floor stretching my foot out before I applied sports tape.

And I was annoyed as hell.

Gritting my teeth, I said, "First of all. I've had a headache since I woke up and it just won't go away. Second, there's a stupid Russian girl who's name I can't even pronounce just trailing my ass on every rotation. She's so close that if I blink she'll pass me."

Kova grinned proudly and took my foot in his hands to carefully flex it. He held my heel and pressed on the center of my arch with his thumb. I leaned back on my hands.

"Damn those Russians and their skills," he said, and I raised a brow. "Taina Mstislav." His accent was so thick as he said her name, I couldn't even mimic it. "It means glorious defender."

"Not what I wanted to hear."

He shrugged. "Russians have always dominated the sport. They view it a little differently. Most girls are plucked from small towns with nothing on their back and the family is poor. They are given a roof and food and all the training they need, but they have to pay it back by winning. It does not matter which Russian girl wins, only that Russia must win. You do it for the love of your country."

My forehead bunched together. "What happens if they don't win?"

"Russia breaks girls." He was silent for a moment, then said almost painfully, "You do not want to know."

I glanced at Taina, who was right behind me in the standings. She didn't know I was watching her.

"Is that her coach?" I asked Kova.

He followed my gaze. "Yes." He said her name.

"You know her?"

"I know of her."

I watched the way Taina's shoulders fell, how her back went ram-rod straight, the way she nodded quickly as she received instruction from her coach. The coach's eyes nearly bulged from her head. Taina's hands were cupped behind her back and she twisted and turned her fingers until the tips were purple.

Kova finished taping my Achilles and watched them for a moment with me.

"I will always have love for my country," he said, "but I do not agree with how Russia handles things. It is cruelty."

"Kova?" I waited until he looked at me before continuing. "I'm going to beat her," I said with resolute determination.

The corner of his mouth tugged to one side and he cupped the side of my face. "You better."

Standing, Kova held his hand out for me. I stood and fixed my leotard so my butt wasn't showing.

"Did you drink enough water today? I can get you some Gatorade if you'd like."

I shook my head. I didn't care for sugary drinks. "I'll be fine. The caffeine withdrawal is real," I joked. "I'm going to get the biggest cup I can find after the meet." All I had was the balance beam and floor left, and then I was free.

Kova studied me. The lights made his eyes sparkle, though I would never tell him that. "Are you feeling okay? Overall?"

"Actually, yes. I'm a little tired but nothing I can't handle. I think when I changed the way I viewed things, it changed a lot for me in general. It just took me a minute to get there."

Holly walked over. "Hey. Do you want to warm up with me?" she asked, then eyed Kova.

"Go," he said, playfully clapping my back. "You ladies have a few minutes until it is time to start."

Kova walked away and we sat down to stretch. After a few minutes, Holly spoke.

"Adrianna?"

"Yeah," I said, reaching for my feet and feeling the burn in my ham-strings. I loved the way my muscles pulled. I stood and turned over into hand-stand pirouettes.

Holly stood closer to me. Quietly, so only I could hear, she said, "You should really be careful with the way you look at our coach."

I froze. The back of my neck burned with guilt but I quickly recovered and pretended like I didn't know what she was talking about.

"I don't understand." But she knew I did. I could see it in her eyes. My heart was about to pump out of my chest. "There's nothing going on," I stated under my breath.

She gave me a knowing smile and tipped her head to the side. "If that's what you want to go with, I get it. It's one thing at World Cup, but at a meet, let alone an international one, you can't let it happen. Not with so many people and cameras around."

I struggled not to panic. "I didn't let anything happen, though."

"You may not have, but he sure did." Holly paused and chose her next words carefully. "Whatever is going on between you two, he's making it very obvious. It's why I asked you to stretch. I was worried someone would see."

I blinked, then blinked again. I didn't know what to say to that.

"When do you ever see a coach look at a gymnast with the intensity that he looked at you? Never. Usually we're all getting yelled at."

She had a point, and I worked on remaining cool and collected. "Holly, but nothing is happening."

Leaning in, she lowered her voice to a whisper. "I had a coach once… but he wasn't like Kova," she said and shivered like it was a bad memory. "If it wasn't for Kova, I don't know what I'd have done."

I frowned. "What does that mean?"

She licked her lips. "Tonight? We'll talk tonight. Just stop looking at each other like no one else is in the room."

Holly walked away while I stood there silently panicking inside unsure of what to do. I picked at my nails and stared in a daze, trying to think about what could have given us away just now. If she saw something, then someone else probably did too.

Shit.

"Congratulations, Adrianna," my dad said, giving me a big hug. The meet was finally over and I got to see him. It would only be for a couple of hours because of the rules, but I'd take it.

"Thanks, Dad." He pulled back and wore a huge smile. "You know, it's kind of funny that I rarely see you in Georgia, yet you fly to Scotland to watch me?"

"This is a big moment. Of course I had to be here and I'm so glad I was. How many medals did you walk away with?"

I smiled bigger, still shocked I'd won even one medal despite everything. "Four. Three gold and one bronze." Naturally the bronze was in beam, but I didn't care. At this point in my life, any medal was better than no medal at all.

Kova walked up to us and placed a cup in front of me. "Coffee," was all he said, and I took it, smiling up at him, so thankful he'd remembered. I sipped it immediately and sighed.

"Konstantin."

I paused mid-sip at the enunciation of his name. I thought I caught a stiffness in my dad's tone.

"Frank. It is good to see you, my friend."

"Likewise."

"Adrianna did magnificent today," Kova said proudly. He was positively beaming, and for a second, I wondered if this was what Holly had been talking about.

"She did. I'm very proud."

"A few university coaches pulled me aside to ask about her future, if she had plans to compete in college. I was not sure if you guys had spoken about that yet or not."

My eyes widened in excitement. I'd been so busy with life that I hadn't had much of a chance to look into colleges the way I should have.

"Really? Who?"

He glanced down. "I cannot say, but there is interest. Do you remember when we talked about prizes and I did not recommend accepting them?" he asked, and I nodded, gripping my cup. The heat felt good in my hand. "If you had accepted, I would not have been approached and there would be no interest."

"Is there interest from anyone I should be concerned about?" Dad asked stiffly. His eyes were fixated on Kova like he was trying to get a psychic reading on him. All three of us stood in awkward silence for a moment.

"Well, I was not going to say anything just yet, but I did overhear the committee speaking and Adrianna's name was mentioned."

Now, I knew this was a lie. He wouldn't have heard them talking freely, because it never would have happened. The committee was very private and spoke behind closed doors, not out in the public. Kova was trying to cover up and brush off Dad's question like he was totally oblivious. I knew instantly to play along.

I gasped obnoxiously loud and bounced on my toes. "No way! You heard my name?" I said, and Kova nodded. I looked at my dad to gauge his reaction. "Dad! This is so exciting! I wish Xavier was here with us now," I said eagerly then leaned into his side for a half hug.

He wrapped an arm around my back and pulled me tight to him in an overprotective manner. My heart thumped against my ribs so hard it was beginning to feel painful.

Clearing his throat, Dad said, "This is fantastic news. Thank you, Konstantin. If it is okay with you, I'd like to have dinner with my daughter. I won't keep her late. I know she has to compete again tomorrow. In fact, after dinner when Adrianna goes back to her room, you can stop by for a drink."

I almost choked on my coffee. That was no invitation, but a demand. Kova had to be dense to miss it.

"Of course," Kova said with a pleasant smile on his face. "I look forward to catching up with you. We have a lot to discuss actually.."

My chest couldn't take anymore tension. I jumped in. "Dad, if we're going to dinner, let's get going. I'm frozen and I haven't eaten all day."

Kova stopped me. "Why have you not eaten?" he asked, looking at me with apprehension.

"I can't train, let alone compete on a full stomach. It has to be completely empty."

"You did not eat one thing today?" Kova glanced at his watch then at Frank before he looked at me again. "We have been here for seven hours, not counting the time since you woke up, and you had nothing at all?"

"No. Just a little water this morning."

Now that I thought about it, the medicine was probably what messed with my stomach this morning and why I felt so nauseous. Some of the pills were supposed to be taken with food and they hadn't been.

"That is very dangerous, Adrianna. That is why you had a headache all day. You need to eat something before you step foot on the floor tomorrow."

"You had a headache?" Dad added, his voice panic-stricken. Color drained from his face. "What else? Anything else bothering you?"

I knew where he was going with this, so I smiled sweetly at him and tried to ease his worries.

"I'm okay, Dad, really. Nothing else is wrong and my headache is long gone. I just hate to eat and work out. I'm sure your room has a fruit basket. I'll take it with me when I go back to my room and I'll eat before I leave the hotel tomorrow."

Dad expelled a breath and I saw the light reenter his eyes. I felt bad for worrying him, but in that moment I finally understood the meaning behind a little white lie.

People lied to protect those they cared about despite was the size of the lie may be. There wasn't much afterthought that went into the future if the lie was ever reveled, instead the conscious decision was made to shield another from the painful reality so they didn't endure the truth.

And I got it because truth was, my body ached angrily, and I fought back the vomit that had been climbing the back of my throat all day. I ignored the cramps and parched lips. I ignored the pain slashing through my chest.

I ignored it all and lied to myself and said everything was all right, when in fact, it really wasn't.

chapter 51

I EYED MY DAD AS HE SIPPED HIS AMBER LIQUID HE OFTEN HAD WITH dinner.

He was reading over some documents he'd brought with him, scanning the papers and flipping them over. Dad never sat still, but was always working.

"What's happening with you and Mom?" I blurted out.

It wasn't often we got to speak, let alone about her. I figured I'd sway the conversation the best I could because I felt like something was on the tip of his tongue about me and I needed to avoid that, especially after how he'd acted with Kova.

"Joy or Sophia?"

That was the first time he'd responded like that.

"Joy."

"We're trying to work things out."

"What does that mean?"

Dad eyed my plate. "Why are you not eating?"

Diversion.

I glanced down. "I ate a little bit. When my nerves are shot, it's hard to eat."

He removed his glasses and pushed the stack of papers away from him.

"Why are your nerves shot?"

I glared and wondered how he couldn't figure it out.

"Dad, this meet is huge, and tomorrow is another full day of competition," I said like it was obvious, because it was.

"Is there anything else going on I need to know about?"

Heat spread through my chest. "Like what? I'm taking all my medicine and I feel fine. I'm going to the doctor as scheduled. I'm just stressed, that's all. What's going on with Joy? I feel like if she never heard from me again, she'd be okay with that. And, Dad, despite everything, she raised me. How can she just let me go like last season's dress she wore once?"

He leaned back and eyed me peculiarly. Whiskey in his hand, he asked, "Why do you not ask about Sophia?"

My jaw bobbed. I hadn't expected that, but it seemed we both had some things to discuss.

"It's not that I'm not curious about her, because I am, I just have a lot on my plate at the moment. Adding another mom to it is not something I feel I should do right now. I figured I'd reach out once the season was over. Before that would just mess with my head and it's not a good idea, considering I have so much going on as it is. Just remembering to take my pills on time is worrisome to me. Making time to see my biological mother is a lot of pressure, physically, as well as emotionally. Not to mention, a little awkward too."

His eyes softened. "I'm sorry, sweetie. You're right. I shouldn't have asked that. When you're ready to talk to her, you can."

"Does she ask why I don't want to?"

"She does, but I'll explain to her next time that you need to get through these next few months first before you do."

"I hope you tell Sophia it's me, not her."

Dad chuckled and the tension in the room relaxed.

"So…about Joy? What does working it out mean? I thought you guys were getting divorced."

"We are. She's just being extremely difficult."

"Why?"

"She married into money and signed a prenuptial agreement. Now she's attempting extortion to get whatever she wants. I've already purchased a home for her, a summer home in the Hamptons, agreed to a monthly stipend, on top of a nice settlement, but nothing more. We had an agreement when you were born, which she's broken countless times that I have record of. I've let a lot slide. I'm not proud of it and it's something I deal with every day, but enough is enough. I'm done letting her get away with whatever she wants because I feel bad."

"She probably hates me," I said quietly. "She probably blames me for everything, for ruining her lifestyle."

"She hates herself more and hides behind it every day with riches. It's why she acts the way she does. Joy is a very insecure woman, so she belittles those around her to build herself up. What she doesn't realize is when she washes that shit off her face every night and hangs up her hideous Hermes scarf, she's still the same person she's always been. I've been patient. I know I've made mistakes, but this latest stunt was the icing on the cake."

I contemplated my next move. With Dad mentioning blackmail, I felt like

I could mention what Kova said to me. I just wasn't sure how without it looking obvious.

I pushed my plate away and stuffed my icy hands into the front pocket of my hoodie.

"Dad, I have a question… Some things have been said around the gym for a few months now. Is it true Joy helped Katja blackmail Kova into marrying him?"

Bringing the crystal tumbler to his lips, he took a long sip with an unnerving look in his eyes. His shifted back and forth between mine, and it was in that simple action that I had clarity.

My obvious response was that I needed to remain unaffected and completely blasé to the conversation. I wouldn't let him hear the anxiety in my voice or see my fingers shaking. The truth was, I was a ball of paranoia.

Dad placed the glass down on the matching coaster. His fingers remained wrapped around it before answering. "Supposedly."

"How?" I groaned inwardly.

"Why do you care?"

"I don't. It's just gym gossip." I responded too fast and now I needed to fix it. I sat back and casually crossed my legs. "I didn't know Joy and Katja were even friends. I always got the impression she didn't like her."

"She doesn't."

I blinked. "I'm confused."

"Joy has never liked Katja. Joy doesn't like anyone more attractive than her, or someone who has the potential to have more than her."

Mean girls were pretty on the outside but ultimately the ugliest of the bunch. The more I learned about Joy, the more I saw just how hideous she was inside.

"So it's true, then? She basically forced Kova to marry her."

"If I was Kova, I'd have married her too."

I tilted my head to the side, unsure how to take that. I studied him back.

"What do you mean?"

His eyes didn't leave mine. "He hasn't been inappropriate with you, has he?" he asked, testing the waters.

I blinked rapidly.

Keep calm.

Don't over react.

Keep calm.

Breathe.

Keep calm.

Fuck!

That was the last thing I thought he'd ask and it rendered me speechless. I should've known better than to even poke at this conversation.

So I gave him a confused look, trying to not let the question fluster me, when in reality my heart was pumping so loud it drowned out any other sound in the room.

"Inappropriate how? Who?"

His eyes were still locked on mine. "Kova. Joy insists Kova has dirty fingers that I should be concerned about. Is he a little more than hands on? Apparently Joy or Katja, I'm not sure which one, found some interesting things out about Kova that's somehow linking to you. Joy refuses to show me anything, but is using it against me for more money. She swears it will give me a heart attack and it's why she's withholding, but she also said if I don't comply that she'll go to the police and the media."

"Dad, that's ridiculous. Please tell me you don't believe her?"

An overconfident smirk slid across his face that rattled my nerves. I held my breath, waiting on his answer, wondering if I should've even asked now.

"Joy would *never* do anything that would taint her image. If what she said was the truth, which I highly doubt it is, she'd still never do it regardless. She wears the Rossi name. She'll always be attached to Rossi Enterprises, whether she wants to or not. If she plays dirty, it would come back to her to haunt her and she knows that." He sipped his drink. "She's being dramatic and most likely exaggerating about what she has. She's trying to intimidate me, but unless she supplies evidence, I have no reason to believe her."

Dad paused, his face slightly softening but his shoulders were bunched tight. "You're my daughter, Adrianna, and I'm always going to side with you first. Vindictiveness is in her blood. I used to think she was a woman with a goal. Now I know she's just malicious and I saw this as another one of her schemes to get what she wants."

"But why didn't you just ask Kova about what Joy said?"

"It's not worth mentioning to him."

"What do you mean?"

"It goes without saying that you're my daughter and if he ever hurt you, I'd break his fucking neck."

I tasted the not so subtle undertone in his words. The way my dad calmly uttered that statement jarred me. I got the feeling he'd do more than that.

Angling his head to the side, an air of superiority surrounded him as he continued. "Adrianna, a man is never going to admit when he lost his sense of pride and was forced into something he doesn't want to be in. A man will also never go to another man with his woes—that's for women."

Reaching for my glass, I took a sip of my water. Tension pulsed on the side of my neck. He had a point, but this was far worse than I could have ever fathomed. Uncomfortable silence filled our table as we looked at each other. Goose bumps broke out over my arms and my teeth clamped down on the inside of my lip.

I chose my words carefully.

"Dad, he's been a good coach to me. There's nothing bad or inappropriate going on with anyone. He's just very dedicated to the sport."

He swirled the ice cubes in his glass. "I think it also goes without saying that I'd ruin him if he did. Money comes with power, always remember that."

I didn't respond. I knew very well how much money could buy. I was out of words and wasn't sure if anything would help the situation.

"Joy put some thoughts into my head that I had always shut down," he said. My brows deepened in confusion. "I didn't believe them, but after today, and the way he touched you, the way you *both* looked at each other, it made me think otherwise for a minute."

My eyes softened. I felt so guilty inside. "It's not like that, Dad, I promise. Take a minute to look at all the coaches and gymnasts tomorrow. What you saw today between Kova and me is a normal occurrence between a coach and a gymnast. You'll see it tomorrow with everyone else. Joy is just crazy."

Dad finished off his whiskey, and once he paid the check, he walked me back to my hotel room. He wished me good luck tomorrow and said he'd be watching.

As I laid down to sleep that night, it dawned on me that he never flat out asked me to confirm anything. Either he was truly on my side and he believed me, or he had a better poker face than I thought.

chapter 52

"**C**ongratulations, Adrianna!" Holly said, squeezing me in a tight hug.

"Thanks! Congrats to you too!" I responded and pulled back, smiling through the fatigue. "Girl, you rocked it! No doubt Kova's phone will be ringing soon with interest about you."

The window to recruit was extremely small and the rules set by the national committee must be followed. During an off period, college coaches could not reach out and speak with any athlete, and they were not allowed to watch competitions. I knew she had the academic requirements—an absolute must since sophomore year—but no one had introduced themselves to her yet, and if they were going to, now was the time to. That's all she needed—an introduction and that was showing interest.

Her eyes were full of hope. "I didn't medal, though."

"It doesn't matter. You made it this far and that's huge. You still have time left, you'll see."

I had a good feeling she'd get recruited, and if not, she could always apply. While Holly hadn't medaled in any of the events, she'd taken fifth place overall, and no coach worth anything would overlook that. It was just the waiting period that sucked in between because a week felt like a month and it made you second-guess yourself. I wouldn't be surprised if interest came from both Division I and II schools.

"You know, we didn't get to talk last night," she said, eyeing me.

When I'd returned to the room last night, she was already asleep, and when we woke up, we were too focused to talk.

"Tonight?"

Even though I would have dinner with my dad again, and I was technically allowed to stay with him, I had opted to stay with Holly since she was here alone. Her parents attended many competitions in the States, but none outside.

They simply couldn't afford it. Being a competitive gymnast required a lot more money than people realized.

"Yes," she said, then leaned in and lowered her voice to a whisper. "You guys looked normal today, by the way."

I remained neutral and just smiled. We had a lot to talk about, and if I was going to reveal any secret, then she would too. And I knew just the one I was going to ask.

Before I went to bed last night, I made sure I would be on point today, but that was because I sent Kova a text last night and told him to get his shit together too.

"Adrianna?"

My name was a distant call, an echo faraway.

Someone nudged my arm a few times until I rolled onto my side and opened my eyes.

I squinted at Holly. "What time is it?" My throat was parched. "Do you have water?" I asked before she could reply with the time. "I feel like I have knives in my throat."

I sat up and my head spun. I knew without checking I had a fever. Fuck my life. I really hoped I wasn't having another flare up.

"You don't look so hot," Holly said, concern coated her words the way parents sound. She handed me a bottle from the mini fridge.

I thanked her. "I feel like shit."

"When did you get back here?"

Taking another sip, I winced as the icy water went down like shards. I recapped the bottle and blinked my swollen eyes a few times.

"We had an early dinner because my dad had a phone meeting." I picked up my phone and glanced at the time. My brows rose. "I've been sleeping for over three hours?"

Holly raised her shoulders. "Don't ask me," she joked. "I just got back and you were dead to the world."

I looked around, so confused. Loud bubbly sounds erupted in my stomach. We eyed each other for a split second before I was up and running to the bathroom. I dropped to my knees and unleashed everything I had for dinner into the toilet.

"Aid?" she said softly.

"I'll be out in a minute," I said before vomit came up again.

God, I hated throwing up more than anything in the world. I'd rather have my period for a month straight than vomit. Luckily it didn't last long and I was soon washing up and stepping out of the bathroom.

Holly's eyes were on me. Without saying a word, I walked over to my luggage and retrieved the small makeup case I used to carry all my medicine. I took it to the bed where Holly was sitting and pulled out the bottles, laying them in front of her crossed legs.

Frowning, she hesitantly reached to pick up one bottle, then another, and another, reading each label.

"What are these?" she asked, her voice soft.

"Not to be dramatic, but they're what's keeping me alive." Holly's head lifted, her pretty blue eyes filled with alarm. "I have lupus, which led to me having kidney disease." When she didn't say anything, I continued. "I have stage four kidney disease."

Her lips parted and she turned sheen white. "Out of how many stages?" she asked, barely audible

"Five," I answered her, and tears instantly filled her eyes. "Don't cry. I'm okay. I'm better than okay, actually. Some days are harder than others. Like today. The back-to-back meets wear me down big time and take a lot of energy out of me. Sometimes I get a little sick. I'm still adjusting."

"How did you find out? Like when?"

I sat down next to her. "Well, I don't know how long I've had either one for, but from what the doctors told me, if both illnesses aren't treated early, it causes long-term issues and the stages get worse. They gather that's what happened with me. I only found out a couple of months ago."

Her brows rose as her hands held two of the bottles. "You take all these?"

"Multiple times a day."

"Wow," she said softly. "Why didn't you tell me? Does Hayden know?"

"No, no one knows. I don't want anyone to know, to be honest. So please don't mention anything to Hayden. Only my family, Avery, and Kova are aware," I said, and she eyed me like she was waiting for more. "My dad told him."

Holly averted her gaze like she was guilty. "And here I thought there was something else going on when he was just trying to help you."

"What do you mean?"

"I thought for sure there was something more than a coach and gymnast relationship happening. All the signs were there."

I swallowed and smiled softly. "He helps me out a lot, and he looks out for me…"

I left out one major detail, but it wasn't something she needed to know. I wasn't going divulge anything that could be used against us.

"But…" She continued.

"He's my dad's friend, you know?"

"Wait. How does this affect gymnastics for you?"

Taking a deep breath, I went into detail, telling her all about the illnesses and how they affected me. I told her Avery's a donor match and that I'd eventually need a transplant.

"I can't believe you never told anyone," she said, her voice a little broken when I was done. Disbelief carved her face and I empathized with her. I'd feel the same as her.

"I considered it. I mean, it would be nice to talk about it, but if I did, what would that change? I'll still have the diseases. People don't want to hear someone always complaining, and I definitely didn't want pity or for anyone treat me differently, so I just keep it to myself. Maybe one day I'll be more open about it."

She nodded, accepting what I said. "Yeah, I guess I could see it from your point of view." She paused. "You're only telling me because I saw the bottles, aren't you?"

"Kind of," I said with a partial smile. "Trust me, I complain a lot to myself. I'm sick of hearing it." Holly laughed, but it was a sad one. "Don't feel bad," I said, "I'd rather deal with it on my own, to be honest. The last thing I want is for someone to worry about it, like baby me, you know?"

"Yeah, I get that. It just sucks."

This time I really laughed. "Just a little bit."

Holly was quiet for a little while. "I just can't believe it. You train harder than most of us, you attend more meets than we do, and you have your eyes set on the Olympics. All while dealing with this?"

"I'm more focused than ever now. When I got the diagnosis, I felt like I had a timer on my life. I was so scared I wouldn't get to live and experience life. I kind of fell into a little bit of a depression because of it and lost my sight, so to stay busy I would just train and keep pushing to take my mind off things."

"You did?"

I nodded. I met her gaze with a pained looked in my eyes. She knew I had a story to tell but I was deciding if I should go the whole mile. I opened my mouth, but she spoke first.

"So before you came to World Cup, there was another coach who Kova ended up firing once he bought the gym. He'd been there for years. We all grew up with him, but we all didn't like him."

Holly shivered, her face twisting in repugnance. I had a feeling what she was trying to tell me was more difficult for her to say than for me to hear.

"Every once in a while I'll see him at a meet and it's as fresh as if it had happened yesterday."

"Who's him? The coach?"

She nodded. "There's a reason why I said what I did to you yesterday about Kova. I know you denied it and all, but I was worried and didn't want you to go through what I did."

My chest deflated. "Holly? If you don't want to tell me anything, you don't have to."

"I want to," she said, still unable to look at me. So I closed my mouth and let her speak. "He was a coach I grew up with, someone my family was friends with, and someone we all put trust into."

She shook her head and mumbled to herself but I caught it.

It's always the ones you never suspect.

Holly took a deep breath and continued. "There was something about him that felt off. He was so mean, but he got results, so I never questioned what he was doing. None of us did. He was the coach and that was that, you know?

"But then…something changed. I can't pinpoint when, or why, but…he… there was this time, no, a bunch of times…" She sighed. I knew where this was going without her saying it, so I did.

Softly, with compassion, I said, "He touched you."

Her uneasy eyes lingered on mine for a moment before she blinked, and said, "Yeah. A lot. I didn't know that he shouldn't. I mean, that's not true. I know now it was wrong, but at the same time he was someone more than a coach, and I thought it was okay because why else would I think it was wrong? We're so isolated, people could never understand this sort of lifestyle is normal for us. Being close with our coaches, traveling alone with them, looking at them almost like a parent. We idolize them. I'm not stupid. I know no parent would ever touch me the way he did, but I didn't think it was wrong either. I know I'm not making any sense, you probably don't know what I mean." She sighed again, resigned, and I was saddened by this news.

I knew exactly what she meant. I'd heard it all before. It was something that happened all the time in the gym world. Now I knew why she was worried about me.

"You don't have to explain it. I know."

Her chest fell. "I spiraled out of control and I went on this crazy boy train. I skipped practice, hooked up with guys from school, snuck out at night, talked back to my parents. I was a mess. All the while my *amazing* coach," she said sarcastically and rolled her eyes, "kept molesting me and making me feel so disgusting. I thought if I went out with boys I actually liked, that it would be okay."

"If he made you feel that way, why'd you keep going back?"

She shrugged helplessly. "Sometimes I felt like I didn't have a choice. I was becoming a really good gymnast. I guess I thought I owed it to him. He was so manipulating, though. I never saw him for who he truly was until it was too late." She paused, her voice dropping like she was embarrassed. "I had to go to therapy for it."

I frowned. "How old were you when this happened."

A tear slipped from the corner of her eye. She quickly wiped it away.

"I was nine when the touching began. It stopped when Kova bought the gym. I was almost fifteen then."

My brows shot up. This was more recent than I was aware. I recalled Kova telling me a story about how he'd fired a coach the day he purchased World Cup for his abusive treatment. I didn't realize it was Holly's coach.

"Can you believe I cried on Kova's shoulder and thanked him? I was mortified, but I was so happy too. Kova threatened him and he never came back." Holly was quiet for a moment, like she was deep in her thoughts. "I wish Kova had come to the gym sooner. He saved me. I don't know what I would've done without him."

chapter 53

I stared at Holly, wishing there was something I could say or do to help her, but I knew there were no words that would bring her comfort. "Kova didn't call the police?"

"He called my parents. Kova wanted to call the police, but my parents begged him not to. He swore he wouldn't. If that wasn't enough, like any parent when they hear their daughter is being sexually abused, they wanted to pull me and my brother from World Cup and basically lock us in our home. They put complete trust and faith into that coach and he took advantage. They didn't want it to happen again. I was devastated. God, I was so upset. I apologized thinking, it was my fault, but looking back, I don't blame them. If it were my daughter, I'd react the same way."

Dread ran through me. I'd heard this story one too many times. "So he got away with it," I said, and she nodded. "And you thought the same thing was happening with me."

She looked up and wrapped her arms around herself. "I have thought that for a little while now. It was strange though, like you didn't look at him the way I did when I looked at my old coach. And Kova doesn't have those creepy eyes when he looks at you," she said, surprise lacing her tone. "I thought something was going on, I just didn't know what, but after what I went through and after all the therapy, I felt strongly about speaking up to you. I didn't want you to go through what I did."

I contemplated how far I should take this conversation, whether or not to reveal a secret that could jeopardize more than one life, or watch her drown in her memories and imagine the worst. I wanted to tell her, my gut said to risk it, but the less anyone knew the better. However, the need to soothe her damaged heart consumed me.

Holly continued, her voice splintered with each word. She reminded me of a crystal vase—the slightest tap would permanently break it.

"You know how there's a strict dating rule?" she said, voice low. I nodded. "It's because of me. There's things you don't know… that no one knows about."

"One time Hayden mentioned something about the dating rule and you, but he refused to say anything more. I tried to pry it out of him. That boy is solid as a rock. He wouldn't budge."

Despair layered her words. "Hayden is protective. I'm kinda glad he never told you. It's embarrassing."

I smiled to myself. Her twin was a giant teddy bear who wanted to comfort and guard everyone. A lot made sense now. Hayden would never accept Kova no matter how much I pleaded my case to him, because of what had happened to Holly. She had been easily manipulated by her old coach, and he assumed I'd been too. It was easy to say I wasn't, but the words were empty when his sister had actually experienced it.

"He's been worried about you, you know."

"I don't think Hayden is capable of not worrying about anyone," I said, and she agreed. "Why is there a dating rule in effect?" I asked.

She glanced at me, then let go of the comforter she was picking at, like she'd finally let go of the shame she carried with her. She dried her cheeks with the back of her hand.

"Before the coach was fired, I spiraled out of control. I skipped practices so I wouldn't have to see him. And like I said, I hooked up with kids from school just to feel normal. I had a terrible attitude. It was too late before I realized that my actions had backfired on me because my coach noticed too. He'd gotten worse than ever with me, and I ended up confessing to Hayden one night. I couldn't take anymore and I broke down. I told him I needed to take an STD test because I had a bump on me that I freaked out over. It ended up being nothing, but Hayden was furious and got involved trying to help. By that point Kova threatened to expel me from World Cup for my behavior." She paused, taking a deep breath. "Hayden went to Kova and pleaded with him, telling him everything that had been going on and how I needed to take an STD test. That's when Kova called my parents. When they wanted to pull us from World Cup, Kova went to bat for us. He told them of his plans to fire my coach the moment he bought the building so we could stay. Unfortunately around the same time, my dad took a job in Ohio. It was an offer he couldn't refuse, but I didn't want to leave and neither did Hayden. They couldn't afford to keep us training here, let alone in a rented apartment, and they sure as hell wouldn't trust another coach so soon. That was when Kova suddenly had a scholarship program no one knew about."

My face scrunched up. That was news to me. "What scholarship program?"

"Exactly."

"The program would pay for me and Hayden to train full time and the meet costs. The only thing my parents had to pay for were the travel, leos, and other needs outside of the gym. Kova said he saw our true potential and that we could live with him and Katja until we got our own place so they could watch over us. It wasn't easy for my parents. They had to come to an agreement, like Kova agreeing not to go to the cops. It took time and money."

It was easily over two grand a month just for both of them to train full-time elite, not to mention the leotards could run as high as five hundred dollars for one. Training at the Olympic level often created financial strain on families, some going as far as to file bankruptcy. Elite was almost as heavy with expenses. With Kova footing the bill, it alleviated the burden on the family with the possibility of securing a future for Hayden and Holly. The whole reason Holly was still competing at an elite level was to hopefully gain a full-ride scholarship to college. Hayden had received one, and Holly was praying she would too.

"In return, we had to sign a no-dating agreement. Kova said his time was valuable and we had to respect it. He was giving us one chance, and one chance only."

I laughed. "I'm sorry for laughing, it's just so Kova."

"I know. I think he felt guilty he hadn't caught on sooner with my coach, so this was his way of giving back. I don't have to tell you how often this happens or how most coaches get away with it. My parents said he even offered to pay for the therapy, but they declined and said he was doing enough for us already. Ultimately, my mom stayed back for a few months until she put us in the trust and care of Kova. We tell everyone that we've lived on our own since sixteen, but it's a lie. My parents were running out of money with the move to Ohio, so we lived with Kova and Katja for a little while. Once the coach was fired, we got our own apartment. That gave my parents the time they needed to get our place situated. Kova knew how much gymnastics meant to me and my brother and he wanted us to have it without worry, but with security. And we did."

My eyes were focused on Holly, my chest aching for the time that was stolen from her. She was the all-American girl on the outside, but on the inside, she was suffering and in a state of anxiety thinking I was being abused like she had been. There was so much I didn't know about the people I spent fifty hours a week with. I knew them, yet they were virtual strangers.

Quietly, she said, "Kova was the one to pull me out of it. He worked with me at my pace until I was ready to train elite. He said if I was never ready then that would be okay, but that we had to try. I owe him so much."

Tears immediately filled my eyes. I blinked them away. He'd done the same for me and it was something I could never repay him for. It was hard to wrap my head around Kova and this story. His generosity, his compassion, why he never told me. It made a lot of sense now. Kova had struggled growing up. The thought occurred to me that he was trying to make a change, possibly trying to give to those who might not have the chance. It placed him in a light that was riveting and took me by complete surprise. It made my heart beat for him and who he was underneath, the layer he kept hidden to the world. After all our ups and downs, I knew there was a man with a big heart there, I just didn't know how big it really was.

Swallowing, I exhaled the worry of telling a secret, and opened up the way she had.

"Kova was the one to pull me out of the dark hole I'd been stuck in too. When the diagnoses came, I shut down and didn't tell anyone. On top of that, I'd been dealing with so many personal things at home I was trying to not let get to me too. I had so much weight I was carrying around every day that I tried to channel into gymnastics. I'd wake up and think, what else could go wrong?" I paused for a moment, thinking. "It took some time, but you know how when you just hold it all in and then you explode and it's usually on the wrong person?" She nodded. "That's what happened. I blew up, and I blew up on him. He let me." Her brows shot up. "Kova knew about it—my dad told him, even though he promised me he wouldn't—and so he'd been trying all along to help me. I just didn't know it because I didn't see it from shutting everyone out."

Holly chewed on her lip for a long moment. "Was there something going on before this? You and him?" Her question was soft and without judgment.

"Yes."

Her shoulders fell. Her reaction part shocked part sad. "I knew it. I had a feeling, but I wasn't sure either."

"It's not like what you and your coach went through. I know it sounds like I'm defending him, but I'm not. I promise. If anything, I pushed him."

"I believe you, it's just hard to accept, you know? There's always a shadow of doubt. I know Kova and I would never put him in the same category of that other coach. It's just…" She let out a sigh. "Yeah, I get it."

I nodded. It made sense. "Do you think the others know?" I asked, praying for two little letters. Holly shook her head and I exhaled in relief.

"If they knew, they'd talk about it."

"Reagan kind of knows." Her eyes widened. "I didn't speak to her about it and I never will, but she caught on the day Katja came to the gym and told everyone about the wedding."

She blinked like she was thinking back to that day. "Yeah, that was a surprise."

"How so?"

"They just never seemed totally in love, you know? I knew they loved each other—like I love you, but not like I love you like that."

The knots in my stomach tightened just thinking about that dreadful day and how I wished I could erase it from my memory.

"He'd been married for months, Holly."

"Yeah, another shock. Especially with the way he always looked at you."

Air seized my lungs. "It's been that obvious since then?"

"No, I really don't think so. After what I've been through and given the fact I know him a little better than others, I can see it."

"How does he look at me?"

"With admiration, almost like he loves you. He sure doesn't look at his wife in the same way." She paused. "I take that back. He does seem like he loves her but it's just different. I can't explain it. Like he tries so hard not to look at you but when he does it's like awe in his eyes. It's kind of funny since he's a man. Usually it's the woman acting like that."

"No way. He doesn't look at me like that."

"It's the truth. Hayden sees it too. Kova looks at you differently. He definitely doesn't look at me like he does you, which I'm glad about." She laughed half-heartedly. "If he did, it might trigger PTSD."

I laughed, and covered my mouth. I giggled way harder than I should have at that comment.

"I'm serious," she said.

"I know it may seem hard to believe, but he didn't force me into anything. It was the opposite, actually. He tried not to but I just kept pushing and pushing until I got what I wanted."

"Even though you knew he had a girlfriend?"

My cheeks heated with embarrassment. I blinked hard, ashamed to open my eyes.

"Yes. I know it makes me a bad person. This might sound cheesy, but he's my other half. I can't imagine a future that he's not in." I inhaled and expelled a weighted breath, then got real with her. "The thing is, I don't know how to stop loving him. My heart beats for him, Holly, every single day. I know it's wrong and I'm not supposed to, but I love him. I don't know how to stop it."

She sucked in a quiet gasp. "Knowing he has a wife doesn't bother you?"

I looked her directly in the eyes and told her the truth. "No, it doesn't."

Her brows shot up, she was taken aback. I didn't blame her. "That's kind of…" Holly didn't finish her sentence.

"Shitty?"

She nodded regrettably. I knew I should feel remorse for what I've done, but the truth was, I didn't. I don't know if I ever did.

"I don't know what I'm going to do. I know the right thing would be to sever ties with him, but I just can't because deep down, I don't want to. My mind gives me warnings but my heart plows them down with nothing but love for him. And love always wins, right? Isn't it supposed to?"

Holly was quiet for a moment. "But he has a wife."

"I know."

"Is he going to divorce her?"

Quietly, I said, "No, not that I'm aware of. But I'd never ask for that either."

"Then what are you going to do?"

I thought about it for a moment before I said, "I can only love him in the dark."

chapter 54

I VOMITED UNTIL I DRY HEAVED.

The back of my throat burned like someone was scraping hot coal down it and my stomach was hollow.

I knew better than to eat airplane food. My stomach revolted just looking at it, but I'd already been feeling sick for most of the flight and figured it was due to hunger and my medications messing with my stomach.

Unfortunately, I couldn't get cleaned up because we had to rush to the next flight. But once we were on the plane, and the seat belt sign turned off, I used the god awful, putrid-smelling bathroom to brush my teeth.

The odor got to me and I ended up throwing up again. I'd never had an issue with flying before, but then I'd never traveled for so long at one time either. I'd have to pick up some medicine to deal with motion sickness before we went to Italy. No way in hell was I going to deal with this if I could avoid it.

I'd slept the rest of the way and when we landed back in Georgia, I excused myself to freshen up.

"Are you okay?" Holly asked, eyeing me as she washed her hands.

I looked at her in the mirror. "I think I'm having one of those flare ups I told you about." Her face fell. "Don't give me those puppy eyes. I didn't tell you so you can pity me."

She turned off the water. "I know. But I still feel bad."

We both dried our hands and walked out to the terminal lobby. Kova's forehead creased as he observed me, his eyes taking in the length of my body. I knew Holly was watching so I tried covertly to give him the look to stop.

He didn't catch on.

Men.

So stupid sometimes.

We retrieved our bags and got in Kova's car. I had Holly sit up front so I could sit in the back with the window rolled down, figuring it would help with the nausea. I slowly breathed in the salty air with my eyes closed. Home. I was home. Thank goodness the airport wasn't too far. Between the jet lag and the exhaustion of the meet, I wasn't feeling so hot.

"Bye, Holly," I said from the backseat.

"See you tomorrow!" she said, walking away. Kova stayed parked until she'd stepped through her front door.

"Want to jump in the front?" he asked.

I faked a groan. "I'm too tired. I'll just stay here if that's cool with you."

"It is cool with me," he said, and I chuckled. "What is so funny?"

"Sometimes you sound like a robot when you don't use contractions," I teased him.

He looked in the rearview mirror, grinning. "*It's* cool with me," he said again.

My stomach did a little flip and I smiled as he pulled up to a red light. Going with the urge in my heart, I unbuckled my seat belt and grabbed onto the seats in front of me to lean forward. Kova's gaze was on me as I stuck my head into the front and reached around to pull his face to mine to give him a quick, little kiss. He responded immediately, his hand to the back of my head while he kissed me deeply as he held me to him. A car honked behind us and I pulled away, our lips making a popping sound.

He shot me a quick glance before he refocused on the road, grinning from ear to ear.

"Minty. I am glad you brushed your teeth," he said, and I playfully slapped him. "What was that for?"

I shrugged and leaned against the side of the passenger seat watching him. "I just felt like kissing you."

Kova laced our fingers together and placed them on the console. My cheek rested on the fabric and I glanced down at our joined hands, feeling really good about us.

I thought about what Holly told me, how generous but discreet he'd been, and it made me swoon for Kova even more. My thumb rubbed the space between his thumb and forefinger in an effort to slow down my racing heart. I thought back to when he told me of his past and how he'd had so few opportunities growing up. It hadn't changed him, only reminded him of where he'd come from and what little he had. He was humble and it said a lot about his character.

"You did amazing this weekend," he said, watching the road. "Be proud of yourself. I know I am."

"You're always proud of yourself."

He grinned and I decided I would tell him my thoughts.

"It took a lot out of me. I'm so physically worn out, it kind of worries me."

His hand tightened. "I know it did."

"How?"

"I can tell by looking in your eyes, at your body. You are trying to stay strong, but your eyes are fighting a war inside and your body language suggests you are extremely tired."

"Yeah," was all I said. He was right. One could tell a lot by just paying attention. "It kind of knocked me down a little, but I'm okay. For once, I really feel okay. I want to give it all I've got right now because I know I'll never have this chance again. I want to know that I fought hard. The last thing I want is to wake up the next day with regret. I know it probably sounds silly, but I don't want to miss this moment."

Kova looked at me briefly. He brought our hands to his lips and kissed them before his gaze was back on the road. He held my hand the rest of the drive and stayed quiet until he pulled into my complex. The fresh air settled my stomach and my nerves subsided and all felt right in the world again. Like a peace fell over us where we finally reached a point in our relationship where we were good and nothing could ruin it. We were turning pages.

"Is everything okay?" I asked, concerned when he parked the car and stayed still.

"I simply do not want to say goodbye to you."

Bittersweet. That's what we were. Beautiful butterfly wings that disintegrated to ashes and floated away in the wind.

"Honestly, I want nothing more than to come inside and just be with you, and I cannot. I want to just drive around holding your hand, and I cannot. I want to wake up drinking coffee with you before the sun rises and then go to the gym together, and I cannot." He was quiet for a moment and I didn't interrupt his thoughts. Kova swallowed, his Adam's apple bobbing like it was a difficult pill to swallow.

"It is so unfair," he said, still looking ahead. "I am already missing you and you have not even left."

The defeat in his words caught me off guard. I was all too familiar with what he was feeling. Life was unfair. We were unfair. A war was raging inside Kova. He meant what he said and my heart ached for this moment when he was true to himself and his feelings.

"Come on," I said, urging him. "Come with me."

He shook his head. "I cannot. I have to go home."

Softly, I said, "Stay with me. Even if it's just for an hour. We can watch the sun set on the beach." Somehow, I knew he didn't want to sit inside, and somehow, I knew he wasn't looking for sex.

He studied me. I didn't falter under his gaze. The emotion in his green eyes was so thick with misery I thought he was going to tell me everything on his mind.

"Okay," was all he said.

That longing tension grew stronger in the confinement of his car. Our chests rose and fell, mimicking each other's, as we tried to steady our breathing. Whatever this was, he felt it too. I couldn't explain why, but after this moment, I knew it would never be the same for us.

We got out of his car and took my belongings upstairs. I grabbed a couple blankets and we made our way downstairs and onto the beach to one of the wooden lounge chairs offered to the tenants of the complex. Kova laid a blanket down. He took a seat first then tugged me to his lap. Chest to chest, I curled into his body, my legs tangling with his, and I used his shoulder as a pillow. I sighed in contentment and looked at the gently lapping waves. Kova draped the second blanket around us, then wrapped his arms around me and held me like he never wanted to let go. He pressed his lips to the top of my head, then nestled closer.

Kova instantly relaxed against me, like he could breathe again. Something was going on inside of him and if this was what he needed, then so be it. We both needed it.

It was only us on an ivory sand beach with the sun setting behind the calm waters. It was enough to lull me to sleep.

After a while, he spoke. "Why does this feel so natural?" he asked. "It is the most ordinary thing, something I have taken for granted living here, though I cannot imagine doing this or being this comfortable with anyone except you. I mean that, Adrianna."

I felt his confusion, how simple and easy this was, yet so hard to process. "I know. I'm trying to figure that out too. I never watch the sunset, but now that I am, it's so peaceful and relaxing." There was something about the whitecaps softly kissing the shore, the way the sun caused the waves to look like diamonds rippling in the distance, the peaceful sound of the vast ocean.

"I wish I could do this every day with you in my arms just like we are right now," he continued, like he was lost in his dark thoughts. I swallowed back my emotion and looked up. The green in his eyes was iridescent against the setting sun and it was startling with his dark lashes. Every time he blinked the hues of green shifted. "All we have is right now. This moment. Tomorrow I will not wake up with you, and tomorrow I will not go to bed with you. I will only have a few stolen hours of the day with you and that is just not enough for me. I want every waking minute to be with you."

I frowned, fear rising in me. I wondered where these feelings were coming from now. The last time he was deep in his feelings, my heart was shattered the following day.

"Kova?"

"Hmm?"

"The last time you were like this, you kept saying *prosti* over and over while we made love, and the very next day I found out you were married." I paused and licked my lips. "Please tell me it's not going to happen again tomorrow. Please tell me I'm not going to find out something shocking that's going to devastate me. I can't handle it right now."

The intensity in his eyes bore into mine. "I am hiding nothing from you. Nothing, Adrianna. I swear it."

I nodded subtly, accepting his answer. "I'm sorry I asked."

Kova shook his head. "Do not be sorry. I shaped that worry within you and it is my fault. But I swear I am not hiding anything. I am just bitter about the hand I was dealt, that is all. I wish I could change things."

Kova looked away, his gaze distant. "I am looking into how I can divorce her, if you want to know. I just have to be careful about the way I do it. It will take some time."

He glanced at me. All I could do was stare into his lonely eyes and know what he said was the truth, and it tore him up. Leaning toward me, he dipped his head and his lips captured mine.

My heart soared. This wasn't just any kiss, and it most definitely wasn't a sexual one. It was a kiss that could only be fortified with honest-to-God love that was bone deep. The kind dreams were made of. The kind we all searched for but rarely received.

It was a kiss that almost made me say I love you.

I clenched my hand around the fabric of his shirt and pulled him closer, breathing in the kiss like he was my life support. I opened my palm and slid it up his chest and around his shoulder to cup the back of his head. My fingers threaded his hair, our bodies flushed together as the passion between two people who had no right giving in to one another grew to a binding fever.

Kova rolled over me, his body half on mine as he deepened the kiss. He reached behind himself and pulled the blanket over his head to give us privacy. It was intimate without even having to try.

We stayed like that until well after the sun set, kissing away our fears and worries, and sealing any distance we'd had between us with a stroke of the tongue.

chapter 55

I DIDN'T CHALLENGE KOVA WHEN HE TOLD ME TO TAKE THE FOLLOWING day off.

For once I agreed, and I think it shocked him more than it did myself. His eyes filled with gratitude and it made me feel good seeing him like that. He kissed my forehead and said thank you before he left.

I shut the door and thought back to everything that had transpired since I'd come to World Cup and how we'd gotten to this point. We had our painful truths and lies, tried countless times to not admit our feelings, tried not to be together. But through it all, we were always there for each other because some force had compelled us to.

And even though he wasn't here, Kova was still all around me. Mixed with the scent of the salty sugary beach air, it was a heightened combo of sweet and dark wrapped in one. I could smell him in every room, and I took comfort in that warmth. It had physically hurt my heart to say goodbye and caused a deep melancholy in me, but I couldn't ask him to stay again.

My body needed the rest, and if I was going to be in this game for as long as I was physically able, then I needed to play my cards right. So I listened to my body, and my coach, and I decided to stay home.

It was a good thing I wasn't defiant for once. I woke up with terrible stomach cramps, and my boobs felt heavy and uncomfortable, so I skipped the coffee and made some peppermint tea hoping it would ease my upset stomach. I toasted a slice of bread, but I couldn't eat it.

A flare up. I'd need to make an appointment first thing with my doctor just to be sure everything was okay. This could really be the cause of a few things compiled together, but I had to make smart choices about my health. After all, I only had one life to live, and I sure as hell wanted to live it to the fullest.

After taking my medicine, I finished my tea and fell back asleep. I felt like crap. Three hours later I woke up and ran to the bathroom. I knew better than to take the medicine on an empty stomach, but the thought of eating made me feel sicker, so I'd skipped it. I figured the tea was fine. Clearly, I was wrong.

"I think I'm dying." I exaggerated a moan to Avery on the phone after I cleaned up and changed my clothes.

"Jesus, Aid, what the fuck time is it?"

I glanced at my clock and frowned. Had I gotten up in the middle of the night and not realized it? Jet lag was messing with me. "It's a quarter after seven."

"Go back to bed." She groaned, and I explained I'd already gotten up twice now. "You're so weird."

"I'm so tired. My period is all messed up and my stomach is eating itself. For once I have big boobs so I can't complain about that, but I'm having a stupid flare up and hating life."

"Your boobs get big during that?"

I thought about her question and palmed one. I winced and gasped.

"What happened?"

"I grabbed my boob to feel the size since I'm so happy they're not bee stings right now and it hurts so fucking bad. My nipples are sore."

"Has Kova been sucking on them?"

I laughed, curling up under the covers in my bed. "No."

"Pinching them?"

"No," I drawled out.

"Then it must've really hurt for you to curse. Are you sure this is normal for a flare up?"

I considered her question. "I mean, I've never really given it much thought, but now that I'm paying attention, I think?"

"What else?" she asked, sounding like she was awake.

"I keep vomiting, but I think that's because of traveling and shitty food I'm not used to eating. I fucked up all my medicine, got my period in the middle of the meet, which didn't help my nerves. Well, not in the middle of it, but right before I left the hotel. I told you, I'm dying. This is it."

"Shut the fuck up, you are not dying. You haven't even gotten my kidney yet. You are literally not allowed to die."

I chuckled. "I hate throwing up."

"I hate throwing up too. I'd much rather have a tooth filled than vomit." She paused. "Wait. Do you still have your period?"

"It's at the end of the cycle."

"So you had it for, like, three days?"

"Yeah, I guess."

"And that's normal?"

"Well, normal for me, I'd say."

"And your boobs hurt."

I was silent for a moment. All I could hear was the beating of my heart in my ears.

"What are you getting at?"

"Have you taken a pregnancy test?" she blurted it out.

Avery was crazy. "I'm not pregnant. Any time I've been with Kova I've used Plan B."

"I would take a test to be sure. Plan B isn't one hundred percent."

"I know that, but I'm not pregnant. What makes you think I am?" Just saying the word was making me tremble.

"Because your boobs hurt, dumbass. You're tired, and hello, you're vomiting." She basically spelled the words out for me and paused between them. "If that isn't a sign, then I don't know what is."

I rubbed my eyes with the heel of my hand. "So? All signs of a flare up and the effects. It's a lot shit it could and could not be, but not pregnant is one of them."

"All it takes is one resilient little fuck to slide on through. Ah, I take that back. An aggressive little Russian fuck to swim on by to the egg."

I couldn't stop the laugh from rolling out of me. "I hate you."

"Aid." I heard the plea in my name. "All jokes aside, humor me."

"I shouldn't have called."

"Don't be stupid. You're getting nervous because now you're actually thinking about it and it scares the shit out of you. I get it, trust me, I get it more than anyone. But the difference is, you have me with you. Get dressed and go to the pharmacy. If it's negative, then you go back to sleep and you don't have to worry."

She was right, and I didn't like it. My stomach was in knots. I threw the blanket off and kicked it away, feeling warmer than usual. Swallowing back the lump in my throat, I glanced down at my flat stomach. Pregnant? No, there wasn't a chance in hell.

"I think I'm having a panic attack," I said, panting into the phone. "I can't have a baby."

Avery sighed like she was annoyed. "Stop being dramatic. Get up and get dressed."

I was struggling to breathe. "I can't, Avery. I just can't." The back of my neck was damp and I felt sticky everywhere. I needed to shower.

"No one is saying you're having a baby, you lunatic. Just go get the test."

"What if I am?" I was only eighteen. Freshly turned eighteen. I couldn't get pregnant.

"I'd say I wouldn't be surprised. Kova is a freak in the sheets, and from what you've told me, you're just as bad."

"Avery! You're not helping."

"What? I'm being serious. It's kinda sexy and hot, but at the same time you guys are both nymphos. It's a good thing you don't live together. I think you'd guys fuck each other to death. Doesn't your vagina ever hurt?"

I shook my head. "What? No. I mean, at first, yes. Sometimes? If you're trying to take my mind off the terror that's consuming me, it's not working."

"I'm not. I was just curious."

I groaned and made sure she heard it. "I'm freaking out over the possibility that I could be pregnant, and you're asking about my vagina. Really, Ave?"

"Bad timing?"

"I know no form of birth control is one hundred percent, and considering how intense our sex is and how much we have at one time, maybe I didn't take the pills early eno—"

I froze mid-sentence. Had I taken them early enough? Had I taken enough? My mind raced through the brain fog back to the first time we had sex again. I blinked a few times trying to remember when it hit me... It was when I had carved an A into his chest during the hurricane, and again a couple of days later.

Tears instantly filled my eyes, but I pushed them back. No, I wouldn't get emotional just yet because I was fairly certain I took the pills within the correct time frame and I wasn't pregnant. Kova would've made sure of that.

Sitting up, I moved my hair off my neck and hunched over to hold my stomach. I was going to be sick and this time it was due to the reality of the situation and nothing else. There was an old wives tale that floated between the Florida-Georgia line that women got pregnant during hurricanes. Now my mind was overthinking stupid thoughts and actually considering them.

"*Ria?*" she joked, to which I actually chuckled sadly. I forgot she would pretend to say my nickname the way Kova did. "What is it?"

Deep breathing, I dropped my head into my palm. "What if I am pregnant? A baby, Avery? I could never admit Kova was the father—he'd end up in jail. No, I take that back. He wouldn't make it to jail. My dad would slaughter him first and no one would find his body, then my child would grow up asking me who it's daddy is."

For once, Avery was quiet.

"Yeah, you're fucked. Let's hope it's negative."

chapter 56

"WHAT THE FUCK DO I BUY?" I WHISPERED INTO THE PHONE. Wide eyes scanned the assortment of colorful boxes. "There's a million of them. Do they all work?"

"Yeah, they all work, but you can buy a few of them to be sure."

"Oh." I hadn't even thought of that. "There are two in a pack."

"Buy three of the two-packs."

"What? Why do I need six tests?"

"Because if you are pregnant, you're going to be in shock and think the test is broken. You'll end up peeing on all of them."

My eyes scanned the boxes. Some had an automatic reading, some detected a pregnancy in five days, some seven. "You're probably right. But let's not say the P word anymore."

"I honestly don't know how I'm friends with you."

"I had a period, though," I said, still in denial.

Trying to steady my nerves, I reached for one of the tests Avery named.

"You can still bleed and be pregnant in the beginning. It's called spotting. A lot of people mistake it for a period."

"Oh." I grabbed one more box and then turned out of the aisle. Head down, I counted the tiles as I walked quickly to the front to pay. "Would it be weird if I peed on one here?"

"I mean, is that where you want to learn you're carrying a future Olympian?"

"I'm hanging up on you."

She laughed. "It wouldn't be weird, but just do it at home. That way you can cry in peace."

"I just want to get it over with. I'm nervous." Heart racing a mile a minute, I paid at the self-checkout then hurried to my truck and jumped in. I threw off my sunglasses and said, "I feel like I'm going to be sick."

"That's because—"

"Shut up. I don't find this funny. My future is going to be ruined."

"Kova should've wrapped up his magic stick because pull out and pray doesn't work."

I fought the smile. "I keep taking deep breaths but I feel like I can't catch my breath. My hands are shaking and I can't stop thinking that I'm going to see a pink line."

"It's two lines, and it's normal. You know I'm just playing with you."

"I know. I just, I don't know." I stumbled over my words.

Sighing, my mind raced with a million different thoughts.

"I took the Plan B, but the more I think about it, the more I think I took it too late. But then I keep thinking about how the doctors said it's supposedly really difficult to get pregnant and I can't figure out how this happened. How are you so calm and cracking jokes?"

"Because I've already gone through this and sometimes jokes help lighten the mood."

I softened at her unmoved tone. She was right and I appreciated that. "I can't believe you did this alone. I feel so bad I wasn't there for you."

Turning into my complex, I was such a mess as I parked. I didn't know what I would've done if she hadn't stayed on the phone with me the entire time, coaxing me to get dressed and go to the store. Remorse reared its ugly head beneath the nerves. I'd been a terrible friend, I didn't deserve this, but I also didn't think I'd be able to do this alone, and I think she knew that. I'd handled everything thrown at me so far, some things better than others, but this, this was the icing on the cake.

"Don't apologize. It was my decision. It is what it is, and I won't think about the past. No good comes from holding onto regrets anyway."

While she had a point, I'd always live with the guilt of her having no one to talk to and the traumatic experience she'd gone through on her own. Letting go and moving forward was a harder pill to swallow.

Once inside my condo, Avery said, "Get a cup you can pee in then throw out."

"Are you going to stay on the phone with me even when I pee?" I asked as I reached into the kitchen cabinet with a trembling hand and pulled out a plastic cup. I looked into it.

"Ah, yeah? I need to know if I'm going to be an aunt or not."

My movements slowed. "Ave…" I couldn't process that thought right now.

"I know," she said, regrettably, and that was enough. She knew. "Just go in the bathroom so we can FaceTime."

Tears climbed my eyes and they immediately streamed down my cheeks. "How could I have been so fucking stupid?"

"I don't have an answer for you, not one that would be an acceptable answer anyway. We both were really stupid, but so were the guys. I hate saying you forget your responsibilities in the heat of the moment, but you kind of do. Still, it's not a good reason to be irresponsible."

Glancing down at my feet, I slipped off my flip flops. The cold tile shot chills up my spine while I stood there wondering how I got myself into this mess.

"Next time tell Kova he needs to tie down that dinosaur. Use some saran wrap."

A loud laugh erupted from me. I wiped away my tears and grabbed the plastic bag and walked to the bathroom.

"I seriously can't believe I'm doing this."

"I seriously can't believe you're going to pee as you're FaceTiming me."

Switching my phone so she could see me, I placed it on the counter and looked at the screen.

"Ave?"

"Hayyyy." She smiled when she saw my face. "God, you look like shit. You're almost transparent."

"I've had better days." I joked. "Okay, let me pee and then I'll be right back."

Turning the phone to face the wall, I grabbed the cup and relieved myself. I flushed, still in shock that I was taking pregnancy tests. I fixed the camera to face me. Avery's faced pinched up. "That's your pee?" she asked once I placed the clear cup on the counter to wash my hands. "It's really dark." She looked closer, squinting. "Is that blood?

I looked at it briefly. "Probably. My pee can range from the color of a banana to cranberry juice."

Her face twisted up. "Gross."

"How long does it take for the test to show results?" I asked, opening the first box. My fingers trembled as I pulled out both tests and placed them on a towel next to the cup.

I expelled a heavy breath. What happened next could change everything and I wasn't sure I was prepared for it.

"They're all different. Mine came up really quickly. Open two boxes. Do the early result one and the automatic. We'll save the seven-day one for like a week from now just to be sure."

I nodded and did what she said. When I had all the sticks lined up next to each other, I stared at them with a weird range of feelings. I most definitely did not want to be pregnant, but what if there was a baby already growing inside of me? Could I get rid of it? I'd always thought I could, but now that I was faced with the seriousness of the situation, I wasn't sure anymore. I had a plan, and that plan didn't include having a baby until I was married and at least twenty-six.

"What are you thinking?" Avery asked softly.

"That everything is fucked up and that my life is about to change. That I don't know what I'm supposed to feel right now. I'm giving myself a headache."

"This is what I want you to do. Dip the stick in the cup for a few seconds, then cap it and place it down. Don't wait, just move on to the next until you're done. Go get a drink of water or whatever it is you drink, and then go back and check the results. Don't hover. You're going to make yourself pass out waiting for the results with the way you're already hyperventilating."

I lifted my eyes to her and paused. Laughing, I hadn't realized I was panting so hard, but man, my nerves were shot. This was a moment of truth, and as eager as I was to find out, I was more terrified than anything.

"I'm scared," I said quietly.

Her eyes softened. "You can do two back flips with a bunch of crazy twists at the same time, run eighty miles an hour toward a table and flip over it, but this scares you?"

I shrugged one shoulder. "Yeah, a little."

Taking one last deep breath, I shook my fingers out and uncapped the first stick, dipping it in the urine for a few seconds. Recapping it, I moved on making sure I didn't look at the previous one until I was done with all four. Avery stayed quiet, watching me. Even though she was hundreds of miles away, I felt like she was right next to me, giving me strength. I needed that more than anything.

Once I finished the fourth one, I grabbed my phone as vomit climbed the back of my throat. I spewed into the toilet, dry heaving until I could barely catch my breath since there was nothing in my stomach to come up.

"This time I know it's your nerves," Avery said, slightly muffled.

Every so often her sassy southern belle side came out and gave me a good chuckle. I turned to look and realized I was covering the phone with my hand. Thank goodness. She didn't need to see me throwing up. Flushing the toilet, I wiped my face and crawled to sit against the bathtub. I brought my knees up and placed my arms on them.

"I don't want to look," I said in all honesty. And I didn't. Tears filled my eyes and I shook my head. "I don't want to look, Ave. I don't want to."

Her face fell, crippling with sadness. "I wish I was there with you," she said softly. "I'd look for you."

"I wish you could. How long has it been?"

"Like thirty seconds."

My jaw dropped. "That's it? It feels like forever."

She smiled sadly. "Yeah, that's how I felt too."

I looked above the phone at the counter and grimaced.

"What's wrong," she asked.

"My pee is more red than yellow from here. Do you think that could alter the test?"

"No, it shouldn't. It's looking for a specific hormone."

"Damn. I was hoping you would say yes."

"Wishful thinking." She paused. "Ready?"

I shook my head, eyeing the counter. My bathroom was so icy cold I started shivering. I held myself. It was the last thing I wanted to do.

"I can't remember a time when I've been so nervous. I'm terrified, Ave. I really don't want to look. I feel like I already know the answer."

I held my stomach. It was so flat.

Avery expressed her sorrow. "Just rip the Band-Aid off and do it."

"I can't believe I called to joke that I was dying and it turned into taking pregnancy tests."

"Definitely not what I expected, that's for sure."

Standing up, I tiptoed toward the counter.

"Pretend I'm there holding your hand," she said, and I swallowed and looked into the phone as I stopped in front of what could change my life forever. "Look at the counter, Aid," my best friend encouraged gently.

My lips were a thin, flat line as I shook my head. Tears spilled from the corners of my eyes into my mouth and I could taste the saltiness.

"Come on, bestie." She had tears in her eyes too.

Finally, I looked.

Chills racked my body as my eyes moved from one test to the other. My lungs ached with each result as I struggled to breathe. I was dizzy and light-headed and staring with wide eyes in absolute shock until my vision blurred.

"Avery?" I said, my voice cracking.

Kidney disease wasn't going to kill me, a heart attack was.

I skimmed the row of tests again and all the lines in utter disbelief.

"What does it say?" she begged, but I couldn't find the words. I didn't want to say it out loud because then it would make it real. "Aid? Say something, please."

I told her.

"Christ on a fucking stick."

chapter 57

I CRIED FOR AN HOUR STRAIGHT AFTER I COUNTED TWO SETS OF POSITIVE lines.

I checked every few minutes hoping they would change. The parallel lines were solid and bright, except for the automatic two that clearly read pregnant.

Pregnant. How was I pregnant? More importantly, how did I let this happen?

Avery listened, and I loved her even more for it. She let me vent through the tears, even though I was a bawling mess of denial and heartbreak. She didn't try to hang up on me. She acted like she was right next to me as if I was crying on her shoulder. She was the perfect best friend, which made me feel even more like shit since I hadn't been there for her in her moment of need.

"How, Avery? How?" I asked for the millionth time and grabbed another tissue.

"I mean, I feel like you know how it happens at this point."

"What am I going to do? I can't tell my dad, and I definitely can't have a baby either. That leaves me with one option."

Avery was quiet for a little while. Gently, she said, "What do you want?"

"It's not that easy to answer."

"If you didn't need a kidney, what would you do?"

"I still can't have a baby. My dad would never accept it."

"If he did?"

My face felt so swollen and the exhaustion from crying and the stress of the truth was a growing pressure on my chest. Her question wasn't cut and dry, and neither was my answer.

"I wish I could go back and change things. I wish I could go back and be smarter."

"Don't think about the past, it'll do you no good. Trust me. Think about the future and what you need to do."

Avery was right, but it was hard to do that when I was staring at all these tests telling me I was carrying a child.

Kova's child.

Our child.

Tears blurred my vision again and I started crying. In a rush, I scooped up the boxes and sticks and dumped them into the trash. The sticks stuck out of the garbage, but I didn't care. I took the last box and placed it between the towels in my bathroom closet. I couldn't stand to look at it any longer.

I rinsed my face with cool water, then dried it. Avery watched but didn't say anything, she just looked as sad as I felt. Lifting my shirt, I focused on my stomach, rubbing it in circles.

"How is there a baby in there?" I asked, more so speaking to myself.

"Technically it's a fetus."

"Whatever. Same thing, really."

"Yeah. Once the heart started beating, I viewed it differently."

I dropped my shirt, wishing I could reverse time. "When's that?"

"Six weeks."

I averted my gaze and thought back to when this could've happened. Staring at the bottles of perfume I never wore, I blindly read over the lush labels without really processing the words.

"How do I figure out how pregnant I am?"

Avery chuckled and covered her mouth. I glanced at her and saw regret fill her blue eyes.

"What? What's so funny?"

"It's how far along you are, not how pregnant you are. You're pregnant. That's it. Nothing more, nothing less. You're totally preggo. It's based on your last period, but since that's all messed up, when did you guys last have sex?"

My stomach knotted. I didn't want to think about that because there was a good chance the baby's heart was already beating, and remaining oblivious was just easier.

If I heard a heartbeat, would it change my mind?

The thought chilled me to the bone and a rush of emotions sucker punched me in my chest.

Licking my dry lips, I sniffled. "Never mind, I don't want to know. That'll just make it harder."

"You should call Kova," Avery suggested with a sugary tone.

"What? Why? No."

Her brows puckered together. "Aren't you going to tell him?"

"No. I think I'm just going to have an abortion."

The silence was earsplitting.

My heart dropped.

Reality set in and we were both still as we looked at each other, our expression mirroring each other's.

I'd already made my decision without processing it until just now.

I was eighteen, and I was going to have an abortion.

My chest deflated, lungs ached for air. The response was so fluid it caught me by surprise. The consequences for having unprotected sex and being irresponsible. Tears filled my eyes again, and my jaw trembled. I knew I'd regret this choice for the rest of my life. Yet the words spilled from my lips because I also knew what I had to do all along.

"I can't have a baby. I'm too young... right? I've come too far for that." A sob escaped me. "I know that's so selfish of me, but I just can't," I whispered, thinking it would lessen my decision. "I just can't," I paused, then told her how I really felt. "I can't imagine actually getting rid of it either."

"You have to tell him," she said softly.

"I don't want to. He's married, and he once said some harsh things about me getting pregnant and what he would do."

Avery groaned into the phone. She knew what I was talking about and she didn't like it.

"Stop thinking about the past. Think about how far you guys have come, how much you guys have grown. Regardless of what his choice is, he still needs to know. It's his right. Don't not tell him. You'll only regret it and then you'll have to live with that regret."

I sighed inwardly. Quietly, I said, "I know I need to tell him. Eventually I will."

"It sucks, Aid. Every day I blame myself for not pushing harder to talk things out with Xavier. It's horrible. Plus, you're going to need time to rest anyway. He has to know."

"Rest?"

"You'll need some time off for bed rest. When I miscarried, I had to rest for a good week or so. I had so much bleeding and my stomach killed me. The cramps are way worse than a period. There's no way you can practice like that."

"Bed rest?" My voice peaked. "But you were further along than me. Maybe I won't need that."

"I think after a specific number of weeks you have to have a procedure done. But I could be wrong. I couldn't just bleed everything out, I had to have it sucked out."

My lips parted in disbelief and I shook my head hastily. Sucked out sounded terrifying and dehumanizing. I wouldn't let it get that far. There was literally no time left in my schedule for bed rest, let alone a procedure. I had one international meet left where the team was selected, and then by some miracle, the Olympics. Two months max until it was all over. No time to rest. Not until after the Games, if I got to them.

"Two months until everything I've worked for is over. After that, I'll figure it out."

Her eyes widened. "Aid, that's a terrible idea. Probably the dumbest one you've had to date. You don't even know how far along you are. Maybe you can just take a pill or something—there are abortion pills—but waiting is not a good idea."

"I can't tell him," I panicked. "I'm not telling him. I'll just go to a clinic or something. I can't go to my regular doctor either. They'll have to tell my dad and he can't know. I'll search for a place online."

I swear she paled. Avery's face moved closer to the screen. "Listen to me. You're making a huge mistake. Tell him, Adrianna."

"I—"

"And you can't just go to some random clinic." Her voice rose, and I felt the alarm in her words. "Don't be stupid."

I rubbed my face, closing my eyes. "What a mess. I don't know what I'm going to do. I mean, I do, ugh. This really sucks."

"Start by telling him and go from there. He has a right to know," she urged softly. "Please, if you never listen to me again, make this the one time you do."

"He's going to be angry."

My stomach knotted tighter just thinking about telling him. I didn't even know where to begin, how to start the conversation, I couldn't fathom a response that would be less than negative. There was no right way to tell Kova I was pregnant with his child.

Avery's voice was strained. "You don't know that. And if you don't do this properly, you could risk having issues with future pregnancies. Don't be stupid."

I looked down. "Maybe that's a good thing," I said, my voice low. "It's what I deserve."

"Don't say that."

"It's true," I replied a little louder. "I fooled around with my coach, I slept with a married man, and I let it happen. I *wanted* it to happen. This is really my fault and what I get. It's Karma."

"You didn't make him do anything he didn't want."

"But I did. That's the thing. I pushed him since the beginning. Since the very first encounter, it was all me. I mean, he's obviously no saint, but I pursued him. In the back of my mind, I was making it so he couldn't say no. I went after him so many times, Ave." My chin quivered with guilt. I was a terrible, terrible person.

"Aid, listen to me. It's easy to blame yourself during a time like this, but it's not all you. Kova didn't do anything he didn't want to do. Even if you didn't make the choice easy on him, he still didn't have to keep it going. One time is a mistake. Two times is reckless. Three times is a choice. A conscious decision at that. He didn't have to keep it going, he chose to."

I looked at my best friend, thanking her for talking it out with me.

Taking a deep breath, I pulled myself upright from the floor of the bathroom and walked into the kitchen and placed my phone near my medicine bottles. I tied my hair up into a messy bun, then picked the bottles up one by one and uncapped them, pouring out the pills into a pile.

Avery was absolutely right, but I still held the fault for inviting it to happen and not stopping it from continuing. There was something too alluring about Kova I couldn't deny, and I didn't know why. He once told me I was the flame and he was the moth, but I couldn't help thinking it was the other way around. If we both felt that way, then a bigger, larger flame spread over time destroyed things in its path and was harder to put out.

I filled up a glass of water and placed it on the counter. Liquid splashed onto the marble. "I'm sure all these pills aren't good to take while pregnant. Maybe that's why I had my period, but it was actually a miscarriage and I didn't know."

"Only going to the doctor will tell you that. I think you would bleed heavily, like more than usual, and you would have severe cramping. You'd know the difference."

I sighed, filled with exhaustion. "What am I going to do? This is all so fucked." I scooped the pills up and swallowed them all at once.

One corner of her mouth tugged up to the side. "You know what you have to do," she said, and I nodded.

She was right, again. I couldn't not tell Kova, but how the hell did I even begin?

"I love you, Ave. I don't know what I'd do without you."

She fake flipped her hair. "Well, duh. That's because I'm the bestest friend ever. So when do you think you will? I hope sooner rather than later."

I shrugged. "I really don't know. Maybe after practice tomorrow."

Her brows rose. "You better text me ASAP the moment you do."

We said our goodbyes and I spent the rest of the afternoon agonizing over my current situation on the internet. It was a terrible idea, but I couldn't stop myself from looking things up, kind of how I did when I'd found out I had lupus and kidney disease. It made everything ten times worse but I couldn't help it.

I tossed and turned all night, sleep evading me, and when my alarm went off the next morning, I almost called in.

Instead, I got out of bed and went on with my normal routine. I was going to muster up the strength to tell Kova, but also make sure I stayed focused on my dream. He'd understand.

One day I'd have kids, just not now.

Until then, I would mourn the child I would soon give up with the man I loved.

chapter 58

MY FIRST THOUGHT WHEN I WALKED INTO WORLD CUP AND SAW Kova was that he would be a hot-as-hell dad.

He had his hat on, this time facing in the right direction, and a heather gray and black baseball type tee that hugged his arms, and paired with his typical black shorts. It was hard not to stare at the cuts and curves of his biceps.

He made my heart pound so hard and a stupid number of butterflies in my stomach swirl ridiculously fast into each other. Kova lifted a folding mat and dragged it across the floor, creating rows for conditioning. I imagined a baby on his hip—not mine—and what he'd look like. He'd be so cute, probably insanely possessive, but deeply in love with his child who he'd teach gymnastics. I could see him explaining his actions and why he was always right, and how he was being a bossy coach with his child because he'd want the best for him.

Kova glanced up and our eyes locked. A different kind of smile pulled at his lips, one that said we were good, like he was happy for once. Go figure. The times that he's happy, I'm dying inside. I swallowed back my emotions and forced myself to return the smile.

He crossed the distance and my chest ached with each step that brought him closer to me. I could already smell his cologne, thanks to my heightened pregnancy senses that I'd learned about online, and it created a steady sensation of desire through me.

I wouldn't tell him today. I couldn't.

"How do you feel?" he asked. "You look a little tired. Did you want to stay home again?"

I shook my head and picked at my nails. I chewed on my lip, trying to fight the panic rising inside me. "Better. I slept all day yesterday."

He eyed me curiously, a shadow from his hat cast over half his face. "You are beautiful," he said softly, accepting my answer. A little smirk formed on his succulent mouth.

Before he could say another word, I stood on my tiptoes and reached for him. My emotions—probably the anxiety of needing to tell him—rose to the top before I realized what was happening. Palming his cheeks, I pulled his face to mine and smashed my mouth to his.

He lifted the lip of his hat and pushed it up, then wrapped his arms around my back and stepped closer to me. Kova let out a little moan as he returned the kiss. He always gave back even better. It was his way of showing me how he felt. His large hands roamed my back, skimming to my butt before he grabbed a chunk and held on. My fingers threaded the hair at the back of his neck as his tongue slipped past the seam of my lips and tangled around mine. He kissed me like he was hungry, like he couldn't get his fill. He was fighting for us and each lap of his tongue was a greater pull to what he wanted but ultimately may never have.

Still holding me, Kova broke the kiss, leaving my breathless. He glanced at my lips, then bit one. It was the little things like this that made me fall deeper for him, but it also helped me decide that today just wasn't the day to drop the ball.

"You're a lover, not a fighter."

He smirked, brows furrowed. "What made you think of that?"

"By the way you kiss. I can feel it."

He seemed content with my answer. "Life is too short to fight. Unless, of course, we fight during sex." His eyes heated with the thought. "Then, I am up to fighting."

My head fell back and a laugh rolled out of me before I could stop it. He dipped his head, his nose tickling my neck. I felt the outline of his smile under my ear. Kova pressed into me and I stepped back until I felt the wall against my back. Heat zoomed down my spine as his chest pushed into me, the warmth of his strong body brought a sense of security and love I so desperately needed.

"Like when we made love again for the first time after so long, when you were throwing things at me, when you tried to cut me..." He emphasized the last words and I laughed. "When you *did* cut me. As much as we both hurt that day, and as much as I loved every minute, I never want to fight with you again like that. So, yes, maybe I am a lover, but I am only a lover for you, and I am only a fighter for you." Kova looked down. "I thought I'd lost you for good during that horrible time. I never want it to happen again."

I swallowed. Yeah, definitely not telling him today.

Quietly, I said, "I don't think it's possible to lose me."

The corners of his eyes softened. "Same. Now, let me fuck you before practice starts."

A loud laugh burst from my chest. "No," rolled off my lips. He made me so happy and I wondered if he even knew that. "Way to ruin the moment with your quick fuck."

Kova whimpered. "You cannot come in like this and kiss me and expect me not to want more. I feel like I just woke up next to you, and you know how much I want that. To see you supple and soft like you are now, and be able to wake up balls deep inside you, to feel you squeeze around my dick, hear your soft little sighs… There is nothing I want more than that."

He made my heart pound wishing for that.

"You only want me for my pussy."

His eyes flared with desire. "Among other things."

I tried not to smile at his response. I knew he was teasing me, but it was doing the trick and making me not think about the larger issue at hand.

"You're such a smooth talker."

"I have my moments. So what do you say, yes? I can pull up your leg like this." His voice dropped as he got lower and hooked my thigh around his hip. "Then I can move your shorts aside and take you quick and fast like this," he said, pulling the material to one side and teasing my bare flesh with his fingers. I'd worn small shorts, a sports bra, and a tank top today. "Or I can lift you up and take you quick but slow right here in my gym." He groaned at the thought of his own words. "Slow because I need to feel every inch of your sweet body. You know I am already hard for you." He pushed one long finger inside and I gasped. "I feel you clenching around me," he said, kissing me. His tongue making me crazy with lust. "Come on, let me have you," he begged, and it was pretty cute.

"No." My response came out a little more breathless than I wanted. "But maybe before I leave tonight," I said, pushing my hips into his hand. Damn traitorous body.

His exaggerated groan was one of epic proportions. "You are going to kill me. How the fuck am I going to wait until then? You should just let me fuck you." He chuckled. "It will not take long."

I ignored his annoyingly right comment and reached between us, slipping my hand beneath the elastic of his shorts to find his bare cock rock solid. Kova grabbed my wrist.

I squeezed. "Still no boxers, I see."

"Never," he said between clenched teeth. "Plus, I like catching you checking out my dick. I will never wear them for that reason alone."

My cheeks flamed. "I do not."

"You do, and you know it makes me fucking hard every time." He tightened his hold. "You had your chance, now you have to wait until tonight."

Frustrated, I leaned in and bit his lip until I tasted blood. I moaned, lapping at the tiny crimson droplets. Kova's cock twitched in my hand and I felt a wave of pleasure roll through his body. I loved that he loved what I did.

"Tonight, I fuck you in here."

"I bailed," I said quietly into the phone.

I don't even know why I whispered when I was alone and no one else could hear me.

"On who?" Avery asked.

"Kova."

"Ohhh," she responded. "Why did you dip out on Fish Lips?"

"We were supposed to have sex after practice. When he wasn't looking, I ran."

Avery chuckled. "Let me guess, you didn't tell him about the spawn."

I shook my head, fighting a grin. I was almost home. "Nope."

"How was practice anyway now that you're carrying a little Russian hothead?"

This time I laughed. "Avery…" I groaned. "It was so stressful, and I don't know why. I'm not keeping the baby, so it shouldn't have bothered me, but I kept thinking I'm going to hurt it, so I hesitated a lot."

She was quiet for a moment. "I think that's normal. Do you think Kova noticed?"

"He notices everything, so I played it off and used my disease as an excuse."

"Who knew kidney disease would come in handy for once. So what are you going to do now when he goes looking for you and you're MIA?"

I sighed into the phone. "I don't know. I guess I'm just going to tell him I'm not feeling well."

"And you think he's going to buy it," she stated, clearly not sold on my lie.

"Yes, but that's only because he knows I'm sick and doesn't want anything to happen to me."

I pulled into my complex, grabbed my things, and made my way upstairs.

"You really need to just tell him, Aid," she said softly.

"I know. I really was going to when I got to practice, but then I saw him, Ave, and I imagined him with a baby. It fucked with my head."

She hummed under her breath. "He would look really good with a baby."

"Drool worthy. See? The words evaded me and I didn't know if I should just blurt it out or ease my way into the conversation, and then I decided to kiss him…"

She giggled. "I know it's easier said than done, but the longer you wait, the harder it will be. The anxiety will eat you away."

I already felt like that now. Once I was in my condo, I dropped my stuff to the floor and sat on the couch. I exhaled a sigh and listened to the silence for a second. "Yeah," I said a little out of breath.

I glanced down at my stomach, still in awe that I was pregnant. I placed my hand on my belly, fearing my next question. "Ave? What if this is the only time I can get pregnant?"

"You can't look at it like that. If it happened while you were training like a damn lunatic, then you should be able to in the future when you're a normal person again. Plus, there's a whole slew of drugs you can take to help you conceive."

I thought about what I had to do and how disheartened I was feeling over the choice I had made. It made me sick. I never really had a view on abortion, not until Avery told me she had one, and now that I was faced with the same decision myself, it was proving to be much harder than I thought. I could not have a baby, but I was quickly learning I didn't like the thought of having an abortion either. I was stuck in the worst predicament of my life with no right choice. Everyone was going to get hurt because of my recklessness.

I sighed inwardly. I felt myself starting to slip into a dark hole of depression and I fought it. There was no time in my schedule to climb my way out of that dingy hole. I'd just done it a few months ago.

"It's going to be really hard, and one of the most difficult moments of your life," she said sympathetically. "You'll feel better about it once you tell him. I can sit here and crack jokes, tell you what to say, but I know firsthand how difficult it really is. The anxiety of it alone will kill you. You're going to try a few times until one day it just comes out."

I wrapped a protective arm around my stomach. "He's going to be so mad."

"I have this really weird feeling he won't be, but even if he is mad, at least you told him. You'll feel better telling him in the long run. Then you can go ahead and schedule whatever you need, and I'll be there with you when it happens."

I swallowed. "You're going to drive over and come with me?"

"Of course, you dumbass. I love you."

My phone beeped and I pulled it away to see a text message come in from Kova. My heart dropped. I knew he'd look for me.

"I gotta go, Kova is texting me."

"Just so you know, I wouldn't recommend telling him over text."

I chuckled. Right before we hung up, I said. "Believe me, I wasn't planning on it."

Coach: Where did you disappear to? I was looking for you.

I chewed my lip trying to conjure up a good lie that would suffice.

I'm not feeling well. I think I'm having a flare up and just needed to go home. I'm sorry.

I held my breath and waited for him to respond. Hopefully he bought it, but I expected him not to.

Coach: Your health is more important. Get the rest you need, and if you need more time, just let me know. Can I bring you some dinner?

I quickly replied with a no thank you and threw the phone down onto my couch. Rolling over onto my side, I cried myself to sleep over the things I had no ability to change.

chapter 59

I PURPOSELY WENT INTO PRACTICE LATE SO KOVA COULDN'T TALK TO ME. Well, twenty minutes late, but it was enough to aggravate him for the rest of the day.

It didn't help that I was terribly nauseous. Either from the pregnancy or because I was nervous as hell to tell Kova, I wasn't sure. All the times I'd thrown up since the last meet could really be from either one. My stomach was all sorts of messed up.

Tonight I'd tell him I was pregnant.

His eyes found mine the moment I stepped into the gym, but I quickly averted my gaze and started stretching. My first thought was that I would play my lateness off since he had said if I needed extra time to rest I could take it, but I also knew I was required to tell him in advance if I was.

"Adrianna. Three miles," he ordered with a bite then turned away from me.

My jaw plummeted to my stomach but there was nothing I could say or do since he was my coach, so I got up, went into the locker room, got my clothes and running shoes on, then went outside. I did a few stretches so I wouldn't irritate my Achilles. It wasn't healed and it wouldn't be until I had surgery, but I would almost go as far as to say it was in remission with the pain and inflammation. No new tears thankfully, and while I hadn't needed a blading session recently, I knew Kova would want to do one before I went to Italy for the meet. It did give me a little pep in my step and Lord knew I could use that right now, and before the biggest gymnastics competition of my life.

The moment my feet hit the pavement, I forced myself to run the three miles straight without stopping. By the time I got back to World Cup, I was winded and in dire need of using the bathroom. I was all cool and collected until I noticed the toilet water was tinted pink.

My sad reality. Either it was just spotting, or I was miscarrying and I didn't know it. I padded myself with some toilet paper but there was no blood.

Confused, I did it again with the same outcome when it hit me that it could actually be my kidneys causing the blood. It was a common symptom of chronic kidney disease.

Anger filled my eyes with tears but I inhaled them back and flushed the toilet. Shaking my head and fingers, I stepped out of the bathroom only to come face to face with a very annoyed Kova.

"Hey," I said, pulling back. I frowned. "Were you waiting for me?"

Kova's green eyes glared down at me and I recoiled. "Do not take advantage of my kindness, Adrianna. You will not walk all over me just because I am sympathetic to your health. If you need something, tell me, but do not show up late and assume you can do what you please without clearing it with me first."

My jaw bobbed. I was a little offended he thought I would take advantage like that, especially after everything. I tried to explain myself, but he cut me off and started speaking again. His Russian accent was thicker this time, and that only happened when he was furious.

"You have ten working days left and that is it. Two weeks until we board the plane." He emphasized the time. "And only one shot left. Let us make it count. We are going to be doing two-a-days until we leave, with the weekend to recoup. Unless you tell me otherwise, you will be here on time and ready to practice."

Mouth shut, I nodded. After all, he was right. I'd purposely showed up to practice late and it worked against me.

He dipped his head and stepped closer. "Inside these walls we are coach and gymnast. Outside, you are Adrianna Francesca Rossi and I am Konstantin Kournakova, and you are my life, but until the day comes when I can claim you in public, we cannot allow anything to deviate us from the goal."

Without saying a word, I stepped around him and walked right into the gym.

I loved him and hated him so much.

All week I'd worked my ass off. Kova and Madeline dished it out and then some. Neither coach went easy on me, which I loved. I hadn't felt that strain in so long, that soreness in all the hidden places. Sure, I'd been uncomfortable and tired and hardly able to walk by the time I got home. Mentally, it was exactly what I'd needed. I refused to allow my exhausting diseases that had the power to cripple me stand in my way. They wouldn't win. There were a few times I'd felt myself slipping and Kova was right there, talking it out of me, but making sure I was okay at the same time.

He'd been right. Now was my time and I had to make it count.

That didn't mean I wasn't dying by the end of the night and nearly crippled in the morning. A little dramatic, maybe, but Jesus, I felt bruised and battered.

I soaked in Epsom baths, had Kova do deep tissue massages, and I even made sure to stay on the special diet for my illnesses. I never missed a dose of medicine either. By night, I welcomed my bed with open arms, and in the mornings I was greeted by the toilet. Morning sickness was no joke. One thing I was looking forward to being over was the constant vomiting that came with the sunrise. It was weird how the timing worked with that.

By Friday, I was counting down the hours until I got the next two days off. I'd looked into cupping, something that was supposed to be divine for sore muscles with lactic acid buildup. It pulled the skin from the underlying muscle to stimulate blood flow, which produced a faster recovery, but I wasn't sure I was ready for the little flaming cups of fire to be suctioned and dragged on me just yet. I'd ask Kova and see what he had to say. We could do a test run and see how it went.

"Hey," Kova said as I was eating lunch in the café. I felt his energy enter the room before I felt him.

I looked up, chewing an apple slice from my spinach salad. "What's up?"

He glanced over his shoulder then pulled out a chair to sit down. My brows furrowed and I eyed him curiously.

Kova leaned over and placed his elbows on his knees. "Come away with me this weekend."

My eyes popped and I almost choked on my food. "What?"

"There is this little town I want to take you to about an hour away."

The creases between my brows deepened and I slowly swallowed the bite I'd been chewing. "Is there something wrong with you?"

Kova released a full grin and dropped his head for a second. His back shook with a chuckle. He looked back up, smiling. "We already know I am not sane."

I tried not to laugh. "Isn't that the truth. But how are you going to slip away without Katja knowing?" I wanted to say Cuntja like Avery had, but I withheld.

He brushed it away like it was no issue. He didn't want to talk about her with me and I didn't blame him, but it was the first thing I thought of. I wondered how he was going to continue his infidelity on his day off if his wife was around.

"So what do you say? Stay tonight after everyone leaves and have dinner with me. I will order whatever you want, and then tomorrow, or Sunday," he offered, "we can go to this little town. Let me take you there. It is just for the day."

I placed my fork down and pushed my salad away. Kova slid it back in front of me. "Eat," he said.

We'd never gone anywhere together. "Why do you want to take me there?"

"You have been very distant with me this week and I do not want that."

"I've been a little busy working my ass off, you know..." I averted my gaze.

I had a reason to be distant, besides trying to keep my focus on gymnastics when the idea hit me.

Maybe I could finally tell him my secret tonight. He wouldn't want to take me anywhere after that, and it would give us a few days apart. There was no way he would receive the news of his child any other way but negative.

He continued, trying to drive his case home. "I know. This is the last weekend before the meet that you will be free for a long time. I am selfish enough to say I want you to myself. Think about it, but at least eat with me tonight. Can you give me that?"

Chewing my lip, I nodded. "Okay."

Kova's hand slapped the table and he bounced up. I smiled at his excitement, feeling a little good to see him so happy over something so miniscule, even though I was going to ruin everything tonight.

Leaning in, he cupped the back of my neck and dropped a kiss to my forehead. I froze with his lips on me, and so did he.

"You can't do that here, Kova," I whispered.

He dropped his hand and took one step back. "I know. I was not thinking. See you later," he said, then walked out of the café.

I watched him leave, wondering what had come over him and if he was serious when he'd said he wanted me to himself for my last free weekend. I knew what he was talking about—he was hopeful I'd be chosen for the Olympic team. If I was, I'd be shipped off to the training center for four weeks—with Kova—to train for the Games with the Olympic coaches.

Thinking about that made me realize I had two choices: Tell Kova tonight that I was pregnant, or keep it a secret until it was all over.

There were a total of seven weeks from today until I left the Games, if I got lucky. Seven weeks of anxiety I had to deal with, or get it over with tonight.

Glancing down at my flat stomach, fear furled inside my chest like a bad omen. I wasn't sure when bellies started to grow, but I prayed mine wouldn't anytime soon.

What was more distressing was I had no idea how far along I was to anticipate such a thing, but that was something I didn't want to know.

My only worry was I hoped the heart wasn't already beating.

chapter 60

"WHY DID YOU WANT TO HAVE DINNER?" I ASKED AFTER everyone left for the evening.

Yawning, I was sitting on the comfy couch in his office. I didn't have an appetite and I wasn't sure how I was going to eat to cover that up. All I wanted to do was go home and crash, not divulge the dirty little secret I was carrying. I glanced down at my stomach feeling a bit of remorse for calling it a dirty little secret.

"Why not?" he responded, as if my question was so odd.

I looked up, feeling defensive for reasons I couldn't explain. "I don't know, because we never do?"

"That is why I wanted to."

I frowned, watching as Kova placed the paper bag on his desk and removed the contents. When he'd asked what I was in the mood for, I'd told him whatever he wanted. Food was the last thing on my mind.

"What else?"

He paused and stood straight. Kova looked directly in my eyes, and said, "Because you have been working hard and I feel a little distant from you. That is why."

My shoulders relaxed. He was being honest and it wasn't fair of me to be rude. "Thank you," I said.

Kova carried over the containers and we sat face to face. There was nowhere to really eat in the gym besides the café, but that felt too sterile.

Once I took a bite, my appetite came roaring back. I didn't eat too much of the steamed vegetables and fresh salmon baked in an almond butter sauce, only until I felt the first hint at being full. We took pieces of each other's food until I was full and Kova polished off the rest of mine along with his.

"This office gets a lot of action," I joked.

I curled up into the corner of the couch and nestled my cheek into the cushions with a dreamy smile. All week I'd been on edge and stressed out. Tonight, I was at peace and I wasn't sure if it was because I knew I had no choice in what I was about to say, or because being around Kova settled my nerves.

Kova got up and placed me in his lap with my back to his chest. He let out a sigh as he wrapped his strong arms around me. He kissed my temple. My eyes closed and I settled into him.

"I have been waiting all day to do this," he said in a low voice, and I chuckled. "What is so funny?"

"I was thinking that same exact thing."

"Great minds think alike."

I smiled and relished in the simplicity of how easy we were, how I totally understood when Kova said he simply did not want to say goodbye, because when there were moments like this, I didn't want to either.

"You have been awfully quiet? What is on your mind?"

My throat tightened.

So much.

Everything.

I didn't know where to begin, but I knew this was it. This was when I would tell him that where his hands were currently on my stomach, there was a life growing inside that we'd created. A life that would never be able to live.

"Nothing, really. I'm fine."

"You said fine. Now I know you have something on your mind," he said with a mixture of playfulness and unease. "Are you nervous about the meet? Because I truly feel like you have nothing to be worried about. You are a shoo-in."

"No," I said quietly.

For once I wasn't panicked about a meet. I was confident. Just thinking about walking out with my coaches, and in my crystal-encrusted leotard, as a top-ranking competitor for one of the four coveted spots on the United States Women's Olympic Gymnastics team caused a flurry of anxious dragonflies to swarm my chest. I was beyond excited for next weekend and the days couldn't come fast enough.

"Did something happen at the doctor regarding your kidneys?"

"No."

He let out a whoosh. "Thank God. Did you have a fight with Avery?"

"No."

Silence filled the room. Kova gave me a little squeeze and settled in closer to me. He was trying to dissect what was going on in my head, but he'd never guess.

I remained quiet, searching for the right words to start the conversation. I wanted to blurt it out just to get it over with, but at the same time, I was terrified.

"Ria?" His voice was thick with worry. "What is wrong? You are worrying me?"

My entire body started shaking, my breathing intensified. Kova tried to turn to face me, but I stopped him and gave him more of my back. I couldn't look at him while I did this. I didn't want to see the look in his eyes when I told him I was pregnant. Would he be relieved I was going to get an abortion? Angry I was pregnant in the first place? Or shock me completely and be disappointed with my decision? My heart raced so fast, my dinner was as heavy as a concrete block in my stomach, threatening to come back up.

"I thought you forgot about that name," I said, my voice thick with emotion.

"Is that why you are so bothered? I can use it more. I worried it came with bad memories, and I was trying to avoid those."

"No," I said, this time tears filled my eyes.

"Why can you not look at me, Adrianna? You are scaring me."

I grew warm, heat bubbling over my entire body. Oh, God. There was no way I could do this. I just couldn't. Avery was wrong. Kova didn't need to know. There was no reason for him to know, it would only cause more unnecessary heartache.

"Please, look at me."

"I…" I started. "I need…"

"What do you need? I will give it to you."

My chest ached from the pounding it took from my heart. I shook my head and dragged in a taxing breath, trying to pull up even a sliver of courage to tell him, but I was struggling to find it. This had to be the hardest thing I'd ever had to do in my life.

"Do you remember when you asked me if my back was up against a wall with a decision that could change my life, what would I do?"

Kova was quiet before he answered in a low voice. "Yes."

"Well…" I began and swallowed as my body roasted with trepidation. "It's my turn to ask that. If you were backed up against a wall with a decision that could change your life, what would you do?"

Kova's body turned to stone under me.

"What do you need to tell me?"

"Answer the question."

Kova rambled in Russian.

"Answer the question, Kova," I said again with a little bite this time.

"No," he said, breathless. "I invented this game. Now tell me what you are hiding."

Tears spilled from my eyes and I shot up from his lap. A gush of air expelled from my lungs. I started pacing his office, staring at the floor wishing it would open up and remove me from this cruel world of anxiety that suffocated me. My chest was so tight, strict with lack of air, and my heart was such a mess I thought I was going to vomit.

Kova stood up and tried to come to me but I wouldn't allow it. I put up my hand to stop him.

Grabbing my keys and cell phone from his desk, I made a beeline for the door. He was quick, though, and slammed it shut. I held my breath and felt his chest to my back and his arm wrap possessively around my hips. There wasn't an ounce of anger coming from Kova and while that was relieving, it was also terrifying, because if he knew the truth, I don't think he'd touch me. I clenched my eyes shut, wishing I had the strength to tell him.

"Let me leave," I begged, barely above a whisper.

He forced me to turn around to face him, but I couldn't look. I stared at his chest, ashamed.

Kova lifted my chin, forcing me to meet his gaze. "What are you hiding?" he asked, his heart clearly holding those words. His frantic eyes searched mine for a clue. "Did you fuck Hayden again? Because I swear on my dead mother's grave…"

Shaking my head, I was offended he would think that, even though I knew he was still sleeping with his wife. "No, you lunatic."

"Then what is it?"

"What would you do?" I asked again, going back to my original question he'd avoided.

Kova exhaled. His gaze lifted above my head as his eyes searched for the right words. Then he looked back down. "I guess I would do exactly what you said to me when I asked you that. Now do you understand why I did what I did? Why I had no choice? Why I hid the unwanted marriage?"

I nodded, my lips a flat line coated with salty tears. Sorrow filled his green eyes. His words dripping like melting wax. I got it, even though I hated it more than anything.

"To tell the person you love that you are marrying someone else causes a stairway of turmoil so bad that no one could ever anticipate. I did not even realize I loved you then, but I could not stand to see you suffer, so I thought I could hide it. I thought I would find a way to divorce her before you could know, but I had nothing. In the end, I was not strong enough to admit it to you." He paused. "Is whatever you are holding in why you have been distant with me?"

My eyes searched his hoping he'd see the truth.

"Stop telling me you love me. I can't handle it."

He looked so wounded. His green eyes pierced me with immense grief and for a split second I felt bad I asked him that. Kova swallowed and his Adam's apple bobbed like he was struggling to breathe.

"No, I will not stop. I love you, and whatever you are scared to tell me, it will not make me love you any less. Just, please, Adrianna, what is it?"

"Stop it. You won't love me after this."

"Impossible. You are an integral part of me now and forever."

I slapped his chest, angry that I didn't have the courage to speak up.

"I'm sorry."

I broke down inside. I hated that Avery had pushed me to do this. I knew I should've just handled it on my own.

Kova's face fell and it crushed me to see him like this. The last thing I wanted to do was hurt him.

"For what? Please, tell me. I cannot stand to see you suffer like this."

Shaking my head, it was my turn to apologize to him. I crumbled in his arms and cried until I didn't have any tears left. Until he finally let go and stopped pushing me to tell him.

Instead, he just held me the entire time.

chapter 61

Knock. Knock. Knock.

Groaning, I dragged my feet across the living room to the rapid knocking that hadn't stopped. My eyes were heavy and drowsy from lack of sleep. Without looking through the peephole, I knew it could only be one person, and opened the door.

"Kova..." I said, and yawned. "What are you doing here?"

I opened the door wider so he could come in, then shut it. He turned to look at me with wide eyes like he was on the edge of something beautiful, but I was too tired to show any interest.

"I know I was not supposed to see you until tomorrow, but I had to come."

I frowned, rubbing my eyes with the heel of my hand. Before I left World Cup last night and my tears had dried, we'd agreed we would go to the little town together on Sunday. It was the perfect plan for me, strategic really. I'd planned to rest all day while mustering up the strength to tell him about the pregnancy tomorrow night after our day out. There was no way we would have another day like that anytime soon, or if ever, so I figured waiting until the end of the day was the best time to drop the bomb. I just had to figure out how I was going to.

I glanced at the clock and noted it was barely seven in the morning. I was beyond worn out physically, and needed to go back to bed.

"Kova, I didn't sleep at all last night. I'm really tired right now. Can this wait?"

"No, it cannot. I had to see you to tell you the news."

He was resolute in his decision and my shoulders dropped. I waved a hand, signaling him to go on and blinked. Kova regarded me, his eyes taking in the length of my body. I was only in a tank top and bikini underwear since I was so hot at night.

"I am filing for divorce."

My lips parted in shock. "What? What do you mean?"

"I found my way out," he said excitedly, almost as if I should know what he was talking about. "I am leaving Katja for good."

My heart raced a mile a minute trying to process the words Kova just delivered. I blinked hard, and blinked again.

"What did you just say?"

He was grinning like a fool. "I am getting a divorce and you will be all mine." He stalked toward me while I stood frozen in place.

His smile was so big and happy and I would've smiled in return if I wasn't in such a state of absolute shock. Kova pressed his body flush to mine and grabbed my face. I stumbled back and he stepped with me. Planting his lips on mine, Kova's kiss was filled with relief, like the restraints had been cut and he was finally free.

My hands were flat to his hard chest. He flexed under my touch and groaned in the back of his throat.

Breaking the kiss, I said, "What are you talking about? What happened?"

Kova gripped my hips and lifted me up. My legs automatically wrapped around his hips.

"Open your mouth and let me kiss you first."

"No—"

With his hand at my nape guiding me to him, he closed the distance. His tongue slid along my lips. A stream of desire roared through me and I kissed him back.

"I need you."

I pulled his hair and he arched his neck back. His eyes glistened with heat and I knew he had one thing on his mind. Sex.

"No, you don't. Tell me what happened first."

"Yes, I do," he said, walking with me in his arms toward my bedroom.

"You're confused."

He flipped on the light and quickly climbed on my bed with me in tow. "No. I am more awake than ever. I see clearly now."

I shook my head, baffled, as he dropped his weight to mine. I tried to move him away so I could get answers, but Kova was quick and pulled both my hands above my head and secured them to the bed in his grip. His other hand glided up my thigh to my ribs. In seconds, his mouth found my neck and his tongue licked a wet trail. All sensible thoughts left my mind when he pulled my tender skin into his mouth and suckled hard. My back arched and a gasp of bliss escaped my lips. His tongue was flat and moving in slow sensual circles. My body shivered and my eyes rolled shut as pleasure hummed through me. He feverously peppered kissed along my jaw until his lips met mine.

"I don't understand," I managed to get out.

But Kova didn't stop the torment when he said, "Katja. The marriage."

"What?" I asked, yanking away in breathless anticipation. "What changed? I don't understand."

"We had an argument and she slipped up. Do you remember when I told you I thought she was up to something? I found out everything she was hiding."

As selfish as that sounded, if I wouldn't give it up for my kidneys, then I wouldn't for Kova.

"You do not understand," he said. He pulled me to sit on his lap and I placed my hands on his chest, feeling the warmth come off him. "I am not asking you to give anything up. I will wait for however long it takes for you to be mine. I just wanted to tell you what happened and how this changes things for us.

I shook my head in disbelief. Tears clouded my vision. "But why? Why? What if we can never be?"

" will not have to report to anyone. What we have is something people search their entire life for. You understand me, I understand you. Do you honestly think a coach and an athlete have never fallen in love? It has happened more times than you can imagine. A coach knows more about his athlete than anyone."

"But, Kova, I'm eighteen."

"I know," he said softly, brushing a lock of hair behind my ear. "And even though I am thirty-four, I will wait for you. However long it takes, I will wait because I love you and I want us to be together one day."

Stupid tears fell from the corners of my eyes. I didn't even know why I was crying, but I was, and they started coming out faster. A gentle smile formed on his full lips. His *kissable* lips.

Kova wiped my tears. I shook my head, staring at his chest. "This is all so confusing."

"Love does not ever makes sense. You just go with what your heart feels. The way you look at me, the pain of wanting something you cannot have, I know that look because I feel the same for you. I know it is there for you, even if you do not tell me."

I chewed on my bottom lip and glanced up to meet his eyes. The corner of my lips tugged up. "I may…"

His lips formed a huge smile. "Admitting you are in love with someone is much harder than it sounds. The most important things in our lives are the hardest to get out. Is this why you do not like to admit your love for me? Because I am important? I did not say I love you for you to say it back, but I can feel it in your touch, the way you grip my skin, the way you reach for me. I know what you feel in your beautiful heart without you having to say it."

I took a deep breath, and asked, "Can I ask what your argument was about?"

"Oh, so much. It was like a domino effect and it could not have pleased me more. After I learned she was pushing for the marriage to get her citizenship, I read an email between her and a friend. Her friend encouraged her to take what she can get out of me. I knew she loved money, just not that much. Even before you came around, I always gave her what she wanted without questioning her. Money is just money. But it hurt to see she was using me for both."

My brows bunched together. "She still doesn't have her citizenship? I assumed she did."

"No, she is on the faster track to receive one, but she still does not have it. Without marriage, it would take much longer for her. The last person we spoke to said she should have it in a year or so."

There had to be more. "What else?"

"I had the strangest feeling she had been cheating on me."

My eyes softened. I wrapped my arms around his shoulders and pulled him down to me. I kissed his lips and couldn't help it, but I smiled at him.

"You can't possibly be upset if she was cheating on you, Kova."

"I know what I do is wrong, and I feel bad about it, but I never, ever used her. I love her, Ria, I always will, but I will never love her the way I do you."

"So, let me get this straight. You're divorcing her because of the citizenship and because you think she cheated?"

Kova dragged his teeth over his bottom lip and averted his gaze. His hands skimmed my thighs and over my hips, the tips of his fingers slipped under my tank top. Leaning in, he pressed a kiss to my chest.

"What is it?" I asked, my voice shaky. My chest rose and fell faster and harder with anticipation.

"Do you recall the night I sent you to my office and she happened to be there?"

Unfortunately. "Yes."

"Do you recall the white envelope she shoved at me that I threw on my desk?" he asked, and I nodded blindly. "I never opened it. I actually placed it in my desk that night and never thought about it again."

Oh, God. Somehow I knew where this was going before he finished explaining himself. My heart was burning. I could feel it in my gut. I tried to scoot off Kova, but he held me in place. I didn't have the strength to fight his hands off.

"She's pregnant," I whispered, chills tightening down my spine.

Something inside me crumpled to dust and I let out a breath of defeat.

I'd never win when it came to him. I'd never be first.

chapter 62

"Yes," he said, dropping his head to my chest.

I cupped the back of his neck. The anguish in those three letters crushed my heart and I realized Kova now had two women pregnant. I was so glad I hadn't told him. This made my decision that much easier.

His hands tightened on me. "I drank a half bottle of vodka straight from the mouth after your father told me about your kidney disease. An hour later I finished it off. I blacked out."

"You had sex with Katja when you found out I was sick?" I stated in utter and complete disbelief.

Of all the things. Of all the things he could tell me, nothing could amount to this kind of devastation now consuming me. Numbness crowded me, sweeping everything else away.

His voice was low, quiet, and surprisingly remorseful. "I do not remember all of it. Just flashback moments of that night. I have tried so hard to remember but my memory is just not there. I woke up naked and disoriented. I could not believe it, and since then it has never happened once."

"You slept with your wife when you found out I basically had a death sentence," I said slowly, trying to wrap my head around it.

Kova didn't respond. His silence was his answer, and his truth would cause me to suffer considerably more.

He tightened his arms around my waist and dropped his chin onto my shoulder. He was warm, but I felt nothing. He was shaking, but I was still. I thought his marriage had been devastating. This was soul-crushing.

"I never planned to tell Katja about us. I was going to eventually leave, but Joy had other plans. She is a woman with vengeance, power, and money. I have yet to know why she is after me. I thought possibly because she was concerned about her name being ruined and the humiliation it would cause." He paused, running a hand over his jaw. "It was Joy who found my jacket in your room on

New Year's Eve and shipped it to Katja. That was how it started, until Joy took it a step further and hired a private investigator to follow us. They have so much against us, Adrianna. So much damning evidence. Joy was able to retrieve all of our text messages from the cell phone carrier. She read every message, saw every image, including the video I sent to you while you were sleeping. They have photos of us at the gym, from meets, my home, your condo. She handed everything over to Katja, and from what I have gathered, used it as bait for your father to get what she wanted. I was cornered."

We were both quiet, lost to our heavy thoughts and the reality of our lives.

"I had no choice but to marry Katja. She had been begging me for years, but I could never bring myself to get down and ask her. After Joy gave her everything about us, she was devastated when I told her I would never marry her. I will never forget the way she looked at me, like she had revenge in her eyes. She was angry, saying I wasted her life and that I will get what is coming to me. She wanted me to expel you from training at World Cup. When I told her no, that was when Joy stepped in. I bargained with both over expelling you from my gym. There was no legitimate reason to kick you out, and you would never just leave on your own when there were coaches after you for the Olympic team. Too many questions would arise and bring unnecessary attention to all. Both of them knew this. It was either marry her, or your gymnastics career would be over, and I would be taken away in handcuffs."

"Joy isn't after you." My voice was hoarse. "She's after me for what my dad has done, and has continued to do. She's taking it out on me because I'm a replica of my biological mother, and because my dad is still talking to her after he promised Joy years ago he wouldn't. Why would Katja go through with this after she found out about the infidelity?"

"When she found out I was cheating, and with you, all she wanted was for me to kick you out because she knew you would go back to Palm Bay. After I refused to, and she spoke to Joy, she threatened to go to the police. She knew I would lose everything if she did that, but so would she because she had no legal tie to me. As the saying goes, money talks, and Joy paid her a large sum. Her heart grew hard from Joy whispering in her ear. Since then she has been just as bad, and it has been two against one."

Kova shook his head in defeat. I remembered my dad telling me Joy had something on me that she couldn't show him because she was actually worried it would give him a heart attack. He thought she was lying. Now that I knew the truth, it would kill him, and I was actually grateful she hadn't shown him, but I was also terrified if I did one more thing wrong, she'd show him everything.

"Dad said Joy's spiteful and jealous, but I find it difficult to believe she would be jealous of me. I think she sees me as the same as my dad, with you." My voice was quiet. "I wouldn't put it past Joy to tell my dad one day, but I don't see her going public with it."

I didn't recognize my own voice. It was as empty as my chest and as dead as my heart. I felt ruined. We were both pregnant, but the difference was that Kova and Katja would be able to raise their child.

For the first time in a long time, tears didn't fill my eyes. Rage didn't fill my blood. Hate didn't seal the wounds on my heart. I was just really sad inside.

I unwound my arms and placed my hands on his shoulders. Kova sensed what I was about to do and hugged me tighter, placing his face on my chest like he was holding on to me for dear life and didn't want to let go.

"Kova—" My voice was cold, distant.

He cut me off so he could rush out his next set of words. "Katja is pregnant, but it is not my child."

I lowered my eyes. Would he deny our baby too?

"Of course it's not your kid. You would say that."

He spoke faster, his eyes hard. "No, it is definitely *not* my child. I walked in on her taking a pregnancy test when she thought I was working out in the garage. The shock was written all over her face, and I know my sudden appearance flustered her. She started stammering and said since she never gave me the test stick as proof the first time she took one, she wanted to make up for that now. I had no idea what she was talking about. When I questioned her, she claimed to have told me she was pregnant, but I had no recollection of that. A man does not forget that vice grip on his heart feeling when he finds out he will be a father. She said it was in the envelope she gave me in my office the night you were there. I was completely ruined when she told me that. So, I drove to World Cup and went through my drawers and found it. I tore it open and sat in silence for hours trying to figure out how it happened when I realized that none of the dates matched up. None of them."

"Maybe you got her pregnant the night you found out about my kidney disease," I spat out.

"Not possible."

My eyes widened. "You said you didn't remember."

He held up a finger. "Just listen to me. I logged on to her accounts and scoured her emails and went through her social media pages. I found conversations between her and multiple men, one of whom I expect is the father."

My brows shot to my forehead. "I didn't take Katja for a cheater."

"Neither did I, so I called her doctor's office and spoke to the nurse since Katja has me listed as an authorized person to receive medical information on all her files. While Katja is indeed pregnant, she is very early in her pregnancy. Just a few weeks actually. My conniving wife had given me someone else's ultrasound photo and was trying to play it off as ours because she knew I did not want her, but also knew a baby would tie us together forever."

"When did all of this happen?"

"Yesterday morning and today."

My heart pinched at his response. I asked, "Why didn't you tell me this last night?"

"I planned to after dinner, but then…"

But then I'd flipped out.

"I'm sorry."

I drew in a breath, feeling the blood drain from my cheeks. I couldn't believe how far she'd gone to keep Kova in her life. I had no words. All I could do was listen in silence.

"Adrianna, I did not have sex with her recently enough for her to be pregnant. I have only been with you. The night when your father called me with your diagnosis, yes, I fell into a state of mind I did not know how to climb out of. The thought of you not being in my life is not something I ever want to imagine, but I did not know how to deal with it either, especially since I could not talk to you. I had to stay quiet and it was killing me. So I fucked off with writing in the notebook, which I am trying to barter with her to get back, and pulled out my old anxiety medication my therapist had given me. I think the shit was expired. I took a couple anyway and opened a bottle of aged vodka. I am not making excuses, but I blacked out that night. Still, I do not think I ever had sex with her. What man forgets when they have sex?"

I stared up at him speechless.

"That is not my baby, but that baby is my way out," he said.

We were breathing heavily, our chests thrust together.

"You're lying," I whispered, my heart racing so fast. "You always lie to me."

He shook his head, his eyes pleading with me. "I told you I would not lie to you anymore. I am telling you the truth. Why do you think I ran over here so fast to tell you everything? I surrendered to the blackmail because I had no choice. Your future was at stake and I was not going to risk it, but there is no way I will put up with this too. Was she going to act like some stranger's baby is mine for the rest of my life and never tell me? That is cruel and heartless. What about the real father? Would he never know? Come Monday, I am filing for divorce. I want her off my hands and out of my life for good. This is… How do you say, the cake's icing?"

I chuckled a little at his words, understanding what he was trying to say. "You mean the icing on the cake?"

His lips twitch, and he continued. "I know what I have done with you is wrong, but this is… I have no words for it."

I had a lot going through my head and I didn't know what to start with first. My stomach was starting to toss, the usual morning sickness I had every day bubbling to the surface.

"Say something," Kova begged. "Please."

Exhaling through my nose, I said, "Get off me."

His face fell. I knew it wasn't what he wanted to hear, but I was about to throw up all over him if he didn't move. Kova released his hold on me and I shoved off the bed and ran to the bathroom, making sure I locked the door behind me. My knees slammed to the floor and I vomited the moment I looked at the toilet water.

God, I hated this. There was no way I could handle nine months of this. I'd wither away to nothing. My throat tasted like acid and my stomach was already empty to begin with, and now it felt like a dry sack of nothing. I washed my face and brushed my teeth, then stepped out to find Kova sitting on my bed with his head dropped between his shoulders. I could feel his guilt from where I stood and I felt terrible.

I walked over to him and placed a hand on his shoulder. He leaned his head into my stomach and wrapped an arm around my butt to pull me closer to him. He wouldn't meet my eyes, but I knew he needed me, was seeking support, and I was more than willing to give it to him. His pain was too overpowering to ignore, not that I could ever do that to him anyway.

Kova was suffering and it was bleeding into me. He looked up, and the vulnerability in his gaze was too much to handle.

chapter 63

THERE WAS NO WAY I COULD TELL HIM ABOUT THE BABY WHEN HE looked utterly defenseless after learning how deceitful his wife had been.

I knew it was wrong, but he was a man devastated, torn, and at odds with his life, trying to find which door was the right one. I wasn't going to beat him down further.

"I'm sorry," I said. My fingers were in his hair. "Everything you told me just made me sick to my stomach and it was a lot to process." Not necessarily a lie, but it wasn't the full truth either. "I don't know what to think, okay? She's so deceitful it's appalling. It just got to me, especially hearing Joy was involved the way she was. I actually spoke to my dad about that a couple of weeks ago, but Joy hasn't told him any of it. I guess it's just really upsetting to see someone go to the lengths she has. I'm already a ball of nerves, you know?"

He nodded, his hand playing with my long hair against my back. "I did not mean to upset you."

"I know," I said softly. "I might have something that could help you. My dad told me whatever Joy has she won't go public with it. She never showed him, but he said she's too concerned about her image to ruin it, and he's right. She won't go to the police because she'll get dragged through the mud too, no matter how hard she'd try to prevent it."

"Why did you not tell me this sooner?"

I shrugged. "I didn't know what she had until you told me. My dad thought she was making it up, and I did too. We had nothing to go on. But now that I know exactly what she has, she'll never tell anyone besides my dad if she really wants to ruin me. It's too damaging to go to the authorities, and I really don't think she ever would."

Kova stared up at me with so much hope that I smiled. Placing my hand on his chest, my fingers spread out. "When will you tell her you're divorcing her?"

"I am not going to tell her, I am just going to file. Let her get served. I am fairly positive she will go back to Russia." He paused. "Although, she really wants her citizenship, so I am not entirely sure. I do not know what she will do about the baby. What I do know is that Katja is no longer my problem."

I swallowed hard, feeling my emotions rise, and threw my arms around his shoulders. I climbed over him, forcing him to lie back onto my bed. Our bodies pressed together and we both sighed like we'd been waiting for this moment, when he would no longer be tied to her. Kova's hands guided me, finding their place on my hips as I leaned down and kissed him hard. Fingers digging into my skin, his body fitted to mine as I melted at the touch of us joined.

I had to wonder if he would still wait for me after I told him about the baby.

"Where is Katja now?" I asked, breaking the kiss.

He blinked like he was trying to process my question.

"Home, I think. I am not sure now. After our second argument this morning, she told me to go fuck myself and that she would not be home tonight."

"Did you say anything else to her?"

"No. I wanted to, but I have already done enough damage and felt like walking out was enough." Kova grinned. "I did turn off access to my bank account and her credit cards. Let her use the money Joy gave her."

I gave him a little kiss. "I know you like to put on a strong front, but I think in here"—I tapped the left side of his chest—"you have a bigger heart than you let on. You care, you're just guarded a little more than others."

He looked at me with a puzzled smile on his face.

"I know what you did for Holly and I think it's the sweetest thing ever," I said, my voice low, and I swear his cheeks deepened in color. "She told me everything you did for her and Hayden, the stupid dating rule and all, the scholarship. Yes, she knows about us, but she will never say anything." Kova froze and I couldn't blame him. I continued. "She won't say anything. Trust me."

"Ria…" he warned, but I placed a finger over his lips. He tried to bite it.

"She was legitimately concerned. She told me what happened with her previous coach and was worried that was happening with me. I assured her it wasn't. I explained what I needed to, of course not going into detail, but she *will not* say a word," I reiterated. I kissed him again, then changed the subject. "Does this mean I get you to myself this weekend?"

Kova's eyes lit up with desire. Sliding his hand up my back and into my hair, his nose touched mine. He pulled the hair tie out, dropping it to the bed, and my hair enclosed us.

"When you are around me, please wear your hair down." He threaded his fingers through the hair at my nape and tugged, causing my back to arch and my chest to push into him. "You are breathtaking," he whispered, pressing a hand to the small of my back. A blast of desire shot down my spine and my body relaxed on his. "I do not know what to make of this, of us, but in my heart it is right. God, I sound like such a sentimental fuck." He chuckled, his breath tickling my neck.

My teeth dug into my lip. "You're totally sappy right now, but it's cute."

Grinning, Kova pressed his lips to mine. My heart felt full seeing him so happy and at peace. He flicked his jaw and slipped his tongue into my willing mouth and devoured me. He kissed me deeply, slowly, with hunger. I moaned, arching my back and pressing my chest to his. I needed to be closer, to feel him everywhere, even though I was already as close as I could be. I widened my hips, shifting to feel more of his erection. He groaned into my mouth and pressed his lips to mine harder, causing a flow of moisture between my thighs.

My hands slid down his shoulders and I dug my fingers into his rigid muscles. My blood was heating, and I suddenly felt like I was wearing too much clothing. Kova wrapped his tongue around mine and tugged on it. I whimpered, nearly crying out as need curled my toes. He ground his cock against me, provoking a response. Wetness coated my panties and I rolled my hips seductively into him. A groan vibrated deep in his throat. His body was warm to my touch, inviting me into his world. Pleasure bloomed through me, my need for him something fierce.

Fisting his shirt, I whispered for him to take it off. I sat up, straddling his hips as Kova arched his back and pulled off his shirt. His hands immediately found my hips, tugging off my panties. My gaze traveled the cut of his abs, loving how each muscle caused a shallow indent, down to that sexy dip by his hips to his groin. This man, with his honey-colored chest that led to strong, curved shoulders, and the letter I had carved into him, was the most beautiful man I'd ever seen. My eyes skimmed lower to the bulge in his pants as a seductive smile pulled at my lips. He was always hard for me and I loved that.

My fingers tentatively traced down his chest, down his sternum, and around his dark nipples. He flexed under me, sucking in a breath through his teeth, watching my every move. His green eyes were filled with desire. Our gazes stayed locked as my hand trailed lower, over his taut stomach to the elastic waistband of his shorts. I dipped my fingertips inside and rimmed the fabric, feeling the hair at his mound. His nostrils flared and he shifted his hips around, his Adam's apple bobbing slowly. Leaning forward, I licked my lips and pressed them to the carved A on his chest. My tongue slid out and lavishly licked the scar, feeling the grooves. Kova's hand came up and gently cupped the back of my head, I could feel him breathing heavily on me. Making my way up his body, I peppered him with kisses until I reached his mouth.

Without asking, I lifted my hips and reached between us to pull out his cock. He was already so thick and ready. He gripped my hips as I positioned his swollen tip at my wet entrance. Looking into his eyes, I sank down on his length slowly, feeling myself stretch wide to fit him. His fingers dug into my skin, his palms hot to the touch. Once he was fully inside me, he tugged off my shirt, his eyes fastening on my breasts. I was throbbing, needing to widen a little more before I could start moving or he was going to tear into me.

His brows bunched together, and he reached for my chest. "Your breasts are bigger." The pad of his thumb traced a circle around my areola and I purred in the back of my throat. My skin prickled with desire, my nipples hardening. "Even here, they are larger."

I glanced down, they did look a little bigger, but I knew why. Emotions clogged my throat and I sucked them back, wondering if we would have this after if he found out the truth.

Placing my hands on his stomach, I let the sensations take over and I began a slow ride, needing him so bad. "Oh," I sighed.

"Lean back and place your arms on my knees."

I did as he asked and let my head fall back as I rode his cock at my pace. It was hot and slow and sexy and just perfect, like a lazy Sunday morning.

"Yes, like that, Ria," he said through clenched teeth.

I glanced down. His finger found my clit and I shuddered, taking him how I knew he liked as I climbed higher from the orgasm that was already climbing. He carefully spread my pussy lips apart and watched as I took his cock. His eyes glowed with a craving so dark my clit throbbed.

"I'm very close," I said breathlessly.

His cock twitched and he grabbed my hips, speeding up the pace as he thrust into me hard. Our bodies slapped together. We moved faster, needing more, my breasts bouncing, my long hair falling over them. They were so tender and the loose strands grazing my nipples tickled a little.

"More," I begged, my eyes closing.

Kova lifted his hips slightly so my clit would hit the base of his cock. It was a different angle and it was exactly what I needed.

Little sounds escaped me and Kova growled. I orgasmed like it was the most amazing high of my life. I never held back when I was with him. Pleasure consumed me and I greedily took all he had to offer. His hand reached up and grabbed my neck. I panicked for a split second and grabbed his wrist until I remembered how much I loved when he did this. Kova took control and wrapped his fingers around my throat and shoved me down roughly, squeezing. Stars exploded in my vision, making me feel like I was coming out of my skin. He released, then squeezed again.

"Don't stop," I whispered.

"You are stunning like this. Take my cock for as long as you like. I am yours."

And I did. Even when our pleasure subsided and he pulled out, we stayed where we were. I rubbed my swollen pussy along his soft dick until I came once more. He loved it.

Kova secured me in his arms. My chest grew with hope and I thought maybe one day we could have more. What we had was more than love. This was a devout connection only two people could share.

I looked into Kova's green eyes and studied his gaze. To have someone behind me, pushing me, seeing and helping me achieve my dream, and more importantly, wanting to be there along the way was special.

But to have someone love me the way he did? There were not enough words in the dictionary to describe that feeling.

chapter 64

A KNOT SAT IN THE PIT OF MY STOMACH AS WE EXITED THE HIGHWAY. Worry plagued me with impending dread as Kova drove us to the next town. Something wasn't right, but I couldn't quite place my finger on what it was that bothered me exactly.

The pregnancy was heavy on my mind, and I one hundred percent planned to finally tell him tonight. The conversation was a delicate one, but that wasn't it. This felt different. I think the unease came from the fact that I'd never been alone with Kova outside World Cup or our homes, and it stressed me out a little, especially since I knew Joy had hired a private investigator in the past. I had no idea if she was still using one after all the damning evidence she had, but I learned to put nothing past her. I never got the notion someone was following me, which only amped up the anxiety even more.

Kova parked his car, then leaned over to press a kiss to my lips. He stepped out and walked over to the passenger side as I rummaged through my purse for a pair of sunglasses. Opening the door, he offered me his hand. Kova looked utterly delectable. Dressed in a pair of distressed dark jeans that hugged his fine ass and a stark white plain T-shirt that accented his biceps, he was simple but insanely appealing. His aviator sunglasses held my reflection and his hair was styled back. He looked delicious. I stepped out and Kova laced his fingers through mine, then lifted his arm to wrap it around my shoulders and tugged me tightly to his side. I rested my cheek on his chest, and he dropped a kiss to the top of my head. We started walking side by side.

Too many emotions hit me all at once while we walked down the boardwalk taking in the salty air. Boats were docked, and people strolled aimlessly like we did. It was a cloudy day but luckily not too humid. We grabbed lunch by the water and chatted about gymnastics, then shopped in some of the small stores. Kova refused to let me buy anything. He paid for lunch and anytime I mentioned I liked something, he purchased it. I fought him tooth and nail on it.

"Stop," I urged, yanking a heavy candle from his hands.

"Stop what?" he looked at me, puzzled.

Kova reached for the glass jar but I pulled back, and said, "I broke it when I threw it at you. You're not replacing it."

He grinned, remembering our fight.

"You threw more than a candle at me, if I recall."

I pursed my lips together, fighting a smile because he looked so damn hot.

"Ria, do not be foolish. It is just a candle. I know how much you love them, so let me get it."

I angled my head to the side and pointed to his hand. He was holding three bags of items he'd bought me throughout the day.

"That Tommy Bahama bag has more than just a candle in it. So does the Sephora one."

"So?" He appeared truly confused.

"So? So stop buying me stuff. Just because I say I like something doesn't mean you have to buy it. That's a lot of money right there, and now you want to add more?"

His eyes softened and he gave me an amused smile. "Give me the candle, Ria."

"No."

"I like buying you things. It makes me happy, now give it to me," he said, but I stood my ground. "I will buy every single candle in this store if you do not give it to me." He waved his fingers for me to hand it over. His eyes glistened with humor.

I held it behind my back and Kova stepped toward me. "I don't even like it."

"You are such a damned liar—a horrible one at that." He chuckled, his eyes gleaming. I loved the playful look on his face. "Just give it to me."

Kova placed the bags on the floor then leaned in to me to reach around my back. I arched, trying to keep it out of his reach, and he pressed a kiss to my exposed neck. I tried to act firm on my decision, but my giggle gave me away.

"Don't be a dick, Kova. I don't like it—or you. Now go away."

"That is not what you said this morning…or last night," he growled in my ear, his hand on the glass jar.

I gave it to him willingly—more in fear that it'd fall on the tile floor and break—as he dropped a gentle kiss right under my ear again. His warm breath tickled my neck. Smiling, I curled into him. Kova hooked his arm around my neck and yanked me to him while his other hand was pressed to the small of my back. He laid a hard kiss to my mouth and just as I was about to give in, he looked up and froze in horror.

"Kova?" I tried to look over my shoulder to follow his gaze, but he swiftly spun around with me. I tried to look past him, but he blocked me.

"Adrianna," he said under his breath.

My smile faltered and my heart dropped at his grave tone. "What is it?"

Kova moved my sunglasses from the top of my head to sit on my nose. He corrected them, then said, "I need you to grab the bags, turn around, and go straight to my car with your head down. Do not turn back, just go and I will meet you there."

Alarm rang through my bones. I knew it. Something in my gut had warned me against coming here and now I knew why.

"What's going on, Kova?"

Kova stared down, begging me to adhere to his request. Reaching into his pocket, he handed me his keys. "Just listen to me, please. I will explain, just go to my car and wait for me."

Dipping my head slowly, I did as he asked. I reached down and grabbed the bags, then turned and quickly walked toward the exit. I could feel Kova's eyes burning on me the whole way, watching me. Just as I was about to leave, I pulled my sunglasses down just a fraction and drew to a stop to peek over my shoulder. I had to look. I needed to see what he saw, what made him go from teasing and fun to somber and serious. Carefully, I twisted around just enough to get a look.

My lips parted.

All sound faded around me.

I was numb, unable to move, unable to feel, unable to hear. I should've listened to him, because nothing could have prepared me for what I saw.

I could only stare at the couple embraced behind Kova. So in love and so…

My dad.

And my mom. My *real* mom.

I couldn't see her full face, but I'd met her once to know it was indeed Sophia. In my heart I knew it was. Her height and hair were similar to mine, and we had an almost identical body shape, only I was much thinner than her. Sophia turned to the side and Dad gave her a kiss on her cheek. They looked up at each other, so in love and so normal. I was stuck for a moment at the simplicity of them, and the blow of betrayal booming through me. I knew Dad was divorcing Joy, but I didn't expect him to be with anyone else, especially not my biological mother. I thought he only gave her updates about me. This was not that. There was a familiarity and understanding with her that came over time, not overnight.

My heart ached, shattered with lies and deceit. With Kova's subtle waving urging me to leave, I turned away and walked out.

It only took me a matter of minutes to get to his car. I sat slouched to the side, hiding in the shadows, silently begging for Kova to hurry up. My nerves were frayed, and my fear was sky high as my heart pounded viciously trying to analyze what I just saw. There were so many thoughts spinning through my head that when two knuckles tapped on the tinted glass, I nearly jumped out of my skin.

Kova got into the car and dropped a bag onto the floorboard by my feet. He'd still bought the dumb candle.

"I can't believe it," I said quietly once we were on the highway. "I can't believe he's with my mom."

"I had a feeling that was your mother."

I turned toward him. "How so?"

"She looks just like you," he stated, slamming on the accelerator. "I just never realized it until now how similar you guys look."

Dread filled my veins. "What the hell are you talking about?"

"I have known for a long time Frank is not a monogamous man."

"Back up. What do you mean you never realized that was my mom until now?" My heart was racing faster than the speed of his car. "Where have you seen her? How do you know her?" Terror filled my blood. "Oh my God. Do not tell me you've been with her."

chapter 65

KOVA'S EYES WIDENED LIKE HE WAS OFFENDED.
"No, I have never cheated on Katja except with you," he spat. "I am not a cheater, and I have never been with Sophia."

I let out a whoosh. Kova exited the highway and pulled up to a red light. I stared straight ahead in a daze.

"You knew he was a cheater," I whispered in understanding.

He shot me a fleeting glance and placed a hand on my knee. Remorse was written all over his face.

"Of course I knew." He lowered his voice, and said, "I have seen him with her before. I just never knew it was your mother until I saw her again just now. I forgot about her, to be honest."

My head spun. I felt like I was missing a huge piece of the story. Kova took note of the expression on my face and continued. "He has brought her to my home in the past for Christmas parties. We have had quick holiday weekends away with them here and there. It has not happened in a while, so I forgot about her."

My eyebrows shot up in anger. "You knew he was cheating and you were okay with it? I can't believe you went along with it like it was nothing. For how long? Didn't it bother you?"

"What he does in his spare time is none of my business. I know it bothers you but do not take that out on me."

I turned back in my seat and looked ahead. He was right. "I'm sorry. I just didn't think adultery was a casual thing."

Kova was quiet. "It is not a casual thing for everyone," he said low, like he was hurt.

I released a pent-up sigh. This day was going all wrong. "Do you think my dad saw you?"

"Oh, he saw me."

My lunch was going to come up. "I'm gonna throw up again," I said, holding my stomach. "What happened?"

He shrugged as if he wasn't fazed. "Nothing. I bought your candle and left."

"I don't understand. That was it?"

"I was not going to strike up a conversation while his daughter was hiding in my car, Adrianna. I said hello and left. What would you like for me to have done? Ask him to have a drink?"

I pursed my lips together but didn't respond. He had a point, so I let it go.

"Did they ask you who you were with?"

"Yes."

My heart stopped. Quietly, I asked, "What did you say?"

"I told them I was alone and that I'd come to pick up candles for Katja since I knew she loved that store."

Kova pulled into a parking spot and turned off the car and looked at me.

"Has she ever been there? With you?"

"Never."

I threw the door open and stepped out, but Kova was already moving toward me. He invaded my space and pressed his body flush to mine, making sure I felt all of him. He cupped the back of my neck and pressed his forehead to mine, breathing into me.

"While I get hard seeing you jealous, I just want to make it clear that I did not take you where I took Katja, you crazy little psychopath. I would never do that. I lied to your father," he admitted before smashing his mouth to mine.

I kissed him back because I couldn't not. He played me, but I let it go. Kova knew how to subdue me with his tongue, his touch, his hold, and that's exactly what he did. He shoved his tongue into my mouth, and I moaned and clenched his shirt in my hand, wanting to push him away, but all I did was tug him closer. He kissed me, his mouth bruising hard, and I sighed, melting into him.

"I really thought you took me where you'd taken her for a second," I said. "I was going to kill you."

Narrowed eyes pierced my heart. "Stop thinking I am always lying to you or trying to hurt you," he said against my lips. I felt the dejection in his words and immediately regretted how I acted. "I told you, full disclosure." Kova thrust his hands into my hair, tugging on the strands at my nape. My stomach tightened when he pulled hard, my body coming to life and aching for him.

Reaching between us, I cupped his swollen length and gave him a good, hard squeeze. His eyelids dropped, heavy with unchained lust. I unbuttoned then unzipped his pants and stuck my hand inside to pull out his hard length. He was bare as usual and rock hard. We were standing so close together no one could see what I was doing. I wrapped my fingers around his shaft and stroked him. Kova groaned, his jaw flexing in an effort to keep it together.

Hands on my neck, he angled my face to his. Goose bumps prickled down my arms as his seductive words circled round me, "Do you know how easy it would be to fuck you out here with no one to ever know?"

My cheeks burned with heat and I squeezed his length without realizing it. I just planned to work him up, not have sex here. He dropped a little kiss to my lips and looked down.

"Look around," he said. "No one will see us."

He was probably right. There were trees everywhere, and in front of the car was a cement wall surrounded by more bushes. There wasn't a person in sight. Leaning down, he nuzzled my neck, his unshaven jaw enticing me to agree.

"All I have to do is lift your dress and slide right in, and your clothes would hide everything," he whispered, drawing in a breath through his teeth. "Let me fuck you out here. No one would know, they would think we are just kissing." Kova was ridiculously hard in my hand, and throbbing. I felt a little moisture and used it to run my hand over his tip. "Let me show you how I barely need to move to make you come." Kova groaned and I knew he'd kill for it to happen. "Let me in that little pussy of yours. I will make it quick."

His hand skimmed up my thigh and under my dress to cup my ass. Cool air breezed past my skin and I shivered. Thankfully it was my thigh that was facing the wall, that way if anyone walked past us they still wouldn't see anything. Swiftly, he dipped his fingers into my panties.

"You're so confident it will happen quickly. No way," I said, my voice a little breathless. "You're not quick—you like to take your time."

"I am a man hell-bent on winning every challenge presented to me. Now stroke my cock, Ria, and do not go light. Do it hard. Use your wrist and twist and squeeze the head."

Heat zipped down my spine as I did exactly what he demanded. Taking me by complete surprise, he leaned forward and licked my lips like he was licking an ice cream cone. I gasped and automatically squeezed my legs together as his finger caressed my clit.

"You play dirty," I said.

"I play to get what I want. Now spread your legs for me, *malysh*."

I shook my head, but my stupid body complied with him once he started rubbing a finger in circles on my clit. I couldn't not. It was impossible. Kova grinned, then slid a finger down my wet crease.

On a lusty whisper, I said, "I'm sure there are cameras out here."

He raised a pointed brow and dipped a finger into my entrance. "Does it not make it that much better?"

My mouth fell open and I struggled to stay quiet, clutching his shirt, pushing and pulling him.

"You do not want to push me away," he teased, "someone might see what we are doing."

My heart was racing, my body on fire for this reckless man who made me do things that were not something I'd typically do. I loved it, though. His gaze was as dark as the devil's and filled me with cravings I wanted him to satisfy. I looked deep into his eyes, inviting him. He could have whatever he wanted. With one pull, he ripped my panties at the crotch. He bit my neck and lifted one leg so my ankle was inconspicuously hooked around his hip.

"I need to be deep in you. Do not deny me."

Bending his knees just slightly, Kova angled himself at my entrance. In one swift motion, he surged inside. We both groaned at the same time, falling into each other. He shoved my hips down and I clenched around him, throbbing from the tightness.

I exhaled a painful breath. "Fuck, Kova. This hurts."

"Eyes on me, Ria."

chapter 66

KOVA CAREFULLY DROPPED MY LEG SO I COULD STAND, THEN FLUFFED my dress on the other side to hide anything that may show.

I winced at the snugness, holding my breath. Little silver stars danced in my vision.

"What are you doing?" I asked, standing on my tiptoes. I glanced around, nervous that someone would see us. He was swollen and thick and it almost hurt to have him at this angle.

"Wrap your arms around my shoulders and fucking kiss me. Let me take care of the rest."

So I did.

I understood what he meant now. Kova barely had to pull out for pleasure to burst through me. It was a slow, hard fuck. This angle made his cock caress my clit with every move he made and hit me deep inside. Warm, powerful strokes, and I was soon trembling on the edge of desire. My nails scored his biceps. I moaned into his mouth, sucking on his tongue, not caring if anyone heard. We rocked into one another, and the hard and shallow drives of his hips worked exquisitely. I wanted to bite him, eat him, devour him until he fucked me senseless. I began panting, my breathing deepening as I felt an orgasm climb almost immediately.

"I told you," he said as breathless as I felt. "I fuck like a champ. Three minutes tops. Maybe less."

"Why… Why didn't you just tell me that from the beginning?" I joked.

Kova placed both hands on my hips and rolled his pelvis into mine. My eyes rolled shut, closing from the bliss strumming through me.

"I need more."

He clucked his tongue. "Always so greedy for my cock. You act like you do not want it and then you beg."

"Just shut up. I'm going to come any second."

"That is good. Because a couple is walking this way now."

My eyes flew open and locked with Kova's. I panicked, but a lazy grin spread across his handsome face like he was pleased with himself.

Dropping his voice, he said, "I am going to come deep inside your pussy when they walk past us." His grin was enough to push my orgasm closer to the brink of insanity. "Try not to make a sound now."

Lips parting, my heart beat rapidly against my ribs. My cheeks flushed as the sound of footsteps drew closer. I placed my hands on his shoulders and chest, hoping it would look like we were talking.

Without taking his eyes off me, he said, "They are getting closer."

Then he thrust two more times, pulling all the way out to where I truly thought we were going to get caught from the way his body surged back and drove in. He shoved my hips down so I couldn't move when I felt him spasm inside me. His jaw flexed and his nostrils flared, eyes a dark pit of euphoria. I started coming just as the elderly couple walked past us. I feigned a breezy smile in their direction as Kova dipped his chin to greet them. I came even harder, pulsing around his swollen cock. As soon as they passed us, Kova leaned in and devoured my mouth as he pushed in one last, hard time as far as he could go. He let out a deep, guttural moan from his chest. My nails dug into his skin and I sighed, taking his cock the way he liked.

"Holy fuck," I said, breaking the kiss.

"Slow and steady wins the race." He grinned, then looked at his watch. "Next time we time it," he said. "I bet I can have you finishing in two and a half minutes."

"You're such an ass. Why do you do this to me?" I teased, still out of breath.

"Do not even act like you regret it," he said, pulling out of me with a pop. He fixed my dress so I was covered again.

I clenched my thighs, hoping it wouldn't drip down my legs as we walked through the building.

Kova leaned down and dropped a soft kiss to my lips. I took a step away but Kova stopped me. "Let me grab your bags."

I'd completely forgotten. I watched as he reached inside the car to get our stuff. He slammed the door shut and engaged the alarm, then reached for my hand. He briefly looked at me with a simple smile. Hand in hand, we walked toward the sliding glass doors. There was an energy buzzing, an excitement spreading inside me, and I wondered if he felt it too. I leaned on him as we went up the elevator in silence and mused over the day, what we'd talked about, what had happened between us.

As soon as the door shut and we were in my condo, Kova dropped everything and slammed me up against the wall. I gasped in shock, my breath lodging in my throat.

"The clock starts now."

"What—" I said but was quickly silenced by his devilish mouth.

"I am not through with you. What happened outside was only an appetizer compared to what I'm going to do to you. This day, being out with you like we were, has made me incredibly hungry for you."

His fingers were in my pussy, pushing his cum back inside me. My hips moved against his hand, desire roaring back through me. A little whimper escaped me.

"After today, you are getting on birth control," he ordered, almost out of breath. "I want you all the time and I do not want to worry about you getting pregnant. It will be better for both of us."

I swallowed hard, choking on his words. All day I'd forgotten I was pregnant until now. Melancholy belted me but before I could react, his mouth was on mine and I let it go. Soon he'd know the truth. Until then, I wasn't going to worry.

My cell phone rang in my purse and Kova pulled back. "Do not even think about it," he warned. His wild eyes holding me captive and I leaned into him, listening. "Take the dress off now or I will rip it to shreds."

It was off in seconds. He reached behind his head and pulled off his shirt, then dropped it to the floor. His mouth was back on mine as he kicked off his shoes and pants.

Both of us completely bare, Kova picked me up and consumed my mouth. I should've known he wasn't done with me. Passion engulfed the air surrounding us and we caved to our decadent desires. I wrapped my arms around his shoulders, my ankles locked around his hips as he carried us across my living room. My cell phone rang again, but I ignored it. Only Avery ever called me back-to-back like that. There was no way I was stopping now that I knew it was her.

Breaking the kiss, my lips moved across his jaw and followed his alluring cinnamon scent I loved, suckling his neck and biting down hard. Kova paused. A low guttural sigh rumbled in his throat and then his hand came down and slapped my ass hard. Sexy as hell, it made my skin tingle.

Kova slid the patio door open and stepped out, my heart racing a million miles a minute. I lived on the top floor and there were plenty of condos around that could see us through the white opened slats. I glanced over my shoulder and noticed some of the balconies were occupied. If I could see them, then they could see me. Which meant anyone could look up and see two naked people going at it like rabbits.

Kova stopped in front of the railing. Looking at me, he said with unyielding resolve, "You are going to be mine out here."

I shivered with steady agreement. The thought exhilarated me completely.

I unlocked my ankles and glided down his body to stand. His erection stood tall between us and the urge to look out to the opening to check if anyone could see us was strong. Grabbing a fistful of my hair, he wrapped it around his hand, then guided me to my knees, forcing me to look up. I was a little nervous, but without hesitation, I opened my mouth and took as much as I could of him. He moaned on contact, angling his hips and holding the back of my head for a good minute. I sucked, swirling my tongue around his length, tasting myself on him. A little salty, I quickly licked it away so I could taste only him. Kova guided my head to his hips, pushing all the way in. His other hand grasped the back of my neck. I couldn't move even if I wanted to.

"Oh, fuck," he breathed loudly. My heartrate skyrocketed, thinking that someone had heard him.

I remembered how he'd taught me to suck it like a Blow Pop so I did just that, making sure I showed attention to that long vein I loved.

"Put one hand on my balls and massage them, squeeze them. Use your other hand and play with your pussy."

Despite the sun shining on my back, anticipation steamrolled through me. I liked touching myself. I knew exactly how to get myself off, and since I was already on the edge, I planned to do just that.

Cupping his sack, I rolled his heavy balls in my hand. I surprisingly liked the way they felt as I tugged and twisted them. I could tell he did as well, especially when my fingers scraped past them. I felt him clench his cheeks as he pushed into my mouth and held still. My eyes watered as I struggled to breathe, and I pinched his sensitive sac between my fingers.

"Oh, fuck me." He moaned long and loud.

I looked up to see his head thrown back, the veins in his neck jutting out. What an angle to see Kova at. I was on the verge of an orgasm and began twirling my tongue around the head of his cock every time he pulled out.

"Keep sucking like that, work that throat."

Oh God, this view of him, my fingers, his balls… I was right there… Right… There. My breathing labored and I rubbed myself hard and fast, my blood rising and my insides quivering. I reached for him and gripped his balls in my palm and squeezed as I came on my fingers. Kova thrust in and hit the back of my throat. My stomach tightened for a second. I was lost on what to do.

"Ria," he yelled, unloading in my mouth. He was so loud I was sure if anyone was outside they heard. I wasn't expecting him to come and almost gagged at the initial stream of the warm, salty fluid. "Swallow it," he demanded, caressing my throat with his hand and fingers. There was so much I squeezed my eyes shut, swallowing it like he said.

Kova pulled out and stepped back, a stream of creamy white fluid dripping off him. "Tsk, tsk, Ria. I said play with yourself, not make yourself come. Get up and on the chair now."

Anticipation seized my chest. My gaze met his. I wiped my mouth with the back of my hand and stood on shaky knees. The beautiful swirls of black and obsessive green in his eyes intrigued me.

"On your hands and knees," he ordered. "Ass up."

I got into position and reared back, placing my chest to the lounge. Before I could blink, a hand came down and stung my ass with a slap.

I didn't cry out. Instead, I chewed my lip and stayed where I was. Kova leaned forward and grabbed my hair and yanked my head back, delivering another pleasure-filled smack. My skin pebbled with goose bumps. I was starting to wonder if there was something wrong with me. Shouldn't I have been repulsed by all the spanking, the biting, the roughness and blood? I was supposed to like it soft and gentle, yet here I was rearing back and wiggling myself in his face.

I loved everything he gave me, and that's what confused me. I could feel my blood climbing and the sensations pouring through me as my body desired more deviant touches and illicit whimpers.

chapter 67

KOVA LET GO OF MY HAIR.
    He pushed on my shoulder blades and forced my face down. My nipples grazed the coarse material of the lounge and shot a zest of bliss down my spine. Grabbing the chair, he slid it closer to the railing. My balcony was enclosed with a screen, but if anyone walked by the building and looked up, they'd see us.

Kova dropped to his knees and grabbed my hips, rotating them upward. He spread my cheeks, and my back bowed, mortification roared through me.

"Your pussy is dripping," he said, his voice thick with desire and it excited me.

He leaned forward until I couldn't see his face. My eyes rolled shut as he ran his flat tongue along my wet lips, all the way to my ass where the tip of his tongue ran little circles.

A moan rolled off my lips and I rocked back into him. My eyes opened just as he swallowed, his throat bobbing. His heady gaze locked with mine. "Had to clean you up before I can play."

"You're such an ass man."

Palming both of my ass cheeks, his hands so large I knew they covered me, he leaned forward and I held my breath as he spread them wide to almost the point of pain. His green eyes were enthralled with me and it sent a shiver of power through my veins. A little sting, and I gasped. I'd never looked at my ass in the mirror, but the next time I was alone, I would. This position was slightly embarrassing, and I hoped I was shaven and cleaned for him.

Kova leaned forward and penetrated my pussy with his warm tongue. I sighed. My back bowed even more and my body relaxed, only for him to pull out and go straight for my ass.

I should've known.

"Arch more for me."

I did as he asked. His teeth clamped down on the skin as he tongued my hole, creating a suction around me. His fascination with that forbidden spot created a frenzy in my blood. I didn't get it, but I didn't question it either, because the truth was I loved it just as much as he did.

"Oh my God!" I screamed, not worried if anyone heard my breathless pants at this point.

Kova gripped my hips and held me to his mouth. My legs widened on their own and my backside pressed embarrassingly hard into his face.

"One day…" he said, his voice a deep husky.

I knew what he was referring to. Anal sex. It was a conversation we'd already had and something that will never happen.

"No, you're not. That's never going to happen."

"Yes, it will."

"No, it won't."

"Ah, but *malysh*," he drew out, his thumb running circles over the puckered little hole, "you have no idea what you're missing."

"There is no way you—or anyone else with a smaller dick—will fit in there. No thanks. Not happening. End of discussion."

Kova's grip tightened on me to the point I knew I'd have a bruise. "No one is ever getting this ass. Do you understand? I will personally strangle anyone who gets close to it. It is mine."

His thumb pressed the hidden spot while he inserted a finger into my pussy.

"I can make you like it, you know," he whispered, pulling out his finger and using the wetness to trace the tight hole.

He applied more pressure, pushing the tip of his finger in. This time he stuck two fingers in my pussy and slowly rubbed along my inner walls, eliciting a low moan from me as he stretched me. I fought back a groan at the double intrusion.

This man knew exactly what to do to my body and I was slightly startled by it because I never found myself saying no, only yes. Body manipulation at its finest. I watched as Kova spit onto his fingers then applied pressure to the tight bundle of nerves. I flinched but held still.

"Are you not worried someone can see you?" he asked.

It was hard to think clearly when my body was a blaze of heat and lust.

"I am, but no one can see my face. So I guess not."

"But those who live in the building can probably figure out what number your condo is."

He was probably right, but I didn't care. "Maybe."

"Take a deep breath," he ordered. My eyes widened, I knew what he was going to do. "A deep breath, Ria." Exhaling, my body softened, and he pressed a finger into my ass, then pulled out. I hope it was a pinky. "Breathe," he instructed, and I did. "Trust me, you will love it when I am done with you."

"It hurts," I said, but he pressed deeper, and when I realized he wasn't stopping, I closed my eyes and took a deep breath and focused on the pleasure. The way he played with my tender lips, working an orgasm up again, was quite remarkable. I was shocked my body was ready for another one.

"Bear down, push back, and relax. Focus on my fingers stroking your pussy."

Surprisingly, he placed a kiss to each cheek, then slid his finger farther into my ass. I clamped together, and my arms shot out in front of me for something to hold on to. My back arched and I rocked my butt into his face.

This hurt. This hurt worse than losing my virginity.

"Kova, please. It hurts," I whimpered somewhere between pain and pleasure as he used a finger to tease my clit and stroke my ass.

Little sparks went off inside of me and I shuddered in ecstasy. I didn't know if I was coming or going. I didn't know what I wanted or didn't want anymore. I was lost in a haze of sex and gratification. Kova was right. He could make me want it, because now I kind of did.

Kova groaned behind me, sliding his finger out but carefully pushing back in. He wasn't aggressive or harsh, but shockingly gentle. He let out a long breath of air and it hit my cheek.

"Just listen to what I say and you will thank me."

As Kova gently worked his finger in and out of me, I glanced between our bodies. His cock was erect and straining to the point it looked painful. The tip of his shaft was purple and almost angry looking. His stomach was rock hard like he was holding on tight to the last bit of his sanity he had left. But he was right. I think he could make me love it because this was better than I'd expected.

I felt myself spasm around him and just as I was about to come, he pulled out and stood.

"Kova... Please..."

With his cock in his hand, he looked at me then angled himself at my entrance, and slid into my warmth that was aching for another orgasm. We both groaned in unison from the sheer pleasure of it all.

Leaning down, he licked a wet trail up my spine to my shoulder and under my ear. He tugged on the lobe. I didn't even know it was possible to have goose bumps outside in this heat.

"I want to hear you scream," he whispered, his hot breath on my face, thrusting into me. "Let everyone hear me fucking you and wish it were them."

I nodded. I'd agree to almost anything at this point.

As he began thrusting in and out of me, my eyes rolled shut and I heard him spit. I cracked one eye open and watched as he rolled his saliva between his fingers and then dropped them behind me.

"Arch back," he ordered. "Exhale."

Then, one long finger slid back into my ass while he was deep inside of me. My body trembled in ecstasy and a raspy moan rolled off my lips. The pressure was almost too much to bear.

I let out a high-pitched moan as he worked me ever so slowly that it almost brought tears of pleasure to my eyes. Like he knew I could only handle so much and didn't want to hurt me. He was careful and attentive and I couldn't stop the sounds escaping me even if I tried. It was impossible.

"Kova…"

"Ria…"

"Why do I like this so much?" I nearly whined. My inner thighs were wet with my pleasure. "I never want you to stop. Can we do this all day?"

He chuckled and teased me. "Oh, *Malysh*. Now you know what I deal with on a daily basis. How I imagine taking you, how it can never be enough. Now you see."

"I do, good God, how I do…" I could barely find my words. "How… Why?"

My body was engulfed with dark desires, cheeks flushed with a tinge of pink, thighs trembling, and shaking from the hunger. I was floating on another level. My body was going to combust from the pressure of pleasure only Kova could give me.

"I don't think I can hold on much longer, Kova. Please, I need to…" I begged.

A dark chuckle enveloped me, and he reached around with his free hand to circle my clit. A loud purr escaped me and I slowly rocked back into him, loving this so much. I wasn't too embarrassed to beg at this point, and I could tell he was close as his dick twitched inside me and his thrusts became harder, deeper, more controlled for both of us.

Kova yanked me up so I had my back to his chest. We were both kneeling, a slave to each other's desires.

"Put your arms behind my neck."

I did as he asked, my breasts swollen and bouncing while he teased and taunted every erogenous area I had. My mind was misty, he took me to new heights. After spending the day with him and our conversations, our connection only grew stronger and it scared me a little. Now I understood what he meant. I wanted this all the time too and I didn't just mean the sex. My heart was his, just like I knew his was mine. I liked seeing his arm across my belly. The vascularity that oozed from him and the vein twirling down. He was strong and rough, and the pleasure so divine.

"Come, come now with me," he said, then sank his teeth into my shoulder, his tongue lapping my skin.

My body exploded with rapture on a throaty sigh, like a huge wave roared through me. I yelled out his name, driving my hips back into his. His pleasure trickled down my inner thighs and I felt tender everywhere, sated from this touch. Our orgasms receded but the content bliss that followed was sizzling between us. We were both panting, a sheen of sweat coating our bodies, but it didn't bother me. Kova reached up to cup my jaw and turn my face toward his. Our eyes locked for a split moment before he gave me a tender kiss that enclosed around my heart. His lips were soft and sweet, his tongue light, as if what he'd just done to my body was normal.

There was nothing normal about Konstantin Kournakova and Adrianna Rossi, but that's what I loved about us.

Breaking the kiss, Kova opened his eyes.

Heart thumping wildly in my chest, the setting sunlight flickered against his compelling green eyes that unveiled an openness with a love so deep my stomach tightened. I was trying to stay strong, I didn't want to say something and regret it, but in this moment, what I felt was love.

Love was a look. Love was a feeling. Love was a four-letter word that held more weight than gold.

Love was clarity.

chapter 68

"Kova," I whispered, like it was the word only he wanted to hear.

His eyes glimmered with awareness and he carefully pulled out of me, then turned me over to lay me on my back on the lounger. His length, still warm and hard, pressed against my thigh. My heart was pounding. We should've been sensible about being so free with our carnality, but we never could control it. It was only us and that's all that mattered.

Our eyes were focused on each other's as he covered my body with his, his mouth with mine, his weight falling onto me. I loved when he did that, when he laid on top of me without abandon and gave me himself. It was one of the rare times I got just him without all the layers, like he was giving himself to me. My arms wound around his shoulders, my fingers through his hair. He kissed me so greedily I could barely keep up with him. Hands sliding down his back, he shook like he was in dire need. He passionately pushed his tongue in my mouth. His hands found my neck and applied pressure, and I went with it. My body unraveled under his. He unleashed on me and I took it all.

"I need to see your face when I make love to you," he said, leaving me speechless.

I didn't question it. I just nodded my head. It's what he needed, and I gave it to him. I knew deep down in my heart that after this weekend, when he found out my secret, it would most likely break the connection we'd worked so hard to rebuild, so I was going to savor it for as long as I could.

Without a second thought, he lifted his hips and pushed his cock into me again. A glaze swept over his eyes and he moaned. He began making love to me like a beast, pumping his hips with ardor. Hard and long strokes, holding himself in me before he was retreating and doing it again, building a maelstrom of desire. An erotic growl vibrated in his chest when he drove harder. My back bowed in response at how deep he was, my nails scoring his back. He shuddered against me and I locked my legs around his waist.

This was lovemaking.

"Kova…" I swallowed, quivering. "Oh, my God…" I moaned against his mouth. "It hurts." And it did. He was so enlarged and hitting all the way in the back.

"Shhh…"

"Kova." I dug my fingers into him, feeling his skin break under my nails.

"Take me. Take all of me," he gritted between clenched teeth. "*Mne nuzhno, chtoby ty byl bez sderzhannosit, bez osuzhdeniya.*"

"Please…" I wasn't sure what I was begging him for.

"*Ty nuzhna mnye.*"

My heart ached at the sound of his cracked voice.

"Just hold on… I need this, I need you. I need to feel more of you."

"You're going to make me bleed, Kova."

He growled, reluctantly slowing his pace. The muscles in his shoulders relaxed, his body loosened, and he cupped my damp neck and held on like I was his salvation. His dominant kisses were almost careless, like he let himself go as he urgently thrust into me. He was getting closer. The little sounds in the back of his throat made me disentangle my feelings for him completely and it scared me a little.

Kova gave one good last stroke, held my jaw in his palms and kissed me so deeply and so desperately my heart contracted and my toes curled. I whimpered, my body shuddering with pleasure. His cock jerked, we gasped, then we were both falling into a blissful state of ecstasy at the same time. The way his tongue enveloped mine, how he used one hand to grip my hip to make sure we were joined perfectly, how I could feel him unloading inside me, made my chest hurt.

"*Malysh,*" he whispered on a groan.

Pulling back, Kova looked down at me and licked his lips. We were nose to nose and breathing heavily. His gaze swept over my face. Sweat trickled the sides of his temples and I wiped it away. The way he looked at me made my heart ache for him with so much affection it was difficult to put into words. We were both sticky and hot. I threaded my hands through his wet hair and locked my fingers behind his head.

"You know that I love you, right?"

Swallowing thickly, I nodded. He was waiting for me to respond. I wanted so bad to tell him I loved him too, because I did. I wished I could give that to him, but something warned me to hold back.

"*Ya vlyubilsya f tyebya s pyervava fsglyada.*"

I waited for him to translate it for me, but this time he didn't. Instead, he smiled, a little sad, but covered it up with a quick kiss.

Cradling me to him, he slid out and stood, taking me with him. I laid my head on his shoulder, a peaceful air settling around us as he walked toward the sliding glass door and stepped inside. I was ready to go to sleep, even though the sun hadn't set completely yet.

"I can walk, you know."

Kova leaned in and kissed my neck. "But I like having you in my arms. I never want to let you go."

"Who knew you could be so sweet."

He chuckled and said, "I am not sweet."

"It's okay to admit you're soft sometimes," I said, egging him on.

He paused right in front of my bathroom. I looked up, waiting. "Soft?" he responded with a confused grin. His hand skimmed over my hip and down my backside and settled over my leaking sex. He inserted two fingers and I clenched around them, drawing in a breath as he pushed his semen back inside me. "This is not from me being soft, *moya lyubov*." He glanced at my lips. "My love," he translated, his voice low.

I blushed. My teeth dug into my bottom lip and I melted a little. I clenched again and his eyes flashed.

"Whatever you say, big boy. Now put me down so I can get cleaned up."

"I will clean you up."

I sighed loudly, faking annoyance. "Why do you have to act like a cave man all the time?"

"Why do you have to be so outspoken? Let me do what I want and we will have no issues," he responded.

I laughed. "You like my mouth."

He raised his brows, his eyes glittering with hunger. "I do *love* your mouth, especially when your lips are—"

I slapped his chest playfully. "Kova! Shut up!" I laughed, squirming in his arms as he walked into my bathroom and turned the shower on. "I need to wash my hair."

"I can wash it."

"You think you can wash it and hold me at the same time? You do realize you need two hands, right?"

He slapped one of his thighs and it echoed against the tile walls. "You underestimate me."

I chewed on my bottom lip. "I need to shave my legs."

"I will shave them for you."

I raised a brow. "Fine. If you can shave my legs, I can shave your balls."

Kova's eyes popped open wide in shock and his jaw dropped in horror. A fit of laughter burst from my lips at his expression.

"Never, ever going to happen," he said clearly.

"That's what I thought," I said. "Now let me down."

"Fine. But I want you back in my arms again right after."

Joining me under the warm spray, his soft tone raised a few flags. "Hey, what's going on?"

He shook his head, unable to meet my gaze.

"Tell me," I pressed, "please."

Kova let out a long sigh and his fingers danced along my shoulder. We stood a few inches apart and I could feel his emotions as if they were my own. We washed up quickly.

"Nothing is going on. I just want you back where you belong. We do not get much time like this together and I want to make the most of it while we can."

Be still my fucking heart. I made Kova meet my gaze and drew in a quiet breath. He was unguarded, water trickling down is face, but it was the pain in his eyes that sucker punched me. There was so much anguish it tore me up. I always thought I would never win with him, but now I wondered if he actually felt that way with me. He was trying and I was holding back.

Blood rushing through my chest, I was trying to stay strong and not cave and admit my love for him, but when it was so rare for him to be this candid with his feelings, I wanted to let go of that last wall I'd put up and run to him.

"We will not be able to have moments like this often," he said, like reality had dawned on him.

A half smile tugged at my lips. Kova picked up the shampoo and lathered up my hair. "I know. Maybe one day, though." I swallowed and decided to finally give a little piece of me that I knew he needed to hear. "I'm yours." I put emphasis into my words, hoping he'd see I meant it.

Without hesitation, he leaned down and wrapped his strong arms around me, pressing his lips to mine. His tongue swept along the seam, requesting access. I gave in willingly, falling into his emotional embrace.

Pulling back, he exhaled a heavy breath and pressed his forehead to mine. "God. How am I supposed to stay away from you when all I want is to be touching you, holding you, just fucking being next to you breathing the same air? I am going out of my mind trying to make this work and I do not know how without fucking it up. I am obsessed with every part of you and never want to let you go."

Breathless, I knew I needed to reassure him as much as I needed the reassurance for myself. "I wish I had an answer for you that was right. For us, nothing is supposed to be right. We just have to take each day as it comes. Always remember I feel the same way as you."

He nodded. "I know. You are correct. It fucking sucks," he said, almost angrily, but not toward me.

I felt bad. "Nothing worth having ever comes easy, remember? That's what makes it so much better." Just then my stomach grumbled embarrassingly loud. "You worked up an appetite in me."

He pinched my hip. "You could stand to lose a few pounds." My jaw dropped. "I am only joking." He chuckled. "Let us finish up and I will cook you something."

I held up my fingers and said, "I'm getting all pruney anyway."

Kova kissed my fingers and laughed. I turned off the shower and he slid open the curtain to step out. "You Americans and your strange descriptions. Where are your towels?"

I stared, riveted with his body the way water trickled over the dips and curves of his natural muscle. It was when he turned to the side that my lips parted and a sigh worked through me. He was physically perfect with a firm, round ass and hot-as-hell hips that led to powerful thighs. But it was the sexy V at his lower abdomen that twisted a need in me to reach out and touch. What this man did to me…

Kova snapped his fingers and my eyes shot up to him. I blushed, and he was grinning like a fool. He loved it.

"Towels?"

I had to think about it for a minute. "Ah, they're in the closet on the shelf."

I stood in the stall shivering as Kova stepped out and opened my linen closet. I glanced at his reflection in the mirror taking in his magnificent backside down to the floor when something caught my eye.

Sticking out of the garbage were the pregnancy test boxes and the four sticks I'd peed on.

chapter 69

I TRIED TO FIGURE OUT HOW I COULD HIDE THOSE WHEN IT HIT ME THAT the closet Kova was opening up contained the last box I'd yet to use.

Oh God.

My heart was beating harder than it ever had before. There was a pounding in my ears, a ringing that shot a shrill of anxiety through me. I felt my emotions rising to the top threatening to break the barrier I'd carefully put up. I felt the tears forming before the words were ever spoken. I felt it all coming, the heated words, the pain that would follow, the accusations. I had no idea what to do. It was all happening in slow motion and I couldn't stop it no matter how badly I wanted to.

Taking deep breaths, I was trying not to choke, but my chest burned, and I couldn't find the words to stop him from going in there. I'd had my chance to tell him and I hadn't. I'd been a coward, too scared to tell him I was pregnant. My hands shook, and my jaw bobbed. I felt my lunch in my stomach slosh around.

I'd forgotten I'd stuffed the box between the towels. I'd been so upset that day I didn't want to look at it or think about the positive tests, so I'd hid it.

I held my stomach, fear crippling me as Kova handed me a towel, then took in my face. His eyes were suddenly filled with concern and he opened his beautiful mouth to speak when I heard the box hit the floor.

Blood drained from my face. I was going to be sick. The room started to spin, the chill filling my veins, making me shake.

I watched him turn back to look at the closet, then down at the floor. His brows furrowed and he bent down to retrieve the box. I pressed the towel to my face, still unable to speak while he picked it up and turned it over.

Kova froze and I felt his confusion pulsating around us. The silence was earsplitting as he stared in shock at the pregnancy test box. I couldn't even hear him breathing.

Droplets of water surrounded his feet. He still hadn't grabbed his towel.

"When were you going to tell me?" he asked so quietly, not looking at me.

Words were lost on me. Oh God, I was going to be sick. My stomach was clutched with pressure and my heart was about to explode.

"When?" His voice was grave, low.

He turned his head to look at me and I still couldn't say anything. His eyes were huge. Color drained from his face too and I felt a tremor of blame in his gaze. My lips parted but nothing came out, because I knew there was nothing I could say that could fix this or justify not telling him.

"When, Adrianna?" Tears filled my eyes. His voice, so severely hurt that I was rooted in place. "Or were you not going to?" I was so guilty, and he knew it. "When?" he asked again, this time his voice rose. His beautiful green eyes were heartbroken.

Somehow, I was able to wrap the towel around my body and rush to my room. I shifted through my drawers and grabbed a pair of bikini panties and a tank top. Dropping the towel, I slipped on my clothes just as Kova walked in wearing a pair of shorts, water still dripping down his body, and the box firm in his hand. He hadn't even dried off.

My heart was racing so hard and fast. I took a step back, scared of how he would react. There was only one way this could go, and that was south.

"I asked you a question, Adrianna."

I glanced at the now crushed box in his hand. That was all it took for me to break down. I started crying profusely, my breathing erratic. I was trying to catch my breath, knowing this was going to kill us both. We'd come so far and now everything was ruined.

"I'm sorry. I'm sorry. I'm sorry," I cried. I didn't know what else to say.

"How long?"

"I don't know."

"What do you mean you do not know?"

I jumped at his harsh tone. "I mean I don't know how far along I am."

I reached blindly behind me for my bed. I was going to fall if I didn't lean on something. I dropped my hips to sit, the sight of my carpet blurry from my tears. Shame filled me. I couldn't even look at him.

"Take the test."

I shook my head, my lips pressed tightly together. Fat tears flowed down my face. "Take it, Adrianna."

I glanced up and a gush of air rushed from me. "I already did."

Eyes hurt, he said, "When?"

"Last week."

Understanding resonated within him and he turned ash white. His eyes dropped to my stomach then met mine again.

"You are pregnant."

It wasn't a question but an assessment. Covering my mouth with my hand, I nodded silently. A strangled cry burst from my lips and I gasped, drawing in a loud breath. The dense air singed my lungs. The pain wracking my heart was unbearable, but it didn't compare to the torture I could see burning inside Kova. I felt it, God, did I feel it, and it was overwhelming. Like a black cloud of smoke slowly killing me. He didn't seem angry. He looked downright devastated, and I didn't know if it was because I didn't tell him sooner, or because I was pregnant. His entire face was that of grief and regret and it was suffocating me. He stared at me like he was reaching out, searching for an answer I was incapable of giving. His emotions were on display for me, so prevalent that I could barely stand to explain myself.

Inhaling a heavy breath, I finally spoke. My voice was very low. "I took four tests. They're in the garbage in my bathroom."

Kova spun around before I'd finished my sentence and I found the will in me to rush after him.

He picked up my garbage pail and turned it over, shaking it so all the contents fell out. One stick was turned up and I could see the two pink lines from where I was standing, so I knew he could too.

"I'm sorry," I said again. "I know I should've told you but I was scared and I didn't want you to blame me and think I planned it. I tried to tell you a few times but I just couldn't do it. I was too scared. Then you started talking about Katja's pregnancy and I didn't want you to think I was lying too."

Kova fell to his knees and picked up the tests, flipping them over. He didn't say anything, just studied them, reading the two that clearly showed I was pregnant.

"I know you probably hate me for this, but I really did try. I don't know what happened… I took the pills like I was supposed to. I didn't even know I was pregnant until we came back from the meet."

Holding the tests, he turned to face me. He squeezed his eyes shut, remorse filling his face. "I could never hate you," he said.

Another sob burst from me and I ran to where he was kneeling. I got down and looked into his eyes. "I'm so sorry."

"You were pregnant at the meet," he said.

"Yes, I just didn't know it."

His face fell. "What made you take the test?"

"Avery. I was so sick, and it was her idea. I just thought I was sick because of traveling and my stupid kidney issues and how it took so much out of me. It never occurred to me I could be pregnant."

He looked down at the tests, staring hard at them like he was looking for an answer.

"You have to be a few months. Two, close to three."

"No," I wept, my jaw quivering. "That means the heart is beating." Fresh, warm tears fell.

Kova looked up, but before he could say anything, I told him what I had already decided.

"I can't have a baby, Kova. I'm sorry but I just can't. I'm going to have an abortion. I've already made up my mind. It's my body and you can't force me to have a kid, not that I think you want one, but I'm not changing my mind. I'm sorry but it's what I have to do."

I don't think I even breathed through that.

"Were you even going to tell me?"

I blinked. I went for the truth because at this point I had nothing left to lose. "I honestly don't know. I was going to, then I didn't know how to tell you. I really don't know. I want to say yes, but I've been a mess and I couldn't find the words. There was never a right time." Exhaling, I said, "No, I know I would've told you. I just don't know when I would have."

Recognition dawned on him. He held the stick up. "This is why you kept pushing me away?"

I nodded.

Kova grabbed all the sticks, then carried me to my room where he sat me down, then placed the throw blanket I had at the end of my bed around my shoulders. He rubbed my arms, trying to warm me up and sat down next to me.

This wasn't what I'd expected. I'd expected rage. I'd expected yelling. I'd expected the worst and yet there was nothing. But he wasn't saying anything, and that terrified me.

"How was I supposed to tell you I'm pregnant?"

Silence.

"I knew you would be mad. I knew it."

Silence.

"An abortion is the only option for us."

Silence.

"I can't have a baby."

Silence.

Silence.

"Say something!" I yelled, breathing heavily.

I could deal with Kova's anger. I could handle Kova's pain. What I couldn't handle was his heartbroken silence. My stomach was a pit of rocks and the fact that he was sitting there in utter silence did nothing to ease the stress I was under.

His eyes flared and he glared at me. "What do you want me to say, Adrianna!" he yelled. "You have already made up your mind. What is done is done," he spat. "That is it. There is nothing left for me to say."

I pulled back and gasped. "You're mad," I whispered, shocked. "You expected me to have this baby, didn't you?"

"No, I did not. If you wanted to, then I would have supported your decision. I would never force you to have a child or get rid of one. I am hurt that you did not come to me," he said, and I got fired up real quick from that. "But I know I have no right to be upset after what I have done to you, so I am dealing with this the best way I can right now." He was quiet for a moment and I started to cry again. "I just wish you would have told me sooner so I did not have to find out this way."

"I'm sorry," was all I could think of saying. I didn't know what to say.

He frowned, looking at the tests again then back to me. His eyes searched mine. There was nothing but sorrow in them.

"I am devastated for more reasons than one. I am mad because I did not ever want a child, but finding out you are pregnant, looking at you and imaging you with my child, it makes me think differently. It makes me want that with you now and it fucking kills me that you will have an abortion…" Kova trailed off and started mumbling in Russian. "What I am, is sorry that I got you pregnant." He looked down, almost as if he couldn't bear to say his next words. "And now you have to terminate our child."

He couldn't even finish the heartbreaking words. We were both paying the price and I wondered how we would ever persevere from this.

"Honestly, it kills me too," I whispered. I'd spoken those words from my heart. "This is going to ruin everything, isn't it?"

"It definitely changes things." He paused, and I held my breath. "If anything, it makes me love you even more than I thought was possible."

My lips parted, my heart shattering down the center. I got up and stood in front of Kova, palming his cheeks. He wrapped an arm around my shoulders and pulled me to him. I felt his breath on my neck, the way his body trembled against mine. I broke down, my heart emptying, and I cried with him. He pulled me tighter and put me on his lap. Kova tried to look at me, but I wouldn't let him and I kept my head down. I leaned in, breathing him in, needing him so desperately. Wrapping my arms around his neck, I placed my face against his chest, and I could hear his erratic heartbeat. I looked up at him just in time to see one lone tear fall down his beautiful face.

"You will never understand how truly sorry I am. For everything I have ever done. To you. To us. For all the pain I have caused you. You must know whatever you want to do, whatever you decide, I will support you. I love you so much, Adrianna, that at times it is hard for me to deal with. Damn the consequences. We are a team—but the truth is, when *you* exhale, *I* inhale. Not the other way around. I might be the beast beneath your beauty pushing you to succeed, but you are the anchor that holds me steady in a churning ocean threatening to drown me. It is how it has been for me since day one, and it will continue to be that way. Always remember that. So whatever you decide, I will support you."

I cried harder than I'd ever cried in my life.

I cried for myself.

I cried for Kova.

I cried for our child we'd never get to meet.

I cried harder, feeling his sorrow as my own.

After a few moments when the tears subsided, I pulled back and took a deep breath. Kova wiped my face and we stared into each other's eyes without saying any more words.

There was nothing left to say. He was right. This would definitely change things.

Easing myself from his lap, I moved to use the bathroom. The emotional stress of this conversation was killing my stomach. I probably just needed to splash some water on my face.

I took one step, but Kova grabbed my wrist and pulled me between his legs. He placed both hands on my hips, then leaned forward and pressed a soft kiss to my stomach. I drew in a quiet gasp, trying to hold back the tears. Kova looked up at me with sorrow in his sad green eyes, almost like he was in mourning.

With his hand splayed on my stomach, he reached forward to press his lips to mine.

"Kiss me, damn it," he fucking begged.

Oh, God, my heart. His gravelly voice made my jaw tremble and the tears to surge again.

"I don't want this to change anything between us," I said against his lips. He started breathing heavily. "I'm scared."

"Kiss me, Ria, please," he begged, his voice completely shattered this time. "I need you to kiss me so I know you do not hate me. So I know you still love me as much as I love you."

And so I did. I kissed him while he kept his hand on my stomach as if he needed to remember this moment, us, and what was growing inside me that we had created. I kissed him back for not treating me the way I'd feared he would. I kissed him back for understanding that while this was our choice, I made the decision and he accepted it. I kissed him back for us and the hope he'd see from this moment on that I was still his and he was still mine and we would forever be Kova and Ria.

As Kova dragged me closer to him, a knock sounded at the door. Our kiss broke apart and our expressions mimicked each other's.

"Are you expecting someone?" he asked.

I shook my head and stepped back.

Puzzled, we both got up to answer the door. The only other person who knew where I lived that ever came over was Hayden, but after the discussion I'd just had with Kova, I prayed it wasn't him.

The rapid knocking persisted and I looked over my shoulder and saw Kova close behind, the pregnancy tests still in his hand. It crushed me to see that because I felt like it meant he was holding onto the only evidence he'd ever have of our baby.

Turning the lock, I didn't look through the peephole before I pulled it open. Hindsight is 20/20, and looking back, I should've never answered the door.

Maybe I'd prayed a little too hard, because right now, I would do anything for it to be Hayden.

chapter 70

"D AD?"
    He didn't hear me.
    He didn't see me.
The silence was deafening, the accusation clear. All he saw was Kova in my condo without a shirt on, fresh from the shower, the water from his hair dripping over the scarred letter I'd marked on his chest.

I was going to be sick. Dad tilted his head to the side, his harsh gaze taking in Kova. I was in nothing but a small shirt and underwear.

It felt like everything was happening in slow motion as my father stepped inside the condo and shut the door.

Dad glanced at Kova's bare chest, then his jaw locked. Nostrils flaring, he said, "Well, this is certainly a surprise. Care to tell me what you're doing in my daughter's condo, Konstantin?"

A chill of terror rolled down my spine. I held my stomach. This was far worse than telling Kova about the pregnancy.

Kova stood completely stone-faced. We both knew there was no legitimate reason for him to be here, and I kind of hoped he wouldn't try to make an excuse. Kova gave nothing away. His breathing was steady as he remained calm under pressure. The situation was fucked up, and even I knew there was nothing I could say to get us out of this. We were both caught red-handed.

"Do you have an answer for me?" Dad asked. He removed his navy blazer and folded it over one of the high-back chairs.

Kova's eyes shot to mine and the tension grew to a thickening level. His Adam's apple bobbed.

"No. Don't look at my daughter," my dad said casually, as he if was asking him to lunch. He uncuffed his sleeves and rolled them up. "I asked *you* a question and I expect an answer from *you*."

Kova put his hands up. "Frank—"

"You know how this looks, right? A man, one I trusted with my teenage daughter—my sick daughter—to watch over her is in her condo. Both of you are wearing fucking scraps of clothing, not to mention, is that a fucking tattoo with the letter of her name?" His jaw flexed, and I thought he was going to pop a blood vessel in his eyes. "So, tell me, what the fuck are you doing in my condo with my fucking daughter?"

My stomach dropped. His cursing isn't what held me immobilized, it was his words spoken with such disgust that frightened me.

"Are you a sick fucking pervert preying on young girls?"

My jaw dropped. "Dad—"

Dad pointed a finger at me. "Shut your goddamned mouth, Adrianna. There is nothing you can say that will help you out of this. I've seen everything I need to. Go pack your clothes. Whatever the fuck this is, ends here."

Tears sprung to my eyes. "No," I gasped.

"Frank, please—"

"You can't be serious," I said, barely able to breathe. My heart was in my throat. "Just let me explain. It's not what it looks like, I swear."

Dad lowered his voice, his eyes narrowing to slits. "Does it look like I'm fucking kidding? I'm not playing games with you."

I took a step closer, but also kept a decent amount of distance. I could feel the heat and rage blistering around him, and it scared me.

"Dad, it's not what you think. It's really not." I tried to think of a lie he'd believe. "I wasn't feeling well. I got sick, and he was helping me."

A sardonic huff escaped him. "Joy was right. This whole time she was right about you and your coach, and I denied it. She showed me a photo of you guys I rejected it, saying she'd Photoshopped it for her own motive. I figured I'd give you the benefit of the doubt and show up for you to explain, but then I find this…" He eyed Kova with repugnance, then looked back to me. "I defended you. I thought you were smarter than this. I thought you were better." He scoffed under his breath. "What a fucking fool I was."

My face fell. I blinked and Dad was standing in front of me. I jumped backward, but he grabbed me in a rough hold and yanked. Pain shot through my shoulder and I yelped.

"Ow, you're hurting me!" I cried out and tried to pull away.

Dad's eyes bulged from his head. "This is what you wear around your coach! Do as I say and get your things now, Adrianna, or I will fucking lose it." He paused. "Now."

Kova stepped in. "You do not need to hurt her because of me. Let her go."

Dad's head whipped toward Kova. His gaze was deadly. "Do not tell me what to do with *my* daughter, you sick fuck. I asked you to watch over her and protect her. And this is how you do it? Get the fuck out of my face, you disgusting piece of shit." He paused, his face getting redder by the second, his grip thickening. "I trusted you! I'm calling the cops—I want you thrown in jail!"

"No! Dad, no!" I yanked away again, but it was a mistake because he only jerked me harder. A breath gushed from me. Something twisted in my arm and it made me weak in the knees. The pain made me lose my breath and I almost fell to the floor.

Kova calmly held his hands up in surrender. My eyes widened at the tests in his white-knuckled fist. Air lodged in my throat. He'd forgotten he was holding them. If there was a God, I would sell my soul for Dad not to see what he was holding. It would only escalate things and make them worse.

"Frank, please do not do this to her. I will leave."

Dad turned toward Kova with fire spewing from his eyes. "Is this what I've been paying for? For you to fuck my daughter?" Then he turned toward me. "Joy was right. I had no idea you were such a slut."

He pulled his phone out with his other hand and swiped it open. I needed to keep his attention on me and away from Kova now.

Kova took a step closer.

"Take another step toward me, Konstantin, and I won't hesitate."

My stomach was a knotted mess. I didn't want Dad to try and hit Kova because as much as I loved my dad, Kova was much bigger and stronger and I worried one punch would knock him out.

"Dad! Stop! Nothing is happening here. Why won't you believe me?" I bawled, but he pulled my arm so hard and high that it forced me to stand on my toes. He twisted it behind my head and a cry burst from my throat. I'd been luckily enough to have never broken a bone, but judging by the agony that took my breath away, I'd say it was fractured or dislocated.

"I'm done with your lies, Adrianna," Dad said.

Kova looked at me. I didn't see the tests in his hand anymore, he must've pocketed them. He was white as a ghost but riled and bursting with the impulse to protect me. I'd never once seen him as I did now, torn from trying to do the right thing and trying to not make it worse. He was holding back from stepping in with reason— he was wrong, we both were wrong—but he also couldn't take seeing me in such pain either.

"My arm, please, let go," I said breathlessly, tears streaming down my face again. "It hurts."

Swallowing, Kova raised his voice. "Do not call the cops. I will walk away from everything. I will sell my gym, I will go back to Russia if I must. You will never see me again, but this is not her fault. Do not ruin her career because of me. Just let her go and I will leave."

Dad's fingers dug into my skin, and my own fingers were numb from his tight hold on me.

Dad ignored Kova as he erratically pressed buttons on his phone. I watched, trying to see who he was calling. My heart was going to jump out of my chest. I was shocked that he'd call the police because it would affect the Rossi name as well as Kova's reputation.

I took one quick glance at Kova, then I turned toward the front of my dad and shoved at his chest with my free hand, pushing as hard as I could. My strength was weak, but I couldn't let this happen. I had to stop him.

Only, I didn't push hard enough.

Dad's eyes flared, a blackness overtaking them. I didn't recognize him. My stomach clenched with fear. He reacted, twisting my arm so hard that I felt another pop. Kova's eyes widened and he rushed to grab me. A scream erupted from my throat and my dad finally let go. The pain took my breath away and I clutched my arm to my chest, closing my eyes in agony as I fell into Kova.

"Adrianna," Kova said. The tone in his voice alarmed me.

I opened my eyes and saw that my dad was about to press the phone icon. Standing up, I lunged with my good hand and reached out, slapping his phone away. It tumbled to the floor and the screen cracked.

Relief coursed through me, but not for long.

The back of his hand flew toward my face.

My head whipped to the side and I flew, my body slamming to the floor with a crash so hard my head smacked it. Kova bent down immediately and tried to help me, but Dad threw him off me.

"Don't you dare touch my daughter!" he roared.

Holding my cheek, I opened my eyes just as Kova got up, but that was all Dad needed. In a fit of rage, he flew at Kova with his fist raised in the air. Kova ducked and swiftly moved to the side, but surprisingly he didn't retaliate. I glanced down, seeing that his hands were balled into fists and his knuckles were straining against his skin.

"Touch her again and I'll rip your head from your neck!"

"I'll tell the cops you hit me," I said hoarsely, trying to stop the fight. I blinked, trying to clear my blurry vision. I don't think I could ever do that to him, but I needed a diversion. My stomach was aching, and it was a struggle to stand. "Your hand print will still be across my face. Not to mention, I can't move my arm. You attacked me. I'll deny anything you say about us because there's nothing to admit."

"Who knew what a manipulating young lady you'd turn out to be. Did you forget you're still a teenager and have zero authority here? You're coming home with me, and Konstantin is leaving in handcuffs."

I shook my head. I tried to get up and whimpered from the throb in my arm. Tears streamed down my cheeks and my eye felt swollen already.

A meaty fist landed on Kova's jaw and his head flew to the side, blood spurting from the corner of his mouth. He picked himself up quickly and took a step toward my father, but he quickly stopped when he realized what he was going to do.

His skin was flushed, damp with perspiration. I could feel the fury in his blood simmering beneath the thin layer. I'd never seen Kova so restrained before. The veins twirling down his arms were protruding, and every time he made a fist they swelled larger. His jaw was locked as he stared at my dad.

"You won't hit me because you know I'm right. You're a fucking pervert," Dad accused, walking toward him. My heart slowed down as I watched. "But that won't stop me," he said, and hit him again.

Kova took another round to the face and my heart broke for him. He put his arms up, blocking a few swings, then he gave my dad one strong shove. Dad stumbled back, and Kova placed the back of his hand to his mouth and wiped the blood away, leaving a smear across his jaw.

I couldn't take Kova being hit again. I knew he was restraining himself for me—and maybe because they were friends—and he knew deep down he was wrong, but I couldn't handle it anymore. It was slowly killing me.

Pushing off the floor, I ran forward and shoved myself between them. Kova saw what I was aiming for and flung me to the side as my dad landed another blow to Kova. I hit the floor so hard my vision shifted to double.

"Stop," I screamed and got back up.

Kova saw, his frantic eyes wide as I pulled myself up. "Stop, Adrianna!" he ordered, but I couldn't.

Dad was in a blind rage and I had to break them up before something worse happened.

"Dad, please stop," I said and grabbed onto his bicep.

He reared back without looking and shoved me with such force that I tripped over my feet. My breath rushed from me as I slammed into the wooden coffee table and my head hit the corner of the couch. Everything went black for a split second as stars danced in my vision, and I crumbled to the floor.

I was suddenly too weak. My body was giving out.

I tried to push up, but I was struggling to find even an ounce of energy. I heard Kova yell something, then, a crunching sound.

I had to get back up.

I was so disoriented, I couldn't tell whose blood was on my dad's fist, and I was sure my arm was fractured. I sucked in a strangled breath and tried to pick myself up, cradling my midsection. A sharp pain lacerated my stomach. I drew in a gasp, feeling like I was going to vomit. Something warm glazed down my thighs, but I was too off balance and fell to the floor again.

"Please! Stop hurting each other," I cried out, and managed to stand on wobbly legs. I was afraid to walk.

I looked up. Dad's back was to me as he threw punches at Kova, who was still blocking them. I took a few steps to reach him, hoping he'd stop when he saw me.

I don't know who pushed me, but my attempt to break them up was foiled. In a blink, I was flying across the room again, this time over the couch and onto the wooden coffee table.

My head whipped back and slammed into the wood with a crack. I slid across the table, taking the décor with me. Glass shattered under my body as I crumbled to the floor in a dead heap. My head began pounding, and I felt warm, sticky liquid all around me.

This time I couldn't move.

This time, I wouldn't be getting back up.

Coldness seeped into me and a metallic taste filled my mouth. I wondered if I'd bitten my lip when I fell.

I tried drawing in a breath only to flinch and cry out in agony from the sharp, shooting pain. A cough erupted out of me that caused my ribs to ache. I whimpered and tears fell from my eyes. I struggled to draw in a lungful of air again without it feeling like I was suffocating.

I could hear them scuffling and I tried to push myself up one last time, only to fall to the floor again.

"She is pregnant." I heard Kova say.

"Pregnant! What do you mean pregnant!"

"Adrianna." I heard my name in the distance.

"Open your eyes!"

"She is bleeding everywhere!"

Their voices began to blend together.

"Oh, my God."

"What did you do!"

"Open your eyes."

"Call an ambulance. Hurry!"

I couldn't move my lips to respond. I couldn't lift myself to stop them from killing each other.

My vision was spotty. I tried to blink a few times, attempting to stay awake and fight the body-draining fatigue that was taking over me. I just wanted to go to sleep.

Sleep sounded like a good idea.

"*Malysh!* Stay with me!"

I couldn't.

All I could do was lay there in agony, my broken body trembling in a warm pool of blood as my eyes rolled shut and darkness consumed me.

To be continued one final time...

dismount

BOOK 5 IN THE OFF BALANCE SERIES

To every Off Balance reader who stayed with me through the good and the bad,
who never gave up on this series and begged for more…
Thank you.
Dismount is for you.

She's standing on a line between giving up and seeing
how much more she can take.
—Anonymous

chapter 1

I FADED IN AND OUT OF CONSCIOUSNESS, MY THOUGHTS BEFUDDLED AND muggy.

I drew in a breath and smelled the pungent scent of chemicals, like a mixture of antiseptic and iron. I tried to move my fingers, but they only jerked. My skin pulsated from the top of my head to the tip of my toes. I felt like I was retaining gallons of water, my body was so swollen and stiff.

I tried to open my eyes, but they were heavy, laden with exhaustion. I took another breath, though it was tighter this time. My brows twitched. I wasn't sure where I was, but I knew I wasn't in my condo.

Alarm was a low vibration under my skin trying to rouse me, but, God, I was so tired. Warmth surrounded me like a cozy blanket, cocooning me in its embrace. Darkness called me back with open arms, and I moved freely toward it. Toward that sublime state where I felt no pain in my body and my heart didn't feel like it was breaking a thousand times over. I felt nothing as I was suspended over the clouds. I wasn't sad anymore.

I only felt one thing—freedom.

"Adrianna, can you hear me?"

A voice I didn't recognize called to me, followed by a beeping sound. My first real thought was that my kidneys had failed, but it was gone just as quick as it came. I was too lethargic to move, to care, to open my eyes.

"Adrianna."

I didn't respond. For a brief moment I wondered if I even could. I nestled deeper under the blanket of serenity, yielding to its pull. All I wanted to do was go back to sleep.

"Adrianna, do you know where you are?"

The question sounded like it came from an isolated location far, far away. I reached for it, but exhaled a heavy, drained breath instead.

"Adrianna."

I stirred. The voice was closer this time. My eyelids fluttered as I struggled to open them, curious of the commotion I sensed around me. What was going on? My breathing seemed to grow denser, and that annoying beeping sound was back. It intensified as I fought to wake.

"She may not be ready to wake up just yet," another voice I didn't recognize said. "She suffered internal injuries and a concussion. She needs time to rest."

Someone was holding my hand. I tried to move my fingers to let them know I was okay, but nothing, no response. I waited and tried again. Willed them to move, twitch, anything. I wanted to convey that I was here. I was okay. But again, nothing.

I released a breath through dry lips. My eyelids felt so warm, like when I had a fever—a telltale sign I was sick. I swallowed thickly, my throat burned. Too tired to fight the pull of sleep, I was ready to drift off when a light shined in my eye. The brightness gave me an instant headache and I moaned in pain under my breath.

"Adrianna, follow my voice."

I wasn't sure I wanted to. I was completely immobilized but content. The exhaustion was too much and the warmth was winning. All I wanted was to go back to sleep and stay in this layer of protection and security without a worry in the world.

I released a tired breath and let myself be pulled under again.

Someone was crying. The whimpering was soft and quiet, as if they suffered in anguish and didn't want to be heard.

Something wasn't right.

I squeezed my eyes tight and tried to figure out where I was. I took in the sounds around me, the sterile smell, the hushed voices. But my mind was still too jumbled to sort it out.

My first thought was to not move—something that had been ingrained into my head since the first time I stepped inside a gymnastics facility. If I'd gotten injured, I could make it worse by moving, especially since I couldn't feel anything.

Slowly and carefully, I started with my feet when I heard that incessant beeping again. A groan vibrated in my throat. I managed to curl my toes, not too much because they were stiff. They moved, though, and then I tried to wiggle my fingers again. Finally, they moved too.

A soft sniffle caught my attention, pausing my movements. My forehead creased as I took in the sterile scent again, then it hit me. I was at the doctor's office.

When did I go to the doctor? I didn't have an appointment scheduled.

Inhaling a deep breath, it lodged in my chest from pulling too hard. I noticed my breathing was different, like I'd been hit by a truck. I was breathing heavier and I expelled every ounce of air like it was my job. My nostrils flared. There was a cool draft of air around my nose. My arm was dead weight as I reached up and blindly felt around my face. A plastic tube was attached to my skin leading to my nose. I was on oxygen. I froze.

A tremor rocked through me. My dry eyes opened, and I squinted, trying to take in my surroundings. I briefly glanced down my body then lifted my gaze to look around the room. Everything was blurry, but I got the gist of it.

There were tubes attached to me that were connected to machines I didn't know how to read. I heard the whimpering again and turned to see a woman sitting with her head tilted toward the floor. She was alone and crying. My heart dropped, and that stupid beeping sound accelerated. Then it all came roaring back.

Kova.

The pregnancy.

Dad.

The fight.

Blood… So much blood.

I wasn't at the doctor's office, I was in the hospital.

The last thing I remembered was flying across the room. I'd landed on the coffee table and had taken everything with me when I fell to the floor. Then my world had turned black.

My brows creased. I vaguely remembered shattered glass. Had I been cut?

A memory of lying in a pool of blood flashed into my mind. A loud gasp parted my lips. Panic surged through me at a hundred miles a minute. Blood. Was the blood from getting scuffed up in the altercation between Dad and Kova?

Or was it from the baby?

I glanced around, disoriented. My head was a little hazy and my vision still blurry, but I finally recognized the woman sitting in the corner.

"Sophia?" I said, trying to sit up.

Tears filled my eyes as bile rose to my throat. My eyes widened in alarm. I felt like I was electrocuted. I looked down to find my right arm in a sling. What the hell happened to me?

Another memory filled my head. Dad had twisted my arm in anger. Was it broken?

A sharp pain sliced through my chest and I covered my mouth with my free hand. Sophia moved into action like she knew what was going to happen next. She jumped up from the chair and grabbed a trash can, holding it for me just in time.

After a few more embarrassing rounds of retching, Sophia took the can from me and walked toward the bathroom. She returned with a plastic cup of water.

"Thank you," I said as she handed it to me. Shit. My throat was raw.

Our gazes met. Her green eyes were bloodshot as they beheld mine. The look in them was both relieved and terrified to see me. I wasn't sure what she knew, or how much she knew, but she seemed so sad, and that upset me.

I averted my gaze and looked down. There was an IV inserted and taped down to the top of my free hand. The inside of my elbow was stressed with shades of blue from injections I didn't recall having.

From the corner of my eye, I saw Sophia take a step.

"Wait," I choked out and she stopped. I had a feeling she was going to get my dad. I wasn't ready for him.

"What's wrong?"

I shook my head, the pain making it unbearable to speak. My arm wasn't in a cast, so it must not be broken. But I prayed my dad hadn't fractured it either.

"How did I get here?" I asked, my throat still scratchy. Maybe I should've asked *when* I had gotten here.

I took a small sip of water and handed her back the cup. The last thing I wanted to do was throw up again.

Sophia placed it on the tray at the foot of the bed. Her brows furrowed. "You don't remember?"

I blinked. "I just remember Dad…" I hesitated, and her lips flattened as she gave me an empathetic look.

"Your father fighting with Konstantin?"

My teeth dug into my bottom lip. I glanced away, nodding subtly. "How long have I been here?"

"Two days."

My brows shot up and I looked back at her. "Two days?" I repeated. "How?"

Sophia took a small step toward me. She fidgeted with her fingers. The chipped paint on her nails caught my attention. I could tell she was being

cautious. Worry prickled my arms. The more the anxiety grew inside me waiting for her answer, the faster the machine behind me beeped.

I'd been asleep for two days. Two whole days.

"I think I should go get your father for you, then you guys can talk."

"Wait. Why are you here?"

She tensed and I instantly felt guilty for my choice of words. I didn't mean
to blurt it out and make her feel bad, but I didn't understand what was going
on either.

Where was Kova?

"I'm sorry. I didn't mean it like that," I said. "I'm just confused. That's all."

"I can imagine you are." I looked at her, waiting for an answer. "Your father and I...well...we had seen each other earlier in the day." Her voice was soft.
"He called me when you were taken in the ambulance. I met him here and have
been here ever since."

My frown deepened.

"You were unconscious and bleeding. Frank didn't know if you'd hit your
head or where the blood was coming from. He said he tried to wake you up and
when he couldn't..." Her voice trailed off, too stricken with emotion to finish.
"Well, you know the rest."

Her words replayed in my head. My chest rose higher and faster. My dad
hadn't known where the blood came from?

I glanced down at my arms. White gauze bandages were wrapped in various
places, including around my arm in the sling. They probably covered injuries I'd
sustained when I crashed into the glass table and took down the décor with me.
I remembered hitting my head. I remembered feeling warm blood pool around
me. At the time, I'd assumed it was from the shards of glass. Now, I wasn't so
sure. There had been too much blood.

Tears blurred my eyes and my jaw quivered. Gripping the starched white
bed sheets in my hand, I trembled as I fought with myself. I didn't want to pull
the sheet back and see blood. If I did, then that would confirm my worst nightmare and I'd know the truth of what had really caused the bleeding.

Sophia walked over to me and placed her hand over mine. I swallowed hard
and looked up at her. I could see the indecision in her eyes and how this was the
last thing she wanted for me. I could tell she really wanted to help me but was
hesitant as to how. What role in my life would she play?

My breathing grew ragged as I fisted the blanket tighter. I didn't have to
ask, and she didn't have to answer. It was a given that if she was here, then Dad
had told her everything. My chest strained with raw emotion as the look in my
birth mother's eyes confirmed my fear. Her face slowly fell.

Silent tears streamed down my cheeks as the truth set in. Sophia's gaze filled with sympathy. I wanted her to hug me, to tell me everything would be okay. I shouldn't feel a sense of loss, and I shouldn't be upset since this is essentially what I wanted.

But I was, and I did.

I'd had a miscarriage. I'd lost my baby.

I didn't need anyone to confirm it for me. I felt it.

Placing a hand over my stomach, I closed my eyes and tried to feel for something, a signal I was wrong and just being paranoid. There was nothing. Had I felt one before?

I didn't want to answer that.

While I may not have intended to have the baby initially, up until I walked into a clinic and had the procedure done, the choice was not final and still mine to make. Mine to keep a child, mine to say goodbye to when I was ready. Then there was Kova's choice too.

But instead this was what I got—my karma. My punishment for wanting an abortion was not being allowed the opportunity to say goodbye.

chapter 2

MY BABY WAS GONE.

I may not have been ready to be a mother, but that didn't lessen the loss for me.

I guess history does repeat itself. I had a child taken against my will, and so had Sophia.

Warm tears blurred my vision. I rolled my lips between my teeth and bit down, fighting the emotion. Sophia took a seat at the edge of the bed. She was on the verge of tears too. My heart felt so damn empty as my world crumbled around me.

Without thinking, I leaned into Sophia's shoulder and rested my head on her. She turned to look at me. I needed someone who wouldn't judge me, but instead help me carry this burden.

She embraced me with open arms, and I closed my eyes. For a split second, it almost felt like this was what she'd wanted, for me to come to her. Her hand ran down my hair in a maternal fashion and I sniffled, bringing her close to me.

"Your dad really wants to see you, Adrianna," she said, her voice soothing. "He's worried."

I hiccupped and pulled away, suddenly feeling weird. "I'm sorry," I whispered.

"Please don't apologize."

"I'm sure he's—"

The door to my hospital room opened and Dad waltzed in. He found me in a seated position and halted, his brown eyes widening. My heart dropped into the knotted mess in my stomach. Considering how we'd left off, I was expecting the worst.

"Adrianna!" he cried out.

My lips parted as he rushed toward me. I wanted to throw my arm around him and tell him I was sorry and that I never meant to upset him. The last thing I wanted was to drive a wedge between us.

Reaching my bedside, Dad put his arms around my body and hugged me like he never had before. An acute shooting pain like a bullet streaking through fire ricocheted through the length of my suspended arm. I gasped in agony, feeling instantly lightheaded from the vicious ache pulsating through my veins.

Dad pulled away and looked down at me as I clutched my arm in the sling. He visibly paled. "Did I hurt you?"

A whimper escaped my cracked lips. I hugged myself to hold in the pain as he cupped his mouth, his eyes filling with regret.

"What happened to my arm?"

My breathing grew dramatically dense, my chest rising and falling at an amplitude that was borderline heart attack inducing. If I couldn't move my arm, how was I going to do gymnastics? Looking into my dad's guilt-ridden eyes, I softly pleaded, "Tell me, please."

I could compete with kidney disease. I could compete while pregnant. I could compete with an Achilles injury. But I couldn't compete with an arm that felt broken.

"Your elbow is dislocated." Shame colored his cheeks. "You're going to have to wear that sling for a while. In a few days you can begin working on little exercise movements to get you back up and running. The doctor said it could take four to six weeks to heal completely."

Four to six *weeks?* I shrunk back. "I have the biggest competition of my life in ten days. I'll take it easy today and tomorrow, and maybe the day after, but I have to be able to regain movement quicker than that in order to compete."

Dad stared at me like I'd grown two heads. His challenging gaze made me feel defensive. My elbow was dislocated because of him.

"You're going to be in excruciating pain, Adrianna," he said. "It's going to be next to impossible to practice so soon."

"I'm sure it's nothing I haven't experienced already."

"You're going to be on bed rest regardless," he countered.

"Trust me, I can handle it. If I'm brushing up against death's door with stage four kidney disease, I can handle a dislocated elbow."

Dad's mouth set into a grim line. "Even so, I can't imagine you're going to be able to practice for a couple weeks, at the very earliest."

My heart sank into my gut. A couple of weeks before I could begin practicing again. No. Not possible. I didn't have fourteen days to spare. I would take a few days off, then start with a day or two of light stretches. Give myself five days total, then after that, all bets were off the table and I was going full steam ahead.

"Other than your elbow, how are you feeling?" Dad tried to change the subject.

How was I feeling? Angry. Hurt. Lost. Empty and totally gutted. I wanted to riot in the streets and then cry alone in my bed. There was a lot to talk about and I wasn't sure where to start or how he was going to react.

"I've been better."

Dad studied me, his eyes flickering through an array of emotions from love to disgust. This was as uncomfortable for him as it was for me.

"I think we need to talk about the extent of your injuries right now and the type of recovery you will be going through."

I swallowed hard. "Okay."

Dad pulled up a chair to my bedside. I glanced toward Sophia standing by herself near the window watching me.

"Aside from the dislocation, and some small cuts and scratches, you have a concussion." He clenched his eyes shut. "Adrianna, you will take the proper time to recover from that, which is around three to five days, and no sooner." Dad lowered his voice to a warning. "I will not take no for an answer."

"I'll take a few days for my head and elbow. I can't really miss more practice time than that."

I knew not to be too defiant when I was still very much in the wrong. I could work through pain, but a concussion was serious. I didn't have a death wish, despite everything.

Dad remained quiet for a long minute, which did nothing to ease the anxiety mounting in my veins. He exhaled a weary huff and leveled a stare at me that made my stomach twist.

"Adrianna," he said, and I knew what was coming next. "You'll be coming home with me."

I didn't respond.

"You'll get the proper rest and recovery there where I can watch over you."

I had no leg to stand on to defend my actions, but this wasn't just any situation where I was caught red-handed and had to pay the price. There were too many separate lives involved that could be ruined if one wrong thing was said. This was entirely different, and I was sure none of us knew what to do next.

"No, Dad, I'm not." His eyes rounded. I spoke low and slow, making sure I made my case clear despite my shaky voice. "I have the Olympic Trials in less than two weeks. I'm not going home. I'm staying here and I'm preparing for it. I didn't come this far just to walk away because of a little elbow issue."

He looked right through me. "I've already made arrangements to have the condo cleaned out and your car returned home. Once you're discharged, you're coming back to Savannah with me. End of discussion."

My throat was tight, I could barely swallow. I'd resent him for the rest of my life if he made me go home now and forfeit a once-in-a-lifetime chance at the Olympic Games. My pulse was pounding so hard it was going to explode. I didn't have much to barter with, so I had to play my cards right. I couldn't let him take this away from me.

"Do you want me to have a personal bodyguard to watch over me and takes me to and from practice? Live with me? I'll do that. Anything you want. But I *am* staying here and I *am* going to practice." When he didn't say anything and continued to stare right through me, my jaw began to wobble in despair. "Can you please at least consider the consequences after this competition? We're talking about the Olympic Trials, Dad. Let that sink in for a second."

I began to feel frantic. There was an underlying tremble in the pads of my fingers. Didn't he understand how huge this was? That every single practice mattered?

Dad's silence simmered like little bubbles of tension in the air. He let out an unnerving huff. His eyes hardened, even though I saw the empathy in them.

"Imagine my shock when that— When he—" Dad's body trembled. "When I learned you were pregnant. Then we get here and the doctor tells me you had a miscarriage and would need to have a procedure done." My cheeks flushed and I looked down in embarrassment. "Do you know they had to use some type of vacuum device to get the baby out?" He paused until I looked back up at him. "And you want to tell me what to do? That's not how it works in the real world, Adrianna."

I squeezed my eyes shut, letting the warm tears fall down my cheeks. My lips were firmly sealed together as I silently cried to myself.

A fucking *vacuum?* The visual made me nauseous. I hadn't known that was how an abortion was done. Not that it mattered now. I knew in my heart I'd had a miscarriage before he'd confirmed it. But hearing it from my father first and in such a way broke me. There was no compassion. Just stone-cold truth that seeped into my bones like black tar and embedded into me forever.

"Was it *his?*"

No. Why'd he have to ask that?

I squeezed my eyes tighter, tears filling them once again. The machine spiked behind me.

"Was the baby Konstantin's?"

I pressed my lips together and my cheeks flushed. There was no way I would answer that question honestly.

"I'm going to ask you one last time." Dad's voice was controlled and quiet, alarming. "Was the baby his?"

Holding my breath, I exhaled through my nose and shook my head.

chapter 3

I KNEW HOW IT LOOKED.

And I knew what Dad was thinking.

I denied the obvious truth, which made me look foolish.

A white lie never wears well.

From the corner of my eye, I saw Dad turn his head to look away. I probably disgusted him and that made me so sad inside, but I couldn't tell him it was Kova's baby. I never would.

"You're barely eighteen and you had a miscarriage."

"It wasn't his," I said low, my voice cracking. I'd rather him think I'd been with more than one person than to know the baby was Kova's.

Dad sniffled and I popped my head up to glance in his direction. Lines pulled tight around his eyes and his jaw subtly shook. I felt his despair a mile away, and a small breath hitched in my throat. My gaze shifted to Sophia, who was watching him with sadness. My shoulders sagged. It broke my heart to see how many people I'd hurt with my lies.

I looked away, unable to handle any more added heartache.

"So that's the reason you'll be coming back. You were heavily sedated and had a minor procedure on top of your concussion. You have to let your body rest."

"You can't force me to go home."

Dad whipped his head toward me. His eyes were as large as I was sure mine were. A mocking laugh bellowed from his chest. "Yeah? And how will you live? What money and connections do you have, Adrianna? Everything you have is because of me."

I sat up a little taller, humiliation burning under my skin. "I'll take the prize money and forfeit competing in college. I can support myself on that." I paused, hoping to seal the threat. "It's not like I'll be in any condition to compete anyway, not when I'm close to kidney failure as it is. I'll even sell my car if I have to."

Dad squinted his eyes and crossed his arms in front of his chest. "Fifty thousand dollars isn't enough to pay for dialysis and a transplant surgery. Now you sold your car but you can't get to treatment. What are you going to do?"

I ground my molars together, fighting back the angry tears. I didn't have anything else to barter with and he knew that.

Dad's gaze didn't waver. How could he hold my illness over my head? I was scared it would consume me before I had the chance to live and he knew that. It hurt almost as much as the vacuum comment he made.

"Don't test me, Adrianna. I have years of experience under my belt that you can't compete against."

"I'll figure it out."

He shook his head. "Not this time. How do you expect to practice when you're bleeding?" he jeered.

My emotions closed in on me. The way Dad was staring made me angrier by the second. Anything I said, he had an answer for. That wasn't fair. None of it was fair. I averted my gaze just as a fresh tear rolled over my cheek onto my arm. I looked down and my brows drew together. My emotions were on severe overload.

With my teeth, I pulled the tape back from the top of my free hand. I needed fresh air. I needed to get out of here.

"Stop it, Adrianna," Dad yelled and placed a hand over mine. I tried to shove him away. I was on the verge of losing it. My chest ached with sharp pains. Everything in me hurt.

"Leave me alone," I cried.

"The sooner you accept it, the better you'll be," he said, wrestling my hand away. I didn't have much strength and he knew that.

"I'm not accepting it," I responded. "I'm staying here. I'm an adult. I'm not missing that competition!"

"That just proves how naive you are. You can't support yourself, and you won't be able to support yourself to get to the competition." He paused and his eyes turned nearly black. "You have nothing."

God, I wanted to scream at the top of my lungs. This was never supposed to happen. None of this was supposed to happen. A concussion, dislocated elbow, and a fucking miscarriage.

"Do you have any idea how sick I am over the fact that he took advantage of you? Someone I trusted. He raped you."

"No, he didn't," I spat back. "He didn't touch me."

Dad glared at me, his eyes wild. "I almost beat him to death." He gritted the words out through his teeth. "He has your fucking initial cut into his chest, Adrianna." His hot breath blew over my face. "Care to explain that?"

"He didn't touch me," I said, as my breathing turned erratic. I was losing control. "He didn't touch me."

Oh, God. I was going to have a panic attack. Christ on a fucking stick.

"You'll never convince me otherwise. You might as well just tell me the truth, starting from the beginning."

For a split second I debated with myself whether to tell him or not. Of course, I wanted to get it off my chest to clear the air, but I knew deep down it wouldn't help the situation. If anything, it would make things worse.

"He didn't rape me," I whispered. "Kova didn't touch me." *Not in the way you think*, I wanted to add.

Dad stood straight. He peered down at me. "You sound like a typical victim," he said full of disgust.

My eyes closed in defeat and I dropped my head back onto the pillow. I shook my head, my voice soft. "I know the difference. I'm not a victim."

I looked up at the blinding white ceiling wondering where I'd go from here. Fat tears streamed down my temples. I laid in a freezing hospital room with my heart breaking.

Dad's hand enveloped mine. Something inside me broke, and suddenly, I wasn't an eighteen-year-old girl anymore with dreams and aspirations. I was just a child who wanted her dad.

Without giving it another thought, I sat up and leaned into Dad's side. I tried to be strong and push for what I wanted, but my heart could only hold so much. My forehead fell into the crest of his neck, and his arm came up to gently wrap around my shoulders. Dad hugged me despite everything. I sobbed softly as he rubbed my back.

I was so embarrassed, sad, filled with sorrow and longing. The anguish was too much to bear

"I'm sorry, Dad."

"I am too, sweetie." God, I hated the remorse in his voice. "What happened that night... Adrianna—"

"I know you never meant to hurt me, Dad."

He held me a few minutes longer as I cried on his shoulder. I pulled back and he reached for the tissue box on the tray.

"When I entered the condo and took in the scene... Saw what little you were wearing, the state of undress Konstantin was in, and that fucking A on his chest... I've never been filled with so much rage. I lost it."

I took a tissue and dabbed at my puffy eyes.

"Then you lost consciousness. You were bleeding and we couldn't wake you up. Konstantin yelled that you were pregnant. I grabbed my phone and dialed nine-one-one." Dad was quiet for a moment before he spoke again. "How long did you know you were pregnant?"

I swallowed. "I'd only just found out a few days before. When we got home from the competition, actually. I was so sick."

"Did you plan to tell me?" I shook my head and stared at the stark white bedsheet. I couldn't look at him. Dad released a strangled breath that eviscerated me. "You were going to have an abortion," he stated.

"Yes," I whispered.

"Adrianna, I wish you would've come to me. I could've protected you better."

I licked my lips. "There was no reason to come to you. I didn't need protection because he didn't touch me like you think he did."

"I thought you were dying." He paused. "I thought you died." He corrected himself, and I finally looked at him. "Do you have any idea what that does to a parent? You wouldn't wake up. You were as white as a ghost. There was blood everywhere."

Fresh tears fell from my eyes. "I'm sorry, Dad." I didn't know what else to say.

"When the paramedics arrived, we gave them a quick rundown of your health and the medications you were on before they carried you out on a stretcher. I thought that was the last time I was going to see you. The police asked questions…" His voice trailed off.

"Police?"

"Yes." He held my gaze. "That's what happens when you call nine-one-one. The police show up too. I told them Konstantin and I had gotten into a scuffle and you tried to break it up but were hurt in the process." He paused briefly before adding, "Then they took him away."

I stared at him in confusion. I'd been wanting to know where he was, but I was afraid to ask.

"I don't understand. What do you mean they took him away? Why?"

"He's been arrested."

Arrested.

I froze, unblinking.

I couldn't move.

I only focused on one thing.

Kova had been arrested.

chapter 4

I HELD MY STOMACH AND BENT OVER.

My heart pounded at the thought of Kova behind bars. The stupid machine behind me beeped erratically.

"Arrested for what?"

Dad was unfazed. "Rape."

"What?" My lips parted in shock. "But you just said you told the police you guys got into a scuffle. I don't understand."

"When the police asked what the fight was about, I told them he'd raped you and got you pregnant. Konstantin didn't fight it. He went with the police willingly."

Oh, God. I was going to be so sick.

The one thing I'd been concerned about was Kova getting arrested and the gymnastics committee finding out about us. If this got back to them… I shuddered. I didn't want to think about it.

My gaze flickered around the room aimlessly, overwhelmed by a million and one thoughts. I needed my phone, but I wasn't sure where it was. I needed Avery to do some digging for me, like arrest records. She was the only person I could trust.

"Kova didn't do anything." My voice was barely above a whisper. "You need to tell the police that, please."

He didn't bother to grace me with a response. My jaw trembled from holding back the scream trying to erupt from my throat like fireworks.

"Is he still in jail?"

Please say no.

"It's where he belongs."

"But he didn't rape me!" I gritted the words out through my teeth.

There went my restraint.

I couldn't handle anymore. My pulse was skyrocketing; my shattered heart was on the verge of bursting from my chest any second. I was moments away from having a stroke, and the stupid machine wouldn't shut the fuck up. This wasn't Kova's fault, and I wasn't a victim of anything. Nothing. For a fleeting moment I thought about airing the truth and telling Dad it was all me.

Screw it!

I leaned forward with fire in my veins ready to burn down the world.

"It was me. I went after him. I chased him. He didn't do anything I didn't want. It's not Kova's fault." Dad hardened to stone. He looked like he was going to explode. "None of this is his fault. I purposely enticed him until he couldn't say no, and I didn't give a shit that he had a girlfriend. That's the real truth."

"That's still no excuse. He's a grown man. He knew better."

"Just like you knew better with Sophia? Like Xavier knew better with Avery?"

"Adrianna Francesca!"

I bowed my head and closed my eyes. I didn't mean to drag others into it my mess.

"He had no *right!* He never should've let it happen. He was your coach, a teacher. He was a friend whom I trusted to watch over you. Not to manipulate you and get you pregnant." Dad stood and pushed the chair back. He glared down at me and pointed a shaking finger. "You'll never see him again."

My jaw dropped to my stomach. "I love him!" I shouted as I shook like a leaf on a tree blowing in the wind. I couldn't control it. "I love him," I repeated. "I love him, and there's nothing you can do about it. You'll never be able to change that."

Dad reared back. Repulsion filled his face. "Puppy love, Adrianna. You're just a child. You don't know the difference."

I rubbed at the ache across my chest, unsure whether the shooting pain was from the tension in the room or my kidney disease. It bothered me that he could disregard my feelings so easily when I'd told him the truth.

"It's not rape when I willingly gave myself to him. I'm eighteen. I'm telling you the truth," I implored him to believe me.

"I don't want to hear another word," he responded with a wave of his hand. "It's making me sick to my stomach to hear this. Say another word and I'll kill him for touching you before any inmate can get their hands on him. You know prisoners hate child abusers. Don't test me, Adrianna."

I was taken aback by his harsh tone. I was losing everything that mattered most to me. "It's not his fault." I wiped the tears away and said, "You can't stop me from seeing him. He's the reason I'm not living on antidepressants and rocking in a corner. He was there for me when my world fell to shit—"

"He took advantage of your most vulnerable state!"

Frantically, I shook my head in disagreement. "He didn't. I know you want to think that, but he didn't." I licked my dry lips. "When is he getting out of jail?"

"Not anytime soon, if I can help it."

All the air seized from my lungs until they constricted in desperation. How was this happening? Chills rolled down my arms as I stared at him wide-eyed in complete disbelief. Dad was really going through with this.

The door to my room opened. A nurse strode in and headed straight for the machine behind me. Dad and I glared at each other. He looked like he was going to ring my neck, but I wasn't backing down.

"All right, what do we have here?" the nurse asked.

"Nothing." I glanced away from Dad's lethal gaze and dried my eyes. "I'm fine, just talking to my dad."

She eyed me for a minute. "I'll be back in a few to change your IV. In the meantime, you need to rest." She turned her attention to my dad. He got the hint and stormed out of the room without a word, and the nurse followed him out.

I stared at the door as it closed behind them. A shadow shifted in the corner by the window, startling me. Sophia. I groaned in mortification.

"I forgot you were there. I'm sorry," I said. "I didn't mean to bring up your past."

"Don't apologize. It's an awful feeling when you think the world is against you." One corner of her mouth drooped down. I nodded in agreement. "He's just angry, you know." Her voice shook as she spoke. "He feels like he failed you as a father."

I closed my eyes and released a sigh. What a fucking mess. Quietly, I said, "He didn't."

"No parent will ever see it that way," Sophia said delicately. I looked up at her and she took a few steps toward me. "May I sit?" she asked, pointing to the chair Dad was just in.

"Of course."

"He just needs a little time to cool off. Frank worries about you all the time. His only daughter is extremely ill. Then he found out his friend was having an affair with her that resulted in a pregnancy. It's a lot to handle. When you didn't wake up yesterday and the hours kept passing, his coloring started to fade and he couldn't stop shaking. He was sweating profusely. I was worried he was going to faint that I had a nurse check his vitals. His blood pressure was high enough that they wanted to admit him for observation, but he refused."

My stomach tightened and shame colored my cheeks. I felt terrible he'd suffered like that. I'd always known if Dad had ever found out about Kova and me it would be comparable to at least a category three hurricane.

I didn't expect it to be catastrophic. That was the last thing on earth I wanted, and it made me feel like garbage because of it.

"Kova didn't rape me. He didn't take advantage of me. It wasn't like that."

Sophia gave me a knowing look. "Has your dad ever told you how he and I met?"

I shook my head. "No, but I haven't had much time to ask him about it. I know you were his assistant."

"We had a whirlwind type romance where the feelings lasted longer than the affair was supposed to. Frank was this big, powerful man, and I was a young girl with big city dreams in her eyes. I'd just graduated from high school early and had plans to attend the community college while working. Frank was this sought after real estate mogul at the time, and he'd happened to be looking for a part-time assistant." She gave me a helpless shrug. "We'd hit it off by accident, really. He would show me properties he was considering investing in, or buildings that were heavily detailed he admired, ones you'd have to have an eye to notice. He showed me the tricks of the trade. It was all very innocent at first.

"I was in awe of what he'd accomplished at his age, and I started talking to him about my future and asking questions and looking for advice. We'd connected and didn't even know it. The more we worked together, the more impossible it was to stop the growing feelings between us." She hesitated. "Frank was married, so I never hit on him, but I couldn't deny what I felt for him either. I wish I could pinpoint when and how, but things just clicked into place one day and we never looked back. We knew this was it." Sophia paused, quiet for a moment as she reflected. "There's a lot of things we would've done differently if we could go back. What I went through alone at the time was one of the most challenging moments in my life. No one understood me. I was labeled a homewrecker. But what people didn't know was that Frank and Joy were already on the verge of a divorce before I came along."

This was news to me. I felt bad for Sophia. She seemed like she had a gentle soul with good intent, yet she lived with so many regrets she still dealt with on a daily basis.

"He was going to leave her until Joy came barreling along and played the perfect part." She sounded remorseful and a little envious. "I don't blame her, though, and I don't hate her. She fought dirty and won."

I, on the other hand, had a fair amount of animosity toward Joy. She didn't just fight dirty, she kicked a dead horse and anyone else who stood in her way.

"I wouldn't say she won if you're here," I said.

A momentary twinkle lit Sophia's eyes, then she said, "Joy never loses."

chapter 5

I FROWNED AND PULLED THE THIN BLANKET TO MY CHIN. I WAS SO COLD and the chills were making their way down my arms.

How could Joy win if they were divorcing? I had so many questions I wanted to ask.

"Why are you telling me this?"

Sophia expelled a heavy breath. It made me wonder if this was harder for her to talk about than she let on.

"My parents were dedicated churchgoers and lived by the Bible. Well, my mom still is, my father passed away years ago. They had reacted in a similar fashion as Frank did with you, except they kicked me out. I was suddenly homeless and pregnant. I only had my sister, and she was sick.

"I know I'm not in any position to tell you what to do or to give you advice, but I want you to know that if you ever need someone to talk to, or a place to run, I'll always be here for you. I remember being your age like it was yesterday. The heart wants what it wants."

She looked at me and I felt like I was staring at myself. It was no wonder Joy hated the sight of me. I must've reminded her of Sophia every day of her life.

"What I'm trying to say is I want you to know you don't have to go through this alone. What happened in my life caused me to fall into a horrible depression I thought I was never going to climb out of. I don't want to see that happen to you. It's a lonely place to be and can destroy you mentally."

I nodded and relaxed into the bed, trying to get comfortable. Over the course of the last year, I'd been in and out of depression and I hadn't even known it until Kova pulled me completely from the black hole I'd been stuck in. He had forced me to face the facts. At the time I hated him for it, but it had also made me love him more because it was what I'd needed in order to move on. That was the day I'd carved a letter into his chest.

Dad would never see it through my eyes no matter how strong I made my case. What hurt the most was knowing nothing I did or said would ever change how he saw the situation. He automatically took me for a victim.

Tears rested on my eyelids. I sniffled. "I don't know what to do. Kova didn't hurt me. He didn't force me to do anything. I swear he didn't take advantage. I know I probably sound young and dumb, but it's the truth and Dad will never, ever believe me. Now Kova is in jail for rape, and Dad wants me to go home with him to rot."

My nostrils flared. I tried to hold back the emotional baggage that came with the territory, but I couldn't. My heart had been ripped from my chest and my future destroyed in a matter of minutes. I wished I had never answered the door.

"Maybe you should take some extra time off for *you*," Sophia suggested lightly. My brows rose. "I think you have a lot going on and need some time to yourself. I did some soul searching after I lost everyone I loved. Frank, you, my sister…even my parents. I'd been kicked out and I was so alone and scared. I hardly had any self-esteem. I wish someone had told me if I focused on myself right then I'd live a happier, longer, fuller life." She paused. "I was too upset to realize that. The most important thing in your life right now is you. That's the only way you're going to get better."

Sophia looked toward the door and back at me, then leaned closer. "I probably shouldn't tell you this"—she dragged her teeth over her bottom lip—"but I think it would help rest your mind." My brows furrowed at her hesitation. "Konstantin isn't in jail for rape. He was arrested for assault."

My jaw plummeted to the floor. "What are you talking about?"

"You have to understand your dad is devastated. People act on emotion first and think later, especially when the situation is dire. Frank only told the police Konstantin attacked him. You're not involved in any of it."

My jaw was still hanging open. I was speechless as a new wave of nausea turned my stomach.

"I don't understand. Why would he let me believe Kova was charged with rape?"

She gave me an apologetic look like she was torn down the middle. "He's your dad, Adrianna. I think if he had it his way, Konstantin would be locked up for the rest of his life." Her eyes roamed my face. "I think rape is easier for him to accept rather than think his daughter willingly slept with someone he trusted…and then got pregnant."

My eyes dropped down to the bed. She was right, and I was sure I'd probably act the same way if I was—

No. I let out a breath. I let that thought go. I couldn't go there.

"I'm going to see if I can get him to think about dropping the charges. I think down the line he'll regret it."

I didn't say anything. I wasn't sure how to respond properly.

"I think he needs to be reminded of how it was for us," she continued. "Then ask himself if he'd want that for you. I'm not saying I agree with your actions, but the situation isn't black-and-white either."

"He's going to say it's not the same thing. He'll never see it like that."

"I can try, right?"

chapter 6

Dr. Kozol stood before me as he looked over my chart. Dad had called him in as soon as I was admitted.

"I highly recommend bed rest until you leave for your next gymnastics meet. You're burning the fuse at both ends. All you're doing is working against yourself," he said, sounding like my dad.

My eyelids were heavy as I looked up at him. I just wanted to go back to sleep.

"I know," I said. "I'm going to. My arm hurts really bad anyway. There's no way I can even do a cartwheel right now."

His eyes bore into mine and he lifted a brow. "Do not take Motrin for that. If you're in pain, or something is bothering you, I need to know first. Not all medications are safe for your kidneys."

"Okay."

"You're in pretty bad shape right now." He flipped to the next page. "Luckily, your kidneys have leveled out since you were admitted. As for the miscarriage," he continued, and my cheeks heated with embarrassment. "Again, bed rest is an absolute must. If you don't heal properly, you'll develop scar tissue and risk your chances of conceiving in the future. Your body could work against you, causing a flare up on top of that. Anything is possible when your immune system is compromised, as yours is right now."

"She'll get the proper rest she needs, Doctor." Dad reassured him.

Dad made it sound like I was going to be on bed rest for the rest of my life. I'd already decided I couldn't spare more than five days, and even that was pushing it. I was hoping by then my arm wouldn't hurt as much.

"You're cutting it close, young lady," Dr. Kozol warned.

I nodded in agreement. I was playing with fate and I knew it.

Dr. Kozol strolled out of the room and Sophia returned to my bedside, reclaiming the chair next to me. Her fingers fidgeted with the sweater in her lap.

I watched her, wondering if me being in a hospital bed brought back memories of her sick sister.

I reached out with my good hand and Sophia took it and gave it a sympathetic squeeze. Her jaw trembled.

I eyed Dad wondering when he was going to tell me the truth about the charges he pressed against Kova. I wouldn't throw Sophia under the bus for telling me, but how long was he going to torture me with his lie?

Dad's cell phone rang. He pulled it from his pocket and looked at the screen.

"It's Xavier. I need to take this," he said, and left the room.

"You're going to listen to the doctor, right?" Sophia asked.

I shifted, trying to get comfortable. "Yes." Maybe I could sleep the pain away during my downtime, then I wouldn't have to think about anything either.

She released a sigh. "Thank God."

"Does me being in this bed remind you of Francesca?"

She nodded, her mouth flat.

"I'm sorry."

"If I could trade places with you, I would," she said, her voice tinged with sadness. Her comment moved me intensely. Joy never would have said anything like that.

"Can you do me a favor and put my hair up for me, please?" I asked. I was hot all of a sudden thinking about Joy and her lack of compassion. Sophia nodded and dug in her purse for a hair tie.

"Francesca had such thick hair like you. I used to wish I had it. She had the prettiest beach waves, while mine was bone straight."

"Thank you." I smiled at her once she was done.

The door to my room opened and Dad strode back in with his phone held out toward me. "Your brother wants to speak to you," he said. I took it as Sophia pulled my hair up into a messy bun.

Bringing the phone to my ear, I said, "Hello?"

"Well, well, well, if it isn't my sister trying to steal the spotlight," Xavier said. It felt good to hear his voice.

"Hey."

"Is it true?"

My smile faded. "Which part?"

"About you being pregnant?" Leave it to Xavier to get right to the point. I didn't answer. "I'll take your silence as a yes."

"I was." I glanced up as Sophia ushered Dad to the other side of the room, giving me a bit of privacy. "I'm not anymore."

"Listen, I know you've gone through a lot these last couple of days. I'm not going to sit here and act like I'm not pissed the fuck off at you and the situation, but I will shut my mouth and save it for when you're able to have that conversation. And, Adrianna, we will be having that conversation."

God, Xavier reminded me so much of Dad in this moment.

"Thank you." I lowered my voice to almost a whisper. "I know I'm in no position to ask for a favor, but I really need something from you."

"Yeah, shoot."

"You have to promise to do it. Say, 'Yes, Adrianna, I promise to do anything you ask,' and then I'll tell you." He repeated after me with a hint of sarcasm that made me feel good inside. "Good," I said. "Now call Avery for me and tell her where I am. I don't want her to worry. I don't have my phone but I'll call her first thing I can, so tell her to be ready for me."

Xavier was quiet for a long drawn out moment. I felt bad asking him to do this considering their history, but I needed him to call her. "Please. I need to talk to her."

He released a deep sigh, which told me him calling her was going to take a lot out of him. "All right, but only because you're my sister and I love you."

I smiled. "Thank you. When was the last time you spoke to her?"

"Oh, months ago. Around the Fourth of July." He was quiet, but I detected the sadness in his tone.

"You're not over her, are you?"

"Avery isn't someone you can easily get over."

I smiled to myself. "Sounds like her. She's hard to forget once she puts her mark on you."

He half chuckled, half huffed. "Tell me about it."

"I better go," I said, my voice small. It was nice talking to him. "I should rest now if I plan to make a huge comeback in just a few days."

"You're crazy, you know that?"

"Yeah, well, what's life without a little madness?"

"A boring fucking life, that's for sure. Stay strong, sis. You got this."

I tried not to tear up. "Thanks, Xavier." We hung up. I sniffled then wiped my nose.

Once Dad and Sophia realized I was off the phone, they stopped talking and walked over to me. I handed his phone back to him.

"Is it okay if I rest for a little while? Alone?"

A shadow crossed Dad's eyes. He shifted on his feet. "Yes, of course. We'll be out here whenever you wake up." He turned to Sophia. "Do you want to go get coffee?" She nodded and they turned toward the door. "I'll just be a shout away," he said right before he stepped out. I thanked him and watched as they exited the room together.

Once the door clicked shut, I waited a few minutes to see if they would return. The silence grew thicker as their footsteps finally retreated. When a fair amount of time passed, I let go and broke down.

I cried for Kova.

I cried for my aching arm and not knowing how the heck I was going to manage when it felt broken.

I cried for the baby I would never meet and the cramps that were eating me alive in its memory.

I cried for all of the hurt I'd caused Dad and for making him feel like he failed as a parent.

And lastly, I cried for my future, for what could've been, but would never be.

chapter 7

DAD OPENED THE DOOR TO MY CONDO. I HELD MY BREATH AS I SLOWLY stepped inside with Sophia following behind me.

I hadn't been here in three days and I was a little afraid of what I would walk in and see. Would there be broken glass? Blood? Furniture that had been turned over?

I glanced around the space, unprepared for what I saw. My condo looked perfect. It was like World War III hadn't happened here just days ago.

"Your dad and I came by yesterday to clean up for you," Sophia said a little hesitant.

She seemed nervous and I wished she wasn't. That desire to be a mother was evident in her eyes and by the way she spoke to me, but she held back. I had a feeling she was worried about overstepping, but, truthfully, I could use a mother right now.

Glancing over my shoulder, I looked at both of them. Sophia seemed hopeful with the way her large round eyes watched me. Dad, well, he just looked sick and torn.

"It was Sophia's idea," Dad added grimly.

"Thank you," I said, my voice quiet.

All the broken glass was gone. There was a new decorative rug on the floor, but the coffee table was missing. I vaguely remembered hearing the wood splinter when I fell on it and felt a pinch on the back of my arm from the shattered glass.

My pace was small and slow as I walked across the carpet. My stomach had been cramping and any sudden movement seemed to make it worse. I'd had some painful periods in the past, but nothing like this. I wanted to bend over and hold myself, and pray it went away soon.

Instead, I sucked it up.

I walked into my room and came to a halt when I looked at the bed and rumpled sheets. Emotions clogged my throat. The sadness that rocked through me filled me with an immediate heartbreak I wasn't prepared for. My heart actually felt like it was being ripped down the middle.

This was the last place Kova and I had been right after he'd found out about the pregnancy.

I could still feel his strong arms around me, smell his cinnamon and tobacco scent in the air when he told me how he felt about me being pregnant. How he asked me to tell him that I loved him, and I wouldn't. I should have. I wished I had. He was my light when my world had been so dark, and now he was gone before I could really tell him how I felt. He deserved to know, and if we ever got the chance to be alone again, I'd tell him.

Thick tears brimmed my eyes, but I pushed them back. Everything was still so raw. I didn't want to cry in front of Dad because that would open the door for questions he couldn't handle the answers to.

"I don't agree with this," Dad said as he came up behind me. I swallowed thickly before turning around to face him. "In fact, I don't like it at all. I'd rather you come home so I can watch over you closely."

I had thought Dad agreeing to let me return to my condo was a sick joke until we'd pulled into Coral Cove.

Dad placed a hand on my shoulder and I had the strong urge to lean into him. Instead, I bit my lip and drew in a breath through my nose. I was so angry at him for having Kova arrested and letting me think it was for something other than assault. He still hadn't come clean, and he'd said Kova was still in jail. Was that another lie?

"I don't want to ruin your gymnastics career," Dad continued, his voice ragged with guilt. "I don't want to be the one who took that from you." His jaw locked tight. "Your safety is my main priority, and that was jeopardized by someone I put faith and trust in to watch over you."

I waited for him to collect his thoughts. He was never going to believe that I'd played a huge part in mine and Kova's relationship. I had so much I wanted to say but felt I should stay quiet.

"This was an extremely difficult decision to make, and not one I'm entirely sure is a good idea. I don't want to lose you, Adrianna. You're my only daughter. I just want what's best for you, but this whole thing has sickened me and brought me to a point I can't seem to come back from. I'll never forgive Konstantin for what he did." I opened my mouth to speak but Dad put his hand up to stop me. "Regardless of what happened or how you feel, he knew better." He gave me a pointed look. "You don't love him, Adrianna. You're infatuated with him because he's been to the Olympics and has the connections to get you there. That's all it is. He played on that."

My jaw dropped and my eyes widened.

"Are you suggesting I slept with my coach to move up higher in rank?" My brows creased when he didn't answer me. "That's insane to even fathom, not to mention literally impossible. You can't fake it to make it in sports. You can't sleep your way up the chain, especially in the Olympics. In your world of business and money, yes, but not in mine."

He shook his head, disappointment weighed heavily in his eyes.

"You don't love him," he repeated, and I wondered who he was trying to convince more.

My shoulders dropped. I wanted to argue with him and tell him I did love Kova, but I'd already told him a few times and got nowhere.

"You're going to be watched. Your phone will be monitored. Your truck now has a tracking device. If you so much as even try to contact Konstantin, or go somewhere other than the gym or the doctor's office, I'll know. Your condo was scoured and cleaned, and that pregnancy test you saved was thrown away."

I swallowed hard. I'd forgotten about that.

Dad shook his head, his eyes becoming glossy. "I trusted you." His voice was a broken whisper and it cracked something in my chest. "I put all my cards on you, defending you, insisting you were mature for your age when others said I was irresponsible to allow you to live alone. I'm furious you put yourself in the situation that you did. I raised you better than that. You let me down."

I winced at his blunt words. All I seemed to do was mess up everything for everyone and that truth fed my guilty side.

"Maybe it's my fault for asking him to watch you like I did," he whispered, talking more to himself than to me. "Maybe I brought it on or just made it worse."

Dad was gutted far worse than I understood. I felt like the situation was amplified by ten for him. The way he looked at me crushed me. His eyes were guarded, and there were blue tinted sacks under them.

"Thank you for giving me this last chance," I said.

His eyes bore into mine. "Don't thank me, thank Sophia. The only positive that came from this is I now know what Joy had on you." He was quiet, like he was deep in thought. "It all makes sense, and I know how to handle her now."

"She couldn't have known about the pregnancy, but I guarantee she knew about the affair." I swallowed, then said, "I'd prefer if you didn't talk to anyone about the miscarriage."

"I wasn't planning on it."

His eyes roamed around my room, not really looking for anything, it was more like he was trying to process it all. Dad cleared his throat and I looked away.

I couldn't handle seeing the disappointment in his eyes. "Come to the kitchen. Sophia went shopping."

My brows shot up. Sophia was really trying.

Holding my stomach, I followed Dad into the kitchen and found Sophia waiting for us. She bit her lip then shot Dad a nervous glance before looking back at me. "I wasn't sure what you needed or could eat, so we got a few basics for you. I also set up your medications and got you a few feminine products that I placed in your bathroom," she said. I assumed she meant pads and such because of the bleeding. I hadn't even thought of that. I was really thankful she had.

I nodded subtly. "Thank you, Sophia. I really appreciate it."

"Figured you could use some stuff. I didn't think you'd want to drive anywhere."

She was right, I didn't.

Dad turned toward me. "I have to go back to Savannah tonight, but Sophia lives off the highway just two exits from here. She wants to be here, so if you need anything, don't hesitate to reach out to her." He blinked. "It goes without saying you're not to have any contact with Konstantin once I leave. None whatsoever. Do you understand me?" I nodded, my lips flat. How did he expect me to train without my coach? I decided I'd leave it for another night.

Leaning toward me, Dad pressed a kiss to the top of my head and gave me a brief hug. He pulled back and looked into my eyes for a long moment. I wished he'd stop looking at me like I'd failed him beyond repair, like there was no coming back from this.

He exhaled a heavy breath before heading to the door and stepping out, leaving me alone with Sophia. She rounded the kitchen counter and stopped in front of me.

"Anything you need, Adrianna, please just call me." There wasn't an ounce of pity in her eyes. "Even if you just want to vent or cry or have girl questions your dad can't answer. I left my number for you."

I nodded as stupid tears climbed to my eyes again. Joy had never been that authentic with me, like she really wanted to be there and help me at the drop of a hat.

Moving on instinct, I threw my good arm around her and buried my head in her neck. Sophia froze, then her breath hitched as she stepped closer to hug me back. She was only a little taller than me.

"Thank you," I said, my voice breaking.

Sophia nodded her head in response and cried with me.

chapter 8

AFTER THEY'D LEFT, I IMMEDIATELY TOOK A SHOWER AND CRIED MY eyes out until the water ran cold.

I couldn't take smelling like a hospital any longer.

I had found my phone in the nightstand and put it on the charger, knowing I would need to call Avery the second I got out. I desperately needed to talk to her.

Not having use of both hands proved to be challenging. My hair had thinned out a lot from the illnesses, but I still had a mop on my head and washing it wasn't easy. Neither was dressing with one hand. I brushed my teeth, then I stood in front of the floor-to-ceiling bathroom mirror and looked at myself. My skin looked ashen, and there wasn't an ounce of life in my green eyes. I looked frail and malnourished. Dehydrated.

I shook my head and stepped out of the bathroom. I climbed into bed and scooted under the covers. The nurse had advised me to take the sling off when I slept. I did a few slow stretches to extend my arm, but I hadn't tried to touch it or move it much before that. The tips of my fingers were numb as I reached, and the ache at the center of my elbow was relentless. It made me nauseous, but I pushed myself to do a few more and deal with it. I didn't want to rely on pain medication if I didn't have to.

Exhaling a heavy breath, I picked up my cell phone and turned it on. All my notifications popped up one after the other. I ignored them.

I pulled up my favorites in contacts and hovered over Avery's number. My thumb trembled as I pressed down.

"Adrianna!"

Jesus. It didn't even ring.

Tears burst out of me and I cried at the sound of her voice. "Ave?"

"I've been waiting for your call!" Avery was frantic. "Are you okay? How are you? What the fuck happened!"

"I'm sorry I couldn't call before," I said in between sobs. "I didn't—"

"It's okay, I don't care about that. I spoke to Xavier and he filled me in. I've been a nervous wreck waiting to hear from you. If I didn't have school tomorrow I'd already be over there."

I rolled my lips between my teeth. "He's in jail."

"No." She gasped.

"Yes. My dad pressed charges."

"What happened? Did he really find you?"

I closed my eyes and pictured his face when he walked into my condo and saw us. I can still feel the shift in the air and his rage.

"Yes. They fought, Ave." I couldn't hide the guilt in my tone. "Well, Kova didn't hit back but I think—"

"Kova would've knocked Frank out cold."

"Yeah, and I think Kova knew that, which is why he didn't fight back. He just blocked everything for the most part."

I told her how Dad was keeping an eye on my phone calls and had a tracker put on my car.

"What's your address again? You need a burner phone. I'm going to have one sent to your condo because this is serious, and when he gets out you need to be able to talk to him so you can get your stories straight."

I hadn't even thought of that. I gave her the info she needed, and she said the phone would be here in two days.

Then I gave Avery a play-by-play of everything, from the news about Katja and the lies she'd told Kova, to how he'd said he was divorcing her, and when we'd spotted Dad and Sophia in that little town. She was shocked that Dad was with Sophia just as much as I was. She asked if they were dating and I told her I didn't know, which was true. I told her how nice and empathetic Sophia had been toward me. I also said how awkward it was too since I wasn't used to it. The worst part was reliving the moment when Dad told me I lost the baby.

"Christ on a stick." Avery was quiet for a few beats. "This is like a soap opera. It's almost too much to believe. Did you really tell your dad everything?"

"I did, including that I love Kova."

"Oh. My. God."

"Yeah," I said, mortified.

"I don't know if I would've gone that far, but at least you cleared the air."

"I went a little further than clearing the air."

"Shit. What did you do?"

"I was dramatic and screamed. Obviously, I wasn't thinking clearly. I do love him, you know that, but I should've left that out. Dad called it puppy love. He insisted I don't love him. Honestly, though, I felt like he was saying that more to himself than to me."

"We'll, ah, just blame your raging pregnancy emotions for going the extra mile. I still can't believe you did that."

"I know, I wish I hadn't." I clenched my eyes shut trying to block out how let down Dad had looked.

She was quiet before she eased her way into the next question. "Did your dad really say they used a vacuum?"

I winced. "Yes."

"That was heartless."

"I don't think he knew what it was called. He just said a procedure was done and the baby was vacuumed out. He was so angry with me, I wouldn't be surprised if he said it on purpose just to be cruel."

"Yeah, but where's his sympathy? Especially since he basically broke your arm. And it's called a D and C. It's not as gruesome as he made it sound. I mean, it is, but it's not. How do you feel otherwise? Have you been bleeding?"

"Nonstop. My shower was all pink and red water. I feel like my insides are falling out."

"That's how I was too. I had severe cramping and had to use a heating blanket. Make sure you don't use tampons or have sex either until you heal properly, not that you'll be in the mood for sex for a really long time."

"The cramping is horrific. I feel like I'm going to throw up. Sophia got me some pads. She picked up all different sizes. Some even look like diapers. I'm not using those. Who wants to sit in blood like that?"

"That's what you say now but they're about to become your best friend at night."

I grimaced. "Really?"

"Oh, yeah. Make sure you put a few towels down on your bed too just in case you bleed through. It's only really heavy the first couple of days, then the cramping will go down and so will the bleeding. If I didn't know any better, I'd say you're trying to copy me. I know I'm amazing and all, but this is just borderline creepy."

"You're terrible." I laughed.

"You know you love me," she said, her voice airy. "Seriously, though, I wish I could be there with you right now."

I glanced down at my white comforter and realized I felt the same way.

I also realized I shouldn't use this blanket until I'd completely recovered.

"I wish you were here too. Who needs high school anyway?" I joked. "My arm is all fucked up and I'm stuck inside for the next few days."

"I can't believe your dad." She blew out a whistle.

"I know he didn't mean to hurt me. His emotions were, like, amplified…" A flashback of the harsh look in his eyes filled my mind. "What am I going to do?" I whispered. "I can't call Kova. I don't know what he's been charged with, or if he's even out. Dad said he was in jail, but he also said he'd been arrested for rape. I don't know what to believe. And what do I tell my teammates when they see me again? Everything is ruined," I said, drawing in a tight breath. "What if I'm not ready in time to go back? What if I can't move my arm and wrist? I'm screwed."

I used the blanket to wipe my tears away. I didn't want to let my mind go there, but there was a good chance I wouldn't be ready. I could hardly flex my fingers. How the hell was I supposed to do gymnastics?

I wouldn't be able to.

I froze.

My throat was closing up, and my body was tightening everywhere. The fingers on my good hand started to tingle. My body lit up like an inferno and I kicked the blanket off.

"Ave—" I gasped, my eyes widening. My heart was beating the shit out of my ribs. "I think I'm having a panic attack."

I felt like my heart was going to explode.

"Aid. Breathe with me. Close your eyes and focus on my voice. Breathe in slowly through your nose." She instructed, and I heard her inhale. "Gently blow out. Let me hear you." I did. "No, you're not blowing out candles. Blow like you're trying to dry your nail polish and not get spit on your nails and ruin them. Do it again with me," Avery said, then gave me the instructions for a new breathing technique she wanted me to copy.

We did a few rounds of these exercises until my body uncoiled and I was crying all over again.

chapter 9

"I DON'T KNOW WHAT I WOULD DO WITHOUT YOU," I said, clutching the phone.

"Yeah, I'm pretty amazing." She was quiet for a moment. "Senior year is a joke. I hardly have to do anything. I wish I could be there with you. Going through something like this is hard, even when you have someone to talk to about it. Sometimes just having someone there makes a difference. Have you considered therapy? I was doing it a few times a week. Now I'm down to one day a week."

My forehead creased. I hadn't known she was talking to someone.

"And it helps?"

"At first I hated it because I had to relive every painful memory over and over. I've learned a lot, and it's helping me cope and move on. It wouldn't be a bad thing for you to consider."

I nodded. "I could probably use it after everything that's happened. Then again, it's not like I can tell a therapist about Kova, and he's a large part of this. Wouldn't the doctor need to notify someone?"

Avery mused over my question. "Well, not necessarily since you are an adult now. But then, people talk…" Her voice trailed off. "Scratch that. You can always call me and vent anytime you need to, you know that."

"Don't text me anything about this in case my dad really is checking my messages, not until I get that phone."

"Noted."

"Practice is going to suck."

"What are you going to do when you see Kova?"

"Try not to cry?" I joked sadly. "I don't know. Obviously, nothing because people will be there, but what if my dad really does have someone watching me? The last thing I want is to provoke him into pressing rape charges. Assault is enough."

"He can't press charges for rape."

I frowned. "What are you talking about?"

"We went over this when you first started training there, remember? The age of consent in Georgia is sixteen."

"But I was still a minor. I just turned eighteen. It happened before I was considered legal."

Avery let out a huff. "Doesn't matter," she said, her voice straining. "Sixteen is the age of consent. You could fuck an eighty-year-old the moment you turn sixteen and the law can't say anything. You're legal. That's it. Your dad can't do anything about it. He can press assault charges for himself, but that's about it."

I stared across the room in surprise. Her words sliced me open and woke me up. A thin ribbon of hope blew through me.

"I can't believe I didn't know this," I said, my voice barely above a whisper. It was a startling revelation.

"You did know it, you just forgot. Honestly, bestie, and this is me speaking from the heart, I think the only thing you really need to do is focus on gymnastics. You're down to the wire, so everything else can wait. Don't lose that focus you've carried with you the last ten years of your life." Avery's voice rose in intensity. "It's inspiring. I was looking forward to watching you go all the way so I can say, 'That's my best friend,' when you're doing flips and shit at the Olympics. Plus, I was hoping to find my future husband there too."

I tried to smile, but I just couldn't bring myself to do it.

"It's really hard, Ave," I said. "I'm stuck between a rock and a hard place." I paused as reality stared me in the face. "I have no leverage."

She didn't respond. Shifting onto my side, I winced at the shooting ache in my elbow. I tried to move back to my original position and clenched my eyes shut. I drew in a long breath and counted to five, praying the throbbing would dissipate soon. Even the simplest movement caused a widespread shot of pain to vibrate through my arm. I exhaled, wondering how this was all going to work out.

I glanced at the clock, it was past midnight. My eyes were heavy with fatigue and puffy from crying earlier.

"I would say allow yourself time to grieve, but I think considering what's on your plate right now, that's going to have to wait. It's time to saddle the horse and mount that beast. You got this. Shelve your emotions and feelings, turn on autopilot, and do what you were born to do."

I moved the blanket aside and lifted my shirt. I needed to grieve the miscarriage, but I'd effectively avoided thinking about it since I got home. I eyed my stomach. It didn't look much different, not that it had before. But it was.

I wondered if I'd regret this loss for the rest of my life.

I bit my lip. Avery was right. *So* right. I needed to grab the reins and hold on, I just didn't know if I had the strength to guide the horse with one hand.

"I feel like I don't know how."

"Turn it all off. Don't allow yourself to think about it. You've done it before, you can do it again. You just have to find that moment of clarity and ride with it."

She was right. I'd shut down the outside noise to become successful, but it took an enormous amount of energy from me in return. The thought of doing that again concerned me.

Shutting down had chipped away pieces of who I was as a person that I'd never get back. It had also taught me strength and shaped me into who I was. But doing that was as emotionally draining as it was physical. How much of myself would I lose this time? Would I turn away people I love forever?

Kova had been there to pull me back right before I pushed myself over the edge for good. He had selflessly let me use him to come back from the dark world I'd locked myself in and had lit the way so I could see again.

This time, though, I was on my own.

"It's getting late and you have to be up in a couple of hours for school," I said. "I'll let you go."

"I'm good. I can still hang."

I smiled to myself, grateful for a friend like her "It's okay. I'm going to lie down and hope this pain in my arm doesn't keep me awake."

"Don't forget to wear the diaper."

I groaned under my breath and she laughed. "Talk to you tomorrow. Hey, Avery? Thank you."

"What are besties for? Later, chica."

After we hung up, I did as Avery suggested. I put a few towels down before I climbed into bed. I made sure my alarm wasn't set and added a note in my phone to contact my private tutor to go over my schedule. I was close to finishing high school a couple of months early and only had very minimal left to complete to graduate.

I switched the light off and then pulled the comforter up to my chin and nestled under the covers. I closed my eyes hoping sleep would consume me soon. That way I wouldn't have to think about anything more, or feel the cold tears coat my cheeks.

I woke from the fiery heat of cramps in my belly at 3:00 a.m. This happened the last two nights since I got home.

I'd followed the doctor's orders. I thought doing absolutely nothing for at least forty-eight hours would help me heal faster, but each night it seemed to get worse and worse. Avery had mentioned it was probably because my body had been through a traumatic experience, and while I was physically fine, for the most part anyway, the emotional duress I was under would tighten my body and make everything stiff.

I let out a whimper and turned over onto my side, curling up into a ball. I wrapped my good arm around myself like I had done the last couple nights and clenched my eyes shut while I held myself. There was an ache in my bad arm that never seemed to quell, but it was nothing compared to the cluster of knots in my stomach tightening by the millisecond. The little balls of hell exploded like fireworks gone wrong. They were intense and I couldn't help but focus on them. I held my breath until my lungs throbbed for air.

God, I wished this would all go away already.

After a few minutes of lying still, the cramps weren't as intense. I sat up and reached for my cell phone to pass the time, knowing it'd be a good hour or so until I fell back asleep. I had a bunch of missed texts from Avery.

BFF: You are amazing. Remember that!
BFF: Be confident in your abilities and remember that's what got you where you are now.
BFF: Keep your head up, gorgeous. WE got this <3
BFF: Okay, you need to wake up already.
BFF: I'm gonna send out an Amber Alert if you don't text me back.
BFF: ...It's been 84 years.
BFF: Fuck the Amber Alert. I'm just gonna find a new bestie.

I sent Avery a slew of texts. She was dead to the world when she slept, but she'd see them when she woke.

I fell into a routine as the last couple of days at home dragged on. I'd rise to messages from Avery that would either make me cry or laugh, sometimes both at the same time. She would send me texts throughout the day to check on me. I knew what she was doing, and it made me feel so guilty for finding any hint of reprieve because I hadn't done that for her. I got the feeling she was trying to engage with me more than usual because she felt like I was going to break soon. She wanted to be there for me, and the thought alone made me tear up.

I attempted to stretch my arm, my wrist, and elbow, but the ligaments were so tight that I grunted under my breath. I wondered how it would feel if I did a handstand, and if I could handle it. I got on my knees and flattened my palms to the floor. Straightening my elbows, I leaned forward and applied a little weight, and winced as pain shot up my arm.

Screw it.

I retrieved a bottle of Motrin and Tylenol from the bathroom cabinet. I'd alternate between them both. I had given myself two days to get back to my original form. It was time to numb the pain. It was the only way I was going to get through practice today.

I knew to stay away from these types of medications because of my kidney issues. It wasn't that I had a death wish, but desperate times called for desperate measures, and all that jazz.

Other than Avery, Dad checked in regularly. He called in the mornings and at night. We FaceTimed a few times just so he could see me. I felt like I was twelve years old again, but I wasn't going to argue.

The last conversation I'd had with him lasted no more than a handful of minutes, but it had carried enough tension that I couldn't stop thinking about it.

I'd asked him if he'd spoken to my coaches, if anyone knew anything. I hadn't dared mentioned Kova specifically, I didn't want to push it. He'd said he'd spoken to Madeline and told her I had a set back with my Achilles and needed to rest it. He'd informed her I'd dislocated my elbow as well. Before we'd hung up, he warned me again about not engaging with Kova. He had even went as far as threatening to press other fraudulent charges to keep him behind bars.

I was an adult. Dad legally had no say in what I did. I didn't understand why he was doing this.

chapter 10

MY DUFFLE BAG SOUNDED LIKE I HAD A COSTCO-SIZE CONTAINER of Tic Tacs in it with the Tylenol, Motrin, and all my other medications.

I wasn't supposed to use tampons yet, but I couldn't wear a pad during practice. Not with how much I was bleeding. I had tested it out before I left home with a pair of workout shorts and decided it was a no-go. On my way to World Cup, I'd stopped at the pharmacy and bought the biggest tampons I could find. I figured they'd hold more. I just hoped using them wouldn't make the pain in my pelvic area worse or extend the recovery time.

With my bag stowed in my locker, I turned around to leave when Holly appeared in front of me. I jumped, startled. She stood there watching me with inquisitive eyes.

"Adrianna!" she shouted, and threw her arms around my shoulders.

I hugged her back with one arm and forced a smile. She squeezed me hard enough to produce a wince, but I hid it.

"Hey, Holly."

She pulled back and eyed me up and down. "Where have you been? Hayden and I were so worried about you. Hayden said he tried to call you but you didn't answer. Madeline told us you were absent but didn't say why."

"My Achilles was flaring up and I managed to dislocate my elbow." I nodded toward my side where my bad arm hung like a scarecrow. She cupped her mouth and gasped in shock. "It's fine now. It was popped back into place, but it's sore as hell and hurts to do anything, really."

Her worried eyes studied me. "How'd you do that?"

"I went to lunch with my dad, and we were walking back to the car when another car came flying around the corner and almost hit me. Dad yanked me out of the way and dislocated my elbow when he pulled." The story Dad had come up with a couple days ago rolled off my lips.

She gasped again, horrified. I had been just as surprised when Dad came up with that on the fly too.

"But what about the meet? What about…about everything?"

My lips flattened at the rising panic in her voice. "I wish I had an answer. All I can do is push through. What choice do I have?"

Her mouth twisted. "Yeah, you don't really have a choice, do you?" Her gaze traveled to my upper arm and her frown deepened. "What's that bruise from?"

I followed her stare and spotted the black-and-blue I hadn't realized I had. I blinked rapidly and squinted my eyes. I needed to quickly come up with a lie.

I took Dad's story a little further. "When my dad yanked me away, I stumbled over my feet and he pulled harder. My arm twisted and I fell into the back of a nearby car pretty hard." She studied me a bit longer before looking into my eyes again. "We were in a parking garage when it happened." I had no idea why I added that.

"Luckily your arm will only be sore for another day or so, then you'll be good to go. That's how it was for me."

My brows rose to my hairline. Holly confirmed we'd had the same injury. "I was working a new bars routine and added a new skill when I did it, only, I panicked because it was my first time trying it." She gave me a knowing look. "I freaked."

I cringed, hearing the socket pop in my head.

We exited the locker room together. Anticipation filled me as we approached the gym. I wondered how Kova would react when he saw me, if he'd try to talk to me later. I was supposed to receive the cell phone Avery had ordered for me today, so maybe I could call him tonight.

As I stepped onto the blue carpeted spring floor, I felt an energy zip through my feet and realign my center. A sensation came over me and I breathed it in, hoping it would guide me in the right direction. It felt like stars were kissing my skin trying to coax life back into me. I prayed it would give me the strength I needed to get through this.

It felt good to be here.

"Madeline is waving everyone over," Holly said, and I nodded.

There was already a small group of gymnasts sitting crossed-legged in front of her. My gaze took in every corner and square inch of the vast room, searching for the pair of green eyes I loved so much. My excitement started to fade when I scanned over the people again and didn't see them.

Kova wasn't here. My anxiety spiked. If Dad had only pressed assault charges, then why wasn't Kova here? I'd assumed he'd be out of jail by now, unless there was something I didn't know.

My stomach tightened. I exhaled a heavy breath and looked ahead. My gaze stopped on Madeline who eyed us as we joined the group. She observed me closely through narrowed eyes and my breath hitched in my throat. I smiled at her, pretending like it was any other day of practice. I prayed she didn't know the truth.

I shook my fingers out and looked to her right. There was a man standing next to her I'd never seen before. He was stiff as a board. His arms were behind his back, his stance was that of a soldier. If I had to guess, I'd say he was a little older than Kova, and he was built a little rough around the edges. His hair was dark and his eyes were a striking black that led to a sharp, pointed nose. He looked of European descent. I wondered if he was from Russia too.

We sat down and waited while Madeline flipped through her yellow notepad. She had one foot propped on a folding mat and was swaying back and forth.

"We have a full week ahead of us and need to stay on track. Since the Trials are right around the corner, I'll be working with Adrianna closely to prepare her while the rest of the team works with Danilo to prepare for their scheduled meets. He's the new coach Coach Kova recently hired. I'll let him give a brief introduction before we get started."

My brows furrowed. Kova had hired a new coach? When had he done that, and why hadn't he told me?

"My name is Danilo Teglia." The new coach began his introduction, and I was caught off guard by his heavy, stiff accent. "Konstantin has been a friend of mine since we were teenagers, though we did not start out as friends. We were first competitors. Where he represented Russia, I represented Ukraine. I have competed in three Olympic Games and have almost as many gold medals as Konstantin." A smile curved his mouth like he was thinking about something. "We became a challenge to each other at meets, always trying to outplace the other. He was my biggest competitor. I currently own a gym back home that is strictly for elite, but also where the Olympic trainees prepare before the Games. I will be splitting my time between here and the Ukraine."

Holly leaned over and whispered, "What's with the lack of contractions?"

I shot her a fleeting look and tried not to laugh. I shrugged.

Reagan looked at us with a grin. She wiggled her brows. "New eye candy," she said, and turned away.

"I look forward to getting situated here. Konstantin has spoken highly of all his gymnasts. I am excited to see what you are all made of. We have similar training methods, so expect the same from me, if not more."

Madeline gave Danilo a friendly smile, then she looked at all of us. "If you need anything, Danilo and I are here to help. Now, let's get started." Her eyes darted to me. "Adrianna," she said, and waved at me to come to her.

"Where's Kova?" I leaned over, asking Holly. She shrugged her shoulders.

Frowning, I got up and walked to Madeline. Luckily the Motrin was keeping the cramps at bay and they weren't as severe. There was a steady warmth of bloating and pressure, but I could deal with it.

"Hi," I said.

Danilo stood to the side. His hands were propped on his hips and his closeness made my heart skip a beat. He was dressed in a plain white T-shirt and navy-blue basketball shorts.

"Nice to finally put a face to the name. Konstantin speaks very highly of you."

I offered him a nervous smile. I couldn't say the same.

"Kova had you scheduled for a blading session tonight. Dr. Hart will be here to take care of it," Madeline said. I turned to her and nodded. "We'll go over your schedule tonight for the next couple of days as well. How's your elbow?"

Slowly, I stretched my arm out to show her. "Honestly, it hurts. It's really sore, but once I start working out a bit more, I'm sure I won't even feel it."

"Can you move your fingers? Raise your arm above your head?"

I swallowed hard. "I need to stretch first and warm it up really good, then I think I should be okay."

She didn't look thrilled. "I'll have Ethan look at it tonight and see what he can do."

"How did you do that?" Danilo asked, nodding with his squared chin toward my arm.

"My dad was playing hero."

His brows drew in like he didn't believe me. "May I?" he asked, and I nodded.

Danilo got on the floor and instructed me to get down next to him. "Flatten your hand on the floor and spread your fingers out. Slowly apply weight as you try to straighten it."

That's what I'd done this morning and it hurt.

I clenched my eyes from the tightness. Danilo placed his hands on my upper arm and elbow and carefully pressed against it to straighten it out. I grunted under my breath, and he halted and looked at me with his midnight eyes.

"It's fine, keep going."

He dipped his chin once. It wasn't fine.

Danilo applied more pressure, counted to ten and then let up. The muscles and ligaments in my arm screamed in protest. I bit the inside of my lip. He relaxed and then did it again, this time the sharp pain radiated from my wrist to my shoulder. Once he did a few rounds of those, we moved onto another stretch.

"Lie on your stomach and prop up on your elbows. Turn your hands up," he said, and I did. "Take a deep breath, then release."

Placing two fingers on the inside of my wrist, Danilo carefully pressed down until the top of my wrist touched the floor. I tensed and clenched my eyes shut. My arm was straining as he held it for a few seconds before he let up and repeated his actions. Something as simple as this caused a series of hot flashes to tingle through my body.

"Are you okay?"

"Yes," I said through clenched teeth.

"How are you feeling, Adrianna?" Madeline asked.

Sitting on my knees, I moved my arm around in front of me. "It's a little better, still tight, but it should loosen up during practice."

"Let's hope it does because with the time you missed, you don't have a choice right now other than to push through it. Your schedule is pretty intense—there's no room for downtime. You need to block it out and work your hardest."

I nodded in agreement and licked my lips. I was going to have to grin and bear it, and pray to every god that I didn't make it worse.

"Lift your arm above your head," Danilo said. I was still on my knees and raised my arm.

He stood next to me and placed his palm to mine. His fingers wrapped around mine and held on while he very gently pressed down to see if I could handle impact. Danilo held my wrist as he did so.

"Lock your elbow if you can," he said, pushing a little harder.

My stomach twisted in agony. God, I wanted to cry from the excruciating pounding that took my breath away.

How the fuck was I going to do vault? Or swing on bars? Tumble?

"Block it out," he ordered. "Pretend it does not exist."

I nodded furiously, teeth pressing into my lip so hard I tasted blood. Clenching my eyes shut, I held my breath as he angled my arm back to stretch it out. My back arched and he noticed. Danilo used his knee to prevent me from leaning back. The jerk.

"You are going to need physical therapy tonight, warm compresses, and an inflammatory to get you through this. I suggest something like this every morning before practice to warm up the arm and loosen the muscles around the elbow, and then again at the end of the day."

"Great, you can do it for her," Madeline said. "Adrianna, I'll see you at beam while I speak to Danilo."

I stood up, giving my thanks to Coach Danilo, then turned around and made my way to the balance beam. I watched the floor as I walked, listening to the springboard at the front of the vault ricochet and the spring in the uneven bars rebound. A prickly sensation spread across my neck. I reached up to rub it away and glanced around the gym.

I felt like there were eyes all over my body. My brows furrowed. Was Kova here and I just couldn't see him? Maybe Dad really did have someone watching me.

The paranoia festering inside me was starting to eat away at me. I expelled a strained breath and wondered if anyone knew anything.

They couldn't… Right?

I'd been absent from the gym for five days. So had Kova. For someone who was going to the Olympic Trials, that kind of absence was unheard of. The same would be said for Kova, and he still wasn't here. It looked suspicious. People were curious, and for the most part, they weren't stupid. I felt like they were putting two and two together.

Stepping in front of the balance beam, my fingers trembled a little as I placed them on the leather. I grazed my palms on the material as I found my center again. My gaze dropped to my hands. There was an indentation on the edge from when someone slipped and hit their mouth.

An indentation like Kova had left on me.

I mounted the beam. The moment my feet touched the four-inch piece of wood, my mind cleared and I set my focus in place.

I knew what I needed to do and let the rest fade away.

I exhaled everything I was holding on to and visualized my routine. The leather beneath my feet called to me, encouraging me. My heart pounded in my chest and my nerves were back to taunting me. But then I thought about how Kova had once said nerves were good and kept the adrenaline going. Lose the nerves, and you lose the love. His words made sense to me.

Despite the flickering agony in every nerve ending in my body, there was not a chance in hell I was going to let anything, or anyone, take this from me.

I could relax when I was dead.

Warming up with connecting back handspring step outs, I blocked out the pain like Madeline and Danilo said.

That didn't mean I couldn't feel anything.

I was silently screaming on the inside.

chapter 11

"COME ON, ADRIANNA." MADELINE GRUMBLED. "THAT WAS WEAK going over. You need to excel after you hit the handstand, then you can push it over."

Weak.

That word left a sour taste in my mouth.

I wiped the sweat from my temples as I walked to the end of the track thinking about Madeline's suggestions. I rotated my arms in wide circles to loosen them. I desperately wanted to rub the ache in my elbow, but I didn't want to show it was bothering me. Instead, I chewed the hell out of the inside of my mouth to hide my discomfort.

Madeline had felt it wasn't a good idea to risk practice tumbling on floor with my arm just yet. So, after we broke down my floor routine and conditioned the dance skills for three hours, we moved to the tumble track.

"Your butt is too low and you're going to knock your teeth out if you land like that on the actual floor. Do it again. Stick the landing," she yelled and clapped her hands.

Using the tumble trampoline had been a good idea after practicing all day. Even though I could feel the strain deep in my elbow, I kept going. My fingers started to go numb but I shook it off. I told myself if I could work through an Achilles strain and a kidney infection, then there was no reason why I couldn't work through this too.

"Faster. You need to rotate faster to build power. Do it again. Get that flip moving faster."

I set my eyes on the end of the trampoline and pictured myself doing exactly what she instructed. Inhaling a deep breath, I placed one foot in front of the other and tapped the black netting. I exhaled and looked to my right. I could feel someone watching me.

Black eyes met mine.

Danilo was blatantly staring at me as he worked with Reagan and Holly on bars. My brows twitched. He wasn't observing me with interest, but more in bewilderment.

"While I'm young." Madeline bit out.

My eyes snapped back to hers. I nodded and shifted my feet.

When I glanced over at Danilo one last time, he had his back to me.

Shaking it off, I hurdled into a roundoff, my shoulder tight as I flipped backward two times before rebounding off the trampoline with a grunt. I reached as high as I could to set a twisting double full out. This was a dangerous tumbling pass on the floor because I was twisting toward the ground and could lead to injury faster.

Blocking out the shooting pain in my arm, I rotated as hard and as fast as I could by bringing my fists to my chest. I told myself to keep going, to push and fight for that perfect landing. I could feel the pull of gravity and squeezed every muscle in my body, twisting until I spotted the giant blue mesh matt to open up for my dismount.

Feet together, my toes touched down first on the floor and I raised my arms above my head to set the landing. After an inconsistent day of practice, I stuck it.

"Fabulous," Madeline said, clapping her hands as she praised me. "Let's move on."

Panting, I flopped down on my butt to scoot off the mat. My chest was a little tight but nothing I wasn't used to, I just needed to take smaller breaths.

"Madeline?" I called out.

She walked over to me. "Yes?"

"I was thinking about something you said earlier. Are you going to be training me until we leave?"

Her head tilted to the side. "I am."

"Oh, ah, okay," I stammered from nerves. "I was just wondering where Kova is. I didn't know he'd be gone."

Madeline studied me. My stomach clenched with anxiety, but I didn't show it. I kept a straight face and didn't look away as if I'd asked a completely innocent question. Her eyes shifted back and forth between mine as if to say, "You already know."

Her lips puckered with false pity. "Don't worry about a thing. I spoke with Kova and I've got it covered. He gave me your schedule until we leave. Go ahead and head to bars now," she said, her lips rolled up firmly. She stepped around me and walked away.

I frowned. I guess we were finished with the conversation.

I hid the slight limp as I walked to bars covered in chalk and my hair a mess at the top of my head. For once, I was looking forward to a blading session. It'd been a while, and they always made me feel brand new…once the aftermath wore off.

I reached the uneven bars and Danilo gestured at me with two fingers. I walked over to him and he reached out for my arm. My hand gently rested on his bicep as his large fingers began kneading my aching muscles. I sighed in relief, my eyes closing.

"Feel better?" he asked.

"Yes," I said, a little breathless. It did.

"I could tell you were in pain."

I looked at him and wondered how he'd figured it out when I knew I'd hidden it well. "It feels numb."

His fingers made their way down the inside of my arm, his eyes inspecting my reaction each place his fingers pressed into me. When he reached the crease of my elbow, I tightened up.

"I will not hurt you," he said. His lack of contractions made me think of Kova.

My lips formed a thin line. I swallowed. Danilo laced his fingers with mine, giving them a good squeeze, then he held my wrist with his other hand and rotated it in slow circles. His hand was warm, and what he was doing felt incredible. He got the blood flowing again. It took away some of the tingling in my arm. Almost like it could breathe again.

"Thank you," I said when he removed his hand and let go. Danilo nodded. "It feels so much better."

"All right," Madeline said, tearing my attention from Danilo. I looked into her eyes, searching for something that indicated she knew what really happened with Kova. Anything. But there was nothing there. The tension in my neck loosened marginally. "We want flat hips, a big cast, and a stuck handstand." She was all business. "Beautiful lines would be a plus. Then we'll move on to the release. Think you can do it?"

A full and a half turn release? No, I couldn't do it right now.

"Yes, just spot me."

I had no idea how the hell I made it through my first day back at practice. All I wanted was to take a hot bath and crash. But I still had a blading session and physical therapy on my arm.

I sat in the cold locker room stuffing my clothes and leftover lunch into my duffle bag while Madeline spoke to Danilo and Dr. Ethan Hart in the hall. I had a few more minutes to spare before I was supposed to meet them in the therapy room. Madeline planned to go over my schedule, down to when we needed to board the plane.

"He was arrested for assault."

I stopped moving. Though Madeline's voice was low, I could still hear her. I wasn't trying to eavesdrop, but the gym had cleared out and their voices easily carried down the hall.

"*Tak*," Danilo said. It sounded like the word was in the back of his throat.

"Just doesn't seem like Kova to fight someone in a bar," Ethan said. He wasn't convinced. "He doesn't go to bars," he said, sounding even more stumped.

Ethan had a point. Kova wasn't a barhopping kind of guy. I don't think he ever went out to dinner, or really did anything for himself. He either was at World Cup, or at home...or with me. My stomach tightened as I held my breath. His life was devoted to gymnastics and those close to him knew that.

I stood up and tiptoed to the door.

"I'm just letting you know what he told me," Madeline said. "He fought in self-defense, but since no one saw the victim hit him first, he was the only one arrested. Things are up in the air as more charges are possibly pending; that's why he hasn't been released from jail yet. Until then, he asked if we could all come together to help. I think we all can agree Kova isn't the kind of person to ask for help, so when he does, it must be serious."

I clenched my eyes shut.

Kova was still in jail.

chapter 12

PICK UP… PICK UP… PICK UP.

    The first thing I did when I got into my truck was call Avery. I needed to talk to her.

He's still in jail.

I clenched my eyes shut at the red light feeling so guilty. How was Kova still in jail? Something wasn't adding up. He should've been released by now.

Remaining indifferent while I'd been in the therapy room had been a challenge. I'd wanted to ask questions, but felt that would've been too suspicious in itself. So, I'd kept my mouth shut while Madeline, Danilo, and Dr. Hart had engaged in small talk.

I lifted my foot off the brake and pressed down on the gas to merge into the next lane. My arm felt a little better. I had more flexibility in my fingers, and they didn't tingle when I flexed them anymore. Ethan had finished up my session with a full-body, deep-tissue massage, and it was exactly what I didn't know I needed. My body was in worse shape than I'd realized. He'd kneaded every knot and had made sure I wasn't as tense before I left.

While I was there, my mind had run wild with thoughts of Kova and how he was doing.

"Besties 'R' Us," Avery answered.

"Ave." I parked the truck and sat back.

"Shit. What happened?"

I repeated what I'd heard at the gym.

"Why is Kova still in jail? Shouldn't he have been out by now?"

I feared the worst. With how distraught my dad was over the whole situation, I wouldn't put anything past him. I had a gut feeling if Dad could get away with murder, he'd attempt it.

"I don't know why he's still in when the charge was so small, honestly."

I pulled the keys from the ignition and grabbed my duffle bag.

"I wish there was a way to look this info up," I said as I climbed down from the truck.

I glanced to my left; the sun was dipping behind the rippling water. The salty sweet scent of the ocean calmed me. Memories of when Kova and I lounged on the beach watching the sunset blew into me. I wished I could go and sit there now, replay the moment when he'd said he was already missing me even though I was in his arms.

"You can," Avery said.

"What?"

"You can look it up. There's a specific website you can use to see when he was charged and if he's out."

My brows shot up. "Really? How'd you know that?"

"Because I don't live under a rock, that's how."

The corners of my lips twitched. "Can you do the search for me?" I asked. "I'm just walking into my condo and I need to take my medicine."

"Already on it, powering up my laptop now. How've you been feeling? How was practice today?"

There was a brown box waiting in front of my door. I picked it up and realized it was the phone Avery had ordered. Hope bloomed inside of me. As soon as I was off the phone with her, I'd charge it and call Kova to see for myself if he was out. I stepped inside and shut the door.

"Well, I felt like my arm was hanging by a thread and going to fall off today. The period cramps suck. They're the worst ever, and I had to use tampons today when I'm not supposed to. I plan to soak in the bathtub tonight. Figured it might help. Overall, I'm just peachy."

"Try to use tampons only if you have to. You don't want to risk anything. I don't know what could actually happen, but since you have such shitty luck, I'd say proceed with caution."

I walked into the kitchen and flipped on the light. I immediately went for my medication. "You make a good point." I chuckled and uncapped a bottle

"All right..." she said, her voice trailing off. I put all my pills in a little bowl, then grabbed a water bottle and took a sip. "Oh, dayum. Fish lips gives a good mug shot."

I perked up. "I want to see."

"FaceTime me and I'll show you."

I did, and she flipped the screen so I could see what she saw. I leaned against the kitchen counter.

My heart skipped a beat looking at the picture of Kova from the shoulders up. His green eyes lacked vitality, and he had a purple fat lip. His hair was disheveled, and there was a small cut near his eye. A series of pangs thumped in my chest. I still couldn't believe Dad had him arrested.

I stared at him, feeling his torment crash over me in waves. There was anguish in his gaze, though resigned, like he deserved this.

This was all my fault, and I would fix it. I just hoped he didn't hate me for this.

"What does it say?" I asked, my voice a little shaky.

Avery scrolled. "He was arrested the night you were admitted to the hospital. No bond has been posted…" Her voice trailed off, then picked back up. "It says he hasn't been released."

Chills coated my arms. I stared in confusion. I didn't know what to think. "Ah, Aid?"

My heart dropped at the dread in her tone.

"He wasn't arrested for assault, he was arrested for *aggravated* assault *and* simple battery."

"What! What does that mean? Is that worse? Why are there two charges? Are you sure?"

"Yeah. That's what it says." Avery sounded like she was in a state of disbelief herself.

"How long do people stay in jail for something like that?"

"No clue. Let me see what I can find." Avery placed the phone in her bra so I could watch while she opened a new tab and typed. "Aggravated assault charges in Georgia…"

She grew quiet. I couldn't see what she was reading no matter how hard I squinted.

"Okay, there's a couple different things… I could be wrong, and don't quote me, but it's a felony. He could face one to twenty years in prison, plus fines and restitution."

"What makes it a felony?" I asked, my voice low.

"Let me see, hang on."

I held on for what felt like an eternity.

"…with intent to murder, rob, or…" Her voice trailed off again. "Or rape someone." She spoke so low I almost missed what she said.

Chills raced down my arms. I moved to a chair and took a seat.

"So your dad did file charges against him," she said more to herself, her voice full of sympathy.

I nodded as if she was sitting in front of me. My mind flickered like a strobe light with thoughts flying to every corner. How had he managed to file rape charges if I was eighteen?

My heart plummeted to my gut. He must've lied. Again. I bet Dad had told the police I was seventeen since I was unconscious and couldn't speak for myself.

This was all sorts of fucked up.

"And simple battery?" I whispered. "What's that?"

I almost didn't want to know the answer.

"It's a misdemeanor," she said a little brighter. "He'd serve up to a year in jail and some small fines, could be elevated to an aggravated nature if..."

Avery stopped speaking and I leaned forward. I wasn't sure how much more my heart could take.

"What is it?" I asked.

"If the victim..." She struggled to get the words out, and cleared her throat. "If the victim was pregnant..."

The silence was deafening.

Neither Avery nor I spoke for a solid minute. This must've been what Dad had meant when he threatened to press other charges against Kova if I didn't keep my distance.

My dad went there. He really, really went there. If Dad couldn't get Kova for rape, he'd get him for something else.

"Want my theory?" Avery offered, breaking the dreary silence.

"Sock it to me."

"My theory is your dad told the police you were seventeen. He'll later say he forgot you just had a birthday because he wasn't thinking clearly. He'll put on a show and they'll buy it. They'll also drop the charges because your relationship was consensual. Plus, you're legal and you'll never press any."

I was momentarily speechless and a bit proud of Avery for coming up with that.

"Not bad. But what about the simple battery? Kova didn't touch me, and Dad already admitted he told the police I got hurt trying to break up their fight," I said, curious to see what she'd say next.

Avery mused over the question. "Daddy doesn't have a leg to stand on. Even if he lied to the police and told them Kova hit you and that's how you got hurt, you can easily set the story straight. The truth is your dad's emotions got in the way and he lost it."

A pulsing throb began in the side of my neck. I needed a moment.

I needed air.

I walked across the living room and slid open the sliding glass door. Beach air breezed around me as I stepped onto the balcony. I inhaled and closed my eyes. The ocean was the place I found comfort in many times growing up.

"I'm sorry, bestie," Avery said, her voice soft and apologetic.

I opened my eyes and kept my gaze focused straight ahead on the horizon. The sun had completely disappeared behind the ocean.

I didn't want to face the music that my dad had taken this as far as he had, but the spasm in my heart forced me to wake up. The fact he'd purposely lied about my age to keep Kova and me apart as long as he could topped everything for me.

Dad knew exactly what he was doing. If this did actually go as he hoped, Kova would miss everything we'd worked so hard for.

The Trials…

The Olympics…

A breath rolled off my parted lips.

I was sick to my stomach at the thought of Kova missing it. That's not how it was supposed to be, that wasn't the plan. Kova deserved to be there just as much as I did.

It wasn't fair.

I took a deep breath, my lungs tight as I struggled not to panic. How was I supposed to do this without him?

I shook my head. I couldn't. I needed him. Kova was my everything.

I swallowed thickly. Tears rose to my eyes at the possibility of that being the outcome. It killed me inside.

"Are you sure there are two charges?" I asked, needing confirmation.

"From what I'm reading, if this is his first offense, they'll release him on his own recognizance." She paused. "Is this his first time?"

I shook my head, overwhelmed. "I… I don't know. I assume so, but I guess I really don't know. I'm guessing since he's still there it's not. Unless my dad said something and wants to actually go through with the other charges without speaking to me, but he can't do that. So, the only issue really is my dad's charge. And," I continued, drawing out the word, "I'll say I don't know who hit who."

My body started to overheat. The last thing I wanted to do was call Dad and talk about this, but I realized I had no choice. Not because I wanted to beg him not to press charges, that was a given, but because Kova had to be at the competitions with me. His absence would raise red flags, and without a doubt, it would hinder my performance.

Dad didn't like bad publicity brought to the family name, so I had an idea.

"Ave? I have to go. I need to call my dad."

"Oh, my God. What are you going to say to him?"

"I have an idea; I'll tell you if it works."

"Just remember that regardless if you wanted the dinosaur dong or not,

Kova was wrong and that's all your dad is going to ever see. Try not to overreact, but I know that's easier said than done."

It was wrong of me to laugh, but I couldn't help it. "Always trying to find a way to lighten the situation."

She smiled from ear to ear, proud of herself. "I try. Text me when you're done."

"Will do. Thanks, girl."

After we ended our FaceTime session, I went into the bathroom and splashed water on my face. I needed to get my thoughts straight and think about my questions before I called Dad.

Expelling a heavy breath, I decided to sit down first and open the box containing the new cell phone. Maybe the website Avery had used hadn't updated their records and he was actually out. Once the phone was all set up, I immediately tried to call Kova hoping he'd answer.

Please. Please. Please.

"*Allo?*"

I stiffened at the sound of Katja's voice. If she answered his cell, then that could only mean he was in fact still in jail.

"*Allo?*"

I bit my lip.

"Is anyone there?"

"Goddammit!" I yelled after I disconnected the call. "Fuck!" The word came from deep in my chest.

The new phone rang and I nearly dropped it when Kova's phone number flashed across the screen. I held my breath and hit the "fuck you" button. In that moment, I was so grateful Avery had gotten me the burner phone. It rang again, and again. I finally turned it off when the ringing wouldn't stop.

Once I didn't feel so shaky, I reached for my actual cell and dialed Dad's number. I steadied my breathing as my emotions and hormones combated each other. I didn't want to explode on him because that would only work against me. However, with the simmering anger inside me, I couldn't make any promises.

"Hello, Adrianna," he said, answering the phone.

My throat swelled. "Hi, Dad. Do you have a minute to talk?"

"That depends on what you want to talk about."

chapter 13

My stomach cramped. Shit. I already had a bad feeling.

"Now, I know you don't want to talk about—"

"Adrianna—"

I sucked in a breath. "Dad, just listen to me, please, for a second," I said quickly.

"How dare you call me and even attempt to talk about this issue. You have some nerve, young lady."

Clutching the phone in my hand, I dropped the niceties and demanded answers from him.

"Kova wasn't at practice today. Why wasn't he there?"

"Of course he wouldn't be there," he responded. "He's in jail where he belongs."

My nostrils flared and I forced myself to breathe calmly. "He has to be here. He's my coach, and I need him." *Steady breathing… Steady… Breathing.* "How long will he be in there? Why do you have to press charges anyway? Why can't you just drop them so he can leave?"

"It's what he deserves for what he did." He ground the words out bitterly. "You have no right to call me and question me on the whereabouts of the lowlife who took advantage of you. Keep this shit up and I will press further charges on that disgusting piece of shit," he shouted.

I was quiet as my anger took ahold of every part of my body from the words he just spit out.

Then I lost it.

"You can't press rape charges because I'm eighteen!" I yelled into the phone and it silenced him. My heartbeat double-timed, I'd never spoken like that to him before. "People are talking. They know he wasn't at a bar fighting a drunk guy. That's not who he is. They know it's just a cover. They know we were both gone during the same time. People are going to put two and two together." I stressed.

"Not my problem. Maybe the world needs to be aware of what kind of man he is."

"I know you lied to the police. If you don't drop the charges, I'll walk into the police station with a photo ID and have them dropped."

I wasn't too comfortable with confrontation, but I was beyond frustrated with the situation and the lies being told. I guess everyone had a breaking point.

Dad didn't respond, and I knew it was because I'd hit a nerve.

"I know what you did. The charges won't stick if I walk in there. Drop them, please. I'm begging you."

I heard an intake of air from the other end of the line. "Adrianna." My name was a warning on his lips. "Do *not* push me or I will withdraw any and all of your assets. You'll have *nothing*. You may have been living on your own, and legal in the eyes of the law, but you can't support yourself or pay for gymnastics. You have no idea the amount of money I've funneled into your gym career, or for you to live like a princess."

"Dad, I know I have no right to ask you." I tried to heed the warning, afraid he would follow through with his threat. "But please think about it. Kova needs to be here. He *has* to be here. The Trials are my last chance at a shot at the Olympics before everything is over." My jaw wobbled. "I need my coach."

"Maybe you should've thought about that before you spread your legs for him."

I flinched, unprepared for his cruelness. "So, this is out of spite? Because you're mad at me?"

He ignored my question. "You have everything you need, including top-notch coaches, to go to the competition. You don't need anything else. You *want* something else, but you're not getting it. If this isn't generous enough of me, then walk away. I'm going to keep you two as far away as possible from each other. I'll do whatever I have to do, just like any father would when a grown man touches his daughter. This is ethically wrong, and not to mention, disgusting. You're too young to understand the ramifications of his revolting actions."

Tears slid over my flushed cheeks. His venomous tone pinched at my skin. I blinked, wondering how he could say such hateful things without an ounce of remorse.

"He's my coach and I need him," I said a little too passionately. "If he doesn't show, people will dig and ask questions, wondering why the former Olympian isn't with his gymnast at the Olympic Games. Is that what you want? Because then the truth will not only ruin everything I've worked so hard for, but it'll expose you too. You won't be able to hide it."

"Fake crying isn't going to get you anywhere, and neither will your idle threats."

I clenched my hand into a fist. "I'm not threatening you. People are going to figure out why he's nowhere to be found. They're nosy, and with a few simple searches, the pieces will fall together. People will discover the fight took place in one of your buildings. Then they'll dig further and find I live here because it's already been registered with several meets. The wheels will start turning. Assumptions and lies will be spread about all of us." I paused. "All it takes is a quick internet search, and *boom*."

Dad stayed quiet. If it wasn't for the sound of the ice from his drink sloshing around in his glass, I would have thought he hung up. His continued silence made me seriously edgy. I took a deep breath and broke down, adding one final thing.

"I'll just say this and then I won't bring it up again. In a few months, all of this will be over and behind us." I reminded him softly, my voice cracking. "I'll have to walk away from gymnastics and never look back. You have no idea what that realization does to me. Gymnastics is what makes me feel alive and happy, because even though I tell everyone I'm okay, I'm really not. I haven't been for a while now unless I'm practicing. In a couple of months, the only thing I'll have to look forward to are endless doctor appointments and a brew of pills and tests. Please," I begged, "let me just have this one thing."

A quiet gush of emotion escaped my lips. I couldn't wipe away the tears fast enough. My lips were trembling and swollen. I drew in a lungful of air and hoped he saw I was bearing my soul to him.

I hadn't lied, but I did get a bit more dramatic than I probably needed to. Though, I didn't feel bad this time. Everything I said was spoken from my raw heart and needed to be said.

"I know I've lost your trust. I know you don't believe a thing I say, but please consider dropping the charges so Kova can come back. Don't make me walk into a police station and do it. Kova has to finish this with me. Not as anything other than my coach, I swear. If you never believe anything I say again, just believe that. I need him by my side to get me through it. He is the only one who can help me."

"I'm sorry, Adrianna, but this time I can't give you what you want." Dad hung up.

I sat there in a daze. Dad hadn't shown an ounce of compassion even though I brought up his lies. I opened myself up and proved I didn't have any ulterior motives. It got me nowhere. I wished he could see it was more than just childish lust, and that Kova and I actually worked well together when it came to the sport. Kova understood my fears and turned them into positives. He saw me as a person and helped me overcome my internal battles while standing by my side.

I needed him now more than ever. Two people like us didn't find each other by accident. Kova was my other half. No one in this world could ever replace even an ounce of him.

I let my phone slide to the couch. Tears leaked down my cheeks and dripped on to my arm. I used my shirt to wipe them away only for fresh ones to bloom right after. I had a horrible feeling I was never going to see Kova again, at least not any time soon.

A sob burst from my lips like a dam breaking free. I cried, and cried, and cried, letting it all out in the loneliness of my condo.

I cried for what Kova was going through.

I cried for our unborn child that was taken away from us with no choice.

I cried for Dad and what I was putting him through.

I wished I could reverse time for a split second so I could rectify this. So many "if only" moments went through my mind.

If only Kova had been wearing a shirt.

If only I hadn't answered the door.

If only I hadn't fallen in love with my coach.

If only…

I yawned. I was so, so tired.

Grabbing the closest throw pillow, I hugged it to my chest and leaned down to curl up on my side. My heart was raw for the taking and I missed Kova so much. I longed to feel his arms around me and tell me it was going to be okay. My emotions were inflicting such destruction on me that I was physically sick from them.

I didn't know how I was going to recover from this—the miscarriage and arrest—or if I ever would. I needed the comfort of someone, anyone with empathy, but I wanted it only from Kova.

My stomach warmed with cramps and a new wave of lightheadedness took over. I curled up tighter, holding myself as I cried alone for the loss of so much more than just my heart.

My eyes fluttered closed as I began to doze off, sinking into a deep, dark hole. I moved my hand to my stomach and held myself where the life we'd created used to be. That was the last thing we had together, and it was gone now… just like he was.

chapter 14

"I feel like I haven't seen you in years," Hayden said as he sidled up to me. Practice was over and I just stepped out of the locker room.

He wrapped an arm around my shoulder and tugged me to him, giving me a friendly little kiss on the top of my head. I leaned into him, soaking him up with half a smile. I didn't have it in me to fake it today.

Bittersweet dreams had kept me suspended ever since the conversation with my dad. Night after night, my mind had played the worst-case scenario. I'd dreamed I'd never see Kova again. I'd dreamed he regretted meeting me and our time together. I'd dreamt I wouldn't be called to stand as a gymnast for the United States women's gymnastics team.

There was nothing more or less I could do. Walking away wasn't an option, losing wasn't either. I'd have to compete without my rock so I could achieve my dream, even if it took every last breath from my body.

I would succeed.

If Kova couldn't do this with me, then I'd have to do it for him.

"It's been a minute," I said, giving Hayden an apologetic look. "Things are just a little hectic right now, you know. I barely have time to sleep." He knew how hard I'd been working in the gym and where my focus was.

"Tell me about it." He paused. "Do you think it's strange Kova hasn't been here?" Hayden eyed me, and I stood up a little straighter.

"Don't look at me. I don't know where he is. Maybe he has something personal going on with his wife."

"He was gone the same week you were, and now he's missing the Trials."

I nodded, keeping my gaze forward. "I do think it's odd, and I wonder why he hired a new coach. But I'm in the dark. Speaking of the new coach, how do you like training with him?"

Danilo was a good excuse to switch topics. I knew exactly where Hayden was headed with that conversation, and I wasn't in the mood to hear or see his disappointment.

"He's going to be a hard ass, probably more so than Kova. I'm kind of glad I'm leaving for college soon." He laughed lightly. "Nah, he's good. Seems angry all the time though."

I laughed. "Like Kova."

"No wonder they're friends," Hayden said. "I can't believe you're leaving for Trials tomorrow. I'm going to be watching and rooting for you, you know."

A sad smile formed on my lips. Tomorrow I'd be on a plane headed to California for a two-day competition that ended with the Olympic team selections on the final night. The upcoming meet would be the most taxing one in several ways but also a learning experience too.

"It's surreal, isn't it? This is what so many of us dream about, and I'm actually doing it," I said. "Sometimes I feel like I don't deserve it."

"Only the stubborn survives."

I shrugged one shoulder. "I guess."

"How are you feeling otherwise?" he asked, gesturing to my arm. My fingers were a tad swollen and my arm wavered between light tingles and itching numbness.

Shaking my head, I grimaced. "Honestly, it hurts so bad that I just want to cut it off." I joked, and he laughed. "The last five days have tested me in every way possible. I'm kind of nervous about this weekend."

"I think you're going to surprise yourself and shock the gym world. You may be older than most of the girls, but they don't have the same passion. It's clear watching you compete. Your dedication shows. I'm placing bets on you. You're sturdy out there, someone they can rely on."

I gave him a friendly bump with my shoulder. "Thanks. How much am I worth?"

He laughed and I found a real smile tugging on my lips.

"Make sure you take a moment to yourself this weekend and realize how far you've come. Soak it up. Think about what you had to do to get where you are, because you may not think you deserve it, but you do. This could be your only time at the Olympic Trials. Enjoy it while you can."

"You're going to make a great father one day, Hayden."

Hayden let out a loud chuckle as Holly stepped out of the locker room. She was wearing a pair of khaki shorts and a crimson shirt with a white A on it and the words "Roll Tide." She finally heard back from Alabama. While she hadn't received a scholarship like she'd hoped for, Holly had been picked to be on their gymnastics team.

Hayden was headed to Michigan State, and Reagan had been accepted to the University of Louisiana on a partial scholarship.

"What's so funny?" Holly asked as she joined us in the hall.

"Hayden was giving me fatherly advice. Very inspiring."

She sighed like she was relieved his advice wasn't for her. What he said was thoughtful, and I actually planned to do exactly what he suggested. Hayden didn't know this would be my only chance at the Olympics, but he was right. I needed to take in the moment because it would all be over before I could blink.

That was going to be my new motto: it's all going to be over soon.

"Better you than me," Holly said, taking me away from my depressing thoughts.

"Someone has to watch out for you," he said to his sister. She rolled her eyes.

"I can't wait to go to college."

"Why? It's not like I can't text or call you," he said.

"You're so annoying. You're going to make an annoying husband one day."

Hayden looked at me with faux shock written on his face. "See what I have to deal with?"

"Go away, Hayden. Let me talk to Adrianna."

"Don't leave before I say goodbye to you," Hayden said. I nodded, and he headed into the locker room.

Holly waited until her brother was gone before turning to me. "I wish we could've had more time together before you had to leave. When you get back, I'll be gone."

I pursed my lips together and pouted. "Me too. Time always feels like it's moving slow but it's actually flying by. Maybe we can visit each other during the summer."

She frowned. "Where will you be?"

Inhaling a deep breath, I exhaled and my shoulders fell. "I haven't decided yet."

"Have you reached out to any schools?"

"Yeah, I actually had some inquiries, but I haven't had much time to look into them with so much going on. Maybe I can next week. Unfortunately, I'll be postponing the college experience. I need to take a year off to get my health in order."

"How have you been doing?"

I beamed at her. "I have a donor."

Holly's eyes lit up and she pulled me in for a bear hug. The last time we'd spoken about my kidney issues, I hadn't found one.

"Best news ever! I've been worried sick about you and was thinking about getting tested."

My lips parted at her generosity. Tears tried to rise to the surface but I pushed them down and mouthed "thank you" to her.

"Avery is a match, actually," I said after a few seconds.

Her eyes widened. "That's kinda cool."

"Yeah, she's excited about it while I'm terrified. So much could go wrong, you know? What if my body rejects it? Then we're both out of a kidney. I'd feel bad for the rest of my life."

She grimaced. "I think that thought is normal for anyone in your position. So, you've been talking about it more, then?"

I shook my head. "No, actually, I haven't. No one here knows anything except for Kova and you."

"Speaking of…"

I averted my gaze. Like brother, like sister. "You haven't told Hayden anything, have you?"

She shook her head, her eyes large. "Not a thing. I swear."

"I didn't think so, but he asked me about Kova too. I know you're leaving soon and will have a new life, but please don't ever tell anyone, okay?"

Holly looked me directly in the eyes. Her brows furrowed in offense.

"I'd never do that. Is everything okay, though?"

I looked away again and swallowed. "Everything is fine," I lied. "Normal, nothing new." I glanced over my shoulders and around us to see if anyone was within listening distance. "It's good," I said, keeping my voice low. "We're both just focused on gymnastics and keeping our distance. It's better that way right now."

Holly was studying me closely. I made sure to wipe my face clear of any hint of emotion as I spoke. I didn't want her to put things together in her head about me and Kova and our absences.

"I'm always here if you want to talk about anything." It was all she said, and I was so thankful. "You can call me anytime. I'll always pick up your call."

I laughed. "I'm going to hold you to that. Don't forget about me when you kill it in the collegiate world."

Holly opened her mouth to respond, but Reagan spoke before her as she walked toward us.

"For someone who is hopping on a plane to head to the freaking Olympic Trials, you don't look so happy."

"Always a pleasure, Reagan," I said. "I am happy."

Her eyes glowed with sincerity and her lips twitched from the smile she was trying to fight. She was going to remain that mean girl she loved to be until the very end. I was okay with that. Reagan wasn't being callous, she was just being her snobby self.

"Hey, girls." Madeline rounded the corner. "How about one final picture of the elites before they leave us to move onto the next chapter of their lives?" Her voice cracked a little even though she was beaming from ear to ear like a proud parent.

We all turned toward her as she pulled her cell phone from her pocket. Hayden rejoined the group just in time. Standing side by side with Holly, Reagan, and Hayden, we looped our arms around each other and pulled in close like we were the best of friends. Because in a sense we were. There was this softness in my heart for them that surprised me. I joined their little family late in the game, and while there were some heated arguments along the way like every family has, we'd all gotten extremely close.

Plastering on smiles, we said "cheese" and Madeline snapped a few pictures. Hayden made a joke and Holly told him to be quiet.

Reagan leaned in closer and whispered in my ear, "Good luck, Red." She winked at me. "I mean that."

Later that night after I'd packed my suitcase and taken my medication, Madeline texted the group of us a picture from earlier. Holly and Hayden were playfully mocking each other like typical siblings, and I was looking at Reagan with heartfelt tears in my eyes while she gave me the realest, kindest smile she could.

If a picture was worth a thousand words, I'd say this one was roughly worth seven hundred and fifty thousand of them.

I immediately saved it to my phone.

I couldn't wait to see where the future would take them.

chapter 15

MY HEART WAS HEAVY AS WE CHECKED IN AT THE AIRPORT.
It was five in the morning, and our plane was set to depart in just under two hours. Dad had told me he was traveling the entire way to the meet and back with me, and had made sure we were both on the same flight. It wasn't enough that I'd be flying with Madeline, he'd insisted he be there too.

I was hoping I could get a little shut eye on the flight to California. Last night I hadn't slept more than two hours, give or take. I couldn't get comfortable because of the little aches pinching under my skin. Motrin was a joke. I'd considered taking one of the stronger prescribed pills I had left over from when I had the kidney infection. I didn't, though. I disliked the drugged up feeling.

My arm ached, and the cramps were worse at night, but I had the notion a lot of what I was feeling was because I was missing someone. The bone-deep heartache was taking a toll on me physically. It was killing me that he wasn't going to be by my side.

Once we cleared security, Dad and Sophia wanted coffee.

"Can we get you a cup?" Sophia asked.

I nodded my head. "Yes, thank you."

I never said no to coffee.

"Any food?"

"I'm good. Thanks."

"If you want to go sit, you can," she said and pointed toward the gate.

I walked to the somewhat empty waiting area and sat down in an open row of chairs and placed my carry-on at my feet. Dressed in a World Cup sweat suit, I pulled my hood over my head and folded my arms together so I could use them as a pillow to rest my head on.

I closed my eyes and tried not to think of how Kova should be here by my side. My entire being was missing him something fierce. It was like a sickness I couldn't shake—lovesick was real. I was already craving the inspirational words he liked to give me before competitions. I wouldn't get them or see the look in his eyes when he told me to be strong.

I clenched my eyes shut, pushing the emotion back. It wasn't fair, and if I had even the slightest feeling I could sway Dad, I would. But I knew there was nothing I could do at this point. Not after what he'd said to me. He'd made his decision clear and that was it. Plus, it was too late anyway.

Curling up into a ball, I tucked my knees under me and covered my face with my hood to block out the light. I was prone to migraines these days, and the blinding light inside the terminal didn't help the pounding on the side of my skull. I drew in a lungful of air and my back tingled with awareness. I shifted in my seat and it happened again, this time stronger. My brows furrowed. It felt like a warning. My arms prickled, and my nose twitched from the faint scent of something familiar.

I felt a presence wash over me, but I hadn't heard any footsteps approach. Maybe I was more tired than I thought. I was in an airport with hundreds of people and my mind was playing with my emotions. I was too delicate when it came to him and his absence. It was the harsh truth, and after this weekend, I was going to try and stop mourning him so much. I didn't have the strength to let go right now. I needed to put all my focus into the sport. It was what Kova would've wanted.

Something in the air shifted and caused the rate of my pulse to increase. I flushed, and warmth pushed through my veins. Electricity danced around me like it was mocking me.

My cheeks bloomed with heat. I was hyperaware of someone watching me.
I held my breath.
The warmth in my chest made my heart speed up with anticipation.
I prayed this wasn't a cruel trick that my subconscious was playing on me.
I took a deep breath, then another, and another.
I knew before I opened my eyes…he was here.
I was terrified. I was scared of what I'd see, or what I wouldn't actually see.
Inhale, exhale.
Every fiber in my body said Kova was here.
Would he be angry with me? Would he resent me and never want to talk to me again after all this was over?
No, he wouldn't. He loved me. He'd told me he did countless times. Love didn't make people feel hate.
My heart was fluttering harder than ever as I slowly opened my eyes… and I stilled.

The first thing I saw was his hand hanging between his spread legs. I blinked to see if it was real. He was moving, pushing his palm toward the floor to signal me. He did it twice, silently telling me to stay. There was a small black duffle bag near his booted feet.

My heart catapulted into my throat. I popped right up and pushed my hood back as my frantic eyes took in his sorrowful ones. My lips parted in disbelief.

Konstantin Kournakova was at the airport.

"Kova," I whispered under my breath. My hands grabbed the armrests. I wanted to jump from my seat and run to him, but I knew better.

"*Stay, Ria.*" He issued the command quietly.

My brows furrowed as I stared at him. I watched him closely, afraid he was going to disappear. His eyes lifted toward something over my shoulder.

My stomach tightened. Kova was eyeing Dad. My fingers tightened around the armrest and I gripped it to steady myself.

There were dark scalloped circles under his guarded eyes as he watched my dad closely.

A vicious ache slashed through my chest. My heart was burning for him.

"Keep your eyes on me," he said. I nodded subtly, my heart hammering against my ribs.

"You're here?" I said quietly.

Tears blurred my vision and my jaw quivered. I didn't want to get caught showing any kind of emotion toward Kova and ruin this, even though I felt like I was breaking inside. That would be like putting us on a platter and handing it to Dad along with a carving knife. I needed to pull myself together.

Anxiousness flickered in my stomach. My nerves were making me edgy again.

I drank him in from head to toe; the demanding need to know what he was thinking and feeling rushed through my blood. He was wearing dark distressed jeans, and I tried to think of a time when I'd seen him in them. All I could remember ever seeing him wear were dress pants or gym shorts. The black military style boots were loosely laced, and the hem of his jeans were haphazardly tucked into them.

My gaze made its way up his body and stopped on his knuckles. They were scraped and bruised, cut with deep red stitching over the creases. It reminded me of when I fell off my bike and skinned my knees. I frowned, wondering if that happened with Dad or while he was in jail.

"Are you okay?" I asked, keeping my voice low.

Enigmatic green eyes bore into mine. There was no half exposing anything in his gaze. He let go and aimed straight at me.

"I am now. And you?"

His eyes dropped to my mouth.

"I'm fine." It was an automatic answer these days, but he knew the real meaning behind the word. "How are you here?" I whispered.

My gaze lowered. His black cable knit sweater looked cozy. I wanted to curl up and burrow myself into him. I needed to feel his arms around me. He seemed so calm and relaxed on the outside, and it made me second-guess what he felt for me on the inside. If he held me, I'd be able to tell.

My eyes traveled back up to his. Kova didn't bother answering me. He didn't need to. His expression told me everything I needed to know. He held my gaze with a depth that wrapped around my entire being. He was asking me to hang on another second, yet to the outside world he remained aloof.

Then he dropped the shroud, and I knew him.

I felt him.

I saw him.

He was anything but cool inside. He was emotionally distraught. He was raw, ribs ripped wide open, bleeding love and despair.

Air expelled from my lungs.

Kova's gaze dropped to my stomach. My nostrils flared and I covered myself, looking away. I felt protective of what was no longer there, protective of my initial choice, but more so protective of my emotions because I didn't actually get a choice in the end. Neither did he. My biggest worry was that I was going to be blamed for the miscarriage. I didn't want to be blamed.

From the corner of my eye, I could see Dad and Sophia walking over to us. I stilled, panicking at the thought of how this would turn out. Did my dad even know he was here?

I turned my attention back to Kova to see if he'd noticed, but he hadn't. The light remaining in his eyes dimmed lower, his gaze staying where my hands were on my stomach. He wasn't angry at me like I'd worried he would be.

He was dying inside, like I was.

I swallowed hard, wishing it wasn't like this, fearing this would change us forever.

I heard their muffled voices before they came into full view.

Dad's eyes were fixated on Kova, glaring at him with hostility. I stiffened. Judging by how tense Dad's shoulders were, I could tell he was irritated, but I also knew he wouldn't make a scene in public. I sat up straighter, my heart beating a little faster. Different scenarios flashed through my mind wondering how this would go as Dad sat down stiffly next to me. Sophia reached over to hand me the coffee cup, then she quietly took a seat next to Dad.

Kova didn't move his head, but he lifted his gaze and nailed Dad with it. "Konstantin."

My eyes widened.

Kova continued to eye him.

"Don't forget what we spoke about and the reason why you're here. Unless it's regarding gymnastics, there will be zero communication between the two of you. You're here solely for her benefit in the sport, and *nothing* more. Do you both understand?"

I held my breath, waiting. Kova didn't reply, and that only skyrocketed the friction between all of us.

I nodded subtly and worried my bottom lip. Kova's eyes softened with guilt as he turned my way. A flash of regret shadowed his eyes before he turned cold. My chest deflated on a hushed breath. Kova grabbed his duffle bag and stood.

My heart stopped.

Gripping the armrests again, I watched him walk a few chairs down. He flung his bag to the floor then dropped into an empty seat. With one leg bent and the other extended, he slouched back and folded his hands behind his head and looked up at the ceiling.

This was hell on earth for us.

Not seeing Kova for nearly two weeks affected me in ways I couldn't explain. Missing him left a profound ache in me that worsened with every second that passed. I thought about him every day. With him sitting so close, I wanted desperately to run to him and never let go.

God, I hoped he felt the same way.

I stared at him, not caring if Dad or Sophia were watching me. Our love was real, but something in my gut pulled on the knots tighter the longer I watched him. He didn't look my way. I stared at him, willing him to look at me. We'd have to choose between being in love and simply breathing. I knew it in my heart we would. We wouldn't get both.

Kova always said timing was everything. He failed to mention our timing would never, ever be right. I looked away. Love and breathing went hand in hand for us. He exhaled and I inhaled. That would never change for us.

I loved my dad. I never wanted to hurt him. But if loving Kova meant I was stabbing Dad in the back, then I'd take the knife and have Dad face a mirror to watch me do it. This weekend was an important one, and I wasn't going to hold back just because he was here and watching like a hawk.

I was elite gymnast Adrianna Rossi, and he was gymnastics coach Konstantin Kournakova. We were going to do our thing. Together.

I allowed a small smile to bare my heart.

❧

"Understand that I'm against this," Dad said, leaning over his shoulder to me. "Him being here doesn't change anything. Do you understand me? You'll still be watched, and you will be coming home after this meet."

We were sitting in first class while Kova and Madeline were in coach. She almost missed the flight but luckily made it just in time before the doors closed.

We hadn't talked about Kova showing up. Of course, it was on the tip of my tongue to ask every question that popped into my head the moment we took our seats. By the grace of God, I stayed quiet. Dad obviously knew Kova was coming, otherwise his reception would've been entirely different. So, I patiently waited.

It wasn't until I'd fallen asleep and woken before our expected arrival, did Dad finally decide to speak to me.

"I've thought a lot about the things you said to me the other night. It stuck with me," he said, angling his body toward mine. He held a glass of whiskey in one hand. Sometimes he was nicer when he drank alcohol. "I've spoken to Sophia about it too. I'm sure she's ready to sew my mouth shut." I smiled at him, though it was small. "She reminded me that girls' emotions are heavier and deeper than boys', that your heart beats differently when you're...in love." He stopped and glared out the window, then looked back at me. "Adrianna, do not mistake him being here for anything other than him coaching you at a gymnastics meet. *Nothing* more. Sophia is not encouraging you to be around Kova, but she is a huge reason why he's here. I can't say that I don't agree, but I don't like it."

All I could do was nod my head furiously. Dad was finally telling me all the things I'd stressed about in my head.

"I'm not okay with this," he continued, "and I never will be, so don't forget that. I'd rather *he* not be here or within a thousand-mile radius of you, but I also don't want to be the one to ruin this opportunity for you by changing up your usual schedule. I thought having any coach with you wouldn't change a thing, but after speaking with Madeline too, she made it clear it's not the same."

I wondered when he spoke to Madeline and what they spoke about. Did she call him to say I wasn't giving my all this week? She couldn't have said I slacked, but I was a little slower...and I was withdrawn and feeling really far away mentally. Being my normal self required too much from me at the moment. I was suffering inside, and I didn't have the energy to fake it, so I didn't. I just kept to myself and tried to turn off everything else. I needed to stow my energy wisely. I had more than an injury and an illness trying to pull me down. I wondered if that was what she told him and why he had a change of heart.

"Does she know about the lupus and kidney disease? And...and what happened?"

I waited with a tight breath.

"No. She just updated me on how your arm was doing, among other things."

I exhaled. "Thank you."

Dad took a sip of his drink, finishing the contents, then signaled to the flight attendant for a refill. "Adrianna... That night, with your arm..."

Instinctively, I hugged my sore arm closer to my side.

He regarded me with grief in his eyes, then turned his gaze forward. "It makes me sick to think of the real damage I could've caused. I hate myself for it. I could've broken your arm." He dipped his chin and angled his head toward mine. "What you said about having to walk away from all of this for good struck a chord with me." Dad paused. "You've worked hard, you deserve this. What you're about to accomplish with your health in the state that it is, is monumental." His eyes softened with pride. "Despite the things I've said to you lately, and what's happened, I want to see you smiling out there, doing what you love to do. We only get one life, Adrianna. I don't want to lose you."

Tears threatened to spill as I took in my father. There were prominent lines around the corners of his mouth, and dark circles hung beneath his eyes. He'd turned so haggard looking from this nightmare. My illness, my relationship with Kova, everything, it had all thrown a curveball his way.

I leaned into Dad, wrapping my free arm around him. He reciprocated the hug. Sometimes less was more, and in this moment, I felt that.

"Thank you, Dad."

chapter 16

YAWNING, I STEPPED FROM THE CAR IN MY WORLD CUP SWEAT SUIT and laid the duffle bag strap across my chest. It was day one of competition and I started it with a low-grade fever, stiff joints, and a lot of shit on my mind. I had a hotel room to myself, which Dad hadn't been happy about. Thankfully, Madeline had reminded him of the rules. Gymnasts weren't allowed to communicate with family or friends the night before. It helped to prevent outside noise from messing with our heads before the meet.

I stepped over the threshold into the main arena. Cool air enveloped me, invigorating each fiber in my body. My eyes were everywhere, trying to take in the room all at once. The place was gigantic and easily housed thirty thousand people. There were massive rectangular banners hanging across the second floor in the middle of the room from the previous years. I blinked in disbelief, not quite grasping I was at the Olympic Trials. So many great hopefuls were in this room. I was among the best of the best in the entire country. I inhaled a deep breath and drew the trace of chalk into my lungs. I held it and smiled to myself. My love for the sport was finally overcoming the shitstorm in my head and taking over.

Following Madeline, I maneuvered through a maze of leotards and slicked back ponytails to look for Kova. I wouldn't deny the fact that seeing him spurred a trail of excitement through me. I'd hoped to see him, or at least talk to him last night, but Dad had quickly doused that with his threat to stick a piece of tape on my door to know if I'd snuck out.

"This is such an exciting day for you. Kova mentioned changing the dismount on one of your routines because of the recent rule change."

I nodded… Then I spotted Kova before he saw me.

His head was bent as he scribbled something onto a yellow legal pad. His wide stance and beautifully carved shoulders combined with his commanding aura capitulated my heart into my throat. He was in the zone and I loved that.

It did strange things to my heart. Would the sight of him ever get old? Or would it increase over time?

"Adrianna's here. I'll see you in a few, Kova. I'm off to get an updated schedule of events," Madeline said, then sprinted off in the other direction.

I drank him in, not worried in the least that someone would see the way my love for him shone. His hand slowed, and he stilled. I chewed on my lip waiting as a veil of familiarity brought me home.

He lifted his eyes, and I caught the faintest curl at the corners of his lips. "*Malysh.*"

Warm-ups had been tough, both physically and mentally. By sheer determination and stubbornness, and a strong bout of tunnel vision, I got through them. Anytime my hips had swiveled a little more than necessary to one side, shooting pain would spear my pelvis, robbing me of breath. And the pressure and pounding my elbow had taken with every tumbling pass or vault felt like someone had taken a hammer to it. The pain had been nauseating. But I'd grinded my teeth and kept going.

Now, as the competition was in full swing, I watched all the young gymnasts who seemed free from restraint and moved as fluid as water, and it messed with my head a little.

"Where did you go?" Kova asked, breaking my thoughts.

I shook my head and stared down at the floor. I think what he really meant to say was, "What the fuck happened out there?"

"Nowhere. I'm just thinking."

Friction radiated off him over my mistake, though he didn't say anything. We walked side by side toward the end of the runway for my second vault of the evening. The first attempt had ended with me on my butt, which would cost me big time. The blind landing was already difficult to begin with, but when I didn't get enough air and dropped my hips and then opened too late, there was no saving it.

"Your form was loose, and you did not block hard enough. Is it because of your arm?"

I shook my head and tapped my feet in the chalk. I curled my toes under to crack them.

"Give me," Kova said.

I glanced up wide-eyed. "Give you what?"

"Your arm. Give it to me." He waved his fingers.

I gawked and moved my arm behind my back. His eyes lowered like he was aggravated.

"Give me your arm, Adrianna," he demanded. "We do not have much time."

I shot a paranoid glance over my shoulder, then raised my arm to him. Kova took it and held me with only the touch of a professional. His thumb pressed on the muscles and joints, then he applied pressure to the crease. He hit a sore spot and I clenched my eyes shut, wincing. My arm was so swollen. Kova extended my arm and made sure my elbow was locked straight.

My teeth dug into the inside of my lip.

"Breathe." He commanded. I hadn't even realized I wasn't. "Flex."

He pushed on my palm and arched my fingers back, then rotated my wrist while holding the inside of my elbow so I couldn't bend it. My fingers were a little tingly and my hand was shaking.

"Do you have extra sports tape with you? If not, I will find some," he said, and I nodded in response. "This is what we are going to do. I will tape your arm after this rotation. It will not completely erase the pain, but it should help. In the meantime, you are going to put everything you have inside of you into that second vault. Give it your all. Do you understand me? We did not make it this far only to crumble when shit gets tough. When you are done, you are going to walk off and come to me like it does not bother you." He paused, then said, "Tonight after the meet, we will do therapy on it. Your father can stand over me and watch for all I care."

I nodded again robotically.

Kova let go of my arm but he didn't move back. He propped his hands on his hips and exhaled a tight breath.

"Talk to me. You have been so quiet."

"I don't want to do anything that will provoke my dad," I said under my breath. I was embarrassed to admit it.

"Believe me, I understand your fear more than anyone, but that is going to cost you everything you have worked for. Do not do that to yourself. I am not telling you to go against your father, but right now, this is about *you* and no one else. You worked hard for this, Adrianna. Do not let anyone or anything take it away from you. Your father knows this, and it is why you are here. Stop overthinking and do what you were born to do. You will live with regret if you do not. You are not reigning champ on vault for nothing."

He had a point.

The warning bell sounded to let us know it was time to go.

Our eyes met. My lips parted.

I watched him exhale, and he watched me inhale.

"Make it count," he said.

Kova turned around and walked to the end of the vault to double check the springboard was in position and the height of the apparatus was correct. He stood off to the side then looked down the runway at me. He dipped his chin to let me know I was good to go. I padded some chalk onto my palms then clapped my hands together. A small cloud appeared in front of me.

I moved to stand behind the taped white line and then stepped back another foot, needing the extra momentum.

Kova was right. I needed to reset my focus. Adrenaline surged through my body as I rolled my toes under me until they cracked, a nervous habit of mine. I raised my arms to salute the judges, then zeroed in on the vault and leaned up on the tips of my toes.

I got this.

I took long strides, building up the power, and envisioned myself flipping over the vault and completing the two and a half twists cleanly.

Fingers spread wide on the floor, I turned my roundoff over, and feet slamming into the springboard, I rebounded backward and reached for the horse to block as hard as I could. Pain ripped through me, but Kova was right. I had worked too hard for it to fall apart now.

Rebounding off with as much force as I could grasp, I soared through the air as tight as I could, twisting and rotating at the same time.

Everything I'd learned from Madeline and Kova flashed through my mind.

I could hear them whispering in my ear where to open up, and I listened, hoping the blind landing was perfect.

The arena came into view as my feet met the blue landing mat. A gush of air exploded from my lungs as I raised my arms to salute the judges. No hop. No bent legs. Just a perfect, stuck landing. The crowd erupted as fans cheered on. From the corner of my eye, I could see Kova's excitement as he clapped his hands and yelled.

Heart racing, I blinked repeatedly…and smiled.

I landed *and* I stuck my vault!

Stepping off the floor and down the steps, I wasn't even thinking when I ran into Kova's arms. It was so automatic and what we'd always done—what so many coaches and gymnasts do. He picked me up and squeezed me to him. Feeling how proud he was of me made me feel so damn good. That told me I'd done my job correctly.

"Magnificent!" he said in my ear, then put me down. Kova high-fived me. My heart bloomed with happiness. "There is the focus you need. That was flawless and what everyone knows you are capable of."

All I could do was smile at him. "Thank you," I said, keeping my voice low, only for him.

"Boy, you had me worried there for a second, Adrianna." Madeline approached us, her eyes twinkling. "That first vault was so unlike you, but this one had your name written all over it. Good job."

I grinned at her. "Thank you," I said when the crowd erupted again.

The three of us turned around to glance up at the scoreboard knowing that was the reason for the cheering. My score had been posted and there was only a third of a tenth deduction.

My eyes widened in shock at the nearly perfect. Madeline tugged me into a quick hug, said a few things to Kova, then walked away. I felt like she was always on the run going somewhere.

Without a worry of who was watching us, Kova stared down at me with a tenderness that synced my heart with his. There was so much love and pride in his eyes that I could hardly handle it. Words weren't always needed to show someone that you cared for them. Sometimes just a look said enough.

One side of his mouth lifted into a crooked smile. My cheeks blushed and I glanced down.

"Come. Let us wrap your arm. It is not going to bring a miracle to you, but it will help a little bit."

"I'll take anything at this point."

"I will work it out with each rotation as much as I can, but expect some pain."

I followed Kova to the seating area where he conditioned my arm, then applied the stretchy sports tape. My fingers weren't as numb, and I was glad about that since I had bars next. I had read online numbness was a cause of nerve damage associated with dislocations. I hoped that wasn't the case, and that this stinging ache that never seemed to go away was because I hadn't allowed myself enough time to heal properly and nothing more.

"Prepare to rotate. I will be back shortly."

chapter 17

"**G**ET THE WHITE TAPE."

I dropped my bag and rummaged through it. I handed the tape to Kova. He began wrapping my wrists for added support and laced some of my fingers with tape too. He applied another layer of tape to my injured arm, saying it may help with the straining. Once he was finished, I took over and slipped on my wristbands and grips then buckled them. Flexing my fingers, I shook my hands out.

"Good?" Kova asked, and I nodded. "Go chalk up."

I turned around and walked over to the stand holding the bowl of chalk and submerged my hands in it. I powdered my inner thighs and then the tops of my legs. Bars was another specialty of mine and one that I usually medaled in. I was confident, but still I visualized my routine and focused solely on that. I sprayed water on my palms, then glanced over at Kova who was spraying the bars with water and then rubbing them down with chalk for me. It provided an added grip. It wasn't something we did often but given how the inside of my elbow was stinging, Kova wasn't going to take a chance.

I walked over to him and eyed the high bar where he applied the chalk.

"Do you want me to spot you?"

"Yes."

"Strong core and stay tight," he said. "Drive your heels way down on the first tap and then drive them again just before the release." I nodded furiously, adrenaline spiking my pulse. I was getting excited to perform. "Hollow through the swing." He instructed by imitating what I needed to do and pointing to his chest. "Just a little longer, then drive to initiate the rotation."

"Got it."

"Straight lines. Stick your handstands. This is your event, Ria. Do not let anyone take it from you. Own it."

Kova clapped my back and then moved to stand parallel to the uneven bars. Piling on a bit more chalk, I blew on my palms and a cloud of white dust appeared before me. I stepped in front of the low bar with my foot pointed in front of me and shook my fingers out. I met Kova's eyes to center my balance, and I inhaled, pulling the air deep into my stomach, then exhaled.

The bell sounded. He dipped his chin.

It was go time.

Mounting the low bar, I did a kip cast to a handstand and let muscle memory take over. I performed my heart out, free flowing from bar to bar in my own element, making sure I stuck my handstands and I had clean lines. As I geared up to release to the low bar, Kova stepped into the side and put his arm out to spot me.

Gripping the bar tightly, chalk dust floated in my face as I came down swinging into another kip, then to a free hip circle before I let go and twisted backward to reach for the high bar. I moved quietly, flowing freely into a handstand. I stuck it, then fell backwards, rotating with only one arm—my bad one—and held on for dear life as I swung around the bar to stick my handstand. This was a skill worth more points than most and it had to be executed perfectly to get the value for difficulty, otherwise it would be all for nothing. My fingers gripped the bar while I gritted my teeth from the strain in my ligaments.

Kova took another step closer to spot me as I completed a pirouette. I rotated my hands once more before I fell forward, tapping into a giant, then tapping again like Kova said to, and reached for my release.

I whipped my hips for momentum to take flight and flew backwards in a pike position, reaching for the bar. My heart stopped for a split second as my toes glided past the bar and I came down. Kova made a fist and pumped it in excitement, then moved out of the way and back to the waiting area so I could complete my routine. I had two more releases that took my breath away before I was circling the high bar to complete two giants. I'd worked on this dismount long and hard with Kova to know when I had to release.

Coming down on the second rotation, I waited until my toes were parallel with the bar and I released my hold. The bar ricocheted violently behind me as I twisted two times with a straight body to complete a double twisting double layout. This dismount was one of the hardest dismounts to complete. It required a straight body going against pressure, and I'd worked endlessly with him to perfect it.

Spotting for the ground, my arms came out in front of me. Feet together, I landed on the mat with only the tiniest hop. Before I could raise my arms, I heard Kova yell his excitement, followed by Madeline shouting. I smiled from ear to ear as I saluted the judges, then I ran off the podium to my coaches. I hugged both and waited with them for my score to post.

I went into this routine with a different mindset than I had vault. I let myself go, living in the moment and loving the sport that had captivated my heart from a young age. I didn't hold back. I didn't worry. I just let my body feel.

I knew it had a lot to do with Kova. It was always him. He sensed my reluctance, my fears, my worries. I had to wonder how I would do without him by my side. I'd like to think I'd perform the same, but honestly, I wasn't sure.

I pulled my buckles back and slipped my grips off.

"How's your arm?" Madeline asked.

"Killing me," I said, panting. "It was the reverse grip and the back giant that did it. I thought I was going to end up tearing my shoulder all the way down. I'm going to need to ice it tonight to compete tomorrow."

"I'll make sure you have everything you need when you go into physical therapy."

Luckily, I had brought a small bottle of Motrin with me. I planned to pop six pills the moment I got back to my hotel room. I couldn't tell anyone, though. I'd probably get yelled at, but this was one of those desperate moments that required it.

I exhaled a heavy breath. I had no idea how the hell I even got through that routine.

"Thanks, Madeline," I said when the crowd erupted.

We glanced at the black screen high above us and looked for my name. With only a few deductions, I was still in second place with a large margin separating me from third. I couldn't believe it. I stared, afraid it would all go away if I blinked. Falling on that first vault was going to cost me today, but I knew in my gut going forward I'd excel from here on out. That was what I hoped anyway.

"Fantastic," Madeline said, smiling. "Keep it up."

She pulled her notebook from under her arm and strode away, writing in it as she did. Probably making a note of the items I'd need for therapy.

"How do you feel?" Kova asked. His hands were clasped behind his back.

I peered up at him and lifted one corner of my mouth into a smile. "Aside from my dangling dead limb, I feel good. Really good, actually. More confident than before."

"Good. I am glad. You should be happy while you are here. You earned it. Pack up and let us move onto beam."

Kova turned to leave, but I called his name.

"Wait."

Anxiety swirled in my blood. I should've waited, but I had to say something.

It was stupid to feel this way when I'd been alone with Kova before, but I was too nervous to ask him to meet me tonight. We hadn't had a chance to talk and I really wanted to. We needed to.

I bit my lip, and his eyes fell to my mouth. "Do you think we can talk tonight?"

Kova drew his lower lip between his teeth. "Come on. Let us go."

A blush crept into my cheeks. I felt like a weight had been lifted from my chest just asking that simple question.

The balance beam had passed much quicker for some reason, thank God, and now I was on my last event—floor. Fortunately, I was still in second place after beam. I'd only had a few wobbles, but nothing to knock me down to third place.

Madeline was rubbing my arms, warming me up. She bent over so she was eye level with me and took my hands in hers, shaking my arms out.

"I want you to go out there and have fun, you hear me? Smile and show this arena who you are and that you're a force to be reckoned with."

My cheeks flushed. Sometimes I was shy. "I'll try."

"No, you *will* do it."

I giggled. "All right." I was high on life right now and really, really happy. I felt like I was bursting with sunshine, something I hadn't felt in a while

She let go of my hands and said, "You're up! Knock 'em dead."

I saluted the judges, then walked up the steps and onto the blue carpeted spring floor. This was a favorite event of mine. My classical routine had a lot of spunk and charm woven through it that had been choreographed specifically to fit my personality and aptitude. It was a lot of fun to perform, a total crowd pleaser where fans of the sport clapped their hands and joined in.

Right before I stepped into position and took my stance, I glanced over my shoulder and searched for my good luck charm.

He was already looking at me.

That was all I needed.

chapter 18

"S o," Avery said, drawing out the word, "how'd you do today? Tell me everything!"

I chuckled at her excitement.

"I need to know if my bestie is going to the Olympics so I can tell everyone at school tomorrow. Then I'm gonna book my ticket so I can watch you in person."

I smiled, my heart beating with so much love for my friend. "It was unreal, Ave! The crowd was so loud the entire time, and there was this big extravagant opening to introduce the gymnasts today. The lights were turned down low while this video montage played above. Each one of us walked onto the floor one by one waving to the people while these huge smoke bombs in red, white, and blue erupted behind us. The announcer said which state we were from and the gym name. We were given matching USA sweat suits too. I can't wait to get a free minute to watch the replay." I hadn't realized how cool the introductions were until I told Avery. Funny how it was a blur until now. "As for the team, I'll know tomorrow. I have one more day of competition, and that's when the team is picked."

"Shit." She groaned. "I must've gotten the days mixed up. I thought it was today. Anyway, that sounds so damn cool. I wish I was there to see it. I'll have to check before I go to school when it'll be on television so I can record it. Make sure you tell me ASAP after tomorrow. Do you think you'll make it? I think you will."

That was the million-dollar question.

"I think I have a good chance, but I'm trying not to get my hopes up even though I'm dying to make it." I chuckled. "I may have placed at Worlds and other major comps, but you just never know. There are so many amazingly talented girls here too. My coaches think I have a chance."

"You mean Madeline?"

I perked up. "Oh, my God. I didn't get a chance to tell you. Kova is here."

"Shut the fuck up!" Avery gasped.

"No, I know. I couldn't believe it myself when he showed up at the airport."

"No shit. Did your dad flip?"

"No. I'm not sure of the details just yet, but my dad knew Kova was coming. He just didn't tell me. Can you believe it? Kova just showed up at the terminal and sat across from me."

"How did he look?"

"Like a wreck, honestly. Horrible. He looked like he hadn't slept in days."

"He probably hadn't."

I told Avery about Kova and how it'd been preparing for the meet without him. I told her I felt as bad as he looked. She made a comment, concerned about how much time I spent thinking about him. I reminded her a gymnast needed her coach. The coach was the only person who understood an athlete's mind and where it goes during competition.

I didn't deny my attachment, I loved him, but I hoped she didn't confuse it for anything more than what it was. When the coach becomes all you know for nearly fifty hours a week times three hundred and sixty-five days a year, a connection is formed that's nearly impossible to break. He knows me better than anyone in the world.

"I'm seeing Kova tonight, but I kind of feel bad because of how much my dad is putting aside for him to be here."

Avery made a sound under her breath like she agreed. "I'm assuming he'll be back at practice. You could always talk then. I wouldn't risk it right now. It's not worth it, and tomorrow is a big day for you. Do you have an alibi in case anyone comes by your room and you're MIA?"

I chuckled. I hadn't thought of needing an alibi, but aside from that, Avery made a good point. I didn't want to risk anything. Even though Dad was putting everything to the side at the moment, it didn't mean I wasn't on thin ice with him. One wrong move and I knew he would take this away from me. I had to decide if it was worth risking everything I loved for him.

There was a light knock on the door. My brows drew together as I stood up from the small chair facing the window. No way would Kova blatantly come to my room like that, not when there were eyes and ears everywhere right now on the floor where all the gymnasts stayed together.

"Someone's at the door," I whispered into the phone. "Let me grab this and we'll talk tomorrow."

"Text me ASAP! I'll be on the edge of my seat waiting. Good luck! Love you!"

After thanking her, we hung up. I placed my cell down on the dresser then walked to the door to look through the peep hole. I was surprised to see Sophia standing on the other side.

When Dad had told me she wanted to come to the competition but wanted to make sure I was okay with it first, I'd been both stunned and secretly elated. It was nice to be supported by a mother who wanted to be there. I had to remind Dad this was a huge competition and they would likely be captured on camera in between rotations since I was competing. I thought he might be concerned to be seen with someone other than Joy. He insisted he wasn't and that I shouldn't be either.

"Hey," I said when I opened the door.

She gave me a hesitant smile. "Hi. Do you mind if I come in?"

"Not at all." I shook my head, happy to see her.

I stepped aside and opened the door wider for her to enter, then shut it behind her and gestured to the little round table by the window.

She took a seat, placing an item wrapped in brown paper she brought with her on her lap. I took the opposite chair and regarded her. It was strange looking at someone who looked eerily similar to me.

"How are you feeling?" she asked.

"Aside from the fact I'm competing on less than half my kidney function and with a gimpy arm, and I'm dead tired, I'm honestly fine for the most part. I have a headache right now, and I'm feeling stiff since everything is settling for the night, but nothing new there."

I scratched the side of my head anxiously, wondering if there was a reason why she was here. A piece of hair got stuck around my fingernail when I pulled my hand away. I glanced down. There'd been so much hair surrounding the drain when I took a shower after I'd gotten back to the hotel room. I'd tried not to read too much into it. I lost hair all the time, but this time there had been clumps. I hadn't lost clumps before.

"I just wanted to thank you for allowing me to come here with you. It was incredible to be able to watch you. I've followed you over the years, and Frank always gave me updates, but witnessing it in person is something I can't begin to explain. You made it look so easy."

My eyes softened. I took that as a compliment. "I'm glad you're here. It's nice to have someone besides Dad who's supportive and actually wants to be part of this."

"I know things are probably a little strange right now with me suddenly in your life. If it's something you don't want, please just let me know. Frank insists you'll be okay with it, but I had to say it myself." One side of her mouth tugged up into a half smile. "I don't want to step on any toes or give unsolicited advice. That's the last thing I'd want. I'll do anything at your pace to be in your life."

There was no way to explain how much that meant to me. Every girl needed a mom, and the only one I'd ever known never wanted me. I didn't want to yell and scream "Yes, please, be in my life," but it was exactly how I felt.

"It was a shock at first." I laughed lightly. "I had no idea you guys were even talking, let alone seeing each other." I paused. "I kind of wished I'd known sooner, but then again, I guess things happen for a reason… I never would've guessed I had someone else out there." I began to ramble and needed a quick subject change. "So, why did you stop by? Something you wanted to talk about?"

Whatever it was, it had to be very important for her to sneak over here to talk to me. I wasn't supposed to have family in my room or talk to them before a competition.

Sophia sat up straighter. She had a small frame like I did and looked petite in the chair. She placed the wrapped item on the table and passed it to me.

My brows angled toward each other. "A gift?" I glanced up to meet her eyes. "You brought me a gift?"

"Yes. It's not much. It's something I was given once and it helped me find my way. Go ahead and open it. I thought you may be able to use it."

I peeled back the brown craft paper to reveal a book. Holding the glossy cover, I flipped it open and glanced down the front, reading over the blurb.

"It's technically a self-help book, but I don't like to call it that. People tend to stray from those." Sophia waited a moment, then said, "I read that book during a chaotic time in my life, and it stuck with me ever since. I was angry at the world and I hated myself because nothing I did was right, only I didn't know it at the time. That book taught me to be gentle with myself, to focus on what I needed in order to be happy, that I needed to put myself first. But more importantly, it taught me how to embrace every part of me."

I looked at her. She seemed a little uneasy. This was the first time she was trying to give me real advice and I think it made her nervous.

"Just say it, Sophia," I said in a friendly tone. "I can tell you're holding back. You don't have to with me."

We smiled at each other.

"Based on what Frank's told me, and what I've seen, I thought it might be helpful for you to read in your downtime, if you ever get any." Her airy laugh caused my smile to broaden. "You're dealing with more than most kids your age, on top of your health issues. Even if you weren't dealing with the other things, you're at the Olympic Trials. That's huge. Do you even realize how big this is? There's a lot for you to process."

I grinned, and looked at the book again before I met her gaze once more. "It'll probably hit me when I get home, and probably at the worst time too. Seems to be how my life is going at the moment."

Sophia took a deep breath. "There's a light at the end of the tunnel, you just have to truck through the mud first to see it. I hope the book is encouraging for you the way it was for me. When you do get time to process everything, it'll all come roaring back and hit you at once."

I'd yet to have time to process what happened that day in my condo, or the days proceeding. My world had crumbled in a matter of minutes and I had to shelve it because I had more important hurdles to jump.

There was a part of me that didn't want to think about it anyway. How many tears could one girl cry? Just thinking about it knotted my stomach. I was better off not having to think about it, but the other part of me knew I'd have to come to terms with it eventually, whether I wanted to or not.

"Thank you, Sophia," I said, feeling slightly emotional. "This means a lot to me. I may start to read it tonight, actually."

I planned to meet Kova down the street at this coffee shop after the sun had set. I could flip through a few pages when I got back while I was lying in bed.

"Can I be frank?"

We both chuckled. She wasn't talking about my dad. I nodded.

"Like I said before, I don't want to overstep, so if you feel I am, please just tell me and I won't say anything." She paused and locked eyes with me. "I saw the way you looked at Kova today." I stilled, and the color drained from my face. "I feel like I need to say it's not a good idea to act on it."

chapter 19

MY JAW WOBBLED AS ANXIETY FILLED ME.

This was why she came here. Dad must've sent her.

Or was she saying this on her own?

I wasn't sure where to start without looking guilty or feeling suspicious.

"I wasn't going to do anything."

Her eyes softened at my lie. "Maybe not tonight, but eventually you will, and no one will be able to stop you." Sophia gave me a sad smile. "You're a young woman in love. I see it because I was your age once and in love too. I remember the feelings and emotions like it was just yesterday. Your eyes light up when you look at Kova. It's not one-sided either, that's what is concerning."

I was stiff as a stone even though my heart was hammering against my rib cage threatening to break free.

"Did my dad send you here to talk to me about this? Like a warning or something? Because I already know the consequences, he made them quite clear."

Her face fell and I instantly felt bad. I wasn't angry, but my words came out a little more aggressive than I intended to.

"No, he didn't. I promise. He has no idea I'm talking to you about this and he never will. He thinks I just wanted to bring you the book." I caught a flash of boldness in Sophia's eyes. "In Frank's defense, though, it took a bit of convincing to get Kova here. I feel like you should know he's trying extremely hard. When he got off the phone that night with you, he was a disaster, stuck between right and wrong. It's taking every ounce of self-control he has for Kova to be here, to allow him near you, to touch you." I opened my mouth to speak but she placed her palm up to stop me, and continued, "Frank knows Kova touches you only with a coach's hand right now, but that doesn't matter. The damage is already done and that's all he can see. You have to know any father would feel this way, right? How Frank is with you, and what he says to me, are two totally different things. He's holding back for your sake, and he's trying really hard, Adrianna."

Her face twisted like she was carrying a burden on her shoulders. The concern she had for my dad was touching. There had been far and few moments where Joy had showed concern toward him in the manner Sophia was. Almost like she actually truly cared about him.

Now I felt like crap for even attempting to see Kova.

I glanced away, and responded softly, "I know he's dealing with a lot right now. I wouldn't want to upset him more than he already is. Why are you telling me this? Why now?"

"I was kicked out of my house when I got pregnant with you. My sister was so sick that my parents pretty much forgot about me anyway. No one knew what was wrong with Francesca at the time, only that she was ill. I think it was easier for them. They had one child to support instead of two with one on the way." Sophia paused like she was hurting inside. It seemed like any time she reflected on the past she drew sadness from it. "I was young and impressionable. There was no parental figure around to advise me when I needed it the most. I just want to remind you I'm here any time you need to talk. I'll never judge you or be angry. Even with guy stuff, been there, done that." She chuckled then sobered up. Large green eyes peered back at me. "I missed out on so much of your life. Now we finally have a real chance to have a relationship, and it kills me to see this web you're stuck in. I want you to know I'm here if you ever need me." She cleared her throat as a way to disguise the emotion filling her eyes. "Anyway, I was going to give that book to you tomorrow, but it seemed like you might be able to use it tonight."

I glanced down at the book again, curious about the pages inside. Sophia was offering her guidance when I'd never really been given any from either parent. Dad was always working. I'd assumed most fathers were like mine since I hardly ever saw any dads at practice, it was always just moms. Joy was another story entirely and not someone I ever asked advice from.

Listening to Sophia brought on a wave of melancholy. A longing. I'd never say I was neglected. I most definitely wasn't, but I had been easily overlooked by both parents with their assumption that I would figure it out. The thought of having a parent figure to come to with questions would've been nice. I mean, just one who wanted me around would've sufficed. I would've taken anything, really.

The creases between my eyes deepened. Even if I'd had that type of relationship with my parents, would any ounce of advice have stopped me from loving Kova?

No. The heart wanted what the heart wanted, and it gave no fucks about anyone's feelings or objections.

"I don't know what to say. I feel like thank you isn't enough. This is more than a book you're giving me."

Her eyes glistened with relief and that made me feel good inside. "You don't have to say anything. Despite your maturity, you're still young. Not that I'm doubting what you have with Kova isn't real, but you should live your life and experience every age while you can." Her eyes narrowed into a knowing look. "I bet you're really consumed with him and you think about him all the time and wonder what he's thinking. Like you have to be with him and can't imagine a life without him." I tried not to squirm. "Find what *you* love and what *you* hate. When you're involved with someone, we tend to think only about what they want and need. It's easy to forget ourselves in the process. Put what you want first. Go to college and attend parties. Stay up until two in the morning with your girlfriends and burn a pizza in the oven. Don't lose out on this time in your life. You'll regret not living it to its fullest. I know I do." She pointed to the book. "Check it out when you can. It might be more useful than you think."

Sophia stood. I placed the book on the table and stood with her. "No one's ever told me that." No one ever spoke to me like that. What she said to do sounded kind of fun.

"Me either, but I think it's something a teen Sophia needed to hear." She waited. "I thought you may too."

I glanced at the book again and reread the tagline. *Don't let this life pass you by.*

"I'm going to read a few pages tonight while I ice my arm. Thank you, Sophia."

"Frank is waiting for me, so I'm going to head out. Regardless of the outcome tomorrow, I'm proud of you. I can't wait to watch you. Thank you for allowing me to be here." Affection swirled in her eyes before they glossed over with remorse. "Francesca would've loved to be here to see you."

While I never got to meet my aunt, the emotion clogging my throat was real. I was so much more sensitive than I used to be.

Nodding, she walked to the door. Right before she left, she looked at me.

"I'm not going to tell you to not see Kova because that'll only make you do it more. If you do, I want you to consider not only those affected, but yourself too. Think about you and your life and the opportunities you have. Take advantage while you can and create your happy ending."

Sophia opened the door and stepped out quietly. I glanced back at the book, debating whether I should open it up and read a few pages now, or go see Kova like we'd planned. Listening to what Sophia said stirred my interest and swayed my decision a little.

Not being able to experience life to the fullest had been a fear of mine since I was diagnosed. I didn't want to lose out and have regrets about things I could've and should've done. The thought scared me.

What Sophia said to experience, I wanted to do. I just hadn't allowed myself to think about it because my focus was on this moment right now and getting through the heartache and pain my body dealt with every day. I didn't allow myself to look ahead, and anytime I had, I assumed Kova would be there. Yet, all those moments she mentioned—college, parties, late nights with friends—sounded like so much fun to me, and he wasn't there.

Gymnastics had always been, and will always be, the love of my life, but it would be naïve of me to not realize it was going to be over soon. I needed to decide what I wanted.

And what did I want? My fingers grazed the cover. What did I truly want?

Thoughts flickered too quickly through my mind like an old film. Some involved Kova, some involved Avery, of course my family, but most of them were of me alone. Happy, but alone, and constantly searching for something no one could give me but myself.

I was angry at the world and I hated myself.

Did I feel the same way as Sophia once did? My skin prickled with realization. I tried to push it away, but…

My breathing labored. My heart started racing. The more I thought about it, the more it hit me that my feelings were nearly identical to hers.

It didn't just hit me. It slammed into me.

I *did* feel the same way. I *was* angry at the world, and I *did* hate myself.

I hated myself for so many reasons, but mainly for how sick I was. I hid it from everyone who cared about me, and in turn, I pushed my body to the brink of total destruction to prove to myself there was nothing wrong with me. Everything about what I did made me angry and filled me with hate, not only for myself but for everything around me, except gymnastics. Becoming sick wasn't anyone's fault, but I couldn't help but wonder if I had listened to my body in the first place, would I have caught the illnesses before they grew into something more? I was stubborn and had assumed it was from overtraining, but I think in the back of my mind I always knew something wasn't right.

A fire burned inside me just thinking about it. Tears burst from my eyes and I covered my mouth. I wondered when my heart hardened and why I became like this, or if I was always like this and I just didn't know it. Tears dripped down my cheeks and my knees shook. It hurt me that I was like this.

An unexpected quietness settled in my chest. It forced me to become aware of the truth, and damn did it hurt. I realized I needed to let go of the resentments I'd built, and the only way to do that was on my own.

The things Sophia said, words of wisdom, were all things I'd been seeking without even realizing it.

My knees buckled and I fell into the chair behind me. After the meet today, I'd done therapy with the other gymnasts to help speed up recovery. Some were getting full-body massages, others were cupping or doing various chiropractic stretches, or wearing vibrating sleeves to increase blood flow. All so we'd be ready for the beating our bodies would take tomorrow for the chance to hold a coveted spot on the United States women's gymnastics team. The faster we healed, the better we'd perform. Lactic acid in the muscles would only hinder the performance and make the joints stiff. It had to be released and that's what we'd focused on. A recovery that would normally take a week for any normal person to heal would take one night for a pro athlete.

I glanced around my cold, small room with two twin beds, and stopped when my eyes landed on the ice pail. I got up and walked over to the black bucket. I checked to make sure I had my room key before grabbing the bucket to go fill. I was supposed to meet Kova in just over an hour. I wanted to, I missed him terribly, but my gut told me to stay in the room and open the book. It was a feeling that resonated within my soul and I couldn't ignore.

I wasn't going to give up Kova, that was virtually impossible. What I needed for myself right now was to rest my body and ice my aching arm.

Maybe cry a few more tears too.

What I really needed to do was heal my heart and learn to love myself again.

chapter 20

I T WAS A QUIET, SOMBER MORNING.
Madeline didn't say much, but neither did Kova. My guess was that
we all were going through the motions and preparing for the long day
ahead of us.

I'd worked my ass off to finish in the top five yesterday, but that didn't
mean anything today. Today was a new day with new scores and new routines.

Once the meet was officially over, both days' scores would be taken
into consideration along with previously required meets standings. Then the
Olympic committee would convene in a private, soundproof room, while
all fifteen gymnasts were placed in a separate room, watching the clock turn
as we overanalyzed our routines, wondering where we could've been better.
Everything we all worked so hard for came down to that moment. Only four
would be chosen plus two alternates.

It was such a mind game.

Later this evening, the final women's team would be selected and
prompted to stand in the center of the floor of the arena. Chills raced down
my arms just thinking about it. For that reason alone, I was a ball of nerves
today.

I hadn't told Kova I wasn't going to meet him last night. I just didn't
show. I couldn't contact him, and he had no way of contacting me either. I felt
bad. He'd probably waited for me. I imagined him looking for me every time
the door opened, getting his hopes up. Eventually he'd realized I wasn't going
to show. He hadn't said anything about it, and it made me wonder if that was
why he was all broody and quiet this morning.

The book Sophia gave me was an oddly interesting page-turner. I wasn't
sure I'd like it at first. A self-help book definitely wasn't my style. But I gave
it a shot and found myself having to force it closed to get proper rest for
today. The author offered a thought-provoking approach to finding yourself

that strangely resonated inside of me. I had to ask myself a lot of open-ended questions that kept going and going. I was oddly excited to read more once we were on the plane ride back home, tempted to try out the different methods to finding inner peace. I had a lot of turmoil left inside me.

"Does being here bring back memories?" I asked Kova, breaking the silence.

A distant smile touched his lips as he wrapped up my wrists for bars. "Yes, it does, actually. Some happy, some bittersweet."

It took me a moment to realize what he was talking about. Kova had been to two Olympics but had to withdraw from the third one because of his mom's declining health. If I remembered correctly, she'd passed away shortly after the Games that he'd missed.

"Is that why you're moody today?"

"I am not moody. I do not get moody."

A laugh gushed from me before I could stop it. He moved onto my other wrist. His movements felt mechanical. "You're the moodiest man I have ever met."

The corners of his mouth curled but he still felt a distance away. Why did he have to smile like that? So sexy and so relaxed and so at ease. Damn him.

"How many men do you know?" he asked, humoring me.

"A lot." I teased. He quirked up a brow. "I know many men."

It took effort not to laugh or smile. I knew no men.

"That so, *Malysh?*"

Blush decorated my cheeks. My heart fluttered with warmth at the sound of the nickname that caused a torrent of feelings inside me. Kova lifted his eyes to mine as he tore a piece of white tape with his teeth. The look in his gaze flooded my thoughts with memories of us together. Doing things I shouldn't be thinking about. It took me back to the day in my condo when the hurricane had hit and I'd carved the first letter of my name into his chest.

Using my other hand, I boldly tapped the left side of his chest twice with my index finger, right over the letter. His hand automatically reached up for mine. My heart sped up and I held my breath. Our eyes locked. Kova held onto my thumb while my fingers softly curled around his knuckles. I didn't have to say anything, and neither did he.

"*Malysh...*"

"I know."

I was his, and I always would be. The same went for him.

But we couldn't act like this in public.

His callused finger stroked the space between my thumb and forefinger. Something so simple pulled on my heartstrings. It was just us until a bell sounded in the background and broke the moment. I prayed no one took notice of us.

"Are you mad about last night?" I asked ever so quietly. He dropped my hand.

"Not at all. But now is not the time for that. Now is the time to show them why you are a valuable player for the team."

My eyes fluttered shut. I knew Kova supported me, but it still felt good to hear it at the eleventh hour.

"The United States is the number one team in the world right now. You know why that is?"

"Because we're the bomb dot com?" I joked. He wrapped one last piece of tape around my wrist.

"You are one of four reasons why that is. Do not forget that. Vault and bars are a given. You are the best out of them all and why you are the reigning champion. You know it too; you just do not like to admit it. Remind them why they need you on the team. Win the crowd over with your beautiful smile and love of the sport."

My lips pursed together. Luckily, I was wearing a leotard and it covered the blush creeping up my chest to my neck. Kova had said really sweet things to me before, but this time his words made me feel a little bashful. He spoke like he was confident of my abilities, and that ignited my adrenaline.

"You ready?" he asked once my grips were on. I nodded and bounced on my toes to get moving. "We are almost to the finish line."

I exhaled and flexed my fingers. All the days that had been filled with tears and aches and hopelessness, the same thing over and over, my diligent coaches who pushed me to the brink of insanity, it was all coming to an end. This was it, and the feeling was something I couldn't describe. Now it felt like it got here so fast.

"It's kind of crazy, isn't it? We've waited for this moment for what feels like forever, and it's finally here."

"It is yours if you want it."

"Are you?"

My lips rolled between my teeth, embarrassment flooding me. I briefly squeezed my eyes shut wishing the ground would swallow me whole. I hadn't meant to say that. Not now at least.

His eyes bore into mine. "I think you already know the answer to that."

The bell sounded again, which meant one more gymnast before I took my turn. Steadying my breathing, I said, "I'm going to chalk up. You're going to be there, right?"

He nodded.

Relieved, I smiled, then made my way to the big chalk bowl and submerged my hands. One event down, three more to go.

I closed my eyes as my fingers shifted through the dry, white powder. I regained control of my inner self as my hands moved over the little chunks of chalk left unbroken. My entire body was swollen from head to toe despite taking all my medications like usual. I wasn't going to let that get in my way. I knew once today was over I could crash hard. It'd be worth it.

That's what I kept telling myself, anyway.

"Ladies, please form a single file line and follow closely."

All fourteen of us got in line wearing our matching USA sweat suits to make our way to the back.

Fourteen now, not fifteen. One of the gymnasts landed wrong on her vault dismount and snapped her knee in half. I wasn't squeamish, but seeing a person's knee inverted and protruding from their leg made my already nauseous stomach churn higher. I felt so bad for her as she was carried off the floor in a stretcher. She covered her face with her hands, hiding her tears and missed opportunity. She was so young, just barely of age to make the Olympic team from what I'd heard. Hopefully, she wouldn't lose faith and would come back fighting ten times harder. She was incredibly good, and constantly trailing my scores.

Day two was in the books, and now we were headed to the waiting room while the Olympic committee met in another room to discuss the team. A man holding a video camera followed closely, making sure to zoom in as we walked by, but he wasn't allowed in the room with us.

I wasn't sure which was worse, the anxiety or the adrenaline pulsing through me knowing that within the hour, six of us would be called to the floor to represent the United States. The anticipation was making me crazy. I didn't want to get my hopes up, but damn it, I really hoped my name was called.

While the meet went exceptionally well, that didn't necessarily mean anything at the end of all this. Gymnastics was so political behind closed doors. I knew from the beginning I needed to prove myself time and time again at the meets. And I had. At least I hoped I had. I prayed it showed that

I worked well under stress, because they were looking for that too. Mistakes could be made, but the committee had to believe in you, had to see you come back with upgraded routines that were more difficult than before. They wanted to see that you were one of the few and strong who could handle the pressure of wearing the red, white, and blue.

Given my secrets, I felt like I was equipped to handle it.

There was nothing I could do now except wait. I'd finished in first place for both vault and bars, fourth on balance beam, and second on floor. My fate was in their hands.

Quietly, we made our way down a chilly, narrow hallway and through a set of double doors. The material of our uniforms swish-swashed as we reached a room with a sign taped to the door that read coaches and athletes only. Ushered inside, we took a seat on the floor and crisscrossed our legs while all of our coaches talked softly amongst themselves. Leaning back on my hands, I glanced over my shoulder and eyed Kova. He seemed to know I was looking for him and glanced at me from the corner of his eye. We exchanged a brief look. He was leaning one shoulder against the wall with his arms crossed in front of his chest as he spoke to another male coach that looked roughly his age.

I looked back at the girls. My nerves were so bad I felt like I was going to vomit any second. I was sure we all felt that way judging by the look of panic written on everyone's faces.

"Is everyone replaying their routines in their head wondering where they could've been better?" one of the pixie girls asked.

We nodded in unison, giggling here and there. The small talk did nothing to hide our jitters.

"Does anyone else feel like they're going to throw up any second?" I asked. Most nodded their heads, and giggled again. Using the back of my hand, I dramatically swiped it across my forehead pretending I was glad it wasn't just me who was a damn wreck.

Time passed painfully slow. Just as we were starting to soothe our nerves, the door opened and five people strode in, three of whom were the Olympic coaches. They carried six large bouquets of roses and sunflowers. It was what the team held in the air once names were announced.

My stomach dropped. I felt like I was going to have a heart attack. My pulse was in my ears and I started sweating. A nervous energy filled the room. There was no denying each of us—including the coaches—felt it. I wanted to unzip my jacket and shake my arms out. I glanced around looking for a bucket because I was sure I was going to vomit any second.

We all came to win, but tonight was the end of the road for eight girls in this room. They'd go home in tears, debating whether this backbreaking lifestyle was worth enduring another four years to achieve Olympic glory.

I knew where my road led if I wasn't chosen.

The door shut with a click, and Romanian Coach Elena, who I last saw at the training camps, held a piece of paper in her hand that sealed our fates. Voices decreased and each of us waited with baited breaths to see who'd been chosen.

chapter 21

"**L**ADIES AND GENTLEMEN..."

Chills kept pebbling my arms. I closed my eyes and listened as the president of the gymnastics committee spoke to the crowd. The team had been selected and announced in the private waiting room, and now the four were just waiting to be individually called to the floor.

The air in the room was packed with tension, anguish, and exhilaration. Tears fell for those whose road came to an end tonight, and for those whose dreams were only beginning. The anticipation was wreaking havoc on all of us. For me, it was a bittersweet ending.

"How does my mascara look?" I heard one of the girls ask another as she hiccupped.

After the team was announced, my stomach had been a disaster of emotions and still was. Now I knew why coaches were brought into the waiting room too—they had to console us after. My knees had buckled, and my heart had crashed to the ground in shock. Kova had been right there when my vision became spotty and I almost fell over. He grabbed me immediately and took me into his arms.

He'd comforted me as I cried on his shoulder, then held my face between his palms and kissed my forehead. It had been both heaven and hell for me.

Heaven, because this was it and what I'd worked so damn hard for.

Hell, because I knew what came after.

I took a deep breath and sniffled, and watched the rowdy crowd with blurry eyes through the tiny window. Coaches were sent to the floor while the rest of the gymnasts stood behind the double doors, waiting. I could see Kova standing next to the other head coaches with his arms crossed in front of his chest as he wavered back and forth on his heels. They were standing near the floor. His black dress pants were custom tailored and fitted to form around his butt and thighs, and the polo World Cup shirt made his biceps stand out. He wore a massive smile, one I rarely saw unless I was alone with him. I loved seeing him like that, though it had been a while since I had. A few feet down were the members of the men's team in matching sweats that'd been selected and announced before us. We'd only been standing there for three minutes max, but it felt like three hours.

"The United States is the number one team in the world…"

My pulse hammered in my chest. I took a deep breath and exhaled. I looked ahead through the narrow windows of the doors and tried to locate Dad and Sophia in the seats. I thought they were somewhere on this side of the building, but I couldn't find them. I probably looked right at them and didn't even notice. Dad was probably on the verge of a stroke waiting for what felt like forever. Even the parents were left in the dark as to who made the team. Any minute, names were going to be called again. And any minute, the tears would start up again.

"I'm sweating right now!" I heard one girl say. I chuckled, so was I.

"It is with great pleasure, I announce the four women who will make up the United States women's gymnastics team…"

The crowd went wild. They were so loud I could barely hear the first name announced.

The double doors were pulled opened by two people with earphones and microphones. Cue the tears. They waved with frantic hands instructing us to hurry up. The coaches turned around and my eyes immediately locked with Kova's.

I didn't hold back the smile on my face. Neither did Kova. The pride in his eyes made everything we'd gone through together worth it. He was so happy.

I pulled my lip into my mouth and bit down. It was hard to believe we were finally here. My chin trembled and I sniffled again. After all the tears and rips, the aches and pains, aggressive coaching and daunting practices, we were finally at the moment we'd worked so hard for. There'd been so many days where I didn't think I could handle another second, yet, somehow, I didn't give up. Sometimes I was surprised myself that I didn't give. I'd made mistakes along the way. A lot of mistakes. There were a few meets where I'd let the nerves get the best of me, but I'd gone into the next meet challenging myself ten times harder to be better, proving to myself and my coaches and those watching that I had what it took.

And it had paid off.

"Go, go!!" one of the employees said.

I drew in a shaky breath as tears filled my eyes again when the second girl was called to the floor. I watched as her arm went into the air and she waved to the crowd, then covered her mouth as she cried and sprinted onto the floor. We were advised to wait before the next name was called.

My teeth chewed into my lip.

"Reigning world champion on vault and bars…" I sucked in a breath and thought my heart was going to burst from my chest "…The third member to join the women's Olympic gymnastics team, Adrianna Rossi from World Cup Academy of Gymnastics!"

There was no stopping the full-blown tears when my name was called next. They hit like a punch to the gut. Suddenly all eyes were on me. A bouquet was pressed to my arms as I stepped back into the arena. I crushed it to my chest, the clear plastic wrap holding the flowers couldn't even be heard over the roar of the crowd. My eyes frantically searched the packed room.

Elena, along with the other two Olympic coaches, believed in me enough for me to represent the United States.

I can't believe I really did it.

All I saw were smiling faces and clapping hands and my country's flag being waved in the air. Emotion flooded every ounce of me. Happy tears poured from my eyes. I was too overwhelmed to really see anything except Kova and the steps I was about to walk up.

My dream had come true.

I made it to the Olympics.

I'd never forget the way Coach Elena had pronounced my name in the small waiting room in her thick Romanian accent to tell me I'd made the Olympic gymnastics team as a specialist for bars and vault, and possibly floor. I practically fainted. Kova was immediately at my side joking that I was in shock and hugged me to him. I *was* in shock and I couldn't stop crying. My hands had been shaking and I was a huge ball of feelings. Luckily, I hadn't been the only one like that. The others named had reacted the same. We all wanted our name to be called, but the real possibility of that was so slim. Being the oldest named to the team with a slew of health issues that were kept under wraps, the odds were not in my favor. Still, I had been optimistic and tried so hard.

My gaze met the two other girls—my new teammates. We all had the same pink rimmed eyes and puffy cheeks from happy tears. Once the final girl was called after I was, and then the two alternates, we stood in a straight line next to each other.

It wasn't real. It had to be a dream.

"Give another round of applause for your 2020 women's gymnastics team!" the announcer said enthusiastically, and the crowd erupted.

Flashes from multiple cameras flickered in front of my face. We raised our wrapped bouquets of flowers in the air as red, white, and blue paper confetti exploded from the ceiling. The national anthem played in the distance. Streamers crisscrossed the air above us. I glanced up and smiled as the colors fell around us like snow. It was the coolest thing ever that I giggled to myself. I couldn't believe I'd made it. I was still in shock.

The men's team, who'd been selected earlier, were welcomed to the stage. We all exchanged hugs under the blowing confetti and congratulated each other. Group pictures were taken, then we were finally disbursed to find our loved ones and coaches.

I walked over to Madeline and gave her a massive bear hug. She was like a proud parent and that made me feel so good to know I made her happy. There were tears in her throat as she sang her praise. Happiness burst through me. She worked with me just as hard as Kova did. She earned this too.

One of the people from the committee came over to speak to Madeline. Just before she left, she looked up and spotted someone behind me. Brows creased between her eyes, she pointed at me, nodded her head, then quickly turned away. It was chaos on the floor and she was gone in the blink of an eye.

I turned around, and through the people crisscrossing in front of me, I realized she was talking to Kova.

Our eyes locked, and something clicked into place. I weaved through the crowd, my feet carting me to him automatically.

Without a care in the world, Kova got down on one knee and I walked straight into his arms. I cried again. His strength I'd needed to get to this point embraced me immediately. Kova gave me a real hug. His hand cupped the back of my neck and his fingers gently pressed into my skin. I drew in a breath, and softly let go, crying into his neck. I'd—we'd—been through so much for this moment, and I wanted to live in it with him for as long as I could. My heart felt full as he held me to his chest.

"*Malysh, pozdravlyayu,*" he said over and over only for me to hear. When I'd finally caught my breath, he said, "Let us find your father." I nodded.

Releasing me, Kova looked at my face. We were eye level. He used his thumbs to wipe away my tears, then without thinking, he took my hand and guided me to where Dad and Sophia were standing. The moment I spotted my parents, I blindly handed Kova my bouquet and then ran to the tall wall that separated the athletes and coaches from the fans.

My father's eyes were glossy, which caused my lips to tremble again. He was beaming from ear to ear like he was going to burst. Saying he was ecstatic was an understatement. I'd never seen a smile like that on his face, one that screamed how proud he was of me and that he loved me. He held his arms open, waiting. I jumped on the white folding chair against the wall with one foot to reach him and wrapped my arms around his shoulders. My eyes closed. He hugged me like he never wanted to let go. His back shook as he squeezed me, and his head was in the curve of my neck. I could hear the clicking from the cameras next to us and my name being called. I felt his hot breath as he released his emotions. Dad gave me a long hug. Despite all the despair we'd both endured lately, none of that was a thought in our minds. It was all forgotten as we celebrated this uphill battle together.

Dad pulled back and that was when I realized he'd shed a few tears himself. My eyes watered. I softened even more.

"Adrianna, I can't believe it!" He laughed somewhere between being happy and filled with so much emotion that he clearly wasn't used to. "I was on the edge of my seat waiting. Congratulations, sweetie! I can't believe it!"

I grinned. Dad was in shock.

"Thanks, Dad."

"How do you feel?"

I shrugged, the massive smile still decorating my face. "I think I'm in shock. I don't really know what to feel yet."

"I'm so proud of you. This is by far the best day of my life. Well, the best day since you and your brother were born."

Giggling, I glanced to my right and caught sight of Sophia. She wore a bittersweet expression that made my heart hurt a little. I stepped onto the next chair and reached for her. She embraced me immediately and I felt the same thing with her as I did when I hugged my dad. Her back was vibrating with feelings.

"Congratulations, Adrianna," she said ever so softly. "I'm sorry for crying," she said, and I laughed lightly.

"It's okay. Thank you," I said in return, smiling sweetly.

I used the back of my hand to wipe under my eyes. I was sure my mascara was leaking everywhere but I didn't really care. Sophia straightened her back while Dad stepped closer to her side. He wrapped an arm around her petite shoulders, pulling her to him. She went willingly. I watched with a gentle smile as they looked at each other like honored parents. Their eyes glistened and my heart felt the longing between them. Sophia closed her eyes as Dad leaned in to kiss her temple. It was so sweet that I stared at them, unable to look away.

From the corner of my eye, I saw Madeline walk over to us and speak to Kova. Behind her, the confetti still floated like something out of a fairy tale. Kova stepped back and gave Madeline a deep nod, then turned to me. She strode away with a clipboard secured to her side.

"We have to go. You are required to take team photos and do an interview with the news station."

I glanced at Dad and Sophia. "I have to go—"

"Go," he said with a nod of his chin. "We'll see you guys for dinner tonight."

I was momentarily caught off guard. Dad answered my questioning gaze.

His eyes glistened with love despite everything. "Dinner with you and your coaches. Both of them."

My nostrils flared as I fought to keep the tears at bay. Flattening my lips, my jaw trembled as my vision blurred. I was overcome with heartfelt gratitude. He didn't have to do that. Dad was extending an olive branch and I respected the hell out of him for that. My heart was pounding so hard. I was relieved this wasn't as tense as I thought it might be. I gave Dad one last goodbye hug, then I climbed down from the chair and turned around and met Kova's emotive gaze.

"Adrianna will be back later," Kova said to Dad.

My eyes widened. That caught me by surprise. I hadn't seen them exchange more than two words since we flew here.

"She has obligations for the team that must be met before she leaves tomorrow," Kova added.

Dad's expression gave nothing away. I knew it wasn't easy for him to speak to Kova, let alone look at him, but he was, and he was doing it for me.

Agreeing, Dad smiled and applauded me one last time.

"Let us go."

Kova opened his palm up to me and I took it without another thought. We walked through the flurry of confetti together toward the double doors with smiles etched on our faces.

There was no turmoil, no heartache, no secrets.

It was just us, together, living my dream.

chapter 22

THE INTERVIEW ENDED UP BEING A LOT OF FUN.
We giggled and smiled the entire time. Our coaches watched nearby but they spoke amongst themselves. I was sure none of us even made sense half the time when we responded to the questions, but the reporters went along with it anyway. There was a blanket of euphoria in the air. Nothing could ruin the biggest moment in the world for me.

Once we were finished, we were ushered into a room for hair and makeup and given new matching leotards. A photographer came in and we were staged and prepped, taking what had to be hundreds of team pictures to use for promo. We tried acting serious and tough, but we were really laughing and giggling the whole time.

There were butterflies in my stomach. My heart was filled with so much joy that I couldn't stop smiling. Happiness was an understatement and I was sure anyone could see that within a five-mile radius. I wasn't the only one who felt this way either. Each of us wore matching expressions and had shaky fingers. We shined and glowed and laughed like we'd been best friends since we were toddlers.

This was, without a doubt, the best day of my life. I never wanted it to end.

Now I was back in my hotel room repacking my belongings to drop them off in Dad's suite before dinner. I still couldn't get over the fact that my dad was going to have dinner with both of my coaches. He was doing it for me, but I was curious to see how he'd be able to sit there without wanting to strangle Kova.

My cell phone rang, and I smiled to myself and quickly zipped up my bag. I walked to the dresser where my phone was charging. I assumed it was Avery, but when I picked up my phone, I saw a name I hadn't seen in a really long time.

My heart froze. The smile vanished from my face. I was stuck, staring at the screen, wondering if I was imagining things.

Mom's cell

·Joy?

Why was she calling me? Creases formed between my eyes and my pulse accelerated as I stared at the name on the screen. I hadn't spoken to Joy since that awful Easter day, and before then, it had been so far and few in between that I couldn't recall when she'd reached out. My first thought was that something had happened to Xavier.

Hesitantly, I accepted the call and brought the phone to my ear.

"H… Hello?"

"Ana."

I cringed. My eyes closed. I hadn't heard that nickname in ages. I'd always hated the way it felt on my skin when she said it, and hearing it again brought a flood of emotion back to me.

"Hi," I said softly. "How are you? Is everything okay?"

"I'm well, thank you for asking. Are you available right now?"

I frowned. "Well, I'm actually at a gymnastics competition right now so—"

"I'm aware." She was curt, then she cleared her throat. "I'm here too and thought I would see if you have a free moment before I have to leave for the airport."

My stomach sank and my frown deepened. "What? You're here?"

Paranoia instantly enveloped me. I was literally across the country and Joy flew to the Trials when I hadn't seen her or spoken to her in months?

That was uncharacteristic of her.

My first thought was that she had a motive. While Joy had been the doting mother attending practices and meets, it'd been a façade and a deal she'd secretly made with my dad. She'd considered me a chore, and once I'd discovered the truth, she stopped caring altogether, which was why I found it so nerve-wracking she was here at all.

"I can stop by your room," she suggested.

I nodded as if she could see me, I was still stunned. "Ah, okay. Do you know which hotel I'm at?" Joy said she did, and that she was actually in the same hotel.

"I'll be there shortly," she said after I gave her my room number, then she hung up.

I stood motionless, staring at my cell phone wondering what twilight zone I was living in that warranted a call *and* an appearance from Joy thousands of miles away like this. She had never come to see me when I lived in Cape Coral, so this visit was an extremely peculiar one.

Quickly, I shot a text to Avery telling her Joy was stopping by and I'd fill her in when I got back home. At least she'd know about me if anything happened. Not that I expected anything would go awry, but seeing Joy put me on edge and caused a severe bout of anxiety to rush through my veins.

A few minutes later, there was a knock on my door. I gave myself a little power talk and then expelled a breath before walking across the room. I reached for the knob, and my spine stiffened as I opened the heavy hotel room door. Joy stood on the other side dressed in a white sleeveless body-fitting dress with matching high heels. She wore a rich navy-blue knee-length coat.

Hard eyes stared back at me. "Hello, Ana."

"Hi," was all I said. "Come in."

Joy stepped inside with her clutch gripped between her fingers. She slowly glanced around the room, her eyes taking in every square inch. I licked my drip lips and shut the door. When I turned around, Joy was sitting in a chair at the little table near the window. I walked over and took the seat opposite, regarding her with confusion as I faced her. Her blond hair was flawlessly styled, but her face seemed different...tighter. Like she'd gotten more Botox in her forehead and cheeks.

"I'm surprised to see you," I said.

She placed her purse on the round table and expressed an exaggerated sigh. "Contrary to what you or your father might think, I do care about you."

My brows shot up. I could easily refute that statement with plenty of examples, but I chose not to. There was a reason she made an appearance, and I needed to know why.

"How long have you been here?"

"I flew in two days ago."

"Two days ago? Why didn't you call sooner?"

She lifted her shoulders in a nonchalant shrug like she couldn't be bothered. "We haven't seen each other in a while. I remembered the rules about parents not visiting before a meet, and I knew how important this competition was for you." She paused. "Congratulations on making the team. I have to say, I'm surprised. You've come a long way, and seeing you perform was...an experience." She grew quiet as she observed me. Her eyes were a little misty. "You really did it," she said, a small smile tried to tug on her over plumped lips. "You made it to the Olympics. I thought it was just a dream that all little girls have, but you made it happen. They say when you're stubborn enough anything is possible."

My eyes widened, brows angling toward each other. Stubborn enough to put my health on the line for it.

"You were there? You watched? Why didn't you tell me?"

"I've been to all your big meets over the year. I just didn't tell you."

My lips parted. "But why? Why wouldn't you? You're my mom."

Her eyes flared with a mixture of sadness and regret. "You shouldn't call me that. I'm not your mother. I did try, though. It may not seem like it, but I did."

She looked away. Her guilt hit me square in the chest. I wouldn't say she didn't try, because she had, it was just toward the end that her heart had hardened and her dislike for me became transparent. To Joy, I was the reason she and Dad split up.

"I'm not equipped to be a mother." Her voice splintered with emotion as she looked back at me. "I never wanted kids, let alone wanted raise another woman's child, one who was the product of an affair my husband had, no less. But I tried for Frank because I loved him. I even gave him a son before you came along. I would've given him anything if only he could've stayed faithful to me."

I pulled back, my chest was tight with hostility. I couldn't disguise the hurt etched on my face. Callous words from a callous woman. She never wanted to be a mother. Who said that to the child they raised? She was the only mother I'd ever known, yet she'd completely discarded me in the blink of an eye.

Taking a deep breath, I shook my head. I couldn't stop the words from flying from my mouth. "Other than to remind me how unwanted I am, why are you here? I know what you did. Dad told me everything. Is that why you've been to the meets and didn't tell me?"

Joy stilled. "Well, if you weren't sleeping with your coach, then I never would've had to do anything."

"You told him out of selfishness and not out of concern for me. You did it to get back at him and nothing else."

She looked me dead in the eyes. "I did. There's no reason for me to lie, but I did. Little did I know what my PI would find once I hired him. I was appalled, disgusted by what he found out about you and Konstantin."

"But why? Why did you go to the length that you did?"

"Regardless, Frank needed to know what was happening. Konstantin was his friend."

"That's not why. You used me as blackmail to get what you wanted."

Joy was quiet. She stared out the window again and it bothered me that I felt bad for her. No, I didn't feel bad. I pitied her. She could wear all the makeup she wanted, but it wasn't going to hide the melancholy that flickered too often in her gaze. The fine lines around her eyes and mouth were taut with anguish. She went with her claws out taunting Dad with evidence to get what she wanted out of him for feeling so deceived. Only she hadn't thought it through, and her plan bombed on her.

"I guess that saying rings true," she said more to herself. "Hell hath no fury like a woman scorned," she said with a fleeting smirk. "I'm sorry I couldn't love you the way a child needed to be loved. It wasn't fair of me to try when I knew all along I never wanted to be a mother in the first place. I sometimes wonder if that's why Xavier behaves in the manner he does…" Her quiet voice trailed off. "You're finally getting what you wanted, though. Frank and I are officially divorced."

My head tilted to the side. I frowned, offended she could ever think that was what I wanted.

"That's not what I wanted. I never wanted that. All I ever wanted was for you to want me the way a mother is supposed to want her child. To be happy for me and not pick on me for every little thing I did. To support me and not body shame me. I tried so hard, but nothing was ever good enough for you no matter what I did. Do you have any idea what that did to me?"

Chest rising and falling, my emotions were getting the best of me and I didn't want to give her that. She didn't deserve my tears anymore. She didn't deserve to see me in pain ever again. I think she'd enjoy that even though her guilty body language and remorse was plain as day.

Joy ignored my truth. "Well, you have a real mother now to give that to you."

I shook my head in disbelief. Joy was hurting. I knew she didn't come here to act bitter toward me, but I could feel it in her words. She was such an insecure woman. I'd never understand her.

"Why are you here if you're just going to continue your mean girl mentality? Why did you want to see me?"

Joy stood up. She straightened her dress and picked up her purse. With a dignified look, she said, "I wanted to congratulate you and tell you I am proud of you, regardless of our relationship and what's occurred. Anyway, I won't attend the Olympics, but I'm looking forward to watching you. What you did, so few can do." There was an awkward pause as tears filled her eyes. "It wasn't right of me to take the issues I had with Frank out on you. For that, I'll forever be sorry."

Standing, I meant to follow her to the door but she shocked me in place with her apology. Right before she opened it, Joy turned around and looked at me. Really looked at me.

"Is that why you came? To apologize?" I asked, my stomach tight with apprehension.

An apology was never something she gave easily. However, there was no resentment in her eyes and her shoulders weren't stiff. The mask was gone, and I saw a woman living with a black conscience covered in guilt and lies.

I saw a person with feelings. Her jaw wobbled and it made my heart ache for her. "Yes. I truly am sorry. I never wanted this for you despite my inabilities. A few times I wished I'd paid more attention to you when you performed. You're incredible, Ana, and I felt like you needed to hear me say that in person."

My lips parted. Her eyes watered and she wiped a tear away that slipped out. I was speechless that she allowed herself to be so vulnerable.

Joy opened the door and I held my breath.

Goodbyes were never easy, and that's what this felt like. We had eighteen years of history together that were coming to an end.

I watched as Joy walked out with the door quietly closing behind her.

In my heart, I knew this was probably the last time I'd ever see her again, and I wasn't sure how to feel other than cry.

chapter 23

THE FIRST DAY WE FLEW BACK TO GEORGIA, I SLEPT THE ENTIRE DAY. In fact, I'd slept for three days straight.

The consequences of pushing myself had set in and I was out for the count. My body kept spasming. Everything tightened up and my body fought against me, trying to take over and bring me down. All I could do was wake up to my alarm going off as a reminder to take my medications, eat something small, and then go right back to sleep. I only had a week until I would be shipped off to Texas again, and my body needed to heal. I may be stubborn, but I wasn't an idiot. Recuperating was an absolute must, or I wouldn't stand a chance. For once, I listened to my body's warnings.

I had yet to speak with Kova privately. After I saw Joy, I went to dinner with both coaches and then back to Dad's suite where I'd stayed until we checked out the next day. Dinner had gone surprisingly smooth and luckily short. No words were exchanged between Kova and me after that night and I hadn't seen him since.

Now, I was back on Amelia Island with no way of talking to him. I could use my burner phone, but I didn't want to risk calling him after Katja had picked up that day, so I stored it in a hidden place in my room where it wouldn't be found. It was so tempting, but somehow, I'd managed to resist.

I didn't want to hurt my dad again either. Something about what Sophia had said when she gifted me the book twisted my stomach with guilt.

Still, my heart yearned for Kova. The longing that was caged inside my chest wanted to break free and run to him. I ached for him, his touch, his words, the look in his eyes when it was just the two of us. I fucking missed him so goddamn much. If this was what a real breakup felt like, then I never wanted to experience it again. It hurt.

While I had to drive down to Cape Coral to pack, there still wouldn't be time to see each other. We were flying together to Texas to train and prepare for the Olympics, but it wasn't going to be possible to talk to him during that time either. It definitely couldn't happen on the plane, and there'd be too many ears around for the type of conversation at the training facility too. We needed time, and we didn't have it. I wasn't sure what the status was of his arrest, or if he was charged with anything.

After I finally climbed out of bed, I showered and ate a normal meal, then I texted Avery to tell her I was in town only to get a ton of angry emojis in return because she was away for a cheerleading competition. She congratulated me on making the team. I hadn't told her—apparently Xavier had. When she got back, I'd be in Cape Coral and then Texas. We promised to fill each other in when we got a chance.

Walking into Dad's office, I asked, "Where's Xavier? Is he here?"

He moved the phone away from his face, and mouthed, "Pool house," and pointed a finger toward the window.

Nodding, I turned around and made my way outside and down the walkway to his mini house.

I knocked on the door and waited. I didn't want to barge in on him; who knew what he was doing and with who. It didn't take more than a few seconds for the door to fling open and his bright smile to greet me.

"Hey—"

My brother pulled me into a bear hug and squeezed me. "Sleeping Beauty finally wakes," he joked. Laughing, we separated, and he invited me into the house. "Dad said not to bother you or he would take my credit card and my truck, so I stayed far away."

I beamed up at him. Xavier's truck was his pride and joy.

"It's all good."

I glanced around. It had been awhile since I was here. His pool house looked nothing like what Avery had described when she told me their breakup story. It looked...livable.

"I really needed the rest. I can't believe how much I slept." His eyes softened with empathy and I pointed a finger. "Don't look at me like that, you loser."

Xavier grinned from ear to ear. "I'm just saying for someone who legit slept for days straight minus five hours, you still look like shit."

I rolled my eyes and took a seat on his couch. "I don't feel like it, though. I did when we first got back and my body locked up. I was throwing up like crazy, but I'm way better now."

Xavier studied me. His honey brown eyes took in my face down to my toes. He grabbed a cigarette out of the pack on the beat-up coffee table and lit it between his thumb and index finger. He took a long drag and exhaled.

"Do you mind?" he asked after he lit it, and I shook my head.

I frowned. His hand holding the cigarette shook, and I wondered why.

"Why are you shaking like that?"

His eyes dropped to his hand. "Alcohol withdrawal. I need a fucking drink."

My brows shot up, surprised he was being so honest. Every once in a while, I had seen his hands shake but I never thought anything of it until now. I had no idea it was alcohol related. Kova loved his vodka, but he never shook.

"But it's so early," I said, stating the obvious. It had to be around noon on a Thursday.

Xavier shook his head and brushed it off. "Nope, we're not going there. We're going to talk about you and how you made it to the fucking Olympics. Do you even know how cool it is to say my sis is going to the Olympics?" He paused, and took another drag. "We have a lot to catch up on."

I let out a light laugh. "What if I say we're not going there?" His eyes turned to stone and I stared right back. Of course, I was going to tell him. I smiled and that seemed to loosen him up. "I'm just playing. What do you want to know?"

"Well, for starters, how the hell do you feel? Your arm okay? Healing...everywhere else?" He used his hand to gesture toward my empty stomach.

I moved my arm around, slowly stretching it. "It aches here and there and it's a little sore, but it's much better. Not nearly as bad as it was. I should be good to go by the time the Games start."

"I couldn't believe when Dad called me. I know he didn't tell me everything because he's concerned about my 'anger issues.'" He sounded annoyed. "I almost drove down there to murder Kova and kick Dad's ass for hurting you. I want the truth, Adrianna. What happened? What's been happening? Has your coach been abusing you this whole time? Did he rape you? Why didn't you come to me? Why didn't you tell anyone?"

My stupid brother had already assumed the absolute worst and it was going to be hard to convince him otherwise. The last thing I wanted or needed was him worrying too.

Xavier's nostrils flared, and the hand that wasn't holding the cigarette tightened into a fist. His knee started to bounce furiously. By the rapid succession, I'd swear he had the questions stored in his mind ready for when he saw me. I don't think he even took a breath. His sudden anger struck a slice of panic through me. Stress cramped my stomach. I hoped I wasn't the reason he needed a drink.

I softened with compassion. I wanted Xavier to see that I was going to be honest with him, but make sure he knew that nothing bad had happened to me. I didn't want him to worry about me like that, or think I wasn't protected and left to be abused. This was going to be tricky because I could already taste his rage.

I sighed and pulled my knees up and crossed them under me. I reached for the blanket on the back of the couch and covered myself. His house was freezing yet he was sweating profusely.

"It's not like that. I know what you're thinking and what Dad told you, and I swear on my life that it's not. I know it's hard to believe, but it's the honest truth. I wasn't raped, Xavier. I wasn't abused. I wasn't taken advantage of. Nothing like that ever happened."

He stabbed his cigarette out in a glass ashtray. "Then what the fuck happened? Because I've been thinking the worst over here ready to go on a murder spree."

"It's not pretty."

"Life rarely is."

I was a little unsure what to do. Xavier threw his hands up before I could even think. He had no patience.

"Well? I'm waiting."

Closing my eyes, I began.

The story took nearly an hour to tell, and during that time, I purposely left the sex out. He knew I'd had sex with Kova, he didn't need the details. I told him how Kova had pulled me from the meet, then he'd gotten married without telling me. How I'd hooked up with a guy from the men's team to spite Kova. I wouldn't tell him who, though. Xavier was shocked over that one and said he didn't expect that from me. I told him how his mom had played a part in the whole charade to get back at Dad, and how she'd roped Katja into it. I'd tried to focus on how Kova and I'd connected through gymnastics and personal stories so Xavier could see it was so much more than lust like Dad had said. Kova and I had a mutual attraction and the chemistry didn't need any friction to begin with. It was already there the moment we'd met.

Just about every little aspect of my illicit relationship with my coach, Xavier now knew. He let me speak, but that didn't mean he wasn't fazed by it.

It was the complete opposite. His eyes rarely left mine, but his body emitted a trail of rage I could feel. Quite a few times I'd wondered if this was what Avery had been talking about because it scared me too. He was like a volcano ready to erupt. His knuckles were screaming white and when they weren't, it was because he was chain-smoking cigarettes. He got up and paced the floor, sat down and grabbed his head and pulled on his hair. I felt bad and stopped a few times only for him to wave his hand in a circle for me to keep going. When I was done, we both sat there for a long moment without saying anything.

I was second-guessing my decision to tell him so much.

"It's kind of similar to you and Avery, you know," I said, breaking the silence.

His head snapped up. Elbows on his spread knees, he dropped his hands and gawked. Wild eyes stared back at me.

"You can't possibly say that."

I frowned. How did he not see that? "But it is."

"Aid—no, it's not. Not even close. He's a fucking adult, what he did is illegal. There's a huge difference."

My jaw slackened. "He didn't do anything wrong." I pleaded with him to understand. "How can you sit there and say that after I told you I pursued him too? I told you I love him. How can you sit there and say otherwise? Who cares about the ages?"

He put his hand up. "Stop. I can't stomach anymore. I'm disgusted. All I can picture is his hands on you, and I want to fucking break them."

Xavier stood and marched into the kitchen, each step louder. I followed him and watched as he yanked opened the freezer and pulled out a bottle of vodka by the neck. He didn't bother with a glass. He uncapped it and took a long swig. I grimaced. How gross. That stuff tasted like rubbing alcohol.

"Xavier, please. I thought you'd be understanding."

He put the bottle back and wiped his mouth on his bicep. "Well, you thought wrong. There's no excuse, honestly." He glared at me, refusing to back down. "There's not."

Hurt laced my eyes as anger ignited inside of my heart. "Avery told me she went after you too. And you're an adult."

He let out a haughty laugh. "Yeah, she's fucking lying, but I'm not surprised. That's all she's good at anyway." He shook his head. "Fucking lies. She's filled with them."

My eyes lowered, and the flame of anger inside of me rose higher with how he spoke about my best friend he'd screwed over. Avery wouldn't lie to me, not after our pact.

"I knew she wanted me, so I chased her until she caved because I wanted that sweet ass too. Only it kicked back and I got attached. Who knew—little fucking Avery." He shook his head again like he was in a state of disbelief. "Karma got me, though, when she got rid of our kid."

"That's right. You got her pregnant then fucked her over and left her."

chapter 24

H IS EYES WIDENED AND ALL I COULD SEE WAS WHITE.
"Don't even go there!" he yelled in my face, spit flying. I pulled
back because I wasn't going to take his aggression. "You have no idea
what you're talking about."

"You're a drug addict and an alcoholic. She couldn't handle that and tried
to help you. I know about all the overdosing too. You were spinning out of control. You shoved her away to hook up with someone else in front of her. You
fucked her over and left her and then ignored her while she was going through
the worst time of her life. You used her. I knew you would too, and had I known
what was happening, I would've stopped it the first chance I got."

It wasn't fair of me to say that, but I was mad and couldn't stop the pent-up
aggression from coming out of me. Damnit. A tear slipped from the corner of
my eye. And then another. I couldn't tell if it was because I was angry, sad, or
just frustrated with everything.

"Don't start with the waterworks. That's the same stupid shit she used to
do, and it won't work."

"You're such a dick," I said and wiped them away. "You got my best friend
fucking pregnant and then walked out of her life like she didn't exist. How can
you sit there and get mad at me and want to kill Kova when you're no better?"

I thought he was going to explode. Xavier put his index and middle finger in the air along with his thumb. It reminded me of a gun. His hand trembled and from that trembling came his wrath that spread throughout the room.

"You better stop, now," he said. His voice was quiet, barely in control. I
wasn't afraid of him. He'd never physically hurt me, but I'd never seen him this
worked up before either. "You're so far off that I'm about to fucking lose it. What
happened is because of her, not me. I didn't do anything wrong but worship the
dirty ground she walked on. She fucked us up."

"Famous last words from a junkie," I spat out and then immediately wished I could take it back.

His chest rose and fell fast, and his eyes flared. "Seriously, Aid? How fucking dare you compare me to your sleaze-ball coach and then call me a junkie. What Avery and I had was really not the same at all. "I don't care if you stood in front of him naked with your legs spread willing and ready, he should have walked away. Dad trusted him. He was supposed to look after you, not fuck you." He seethed. "I can't believe Dad didn't kill him."

"He almost did."

"Good. I wish he had. I wish that fucker was six feet under and rotting. I wish I could pull each fucking limb from his body."

My jaw trembled violently. Before I could stop them, tears gushed from my eyes. This was not what I wanted to happen when I came in here to see him. I didn't want to fight with my brother. I missed him and wanted to talk to him.

I covered my face with my hands and cried, sobbing quietly. A loud sound erupted in the room, like an explosion, and I jumped. Glancing up, I saw Xavier had punched a wall. There was a massive hole.

He stalked over to me and I stepped backwards quickly. My heart was racing. His knuckles were bleeding and when I stumbled, he grabbed me by my elbow.

"Get the fuck over here," he said, and hauled me to his chest.

Xavier released a deep, slow sigh that was dripping in regret, and hugged me. I broke down, crying hysterically against him.

"I'm sorry for calling you a junkie." I whimpered. "I didn't mean to. I know you're not."

"Just shut up. I am one, and I got pissed. I'm your big brother. I'm supposed to protect you and all I ever do is fuck up every damn day. I'm not mad at you, I'm mad at myself and feel like all I do is let people down." Cupping the back of my head, my brother held me, letting me cry as much as I needed to. "I wanted to kill him, sis, when Dad told me what happened. He had to hold me back because I fucking lost it and I was ready to get my boys and go after him. I feel like I let you down and didn't protect you when you needed it most."

His apology wasn't helping my emotions because all I could do was feel the weight of his words and the regret lining them. I clenched my eyes shut trying to hold in the tears. We both felt bad. Maybe we both had shit built up inside we had to get out, and it just happened to be with each other.

Guilt ate away at my heart. All I did was hurt people and sometimes I didn't even know I was doing it.

"I promise, Xavier, I promise nothing like that happened. I swear." I sniffled.

"I have no reason to lie anymore. Please believe me. He—Kova—he was sick over it when it happened. I didn't care that he was, and I found myself purposely tempting him and trying to be around him."

Xavier pulled back and lifted the hem of his shirt for me to wipe my tears. I tried to smile but I couldn't bring myself to as I took it and dabbed my eyes. I was hurt, but so was he. God, I wished we could go back and redo this conversation from the start.

Exhaling a large breath, I glanced up and was taken aback by the way he was looking at me.

Xavier was in a bad place. I had a terrible gut feeling no one knew just how messed up inside he was. His pointed nose flared. His dirty blond eyelashes framed the glowing amber of his eyes. He was going through some deep stuff too.

I didn't say anything. All I could do was hug my brother. He was emotionally suffering just as much as I was, possibly more, and maybe, just maybe, he needed this more than I did.

My heart pounded against my chest for him. Squeezing my eyes shut, I prayed that whatever he was dealing with inside would get better.

Xavier rested his head on top of my shoulder and we stood in silence as tears streamed down my flushed cheeks. He dipped his head and I felt his back shaking. It was a subtle shake, but I could feel it.

After a few good minutes of us dealing with our struggles in quiet, I said, "I know you're mad at her, but I hope you can come to terms with what happened between you guys. Not only is she my best friend, but she's my match, Xavier. She's always going to be in my life."

"I know. What are the chances that would happen?"

Xavier seemed much calmer now that he released whatever he was holding in.

"I was just as shocked. She surprised me on my birthday with the news."

"I know. She told me," he said, and I glanced up with my brows drawn together. He answered my puzzled stare. "When she got the news, she was bursting to tell you. I'm sure you know she's terrible with surprises. So, she told me and talked my ear off for days and said she was going shopping for you."

A dim smile tugged at one corner of my mouth.

"She got me some really funny things," I said, thinking of the shirts and mug. "I loved them."

"Yeah, I saw them. I helped her pick them out."

Surprise was written on my face. She hadn't told me they'd spoken or that he'd helped her, but I guess that didn't really matter in the grand scheme of things anymore.

"It'll never work out with her," he added, his voice as far away as his stare. He was looking at something over my shoulder, but I could see he was lost in his thoughts.

"You don't know that."

He looked back at me. "No, I do."

"Do you love her?"

His long silence was my answer and I didn't like that. It was like barbed wire around my bleeding heart.

"I don't want you to worry about me and her. Everything'll be fine. I'll be real with you that I still fucking love her even though I want to wring her tiny goddamn neck. I know she feels the same way. But sometimes love just isn't enough, some things just can't be forgiven."

"Crazier things have happened."

He ignored me. "The last couple of years have been really…disturbing, but I'll always be here for you. I love you, but you better not ever think about hooking up with that man again, Adrianna, because I will kill him."

A sad chuckle rolled off my lips. I knew he wasn't serious. At least I didn't think he was.

"I love him, Xavier. How does one stop loving someone when it's killing them? I don't want to let go of him, and I know he feels the same way about me."

"Even with everything he's done to you, you still would hold on and love him?"

Before I answered, I took a hard look at him. Something in my gut said he was asking more for himself than to question me. I had a feeling this had to do with him and Avery.

"I do." I looked in his eyes and told him the truth. "If it's worth it, I have to forgive to move on. Kova's worth it." I nodded. Xavier didn't say anything. He seemed surprised and slightly hopeful. "Please, *please*," I said, stressing the word, "don't tell Dad. It's the honest truth, though."

He lifted my side braid and ran his fingers over it. Still looking at my hair, he said under his breath, "When you find out how to stop loving people when it's killing you, let me know."

chapter 25

I'D ALMOST FORGOTTEN I HAD TO SEE MY DOCTOR FOR A FULL CHECKUP before I left.

Lupus brain fog was real.

I drove south to Cape Coral the day of the appointment.

Before I'd left, Dad told me Kova had called him and said he needed to speak with me because a couple of colleges had inquired about me. I had been thrilled, thinking I could put my focus on my next goal to keep my mind busy, but Dad had been reluctant. He didn't want me going back to World Cup for anything without him, especially where Kova was involved. But he also knew how important it was to discuss this matter. As gradually as I could, I'd reminded him Kova wasn't going to college with me.

With a little over an hour before I had to see my doctor, I was currently sitting in Kova's office with Madeline next to me. They'd already been in his office waiting for me when I walked in wearing light denim skinny jeans and a boho chic top with my leopard flats.

Looking at him but not being able to touch him, physically hurt me. I was getting to the point where I was unable to tell the difference between heartache and the tightness from my illnesses anymore. Both hacked my chest open with bare hands. I swallowed, wondering if he felt the same. I thought this would be easy—come in, have the conversation, leave.

But it wasn't like that at all.

The anguish in my chest at seeing him again in his element consumed my heart and took over all feeling. His fingertips tapped the top of the wood desk and my eyes dropped to the motion. Memories of us in his office flashed through my mind. My eyes lifted to the wall he took me against when Hayden had walked in and found us. I looked back at the desk he was still tapping, and I pictured myself hidden under it naked when Katja had walked in. I shot a quick glance over my shoulder to look at the couch where we had shared many intimate moments together and did a double take. My stomach plummeted.

It was a direct blow to my gut.

The couch was gone. My brows knitted together and hurt lacerated my tender heart. I wondered when he got rid of it, and why. My instincts told me it had to do with us, but the bigger part of me fighting for us was more optimistic about it.

I turned and faced forward. Madeline was still writing stuff down and checking her phone while she did, mumbling to herself. Kova was peering straight into my eyes with a helpless look.

I needed him. I needed to touch him, to feel his arms wrapped around me. I needed him to demand I tell him I love him so I could say I hate you. I just needed him to breathe against me and I'd know how he felt about us.

Absence did not make the heart grow fonder. It made the heart ache for something that might never be.

I didn't believe in soul mates. I thought the saying was cheesy, it made me laugh, but I got it now. I understood it, because I felt the two words come together.

Not attempting to see Kova later was going to be a struggle. I was trying to respect my father's wishes and not hurt anyone else, but when my stomach was in knots and my heart was screaming out for him, it was difficult to consider anyone else's feelings but my own.

I looked at Kova. Our eyes met and he took my breath away. His hat was missing—I loved seeing him in it. The half-moon crescents under his eyes and drained expression told me he hadn't been sleeping much. I briefly wondered if he was writing his thoughts away or finding solace at the bottom of a vodka bottle. Sometimes he did that when his thoughts were dark.

My gaze drifted further down and I noticed Kova wasn't wearing his wedding ring anymore. I glanced away, trying to think back to the Trials and whether or not he had it on then, but it was all a blur. I wanted to believe he hadn't worn it, but I just couldn't remember.

"It's good to see you, Adrianna," Madeline finally said. She looked up from the binder she'd been writing in. "It felt strange not seeing you all week."

I gave her a sincere smile and cupped some loose strands of my hair behind my ear. "It was strange not being here, actually. I didn't know what to do with myself. All my schoolwork is done. I finished early, so I just slept the whole time."

Her gaze softened with a knowing look I didn't like. She knew why I'd slept the week away, I was positive she knew. Though, it became a question with multiple choice answers. Did she know about both diseases? Or about the abortion—could I call it that if I'd already started to miscarry?

I didn't want to think about it.

"What did you do with your medals?" she asked me.

Now I was grinning from ear to ear. "I hung them up in my room at my dad's house along with the flowers. I placed the bouquet upside down to dry so I could keep them forever."

"That was such a great idea. You can spray them with hairspray and they'll hold."

"Thanks. I'll do that."

Just as I looked at Kova, Danilo walked in. Glancing over my shoulder, I watched as he took a chair that looked too small for him to sit in and pulled it right next to me. He was a beast of a man and looked like someone on steroids. I bet he crushed soda cans between his meaty hands for fun.

"As you know, Danilo is now with World Cup," Kova said. "I felt he should sit in with us to go over a few things as he will be the new head coach."

I frowned, and looked back at Kova. Head coach? But what about him? Or were there two head coaches?

I studied Kova's gaze, trying to see what he meant by that, but he gave nothing away. Zero. Was he going to have to go back to jail? The thought made me queasy and now I had even more reason to talk to him privately…if we ever could, that was.

"Congratulations, Adrianna," Danilo said, putting my attention back on him. His Ukrainian accent was stronger than Kova's Russian.

"Thank you."

"Yes, let us get started," Kova said and stacked a few papers together. "A few universities have interest in you. They are top ranking division one schools in gymnastics. Now, while we are unaware as to what you plan for your future, it would behoove you to consider their offers, and to do it soon."

My lips twitched at the way he said "behoove.".

Kova continued. "They are aware you are a member of the Olympic gymnastics team and that you may postpone for one year. This is very common. Should you commit to a school, you have a place on any of the teams whether you postpone or not, except for one."

I was curious. "Which schools?"

Kova's eyes scanned the papers. "University of Florida, UCLA, University of Georgia, and University of Oklahoma. They are all offering full gymnastics scholarships. The head coach at UCLA feels she can work with you enough on beam to have you as an all-around gymnast, and not just a specialist. Georgia and Florida want you as a specialist on vault and bars. The difference between them is Florida wants you to commit this year. They will have to reassess you the following year. Oklahoma wants you as a specialist on vault, bars, and floor." He paused and looked me in the eyes. It was hard to focus on his words when I was looking at him. "You have options."

"All the schools are the absolute best. You can't go wrong with any of them," Madeline said. I turned toward her and she smiled. "I'm partial to Florida—Go, Gators!—since I went to school there." She put her arms out and did the gator chomp. It made me smile bigger.

"I have no preference," Danilo added blandly, and I stifled a giggle. He just shrugged when I looked at him. "I am not familiar with any university here."

I sat for a moment thinking as I looked back to Kova. Madeline and Danilo gave me their opinions, but Kova hadn't and I was curious what he thought.

"What do you think?" I asked him.

Kova's opinion mattered most to me.

"It does not matter what I think. The choice is yours to make."

My brows furrowed, my smile faltering a bit. I was overcome with emotion. Uncertain which choice was right, grateful that I'd been offered at all. I swallowed, feeling a little stressed out but happy. If we were alone, I would ask again and make him tell me.

"When do I need to make a decision by?" I asked.

"Your commitment will be announced after the Olympics so you can focus. I believe the schools will be emailing you and your dad with documents to review."

Being offered a place on the team from any of those schools was an honor. I was flattered they recognized me. Kova had said they were watching, but I never believed it when there were so many other athletes better than me.

"You have a big decision to make," Madeline said. "You'll have to weigh the pros and cons and really think about where you want to call home for the next four years or so."

Danilo added, "They will do a full medical sweep on you as well and check you for ailments. It is wise to be honest and up front before any contract is signed."

I nodded reluctantly, aware of what he was hinting at. Eventually I'd have to share my secret and pray the school wouldn't withdraw their offer. Until then, I couldn't worry about it. I had enough on my plate as it was.

"Before you leave today," Madeline said, "you'll need to clean your locker out since you won't be returning to train here."

I was quiet. It never occurred to me that I needed to take everything with me, but she was right. I would never train at World Cup again. Tomorrow I would leave for Texas, and then I was Olympics bound. After that, I was going back home to Amelia Island.

I glanced down at my hands. My palms were dry, and the skin was ripped a little. A bittersweet sensation climbed to my eyes. I hadn't grown up in this gym training, but I spent enough time here to consider it a home. I matured as a person and athlete. I formed friendships and relationships within these walls. I cried and laughed.

I'd take the memories with me and hold them close to my heart. This was another chapter of my life I was about to finish.

"You didn't realize, did you?" she asked softly. I shook my head.

Still looking at my hands, I said, "I guess I'll be saying goodbye, then."

"Take all the time you need."

Madeline and Danilo rose to their feet. "Make sure you come say goodbye before you leave. The girls are waiting on us, so we need to get out there."

Danilo stared down at me a moment, then said, "Second place winner is first place loser. Bring home the gold." My lips lifted at his words of wisdom.

I sniffled back my emotions and thanked Danilo, then told Madeline I'd find her. The door shut behind them as they left, leaving Kova and me alone.

The moment I'd been waiting for had finally arrived.

The air in the room became dense, that awkward silence filling the space between us. It was just the two of us, a ticking clock, and many, many words left unspoken.

I blinked my eyes rapidly trying to fight the tears when I decided to stand. I needed to get out of here, but I wanted to ask Kova questions. My pulse kicked up a notch and beat like a drum in my throat. I was jittery, feeling too vulnerable at the moment. I wasn't prepared for these emotions when I came here and now that they were baiting me. I needed to leave or I was going to cry any second.

"I'll see you later." My throat tightened and my words sounded mumbled. I couldn't even look at him.

Saying goodbye to World Cup meant saying goodbye to Kova.

My heart was not ready for that.

My. Heart. Was. Not. Ready.

I couldn't breathe. Oh God. My chest was so tight. I struggled to get air into my lungs.

"Wait," he said, but I was already at the door and reaching for the knob. "Please." His hand appeared in front of me. He held the door closed, and I immediately dropped my hand.

We were alone. He was right next to me. My eyes closed shut as my breathing deepened. I could feel the warmth of his presence, the smell of his sultry cologne, the dire need pulsing through me to reach out for him. I couldn't walk away when we were made for each other.

I shook my head before he could say anything. My eyes were filled with tears now. There were pieces of my heart embedded here that I couldn't take back with me. How was I supposed to leave?

Kova didn't say anything.

I didn't say anything.

Did he know how much I needed him right now? How close I was to breaking inside?

Of course, he did. Because he was Kova, and I was Ria, and we understood each other in ways no one else could.

He reached for me…and that was all it took.

Kova cupped my arm and pulled me to him. I went willingly and let out a cry against him. My hand found his chest and I fisted his shirt as soft tears fell from my eyes. I hugged him so tight, like I was afraid to let go, because I was. I was scared to let go because I wasn't sure what would happen to us next.

"Ria," he whispered. His fingers brushed the hair away under my ear and draped it over my other shoulder. He tried to tip my face back to look at him, but I shook my head. "Please, I need you to look at me."

"I'm so sorry." I whimpered. "For everything. I wish I could take it all back."

"No," he said on a strangled gasp. "Do not say that. I do not regret a thing, and I know you do not either."

Taking my wrists gently into his hands, he brought them up and over his shoulders so I had no choice but to hug him, and it broke my heart even more. He let go then placed his hands under my shirt and on my hips like he needed to feel me. Kova hugged me to him. A sigh rolled through my lips at the touch of his warm flesh on mine.

Kova needed me too.

Rising up on my tiptoes, my heart beat wildly against my ribs. With trembling fingers threading through the hair at the back of his neck, I finally looked up.

My heart was in his hands.

chapter 26

I WANTED TO KISS HIM AND TELL HIM THAT I DID LOVE HIM, THAT I WAS going to do whatever I could to fix this and make it right, but something felt so off that it caused a tide of anxiety to wrap around my heart and hold back.

I could hardly breathe. Kova's eyes were on mine, but he wasn't looking at me. He seemed distant even though he was right in front of me. My chest rose and fell, tight with the panic that he no longer wanted me in his arms.

"What…what's wrong?" I asked.

I'd never felt him like this, so withdrawn from even himself. It scared me.

"Nothing," he said under his breath. "I just want to look at you."

His hands squeezed my hips, his fingers clenching my twisted shirt in his hands now. Kova was nervous. I didn't like the feeling closing in on me at seeing him like that. It made my stomach ache, like a negative intuition I feared to acknowledge. It lit up through me, but I doused the paranoia and pressed closer to him. I wasn't supposed to hurt when I was in his arms, and I was going to prove to myself it was all in my head.

"Kiss me," I said quietly. I wanted his lips on mine, but I wanted more to see his reaction.

Kova let go of my shirt and placed his palm around the side of my neck. My knees were weak with him this close. Something so simple caused a surge of feeling to rush through me. His thumb caressed my jaw, and his lips parted, but he didn't move. All Kova did was look at me like he was suffering inside.

If he wasn't going to kiss me, then I would kiss him. I would show him that despite everything, I was still his and he was still mine and we would get through this.

I leaned into him and felt his palm press against my chest.

My breath hitched in my throat.

I blinked, and frowned.

Kova. Stopped. Me.

My frowned deepened.

Kova didn't want to kiss me.

I reared back, my eyes as round as a full moon. I stared at him. Surprisingly, his gaze didn't waver, but he was sad and confused, filled with indecision.

We'd come so far. This didn't make sense. He wasn't supposed to look at me like that.

Oh, God.

I was going to be sick.

It wasn't supposed to be like this.

He was supposed to crush his stupid fish lips to mine and kiss me like I meant everything to him. He was supposed to tell me we'd get through this. He was supposed to tell me he loved me, damn it.

My hands fell from around him and I stepped back. My legs shook. A numbing low vibration spread beneath my skin. It made me jittery as hell. I needed to get out of here before I threw up. Kova didn't want me anymore, and I wasn't sure how to handle it.

"I have to leave," I said.

A string of Russian flew from his lips as I reached for the doorknob behind me. Kova's arms flew up to the sides of my head and caged me in. I looked up at him, confused, and held my breath. He couldn't tear his eyes from mine. Kova stepped closer until I was forced to press against the door. I was confused, yet I couldn't stop myself from relishing the feel of his body on mine. A gush of air rolled off my lips. He was touching me, he was right in front of me, and yet he wasn't, but now he wasn't letting me leave.

Kova pressed his forehead to mine and let out a shaky sigh. He was struggling and I hated that after we'd come so far.

"Do not ever second-guess my love for you again," he said, then smashed his lips to mine.

Tears climbed my eyes. My jaw trembled and I broke down seeing the insult in his wounded gaze. I couldn't help but cry against his mouth. I felt guilty for doubting his love after he'd told me countless times how much I meant to him. The first opportunity to question him, and I slipped into a coma of insecurity.

"Please, do not cry," he said, then kissed me again. Kova's lips were on mine, but he wasn't there.

"Then kiss me like you mean it," I begged.

"Devil, strike me down," he whispered so low that I almost missed it.

His lips stroked mine with despair, but his tongue didn't penetrate. He breathed against me, and I begged for any ounce of proof that he still loved me.

Kova tugged my top lip between his as he wrapped his arm around the small of my back. He pulled me flush against him and held on to me with his warm body. I wanted so badly to take the lead, but I needed some sort of signal from him that we were okay so I could put those thoughts to rest. I needed to see if what I was fearing was all in my head, or if my worst nightmares were true, and I was losing him."

He proved me wrong.

Kova's tongue licked past the seam of my lips with a sigh. He leaned into me and let go of whatever he was holding on to, kissing me like he meant it. His tongue fondled mine, his teeth were sharp nibbles on my lips. He made sure his mouth consumed every breath of air I had. He took and took and took, and I loved that he did because I loved his fiery passion and the way it made me tingle everywhere. His shaking hands gripped every inch of skin he could touch, his nails dug into my skin as he lost himself in us.

This was my Kova. The Kova my heart beat fiercely for.

His hands slid down to the back of my thighs. Kova lifted me up and pressed my back to the door. I melted against his strong chest, loving how he held me in his arms. Sex with Kova was electrifying, but kissing Kova was something entirely different that I wasn't sure how to put into words. A kiss was more intimate. A kiss was unspoken words tangled with raw feeling. It brought you closer to someone. It was how I learned to understand Kova.

We needed this moment to know that we still had each other to get through this.

My legs wrapped around his waist as he deepened the kiss and made love to me this way, telling me he was still there when I thought for a moment he wasn't.

"I missed you so much," I said in between kisses.

His hand came up to press against my throat. I swallowed, remembering how much he liked that. Vibrant green eyes stared back at me before roaming over every inch of my face. His jet-black lashes lowered, his thumb smoothed over my neck and jaw, then to my lips, like he was finger painting them. His tongue dragged over his bottom lip as he leaned in to steal another kiss from me.

"Not more than I missed you," he said.

"I thought you might hate me for what happened."

His eyes snapped to mine, his brows angled toward each other. "Impossible."

"Where's your wedding ring?"

His callused thumb was still on my throat like he wanted to feel me talk. "I do not know." When I didn't say anything, he said, "I threw it out the window while I was driving." His voice was low, guttural when he spoke. "It is of no value to me and a reminder of the mistake I made."

"Oh." I wasn't expecting that.

"I know you have your appointment and a few things to wrap up here, but I need to hold you for just a moment longer." He paused and carried us to his desk where he sat on top of it with me wrapped around him. "We have to talk."

Dread coiled inside of me.

Four words, that when put together, could quintessentially make or break a relationship. I tried not to think the worst like I had earlier, and hoped for the best.

My head fell forward and rested on the honey curve of his neck.

"When we arrive in Texas tomorrow, there will be a full health scan by the Olympic coaches and the governing bodies. They look for all unauthorized medication that enhances performance." He tightened his arms. "I know you do not want anyone to know about your health right now, but they will discover the medications in your blood. They are going to question you."

I stared at his neck, unblinking. "What if they think I'm using steroids or something?"

"They will not. I have already checked all of your medications against the list."

My brows furrowed. Lifting my head, I looked at him. "How? You don't know them."

His fingers twirled a lock of my auburn hair. Tugging on the strand he was looking at, he said, "When I called Frank and spoke to him about the universities, I mentioned this issue as well. He gave me a list and we both agreed that you need a printed copy of your medical records from all doctors. I informed him that the Olympic doctors and media news stations will learn of the kidney disease and lupus. They will no doubt talk about it."

I swallowed hard. "What do you think the worst is that can happen?" My fingers rubbed over his skin. "I'm nervous now. I didn't even think about them finding out."

One corner of his mouth twitched. "Nothing other than you will most likely have more cameras in your face than other gymnasts, and more questions to answer. Probably more screenings. I do not want you to fear the worst or think that you will be treated any differently when we get to Texas. Believe me, the coaches will not go easy on you and they will not feel bad in the least. They have a one-track mind and all they see is gold. They will demand your blood and sweat. But I want you to be prepared beforehand to talk about it."

"Thank you for warning me. You know I don't like talking about it. It makes me feel like a walking disease. I mean, I am, but I feel like all eyes are on me now and I hate that feeling. I think this might be harder for me than the actual Games."

Kova eyed me cautiously.

"I want you to think of it as a story of both survival and inspiration, nothing else," he said, but his voice was too distant again for my liking. "That is what you are, Adrianna. You are an inspiration. You may not see it now, but one day a young gymnast will look up to you for your strength and fight, using your story as her motivation. Do not get caught in your emotions thinking the worst. Not only did you make the team, you made it while having lupus *and* kidney disease. That is not something to just be proud of, but to wear with pride. People will talk regardless. Who gives a shit? Do not let that take away from what you are about to do."

My lips twitched for a second. He said shit with a heavier than usual Russian accent.

"Why didn't you give an opinion when I asked about colleges? You know what you think matters to me. I want your insight."

He kissed the top of my head. "I don't want you to make a decision based on what I say."

"I won't. I'm just curious. I'm sure you know more about the schools than I do anyway."

Kova sighed deeply. "UCLA is a fantastic school, the team is top-notch. The head coach is someone I could see working well with you. She is known for bringing out the best in gymnasts and giving them time to find where they shine most. However, after all you have been through, what you will undergo soon, I am not sure competition on all four events is wise. You hate balance beam. Why waste your time and energy on something you dislike when you can spend it on something you love and excel at?"

Kova made a valid point, but I also liked to challenge myself. Plus, if I was taking a year off to recover, then I could possibly do all four events.

"Florida and Oklahoma are both neck and neck," he continued. "I personally love watching you on floor. Yes, vault and bars are where you outdo every competitor, but you come alive on floor, so I am leaning toward Oklahoma. With that all being said, given your health, Florida is an ideal choice for you."

My finger traced back and forth over his collarbone. I noticed he didn't suggest Georgia. My intuition told me he didn't want to make it seem like he was asking me to stay back and that was why he didn't bring it up.

Goose bumps prickled my skin as I touched him. Kova rested his cheek on the top of my head. I realized this was all it took for me—a stolen moment with him that settled my nerves.

chapter 27

"I THINK YOUR BEST OPTION AT THIS POINT IS TO FORGO DIALYSIS and schedule the transplant surgery immediately following the Olympics."

Puzzled, I sat staring at Dr. Kozol as if he'd just spoken a foreign language and expected me to understand *and* respond to it. The plan was originally to begin dialysis so I could allow my body time to rest and heal from gymnastics before I jumped into surgery. I knew eventually I had to get the transplant, just not so soon.

"I don't understand," I said, confusion shifting through me. I thought I was doing okay, better than I had in a long time. I felt okay, not worse. "I was going to move after the Olympics, possibly to another state. I thought I would continue our treatments there, just long distance. Now I need to schedule surgery immediately? What happened to dialysis?"

While I hadn't had time to give it thought considering how fast my life was moving lately, I knew accepting a place on one of the college teams was next on my list. If I had surgery, the offer might be retracted. A decision needed to be made soon even though I'd only just learned of the proposals.

It'd be what I worked for, my incentive to get better.

Not to mention, Avery had to prepare too. Was there even enough time for both of us to get on the same schedule? Anxiety gripped me. This was getting more real by the minute.

Avery was going to college. Did that mean she needed to take a leave of absence? I couldn't do that to her, especially not her freshman year. Maybe a summer surgery would work. That way we both could rest and heal properly. This summer was too late, it would have to be next year.

Clearing my throat, I continued. "Were my test results not what you expected?"

"They're not where I hoped you'd be at this point. You're responding to the medication, but your body is fighting it, and though the decline is slow, it's steady. The longer you go without surgery, the more wear and tear you're doing to your body even though you can't physically see it. You need to really consider surgery immediately upon returning. You don't want to get to the point where you'll be too far gone."

While Dr. Kozol had seen me when I was in the hospital, he hadn't been able to run the tests he typically did. When I got here, he had vials of blood drawn and tested in his office, some sent out to the lab, along with X-rays and ultrasounds on various organs. He left no stone unturned. I'd sat for hours in his office thinking he'd tell me one thing only to surprise me with something else.

I glanced down at my lap. My fingers were twisted together, my nailbeds a pale pink. This was not what I was expecting. That changed a lot for me. I wouldn't be able to do that *and* move at the same time.

"How would this work if I move out of state?"

Dr. Kozol stared at me for an uncomfortable moment. "Where are you planning to go?" I listed the schools I was offered a scholarship to and told him the training hours were not nearly as grueling. His bushy brows rose. "So, you're going to continue with gymnastics?"

I nodded, and his eyes bore deeper into mine. I felt like he was silently ridiculing me, that I was reckless for my choices. He wasn't happy with me.

"If it's possible, I'd like to. It's really the only motivation I have right now."

"Have you considered speaking to a psychologist?"

I grimaced. "No, I don't want to do that."

The last thing I wanted to do was tell some stranger my problems and have them give me more pills to take. I was already on a daily cocktail of medication. I didn't want to add more.

"I'm concerned the illnesses have skewed your vision. You're not making wise decisions, Adrianna. Maybe you should really consider speaking to someone. You do realize you won't be able to do gymnastics this year if you have surgery, right? It's not physically possible."

Of course, I was aware of that. I was aware of everything against me.

I wasn't going to answer him. If I could do dialysis, then I'd be okay for a little while. He had to know that was the door I was going to walk through. At least that way everyone can get prepared and adjusted. That's what I told myself, anyway.

"Wherever you decide to live, I'll put a team together for you. Everyone knows someone in this field, but I'll make sure I'm personally part of the new team, if you like." Dr. Kozol grimaced as he stacked the papers together. "Medically speaking, however, it's not wise. I just don't see how you're going to be able to come back with the thunder you need to train, even if the hours are less and the routines are not as demanding. Transplant recovery is going to take months for you to heal. Then you have to build yourself back up, and then start training. I'm concerned you're going to break your body back down and we'll have to start over. We don't want that. We only want to go up from here."

"But it's doable?" I asked, hopeful.

"I can't recall seeing anyone do it, but that doesn't mean it's not possible." He paused. "I just have to ask something." I nodded, curious about what he wanted to know. "Is gymnastics really worth risking your life for? Really think about that question. You're young. Why are you trying to destroy yourself? You wear yourself down by playing a sport. Once you reach stage five, which you aren't far from, that's it, Adrianna. You can kiss gymnastics goodbye and live out your days in a hospital bed." He studied me. "I don't understand why you want to do that. You'll make your life so much harder."

My eyes dropped to the floor. I didn't have a death wish. I guess I just didn't like my life and strived for a better life. It bothered me that something that couldn't be seen could dictate so much in my life.

"If we're not going to schedule your transplant right after, then we need to start you on dialysis. I want you on a plane back here within two days after the Olympics. Otherwise, I'm going to have to resign as your doctor. The risk is too great, and you've not yielded to the treatment I've devised for you. I've done everything I can for you up until now—I've waited long enough."

If I did what he said, that meant I wouldn't be able to do the promo tours with the Olympic team after. My heart crumbled a little.

"I'm not trying to be defiant and I don't want to die. I guess it's the one thing I have control over. It's the one thing that truly makes me happy. Without gymnastics, I don't know who I am. I don't know how to live or what to do."

"That's because you haven't given yourself time to live," he said sympathetically. "Give yourself time to recover properly and then weigh your choices. After that, you can decide what you want to live for. You'll have all the time in the world during recovery to find who you are and what you want to do."

Quietly, I said, "I don't know how to live without gymnastics if I quit. Gymnastics is who I am."

"You don't have to quit. There are other ways to be involved in the sport. You need to get better first and then sort out your future. But with these kind of results after months and months of powerful medications"—he tapped the paper—"you're knocking on death's door. Your kidney function is already extremely low. You're pushing the limit. If you drop to fifteen percent, you'll need emergency surgery. Just attending college is going to be difficult in general with the side effects of dialysis. You need to seriously weigh your pros and cons."

I nodded. "I have a question. Realistically, say I start dialysis shortly after I come home, and say I respond well to the treatment, how long do I have before I would need a transplant?"

Dr. Kozol chuckled under his breath. "I feel bad for your future husband," he joked, which made me laugh. "If, and that's a big if, you have a positive response, I'd say no more than two years to be safe. Four would be ideal, but given where your health is right now, that's highly unlikely. We'd rather be prepared early. I hesitate to tell you this because I don't want you to focus on that."

I perked up. I could work with a two-year timeline for both Avery and myself. Even though she was selflessly giving me a kidney, I had to take her time into consideration too. I wasn't going to chance my life like everyone around me assumed I was. I felt in my heart of hearts I'd get better enough to compete again, and that's the kind of mentality I went with. I could hire a personal trainer and do light workouts while recovering with dialysis that way I didn't lose what I'd worked so hard to attain.

Biting the inside of my cheek, I said, "Let's schedule the dialysis now. I'll be here with bells on first thing when I get back." I stopped when something dawned on me. "Wait, I'm supposed to be going back to Amelia Island after the Games."

"That's not an issue. I have an office about thirty minutes west of there. I'll make sure your file is transferred and everything is in place when you come in. In the meantime, once you decide where you will relocate to, let me know so I can put together a reputable team. How long will you remain in Georgia?"

"I'm not sure."

Dr. Kozol began writing while he asked me questions. Since I was deferring school to recover, I had roughly nine months before school started again, which meant I had about six or so to prepare for the collegiate team, and three months to get my health in order.

"Right now, you're retaining fluid in your feet, which isn't good."

"Is that why they felt stiff and swollen this morning? I almost had to change my shoes."

"Yes. Luckily, it hasn't reached your face. Any nausea or confusion? Irregular heartbeat? A change in urine?"

I shook my head. "Honestly, no. I've been feeling really good. Other than the usual joint pain and more hair loss, nothing out of the ordinary. My headaches have been pretty bad, but I think those are due to the fact I'm stressed out and running on anxiety because of the training camp and the Games."

His eyes met mine above the rim of his glasses. "Don't ignore what your body is trying to tell you."

"I'm not."

The room grew quiet as Dr. Kozol made his notes. I wasn't too thrilled about starting dialysis.

"You're going to be monitored for heart disease since you already have severe kidney damage that's progressing. I'm going to switch out one of your medications for a stronger steroid. This'll help with the wear and tear. I implore you to take the medication exactly as it's stated on the bottle. You cannot miss a dose."

I sat up straighter. "I'll fill the prescription, but I need to see if it's on the list of banned medications before I take it. I'm going to be given a full health screening by the Olympic Committee, so I'll need a full copy of my file."

"I spoke with your father and already have it prepared for you. I've included my personal phone number for their physicians. Everything is right here," he said, tapping the thick folder next to him. "I also told Frank I'd be willing to attend just to be safe. He felt like it was a good idea."

A huge sense of relief washed over me. I smiled, actually liking the idea. There would be doctors chosen by the Olympic Committee, but they didn't know me, and if I was cutting it as close as I supposedly was, maybe this was a good thing.

I hadn't made it this far just to collapse now.

chapter 28

"**E**VERYONE IS GOING TO KNOW." I WHINED INTO MY CELL PHONE. "Why is that a bad thing?" Avery asked.

"When you found out, how did you feel?"

She was quiet for a moment. "I guess I was really sad and just felt so bad. I started thinking about all the negative things. I got really down inside and cried."

"Exactly. I don't want that. I don't want anyone to feel that way about me. I'm fine. I'm not going anywhere anytime soon. Now people are going to look at me differently. They're going to be like, 'Oh, that's the girl with lupus and kidney disease,' or 'Why doesn't she look sick?' What if they call me names for pursing my dream instead of getting better? Then the digging starts, and the questions follow. Then there's the pity looks. I just don't want to be made to feel any different, because I'm not. I'm just a little sick. Others have it worse than me. I'll be fine."

I was in my room packing for my early flight and stopped to sit on the bed. Lying back, I stared at the celling.

I started to panic about one thing, then all the little things followed that didn't bear a thought in my mind before this. The walls of my chest began to feel like they were closing in and then the pressure started. I didn't like when my pulse pumped harder in the next beat. It shook me up. My hand flew to my chest and I closed my eyes, inhaling through my nose and exhaling through my mouth. My fingers shook and my body began to warm all over.

"Yeah, but they're not going for gold either." Her tone softened and I opened my eyes. "Maybe it won't be such a bad thing. Talking about it is good, chica."

I let out a dramatic sigh. "I can't believe I didn't see this coming."

"I can't believe I get to go to the fucking Olympics and watch my bestie!" Avery said.

I chuckled and sat up. Glancing over my shoulder at my suitcase laid open on my bed with clothes and leos strewn across it, I reached for my favorite leo and fingered the material. I'd gotten this one shortly before I went to World

Cup. It was all black with tons of fuchsia Swarovski crystals in different sizes across the chest. It was the leo I wore to warmups right before my big meets. Joy had gotten it for me.

"Will it be weird with Xavier there?"

"I don't have an issue with him, he's the one who hates me. You know that."

"True, but didn't he call you when he found out I made the team?"

Her giggle made me smile. She was giddy. I was surprised when I found out Xavier had called Avery and told her the news considering how he supposedly felt about her.

"He did. He's so excited for you. I honestly hadn't heard him like that in so long." She paused. "It was good to hear him so happy for a change."

"Do you think you'll talk to him, like hang out at night? You know I have to room with my team, so I won't be able to stay with you."

"I'm not worried in the least. If he wants to chill, I'm cool with that. If not, then that's fine too. I figured I'd walk around and check out the eye candy. I know all"—she drew out the word—"about the Olympic Village and what goes on. I read online that over a hundred thousand condoms were ordered just for the Village, and nearly five million for the whole city. That's a lot of fucking for just two weeks."

A loud laugh burst from my throat. The Olympic Village had super tight security to protect the athletes and help keep them focused on their events without distraction. That meant no reporters or parents or friends were allowed behind the gates. Only those competing in the Games. With a variety of ages and bodies primed, and all the tension and stress, athletes needed a way to let loose. From what I'd heard, nothing was off limits and anything was possible. There had been numerous rumors surrounding the last Games about orgies and dating apps used for sex. Honestly, I couldn't imagine doing any of that.

"So, what do you think you're going to do? Just sneak inside and people watch?" I laughed picturing her walking around like a little kid in a candy store. "Are you going to walk up to a dude and say take me for the night, no name needed?"

"Aid… Stay innocent. I know a lot of the guys visit bars and venture outside the Village after they're done competing. I just want to see them in all their glory. Nothing more. Look, but don't touch."

"Right," I said, not convinced in the least. I placed my cell on my shoulder and held the phone with my ear. Folding my leos and gym shorts, I stacked them in my suitcase. "Make sure you tell my brother first. I bet you won't make it through the hotel doors."

"He won't care."

"That's what you think."

I thought back to how he acted over her while I was home. Fat chance she was doing anything without him. Xavier could deny all he wanted that he was done with Avery, but after speaking to her and him, they were both so totally head over heels for each other still. It was too bad they were hiding their pain and not dealing with it together.

"You're so crazy."

"And you love me for it."

"True." I smiled to myself as I walked into the bathroom to place my toiletries into a separate bag. "So, I had to see my doctor today before I could board the plane tomorrow."

"And?" she responded quickly, her voice tight. "What's wrong?"

Now it was my turn to laugh. "Nothing is wrong. He did a thorough body check." I paused, swallowing hard for what I was about to say. "He wanted to plan the surgery after the Games—"

"Let's do it!" I frowned, caught off guard by her response. "Tell me when and where and I'm yours."

"I told him I would start dialysis instead."

She groaned under her breath. "You know, if you were in front of me right now, I would shake you. Why did you do that?"

I walked back into my room holding the little Louis bag. "You'd have to take time off from school your freshman year of college. I'm not doing that to you, and he said I could probably get by two more years with dialysis. Maybe even four. I figured if it all goes well, that's what we'd do."

Avery made a sound under her breath. "I don't understand you. I'm willing and ready now. You are well past ready and needed a damn kidney a week ago. What's the hold up? Are you scared your body is going to reject it? Because I'm not. I think it's going to be a success."

I sat on the edge of my bed and slid down until I was on the floor, and pulled up my knees. My lip rolled between my teeth. I picked at the carpet, feeling that gloomy sense of despair swirl around my chest again. I hated when I got down and out like this. It was hard to breathe, hard to focus, hard to just think because of the guilt I was dealing with inside. Avery would have to give up a lot for me. She'd have to alter her life for a while for mine. I really felt like I needed to let my body cool down from all the intense training before jumping straight into surgery. They all seemed to say otherwise.

"I'm not going to take away your first year of college like that. The recovery time is long. Plus," I said, hesitating, "it would have to be well planned and more organized since I won't be here. I don't even know which doctor will be doing it. It's not that easy."

Was I trying to convince her, or me?

"What do you mean you won't be here? Where are you going, and why am I just now hearing about it?"

"You're going to need months off. A summer would be ideal."

"Aid," she said. "What do you mean you won't be here? Where are you going?"

Exhaling a strained breath, I told her about the offers I received from the colleges and broke it down for her. "They couldn't have come at a better time," I added. I truly believed that.

"Hold the phone. Florida wants you, and you're going to say no? Are you serious? But that's where I'll be going, and we always planned to go to college together." She mock whined. I swear I heard her stomp her foot.

My shoulders slumped forward. "I don't know. I feel like I know, but I don't. I'm really so torn."

"Ugh. You'd rather live with tornados or earthquakes?"

I paused, unblinking, trying to figure out what she was saying when it dawned on me. A small laugh rolled off my lips.

"Well, when you put it like that, neither. Seeing as my gym future is so uncertain, I have to think about where I'd want to go to school if I don't end up doing gymnastics. Where I'd be happy living and possibly one day having a life there. The plan is to have a place on the team, but there's a good chance I won't be able to handle it in the end."

She was quiet. "Yeah," she said softly, agreeing with me. "What about Kova?"

My eyes closed. Her question was a straight shot to my gut. I tried not to think about him when I thought about my offers, but the truth was, I did. He was very much sewn into the layers of my heart. He always would be, and I'd be lying if I said living near him wasn't high on my list.

"You're going to leave him? I find that hard to believe."

"I can't walk away from him."

"Then what will you do?"

I contemplated my answer. I had a feeling that what I wanted to do, was not what I would do.

"How do you walk away from someone you love?" My jaw began to tremble at the thought of leaving that I had to stop talking for a second. "It's impossible."

"What?" Avery yelled, though she'd pulled the phone away. She gasped. "Be right there! Can I call you back in a few, Aid? My dad literally just said my ass is grass, so I have to go run and hide now."

A slow smile curved my lips. "Ave," I said. "What did you do?"

She snickered into the phone, which made me laugh in return. "My brothers were pissing me off. They got what they deserved."

I shook my head. "Which was what?"

"I put that temporary hair dye that's all the rage in their shampoo. Now Connor has electric blue hair, and Michael's is corn yellow. Or maybe it's the other way around. Either way, they deserved it."

I covered my mouth. Xavier would straight up murder me if I did that to him. He was all about the hair right now, which was probably why her brothers were too.

"Text me later," I said, then we hung up.

Rising to my feet, I finished packing everything except for a few things I'd add in the morning. It wasn't late, but the flight departed very early, so I figured I'd just go to sleep since I didn't have anything else to do. I was always tired anyway.

Lifting my suitcase off the bed, I spotted the book Sophia gave me. I reached for it. I gazed down with the sudden need to flip through it, wondering if this was a sign too.

I climbed into bed and pulled the blanket over me. I read countless passages about stepping forward into growth and that I was to trust in myself to see my true beauty. How I had to train my mind and heart to be stronger than my emotions or I'd risk losing myself. That I needed to prove myself to me, because I mattered most to me. Then there were the reminders that I'd been given this life because I was strong enough to live it.

Sometimes I didn't feel like I was strong enough to live it.

There were so many motivating pages that I connected with. Who knew words could breathe inspiration into me like this, like maybe I was strong enough to handle anything.

It wasn't until I read the last page of a chapter that it really hit close to home. *When you change within yourself, the world around you will follow suit.*

I had to close the book otherwise I would cry. The words rang with too much truth. Somewhere along the way I'd felt the change and had been trying to fight the pull, not accept that it was okay like the book suggested I do. I *was* a different person, and that meant I would have to let go of who I was comfortable with to find the new me. Accepting this also meant there would be a domino effect of change coming into my life. Was I ready for that?

I placed the book on my nightstand and turned off the light. I'd had enough reading for one night. Going to sleep sounded more appealing than mulling over my thoughts. Curling up on my side, I was on the verge of dozing off when my cell phone rang and startled me. I reached for my cell and frowned.

"Avery?" I said. She was sniffling into the phone. "What's wrong? Are you crying?"

"I'm just so happy for you. I only want what's best for you, and I feel like you're starting to finally see your worth and what you're capable of. I'm so happy you're my best friend."

I nestled the phone closer to my face and smiled. "You're so corny. I love you."

"I know. I just had to say it. Wherever you end up, it's where you're supposed to be. Even if you are hundreds of miles away from me," she added. I could hear the smile on her face. "I can't wait to see you soon."

We both hung up and I drifted off to sleep, feeling much more optimistic and truly fortunate that I had a friend who'd stuck by me through all the shit I'd been through.

chapter 29

KOVA KEPT TO HIMSELF AS THE CLOUDS PASSED BY. HIS BLANK STARE was reflected in the glass, a look I couldn't recall ever seeing in his eyes. He seemed lost. Usually there was a feeling in his eyes, or an emotion he was trying to hide that I could typically see through.

This time there was nothing. That's what worried me the most, because he was the same exact way when we flew to the training camp a couple of weeks ago.

When we had first arrived at the Olympic training camp, I thought Kova's distance was due to us keeping everything strictly professional. We hardly spoke during then, not that we had time to. It'd been more intense than the last time I was there.

I wanted so badly to reach out and take his hand and just ask what's wrong. He didn't look at me very much, and when I did actually catch his eyes on me, he'd quickly look in the other direction. It bothered me to see him hide his emotions from me when he rarely ever held back before.

I knew it was the last thing I should've been concerned about, but before life had flipped upside down, we were in a really good place. I wanted to go back to that time. To when Kova had picked me up from the training camps and took care of me. I'd been in rough shape, probably having flare ups if I could remember properly. Funny thing, though, the camp I attended this year made Nationals feel like a walk in the park. Located in a secluded area of woods with hardly any cell phone reception, the coaching had been borderline emotionally and physically abusive. Food had been carefully calculated and washed down with laxatives once again. I'd forgotten how much I hated that part with a passion until my stomach had cramped in the middle of training from the pills. We had been weighed every day. I knew nothing about my new teammates except for the injuries they'd hidden and been forced to train on. Not one girl was in working order, each one of us brought something more painful to the table. One gymnast had trained on a foot that had broken bones. Another girl had landed wrong and fractured her back, resulting in an alternate taking her spot. Still, we hadn't complained as our bodies were manipulated during the day and therapy was applied at night. We were brand new come morning.

Those two weeks were probably the most intense weeks of my life and I hadn't even realized it at the time. Not only had I trained with a whole new team, but I'd been nervous about my medical file. The tests had come back clean like I knew they would, but I'd started to harbor animosity from the constant interrogation into me regardless. Each time I was interviewed, the anticipation mounted inside of me. I kept thinking the next question would be about Kova.

The doctors couldn't comprehend how I was training like the others who were relatively healthy, let alone hid my illnesses the way I had. Kova had reassured them it was under control. I'd told them I trained like I always had because I didn't know any other way, and Kova added that I actually challenged him as a coach while he was training me to see how far I could go. They'd seemed to like that and told me they could recall only three other athletes with health issues similar to mine who persevered against the odds. That gave me hope. But the two weeks after we arrived until now, was where things really started to shift.

It was crazy to me that I could be sitting right next to Kova yet feel miles and miles apart from him. Even crazier was it happened in the course of a month where we worked so near each other. The change in his demeanor left me confused. He was here, but he wasn't. Detached. He stood in front of me, but I couldn't feel his essence surround me like I usually did. Kova was never rude. On the outside he looked normal, like every other coach here. But when he looked at me and our gazes actually had the chance to meet, Kova appeared depressed for that brief moment. I tried to tell myself that we both were in the zone and he probably didn't even realize it. I had no real reason yet to believe otherwise since we hadn't talked.

My heart could only believe so many lies until it started to weep for the truth.

Reaching for the bag near my feet, I rummaged through and pulled out the notebook I got just for documenting my life once I had made the team. I'd done a little writing here and there, just not as much as I had hoped. Now I had time to kill.

I flipped open the notebook and ruffled some pages. I hoped the sound of the papers would make him curious to see what I was doing. At least initiate a conversation. But it didn't. Kova just stared ahead at the clouds, stuck in his thoughts. The look in his dead eyes made my stomach clench. This would've been the perfect opportunity to push him like he'd once begged me to, if only we weren't on a private plane filled with Olympic officials and athletes.

I wrote for a little while. Mostly things about Kova, and the feelings I was dealing with inside. How I fell for his flaws, my fears of the future and what I was up against. Where we would end up—yes, we. There was no fooling myself—I knew in my heart I would be wherever he was.

Closing the journal, I put it away safely hidden and took out the book Sophia gave me. I didn't want to be lost inside of my head anymore, and lately these words were an escapism for me. They gave me cause and a drive to be a better me.

I read for a little while then started to nod off. Kova still hadn't looked over at me, so I put the book away and shut my bag.

I couldn't stand another second of seeing his head pressed against the glass any longer. Lifting the divider between us, I pushed it between the seats then pulled my legs up under me to get comfy. Without asking him, I leaned against his arm to rest my head on him.

That got his attention really quick.

Startled, Kova sat up straighter and immediately looked above my head. The tension in his shoulders loosened as he glanced around. I took that as a hint and nestled closer to him. Kova's gaze fell on me. Seconds ago, his eyes were vacant, now they were overflowing with turmoil.

I held my breath hoping he wouldn't shake his head or push me away. Kova slouched at an angle in his black dress pants and stretched his legs out. His crisp, white long-sleeved shirt that'd been rolled up at the sleeves was wrinkled from sitting in the same position for so long. A few buttons were left undone and the collar bunched around his jaw. Muscular thighs filled out the material of his pants, and I couldn't help but notice his bulge when he shifted again. His length strained against his pants and it left nothing to my imagination. I stared longer, picturing how his cock looked bare and how it looked right then. My cheeks flamed and I clenched my eyes shut. I felt like I'd looked too long.

When I opened them and met his gaze, his eyes were a brilliant green from the way the golden sunlight was reflecting off them. A breath caught in the back of my throat. He studied me for a quiet moment, his softened gaze taking in every inch of my face. Truthfully, I was afraid I was going to lose him.

Kova turned slightly to the side and pulled the screen down to block the light. He reached for the blanket hanging off my chair and surprised me by fluffing it out before draping it around both of us. Kova raised his arm that I was leaning on and wrapped it around my shoulder. He snuggled me as close as he could get me until I repositioned myself. I was lying on half his side and half of his chest, so we had more of each other now.

I closed my eyes, and for a good moment, I didn't move. My thoughts were on him, how I felt at peace in my soul while in his arms, the way his warmth spread through me. I was secure and safe. His fingertips pressed into my upper arm and it just solidified how I felt. His body relaxed against mine and I heard him let out a long, relieved sigh under his breath.

We both held still for a long while. Together.

To my complete surprise, Kova's other hand slipped under the blanket. I stilled as he laced his fingers on top of mine and then curled them over to bring us to rest against his stomach. Kova exhaled slowly and I felt him unwind. Without moving, I lifted my eyes just enough to catch a glimpse of him. His eyes weren't squinting, and his jaw wasn't so tense. He looked…almost at peace.

I molded against the length of his body. Something in my stomach was warning me this was the calm before the storm. I blocked it out, not wanting to ruin this moment we both needed by overanalyzing it.

Kova shifted ever so slightly.

"I still love you, *Malysh*," he whispered, his lips brushing the shell of my ear. "Forever."

We stayed like this for the remainder of the flight and didn't move.

chapter 30

"THIS IS WHAT YOU WORKED FOR. ARE YOU READY?" KOVA ASKED, running his hands up and down my arms. I nodded, blinking a little faster and breathing quickly through my nose. "Look at me." My eyes snapped to his. I was feeling a little frantic. Kova was kneeling on one knee in front of me. For once I stood a little taller than him. We were standing in the back where only coaches and athletes were allowed, waiting to be called by country for introductions.

"Now take a deep breath and exhale."

I looked right into Kova's unwavering eyes and showed him how nervous I was. He glared back and shook his head, silently telling me to let it go. His gaze didn't waver until he felt I had. I expelled a tight breath and rubbed my chest.

The nerves from being in the Olympic arena were impossible to ignore. The moment I stepped off the plane, I felt the eagerness in the air. So much hope was packed into the city of Athens that would host seventeen days' worth of sporting events. It had been decorated and cleaned for the arrival of those participating and those who traveled to watch. There were rainbows of colors everywhere, each participating country brilliantly represented, and attendants walked around with massive smiles. The Olympics were the one place where every nationality came together and let bygones be bygones.

"Do not let this experience pass you by like most of us do. This is your moment and you need to enjoy it. You trained, you worked hard to get here. Nothing, and no one, can take this away from you. You may not realize it yet, but you are an inspiration to me and to people of all ages. So, take this moment in as much as you can, and let your body take over and do what you were born to do—perform. Do not let up here"—he pressed a gentle finger to my temple—"take away what is in here." He laid his finger over the left side of my chest, right over my racing heart. "You bloom under pressure where most crumble, Adrianna. You are so incredible to watch. Believe me when I say, the world is waiting to see you walk out there today."

His eyes bore into mine. I could tell by how tight his words were and how stiff he spoke that he wanted me to believe him and trust what he said.

Like I'd done many times in the past, I trusted him.

Behind the glitz and glamour of one of the most esthetically appealing Olympic sports, were hours and hours of tears, blood, and sweat I'd put in for this moment. All the preparations, the mistakes I'd made that brought on a series of ups and downs, the rigorous long training that sometimes made me want to give up, outrageous coaching methods that ended with positive results because my coach demanded nothing less than perfection, it all came down to this. This was it. This was what it had all been for.

"Gymnastics is seventy percent mental, thirty percent physical. Your body already knows what comes next. All you need to do is have trust in yourself." His brows rose. "Prove yourself to you," he said, and it reminded me of what I'd read in that book Sophia gave me.

I nodded again.

"Talk to me, Adrianna. Tell me what is on your mind."

Taking another deep breath, my shoulders fell when I exhaled. I looked at him and said, "I'm nervous. I can't concentrate. All I keep thinking about is what if I mess up. I think about my routines. Who my biggest competitor is on each event. My mind is all over the place."

I clenched my fingers into a fist and felt how swollen they were. I was beyond anxious from the moment I opened my puffy eyes in the tiny room I shared with one of my teammates in the Olympic Village. My bones ached, my skin was tight and inflamed.

When I woke up, I'd immediately taken all of my medications, then I ate a banana. I wasn't supposed to have them, but it was all there was in the room since the cafeteria was too far to walk to with the little time I had to get ready. This was the first time I didn't have to hide the bottles, and it felt good.

My teammate didn't stare at me like I was contagious while she watched from her bed. She didn't question me. She didn't even bat an eye when I threw back eight different pills, and dramatically said, "Make way world, here I come." She just laughed. She was a freshly turned sixteen-year-old, but she looked twelve. She was also the alternate who'd been given a chance.

The four of us had decided to get ready in one room this morning. My chest had been so tight that I couldn't even get in a proper deep breath. Nerves hung in the air like black dripping tar. We joined hands to form a circle and prayed together silently to our higher ups, preparing to take on the biggest event of our lives. The confidence shone brightly, quietly, as we bowed our heads and closed our eyes.

The United States had won gold in the last two Olympics. The pressure was on. Determined to take the prized medal home, we dubbed ourselves the Phenomenal Four.

After our prayer session, one of the girls had played Beyoncé's "Run the World (Girls)" and the mood instantly changed. Giggles and smiles replaced the distressing fear. Our hair was intricately braided into stylish ponytails topped with spray glitter, and our makeup was naturally done. Sports bras and bloomers were tucked in and hidden, hairspray was applied to our butt cheeks and thighs so the leos didn't move too much. After shedding a few more tears, we took turns posing for pictures solo and grouped together.

The most emotional part of the morning had been when I stepped into my leotard with USA stamped on the back. There were swirls and swirls of red and blue crystals against a white background. I ran my hands down my flat stomach and then over my long sleeves, feeling the decorations under my palms. I had allowed myself to take in the moment and smiled, hugging myself.

Nothing, and I mean nothing, could describe the feeling that had rushed through me as I pulled up the sparkly, stretchy material for the first time.

I had done it.

By some miracle, I had made it to the Olympics.

"It is not only about how good you are as a gymnast physically, it is about how good you are here, too," Kova said, his fingertips back on my temples, pulling me from my thoughts. "You have shown there is no limit to your dreams. You rose to the challenge. It has been a privilege to coach you. Watching your growth in the sport has been the highlight of my career. You are my biggest accomplishment. You withstood the pressure and odds and proved everyone wrong. I am proud of you and cannot wait to watch you out there."

Damn it. Tears filled my eyes. I blinked rapidly, trying to hold them in, but his words, they were spoken from his heart and not because he was trying to encourage me. I knew by his intimate tone that Kova meant them. Without another thought, I wrapped my arms around his shoulders and leaned down for a hug.

It was hard for me to talk. I wanted to say something back to him, but my emotions were too strong and I couldn't find words good enough for him. I'd only been with Kova and his gym for a few years now, but it felt more like a lifetime when we worked so closely together. He motivated me. He critiqued every little thing I did to help me perfect it, knowing I wanted nothing less. Kova helped me see that I could resist the fall that so many easily succumbed to on this journey.

This was our last competition together. The final show.

The last time that Kova would stand before me and make sure I was mentally prepared.

My heart pounded against my ribs so hard, I could feel it in my throat.

It didn't hit me until right now that this truly was the end in so many ways. Even if I hadn't wanted to train in college, I wouldn't be walking into World Cup again to prepare for another Olympics.

While I could mentally handle the training, my body could not physically endure another four years. I didn't want to ever admit it, but the truth was, I was too weak to continue. I'd maxed out. Stubbornness, willpower, ambition, call it what you wanted, it's what got me here to this moment, but I didn't have a death wish. I knew that after the Olympics this really was the last time for us.

One last squeeze, I missed the comfort of his arms so much. If only after the competition I could end the night with him just like this. Kova meant so much to me, he gave me more than he realized. Without him by my side, I don't think I would've made it this far.

Sniffling, I pulled back and looked at him. Before I could wipe away my tears, Kova's thumbs were already there. He dried his hands on his pants. I expelled a tight breath, trying to exhale the nerves and shook my fingers out.

My jaw trembled as our eyes met. My teeth dug into my lip as I fought the surge of feelings flushing through me. There was so much commotion around us as staff instructed the athletes where to line up and where the coaches needed to be. We were just getting ready to walk out to be introduced.

"This is our last competition together," I said.

Kova's tongue ran over his bottom lip as he studied my eyes. "Let us make it the best one yet."

I nodded, and he stood.

Bending down, Kova picked up my duffle bag and placed it over his shoulder. Just as he was about to walk away to stand with the other coaches behind us, I reached for his wrist. Kova glanced down.

"Thank you…for everything," I said.

Kova shifted his hand over mine and gave me a little squeeze.

I dropped my arm then turned around to find my place in line. My teammates and I bounced on our toes waiting to be announced in our matching royal blue sweat suits with USA printed down the spine in white and then over the left side of our chest in red.

This was my proudest moment.

I drew in a deep breath and closed my eyes, taking it all in as I tried to steady my racing heart.

"Team USA, they're ready for you," someone yelled. She had a microphone attached to her head and a clipboard glued to her chest. She dipped her head then waved her hand at us.

I exhaled slowly and a smile that I wasn't prepared for spread across my face.

I still couldn't believe I'd made it.

chapter 31

OUBLE DOORS WERE HELD OPEN AS THE FOUR OF US WALKED BEHIND an employee who held a white sign high in the air that read USA in black, bold letters.

The crowd exploded the moment we stepped inside the stadium. It was loud. A massive smile split across my face at the jolt of excitement it gave me. The fans had to reach an octave that was earsplitting. It was really cool and made me feel alive. My eyes ran over the crowd in a blur. The fans stood waving flags, air of enthusiasm surrounded all of us, welcoming us… I was still in shock. I couldn't believe after all the hard work that I was actually here. We followed the woman in a straight line to the floor. Walking up the three steps, we stood next to Team China on one side, and Team Romania on the other. My eyes skimmed the gymnasts. Some exchanged smiles, some didn't. I smiled brightly, though, feeling the thunder of adrenaline course through me. It was empowering to look around at the faces of girls who gave up so much of their youth to be here, fighting for a dream just like I had. We may not have a lot in common, but we had that, and it connected us for a moment in our lifetime forever. I may have missed out on football games, high school dances and prom, making memories with friends, but I didn't regret it because nothing could top this moment. How often did one get to say they went to the freaking Olympics?

Music blared through the speakers and my smile grew larger, happiness taking over me. The crowd clapped and shouted as introductions were made by team before we departed to the first event. I was eager and couldn't wait for the Games to begin.

The countries were split up on the four events, with USA starting on the balance beam. Considering my nerves were already wired, I was both thankful and anxious as hell to start with this event. I'd rather have started with bars, something I had more confidence in, but maybe this was a good thing. That way I got beam out of the way and I could loosen up a little.

I wasn't supposed to compete on beam, but when my teammate fractured her back during the training camp and the alternate was chosen, the committee made a decision between the both of us. After some deliberation, they chose me to compete on beam, which meant I was competing on all four events now while she had two. My routine had the higher execution score, but hers had the difficulty.

Because of the governing rules, the Olympic coaches were not permitted to be on the floor while gymnasts competed, only their coaches were allowed. However, they could instruct from the seats. Each of us had our coach with us and we were allowed a quick warm-up with them before the competition began.

"I know you were not prepared to compete on beam, but the coaches believe in you. They believe that you also have the ability to help carry the team to gold."

I nodded as I powdered my feet then stomped on the floor.

"Look at me." I looked right into Kova's green eyes. "Center your focus. Concentrate on your routine and know you have what it takes. I want you to take a deep breath before your connection series, and keep your chest high when you execute your jumps because those completed in a clean succession will increase your score. Keep that ankle locked in your turns."

Expelling a tight breath, I nodded. "I got it." I paused. "I can do it." I paused again. "I got this." Balancing for ninety seconds on a four-inch piece of wood. I could totally do it.

Once we took turns warming up and it was time to begin, we came to stand in a close circle. We placed our right hand out in the middle of us, and yelled "Phenomenal Four" just as the bell sounded letting us know it was time to start the first event of the Olympics.

I watched as my teammate stepped onto the podium and walked up to the balance beam with her shoulders squared back. There was something exhilarating about watching this tiny little fairy-like girl mount the beam and dominate it like a queen. She was inspiring, and she was also the front runner with the highest difficulty of the meet. The only other gymnast who was capable of executing a routine similar to hers was a girl from the Ukraine. The Ukrainians were trying to make a comeback after not winning any medals since the nineties.

I couldn't sit still, none of us could. We paced the floor and cheered on our teammate in between doing various stretches to keep our muscles warmed up. When she stuck her dismount and the crowd cheered, my heart dropped a little. Now it was my turn.

I powdered my feet again and applied more chalk to my palms and the tops of my thighs. Kova stood behind me, massaging my shoulders and arms to keep me warm. My heart was fluttering and my fingers shook. I drew in a large breath

530 | LUCIA FRANCO

and inhaled the chalky air, coughing when I exhaled. That made my lungs burn. I swallowed, wincing because of my sore throat.

I could do this.

"Stay focused," he said, turning me to stand in front of him. "Positive thoughts. It is just like any other meet."

"Only it's not." I half joked, eyeing him.

Kova smiled halfway, but I'd caught it. "Your biggest competitor is yourself. This is you living your dream, and me living it with you."

It was only us in the arena despite the thousands of beating hearts surrounding us. *Let me live with you*, was something I'd never forget he said. It was woven into my soul for eternity. The happiness I felt was a seed soaking up his words and blossoming inside of my chest.

A smile slowly, contentedly, fell over my curved my lips. I knew what he was doing. I made a mental note to remind myself of what he said so I could write it in my journal. I wanted to remember it forever and explain in detail how I felt, that way when I looked back on this day many years from now, I'd get that same feeling again when I reread the words.

"You better go," he said. There was a spark in his eyes. He seemed content, and that pleased me.

Turning around, I walked over to the stairs and took a deep breath. Then I proceeded up the three steps and made my way toward the sixteen-foot piece of wood that was either going to make me or break me. Right in front of it sat four official judges wearing matching navy-blue suits and unsympathetic stares ready to critique every little thing I messed up on.

I stopped in front of the apparatus and breathed in positivity. Before I saluted the judges, I looked over my shoulder and made eye contact with Kova. He gave me a deep nod, and mouthed, "You can do it."

That was all I needed. Turning back to face the judges, I drowned out all the noise around me and let the countdown begin.

I raised one arm to salute them with a thin smile on my face. Fingers twinkling over the beige material, I mounted the beam into a straddle press handstand and swiveled my hips until my split legs were parallel to the balance beam. Clenching my stomach, my inner thighs helped center my hips as I balanced over the beam with every muscle squeezed in my body. I arched further to stand and finally took a breath. It was so easy to forget to breathe during competition. However, if I breathed even the slightest breath at the wrong time, I could easily slip up.

I sashayed across the apparatus from one end to the next, staying focused on only what I was attempting and what came next. Muscle memory kicked in and I completed turns on my toes with finesse. I completed a double back hand-spring full-twist like a silk ribbon floating through the air. Then the courage came and I felt confidence bloom through me.

I lowered my arms; I was almost finished. After another exhale, I gracefully stepped into a succession of jumps with turns, adding a back tuck straight into a bonus jump. My arms came down and I prepared for a standing back flip twist. I looked at my clear painted toes between the four inches of wood and tried to center my hips. If I went backwards, I could swing my arms behind me to gain the momentum I needed to flip back and twist at the same time. If I went forward, I didn't have the arm swing, and I could only hurdle so far into a front flip twist. Going in a different direction was what made it so difficult and upped the score.

My routine had me flipping forward.

Inhaling, I stepped into the barani and pushed off the balance beam into the front flip full twist. I came down and felt the leather scrape against the arch of my foot.

Eyes wide, my heart dropped.

No.

My heart sank.

I clenched my muscles and curled my toes around the four-inch piece of wood, my entire body fighting to hold on. I stiffened, pushing against the pull of gravity. If I fell off completely, I would lose one full point. If I could save it, even if a little messy, it would be a lesser deduction.

Digging deep, I pulled it together and raised my arms in the air to attempt to save it. *Thank God,* I thought to myself. I blinked and realigned my focus once again. I thought I saw stars for a second there.

I made my way across the beam in a series of required dance skills, then straight into a standing back pike that I landed with ease. Stepping toward the edge, I glared at the apparatus, determined to make it mine. I wasn't going to lose, not after I'd come this far.

I licked my bottom lip, then stepped into a roundoff back handspring, then into a double twisting double back. Fists pulled tight to my chest as I rotated backwards, double twisting at the same time, I spotted for the ground.

My feet landed together, my stance steady as I raised my arms and stuck my dismount. A massive smile filled my face. I held my landing for a moment longer and then turned and raised my arms to the judges to salute.

It was the longest ninety seconds of my life.

I turned around and found Kova's thrilled face immediately. I skipped over to him quickly and threw my arms around his shoulders as he caught me from the steps. He pulled me into a swift embrace then released me.

"Excellent dismount and routine."

My eyes narrowed. "Aside from the slip, you mean."

Kova smirked but he didn't get a chance to respond as my teammates came over to congratulate me with hugs. We were all smiles and hopeful eyes. My score went up pretty quickly and the crowd yelled with enthusiasm. I gasped and my brows shot up. A shot of electricity zipped down my spine as I stared up at the television screen with my name next to the flag.

It was my first Olympic score, and it wasn't bad.

The two other gymnasts from my team took their turns. Each time one finished, we congratulated her, praising her and lifting her spirit regardless if she needed it or not. It brought morale to our small group and helped quiet our loud thoughts. We we're panicking on the inside and going through the same thing together, we just didn't talk about it.

One gymnast from my team had more balance checks than I had, while the other had a near perfect score. Both had high scores in difficulty, which made a difference. Along with my score and after the first rotation, Team USA was currently in second place, a tenth of a point from being in third.

chapter 32

"BEAM WAS JUST A WARM-UP. NOW YOU GET TO SHOW THE PEOPLE one of the reasons why you are here," Kova said. "The Amanar." Vault.

I smiled proudly. I was one of the few who attempted this skill. I'd worked hard to perfect it.

"Remember," he continued, lifting one arm to demonstrate, "when you block"—he arched his chest and tapped it—"get to the front and middle of the table to gain proper flight with a vertical takeoff."

I listened closely as I put on my wrist guards then flexed my wrists and fingers. The block was going to hurt. For the most part, my elbow had healed from the dislocation. It was still tender here and there, but not all that bad. I was careful during qualifications, but I knew after this event it was going to be sore. All my power was going into my block that required straight arms and a strong pop throughout the arm. I was going to put everything I had into this block.

"Strong run, low and long, we want power when you take off."

"Got it."

I did. I had it. I imagined myself doing exactly what he said.

I was the last to take my turn for this rotation. The other athletes from my team had competed already with USA dropping to third, just a fraction of a point that separated us from second. It wasn't due to my teammates, though; they hadn't made severe mistakes. It was quite the opposite, actually, and they'd done very well. The other countries were just better in that rotation. Plain and simple.

I didn't want to let my hope slip, so I stayed blindly optimistic. My vault would be the deciding factor if we'd go up to second or stay in third. I was confident enough to carry my team to second.

I pulled back the Velcro to loosen it for a moment so my hands could breathe. I woke this morning to swollen wrists but ignored them. I could crumple when I got back to the States.

Not today, kidney disease, not today.

"Go chalk up," Kova said. "I will adjust the springboard."

"See you on the flip side."

I turned around to walk in the opposite direction but halted when I heard Kova laugh under his breath. I glanced over my shoulder and saw that he was already watching me with genuine pride in his eyes. His hands were propped on his hips and his expression radiated with content. He was looking at me.

My lips twitched. Turning back around, I walked to the end of the runway. I bounced lightly on my toes and shook out my fingers, my head bobbed from side to side. I refused to look into the stands and only kept my eyes on the vault and my coach. Bring on the tunnel vision. My fingers felt a little numb, so I re-tightened my brace. I swung my arms around in circles and shook my legs out. The green light was given, and I took a deep breath.

This was it.

Exhaling, I drowned out the sound again and pretended I was the only person in the room. I looked down and double checked I was standing eighty-seven feet back. I lifted my right arm to salute the judges then looked only at the vault and exhaled again. My heart was pumping so fast it was all I could hear. I had one chance to stick this dismount and only a few seconds left to complete it as perfectly as I could. I stomped my feet in the chalk once more, then tapped one pointed toe in front of me and lifted my arms in front of me.

Inhale, exhale.

Rising up on my toes, I licked my lips and swallowed. I leaned forward and drew in a lungful of air, then took off running as fast as my legs could take me. The room grew eerily quiet as I neared the apparatus, the cool air kissed over my skin.

Kova's last-minute suggestions played back in my mind. I heard his voice and applied what he said. My body moved of its own accord the moment my feet slammed into the springboard, rotating back onto the horse. Chest arched and hips flat, my legs were glued together as I blocked the hardest I possibly could manage, grunting from the impact. I took flight and reached as high as I could for maximum height and began twisting while I rotated two back lay-outs at the same time. After thousands of hours of practicing this skill, my body could do it on its own. I stayed tight and timed the right millisecond to open up, praying I got it right.

Core muscles tight, I opened my arms as my tiptoes touched the landing mat. Knees bent slightly for impact so I didn't hyperextend them, I stuck my landing perfectly and raised my arms in the air, holding my position to prove no hop was coming next.

The crowd exploded and a huge smile spread across my lips. I was so ecstatic that I almost started to laugh. I saluted the judges once more then turned and spotted Coach Elena in the stands behind a wall where the Olympic coaches were, right behind where Team USA was currently sitting. She was pumping her fist and shouting her happiness and showing the first smile I'd ever seen her give me.

My cheeks burned with joy as I made my way down the stairs into Kova's bear hug. He kissed my temple and said a slew of things in Russian that I assumed were praises before putting me on my feet. My teammates rushed over, squeezing hugs and cheers and clapping from all around. They were already dressed in their sweats to rotate.

Glancing over my shoulder, I turned around waiting for my score when I spotted Kova standing on his tiptoes talking to Coach Elena who was bent over the railing. She looked my way as she spoke to Kova, who nodded his head in return. He tapped the railing twice with his palm and pushed off, walking back toward me with determination. Before I could ask him anything, my score was up.

My jaw dropped in total shock. Not only was it nearly perfect, I had the highest scored vault of the competition so far. Only two tenths away from perfection. I'd take it.

I was still in shock when the girls gave me a group hug, springing on their toes. Gymnastics was an individual sport as much as it was a team sport.

Giggling, I covered my mouth with my hands and shot a glance around the room. Home flags waved though the air, faces were painted various colors, and signs raised above heads to show support for a sport that easily created so much doubt. It was my first real time looking at the beaming faces who'd traveled across the world to be here. I took it all in, appreciation invigorating my heart. I still couldn't believe I had made it to the Olympics.

Since I really wanted to compete in the all-around tomorrow, I had to compete on vault twice today. One for the team, the other to qualify for the all-around.

"Number one, Ria," Kova whispered, patting my shoulder after I executed my second vault and finished with nearly an identical score. "Get your bag and let us go to floor."

I grinned. I was first in vault by a large margin. A few steps and I was grabbing my duffle and quickly speeding up my pace. Coach Elena was hanging over the ledge and put her hand out when she saw I was coming her way. I smiled and rushed over to her, slapping her palm with a high five.

"Excellent job, well done," she said, her words stiff through her Ukrainian accent.

This was the best day of my life. I wondered if I'd ever feel anything like this again one day.

Still trying to catch my breath, I skipped over the black wires on the floor and met up with my team that was now on floor. I dropped my bag, and Kova squatted next to me. He leaned over and unzipped it, rummaging through it for my sports tape. He pulled it out and I turned toward him to give him my ankle.

"How is your foot?"

I thought about his question for a minute. "It's fine. Nothing I can't handle for a few more days."

He smiled but was looking at my foot as he taped my ankle. Once he was done, he ran his hand over the kinesis tape on my calf and Achilles. He nodded to himself, pleased. He was checking to make sure it was still on good.

"You are incredible to watch. The crowd loves you."

My cheeks blushed. I playfully rolled my eyes. "They love everyone, Kova."

"True, but they are much louder for you."

"You're just saying that."

"No. I am not. They see what I see."

My teeth dug into my bottom lip. Kova stood up, and I asked, "And what do you see?"

He studied me for a moment, then placed his hand out to help me up. His jaw flexed, my gaze fixed on his full, kissable lips.

"I will tell you tomorrow night." My brows furrowed, waiting for him to explain. "Tomorrow night, Adrianna. Now go warm up. Elena altered a tumbling pass."

Nodding, I squinted at him as I walked up the steps to the blue carpeted floor. I had questions, but I didn't want the thoughts to be stuck in my head for the rest of the day, so I shut them out and placed the questions in a drawer for tomorrow.

Each team was given a specific number of minutes to warm-up with tumbling passes. I stepped closer to the corner and looked ahead for Kova who was standing in the opposite corner ready to spot me.

He looked both ways then waved his fingers for me to come.

I turned over my first tumbling pass with Kova spotting right next to me. He halted my body with the palm of his hand so I didn't over rotate.

"Good. Delay the twist for another second and a half the next time," he said, and I nodded.

This was another last-minute change from Elena. I only knew this because I'd had the same passes for almost a year. They were just a little more difficult, especially on my endurance and lack of kidney function. I tried to remain calm as I drew air into my lungs, but they were so tight that it caused me to breathe harder. I stomped in chalk and powdered some on my palms. Kova reached the other corner and it was my turn again. I waited, watching his eyes, then he turned to me and waved.

I swallowed back my nerves and sprinted halfway across the floor. I hurdled into a front handspring, flipping over and punching my feet together into the floor to rebound into a hand-free roundoff, then finally double twisting backwards to land. My feet pounded into the spring floor and I felt the impact grind down my spine. Kova was right there to catch my chest from leaning forward too much. A gush of air rushed from me and I started coughing.

"Are you okay?" he asked, a slight shadow of concern in his eyes.

"I'm fine," I said out of breath. I winced and grabbed the inside of my elbow. I knew vault was going to make it hurt. "I'm just a little out of breath. I'll be good."

Kova's eyes were fixated on mine. I shook my arm out like it didn't faze me, but the truth was, there was a burning pain shooting up my arm. "Okay, because you will need to add a front tuck to the end of the pass for bonus. You will also switch your first tumbling pass."

This time I returned the concerned look. He was adding a bonus front flip and changing my tumbling pass. I waited for him to tell me which new tumbling pass I would do.

"Coach Elena believes that after she watched the other countries perform, if we increase our difficulty right now, it could push us to first."

chapter 33

THE FOUR OF US STOOD IN A CIRCLE WITH OUR HANDS IN THE MIDDLE again.

Each coach told us what to do and where we needed to make small tweaks to our routines. Some coaches even suggested pointers to the others. We knew the risks involved with a last-minute change even though we were still prepared if it came to this. Stepping out of bounds, twisting an ankle, over rotating. Anything was possible if your body is out of sync for even a millisecond. We came together and discussed what we had to do in order to take gold.

"Ready, girlies," the smallest one said with the brightest eyes. She sounded like she still hadn't reached puberty even though she was fifteen. "On the count of three."

"One... Two... Three."

"Phenomenal Four!"

We split up and I stood to the side, cheering on my teammate. I was third to go in this rotation.

The music started and I watched as she began, holding my breath when she executed her first tumbling pass like it was second nature to her. I could breathe.

There was something about seeing someone else do a trick first that brought a sense of relief to me. Now I knew I could do it too. Seeing her skip and leap across the floor to the other corner and then complete another extremely difficult tumbling pass, one that even I couldn't do, made me feel even better the second time. I was eager to get out there and perform.

"Is it true?" one of my teammates asked. "Do you really need a kidney?"

I blinked, confused for a moment until I remembered that the world knew about my secret now.

I nodded hesitantly. "It's true. After the Games are over, I'm on a flight back home to start dialysis immediately."

Her eyes softened, but not with pity like I expected. There was a sparkle of admiration that caught me by surprise. My head tilted to the side.

"Wow," she whispered. "You're, like, really tough."

My cheeks warmed and I laughed, feeling slightly embarrassed. "I wouldn't say I'm tough, just hardheaded."

"Do you hurt? Like are you in pain now? You don't look like you are."

"Not really right this minute, but once I sit down and unwind is when I'll start to feel the side effects. Everything tenses up and the pain sets in. It makes me feel like I'm an eighty-seven-year-old and strips me of me. Doing gymnastics numbs that feeling. It makes me feel like nothing is wrong with me."

She stared at me for a long minute like she was trying to figure me out. "When I heard the news, I didn't believe it. I honestly thought it was a hoax to drive attention. There was no way, not after I saw how hard you trained at camp with everyone. And then seeing you here? I still didn't believe it even though I'd read about it numerous times. Sorry if I'm being rude, but I had to ask. You just seem so…normal."

I am normal, I wanted to say.

I wasn't sure whether to smile or not, and that was because I wasn't sure how to feel. She wasn't pitying me, she wasn't being cruel about my illness, she was genuinely curious and somewhat in awe. It was kind of a…normal conversation.

I glanced at my chalky toes and allowed the smile I wore to hide the imperfections and sins of my personal life tug into a real one. I looked back at her.

"You're not being rude. I was just caught by surprise is all. I've kept it a secret for what felt like forever and then suddenly everyone knows overnight."

Her eyes widened. "Yeah, I can see that now." She began to frown.

"Don't feel bad," I said, trying to reassure her. "Really, I don't mind."

"You seemed out of breath when we were practicing earlier."

My cheeks warmed again. "I was. The shortness of breath is daily for me and kind of annoying. I'm missing like seventy percent of my kidney function which means I'm depleting all my stored energy and oxygen at a much quicker rate. Sometimes it's hard for me to catch my breath when I'm in the zone, my chest gets all tight and sometimes I get nervous thinking I'm going to have a panic attack from it."

She stared at me, a little disturbed. I averted my gaze to the floor where a gymnast was completing her final pass. "Well, that escalated quickly." We both laughed. "As you can see, I don't talk to people a lot about this."

I was so awkward about it. I'd have to work on my rambling if I was going to respond to questions from others.

"It's all good in the neighborhood."

"When I crash tonight in the room with a pillow over my head, don't worry. I can breathe just fine, so don't pick it up. I'll be recharged by tomorrow, well, ah…" I hesitated. "If I make it that far."

She gave me the thumbs up and smiled. "Done. And you totally are, at least for vault anyway."

The classical music we all performed to ended with a round of applause.

"Wish me luck." She smiled over her shoulder.

"Good luck," I said enthusiastically.

Just before her routine ended, Kova strode over to me. His arms were crossed in front of his chest as he watched. She'd completed her last-minute adjustments with ease and perfection too. I was next.

"Excited to watch me?" I asked, the implication was obvious. I was in a really good mood.

Kova tried not to look at me, but I could tell it was a challenge by the squint in his eye. I knew Kova liked to watch me perform on the floor. He dropped his arms behind his back and grabbed his wrist.

"You think changing the tumbling passes will really help?"

He wavered back and forth on his toes and heels. "I do. USA is very close to being first. We may not make it there in this rotation, but with everyone's upgraded skills, I believe we will in the last event." He paused for a moment, then lifted one shoulder. "Well, I am sure we all here believe that," he said more to himself.

I cracked my knuckles. The floor music ended and my heart beat spiked. Butterflies swirled in my stomach and I inhaled slowly. I loved floor, but it'd always caused me a little trepidation. There were many risks involved in doing gymnastics, but I didn't really ever feel like I could become paralyzed on the other events as easily as I could with floor.

"This is for you, Kova," I said, and stepped up the stairs to the floor. I saluted the judges then walked to the center of the floor, taking my stance. I positioned my arms like a delicate swan out to my sides and exhaled before I bent over and dropped my head dramatically.

Five seconds later, I began. I lost myself in my element, flouncing from one corner to the next in a sequence of whimsical leaps and delicate jumps. There was no faking the smile on my face—I truly loved performing on the floor. I danced the way I felt, so alive and free. As I made my way to the corner for my first tumbling pass, I took a deep breath and turned around, counting the music in my head. My heels met the edge of the tape and I brought my hands down and rose up on my toes. With my last-minute change, Kova stood in the corner that I was running to simply for peace of mind.

I turned over my roundoff, punching my feet out of the wide back hand-spring and set the first flip, rotating in a snug twist. I decided midair I wasn't going to add the bonus leap like Coach Elena wanted.

Spotting the ground, I landed with the force of ten times my weight into a graceful lunge and smiled from ear to ear. Or, as Kova had once put it, "Become a gentle ripple in the ocean when you lunge." I'd made fun of him for that one.

My arms spread out as I danced to the next corner like a feather billowing through the air, my toes hardly touching the floor. I could see Kova from the corner of my eye make his way to the opposite corner to spot me again. It was silly, if I really thought about it. The comfort of a coach triggered bravery for the athlete to attempt something outright intimidating. A lot of gymnasts chose to have their coach nearby. It was the psychological part of the sport. Kova couldn't step onto the floor, but just knowing he was there made all the difference.

Kova dipped his chin once. I counted the music beats in my head and hur-dled into the center of the floor to do the front flipping tumbling pass I warmed up earlier. Forward flipping was more terrifying for me, not to mention, exhaust-ing. It took a lot of energy out of me. I stepped into a front handspring and dug deep. I pushed away any type of mental and physical fatigue and ran on auto-pilot, releasing every ounce of energy I had left in me. I knew this series of flips were worth more if executed properly. It was why I didn't do the bonus jump a few seconds ago. I wanted to conserve my energy for this tumbling pass.

My figure breezed through the air, defying gravity with completely straight body twists every three seconds until I reached the corner. I paid attention to the tightness of my muscles and centered my hips in rotation. Feet punching the ground in the blue spring floor, I immediately rebounded with the bonus jump and then stepped into another front handspring without taking a breath and into a roundoff, a full twisting layout, and then flipped to the other corner in a series of back handsprings to complete a double layout.

Rippling like a wave, I smiled and let out a huge gush of air as my fingers fluttered for effect. I could faintly hear the crowd clapping and cheering, but I wasn't sure for who. My lunge was completed with finesse and ease and then I was skipping around the floor until my last tumbling pass came. It was a simple one, a double twisting double back.

Counting down the beats, I drew in a breath and leaped to the center of the floor to finish my floor routine with a flare from the ground, my body contorted like a pretzel. My heart was racing so hard my chest physically hurt.

As the music came to an end. I exhaled and held my position, then I was standing up to salute the judges twice.

Panting, I spun around and clapped my hands excitedly as I exited the floor.

Coach Elena was waving her flag in the air. Her excitement was contagious and I found myself smiling in return. Guess she wasn't too mad I skipped out on the extra points. All those around her watched her cheer with the crowd, her pride obvious. Floor was always so much fun to watch.

I stepped down right into Kova's arms and pulled my feet up behind me. The smell of his cologne lured me closer to his neck. I wished I could give him a little kiss on the lips to the ending of a great routine. I'd performed my heart out for him and I could tell by the way his fingers pressed into me that he was indebted by the gesture. He hugged me tight to him as he took a few steps. He said something in my ear, but I didn't catch it.

Kova released me and my teammates came running. As much as I loved training at World Cup, it would've been nice to have camaraderie like this when we competed together. The girls got dressed to rotate to the final event, but my body was too warm to put clothes on just yet.

My breathing labored a bit. I took huge breaths when I knew I shouldn't because I just couldn't help myself. I paced the floor waiting for my score while holding my neck. Time always slowed waiting for the numbers to populate. Inhaling, I could feel the low-pitched wheezing sounds in my chest as I struggled to pull air into my lungs.

I stared at the screen and I didn't blink. Goose bumps broke out over my body as the black, bold letters finally appeared.

My lips parted. I held first place for vault, and now I was in third highest overall for floor too. Now I had medals for two of the four events.

A sated smile split across my face. Now that I had the third highest floor score of the entire meet, Team USA was only five tenths of a point away from gold.

Easy peasy.

Maybe Kova had been telling me the truth all this time. Maybe I do work really well under pressure.

chapter 34

ONCE WE ROTATED, I SAT DOWN ON THE FLOOR TO REMOVE THE TAPE from my ankles just as Kova squatted in front of me.

He didn't speak. He was waiting to wrap my wrists for me. After I balled up the tape from my ankles and dropped it into my bag, I glanced down at my hands and my brows furrowed. Kova reached for my fingers and turned my wrists over. He inspected them the way I had. He pressed gently and flexed a digit back. They were much more swollen than normal, and my fingers were puffy. This could've easily been from how much of an impact my bones took today, though.

I took my hands back and shook them out. I looked ahead, acting like it was normal, then gave Kova my wrists again with steadiness this time.

Kova ripped a piece of tape with his teeth. I asked, "What did you say to me when I got off the floor? I didn't catch it."

He was quiet for a moment. Kova didn't raise his head to look at me, he just kept winding fresh white tape around my wrists.

"What did you say?" I asked again, leaning closer to him.

"Nothing."

"Yes, you did. I heard you."

His nostrils flared. "It was nothing."

Now wasn't the time to push, but I had another idea. "What's tomorrow night?" I whispered.

"Tomorrow night," he said, more so under his breath, "is when you and I are going to be alone to finally talk."

Somewhat accepting of that response, I glanced around wondering how he was going to pull that off with my family here.

I shelved that thought for later. I was starting to get a headache from everything I'd been shelving lately.

This was the final rotation, and then we'd know if we got back what we put in. We were holding the silver, and as much as I wanted gold, I was still very pleased with second place.

"I can't believe it's almost over," I said, wonderment in my tone.

Kova's lips twitched. "It goes by fast. All that time and work for one day."

"Yeah."

He wrapped my palms up next. "How are you feeling otherwise?"

"Great," I said, and shrugged. "I'm really great."

I *was* really great, and happy.

I drew the chalky air into my lungs for it to revive me one last time. Kova finally lifted his eyes to mine. My thoughts were quickly forgotten when I caught view of his smile. His lips were pressed together and there was a flirtatious glow that surrounded him. I found myself giggling just as a photographer took a picture of us. There was news media everywhere we turned, but they weren't allowed to interview us or call our names. All they could do was video record and take photos.

"Why are you laughing at me?" I asked.

Kova shook his head. "The way you said that, I am not sure what I found so funny. Maybe it was the sound of your voice." He paused, then said, "Great. I'm really great," the way it sounded to him, and I erupted with laughter. "You did not respond like I expected."

My smile widened. "Oh, and how's that? Like I'm going to talk about how stressed I am? We both know that. How my nerves are totally shot and I can't stop shaking on the inside. I don't want to be a broken record today."

He studied me, then he stood and held his palm out. I pulled on my cotton wrist wraps and Kova guided the grips to my ring finger and middle finger, slipping them through the little holes.

"Everyone is going to be watching you," he said, engaging in a conversation.

I was the last one to compete on the team, with my routine being the highest in difficulty. Once my score was added into the team's final score, we'd know what place we'd finish in, but that didn't mean it was the medal we'd receive. If we did.

"I know," I said softly.

"You should be proud of what you accomplished to get here, and that your routine is the hardest one here." He nodded and spoke with his lips hardly moving. "The others who competed before you had either the same starting score as you, or were close to it. From the looks of it, the one who was in the lead, her routine was adjusted at the last minute, or she lost the difficulty points during execution. Which means, you are a full point ahead of her."

My eyes lifted to his.

"I could take the lead in bars."

Kova's hands stilled. We both understood the magnitude of this moment and didn't look away. My chest housed a wild frenzy of heartbeats at this realization. I couldn't contain the smile that started spreading on my face.

I licked my chapped lips. "I can do it. I know I can."

Kova moved onto my other hand. "I do not want you to think when you are out there. I just want you to let your body take over—it knows what to do, trust it. Do not overthink it. We will do our standard warm-up like always."

I glanced around his body. The other girls were warming up with their coaches. We would be up soon.

"Okay. Okay. Okay. I got this."

He looked into my wide eyes. "If you secure this event, you will be headed into the all-around tomorrow. Too many mistakes on beam from gymnasts after you that you are surprisingly still in the running for a spot tomorrow. Between vault and floor, I have a feeling bars is going to be another medal for you."

My brows shot up. "What makes you so sure?"

Some of the gymnasts were already granted entry based on other qualifying requirements that I hadn't been able to meet at previous meets. That made the entry margin even smaller for me.

"I have been keeping track. I firmly believe you will secure a spot."

It was all Kova said. Like he was so sure of it and I had to accept what he said.

I was at a loss for words and smiled to myself. I was so giddy inside I couldn't stop smiling. Shrugging, I said, "Sweet."

After my grips were on and tightened, Kova and I warmed up on bars, loosely running through the routine and practicing some release skills. A few handstands and pirouettes, then my dismount. A couple of quick pointers, Kova reminded me not to overthink and just let my body do what it was made to.

"Let gymnastics live with you," he whispered from behind me.

I didn't move. I just nodded my head. We both knew what those words meant.

Be still my sick heart and listen to him already.

Within five minutes, I was standing in front of the low bar preparing to mount it. This would be the last time I would compete wearing a red, white, and blue leotard, and the final time I'd compete at the Olympics. Kova was right—I was going to let gymnastics live with me in my final performance.

Drawing in a deep breath, I looked over at Kova who stood to the side of the apparatus prepared to step in and spot me like we'd agreed. I was the last one to compete now. Team USA was teetering back and forth between gold and silver, only a tenth of a point away from slipping into silver again. I would either lead us to victory or we'd become first place loser, as Kova had put it once and Danilo had reiterated the last time I was at World Cup.

Funny how I didn't feel like a first place loser anymore like I once had. Not after the struggle I was forced to bear this past year.

"You got this," Kova said, focusing solely on me. "Do not think, just feel," he said, using his hands.

I exhaled and felt the crowd's enthusiasm around me. I used what they were giving as my reason to be strong and help my team take home gold. I had this.

My teammates cheered my name from the sidelines where they stood, just like we had for each one before me. I chalked up one final time on my palms, thighs and feet, and then, I saluted the judges.

One minute and thirty seconds, and it would all be over.

My hands reached for the low bar, my hips swinging forward into a kip cast to a handstand. I stuck it for a second with my hips flat and toes pointed, then swung down into a back hip circle straight to a handstand again. I did this once more then brought my body down and around the bar for a second time. At the angle I'd been trained to release the bar, I did. The bar ricocheted as I reached for the high bar and swung up to a handstand. Switching my grip so it faced backwards for added difficulty points, I fell forward into a full giant and closed my eyes, feeling the wind against my cheeks and tasting the chalk in the air. I knew Kova would be standing right to the side ready to spot as I completed another pirouette holding my body stone still.

I swung down into a giant to gain momentum as Kova stepped closer. Tapping at the right timing, I hollowed out my chest and swung my body around, bringing my hips parallel to the bar and then whipping them as hard as I could into the air as I released the bar at the same time to fly backwards and over it in a pike position. Kova's arms went up as my body came down. I gripped the bar with all my might and moved swiftly into another release skill that we'd worked hard on. Nothing mattered but this routine and the way I felt as I soared through the air from bar to bar like a snowflake delicately drifting in the wind. My heart was on display, my undying love for bars and this sport, it was all there as I performed my routine. I did a total of three releases back-to-back when Kova stepped down and let me do my thing for a couple of seconds until he was standing there again, this time gearing up for my dismount.

I took a quick breath. This was it.

Licking my lips, I spotted the landing mat that had clouds of chalk on it.

My mind went back to my first day at World Cup.

To the excitement and hunger for this moment.

To the pain.

To the anger.

To the betrayal.

It all lead to right now.

My fingers tightened around the bar. Stuck handstands with flat hips and pointed toes, I could vaguely hear the exploding crowd as I circled the bar two and a half times gearing up for my dismount.

And then…

I let go.

chapter 35

THE SUDDEN SILENCE FROM THE CROWD WAS THRILLING. IT WAS AS if they held their breath with me. Slowly, like in slow motion, they came into view with every rotation and twist. They stood motionless as I squeezed my body and completed my last half twist. My heart spiraled as I descended and spotted the ground.

Feet together and knees slightly bent, I extended my arms in front of me and closed my eyes, knowing immediately how this would end.

Chalk floated up around my ankles as I squeezed every muscle to stick my dismount. The crowd erupted, breaking the quiet. I opened my eyes and raised my arms to salute the judges twice. My chest rose into the air as I dragged in a ragged breath, and I turned toward my team with a massive smile splayed across my face.

I knew in my heart that we had done it.

All three girls were waiting for me, jumping and chanting as I ran toward them with open arms. I was enveloped in group hugs and happy tears.

The four of us spoke at the same time, and we giggled.

"Do you think it's enough?"

"I'm going to be sick."

"What's taking so long?"

Our questions and worries flew out of our mouths. We were currently holding first, but only by a thread. If I was given the full points for difficulty, my score would make it almost impossible for another team to beat us.

Tears streamed down my cheeks, and I held my breath, waiting, praying that we wouldn't get bumped to second. My score lit up the screen and my jaw dropped. Shock rendered me immobile.

I couldn't move. I was stunned, unable to do anything but stare and feel the chills wrack my arms. The fans exploded in a wild frenzy, and that got me in motion. My teammates and I hugged each other as happy tears fell down our cheeks. We were in a state of disbelief and total shock. Of course, we'd hoped and dreamed, but never imagined it would actually happen. It was absolute mania where we stood. The screen changed to show the current standings.

I blinked, and blinked, and blinked.

My jaw plummeted to the floor.

Team USA was in first place by a full three points now.

I looked around frantically, unable to control the abundance of feeling rushing through me. Happiness. Disbelief. Shock. My heart was in my throat. Cameras were everywhere. Their flashes reminded me of fireworks as excitement in the arena spread. There were still gymnasts who hadn't competed yet. The remaining teams were now fighting for silver and bronze, and they were aware of it. No team would be able to take the gold from USA.

I always thought the girls looked a little maniacal on television when they realized they'd won. Now I got it. This moment was worth every ounce of heartache I'd gone through. Whether it was from those I loved or due to my health, it was worth it.

I'd wanted this my whole life.

Gold. Team USA would win gold. *I* would win gold.

I held my chest. This wasn't real. It was too good to be true. I tried to catch my breath and slow down my heartbeat when someone pulled me into a hug.

I didn't have to guess who it was. I knew the moment his hand touched me.

A smile spread across my lips. I threw my arms around his shoulders and jumped into him. My feet kicked up behind me as he snuggled me to his chest and hugged me tight. His happiness surrounded me.

Being in Kova's arms while Team USA took home gold was how it was meant to be.

My arms tightened around his shoulders, and my heart pounded so hard I was sure he could feel it against his chest. No one thought I'd make it this far, but he did. Reluctant at first, Kova was the only one who thought I had a fighting chance if I put the work into it. And I had.

My tears continued to flow as I cried in the curve of his shoulder. This moment was more than just winning gold.

"Congratulations, Adrianna," Kova whispered in my ear.

I clenched my eyes shut. Normally I'd step from his arms so bystanders didn't give us nosy stares, but I didn't care who saw us this time. This was something I never wanted to forget. I wanted to remember how this moment felt for me, Kova, and us. Plus, we were at the freaking Olympics! No one was going to say anything, especially when we looked just like other coaches and gymnasts.

"Is it real?" My voice shook as I asked. I didn't want to look and see that I'd made it up in my head.

Kova chuckled under his breath. "It is real, *Malysh*. Team gold, and you move onto the all-around tomorrow with the highest vault and bars scores of the Olympics. I think you will take floor too tomorrow."

My head popped up and I looked at him. I probably looked a little crazy with how wide my eyes were.

All I could do was respond with a dropped jaw.

Kova nodded, his gaze falling to my mouth then back to my eyes. He released me, but neither one of us moved. We were so close we were still touching.

"You did it," he said. There was a soft smile behind his eyes. "Even when the world was against you, you showed them how resilient you are. That is bravery not many are granted with. It is one of the things I love about you, you know. You are steadfast in the pursuit of your dream. You are so much stronger than you realize. Your willpower makes me look weak, but I aspire to have the heart and drive you do one day. I hope you are proud of what you have accomplished. I know I am."

I blushed. Kova made me sound like such a strong person, but I was only as strong as those I surrounded myself with. He was my strength. He was the reason I pushed myself so hard. He pushed me to push myself because he knew I could handle it. He loved the adrenaline and so did I. He evoked motivation in me and made me want to be a better gymnast and human. I had learned a lot from him in these few years I'd been at World Cup, and probably even more than I realized until years from now when I look back on my experience.

Kova made me the best version of me, the elite gymnast I only ever wanted to be. He dedicated countless hours of selflessness and coaching because he believed in me.

"Where do you think I learned it from? It's a reflection of you."

His eyes softened. "Get dressed. We have to go."

Nodding, I turned around and went to my duffle bag. I quickly pulled on my sweat suit and strung my bag over my shoulder. I sped up to rejoin my team, and Coach Elena and the entire U.S. Olympic Committee held their hands out over the railing again. I slapped them all with a giant smile on my face, grateful that they also believed in me enough to give me this chance.

Most days I was my own worst enemy because I knew what I was capable of in my heart. When I didn't meet my own expectations, I beat myself up. It was an incredible feeling to see that I had people supporting me all along.

"In third place, winning the bronze medal…"

The crowd gave a vivacious round of applause. Third place at the Olympics was a huge accomplishment, but I knew those girls felt defeated inside and my heart cried out to them.

Second place was announced next, and my pulse skyrocketed as I awaited our turn. My knees shook and happy tears climbed my eyes for the millionth time. I was an emotional mess. Every time I dried my tears they started right back up.

"Ladies and gentlemen," the announcer said, his voice booming through the speakers, "please welcome your Olympic gold medalists, Team USA."

I stepped up onto the center platform with my team and waved toward the crowd. Chants of "USA! USA!" came from the stands. My jaw trembled as an abundance of happiness filled me. I couldn't stop smiling.

A woman came forward holding an open box with four shiny gold medals. They lay flat with the multi-colored ribbon folded underneath. They were brighter close up and beautifully engraved with an image of Nike, the Greek goddess of victory. The woman was met by a member of the International Olympic Committee who reached for the first medal then draped it over my teammate's neck as the announcer called her name.

"Adrianna Rossi."

I sniffled when my name was announced next. The IOC member lifted a medal and I bent at my waist. Carefully, she adorned my neck with the surprisingly heavy accolade.

"Thank you," I whispered.

I straightened and stood tall, drawing in a deep breath and exhaling. Glancing down my stomach, I picked up the award and held it in my palm. I had the strongest urge to take a bite. It reminded me of a gold wrapped chocolate coin I got one Easter.

Of course, I didn't bite it. I'd do that in private.

I gave it a little toss to feel the weight in my hand. I'd given up so much of myself for this, and it was so worth it.

After the last medal was placed around my teammate's neck, another member of the Olympic committee came forward to hand us small bouquets custom to Greece. Bushy olive branches cupped the beautifully bloomed orange, red, and yellow flowers. I smiled down at the bouquet then bent my knees to receive the laurel wreath on the crown of my head. The interlocking olive branches represented victory, power, and glory. I was proud to wear it.

I searched for Kova, but he was lost in the sea of faces. Then the three flags representing the medaling countries rose high in the air, and "The Star-Spangled Banner" began to fill the room.

My eyes glistened at the sight of the flags. I was in awe. I couldn't tear my gaze away. This night was emotional on so many levels. Everything I'd worked hard for was all for this moment in time that would live with me for the rest of my life. Being in a room surrounded by hundreds of thousands of people who loved this sport just as much as I did was no better feeling in the world. These were my people.

I peered down at the medal again and held it closer wondering if I'd feel the same way if we hadn't medaled. I realized I would because it wasn't about winning. It was about the journey and the drive to achieve my dream. My determination had completely overtaken every molecule of air in my body, making the chase worthwhile.

A soft smile moved my lips. I wasn't going to lie to myself anymore. I was going to be open and honest with myself and accept what I couldn't change.

I looked up at the American flag and stared. I was proud of myself. I didn't feel like there was a crushing pressure on my chest anymore, or this need to improve myself all the time. There was freedom that came with this moment. I was free from the restraints of myself.

Standing underneath the gleaming lights, I felt different. Older, newer. On the mend. I felt that after today, I could take on anything my future held.

Gymnastics made me strong. It made me brave, and if I really let myself think about it, gymnastics prepared me for the next phase of my life by pushing me to fight for something I really wanted. It gave me strength.

I thought I'd be bursting with joy standing on this podium, but what I felt more than anything was a sense of relief.

I could breathe again.

As the anthem drew to an end, we raised our flowers in the air to give one final salute. I smiled as rainbow colored confetti shot from the high corners of the room and balloons fell upon us like fresh snow.

chapter 36

AFTER THE TEAM USA CELEBRATORY DINNER LAST NIGHT, I DIDN'T get to talk to my family for more than a few minutes before I was ushered to the village for therapy, then sent back to my room to decompress and prepare for today. I'd stuck to the same schedule of eating and meds, hoping to relive what I did yesterday.

Not even twenty-four hours later and it was a totally different sporting event.

Inhaling a deep breath, I looked down at the leotard I was allowed to design myself for this competition in preparation of making it this far. Every gymnast did. Over two thousand jade Swarovski crystals in several sizes were attached to the deep mahogany material in fiery flames, overlapping each other. It was a color I didn't typically wear.

Yesterday I was decorated in stars and stripes that represented independence and freedom. It took two years for that design to mature at the imagination of Coach Elena, all for one day of glory.

But today's leotard was by far my favorite for two reasons. The base was a color that complemented my dark red hair and sun-kissed dusting of freckles on the bridge of my nose. The green was for Kova's eyes, a color most redheads just so happened to wear too.

Intertwining colors. Strength in darkness.

I smoothed my hands down the front, my palms catching the three-dimensional stones. He didn't know what I'd done, and I wasn't sure if I was going to tell him.

I glanced at Kova standing next to me. He seemed focused. Almost too focused. My eyes raked down his body. He was dressed similarly to yesterday, only this time he wore a black polo shirt with his dress pants. The shirt strained around his biceps. I moved my eyes upward and found Kova still deep in thought.

I bit my lip, then said, "Where's my pep talk?"

He didn't hear me, so I gently backhanded his arm. He jumped and glanced at me with confusion.

"What is wrong with you?" he asked.

I almost laughed because he was genuinely confused. "Did you hear what I said? Any last-minute pointers?" I paused. Now I was worried. "Are you okay?"

He stuffed his hands into his pockets and turned his body toward me. "There is nothing wrong, I am sorry. I was focused on trying to read Coach Elena's lips. There are no last-minute pointers today."

I looked over at her. She was waving frantically, trying to get his attention. I tapped him and lifted my chin in her direction. He glanced her way and nodded, then held up one finger.

"How come you're not saying anything positive today?" Kova smiled at me, and I continued, "It's almost like tradition for us. I'm trying to recreate my past meets. I'm feeling a little superstitious I guess..."

Kova chuckled. "You are as far as you could possibly go. Today is about you, your talent, and your accomplishments, and being awarded for them." He paused, then smiled and said, "But if you want me to tell you what I am thinking, I will."

My cheeks bloomed with warmth. "I do."

"Do not beat yourself up tomorrow for any mistakes today. Of course, the goal is not to make any," he said, and my lips twisted. "But try to remember that you worked really hard to get here and this competition itself is a gift. You made your dream a reality, and you took it a step further. Not many people are able to say that. That is a beautiful thing to witness."

He didn't say that to appease me, Kova spoke from his heart. If it wasn't for his nostalgic tone, I might have thought otherwise. This was a big moment for us as coach and gymnast. He knew it, I knew it. I wouldn't return to World Cup, and once we arrived home, he wouldn't be my coach anymore.

I was unprepared for the sadness in his eyes. I acted on impulse and wrapped my arms around his shoulders. Kova reacted immediately and hugged me back just as a few flashes flickered around us. He dropped his face into the crook of my neck. His body was so warm pressed to mine. I didn't want it to end and the thought filled me with melancholy.

The bell chimed and we pulled back. The crowd bustled with excitement again and I felt it. I cleared my throat about to speak when Kova eyed me and said under his breath, "Tonight."

I nodded. I still didn't know what that meant. I just assumed I'd see him somehow.

Kova turned around and made a beeline for Coach Elena. They spoke for a moment. I glanced at the judges' table down the runway and powdered my palms then slipped on the wrist guards. The green light flashed, and I licked my lips and swallowed.

Stepping behind the white line, I asked myself what the one thing was that separated me from my competitors.

I had more to lose than them.

The all-around was a perfect example of how everything can change in the blink of an eye when it came to gymnastics. After the second rotation, I'd teetered between third and fourth place because of the balance beam. In the end, I'd secured the silver medal. I had been only five tenths of a point away from gold.

I smiled and told myself I wasn't allowed to be upset. I had so much fun that it was virtually impossible to be sad. I considered myself fortunate to be here.

Dressed in my Team USA sweat suit, I took it all in for the second time as I stood on the podium with Russia and China. Emotion consumed me when our flags were raised. The rich colors of my flag evoked a powerful reaction from me that was electrifying. The butterflies that had been swarming in my stomach the last two days were sprung from the restraints of my ribs and fluttered away. Quiet tears spilled down my cheeks. My heart was overloaded with feeling knowing I'd leave the Olympic Games with a handful of medals.

I glanced around. My eyes browsed over the faces who helped make this event possible. I was still in a state of disbelief and clutched the medal in my hand tighter when I saw him.

I held his stare, afraid to let go.

I had officially achieved my dream. Now I had a bigger battle to face.

chapter 37

"How'd you do it?" Dad asked, his jovial tone causing me to look up.

He had a crystal tumbler in one hand and Sophia's hand in his other.

I shrugged nonchalantly and couldn't help but smile. Gymnastics was all I'd ever known. It was like breathing to me. When I stepped onto the competition floor, my soul came alive and I felt like I was where I should be.

"Seriously. How do you do it?" Avery asked too.

"I don't know. Guess I was born to do it." I joked.

Dad was still looking at me. There wasn't any hardness surrounding his eyes and he didn't look like he was as stressed as he had been. He just looked... happy. Really happy.

"I'm in awe of you," Dad said. He couldn't stop smiling.

I blushed. "Stop looking at me, Dad."

He mocked confusion and I couldn't help but giggle. "What? I can't look at my daughter who won a bunch of medals at the Olympics? I was captivated watching you. Now I wish I'd attended all your meets."

I didn't want him to feel bad. "You were at the ones that mattered the most."

Sophia patted the top of his hand and he looked at her.

"I can't believe the village was boring," Avery said only for me to hear.

I turned my attention to her.

"It definitely wasn't as glamourous as I thought it would be." I told her how lackluster it was. "It was like a giant schoolyard and everyone was waiting for the bell to ring. I definitely didn't see or hear about any sex orgies that supposedly happen."

"I think that happens after they compete."

I mused over her response. "I guess, but we're asked to leave to allow the other athletes to prepare. I'm thinking it happens in a hotel and not there." Not that I was looking, but I was curious after all the rumors I'd heard.

"Let's take a selfie," Avery said, and held up her cell phone.

I was sitting next to Avery with Dad and Sophia across from us. Xavier was next to Dad, but he mostly kept his focus on his cell phone. We were at a round table in a private dining room for another night of celebrating Team USA. All coaches and family were invited. Everyone was decked out, ready to celebrate. The room was filled with people mingling, and happiness permeated the air, putting a permanent grin on my face from the moment I'd walked in.

Avery held her phone up high. We said, "besties," and smiled. She took a few more pictures and then we looked at them together. She posted one on social media with the hashtag "my best friend is cooler than yours." Then she posted another with the message, "A redhead's perfect accessory—a gold medal." It was a funny one of me trying to sink my teeth into the medal.

I glanced around searching for one person.

It didn't take long. My eyes found him immediately.

Kova was leaning his elbow on a highboy table talking to a woman. He took a small sip of what I presumed was vodka in his clear glass, and I watched him like I was thirsty. He nodded a few times before he let out a real laugh and a real smile. My eyes softened with longing. I hadn't seen that type of reaction from him in months.

God, he looked so damn delicious dressed in all black. His sleeves were rolled to just below his elbows and the top few buttons of his shirt were left undone. Matching dress pants and shoes, he looked like sin in the flesh. Kova was oozing sexuality. I'd watched as he moved across the room like a social butterfly for the last hour talking to people. He never once looked in my direction. I tried not to take it personally considering my dad was here, but we had just accomplished something huge together.

"What's wrong?" Avery asked.

I bit my lip. "I feel like Kova's acting strange."

"It's probably because your dad is here."

"Yeah, you're probably right, but still. I feel like he's purposely ignoring me. Something's off. I can feel it."

"I wouldn't worry too much right now. Things are hectic here. Don't read too much into it."

I nodded in agreement even though I didn't like the negative feeling churning in my stomach. "I still can't believe you're here," I said to her, grabbing her arm. I was so happy Avery was granted permission from her parents to attend the Olympics.

"I know. I was ready to sell my soul to fly here when your dad talked to mine and said he'd watch over me. It was smooth sailing after that." She finished with a cheeky smile.

I glanced around the table making sure my brother wasn't listening before asking, "Has it been strange being so close to Xavier?"

Avery shot a fleeting glance his way. She puckered her lips before she spoke. "Yes and no. I think I make it really difficult for him. Like one minute I'll catch him looking at me like he likes me again, and I'll smile a little at him. Then the next second he looks disgusted with me. It's a little unsettling but I remind myself he thinks I aborted his baby. It keeps me from getting mad and reacting."

My heart was sad hearing this. There wasn't one person who had caused the miscarriage, but they'd never see it that way. She felt responsible, but if Xavier knew the truth, he'd feel even more responsible than her. Their truth was a double-edged sword.

Her mouth opened, then closed. She frowned and wet her lips. "We stayed up talking last night until three in the morning."

My brows shot up. I swear Xavier had multiple personalities. "You're kidding me. What happened?"

She shrugged one shoulder. "Nothing happened, we just talked about the transplant surgery, actually."

That was all she said. Nothing more. Nothing less. I waited patiently until I couldn't take it anymore.

"Okay, you're going to make me drag it out of you, aren't you?"

A sly grin spread across Avery's face. She picked her head up and looked at me with round blue eyes.

"Tell me what happened," I urged.

When Avery blushed, it was so obvious. She was light-skinned and her cheeks turned into red apples.

"He asked me to come to his room. Of course, I went. I basically fucking sprinted there. I was shocked at first because he'd hardly said two words to me since we left the States. When I got to his room, he had the fake fireplace lit up on the screen and blankets on the floor in front of it." My brows creased. That was the last thing I'd expected. "I once told Xavier I loved sitting in front of the fire and listening to the crackling wood. He had his cell phone playing the wood burning sound. It was like a beacon calling me. I went right to the floor and laid down. He did too."

My lips parted and my brows angled deeper toward each other. I was puzzled and I was sure it showed. "Who knew he had a sweet side to him? I'm surprised he did that."

She blew out a huff and said, "Me too. He said he didn't get a chance to thank me for testing to see if I was a match for you. He seemed…indebted over it."

I pulled back. "My brother?"

"Yup." She nodded. "I swear he was on the verge of crying he was so happy that we matched up. He just kept thanking me over and over. He was really sweet, and he reminded me of the old Xavier." She paused and her voice lowered even more. "I miss him."

"At least you guys didn't fight." Her eyes rolled toward mine. "Oh, did I speak too soon?"

"Girl, yes. He insisted that he's going to take care of me the entire time I'm in recovery until I'm back to myself. I told him that wasn't necessary, that I didn't need him because I had family to help. We bickered about that for a solid minute. You know what he said? He yelled in my face that he's my family and only he's going to be allowed to take care of me." I frowned, my feelings torn over his behavior. "I wasn't sure whether to swoon or be turned off," Avery said, sounding torn herself.

I glanced across the table at Xavier, who was openly studying Avery. He couldn't tear his eyes from her. My head tilted to the side as I took in his appearance. Xavier rocked that pastel preppy style well, not giving a shit if he was wearing "girl colors," as Avery's twin brothers had put it many times to taunt him. His disheveled hair complemented his lax shirt and loose tie. Funny that he loved preppy clothes when he was anything but a prep boy. He was in trouble with the law often, defensive, abrasive. There was an underlying aura of danger that followed him. He was a walking hazard. All it took was the wrong look and he'd detonate. He'd be better suited in all black, not a soft salmon color. Yet, sitting across from me, Xavier looked at Avery like he was a man drowning in love over someone he'd never have.

"How did you guys leave off?" I asked carefully, looking back at her.

"He said he wanted to see me again tonight, but I told him that's a negative because I get to hang out with my bestie," she said with a beaming smile, her shoulders shifting from side to side. I had so much love for her.

"Have you guys seen each other every night since you got here?"

She peered down then chanced a guilty side-eye glance at me. "Maybe," she drew out shyly. I laughed. "We have, but only because in order for me to go anywhere, your dad makes Xavier come with me. It's *so* annoying. Last night was the first night I was alone with him, though, like in his room alone. My heart was racing the entire time. I couldn't believe he asked me to come over, let alone set up that fake fire."

I giggled, not surprised Dad had done that. "We're in a foreign country, what did you expect? You know my dad sees you as a daughter too."

She gave me a droll stare. "I felt like I had a bodyguard. He was on top of everything I did. I couldn't breathe without him questioning me."

I grinned. "You have no chance in the Olympic village with Xavier around."

"Fucking right, man."

This time I chuckled. I didn't think I'd ever understand those two. They either had something toxic together or something profound. There was no middle ground with them. Like I'd told Xavier that day in his pool house, they were similar to Kova and me.

Hesitantly, I asked, "Do you want to see him tonight?"

Avery lifted her gaze to mine, but I stopped her just seconds after our eyes locked. Her face was blank but her eyes gave her away.

My lips twitched. "I have an idea…"

chapter 38

I APPROACHED KOVA, WHO WAS FINALLY ALONE FOR THE FIRST TIME tonight. Throwing a quick glance over my shoulder to make sure Avery was still covering for me, I stopped in front of him. He looked up in surprise and quickly surveyed the room before turning his attention to me.

"Hey," I said, feeling my cheeks rush with blood.

Kova's eyes moved down the length of my body in a sensual sweep. I wore a crimson designer dress with gold glitter scattered throughout the slinky material and matching high heels that made me feel like a goddess. The dress and shoes were one of Avery's many outfits she'd packed for the trip. She had insisted I wear them tonight.

Kova's jaw flexed and his nostrils flared as he exhaled. I was pleased with the way he looked at me.

"You look beautiful," he said, but the compliment didn't reach his eyes.

"Thank you," I said, then I got right to the point since we didn't have much time. "So… You kept referring to tonight. Did you want to meet?"

"Ah, yes," he said, his jaw stiff as he swirled the ice in his glass. "I know you will not be returning to Cape Coral for a bit." He stared down at the ice avoiding my gaze. Kova kept his elbows locked to his sides and his stance unwelcoming. I wondered if he was worried about my dad seeing us. I almost regretted coming over here now. "We have a few things that were left unsaid that I feel need to be discussed. However, if you cannot get away for, say, thirty minutes, it is no problem."

I shook my head even though he wasn't looking at me. Why wouldn't he look at me? His standoffish attitude left me with this unbearable feeling I didn't want to acknowledge. I didn't like the sudden twisting of dread in my chest.

"Avery will cover for me. What's your room number?"

That got his attention. Kova glanced up to tell me what room he was staying in, but he was so disengaged with our conversation that I had to say something.

"What's wrong?"

He looked straight into my eyes. "Nothing at all. Just catching up with a few old friends."

I nodded slowly, not believing him. I couldn't shake the unsettling feeling under my skin.

The back of my neck prickled with heat. Kova didn't say anything more. I offered him a shaky smile, but he didn't return it. There was an awkwardness hanging in the air between us. All I could do was turn on my heels and walk away.

∽

I kept my head down as I walked toward Kova's hotel room. I couldn't shake the gnawing feeling in my stomach the closer I got to his door. My nerves were shot after the tense moment I'd had with him before I left the dinner. Kova hadn't looked my way for the rest of the night, and I had the strangest notion that he didn't want to see me.

Maybe it was all in my head and the paranoia was getting to me. We both were risking a lot to see each other. Longing filled me. I looked forward to the day when I didn't have to hide how I felt about him.

Avery had agreed to tell Xavier that I crashed early when she went to see him. She would mention the adrenaline wore off and I just wanted to sleep. It was the perfect cover, and it wasn't a lie. It was *exactly* how I felt. I was coming down from the high of being here, and I knew everything would start to settle in my bones soon.

Standing in front of Kova's hotel room, I looked down both sides of the hallway then hesitantly raised my fist to rap on the door. My heart pounded in fear of being seen walking into my coach's room after midnight alone.

The door opened immediately and I stepped inside. Before I could say a word, Kova grabbed my elbow and kicked the door shut with his foot. He pushed me up against the wall then pressed his body to mine. With one hand gripping my hip and the other angling my jaw up to his, Kova's body was fiery to the touch and seething with something a little darker under the surface. My lips parted and I gasped as his cool lips slanted over my needy ones. His tongue slipped into my mouth and I moaned at the connection, fisting his shirt, desperately needing more of him.

I most definitely was being paranoid earlier.

My palms slid up his chest and around to cup the back of his neck. I rolled my hips against his and felt my body come alive. I relished the feeling of how strong and powerful he felt while I was in his arms. I gripped his shoulders, feeling his muscles contract under my fingertips. Kova was like a caged animal that needed to be freed. And I loved it.

Skillful lips made my knees weak. Kova devoured me with a kiss he was more than eager to give. His passion engulfed me and I reveled in the way his mouth moved over mine. The man was a damned good kisser.

Kova's hand slipped over the small of my back. A shot of electricity shot up my spine. His erection pressed into me and I sighed into his mouth.

Cupping my butt, Kova lifted me up, and I wrapped my legs around his hips. A cool breeze blew across us and I noticed my panties were damp. His palm slid into my hair, and his fingers curled around a chunk of the locks and tugged near the root. My chest pressed into his and I groaned in the back of my throat.

I broke the kiss, needing to breathe. "Kova," I said after drawing in much needed air.

My lips were swollen. His hungry mouth found my neck. I shivered as chills danced around my entire body. Kova clenched my hair and tugged it harder, exposing more flesh for his tongue to lick a wet trail to my ear. His teeth nipped my tender skin and I gasped before a sigh rolled off my lips.

"I've missed this," I whispered.

I rolled my hips in a smooth, slow wave against his hard body, silently begging for more. His hold on me tightened, and his cock teased the top of my pussy as I arched my hips back. I melted inside. I loved when he had control over us like this and still felt like an animal under my touch. Kova lifted his gaze to meet mine. His eyes gleamed. He peered at me in awe.

Kova studied my mouth. His palm cupped my jaw as his callused thumb dragged across my lower lip. I slipped my tongue out and wrapped it around his thumb. I drew it into my mouth and bit down. Kova's nostrils flared. His body went rigid against mine. He pulled his thumb from my mouth, and my teeth cut into each crinkle of skin as he slipped out.

This intoxicating friction between us was too alluring, too dangerous. We hadn't been this close since the day we were ripped from each other. Now that we were alone, we were much more combustible than ever before.

"I wanted to do that the moment I saw you tonight in that red dress," he said, his voice raspy. "*Kravisyata.*"

Why did my chest ache hearing those words?

His hand shook as he smoothed my hair behind my ear. One more glance into my eyes, then Kova stepped back from the wall and walked us over to the bed. He lowered me down. I sat on my knees and adjusted my linen cornflower blue shorts and white, flowery chemise.

"I didn't think you saw me until I walked up to you."

I lowered my eyes, not wanting to look at him, because the truth was, the way he'd acted toward me in that room made me feel invisible. Kova had treated me like a stranger, not someone I'd made a baby with.

Two fingers tipped my chin up until I was forced to meet his intense stare. He exhaled and I caught the faint scent of vodka on his breath. I wondered if he could hear how hard my heart was working right now.

Kova ran his tongue over his bottom lip, his front teeth dragging over the plumpness. "All I ever see is you. Everywhere I look, I am reminded of you. I knew the moment you walked into the room. I just did not expect to see you the way I did. And, honestly, what did you expect? I could not talk to you. I definitely could not have acted like we were more than coach and gymnast."

"That's why you ignored me? You didn't look my way once." I was still a little bothered over that. "I didn't think you even thought about me. You acted like a stranger."

Kova snorted under his breath and backed away from the bed. He dragged his hands down his beautifully tormented face as he turned and gave me his back. My body instantly missed his warmth as he walked over to the round table in his room.

I climbed off the bed and stalked after him. He glanced at me and his expression shifted into a multitude of emotions. Right versus wrong. Want versus need. Sin and morals conflicted in the storm clouds of his eyes, and my brows furrowed. I didn't like what I saw.

Kova reached for his glass and downed the rest of its contents. I watched his throat work the clear liquid, the slender muscles and veins contracting with each pull. The ice clinked together and Kova all but threw the glass back on the table.

"I'm right, aren't I? You did ignore me like a stranger." When he didn't answer, I pushed my next question through my teeth. "How do you manage to do a complete one-eighty in the span of a couple of hours? How do we go from being this close"—I crossed my middle finger over my index finger—"to this?" I separated my fingers into a peace sign. "Explain to me why you decided to put space between us, because that's what you did when you started this whole 'let us ignore Adrianna now that Olympics are over' campaign three point five seconds after it ended," I said, mocking his English. "You acted like you didn't even know me."

I was getting myself worked up and I didn't want that. I wanted to remain in control of my emotions. Being this close to him yet feeling so far away completely blindsided me. I took a deep breath. Kova had ignored me, causing my past insecurities I'd fought so hard to ignore to come roaring back in full force. And he was lying about it.

"I did not ignore you, Adrianna," he said a little stilted.

I gawked. "Yes, you did. I don't understand why you acted like I was invisible when you suggested I come here to talk. Even now, I can see the look in your eyes when you look at me. You're not as impenetrable as you think you are. I see right through you, Kova."

Kova scowled, his gaze narrowing. "You do realize your father was in that room, yes?" He stepped closer and I felt his hot breath on my face. "You do realize that I went to jail because of us, yes?" I nodded, and he continued. "Then answer me this, why the hell would I put myself in jeopardy like that again, on top of being in another country? You cannot be serious right now, Adrianna. We had a role to play. I played mine and you did too. The *Games* are over. That is it."

chapter 39

HE WAS GLARING AT ME.

I felt his words, but I didn't feel like they were coming from him. He wanted me to believe they were his, though.

It was disheartening the way he was acting toward me after our Olympic win. It wasn't an idiotic thing of me to ask him. We didn't pretend out there, there were no roles. My medals were just as much his as they were mine.

Tears climbed up the back of my eyes. I wish I didn't get so emotional. I shook my head and walked away for a second then turned back around to face him.

"If you're so worried about my father, then why did you want me to come tonight? Was it so you could tell me we're officially done working together and you have to act like you don't know me now? Is that the point you're trying to make? Because guess what, *Coach*, I fucking got it."

His eyes blazed with fire. Still, he didn't say anything.

"You've been sending me mixed signals since you got out of jail. At first, I understood. Trials came and you showed me a glimpse of the old Kova. I thought everything was okay, but really you were just giving me this false sense of hope for us. You act like you don't know me and make me think you've changed your mind about us. Then in the next minute you rip me into your room and kiss me until you steal my breath and then feed me lies. You're back to being this cold, distant man that seems to want no part of me." I pause, my jaw quivering from the tears I was holding back. "Can't you see what this does to me?"

Kova cast his eyes away. He lifted his backwards hat and ran his fingers through his hair before he replaced it. I poured out my feelings to him and he didn't even do a double take.

"Nothing has changed, Adrianna."

"You're such a liar." Kova didn't flinch. He didn't even respond, and that told me everything I needed to know. My heart pumped faster. "Kova, you're scaring me. What's going on?"

Again, no response. He just looked down and avoided my gaze. My pulse rate increased. That bridge we'd worked so hard to build was collapsing plank after plank.

"I shouldn't have come here. This was a mistake—" My heart clenched at the word. I looked at the floor and frowned. "This was a giant mistake. Everything was a mistake. I can't do this anymore." I started to feel a little frantic.

I stepped around Kova and headed for the door.

"Stay," he finally said.

I stopped immediately, wishing I was stronger when it came to him. I turned around and met his stare. He looked defeated.

"What am I doing here, Kova?" The last thing I wanted to do was fight, but I couldn't keep it in. It wasn't healthy for me or us.

I wanted to be able to talk about the past, the present, and the future with him tonight since tonight was all we had for a little while. We didn't have to sign anything in blood, but we could at least talk a little bit so there wasn't a total break in our chain.

Feeling dejected, I asked, "Help me understand what is going on. I know we haven't seen each other in about a month, but the last two days you were my supportive coach and it made me think we were okay. But now with this feeling in my heart, it's like I don't even know you."

"I was your coach because that is who I am supposed to be. I did what I had to do to help you get to the finish line. I was doing my job. I did not want to ruin your moment."

I frowned, not liking the bite in his tone. I moved closer to him. I studied Kova, but his eyes gave nothing away.

"So, you faked it? All those encouraging words, going as far as 'living with me,' they were just part of your job description?"

Kova ran his hands over his face and groaned. "No, I meant them, Adrianna, but I wish I did not."

I blinked rapidly. "How could you say that?"

He placed his hands on his hips and stared up at the ceiling for a brief moment. "I got arrested and almost charged with rape," he said after expelling a long sigh.

"I'm eighteen. It wouldn't have happened."

"Katja is still on my case. Your father..." He paused, and his eyes lowered to slits. "He still has the option to proceed with charges. There is a lot to be settled and it is far from finished. It is not so easy like you think to just jump right back to what we were."

"I knew it," I whispered, my voice hoarse. "I knew it," I said again with more conviction. Kova straightened his back and leveled a stare at me that fanned black smoke around my heart. "Keep going."

Kova's gaze hardened. His lips pursed together. There were a lot of things I'd mentally prepared for on my journey to the Olympics; however, never had I anticipated the next words to fall from Kova's beautiful lips.

"Adrianna, we cannot go on like this. I think it is best if we do not see each other until everything settles."

I reared back. The silence in the room was earsplitting. "You want time?"

He looked me in the eyes and flattened his lips in response.

My heart sank.

How could he think after something as catastrophic as what we went through that more time away from each other would benefit us? Time would ruin us. People didn't separate when things got tough. They came together and worked through their issues as a team. Their bond was unified with each challenging moment, not split down the center because there was a breach.

We are a team—I exhale, you inhale.

I had been so ridiculous.

My blood ran cold and my throat swelled. Kova had been putting distance between us. What I felt wasn't due to paranoia. It wasn't in my head. It was real. Really fucking real, and what he wanted.

I stared at him, unblinking.

My world crumpled before me.

My heart stopped beating.

All those things he had said to me that day in my condo, how he was going to leave Katja to be with me, how he wanted to live with me and my stupid fucking disease, he took it all back in the blink of an eye. All those miles we had crossed together to get where we were, they were swept away like it never happened.

Angry tears brimmed my eyelids. Kova's gaze softened and he took a step toward me. My hand flew to my chest and I clutched my throat. My brain was telling my body to breathe, but I was stuck in a state of panic. I couldn't focus enough to breathe.

He had sworn he wouldn't hurt me again. He'd promised. Yet, he did.

Then it hit me.

This was why he'd wanted me to come to his room.

He wanted to break up with me.

I leaned toward him, my heart beating frantically. His gaze didn't waver from mine. He didn't back down. He didn't say anything either. Kova was slipping away. I looked at him with resentment that he wasn't fighting harder to be with me like I would for him. I wanted to let go of him completely *and* still reach for him because I couldn't not.

"Time. You want time?" I stated again, fighting the tears. "I literally don't have the time to give you. Do you understand that? I don't have all the time in the world like you do. I'm sick, Kova. I only have now." Jesus. The look on his face matched the gutted feeling inside my heart.

His shoulders sagged and he dropped his hands from his hips in defeat. He didn't want time and yet he told me he did. I shook my head. This back and forth wasn't something I was going to continue doing. I didn't have it in me. He could either have me now or he couldn't. I was only going to get sicker, not better. I didn't have the kind of time he wanted.

I stood straight and exhaled a ragged breath. I didn't want to be hurt anymore. I didn't want anyone to make me hurt anymore. And that started with *my* choices.

I shook my head and took a step back. "It's now or never with me."

"Ria," he said, his face fell. "Please…"

I put my hand up. "Don't. I know our relationship isn't normal. I'm aware of the major issues surrounding us, but that doesn't mean you can push me away because of them." My voice shook. "I know what my dad put you through and it disgusts me you had to go through that. I'm not being unsympathetic toward you or the legal issues you're facing, but was I stupid to think we'd work through what happened? I guess so," I said, more to myself than to him.

I clenched my eyes shut, regretting that I'd snuck out. When I opened them, Kova was standing in front of me looking utterly destroyed. The miserable look in his green eyes made my heart twist with grief. He was hurting as much as I was, yet he was the one who was causing our pain. I didn't understand why he'd do this to us when it devastated him just as much as it did me.

"That is not what I am saying, but I think we need to wait for this storm to weaken before we can be anything more."

"That's not what you told me in my condo that day when you said we could be together because you had a plan. Even before that, you knew it was eventually bound to happen." I felt like I was going to shoot steam from my ears any second. "You can't look me in the face and tell me you didn't anticipate any of this. What happened for you to change your mind? I know you were arrested, but I'm eighteen now. No one can stop us."

There was so much more I wanted to add, but I stopped when I felt tears streaking my cheeks. There would always be people who wouldn't approve of us, but I never once thought that us not being together was an option. I always put him—us—first, and I thought he would too at this point.

My spine bowed, and I looked at him helplessly. "Why can't you ever put me first?"

"Adrianna, you know my feelings for you, but I have to keep your father in the back of my head. When I got out of jail, we had a meeting." I squinted at him, stunned over this news. Dad never told me about this. "Frank threatened to ruin me if I went near you beyond being your coach. He knew he did not have a leg to stand on legally, but he said he would go to the media and claim that I sexually abuse my gymnasts, and he would provide proof for people to dig deeper. He said he would release pictures of us but blur your face to protect you. He said he has connections and will make sure the story goes worldwide. I have worked with your father in the past, I do not doubt him."

I stared up at him, dumbfounded. My eyes widened and I took a step closer, angling my head to make sure I heard him correctly.

"You're scared of my dad and his empty threat? He'd never do that because it would implicate me, not in a million years, no matter how mad he is." I stared at him. "So quick to believe him," I whispered in shock. "You bought his lie. You made it your out."

Kova widened his stance. His brows lowered and his gaze turned defensive. "Everything I have worked for since I came to the United States will be taken away if we continue a romantic relationship. How would we work out if I have no gym? No name? Nothing? How could I support you, support us? I cannot make mistakes right now." The color drained from his face. "He can ruin me and you, and that is not something I am chancing."

I ground my teeth. I was frustrated because I knew my dad was using this as a scare tactic and Kova was buying it. He edged closer to me and I stayed exactly where I was.

"I have to walk a straight line and I have to do it for us. You think I want to leave you? You think I do not care about you? My fucking heart beats only for you, Adrianna. It kills me inside. I want to ram my fist through a wall over and over because of this shit we have to go through. I am trying to do what is right. Whether you like it or not, the right thing is time. Are you not sick of living in this fantasy we have created? Do you not want the real thing? I do. And I will do everything I can in my power to make that happen for us."

"I'm not trying to be dramatic, but you don't seem to comprehend that I don't have that kind of time. I was supposed to go home and start treatment. What if the dialysis doesn't work, or I have the transplant and my body rejects the kidney? I know these are slim possibilities, but that's how my life is at the moment and how I have to think now. I can't wait around for you because that's not fair to me. If we're careful, we could have now, you just don't want to."

My heart was about to jump out of my chest. I was going to be sick any second.

"You only want me when I'm at my best and not at my worst," I said, my voice shaded with disdain. "That's not what love is. I stood by you at your worst. I never gave up. I took everything you would give me, and I gave myself to you ten times over because I knew you needed me when you were going through something. Now when I need you the most, when my body is literally fighting to kill me, you feel time between us is best."

Kova opened his mouth to speak, but I wasn't done.

"You want time, Coach?" I said, bitterness dripping from my tone. "Time is exactly what I'm going to give you." I turned toward the door and shot one last response over my shoulder. "I'm leaving for the University of Oklahoma shortly after I get home. You're getting exactly what you wanted."

chapter 40

"**A**DRIANNA," KOVA CALLED OUT. "LET ME FINISH."

I wanted to lift my middle finger to him. I'd been living a dream expecting to luck out in the end. I'd set myself up, and that hurt my heart more than Kova ever could. I really was just a stupid, naive, lovesick girl.

"Come here," he demanded, and I ignored him. A string of Russian flew past his lips as I wrapped my hand around the doorknob.

More tears filled my eyes and I fought to keep them back. I was so sick of being this heartbroken girl fighting for someone who would give up on me so easily. I had allowed my view to be clouded by the illusion Kova had painted for me.

I pulled the door open a fraction and Kova slammed it shut then spun me around. He pressed his back to the door, blocking my escape. A gasp lodged in my throat. I was unprepared for the passion in his touch or the heat of his breath on my cheek.

He blinked and something adjusted in his gaze. "You are angry with me because I said we need time for everything to settle down, but you were planning to move to another state? Do you see the hypocrisy here?"

My jaw dropped. "Excuse me for assuming we would continue to be together regardless of which school I went to. We could drive or fly to each other, talk all the time, even spend time together on holidays or weekends. There's no one stopping us. It's really not that hard if you want it bad enough." I paused and shook my head. "But you don't want that and there's no reason for me to stay now."

Kova gnashed his teeth together as fire ignited in his eyes.

Finally, he displayed an emotion I could understand and handle from him.

I breathed it in and found the strength I needed. He stepped forward and pressed his body to mine, his fingers gripping my bicep. Kova was breathing as hard as I was, but it was the way he was staring at me that reduced me to a brokenhearted mess. He looked so powerless. I didn't not want him in my life, but I refused to be put aside until the time was right.

"I never said I did not want to be with you. Do not put words in my mouth, *Malysh*." He said the words slowly and they set me on edge. "How can we be together with your father watching over every little thing we do? Please use your head for a minute and think about this. Our livelihoods are at stake."

I didn't say anything. My dad would never, ever accept us. But we could make it work if we wanted to, I was sure of it. How long would I be waiting for Kova? Until he felt like it was okay for us? The thought of watching time pass like that was asphyxiating on so many levels. I didn't want to lose him, but I had to put myself and my health first.

I lowered my eyes and grew insanely angry that this was where we were in our relationship after everything we'd been through together. "I'm sick of you," I spat, pushing at Kova's chest. He grabbed my good elbow and I fell into him. "What a regret it was to come here."

"I am right," he said, his voice filled with arrogance. "You know I am right, and you hate it. You think I want to be away from you? You think I want to even consider the idea? Never, but I am doing what I can to help you, to help us."

I needed to get out of here. I tried to shove away from him, only I didn't have the strength to, so he stayed right where he was. My chest rose and fell with rapid breaths.

"No, not this time. This time is different," I said. "You're a coward. If you weren't, you would do whatever it took to be with me."

Kova drew in a long breath. His eyes flared wide. Tension brewed between us. Men didn't like to be called a coward. It was probably one of the most insulting things to say, and I'd said it. I could feel his temper rising with each breath he took. He released my arm and I stepped back. The back of my legs hit the bed. I drew in a breath and tried to not let him affect me.

"What's the next excuse once the smoke clears? There's always going to be something working against us, Kova." I was disgusted with him and myself. "By the time you're ready for me, I won't be here."

"You are not in the position I am," he said through clenched teeth. "You have not a clue."

That set me off. I too was risking a lot to be with him.

"I don't have to be in your position to know it wouldn't matter to me!" I screamed. "I'd do whatever it takes. I *have* been doing whatever it takes. You told me you were divorcing Katja to be with me. Here I was thinking we were still okay because what we have is so strong, but really you're over here ready to let it go because you got scared." I was winded, on the edge of exploding. I wanted to punch something, and I wasn't the violent type. Kova brought out that side of me.

"You're not that weak," I continued. "You're the strongest man I know. You're just scared. You know what? So am I. I have a hell of a lot more to be scared of than you and I'm *still* fighting for us." This rage building inside of me needed to be let loose. "Tell me." I stepped forward and pushed at his chest. My eyes lowered to slits. "Tell me what it was that changed your mind. At least give that to me. I know there's more, because there's *always* more when it comes to you, Kova!" I yelled in his face, trying to rid myself of all the hurt he continued to cause me.

Kova shoved me onto the bed. I tumbled to the side and he reached for me. He grabbed my ankle and yanked me down the bed until my legs we're hanging off. I quickly sat up as he leaned over me. I breathed into his face, panting from the unexpected action.

"I cannot stand the thought of hurting you anymore!" he shouted, his eyes wide and bright.

A vein strained along the column of his neck leading down under his shirt. Finally, Kova let go.

"I will never forget seeing you on the floor that day, the blood every-where as your fucking eyes closed shut. I thought I lost you, and I vowed to myself that I would never hurt you like that again."

He shook his head like he was reliving the moment. He looked terrified. Kova stepped away and paced the floor, but he kept his gaze on me. His aggression ate up the space between us.

"Your life means too much to me for that. I sat in jail, overanalyzing everything, realizing how much negativity I brought to your world. I decided it was best to put distance between us, except when I saw you again, I knew there was no way. Just like right now, I cannot handle the thought of not being with you everywhere you go."

I blinked and he was inches from me. Kova lowered his face and dragged the tip of his nose over my cheek until his lips hovered above mine. I found myself leaning into him, hoping he'd kiss me.

"I would give everything up for you because you are *mine* and I am *yours* and that is all that matters. We will always be each other's. No one can change that."

I leaned in closer and Kova sucked in a breath. He stepped back but I reached out swiftly and clenched the center of his shirt. I yanked him toward me and we fell back onto the bed with my legs tangled with his. I held my breath praying he wouldn't move.

He cupped my cheek and my jaw in his palms. There was a sudden tenderness in his touch. Kova looked at me. "I hate that I hurt you, and I hate that you miscarried our child. It sickens me. I hate that your father will always be between us. He will not accept us, and you cannot decide between the two of us either. A good man would have never put you in this position. I try to do the right thing, but all it ever does is backfire. You get angry and try to inflict pain on me. I bite back because I like when you push me and fight me. But this is too much for one couple."

Beads of sweat pebbled his forehead. Kova was breathing heavily, and I could feel the heat radiating from his body. I leaned up on one elbow and Kova stayed where he was on me. I took pleasure in the weight of his body on mine.

"I am better off alone." Kova lowered his voice; his distraught eyes searched mine. "And so are you. But that can never be now, can it?"

My lips parted as his words slammed into me. I let out a small whimper then flattened my lips between my teeth.

Kova stood up and reached for me, but I moved out of the way and got off the bed myself.

"Ria—"

"I'm leaving." I walked around him, but Kova was quick.

He grabbed me, his fingers pressing into my skin. I wrestled him and felt this burst of angry energy explode through me. Kova was so much stronger than I was, and I took satisfaction in the knowledge I could use as much strength as I wanted and I wouldn't hurt him. Not unless I had a knife, which I didn't.

Kova grabbed my wrists and tried to pin them behind my back. When that failed, he spun me around so my back was pressed to his chest and he had both of my arms crisscrossed in front of me. I tried to squirm away, but he held me secured. I wished I didn't like how he held me to him.

"Let go of me."

Kova ignored me. I was no match for his strength, but still, I tried.

"Let go, Kova."

A grunt escaped my throat as the frustration mounted inside of me.

"If you don't want to be with me now, you can't have any of me later." My heart broke saying those words. "Let. Go."

Kova held me tighter. I found it therapeutic trying to fight him. It released something inside of me. My head fell back against his chest and I let out a little whimper. His face dipped down and his nose brushed my neck. His warm body enveloped me, and I stupidly relished in it. Tears filled my eyes and my body relaxed enough so Kova could let go of my wrists and bring his arms up to hug me. He embraced me with warmth and love.

"Kova."

He pressed a soft kiss under my jaw. "I love you, Adrianna."

I broke down, unable to handle a second more. "I know we're no good for each other," I whispered, admitting the truth. I leaned back into him as a tear slipped down my temple. "I know we'll never be good for each other, but that doesn't stop me from wanting to be with you."

I felt Kova shake his head. His lips brushed tenderly over my skin.

"I cannot let you go, just like you cannot let me go," he said.

The truth was like gravel on my raw heart.

chapter 41

"WHY IS THIS HAPPENING TO US?"

Kova lowered his hips to the bed and took me with him. He turned me sideways to face him. I sat on his lap with my knees pressed together and my legs hanging over his. He kissed my temple and hugged me close. I missed the feel of his arms and nestled closer. I fit like a puzzle piece against him. I could stay here for hours if he'd let me.

"All I know is that I am tired of hurting you. I will do anything to see you live a happy life. You must believe that."

I shook my head. I couldn't look at Kova just yet. What he said wasn't wrong, I just didn't agree with it. When there's a will, there's a way. Gymnastics had taught me if I wanted something bad enough, then I had to put the work in to get it. And that's how I felt about us. I was willing to do what it took. I wished he'd fight for us the same way.

"Don't you understand that time is not on my side right now? Nothing hurts more than you leaving."

Kova cupped my cheek and I finally looked at him. The anxiety encasing my chest intensified. He leaned down and kissed my tears away as they fell in rivers. I wound my arms around his shoulders and threaded my fingers through his hair. I closed my eyes as I inhaled him into me. My heart felt like it was shattering into a million tiny pieces. I was afraid to let go, afraid we wouldn't ever have this again.

Kova was my everything.

"I have thought about you nonstop since that day. I drove myself crazy when you were in the hospital and I could not be there with you." He pulled back and paused like he was struggling for words. His fingers skimmed over the hem of my shorts. "I have never felt more powerless than I did in that moment. All I felt was rage, and it resulted in a few fights while I was waiting to be released. It was part of the reason I was not released when I should have been. You mean everything to me. I resent myself every second of my life after seeing what you went through. You deserve better."

I shook my head frantically. "I'm so sick of everyone telling me what's best for me. I don't need you, my father, or anyone for that matter to make decisions for me. Let me make them, and if I'm wrong, I want to experience that for myself too. I'm the one who gets to decide what to do with my life and who I want in my life. And what I want is you, Kova. I just want you in my life."

Kova exhaled a heavy breath as his gaze bore into mine. His back bowed. He was struggling again. I could feel him wavering beneath my touch. Tipping my jaw up, I parted my lips toward his and lowered my eyes. I peered at him through my lashes. He exhaled through his nose and his chest heaved into me. Kova dropped his gaze to my mouth. I drew in a soft gasp as he leaned toward me, his tongue delicately tracing over my lips. Without hesitation, he slipped inside and stroked across my mouth in a deep kiss. Our lips fused together, and that was all it took for my body to come alive. Heat exploded around us. Flashes of desire tingled down my skin. My back arched and I moaned.

I straddled him without breaking our kiss. Kova's hands were on my hips in seconds, his palms cupping my butt as he guided me over him. Our bodies met and everything locked into place. My arms tightened around his shoulders and Kova deepened the kiss. He embraced me, clutching me desperately.

My thighs clenched around his waist and I felt his hardness press between us. It wasn't about that, though. We had something everyone dreamed of having one day, chemistry between two people that only increased the passion each and every time they were together.

Kova broke the kiss, panting heavily against me. "This does not have to be difficult. I am trying to do what is best for you, Adrianna." He paused. "Fuck," he said through gritted teeth. "I'm trying to do what is best for us."

I looked deep into his eyes. They were brimming with raw emotion. I wanted him to give into me the way I was giving into him.

"Let me decide what's best for me."

I smashed my mouth to Kova's. He kissed me back hard, brutally, putting all his feelings into the way his lips crushed mine. He kissed me like he was giving me hope and breaking my heart at the same time. This wasn't a man who wanted to leave me. This was a man who was on his knees madly in love with me, trying his hardest to right his wrongs.

"Tell me you love me," he said.

My breath hitched in my throat. I looked back and forth between his eyes, suddenly scared to tell him I loved him. My heart pumped hard and fast as he watched me, waiting, silently pleading for something he wasn't sure I could give him.

With tears streaming down my cheeks, I finally said the words he needed to hear. "I love you." I released a loud sob as soon as the words left my lips. "I've loved you for a long time."

Kova studied me, the black flecks in his probing green gaze cut right through me. My declaration stilted him into silence and his stare filled with a mixture of wonder and heartbreak. I think he always knew I loved him, but saying the words changed his reality. He wasn't prepared for the weight of those words to actually leave my lips.

Kova lifted my hand and brought it to his chest. His heart beat wildly under my palm. "Do you feel that, Adrianna? My heart will only ever beat for you. This is what you do to me when I think about how much I love you."

I felt his pulse and wondered if he knew the rapid thumping of his heart mirrored my own.

My fingers moved over the raised scar beneath his shirt, tracing over the letter. I softened. The mark was more than a binding of two people. It represented our agony and connection. Proof there was no length we wouldn't go to for each other. How were we supposed to walk away from one another when it was agonizingly clear we didn't want to?

"I love you, Kova," I said, my voice soft. "I love you so fucking much." My jaw trembled from the magnitude of emotions coursing through me.

Saying I love you was so much harder than saying fuck you or I hate you. Love was putting themselves out there to risk everything one had to give. It was the strongest emotion there was. Hate dissipated over time. People didn't reminisce over hate, they reminisced over love and the way it made them feel. Love grew and intensified over time. Love also wrecked lives.

Kova drew in a quiet breath and nestled me closer to him. Being wrapped in his arms was something I reveled in, but this time he was finding solace in holding me. His eyes closed and he took a few shallow breaths. I didn't know what the next five minutes would bring us. All I knew was that we couldn't lose each other.

"Loving you scares me," I said, opening myself up to him and the truth. "More than anything in the world."

He opened his eyes and looked at me. I cupped the back of his head and brought his lips to mine. Soft and pliable, his kiss eased the tension around me. My body pressed into his, his chest against mine, and I expelled a breath knowing this was right where I needed to be. My mind was a muddled mess, and the more I thought about our future the messier it became. There was only one thing I wanted tonight.

"Kova?" I waited until his eyes met mine before I continued. "Make love to me?"

"Are you sure that is what you want?"

I nodded. "I think it's what we need. Just…just go slow."

His brows angled toward each other. "I do not have any protection with me."

Crazy how we never really cared about protection until I got pregnant. It wasn't like we didn't know unprotected sex led to babies, we knew, we just got too lost in the passion to really care.

"I'm on birth control now."

A shadow formed in his eyes and it hurt my heart. I'd gone on birth control before I left the hospital.

"Are you upset I started the pill?"

"No," he said, shaking his head. "All of this happened because of me, and it sickens me."

I wished he'd stop blaming himself. If he didn't let go of the guilt it would eat him alive.

Kova pressed his forehead to mine and looked between us. He stilled. I fisted his shirt tighter and followed his gaze. My heart nearly stopped when I realized he was looking at my stomach.

A million thoughts ran through my mind.

I wondered what he was thinking.

I wanted to know if he felt like his chest was caving in the way mine was too.

I was scared to know if he wanted this for us, or if he was truly trying to put me before him.

His brows knitted together, and I prayed he didn't turn me away because of what had happened.

"I'm sorry, Kova. I understand if you can't…be like that with me anymore. I'm sure I disgust you after what happened—I disgust myself."

God, how I hated myself.

Kova's eyes snapped up to mine. "What the fuck are you talking about? I love every single thing about you. Everything." Kova pressed me back onto the mattress. He dropped a quick kiss to my lips then one over my collarbone. He slid further down my body and I watched him. "I loved that, for a moment," he said, kissing the spot next to my nipple, "no matter how brief it was"—he kissed just above my bully button—"my child was growing inside of you. And it makes me want you more."

I clenched my eyes shut. Kova gently placed his lips right next to the crease of my hip and thigh. It nearly ruined me when he pressed one last kiss to the center of my pelvis. My fingers threaded through the hair on the back of his head as I fought the feelings rushing through me at his unexpected tenderness and just how wrong I was.

There was this deep-seated need inside of me to know that he didn't hate me, that he still wanted me intimately, that he didn't find me repulsive after what had happened.

chapter 42

PRESSING MY LIPS TO HIS, I PUSHED AGAINST KOVA'S CHEST TO ROLL him onto his back before he could say another word.

I sat up and straddled his hips. Kova peered up at me, his vulnerable gaze probing mine. His hands found the tops of my legs and grabbed me.

This man loved me so much and it was ruining him. He was willing to suffer for a better us one day.

I gripped the hem of my shirt and pulled it over my head and dropped it on the bed next to us. As I reached around my back to unclasp my bra, Kova sat up and stopped me with his hands on mine. I looked at him and froze, afraid he was going to stop me completely.

He didn't. Kova unhooked my bra and the straps fell down my shoulders. I quickly fisted his shirt and pulled it over his head. The corners of my lips curved slightly at the sight of the A on the left side of his chest. Delicately, as if it were still fresh, I grazed my finger over the jagged skin. I leaned forward and pressed my lips to his chest. I was curious what Katja had thought when she saw it, because I was sure she had, but I didn't want to ruin the moment by asking him. This was about us. Our love. Our healing. Nothing and no one else needed to be brought into it at this time.

Kova's palm cupped the back of my head as I kissed my way up the curve of his neck, peppering more kisses along his jaw until I found his lips. His shoulders contracted under my touch as I rose to my knees and looked at him. His fingers pressed into the space below my butt cheeks. We stared at each other, unblinking, drinking each other in. Every lesson learned formed a new scar. I just hoped this one wouldn't hurt as much.

I stroked his jaw. His stubble was rough against my hand. My thumb brushed over his full bottom lip as his hands roamed the back of my thighs. Leaning into his mouth, I whispered, "I love you, Kova. I want you to always remember that." Then I pressed my lips to his and savored the feel of his lips on mine, and I kissed him longer.

Kova deepened the kiss. I moaned when his hand came up and the tips of his fingers gripped the sides of my neck. He hauled me closer to him in pure desperation. His devious mouth overpowered mine. He took control of the kiss and set the pace. I panted, my lips parting. Kova wasted no time delving his tongue into my mouth with a flair that weakened my knees. He was a skilled kisser and I was needy for him.

Lowering my hips, I scooted closer, needing to feel his bare skin against mine. My nipples pressed into his chest. I sighed into his mouth from the warmth exuding from his body and wrapped my arms around his shoulders only for Kova to break the kiss.

He quietly repeated what I'd just said to him. "I love you, Adrianna. I want you to always remember that."

I reached for the elastic of his shorts. My eyes caught his Olympic ring tattoo. I could get a matching one now. He watched me, then grabbed my wrist for a moment like he was nervous. I glanced up and swallowed thickly, meeting his gaze.

Kova let go and I shifted off his body to pull his gym shorts down. His erection sprang free and laid above his hips. My eyes widened. Thick with my favorite vein, his length hung a little to the side when he laid on his back. I dragged my teeth over my bottom lip feeling the desire awaken inside of me after it was dormant for so long.

"Come here," he demanded.

Kova grabbed the sides of my face when I climbed back up his body. He kissed me as he rolled us so I was underneath him. He crushed me with his weight, and I rejoiced quietly knowing he was reaching his breaking point. My hands found his back, suddenly greedy to touch him the way I wanted to after so long. I loved feeling how his muscles contracted under my touch. He was so strong. Little sounds from me melted into his mouth. My nails scored his skin. Kova flexed against my fingers then reached between us to unbutton my shorts.

Moving to his knees, he pulled off my shorts and panties in one swift move and then halted in his tracks.

His brows lowered into a harsh frown. I followed his gaze to my stomach and my heart sank.

"Kova," I said softly. He looked at me with blank eyes. "I'm okay."

He was hesitant, then dropped my shorts on the bed. He regarded my body with contemplative eyes then looked at me again. I smiled at him with affection. We were both bare to each other now.

Kova surprised me by kissing my stomach again. I pressed my lips between my teeth and bit down. I glanced at the ceiling, fighting the emotion from his tenderness. I wish he hadn't done that. My knees pulled up and my nails dug deeper into the sheets. I expelled an audible breath trying to find the strength for this—for us. I was shaking on the inside, unprepared for the emotional aspect to hit me the way it was. Kova placed his hand over mine and loosened my fingers that were twisting the sheet. I sucked in a breath. He climbed up my body, my knees spreading wide for him.

"Ria," he said.

I shook my head. I wasn't ready to face him now.

"Adrianna, look at me," he begged.

I couldn't. I was afraid to see that he regretted me, us, this. It was too much for my heart to handle.

"My love." His voice softened, and I broke down.

Tears streamed down my temples and I sniffled, still refusing to look at him.

"I can't," I said. "I can't look at you. I don't want to see the regret in your eyes again. I already saw it once tonight when you first looked at my stomach." I flattened my lips for a second. "I don't want to see that you'll never want me like you used to."

Kova positioned his body over mine and laid on me, forcing me to look at him. "Even when I am dead, long buried, and forgotten about, I will still love you, I will still want you. That will never change. You are a part of me now, just like I am of you. We are connected for the rest of our lives." He leaned down and swept a sensual kiss across my lips. "And I am going to show you just how connected we are, *Malysh*."

Taking my arms, he bent them above my head and held both my hands securely in one of his. He captured my lips with his own and drove his tongue into my mouth determined to make me stop overthinking. He grabbed my thigh and hiked it over his waist to seat himself more comfortably between my legs. A moan purred in the back of my throat. His straining cock pressed against my hip as his kiss did wicked things to me. He moved his hand to my breast and my back arched in response. I let out a small sigh. He gave it a gentle squeeze then teased my nipple between his fingers. My body pressed into his, already begging for more.

Kova devoured my mouth, not giving me more than a second to take a breath before he was consuming me again. He tugged my nipple harder, so hard that I felt a zing hit my clit. I gasped in response and tried to wiggle my hands free so I could touch him. I needed to, but he held them down with more weight and deepened the kiss. His silky tongue twirled around mine and tugged before he let go and ran it along the roof of my mouth. Each and every time he kissed me like this, I was weak.

He slowed the kiss, then pulled back, allowing me to inhale needed gulps of air. I looked at him and my breath caught in my throat at the look of love in his eyes.

I'd been stupid to worry about how he felt about me and us. This man clearly loved me like he claimed.

chapter 43

I WHIMPERED, ALREADY MISSING HIS TOUCH WHEN HIS HAND FOUND MY throat.

My eyes widened as his fingers encased my slender neck. I may trust him and get turned on when he does this, but it was still a little intimidating when I was helpless.

My body writhed against his. Kova shifted to the side and his cock pressed against my pussy. He leaned down and closed the distance, kissing me painfully slow. His tongue stroked mine too sensually and I shuddered. His thumb smoothed over my pulse and carried me to another level. Kova's hips rolled into mine. For a split second my heart skipped a beat and my body tensed, but then Kova slipped his tongue around mine and I exhaled into him.

I didn't hold back the pleasure filled moan and let it roll off my lips. God, I loved this. There was something thrilling about being at his mercy and the way he manipulated my body. Silver stars danced in my vision. Little black dots floated in the distance the tighter he squeezed around my neck. It was getting harder to breathe. Still, I didn't tell him to stop. There was a dark part of me that took gratification in being choked. I liked the way he made my body go in and out of tunnels of pleasure. I liked the way he set what my body could do and couldn't do. I let him and craved it.

My mind went blank as he thrust his hips, his thick erection teasing my entrance. I attacked his mouth with mine and he growled his approval, nipping my lips and kissing me like the untamed animal he was. My heels dug into the back of his thighs. I needed more of him.

"Kova," I whispered. "I need you."

His eyes dilated. He released my wrists and reached between us to grab his cock. Kova looked down as he used the head to stroke my lips until they spread open. I was swollen and so pink. Kova's nostrils flared as he teased my wet entrance. My hips rolled back and I angled my body to get more of him. He pressed his fist against my pussy and pushed the tip through his hand to enter me.

His hand grinded into my clit. My toes curled and I let out a long moan. "Please..."

He applied more pressure to my neck, and I could feel his palm gripping my esophagus. My chest rose, and a squeak escaped my lips. I was filled with aching pleasure it was nearly painful. Kova released his hold and all the oxygen roared back into my lungs as white-hot pleasure exploded inside of me. Euphoria barreled through my veins and I turned into an animal. I needed him desperately.

I grabbed his face and slammed my mouth to his. I dug my heels into his backside, trying to get him further inside of me. Our teeth gnashed together, but that didn't stop us. We were two passionate people and our sex only multiplied it. I turned him over and we changed our positions so we were sitting up and I was straddling his hips. Kova aligned his cock with my entrance then fisted my hair. I yelped from the initial pull but loved every second. He wrapped my hair around his fist tighter, making me arch into him.

"Only you, Kova. Only you will ever have my heart," I said honestly.

We were both on the edge yet it was painfully obvious we were hesitant to take the next step.

"I will go slow," he said under his breath, and I nodded.

Breathing heavily, he breached my entrance and pushed past that initial tight bundle of nerves. It burned a little as I stretched to fit his size. I tensed, scared it was going to hurt since it'd been awhile. My nails scored his shoulder blades and he flexed.

"Relax for me, *Malysh*," he whispered in my ear, then kissed my neck.

Kova slid inside of me a little more. My cheeks blushed as my body grew warmer. I felt like I was having sex again for the first time.

He nipped my neck. "It is me and you."

I smiled weakly at him, trying to control my breathing. Me and him. I liked the sound of that and eased myself down, taking him inch by inch.

His hand in my hair loosened and his mouth seduced me with a sweep of his lips over mine. He pulled me closer to him and rocked into me provocatively. I felt myself getting wetter for him.

He wrapped his other arm around my lower back, and I reveled in the feel of my chest pressed against his. Kova plunged his tongue into my mouth and let go of my hair. I moaned softly around his lips, madly in love with this man who was so wrong yet so right for me in every way. Kova seized my throat again and deepened the kiss so it was all I could focus on as he drove into me. With each sweep of his ravenous kiss, I surrendered myself until I let go. It was me and him, like he said, and that thought released me completely.

Kova evoked power and control through his touch, enough to distract me so he could thrust his hips against mine and drive in as deep as he could get. I gasped at the intrusion, but our kiss muffled my moans. He let go of my neck to palm the back of my head. My body tensed and I flinched, trying to move, but Kova held me snug to him and grinded me against him, creating this unbearably hot friction between us.

My thighs quivered around him. Kova let out a long, deep groan as I dragged my nails over his scalp and through his hair. I bit down on his lip and drew in a lungful of air at the same time. Kova hissed, then drove his hips harder into me. He held me down on his cock for a second. I could feel his balls tighten against my ass. His cock twitched inside me and I undulated on him.

There was this burning sensation where our bodies were joined. It was from that glorious push and pull we craved. I clenched when he drove in deeper because it hurt and he did it on purpose, but I also loved that bite of pain mixed with pleasure only Kova knew how to give. I relished it.

Kova brushed my hair away from my shoulder then leaned in and pressed his lips to my neck. I rose up on my knees, feeling how raw I was and still so tight. I sank back down on him, pushing past the pain I knew would go away soon.

His tongue dragged a wet trail up my neck. My arms wrapped around his shoulders and I delved my fingers into his damp hair, feeling his heated breath tickle my skin. I held him to me, cradling his head as he brought me higher. Kova's hands kneaded my hips. His cock was so hard and rigid, wide inside of me after so long. I thought about where his hands were, how he was kissing me, how his body felt against mine, how I loved him. My pulse hammered through my veins from the erotic note of pleasure streaming between us.

"I have missed you being in my arms," he said, looking at me like he was already lost to us.

I could feel the strain under his skin and how he was holding back. He was trying to be gentle with me.

"So have I. More than you can ever know."

I did miss him, and it was why I was suddenly so emotional. I fucking missed this man.

"Are you okay now?" he asked, and I nodded. "Are you sure? I am going to try and be gentle right now, but I do not know if I can hold out for long."

I smiled. "Don't ever hold back. I want you, and all of you."

Kova slammed his mouth to mine. Each thrust bringing us closer together, our heavy breathing the only thing we could hear. His tongue caressed me the way his cock consumed me, both taking me to new levels of gratification. He deepened the roll of his hips, reaching every depth of me he could, and tightened his arm around my back to hold me still. I reveled in his power, the way he made me feel like I was the only thing in the world that mattered to him. Sex was a way for Kova to express himself, and I opened myself willingly for him to do just that.

The friction between us heightened from the way his mound hit my clit. I trembled around him, feeling the little sparks of desire lick over my body like a firecracker each time. I could feel Kova swelling, getting harder as he was almost there. I felt every rigid inch of his cock inside of me as he increased his speed and lost control. I gasped and shuddered around him as he held me immobile then made me look him in the eyes.

"I need you." He grunted as he pushed into me. "I need you forever. How can we give this up? Do you feel this?" he asked, then slammed into me passionately and I lost my breath. "How are we supposed to walk away from this?"

I couldn't respond. Not without him hearing the tears in my voice. This beautifully anguished man was at my mercy and giving me everything I could ask for. I was a risk, we were the gamble of a lifetime, but he let caution fly because he loved me, he loved us, even though it killed him to do so.

chapter 44

KOVA LEANED INTO ME AND PRESSED MY BACK TO THE BED. He hovered above me and I held my breath when I met his defenseless gaze. My lips parted as he slid into me with precision and held himself there like he needed this more than I did. My back arched, my nipples pressing into his bare chest.

"I do not want to be the one to ruin your life," he said, and the hitch in his voice sent a shiver down my spine. His honesty broke my heart. He couldn't ruin my life even if he tried. "I do not want it to get worse for you, but fuck, Ria, how do you go on without your other half?"

"You don't."

He kissed me deeply. His tongue was wicked, his kisses devouring me until I was breathless. My hands roamed over the strength in his back, and I took pleasure in the firm muscles and how beautiful his body was.

Kova hiked my leg over his back to drive deeper inside of me with ease. My thighs quivered and he went even harder. I gasped and clenched my eyes shut as he reached so far back it actually hurt. My breath hitched in my throat and I tensed for a second from the pain in my stomach. Kova took me with purpose. He was on a mission to not only have me, but to take what he could. He was a desperate man.

His hips bucked against mine like he was in dire need to be deep inside of me. My nails marked his back as I took what he gave, and I gave him what he so clearly needed of me. I tried not to think about the fact that this might be our last time together.

Kova muttered in Russian but I couldn't make it out.

For the first time in a while, pleasure rose in my blood. My hips surged against his, and the feeling intensified inside of me. We both moaned at the same time in breathless anticipation at the connection. We felt too good together.

Holding onto Kova's biceps as he took me, I kissed his shoulder, the honey curve of his neck, and every inch of his skin I could reach. My inner thighs were wet with both of our desires. His lips found my neck, and my head rolled back in euphoria. My body tingled. I was on the cusp of craving and need. I found myself chasing what only he could give me.

"I cannot lose you," he whispered so low I almost didn't catch it.

Kova's fingers pressed into me. He was speaking in Russian again, but it was a mumbled mess. His body was like this emotional wave crashing into me, shaking violently as if he was lost to something bigger than us.

He pulled out and dropped his weight onto me, then he laced his fingers with mine and stretched our arms above my head. I felt that telltale feel of an orgasm climbing. My mouth fell open and I moaned in pleasure. This man... What he did to me... My toes curled and I wrapped one leg around his from the pressure between my hips.

"Tell me you love me." Kova demanded, but I flinched when he surged back inside me. He was going so deep. "I need to hear it, Adrianna," he said, his eyes clenched shut like he was the one in pain. "Tell me you love me the way that I love you. It is me and you, *Malysh*." His forehead creased with harsh lines. "Me"— he withdrew and surged in slowly, then let out the sexiest moan yet—"and you."

I attempted to speak, but Kova kissed me ruthlessly, pulling my bottom lip into his mouth and tugging on it. We were two passionate people who were both the best and the worst kind of people for each other. And yet, we couldn't stop. We were addicted to one another.

He squeezed my fingers tighter and brought our joined hands to the sides of my head. My back bowed in response, and I clenched around his fingers, holding on for dear life when I felt the burst of pleasure slice through me.

The orgasm rippled from me and I exploded around his cock. My hips began thrusting into his, desperation glided my clit over his dick, fast and quick. I inhaled. Kova hovered over me, riding me until I saw stars and felt the bursts of energy kiss my skin. He dropped his head to my breast and tugged on my nipple with his teeth. His tongue twirled around it and latched on, pulling on the sensitive tip. A blooming heat spread through my limbs. My pussy clenched around him again, and I was floating down from oblivion.

His cock twitched and his thrusts quickened. Kova ran his nose along the line of my jaw. He grunted in bliss, and I could tell he was getting close to finishing. His back bowed as he fought his release, but I wished he would just let go already. Kova withdrew from me and sat up. His hands reached for my hips and guided me onto his lap. He glanced down to line himself up with my entrance, and froze to a standstill.

I frowned and followed his gaze, curious as to why he stopped. When I looked down, my heart dropped. He was staring at my stomach again.

His lips tugged down.

"I'm okay. Keep going." When he didn't move, I lifted his chin and nipped at his lips. "Kiss me. Kova, please kiss me, I need you."

He finally met my gaze. My stomach tightened at the pure anguish in his eyes. Color seemed to drain from his cheeks.

"I cannot do this to you."

No.

He looked down again. The back of his knuckles grazed gently over my skin. His eyes lifted with an unspoken apology and I felt the final straw snap inside of me.

He exhaled a swoosh of air, then said, "*Prosti*—"

"No," I said firmly even though emotion clogged my throat. My heart dropped into my gut. "Do *not* say that."

"I am sorry," he said, his chest heaving rapidly as if he was struggling to breathe.

I gripped his arms tighter and held onto him for dear life. "Kova, I'm fine. I promise I'm okay. Please don't stop." I pleaded with tears in my eyes now. "Please, Kova. I love you. We need this. I need this. Don't let your mind go there. We're here, we made it." When he didn't budge, my voice shook with panic. "Kova, I'm begging you, don't do this to us."

He looked at me, but it wasn't enough.

Cupping my face, Kova pressed a kiss to my lips before laying me back and rolling over off me. He placed his hand on his stomach and stared up at the ceiling, looking like he was absolutely wrecked. I broke down and covered my face as I lost myself witnessing his state of emotion.

"I am always going to be a source of pain for you," he said, more to himself than to me. His voice was gut wrenching.

I cried harder, quieter, consumed by the obvious shift in our relationship that struck with force. Pressing my knees together, I drew in a long breath as I watched him sit up at the end of the bed. Kova dropped his head into his hands and didn't move. Each second that passed with his back to me was another layer stripped from my heart. Every breath he took was one he chose to take without me.

I pulled the blanket over to cover my chest and then wiped my eyes with it. I sniffled when he stood up and pulled his shorts on.

"I love you, but this is too big for us to overcome this time, Ria." He faced me with tears in his eyes. "It is only going to get worse. Oklahoma is a good idea. Knowing you are close to me, I would have to find you."

I couldn't take another minute of this and cried out. My heart was about to pump out of my chest and explode. All I could do was try to catch the shattered pieces with slippery fingers.

"I do not want this to end, but I do not see another way for us any time soon. I cannot—*will not*—keep putting you through all this hurt. I refuse to continue doing that to you. Being in your life while you are going through treatment would only bring more agony."

"You think leaving will make me happy? Don't you understand that the thought of life without you breaks my heart? I don't think I can survive without you, Kova."

He studied me for a moment before replying. "You are much stronger than you think." He was shutting down, withdrawing from the conversation, but his next words obliterated my heart. "I think you should go back to your room."

Kova stepped into a pair of shoes after putting his shirt on, then reached for his cell phone and room key on the dresser. He slipped them into his pocket. I curled onto my side, the chilly comforter cooling down my cheek. Pulling my knees up, I hugged myself as I watched him walk toward the door.

This didn't feel real. This wasn't us. Not after how far we'd come.

Kova was walking away from me. He was taking everything that I willingly gave to him with him. I allowed it, though, because I loved him. I loved him with every bone in my body, and there was not a single thing I could change about that, or would change.

The further he got from me, the more I held my breath. Stopping with his hand on the knob, Kova tilted his head down then to the side. He lingered, then looked back at me.

My lungs seized from lack of air. My stomach was a mess. I wanted to scream at him or call him a coward again, anything to make him stay and fight through this hardship with me.

"Please don't go," I whispered.

He turned back to the door and opened it. A gasp of air expelled from my lungs.

I closed my eyes shut and broke down in his room after hearing the soft click of the door shutting. I knew he wanted us, that wasn't a question. He just didn't want us bad enough to walk through the fire to get there.

chapter 45

S OMEHOW I HAD MADE IT BACK TO MY HOTEL ROOM.
I had no memory of how, or changing out of my clothes, or retrieving my notebook. Everything had blurred into one.

I'd been writing for over an hour, sobbing my eyes out. My tears smearing some of the ink, but I couldn't stop my hand flying across the paper.

I wrote down every emotion I felt from the moment I walked into his hotel room to now and described what it did to me. Writing was cathartic. I understood why Kova liked to write. It was private, intimate, real. No one judged me, no one gave terrible advice. It was just me and a blank page, allowing me to express whatever the hell was going through my head. I realized through the painful words how much I held inside of me.

Pages and pages later, I was still shedding tears trying to understand how it came to this. It was nearly two in the morning when the door opened and Avery walked in. Our eyes met. I was still a sobbing mess and the sight of her devastated me further.

Avery rushed over to me just as I covered my eyes. My head tipped back. I released a tight breath, suffering all over again.

Wrapping her arms around me, she held me as I cried on her shoulder. She comforted me without saying a word. Avery had been with me through everything from the beginning. She had a notion of what I felt right now. There was no need for me to say anything, she knew.

"Oh, Aid," she said, her voice full of sadness. "Don't cry. Trust me, crying will get you nowhere. You'll realize it wasn't worth it."

I wanted to believe her, but I couldn't, not with this agony pulsing inside of my ribs. It told a different story. I was completely blinded by heartbreak and couldn't see anything beyond my pain.

After a few moments, I pulled back. Avery reached for the box of tissues on the nightstand and plucked a few then handed them to me.

I kept my head down and blotted my eyes. "I just don't understand," I said. "It doesn't make sense. He wanted me to wait. Why would he want to wait? It's not like he said give me six months to clean this up, or one year, he just said we needed time. Time is an infinite number, and a self-imposed deadline can be pushed back. Kova is a perfectionist. By the time he comes to me, I'll already be dead and buried."

I could feel Avery studying me. I looked up at her through my lashes. Her lips were flat and twisting with sorrow as she looked into my eyes.

"I tried calling you. How long have you been here? I would've come back in a second if I knew you were like this."

I blinked. I didn't recall hearing my cell phone ring. "I don't know where my phone is," I said. God, I sounded so empty.

Avery frowned. "Are you sure you brought it back with you?" I nodded. Avery got up and looked around. She came out of the bathroom holding it and looking at the screen. Her thumb moved up and down as she read.

"You have a bunch of messages."

I didn't care.

"Hayden and Holly both sent you congratulations." Her voice trailed off. "Wow. Homeboy gave a play-by-play of you as he watched the event on TV." Her eyes widened. "Okay, now Hayden's just annoying me with all these messages. Holly said congrats and that she loves you. She said you looked so happy on the podium. You even have a message from Reagan."

I sniffled, trying to be grateful I had friends like them, but I felt nothing.

"Congrats, Red, I knew you had it in you all along. Too bad you didn't medal in beam. Nice job, though." Avery observed me with a blank stare. "That was from Reagan."

A partial laugh escaped me. "I figured that."

"Do you want me to message them back for you? I can pretend I'm you."

I nodded. "Thanks." Even though I was upset, that didn't mean it was okay to ignore their messages. I felt bad, but I didn't have the mental fortitude to handle responding to them right now.

Avery put her knee up and sat on the edge of the bed, typing away. After a few minutes, she put the phone down and looked at me. The air was chilly, yet I didn't move to pull the blanket over me. I felt like in some way I deserved to suffer in the cold when I despised it wholeheartedly.

"I'd give up my medals not to feel this heartbreak anymore." I blinked, staring straight into her eyes. "I'd even give up going to the Olympics."

Her shoulders slumped forward. Avery frowned, then said, "Hey. You worked hard for those. Don't say that."

"What happened with my dumb brother?"

"Don't change the subject."

I eyed her resolute expression and knew I wouldn't be able to turn the topic. After a few quiet seconds, I said, "Then how do I stop feeling like this? I feel so empty inside, yet I feel everything all at once. This is worse than when I found out about the marriage."

That took me so long to accept and get over. I couldn't imagine how long this would take.

Her brows furrowed like she was bothered. "I don't like that you'd give up something like your medals in exchange for him after how hard you worked for them. You almost sacrificed your life for them." She took a deep breath and exhaled. "You're my best friend, and I feel it's my duty to tell you that if Kova makes you feel this way, then I think you need to reevaluate what *you* want. He clearly has other plans right now, not that I agree or disagree with them, but you need to think about you where he's concerned. What do you want? You know what he wants," she said, hitching her thumb over her shoulder. "The *you* that I know, would never think like that. Those medals are your whole life, and you'd give them up because of a guy?" Avery gave me a droll stare. "No. Nope. Not happening. I know right now is hard for you. I'll be here every step of the way to help you, but you need to change that attitude right now."

"What do I do, then? I feel so hopeless inside, Ave."

I sniffled again and leveled a stare at her. My stomach was hollow from anguish. It'd been hours since I had dinner. The thought of eating now or anytime in the near future made me sick. Hello, emotional stress.

"What did you do?" I asked. "I'm sitting on the edge here wanting to erase every memory so I never have the chance to feel like this again."

Sympathy filled her crystal blue eyes. "That's what happens with your first love."

My jaw trembled. Kova was my first everything. He was a devastating love I'd never regret.

"It took me a while to realize the only way to stop that emotion gnawing away at you is to live with it. Receive it, accept it, and move on. I'm not saying tomorrow, I'm not saying to never think about it, I'm just saying you don't want to waste your days away pining after something you can't have. You need to live your life and find something new that makes you happy. We fell in love, we had our hearts broken, and we'll move on like so many others have."

"Why does anyone want to fall in love if it ends like this?"

Avery smiled sadly at me. "Sometimes the most heartbreaking memories are the most heartfelt ones we can never let go of. You had a good time, and you'll remember that feeling it gave you. You'll smile and wonder where that person ended up and how their life is going. Nostalgia will hit and you'll smile. There's something to be learned. It's why you hold onto them."

I glanced down at my hands, musing over her words. I was twisting one end of the tissue into a sharp pointed edge. There was something somber about that. People wanted to remember the good times that were filled with kisses under the rain. It was when one felt the most alive.

"In some strange way that helps," I said. I glanced away, feeling the sorrow settle over me once again.

"I can't stand to see you like this. Yeah, I like Kova, and I think you guys would be good together. But seeing you like this kills me. It makes me despise him. Honestly, I want to kill him. He isn't worth this, Adrianna. Not to see you like this, ready to give up your Olympic medals."

I fought back my tears. I heard Avery loud and clear. I thought about what Kova had said to me and how I felt his tone in my heart. He mimicked my feelings exactly, yet he'd still walked away. I didn't understand.

"Why didn't he fight for me?" I asked, my voice small. "He didn't even try. I wanted him to so badly. All he kept saying was that we needed time. Time is the same thing as walking away. Seriously, Ave, do you really think my dad is going to be cool with Kova even in a year? Obviously not."

Her shoulders fell. "Would it have changed your mind if he had?"

I bit down on the inside of my lip. Avery sensed my indecision and leaned in to hug me. "You know, sometimes I feel like I'm stuck in the twilight zone when it comes to you and Kova. I find myself cheering for him when I know I shouldn't. Call me crazy, but I don't think he didn't *not* want to fight for you. You guys have been through a lot, and I've seen the way he looks at you when no one is around. That's not someone who gives up easily. I think Kova is really trying to do what he thinks is right for the both of you. I think he would've fought for you only if he knew he could win. He can't win right now. Why drag out the bad time? It could only make things worse."

I pursed my lips together, fighting the emotion and shifted my eyes to Avery. Her crystal blue eyes weighed into mine. That sounded like Kova. I wanted to believe her, but it was hard to when I was so passionate about us. It went back to that whole "if there's a will, there's a way" thing. I felt like he had no will, and I think that's what crushed me.

"Kova doesn't know that for sure. That's a huge risk to take."

"As much as it hurts to hear this, I think he did the right thing, even though it's killing the both of you. You're strong, he knows that. He knows you'll get over this." She paused and pressed her teeth into her lower lip. I could sense her hesitation when she sat up straighter. "The next couple of weeks are going to suck monkey balls, not just because of Kova, but because of your health too. Your life is about to take a huge turn. I feel like you should take that time to go through the motions and think about yourself and what you want. Reflect, heal, and all that shit. That way you give yourself time to figure out how to navigate your new life. Find who you are." She stared me in the eyes. "That's when you'll see just how fucking amazing and worthy you are."

Tears filled my eyes. I seriously loved my best friend. My jaw wobbled as I let out what I'd secretly been holding in. "I think… I think I'm really just scared, Ave. I'm scared I'm not going to get to live a full life. If I wasn't sick, then I feel like I'd be more understanding, but that's not the case. I want to live right *now*. Tell me I'm insane—we both know I am—but I think I need to live to get me through what I'm about to do, and that's with the people I love most." Tears streamed from my eyes and my voice squeaked. "I'm not asking for a lot. What if he comes around when it's too late? All that wasted time."

Her eyes hardened and she pointed a finger at me. "Don't even utter shit like that. I'm serious, Adrianna. You know I'm always going to be Team Ria, even if you're wrong, but you have to give Kova a chance to come back from this too." She was a little upset with me. "You know I'm right. Just say it," she said, grinning now. "Ave, you're always right."

A smile twitched my lips. I regarded Avery in a different light tonight. We'd always had this funny, easygoing friendship. The last couple of years we'd grown a lot, and now I was seeing her in a way I never had before. My head tilted to the side. Avery had this fiery ball of courage that she hid in her back pocket. There was a tenacity about her, and she inspired me with it.

"Did you let go completely?"

Avery looked away for a long moment, then back at me. I knew her answer before she even said it.

I smiled sadly at her.

"He's got one chance left. When he's ready, he's ready."

"Are you just going to wait?"

"Psh," she said. Her smile was filled with amusement. "That's a negative. I'm too young to wait around for love. If it happens, it happens."

I smiled back, but I didn't believe her. Avery was putting on a strong front, but I'd give it to her. She was trying to lift me up, and it was working.

When Avery spoke again, her voice was low, and there was a slight tremble to it. She couldn't look at me. "I feel like when people are looking for love, it never happens. I also feel like when they're waiting for it to knock on their door, it'll never happen either. I don't want to be like that, so I'm just gonna live and see where I end up and have fun. I want to spread my wings and fly against the wind. Life is too short to eat fat-free ice cream and sugar-free cake."

She was seriously winning me over.

"Did you think it would come to this?" I asked her. Tears blurred my eyes once again. I wanted to stop crying.

"No," she said quietly, and grimaced. "Honestly, I never saw this coming. I feel bad about it." Leaning into me, Avery gave me a big bear hug, then looked at me and said, "I think you need to ask yourself who you are without Kova."

chapter 46

THERE WAS AN ENORMOUS FEELING OF LOSS THAT NO ONE HAD prepared me for after the Olympics.

It had hit at the end of the first week.

An emptiness settled in my chest and built a fortress around the outer layer. I didn't like the barren feeling that spread like black smoke through my heart chambers, and I used sleep as a way to avoid it.

This time three weeks ago, I was standing on the podium accepting the team gold medal. Now I was getting out of the shower hardly able to stand because of inflammation in my body. My ankles were sore, my toes looked like sausage links, and my cheeks were often warm to the touch. I was *so* out of breath, and the exhaustion wrecked me. I couldn't catch a good deep breath no matter how hard I tried. It was like my body had said that's enough and took over and released everything I'd been fighting to keep at bay for the last few years and unloaded it.

I'd achieved my dream…but no one talked about the after.

The first week home was spent sleeping, and then more sleeping. Dad was staying at Sophia's, but they both came over throughout the week to check on me and have dinner at night. We hadn't gone back to Amelia Island because I had a doctor appointment set up two days later and Dad felt it wasn't necessary to drive to Cape Coral right after. I was glad. I didn't want to be stuck there. Surprisingly, I felt more at home here than I did there. I'd missed my appointment, and the ones scheduled after that. Dad had reassured Dr. Kozol that I was okay and that I would be in within the next few weeks.

The second week I still hadn't cleaned anything or even unpacked my bags. Sophia actually came over and did that for me. She offered to hang up my medals, but I told her it wasn't necessary since I needed to start packing up my condo anyway and wanted to bring them with me. I slept a little less but not by much.

Today marked the end of the third lonely week home, and the deadline of when I was supposed to announce to the gymnastics world that I was committing to the University of Oklahoma.

The school was aware of my health and was still willing to take a chance on me after I'd told them I couldn't take a full load the first year. They even granted me a late start due to competing in the Olympics, so long as I could catch up on my assignments. I should be elated, but I couldn't find a smidgen of joy. There were no rays of sunshine in my veins. No excitement when I got a swag package of clothes in the mail from the school. Not after how depressed and alone I'd been lately.

I'd gone through spurts of depression in the past, but I'd never felt depression quite like this since I've been back. It made me think I'd never truly experienced what depression was until now.

My ache for Kova increased with each moon. It was worse in the middle of the night. I missed him so much and longed to hear his voice. Tears fell at any given moment. I was alone, missing my other half.

There was no more Kova and Ria.

I wondered if his heart hurt the way mine did.

If I was on his mind the way he was on mine.

If he felt my loss the way I felt his.

I wondered if he'd picked up his phone to call me like I had him numerous times only to not go through with it.

Kova had been on my mind more so this week than the last two, and I think that was because my time here was coming to an end. He had known about my commitment to Oklahoma before anyone else had, but he didn't know that I hadn't left yet.

It was strange. I hadn't felt the need to tell him I was actually here. We'd both made a decision that night in his hotel room. Being home and looking back on that night, writing and reading my journal, it killed me to accept that our minds were set and we weren't budging.

I don't think it would've mattered if he knew I was here or not. Kova wanted time, but I didn't have it to give.

Seven days from now I would be in another state living on my own again. I was both anxious and nervous about that and thought Dad would initially be against me moving so soon, but he was actually relieved. He figured the further away I was from Kova, the better.

I turned off all the lights then locked up my condo, finally leaving for my very much delayed appointment. I made my way downstairs and stepped outside. Dad was already waiting for me with Sophia. Pulling my jacket tighter, I opened the door of his sleek Mercedes and slid into the back seat.

Within the hour of arriving, I had vials of blood drawn, ultrasounds completed on various parts of my torso, and numbers were input into the computer to track my overall health. We were sitting across from Dr. Kozol ready to go over my new treatment plan. It was like any other appointment I'd had with him in the past, only it wasn't. Dad and Sophia were here, and something about that made this appointment feel so much more final.

"Congratulations, Adrianna," Dr. Kozol said, taking me away from my thoughts. "The whole office was cheering you on. We're so proud of you, even though you defied doctor's orders."

I chuckled and dipped my chin to hide my blush. I was honest and told him I'd taken lots of Motrin while I was away. He continued, "We had every television on in here, holding our breaths. You had quite a few people in tears watching you accept the gold medal. I must say, for someone who is as ill as you, you're a true fighter and a sight to watch. You made it look so easy, like nothing held you down. I'd never guess you're as sick as you are."

"I've been sleeping since we got back. Believe me, it came with a price, but it was so worth it."

He angled his head, giving me a knowing look. "I bet. Your exam tells me you had a pretty bad flare up. Luckily it happened after you got back."

Dr. Kozol asked me a handful of questions, then went on to address that he'd found a doctor in Oklahoma he felt was capable of handling my case. He told us how he'd spoken in depth with him multiple times and what his plan of attack would be. It was similar to my current one before I'd decided to move. Though he was confident, he also suggested we get a few opinions of our own, just to be safe.

I listened to Dr. Kozol tell Dad step by step of what to expect within the next few months. I'd read about this phase online so many times I was having nightmares about it and it hadn't even started yet.

"Expect dialysis three to four times a week, lasting anywhere from three to five hours each time." Dr. Kozol stacked some papers together. He pulled a pen from his coat pocket then began writing something down. He looked up at me when he was finished. "During that time or after you leave, your body will cramp from the fluid being pulled from your body during dialysis. That's the stuff your kidneys couldn't process any longer. Most patients complain of leg cramps, though some say their entire body aches. Everyone is different and only time will tell." He tipped his head and bore his eyes into mine. I felt like I was about to get yelled at from my dad. "Make sure you take it easy and don't overdo it. If you're postponing the transplant surgery, then you need to treat your body like a temple during this time."

"Okay." It was all I could say. I swallowed, though my throat was dry. That was a lot of time to sit and do nothing while my body was cramping up.

"Take the nausea pills I prescribed you since we know they already work. You'll have nausea most of the time, and drugs will be given to hopefully prevent flare ups. Your blood pressure will likely dip. That'll be monitored so you don't pass out from not being able to catch your breath from something as simple as carrying groceries to doing a light jog."

That worried me. I already had a hard time catching my breath, which he was aware of. Now I was going to need to be extra cautious that I didn't pass out and hit my head and die in my new apartment alone.

"She'll be taking a year off from sports to work on her health," Dad said to Dr. Kozol, then he turned to me. I told him I would take a year off. That didn't mean I actually would. I was estimating six months, at most. "Your priority is your health. Nothing else. There should be no reason for you to exert yourself. All you have to do is get up and go to treatment. That's it."

I nodded vehemently. Dad was right, and I had to remind myself that I had a very strong and solid support system. He was making it possible so that I wouldn't have to worry about anything except my health and attending the few classes I was taking.

Dr. Kozol continued. "Some people will either gain or lose a substantial amount of weight, so watch for that. Some patients claim they have newfound energy after dialysis starts. No two patients are the same. Log your symptoms in a journal so you can track how you're feeling." He looked at Dad. "If you want to have a driver on the back burner for her, it wouldn't be a bad idea. Occasionally there've been patients who are too physically tired to drive after."

Of course, Dad loved the idea and said he'd set something up just in case.

I thanked Dr. Kozol and apologized to him for all the times I had been difficult. He chuckled and said he liked the medical challenge I brought to his desk. He also added that I probably aged him ten years while I was under his care.

My future wasn't going to be pretty for a bit, but one day it would be again. I was confident that it would be, even if the only thing I had to look forward to wouldn't start for about eight months or so. I wouldn't give up sports completely, it just wasn't possible. However, I would be smart about my decisions. Light jogging maybe, and some light weights. No actual gym, though. No Motrin, nothing that could hold me back. I only wanted to go forward from here. Moving to a new town alone would be a challenge too, but I was a little excited about that. I wasn't sure how I was going to handle everything on my own in the beginning, yet I knew exactly what I had to do in order to live.

I was going to live. I had to for me. I hadn't achieved my dream of Olympic glory only to give up now.

chapter 47

LIKE EVERY OTHER NIGHT OF MY LAST WEEK HERE, DAD AND SOPHIA brought over takeout.

They made sure it was food I could eat on my special diet. Dinner was really the only meal I ate since I slept most of the day, so I made sure to eat everything they brought over.

"Did I bring enough boxes?" Dad asked, taking the last bite of his steak.

After we ended with Dr. Kozol, my dad picked up boxes then dropped me off at my condo. He was flying out in a few days to negotiate a new business deal, and Sophia was going with him.

They both planned to meet me in Oklahoma two days after I arrived to help me get settled and go to my first doctor's appointment. Dad had insisted that Sophia stay and be there for me after he left until I got used to the side effects of the treatment, but I wanted to do it on my own. It was something I needed to do on my own. Maybe she could stay a few days, but that was it.

"Yes, I have plenty. I should be able to have this place packed up in a couple days with a day or two to run last-minute errands."

"How have you been feeling…otherwise?" Dad asked, dragging out his question uncomfortably. I watched his eyes do a quick sweep across my body and I knew what he meant by that. "Every time I see you, you look like you're hardly sleeping."

Though the part of my life that haunted his eyes was in the past, it was still very much in the present for me and lingered like a bad odor in the air. It was going to take time to dissolve.

"I'm honestly doing well, just catching up on all the sleep I missed out on. Dealing with the aftermath, of course, but otherwise, I'm really okay."

Dad regarded me. I held his stare, willing him to believe me.

"I can help you pack, if you'd like," Sophia offered. I looked at her.

"I'd like that. Thanks," I said, giving her a smile.

I didn't want to pack, and I sure didn't want to do it alone where I was lost to my thoughts. I'd either get nothing done from being depressed and not having the energy to do it, or I'd cry over the shitty hand I'd been dealt.

Dad's voice caught my attention. "When you get off the plane, look for the chauffeur to take you to your apartment. Your SUV won't arrive until the following week. Your apartment is right outside of campus and within walking distance of everything you could need, at least that's what student services told me when I spoke with them. The driver will have your house key, and the place will already be stocked with food."

I smiled, grateful that Dad was still willing to support me after everything. He could've kicked me out. I was eighteen, after all. Standing, I took the plates to the sink. They didn't usually stay after the sun set.

"Let me get this," Dad said quickly, and stood with me. He waved my hands away. "Go relax with Sophia on the balcony, or something. It's cooler out now."

"Dad, it's still like eighty degrees outside."

"It's better than ninety-three."

Dad carried the empty containers and plates to the kitchen. I was kind of happy that he suggested I hang out with her. Sophia came into my life at the worst time, and I've been wanting to thank her for everything she's done to help me.

We both took a place on the love seat on my patio. Sophia angled her body toward me and brought her knee up.

"How do you feel about the move? College? Are you getting excited?"

I nodded and shrugged at the same time. "A little bit. I think I'm starting to be okay with it…with things."

Sophia's eyes softened with compassion. She knew I wasn't just talking about going to college.

"Whatever is meant to be will always find its way," she said like she was so sure. "You'll see. I know what you're about to do seems scary, but I think you're going to discover just how strong you are."

My voice was small. "I don't feel strong. I feel really weak." I swallowed and opened up a little. "I'm scared."

Her eyes were empathetic. "Francesca used to tell me the same thing. She had a fighter's heart and I envied that about her. I didn't have the same ambition as her, obviously."

I felt bad that she viewed herself as someone weak. To give up a child because she knew she couldn't give it a proper home is not something a weak person did; however, I understood her sorrow completely.

Sophia continued, her brows smoothing out as she thought about Francesca. "She'd say she didn't know who she was or what her purpose was in life anymore.

She was physically weak all the time, said her head was foggy a lot. She forgot things so easily, or couldn't focus on one task long enough to finish it. She was much sicker than you, though. Much sicker." She paused, staring off like she was stuck in the past. "It's going to take time adjusting to this new lifestyle of yours." Sophia rolled her lip over her bottom teeth and worried it a bit before returning her gaze to me. "I didn't mean to ramble and tell you a morbid story about my sister."

I shook my head, letting her know I appreciated it. "It's totally okay. I'd rather know what to expect, even if it is kind of sucky." She gave me a small smile, and I reassured her once more. "Tell me whatever you think is helpful. I know Francesca and I have different illnesses, but they're still similar in many ways. At least I won't be going crazy over the side effects."

Sophia nodded her head, her tender doe eyes expressing her feelings. I studied her. She appeared apprehensive about something. I decided I would start a conversation and open up a little more to her. She was trying…and so was I.

I licked my lips nervously. I wanted to tell her how I was really feeling inside. I wanted to make sure what I was feeling was normal and that I was supposed to go through these motions. A part of me hoped she had sound advice to give.

"I've had a lot time to think since I got home. I should've gotten up and gone about my usual day. I should've started packing and preparing to move. I should've had deep tissue massages post training so I didn't lock up. Instead, I let myself go. I couldn't do anything because all I did was think about *him*." I eyed her to see how she'd respond to mentioning Kova in the way I did. "Every day, all day, my thoughts have revolved around him. I wasn't even awake long and I still managed to think about him the majority of the time. I even dreamed about him. The strange thing is, he would be so angry to know I wasn't taking care of myself, that I'd gotten weaker. He wouldn't have wanted me to feel the way I have been." I sighed heavily. Saying these things aloud was vastly different than thinking about them. It made me reflect on myself. "I normally never succumb to these feelings, but I've been having a really hard time lately. All I do is lie in bed." I blinked rapidly, feeling the tears climb my eyes. "As the days passed into weeks, I realized that the reason I was sick was because of me."

Sophia had tears brimming on her eyelids. She didn't respond just yet, and I had more to get off my chest.

"I wasn't trying to make myself sick, I just missed him so damn much that I couldn't do anything else. How did you do it? How did you get over my dad if you loved him so much? How did you not think about giving me up? How do you wake up and not allow yourself to think about it?"

Sophia angled her head to the side. Her eyes were guarded. "I never got over him, and I never stopped thinking about you. Why do you think I'm here?" She smiled softly. Now I felt bad for asking her that. "You don't have to stop thinking about him, but you can't wallow in your feelings the way you have been either. That's not healthy. You have to pick yourself up and heal, and the only way you can do that is by learning to love yourself first. After that, you take each day one at a time."

I shook my head, not understanding how it could be so easy. "One second I know I need to leave and the next I want to stay. I know what I'm supposed to do, but I'm scared of the unknown. How did you leave the person you loved?"

She shrugged one shoulder and shook her head slowly. She wasn't even sure herself. "It's easy to fall in love when it's not the right time. Walking away is another story."

I let out a breathy laugh and glanced down. "It sucks when it's the first time."

Fuck. I hated heartbreak.

"Your time may never come, or maybe the stars will align when you least expect it and it'll happen. It took me too long to see that I had to do what was right for me to be happy and healthy in order to attempt a life with him or you again one day. I think you already know what you have to do, Adrianna."

I glanced away, my jaw was trembling. "Then why do I feel like this? I'm so torn. If I think it's right, then I'm wrong. My gut is just making me sick."

She blinked and her eyes lifted to mine. "You feel doubt."

"Yes," I said immediately. I was totally doubtful, and it was wrecking me inside.

Sophia shook her head. "You're not doubtful, you're emotional. You shouldn't doubt your decision, but you should be emotional over it."

Tears fell from the corners of my eyes. She was right. I twisted my fingers together.

"That feeling you have deep inside of you? Go with it. Trust it. It's okay to be emotional, even upset."

"I feel like I have two gut feelings." I laughed but I was being serious.

"You have to work on trusting yourself more."

I looked at Sophia. It was still strange to me that this woman was my biological mother and I had only just met her. She helped me at my lowest and was willing to stay by my side despite the baggage I carried. She didn't judge me or humiliate me, or make me feel bad for my choices. Sure, she probably had tons of thoughts running through her head, but she kept them to herself. She just listened and gave advice when I needed it most.

I couldn't recall one time Joy had ever been there for me in the way Sophia had. Before recently, I couldn't recall my dad being there much either. I realized during my time with Sophia that I longed for guidance, to have a parent tell me what I was going through was normal and that I was going to be okay. My heart was pounding in my throat. I wanted a real relationship with Sophia, and I hoped she wanted that too.

"There are no words that describe the gratitude I have for you." Taking a deep breath, I released it, and said, "I want to have a relationship as mother and daughter…if you want one with me. Even though you weren't part of my life until recently, you still didn't have to help me and be there for me like you have been." Pausing, I licked my lips nervously. "Thank you for coming into my life when I needed a mom the most."

"If it were up to me, I would've been in your life since day one. With that being said, I'm not going to focus on what I lost out on. I'm going to focus on the present and what I have in this moment and every day after. If you want me in your life, I'll be there. I want it more than anything, but I want it at your pace and when you're ready. I'll always be waiting. Do whatever you need to do for yourself. Don't worry about me, your father, your coach, your friends. You have to live the life *you* want. It's okay to not have all the answers right now. As long as you're trying to be the best version of yourself, that's all that matters."

My eyes dropped to my hands. Sophia's words moved me deeply.

"You have no idea how much I really needed to hear that." I smiled bigger and then sniffled. I looked up at Sophia.

Leaning closer toward me, Sophia said, "We lost out on a lot of time, and while I try not to think about it, it still breaks my heart. I don't want to waste another second with you."

I hoped she understood just how much I wanted a mom and one who wanted to be there. I'd take anything at this point. It would be so nice to be able to call her up and just talk. Avery had that with her mom, and I longed for that myself. Now that she was in my life, I wanted to know everything about her. Everything I missed out on.

"Tell me about your sister, about your parents. I want to know everything."

Sophia laughed. It was a full-on belly laugh that caused a wide smile to spread across my face. This was good, really good.

I sighed. My heart felt like it was in a good place for the first time in a while. I definitely couldn't open up about Kova to Sophia the way I did to Avery, but that's why Avery was my best friend, and Sophia was my mom.

"All in good time," Sophia said, growing serious. "Have you finished reading the book?"

Before I could answer, Dad opened the sliding glass door and stepped outside to join us.

"Not yet. I've been saving it to read on the plane." I paused, thinking about the hours I was going to spend at the dialysis center. "If you can recommend any more books, let me know. I'm going to need them."

Her eyes lit up. "I have plenty to recommend, and even a few at home I can give you. Reading is good for the soul and helps you escape reality for a little while." Sophia looked up at Dad. "Ready to go?"

Dad nodded. "I've got a late-night conference with Asia I can't miss. I need to head back to your place soon and use your office."

Sophia stood up and straightened out her shirt. She looked at me and said, "I'll be here around nine tomorrow morning to help pack."

Until then, I was going to lose myself in my journal and just write out what I was feeling.

chapter 48

Coach: Can I see you?

M
Y HEART LODGED IN MY THROAT.

I was pretty sure I stopped breathing for a whole minute.

Rolling over onto my stomach, I crumpled up my blanket under me and held my phone between both hands. I reread the single text message over and over until my eyes were blurry. It was still early in the morning and I didn't sleep well last night with everything on my mind. I could be hallucinating.

This was the message I'd been waiting on for weeks.

Now I wasn't sure how to react to it.

On one hand, I was excited to see that Kova was finally thinking about me. On the other, I was apprehensive to see him after the way we had left things.

Without wanting to look too eager, I put my cell phone down. If I responded immediately, then he'd know I was waiting. I didn't want to give that to him. We'd gone a month with no contact, I could hold out a little longer.

Not reaching for my phone was more of a struggle than I thought it would be. I turned over and got out of bed. My bones cracked and my lower back ached a little when I stood. I groaned inwardly and stretched my arms above my head. I took a long shower, then poured out the first nine pills of the day, and his message was still there.

I guess I wasn't hallucinating after all.

I stared at the screen trying to think of the right response. Butterflies took flight in my stomach knowing I'd be seeing him again.

Biting my lip, I finally texted back.

Me: How about tonight? My place?

He responded immediately. He'd been waiting. I smiled, taking satisfaction in that.

Coach: I will be there at 8.
Coach: See you later.

I checked my watch.

It was 7:57 and I was edgy with impatience. Kova would be here any minute.

I shook my fingers out. My nerves climbed as the clock ticked by. I'd dropped Dad and Sophia off at the airport earlier. We'd said our goodbyes, and I drove back to my condo, sweating to death from anxiety that I was going to see Kova. Would he still be *that* Kova? Would I still be Ria to him?

I had kept busy with the last of the boxes I had left to pack, then took a quick shower since I'd gotten so clammy after the drive home from the airport. I'd dressed and even added a touch of mascara to my lashes and a plum tint to my cheeks. The blush helped offset the dusting of freckles on the bridge of my nose.

I walked into the kitchen and grabbed a bottle of water. I'd been so parched lately, but that was due to not getting the daily ounces of water I needed since I was sleeping twenty hours a day. I'd have to start counting my meals and fluids again just to make sure I was getting the proper nutrients. Uncapping the bottle, my hand shook a little as I brought it to my mouth. I took a long pull then recapped it. Kova was going—

Knock. Knock. Knock.

My eyes widened as heat instantly prickled down my spine.

My heart froze.

I stared at the door for another long second then walked around the kitchen counter, nervous to answer it. While I had no idea which version of Kova stood on the other side of the door, I was excited and couldn't rub the smile off my face. I brushed a lock of hair behind my ear before I reached for the knob. Inhaling a deep pull of air, my heart was pulsating in my throat as the door opened and our eyes met.

He was still as handsome as ever.

I wasn't going to hide how I felt toward him. Not at this point. He could see through my gentle gaze and soft smile. I was looking at him with a love no one would ever stand a chance against. Kova was my everything and he'd never doubt it.

Sophia was right. I was emotional over my decision.

It'd been almost one full month since I'd last seen Kova. I didn't love him any less. He was similar to the ruined man who had left me behind in his hotel room, only he wasn't. Something was different about him. He looked ragged and worn down, but there was a peaceful aura around him in the midst of my chaos that soothed me. I was drawn to it.

All these feelings hit me at once as my eyes shifted back and forth between his.

The stupid man that I loved so much was looking at me with a stare I hadn't felt the weight of in so long. The plea in his gaze made me want to do anything for him again. He blinked and the struggle was there. He was dying inside without me, like I was without him. Kova was trying so hard to do what was right. The problem with that was he forgot about himself and what he wanted too.

I pushed the door back and welcomed him in.

I had to break the craving I got when Kova looked at me. I was all the things he needed from someone to give him, and I liked that I was. It made me feel good about myself because I grew stronger when he did. He was an addiction that I would always chase first.

"Adrianna," he said, and I felt my cheeks blush.

I locked the door, then slowly dragged my eyes up to his. "Hey."

"It is good to see you. I have missed you." Kova raked his eyes down the length of my body. "You look good."

"Likewise."

My ears were warm. I slipped my hands into the back pockets of my shorts and rocked on my toes and heels. I was nervous to take the step toward him even though that stupid organ in my chest was begging me to.

"How did you know I was here? When we were in Greece, I told you I was leaving."

Kova's response was a subtle curve to one corner of his lips. I didn't bother pushing the question. He had known I was here, he just took his precious time.

"What did you want to talk about?" I asked, changing the subject. I gestured toward the chairs at the breakfast counter. He raised a brow. I had boxes sporadically placed around my condo. "I actually have something I wanted to talk to you about too."

Kova took a seat and angled his body toward me. I caught a drift of his cologne and faltered in my step. Desire prickled down my arms and I blinked. I exhaled a breath. My palms were clammy, I was restless for his touch. My chest rose and fell so quickly as a flood of emotions came roaring back into my heart. This was going to be much harder than I'd thought.

Just as I was about to sit next to him, Kova reached out and hooked a finger around my belt loop. With a tug, he spread his legs and pulled me to him. I inhaled a gasp. My hands came flying up and pushed against his chest when our eyes met. The connection was automatic for me. My fingers curled around his shirt and I felt the pull. I leaned into him, needing to close the distance.

Hugging me with his legs, I was just inches from Kova and eye level with him. My lips parted as I peered through my lashes at him. His stubble was much thicker than he usually wore it, and there were faint purple circles under his eyes that I hadn't noticed at first. The tips of my fingers brushed across his collarbone. I did it again, and Kova's palms warmed against my back, pulling me toward him. His touch scorched my skin, flames of desire coaxing me to let nature take its course. The back of my hand grazed his facial hair.

Our lips were seconds away from meeting. "*Malysh*," he whispered.

I pulled back and frowned at him. The curtain lifted, the smoke cleared, and I blinked. That was why I was in this predicament in the first place. He called my name and I came running. Over the past month, I was forced to reassess a lot of the choices I'd made. I felt different inside now. My views had shifted.

I took a small step back, but not so that we had to stop touching. "What did you want to talk to me about?"

His head dipped to the side and he peered up at me with alluring eyes. "I spoke with an attorney on what the best course of action was for my marriage. I filed for divorce."

I blinked. Wow. *Not* what I'd expected.

"I don't understand," I said, my throat a little dry.

"I told Katja I no longer cared what she had on me. I was running worried and she thrived off that. When I showed her I did not care about her threats and actually filed, it was not a thrill to her anymore. I have a long way to go, but the divorce process has been started."

His brows knitted toward each other when I didn't respond. Kova had already told me he was filing for divorce because Katja had gotten pregnant by another man. It was his way out for all the blackmail she had on him. It wasn't for *us*, though. "I told you before Frank found us that I was going to," Kova added when I'd remained silent.

Kova filing for divorce should've relieved me, even made me feel giddy, not this sense of indifference unfurling inside of me. I was supposed to leave, and he just threw a curveball at me.

I studied Kova. Was I supposed to say congratulations?

"When did you file?"

"Two weeks ago."

He'd filed two weeks ago and it took him that long to reach out to me. Something about that crushed me.

"Where is Katja? Where does she live now?"

He shook his head, confusion filling his eyes. "At my house," he said, then he sobered up. My hands fell from his chest and I tried to take another step back, but Kova caged me in. My pulse sped up.

"And that's where she's been with you since you got back, right?"

The happiness Kova had walked in with was slowly dissolving into thin air. His shoulders hardened and his brows creased together like he was offended I could insinuate anything more.

"You question my love for you," he stated, quiet and low.

I shook my head. "Never."

I knew Kova loved me, and that no one would ever love me the way he did.

"What do you want me to do, Adrianna? I am trying to make the necessary changes for our future. Is that not what matters?"

I wasn't expecting the knife to slice through my chest the way it did. I wanted to yell back and demand to know why he waited two weeks to see me. If he wanted time knowing that I didn't have much of it to give, why didn't he move quicker if he was sticking to his plan? I was trying not to be nitpicky but that was weeks wasted that we'd never get back. Weeks we could have spent talking things out and figuring out life together. Hearing that he was still living with Katja hurt me. It didn't matter that he'd filed for divorce if he was still living with her.

If Kova was serious about us, he could've gone to a hotel or rented a condo. Anything to prove he was putting me and him first because it was something he wanted for us. But he hadn't.

Without an ounce of emotion, I said, "If the divorce is what you want, then I'm glad for you."

chapter 49

KOVA PULLED BACK, A TINGE OF WORRY ETCHED HIS FOREHEAD. His eyes shifted quickly between mine. "It is what you wanted too, yes?" he said.

"What I want shouldn't sway your decision. The decision should only be yours, Kova."

His worry deepened. "The decision *is* mine. You knew I needed a way out and why I had to stay married. We talked about this and you agreed with me. Now that I have filed papers you have a change of mind? What happened? I do not understand why you went backward instead of forward."

I was one of those angry criers. I could feel the tears rushing to the surface threatening to spill over. The last thing I wanted to do was to shed more tears.

I couldn't figure out what I was most angry about, though. Was it that Kova wanted time? Or the fact that I was sick and I resented myself for it?

My hands were resting on his spread thighs. I could feel the tears clogging my throat. I didn't change my mind, we just didn't agree with what the other wanted. I drew in a breath through my nose. My eyes closed shut and I clenched them to hold in the tears.

"What is it?" he said, his voice grave.

"Did you just think you could ignore me for however long you needed to, then come back and act like time didn't pass and everything would be fine and I would be waiting here?" A sharp ache shot through my chest. "A quick update and then it's goodbye for a little while again? Because I had a lot of time to think during these four weeks, and after the way we parted, I was under the impression you were completely done with me."

His brows shot up, his eyes widened. Kova's voice was bold. "I said I needed some time. We both do."

I shook my head in disagreement. "Time is infinite. You can't tell someone you need time and expect them to wait until you get your life together."

My pulse hammered away in my neck. I was proud of myself for standing up. We both remained quiet until Kova spoke.

"I want you. You want me. Is that not enough for us to hold on to for now?"

He looked at me with his heart on his sleeve. I shook my head, regret filling my veins. It simply wasn't enough. We'd learned that the hard way and we'd both suffered. It was now or never. It had to be.

"You've had me on your time since we started," I responded, my words were just above a whisper. "You had me when you pulled me from the first meet. You had me when you got married. You had me the months following when I was devastated that you could lie to me the way you did and hide your marriage. I don't think you understand the magnitude of what that did to me." I paused. "You had me when Katja paraded around your gym humiliating me, rubbing your marriage and my poor health in my face. Still, you had me when I got pregnant. But now that I have to step away from gymnastics for a little while to work on my health, you want more time..." I shook my head and said, "It's always when you're ready for me and never the other way around."

Blood drained from his cheeks. He leaned back. "That is not true," Kova said, his green eyes flaring. "I want you always. There is much unfinished business left to take care of and too much outside noise. We would be fighting every day like we are now and grow to hate each other. I cannot stomach the thought of that."

We'd always had shit between us and still managed to make it work. I wanted to stomp my foot because it was no different now.

"You had me through the good, the bad, and everything in between. Anytime you needed me, I've been here. Where were you all the times I needed you? That's right. You were playing house with your wife."

His back straightened with indignation. "That is not fair, Adrianna," he said, his voice low but steady.

"Maybe not. But I've given you more than enough time. I've been waiting for you to choose me since before you made Katja your wife, because even back then when it first started between us, my feelings for you were that strong. I waited, though, for different reasons. Mainly because I was so young. I thought that was the issue, but I'm learning it's more than that."

Kova's eyes softened with pure unfiltered rawness. His face fell. I think it was starting to really hit him that I wasn't changing my mind. He couldn't give me what I wanted, and that killed him. It killed me too.

The barefaced truth was I would do anything for him.

It wasn't that I thought he wouldn't do anything for me, but he had to think about it first. I didn't.

That was the difference.

"I am trying, Ria," he said dejectedly. His fingers let go of my belt loops and found the back of my thighs. His palms were warm to the touch. Kova leaned forward, his back bending over so he could look into my eyes and plead with me. His eyes were so vibrant and green. "Please believe me. You have every part of me. No one has ever had me the way you do, and no one ever will. I am doing the best I can, given the situation."

Guilt ate through my lungs, squeezing them tight. I moved my hands from his thighs to his biceps. My thumbs glided over the veins. I pressed and watched the vein compress and expand.

"I want you now. I want you on my time. I don't want to wait around anymore for you. I love you and you love me. Couples fight and then they make up. They learn from mistakes and it brings them closer. Isn't that how it happens? I really think in the end we would be okay.

"I want you to be mine and only mine, and that means not living with anyone else if it's not me in the meantime. I want you to be committed to me unconditionally. Can you give me that? Give yourself to me completely the way I can give myself to you?"

God, the look in his eyes was going to ruin me forever. It was seared into my heart. I knew his answer before he did.

"I didn't think so," I answered quietly for him.

There was no animosity between us. Just brokenhearted words neither of us expected. Kova was trying. I just couldn't give him more than an inch without it eventually leading to another heartbreak. That would require more than I had to give.

"I didn't hear from you for a month. Is that what we are now? A monthly check-in?" I said, trying to step away again.

Kova pulled me closer and dipped his head into the curve of my neck. He exhaled a heavy breath and it prickled my skin. He held me tight and I let him because even though he'd hurt me so many times, I didn't know when I would see him again. My arms wound around his shoulders and it was my turn to dip my face near his.

"Do not dare reduce us to that."

"Actions, Kova. I can't give a title to something without cause. You gave it to me."

"Adrianna, you are not being reasonable." He stressed against my collarbone. "Sit back and think about what you are holding against me. My hands are tied."

Pulling back, I had to look at Kova when I said what I needed to say next. He had to see how much his decision had crushed me, how it ultimately changed me. I hoped one day I'd be able to forget it, but I wasn't sure how when anytime

I thought about my time at the Olympics and who was on that journey with me, I'd always, and forever, think of Kova. He didn't just leave a footprint on my heart. As always, Kova went the extra mile and carved it out of my chest with his chalk-covered hands and took it with him.

"When you saw me break down in that hotel room… When I finally needed you for once, you walked away."

His eyes hardened and his body tensed under my hands. "Let me refresh your memory that I was there for you after training and during recovery. I took care of you when you could not on those nights. I even became certified to treat your Achilles injury and bought proper equipment just for you. You hid your illnesses from me and would not let me be there for that, so I had to be a piece of shit and push you to open up to me because I knew you needed me. I let you use a knife on me because you needed me. So do not dare tell me I have not once been there for you. I have plenty of times. We are not so different, Adrianna."

Warm tears fell from my eyes. I burst out crying. Kova knew more about how I felt about my illnesses than Avery. He knew my darkest fears and how I was scared it was going to kill me at a young age. That was the hardest reality to accept, that I was going to live this next chapter of my life on my own.

Kova dragged me a little closer again. He was right. We weren't so different, and he *had* been there for me.

Wrapping his arms around my back, he pressed the tips of his fingers into my sides as he hugged me. I whimpered softly until I got myself together to look at him again.

Kova reached out and used his thumbs to wipe away my tears as I said, "I can't keep getting caught up in us holding out for more when all it does is make me sicker in the end." Exhaling a deep breath, I said, "I put too much into us."

He looked at me, his brows lowered. He seemed concerned. I gestured to the space between me and him. Emotion cracked in my voice and my chin wobbled.

"The old me wouldn't have hesitated to give you exactly what you wanted." My lips pressed together. Kova squinted at my mouth. "I had to make a choice." I shook my head, feeling miserable. Kova finally dropped his hands from me, mine fell to the tops of his thighs again. His lips parted in what I would assume was disbelief. "You mess with my mind too much. You're all I think about almost every second of the day. I get so consumed in *you* that I forget about *me*. It's taken enough of a toll on my life." My voice shook. "I love you—"

Kova pushed the barstool back and swiftly stood. He looked terrified. Utterly terrified. I could feel the fear pumping in his chest.

"Adrianna, stop," he said. "Do not say another word," he warned.

I kept going even though it was going to hurt him. I had to get it out and this was the only time we had.

"I love you, but I need to get my mind right and my health right, and I realized I can't do that near you. The more I stay around you, the more destruction it causes to my life." I paused, and he held his breath. "I wanted you to be all in, but you wouldn't. I didn't want to have to question us as a couple in between dialysis appointments. It had to be all or nothing for me. You made your choice, and so did I."

His eyes widened and his lips parted. I swear I could hear his heart beating. "What are you telling me?"

My heart lodged in my throat, and more tears brimmed my eyelids. I took a step back. Kova looked down, confused, then back at me. This next part was going to be so difficult.

"I need to focus on me."

"What are you saying?" He demanded through a harsh whisper. "Say it."

I stared. With tears streaming down my cheeks, my voice was so small and dripping in defeat.

"This is goodbye."

His hand came up slowly to cover his mouth, his eyes bore into mine. "I refuse to accept this." His words exposed the shake in his voice, and once again, I almost yielded. "Absolutely not."

"You have no choice but to accept it. I've already made up my mind." I paused. "In two days when I board my plane, I'm leaving us here and saying goodbye to what we once were."

The anguish filling my chest was almost too much. Whoever said "sticks and stones may break your bones but words will never hurt" was a total fucking liar.

Kova's lips parted and I felt his shock reverberate through me. His wild eyes held me immobile. He ate up the space between us in three strides, his gait heavy with determination. He closed the distance and I placed my hand on his chest to stop him. A gasp escaped my lips as he cupped the back of my head and brought his mouth to hover above mine. Kova leaned into me as he pulled my body to his.

"Don't make this harder than it needs to be," I whispered. "Please." He shook his head, his beautiful eyes pleading. Hot air swept across my cheek as he exhaled through his nose. I knew what he was thinking—we were already passed that point. Kova pressed closer to my lips and I arched back, curling into him.

"No." It was all he said. "No." His voice shook a little this time. "Not this."

Kova pressed his nose into my cheek, and his hands traveled my back. He picked me up and wrapped my legs around his back. His fingers threaded through my hair and cupped the back of my neck. He held me to him for dear life. Heat flooded my body, and a soft sigh rolled off my lips. I felt his sorrow and it consumed me. I exhaled and melted into him, missing him so much already. He swept frantic kisses across the slope of my neck. My thighs squeezed around his waist in response and I held him to me just as tight.

I loved this man with every part of me, but that wasn't enough to stop me from executing the hardest thing I had ever done in my life.

Kova pulled back and met my gaze. He couldn't take his hands off of me. The startling revelation in his eyes was much harder to witness than I'd expected.

"You are leaving me," he stated.

My lips puckered and tears blurred my vision. The creases between Kova's brows deepened with each second I didn't respond.

"I'm leaving us."

Kova shook his head. His gaze bore into mine and it twisted my stomach. This was a total blow to his gut and it showed.

"What does *us* mean? Define it, Adrianna."

My shoulders fell. "Why are you bothered by this? It's what you wanted, isn't it? The time you so badly needed?"

He pulled my lips closer to his. "Not if there was a chance I could not ever see you again," he responded immediately.

My nostrils flared. "While you were making decisions that worked for you, I made a decision for myself. The time you needed away from me was enough time for me to reevaluate my life."

A breath hitched in my throat. The moment the words left my mouth I regretted them. I was finally understanding why people lied to their loved ones. Sometimes the truth hurt more.

Tormented eyes regarded me.

Shaking my head with regret, I said quietly, "Times up, Kova."

He didn't hesitate.

Kova pressed his lips to mine in a no-holds-barred kiss. He inhaled me deep and drew me into him like I was the air he breathed.

Like he didn't want to let go.

chapter 50

Kova's fingers pressed into my waist, and I clenched his shirt in my fist. I kissed him back without reservation.

Our lips fused together too perfectly, the stars only ever aligning for us when our bodies did. It wasn't fair, it was a cruel existence that tortured our emotions, but it was how we communicated.

Kova's grip on me tightened. I arched into him with a small gasp as his tongue delved into my mouth. A moan vibrated in the back of my throat causing Kova to escalate his assault on my mouth. I kissed him back with just as much vigor, arching my hips against his. Kova noticed and responded with a skilled stroke that made my toes curl. I was getting lost in the man who was my everything and that I was inevitably walking away from. He was my awakening and my reckoning.

Breaking the kiss, I whispered, "I'm sorry."

"You are just going to give up on us? Just like that?" His grip tightened like he was afraid of my answer.

My jaw trembled at the defensive tone in his voice. "I'm not giving up on the idea of us, but I am letting go of us right now."

"No," he whispered sharply and shook his head. "I know what that means. Please," he begged, "do not do this. Whatever you want, it is yours. Tell me and I will honor it."

Tears trickled over my pressed lips and down my chin. His gaze was a kaleidoscope of emotions. It hurt to see him in pain like this, to know that for once it was me doing the hurting.

His eyes were glossy with tears. This was the second time I'd seen an emotion this powerful on Kova. It rattled me. The last time this happened, he'd found out I was pregnant.

"It's too late," I said, my decision final.

Without saying another word, Kova slammed his mouth to mine. He savagely kissed me like his life depended on it. His hands were all over my body, the warmth creating a carnal glow throughout me. I jerked forward to kiss him back and bite his lip. He touched every inch of me he could. The desperation in his touch was what took me by surprise and revived the flame I'd gone breathless to blow out. His tongue plunged into my mouth and wrapped around mine in a sweep of untamed passion. His kiss was a feeling, an erratic pulse. Kova's hand captured mine. He squeezed my fingers, pressing our joined hands against his heart where the letter A would be for the rest of his life.

"Fuck everything. I am going to sell the gym and come with you. Where you go, I go. It is us, Adrianna. I would rather fight with you every day than risk never being with you again."

I gasped, shock ricocheting through me. Burning stones were tossing around in my stomach. Kova was going to give up what he loved. Had I been wrong about how he felt about us all along? My heart clenched at the thought.

No, I wouldn't go there. I wasn't going to backtrack because he said something I wanted to hear.

"You can't do that," I said. "You can't, Kova. I won't allow it. You love that gym."

He pressed his lips to mine. "I love you more, and if that is what it takes, then so be it. I do not care if you tell me every hour that I am being a dickhead, or that I am terrible at expressing myself, or that this was a mistake. As long as we are together, then say all you want. I know where your heart lies for me. But if it will chance ever being with you again? No. Absolutely not."

He kissed me again until I was breathless. I allowed it by pressing the back of his head so his lips crushed mine. Desperate lips and painstakingly slow hands showed that what we had was real. I never wanted to let go of him. What I wanted, now, was to change my mind.

My breathing labored to wheezing and that worried me, but not enough to stop. And that was my biggest flaw right there that could eventually cause me my life—I stopped thinking about *me* when I was with *him*.

This feeling, though, this connection, the chemistry driving us together, it was once in a lifetime and why I allowed it to devour me.

"You're just making it harder," I said, breaking the kiss, and Kova groaned.

Flattening my hand, I pressed on his chest to push him back to put space between us, only I fisted his shirt and tugged him to me.

"Fuck," I whispered under my breath and dropped my head on the curve of his shoulder. I couldn't let go, damn it. I was scared to, because the truth was, I didn't want to. I honestly didn't want to let him go.

Taking my jaw into his hand, Kova tipped it back until I was forced to look at him. His thumb pressed under the center of my chin and his palm cupped my throat. The gesture was tender but his touch longed for love. Kova stared into my eyes. He fought to steady the tremble in his hand, but I felt it.

He exhaled, and like always, I inhaled.

Then Kova gave me a soul-searing kiss that almost made me change my mind. His lips suctioned over mine and he breathed me into him like I was his last dying breath. His kiss evoked the unusual love we had for each other, and I loved that it did. It made it that more ours and ours alone.

"Do you not see it yet, *Malysh?*" His eyes were frantic. "I bleed my emotion silently, and you express yours with hunger. It is a give and a take, a perfect balance, which makes us right for each other. We need each other."

Just not right now, I thought as more tears surfaced. He'd only changed his mind because I set the ultimatum.

Kova placed me on my feet and turned away. I watched as his hands came up to the back of his head and he laced his fingers together. Frustration bloomed a shade of red under his white knuckles.

He turned around and I almost lost my breath. Konstantin Kournakova was a beautiful tragedy I'd never forget.

"I am going to accept the offer I got for World Cup from Danilo. He can have it all," he said with determination. "I will talk to my attorney about rushing the divorce, and I will give Katja whatever she wants to be away from her. You want to say goodbye forever? No, that is not happening. It is a done deal, the gym will be sold. I had already started the preparations. I will just move it along quicker." Kova paused, then caught me by surprise. "I am coming with you."

I shook my head, he wasn't understanding.

chapter 51

M Y CHEST ACHED. I DIDN'T WANT HIM TO MAKE THESE DECISIONS because of my tears. I wanted him to make them based on his own feelings and experiences, the way I had.

"Don't. Don't do that. Don't give up what you love for me," I argued.

"It is done. I am selling World Cup."

Goose bumps broke out over my arms. He made it sound like he was so sure about it.

"It's too late for that," I said miserably. "I'm going alone."

The look on his face had me drowning in grief. Kova hung his head between his shoulders. I could feel his suffering pouring into me and it was wrecking my heart. I walked over to him. He wrapped his arms around the small of my back and hugged me so tight I could feel the subtle shake under his muscles.

"I do not want to live without you."

My eyes closed shut, seeping with tears. "Our love makes me sicker, Kova."

My face was folded into the column of his neck as he gave me a hug. Kova didn't respond for a long minute, maybe two. He was sinking in anguish with me. We stayed in each other's arms as reality fell upon us.

Our love made me sicker. Our love ultimately tore us apart.

I wiped away the tears under my eyes and took a deep breath. His suffering mimicked mine and it made this that much tougher. Kova's gaze was glossy, brimming with dread.

"I know it is selfish of me to try to stop you, but love is selfish, and, *Malysh*, I have never loved anyone or anything as much as I love you. If you are leaving, then so am I."

My stomach clenched. The words I longed to hear were too late.

Shaking my head, I was brutally honest. "I don't want you to come with me."

He didn't blink. He didn't even move for a long moment. His lips pressed together and he subtly nodded his head. His form became blurry in front of me.

"Can I at least take you to the airport?"

I sniffled. "Yes."

Cupping the sides of my face, Kova bent down. My hands found his hips just as he pressed one last kiss to my lips.

"Just know that this is not what I want. It is going to be the biggest challenge of my life to see you walk away, but I will. I will give you what you want and hope our love only grows from the distance into something that will force us to come together and be impossible to walk away from again one day."

He kissed me hard, then briskly pulled back and spun around. Kova didn't stop, not even when he flung the door open and marched out with my heart did he turn around and look back at me.

❦

"Tell me I'm doing the right thing," I cried into the phone a couple minutes later. "Because if I am, why does it hurt so bad?"

The first thing I did was call Avery. I could barely see the screen from the fat warm tears pouring out of me to find her name. The waterworks were turned up high and I was hiccupping into the phone.

"You had one job, and you ended up screwing your coach." A sad laugh escaped me at her dry humor. "What happened?"

I sniffled and pulled my knees up to my chest, nestling further into the corner of my couch. I stared out the sliding glass door at the swaying palm trees, rewinding the story from the beginning for Avery. I broke down multiple times and asked her repeatedly if I was making a mistake. She insisted it was par for the course and encouraged me not to feel bad about it.

"You're doing the right thing. It takes courage to defy your heart. If your health wasn't in jeopardy, then I'd say you need to give yourselves a fighting chance. But I can't. There's too much at stake, and if Kova did anything to risk your progress, I would personally kill him."

My teeth worried my bottom lip. "It just feels… I don't know…" My voice was distant.

"It's going to feel like that for a long time," Avery said, knowing what I meant.

I was nauseous. My nerves were so bad I felt like they were burning a hole through the lining of my stomach. How long was a long time? He hadn't even been gone for more than an hour and I wanted to run to him.

"I told him he could take me to the airport."

Avery groaned.

"What does that mean?"

"It means there's a ninety-nine percent chance you're going to change your mind now. I kind of wish you didn't agree." She half joked, half laughed. "Tomorrow when the movers are at your house, all you're going to be thinking about is saying goodbye to Kova the following day. That anticipation is going to build and you're going to give in."

"Maybe I'm supposed to cave." I countered. "Everywhere I look, I see him. I smell him. I *feel* him, Ave. My heart is saying don't do it." I was drowning in heartache and beginning to doubt my choice now.

"Now's not the right time to think with your heart, chica. Look at where your heart's taken you the last few years," she said sympathetically. "Yeah, you're essentially walking away from someone who can never be replaced. You'll never have what you have with Kova with someone else. And you know what? You don't want it with anyone else. So in a way, you're walking away with assurance that this is how it's supposed to be for now, and that one day it will be worth it because there isn't a world that exists where you two aren't together."

My stomach was churning into tighter knots. "This is going to suck," I muttered.

"Tomorrow when the movers are there, just call me. Call me eighty-seven times if you have to. I just want you to think first before you make any decision."

"I will. Do you think he'll show up tomorrow?"

"I think when you told him everything, including your love is making you sicker, that put shit into perspective for him. Aid, even *I* felt that, and I don't even love you like that." We both laughed. "But you know why it hurt when I felt it? Because it's the damn truth and it fucking sucks. Kova knows that, that's why he didn't argue with you. So, no, I don't think he'll show up."

"Aren't we too young to feel heartache like this?" I joked, then rubbed at the tightness in my chest. Wiping my eyes with the back of my hand, I sat up a little straighter and exhaled.

"I'm learning that there are no rules in the game of love." Avery was wistful.

"I'm forfeiting now."

We both laughed again then said our goodbyes, with a promise that I'd call her first thing tomorrow. I was still suck in the corner of the couch with no will to get up.

Slouching down, I clicked on the picture icon on my phone and scrolled through photos I'd saved of Kova and me, looking for a specific one. I didn't have many, but I had enough that even in spite of my broken heart it still held memories I never wanted to forget.

I stopped scrolling when I found it. I stared, unblinking at the image that brought tears to my eyes. Only, I wasn't looking at just the image. I pictured myself standing in the room watching the pair take a selfie together. They were at ease with each other and I found myself longing for it. She was a tiny, happy thing snuggled in his strong arms. He was protective over her, though she didn't know it yet. Laid back and in love were a few words I'd use to describe the feeling on his face as he lifted the phone, and with a few clicks, he captured this photo.

It was the day he came to my hotel room after I had to attend and watch the meet he wouldn't allow me to compete in. He'd pulled me onto his lap after and asked what I'd learned. I'd resented him leading up to that day until understanding had dawned on me. His motives were genuine, the outcome constructive, but the way he delivered them was usually questionable. It was a day I would never forget. I thought it was when I really started to feel something for Kova.

It was also when he'd said we were a team, exhaling and inhaling together. I was his weakness and he was my strength. We inspired each other, and we pushed each other to be better people than the day before. He was the beast beneath my beauty, pushing me, he'd said.

It was all true, and that's what broke me down.

Tears filled my eyes. The longer I stared at the picture, the more I longed to feel safe in Kova's arms again.

Pressing down on the image, I saved it as my wallpaper.

chapter 52

I STARTLED AWAKE AND SAT UPRIGHT, LISTENING.

I thought I heard a bang.

Blinking my blurry eyes, I glanced around and yawned. I must've fallen asleep on the couch. I spotted my cell phone on the floor and realized that was the sound that woke me. I picked it up and checked the time. It was close to midnight. I tucked it into my stomach then curled onto my side. That space in between just falling asleep and really sleeping was—

Knock, knock, knock.

I froze, my hand clenching my cell phone tighter. My body instantly warmed. Staring at the front door, I knew who stood on the other side without having to guess. I breathed and felt goose bumps pebble my skin.

There was a small part of me that secretly hoped he'd show.

I placed my phone down and stood on unsteady legs. I crossed the carpet and reached for the knob. I stilled for a moment. My heart was pounding in my throat. I didn't have to open the door. I could pretend I was asleep. It would be the right thing to do, and then I wouldn't feel guilty about lying to people about him. He knocked again, this time a little heavier.

My heart was racing.

I swallowed thickly and asked myself what *I* wanted.

Without a second thought, I reached for the lock and unbolted it.

Holding my breath, I pulled the door open and found Kova leaning against the frame. Both of his elbows were pressed against the sides to hold him up and his legs were crossed at his ankles. His head hung miserably between his shoulders and he was staring at the floor.

I didn't have to say anything, and neither did he.

My stomach was a knotted mess seeing him like this.

I felt his despair coming from a mile away. I was sure he felt my sorrow when I was looking at our pictures earlier and reminiscing. My fingers twitched.

I knew if I took one more step it would change the course of the night for us. The knots in my stomach were growing. I could be strong in my personal pursuit, but I could also be human and allow us one more night. Kova came to me. He was leaving the choice up to me.

I reached for him.

Stepping forward, I wrapped my arms around his lower back and hugged him. His elbows fell and he engulfed me with his body. I pressed the side of my face to Kova's chest and closed my eyes. I heard his heart beating rapidly and tasted his bitter anguish on my tongue. Stepping closer, my arms tightened around him.

Kova rested his cheek on the top of my head and hugged me with a passion that pushed down my walls. I inhaled and felt his heat spread through me.

Home.

This was home for us.

"I wish I did not love you the way I do, Adrianna," he whispered. "I wish I was a stronger man."

Tears sprung to my eyes and I clenched them tight. His tone almost brought me to my knees. Kova was gutted. There was a rawness in his voice that sounded like he'd been crying all night. I knew exactly what he meant, though. We had no right to love the way we did.

I lifted my head from his chest to finally see his face. My stomach twisted as our eyes met.

"You're the strongest man I know."

His eyes were rimmed a pale pink. Kova was a robust man but the weakness in his indecisive gaze left me feeling for him. I had the notion that he was ashamed he was here, but not embarrassed. It was an inkling in my gut, but I'd feel the same way if it were me.

Rising up on my tiptoes, I ran the pad of my thumb over his lower lip and tugged it to the side. I watched it plop back and did it again, feeling hungry for his lips on mine.

My other hand cupped the side of his jaw and I brought his mouth toward me. My body arched perfectly along his. Kova held me closer. Need surged through me and I pulled in a deep breath. Just before I pressed our lips together, I whispered, "Let's finish what we started."

Our lips met. The words burned my throat and my heart sank with reality.

This would be our last night together and I realized how much I wanted this for me, for him, for us. But I also realized how deeply it would hurt in the end.

The kiss deepened and I held my breath, my heart racing with desire. Kova nodded without separating us and I almost fainted with excitement. I couldn't hold back and plunged my tongue into his warm mouth. Kova met me needy stroke for hungry stroke. His silky tongue was the most illicit.

Our bodies aligned and he tightened his arms around me. This kiss wasn't a painfully hard one, it didn't fill me with anger or sadness. It was a kiss that longed for more days watching the sunsets together.

It was a kiss that was supposed to be felt forever. And boy, did I feel it in my chest.

My back arched and I lifted a leg to hook it around Kova's leg for more stability. He got the hint and hoisted me up instead. My legs wrapped around his waist and I gripped him between me. I felt so tiny, protected, and loved in his arms.

"Come inside and lock the door," I said quickly before my lips were back on his. "Don't forget the chain," I added.

I knew where this was going, and so did he.

There wouldn't be any talking, just breathless pants and naked bodies making sweet harmony together between damp sheets.

And I was okay with that. I needed it, he needed it. I was impatient for him and squeezed my thighs around him. The only time we were ourselves and open with each other was when he was deep inside of me and I was at his mercy. It was carnal and it was glorious. I loved what our bodies did when no one was looking.

Kova walked inside and kicked the door behind him then turned to secure it before he carried us away to my bedroom. Our lips didn't separate and his tongue never stopped caressing mine as he held me with one arm under my ass and the other hand tangled in my hair.

He didn't bother to flip on the light, we didn't need it, I'd accidentally left the bathroom light on earlier and it provided a soft glow in the bedroom. He brought us to my bed and held me closely as he leaned over and laid me down in the center. He covered me with his weight and twisted his tongue around mine. We moaned in harmony at the feel of our bodies pressed together. I ground my hips erotically against his, not holding back tonight. Kova reciprocated, and he let out a hearty groan when I rubbed my pussy down his thigh. I was already so wet for him.

Only Kova could intoxicate me with a kiss.

His elbows boxed me in. My hands gripped his backside with need. I pressed my fingers into him and felt him contract under my touch. The only sound in the room was that of our lips. Kova kissed me with a sensuality that I was sure was only seen in movies. We had a full-blown hot and heavy make out session that was probably some of the best foreplay we'd ever had while he still had his hat on backwards and we were both fully clothed.

"I want you all night."

Kova dusted kisses on my jaw and sloped down to my neck. He moved the collar of my shirt to the side and kissed whatever he could put his lips to.

"Yes." I sighed, arching my chest into him.

My fingers reached for the hem of his shirt and pulled it up. Kova moved just enough for me to drag it over his head and then his mouth was on mine again. I got the feeling he was scared to stop kissing me and made sure to meet me stroke for stroke until he took my breath away.

Blindly, I felt around my bed for his hat. That broke the kiss, which almost made me giggle. He looked at me and I answered the question in his eyes.

"I always loved the hat on you."

Kova replaced the hat and regarded me. Soft eyes roamed over my face just as my hands found the waistband of his shorts. I didn't pull them down yet, I just wanted to feel the planes of his back one more time.

Dragging my hands down the length of his back, his muscles contracted under my fingers as he kissed me. I reached around to his lower stomach, running my fingers along the crease of his flesh and the seam of his elastic shorts. His hips flexed as I glided my nails along the deep grooves of strength.

I pulled back and ran the tip of my tongue over my bottom lip then pressed my teeth down. I dragged them over and glanced nervously into his eyes.

"What do you want to say," Kova asked gently. "Tell me."

I became shy, but for a valid reason. He could reject me and I wasn't sure I was prepared for that.

Kova adjusted his legs and I felt his cock slide against my thigh toward my pussy. My back bowed and my legs spread wider to feel more of his length.

"Will you stay the night?"

He smiled faintly and dropped his gaze to my lips. Kova nodded then found my lips again. Relief coursed through me and I could breathe. I twisted my legs around his and gasped as he surged forward and crossed over my clit. He kissed me until we were both panting in desperation, then he pulled back and climbed off the bed.

I watched him, curious what he would do next. I was hungry for him and already missed him on me. He toed off his shoes, then hooked his thumbs in his shorts and shoved them down. I pushed up on my elbows and watched in fascination as he stepped out of his shorts. His cock sprang free, the crown glistened in the dim light. Desire pulsed through me, and I pulled my knees up and my toes curled under me.

Kova cupped his sack and adjusted himself. I drew in a shallow breath, still in a bit of disbelief that he was here. He palmed his length and my lips parted as he twisted his wrist and gave himself a good squeeze. I pressed my thighs together and wetness coated my pussy. I drew a breath in through my nose and arched my back. A soft moan rolled off my lips. For a brief moment I wondered how I was going to live without him and why I was doing this to myself when I felt so strongly toward him. Kova waved two fingers at me to look up. Heat bloomed under my cheeks as our eyes met.

"Are you sure this is what you want?" he asked.

I swallowed and nodded.

"Say it."

"I want you," I said, curling my toes tighter.

His eyes bore into mine. "Tell me again. Once I start, I will not stop."

A smile tipped my lips. This was one of my favorite sides of Kova. "Make love to me."

His gaze darkened. That was all the confirmation he needed. Kova extended his arm and grabbed my ankle. He yanked me down the bed, and in the blink of an eye, he had my shorts and panties off and on the floor. He climbed over my body and I sat up, putting my arms in the air for him to remove my shirt. He tore it off and unhooked my bra in a flash.

"I am desperate and crazy for you." A gasp lodged in my throat. My heart ached. "This is not goodbye sex. Do you understand me, Ria?"

chapter 53

KOVA GAVE ME A QUICK KISS THEN REARED BACK AND GRABBED MY hips. He flipped me over to face the bed and jerked my ass up. Heat zipped down my spine. My arms moved to the sides of my head and I spread my fingers out for balance. He tapped the back of my thighs and my knees automatically spread wider. A sigh rolled off my lips. Moving the hair from my face, I peered over my shoulder and caught a glimpse of Kova. His eyes were on my exposed sex. He made me feel desired the way he stared. I clenched and imagined his fingers on my clit. My pussy contracted and his eyes lowered.

"Arch your back." I did, and he growled. "More, Adrianna." He demanded. "I know you can do better than that."

A wistful grin spread across my face. Of course, I could. I just wanted to hear him say it.

I curved my back and gave him the view he wanted. He palmed my ass cheek and goose bumps pebbled my skin. I pushed my ass into his hand wanting more and watched as his jaw flexed in appreciation the sharper the angle was. His thumb grazed over my swollen lips. Pleasure glazed my pussy and Kova used it to tease me. A moan escaped my throat.

Lowering himself, Kova gripped the top of my thighs to hold me still. He disappeared from view and placed his flat tongue on my pussy. My jaw dropped and I gasped, feeling pleasure drip from me toward his mouth.

"Yes." I sighed.

His fingers dug into my legs as he pulled me to him and gave me a long, thick lick with his tongue. Chills danced over me and my eyes fell shut. He caressed my clit until my hips were moving into his face, then he penetrated my entrance and stroked me until I was reaching behind me and wrapping my fingers around his wrist. He was tormenting me.

Dragging his tongue higher, my pussy clenched knowing where he was going. One of his hands left my thighs and he pushed down on my lower back to spread my knees wider. It felt different at this angle, more intense and better. I liked when he put pressure on me so I couldn't move much. There was something arousing about it.

With a last sweep over my pussy, Kova kept his hands where they were to hold me steady and dragged his wet tongue that was mingled with my pleasure and his saliva toward my ass. I fisted the blankets as mortification burst under my cheeks. I was beyond embarrassed I liked when he did this to me. A squeak pushed past my lips and he tasted me slow and deep. I rocked into his face, sighing and moaning, wanting him to tear me up like the animal I knew he could be.

His mouth left and clamped down on my backside and bit me. He quickly released my skin and lapped at the sting with his tongue. He did it again, this time tugging my skin between his teeth until he heard my small inhale. He let go and moved his way up my back, biting me and pulling my skin between his teeth. He left me gasping and breathless, feeling the zing all the way to my clit. I shivered.

I watched him stand from the corner of my eye and his hand slipped between us. His fingers found the sensitive nub and I whimpered, needing him desperately to fill me. Kova leaned over and pushed my auburn locks away from my face. He fisted my mane and wrapped it around his hand. My neck kinked to the side and I waited. He leaned in and the warmth of his chest heightened the chemistry between us.

"I am going to fuck some sense into you." He bit my ass again. "Then I will make love to you, and knowing I cannot change your mind, I will still try to prove that you and I are it, Adrianna."

Kova pulled back and palmed his cock. Dragging the tip up my wet pussy to my entrance.

"There is no way I am putting one more thing between us tonight, *Malysh*." Then he drove into me bare and pressed down on my lower back until I was in a butterfly position.

Thank God I was flexible, and not just because my hips were flat to the bed. He hit a different angle and the pleasure was too intense for my body to process. Low hips caused my clit to grind into the sheets. I felt pleasure seep from me, and I exploded. I orgasmed immediately, spasming around his cock. The sheets were bunched in my hands and I was trying to hold onto the bed from how extreme the pleasure was. Lips parting, I moaned as I rocked into him shamelessly soaking up my climax.

"Beautiful," he said, the heel of his palm gliding up my spine.

I shivered when his fingers wrapped around the front of my neck and applied pressure. My back bowed and he dug his fingers into my throat to draw out the orgasm. A very pleased sigh spilled from my lips and I smiled lazily.

Kova was pressed to my back, his cock still deep inside me. "Nothing like being able to watch you use my cock to come on me." My pussy spasmed in response to his dirty talk, and his dick twitched. I was so soft and wet for him and I didn't want him to leave my sex. "I bet you needed that." I nodded, panting. He pulled out just a fraction then pushed in too hard. "I bet you need more, though. Am I right?"

I tried to look at him as much as I could from this angle. Reaching behind me, I felt for Kova's face and guided him to turn so he had to face me. I lifted up just enough to capture his lips with mine and kissed him with gratitude. He loved me so good and I was thankful. It'd been so long since I had a proper orgasm, and with everything going on the last couple of months, I was overdue. I felt drunk from coming so hard. I pulled his tongue into my mouth to suck on it. Kova growled into my mouth and squeezed my neck until my lips popped off his with a pant and I was falling into a black hole of pleasure.

"Move down just a bit." Kova instructed. "There. That is it." His hand reached under to feel where our bodies were joined and then higher where my tender clit was. My teeth bit into my lip and my feet flexed in pleasure. I bent my knees to my sides, and our joined bodies just hung off the bed. I shivered. If it weren't for Kova's strong thighs to stop me, I'd fall off. I was at his disposal to do as he pleased, and it excited me.

Kova leaned over me again, this time bringing his knee up and resting it over mine. He adjusted himself inside of me and got seated deeper than usual. At least that's what it felt like. I savored the feel of his body on me, hoping this night would pass slow. If what I was imagining was what Kova planned to do, then it was going to be incredible.

Bent at his hips, he stood on one leg as his hands reached for mine. He moved over my wrists and interlocked our fingers together, then brought them down to our sides. He positioned me on the mattress with his weight and rolled his hips into mine with a slow, divine tenderness that made my whole body quake. His fingers tightened and I heard the whisper of a grunt in my ear. Kova exhaled in bliss, and I felt it wash over me. I wish I could see his eyes right now. I bet they were closed, and he was deep in the moment.

His legs were long enough for him to stay bent over me and his cock fully seated inside. Something about this position made me defenseless. It evoked too much emotion from me and I couldn't process it all at once. Being under Kova was a thrill. His movements were animalistic the way he mounted me from behind. His hunger was deep, and I was anxious for him to devour me. His hips surged above mine, dragging them to thrust into me until I felt the top of his sack at my pussy. I clenched around him, my stomach tightening. My clit rubbed the bed as he pushed forward, and I sighed loudly. Kova's lips found my cheek and he pressed frantic kisses to me while he drove his hips painstakingly slow into me. He bit my puffy bottom lip and I reacted by wrapping my lips around his into a breathless kiss. Nose brushed nose while tongues danced erotically around the other.

My body was shaking under his. Kova bent the leg he was standing on to get under and ground in deeper. He reached the peak and we gasped at the same time. We both held still, unable to move as we lost ourselves to the exhilaration. I was aching for release and I kept contracting around his shaft. I was trying to wait for him, but I wasn't sure how much longer I could hold out before I started screaming his name.

Kova turned our joined hands over and placed our wrists under my chest to prop me up a bit. It gave him leverage to drive into me. My heart sped in anticipation. I couldn't think properly *and* try to fight release at the same time. Kova leaned up behind me and dropped kisses to my shoulder blades. He pressed his lips to the center of my back and stilled. I held my breath as he dropped his forehead to the back of my neck. He let out a heavy sigh and it blazed down my spine.

We didn't move. The only sound was heavy panting and damp bodies grinding back and forth.

"We cannot get closer than this, *Malysh.*"

His voice… The anguish in it seized the oxygen in my lungs. Kova wasn't just talking sexually. I felt the depth of his words and the way he held me under him as he said them. He believed it and there was something so incredibly fulfilling about it. Something flashed in my mind and I got emotional for a second. I wondered if it could ever be better than this, and if I wanted it to or not.

Kova had experienced a myriad of life events with me in a brief period of time. Emotional highs and extreme lows, the way we tried to disentangle ourselves only to keep running back. Tears began to climb my eyes.

Kova was right. We were closer than ever before and the energy in that alone made the blood in my veins rush for him. My body tingled and my neck arched back wishing I could make this exact moment last forever.

"Kova," I whispered. I didn't even recognize my own voice. I held our hands closer to my chest. "I… Oh… I…"

"Tell me."

My pussy clamped down on his cock and I squirmed under him. His groan was deep, sensual and it heightened the chemistry. His chest was damp on my back. Kova was a man who was lost to pleasure.

Drawing in a nervous breath, I needed to find relief. "I love you."

Kova pushed back and that only made the moment that much more intense. He exhaled and his breath tickled down my back. His cock twitched and he dragged a breath in. My clit touched a different part of the bed and I moaned at the coolness. I was on the edge and needed him to finish us already before I exploded.

"I am coming inside you," he stated.

"Yes." I sighed in euphoria. I imagined him coming inside me and I gasped.

His width felt larger than usual and I briefly wondered if he'd had sex since after us. The thought disappeared the second I felt the spark of pleasure deep in my pussy. I gripped our hands so I could buck my hips back. I almost squeaked when he hit a new spot. I wanted more. I *craved* more. Little moans spilled from my throat and then he was rearing back and moving his hips forward into me, driving them with a one-track mind. I was going to be raw by the time we were finished.

"The last time I came inside of you was right downstairs." My heart clenched. "Remember that, when we were outside? My cum was dripping down your leg," he said, his groan guttural, and that was it.

I exploded around his cock for the second time. "I'm sorry... I can't hold on."

Kova tensed, he held his breath, and then he was rocking into me with a swift hardness. His dick jerked and he was coming inside. He let out a loud sound between a pant and a guttural groan, and it made my pussy tighten so I was riding the swell with him. Another pant, and it was in the back of his throat and filled with so much pleasure that I was almost jealous.

My flesh tingled with rapture. I closed my eyes and allowed myself to fall in a cave of depraved thoughts with him. It was decadent and tempting, and where I came alive. The intimacy wasn't a casual affair. Far from it. The intimacy between me and Kova was about truth and what would ultimately connect us forever. We could tell each other anything, and he told me his truth the way he made soul-searing love to me.

I could feel Kova's orgasm as he unloaded inside of me. My pussy was slippery from his thick fluid. Hearing him find release was orgasm inducing. Feeling his cum spill out of me as he mounted me from behind was an experience I'd never forget.

I was free-falling still when Kova finished and swiftly pulled out. He grabbed my hips and shoved me further up the bed and flipped me over. A breath escaped me and my body opened to him. Kova climbed over me and crushed me with his weight. His lips devoured mine and his tongue was needy. I kissed him back and cradled myself around him. The inside of my thighs were sticky, and his heavy cock lay pressed between us, wet and burning hot. There was something about the way we were tangled that made my heart rush with love.

His kisses would be the death of me.

Fingers in my hair.

Damp bodies.

Starving kisses.

Legs straining in ecstasy.

He. Did. Not. Stop.

Kova's passion was all-consuming. He was going to make sure I felt him for eternity.

chapter 54

KOVA TURNED OVER AND TOOK ME WITH HIM.
I laid on top and felt the cool breeze blow against my back. I shivered and Kova wrapped his strong arms around me. His warm embrace transported me back in time when we had experienced this a time or two when there was no outside noise and it was just us.

My eyes watered. I was beginning to understand what Kova was trying to explain to me that I was so bent against. Because right now, when there was not a single thing that could interrupt us, it was harmony in the soul. This was peace. This was true bliss in every aspect, and really, how it should feel.

It was how it needed to be.

I lifted my gaze to meet Kova's. Sparkling emerald green and gunmetal gray stared back at me. He released my legs from his and I dragged them up to straddle his waist. My tongue ran over my swollen lips and heat flamed my cheeks when I felt myself leak his pleasure onto his pelvis. It was so warm and thick.

A smirk tugged at Kova's lips that made my heart stumble. He lifted his hips slightly to glide over my clit. I gasped then clenched, feeling more of his cum ooze from me. He liked it and my cheeks deepened in color. I wondered if I had ever seen his filthiest side.

Palming the back of my head, he brought my lips to his and gently kissed me. My body was exhausted and I was beginning to feel tired. The tips of his fingers dragged lazily up and down my spine. I purred into his kiss. Kova used his other hand to reach behind me and drag two fingers coated with his release over my clit.

"Kova, I'm a little sore," I said against his mouth. "Give me a minute."

He ignored me and rubbed the sensitive ball in circles. I squirmed on top of him, feeling out of breath. My nipples brushed across his and my body was on fire when he traced my folds. My toes curled and I tried to hold back from feeling too much. His fingers dipped into my pussy and pressed along the walls of my sex. He withdrew and dragged them up to my ass. I clenched.

"Let me play with you," he asked gently, his voice rough. I nodded and rested my head on his chest. "I like touching your pussy. If you need to come while I am, go ahead. Rub your clit on me, *Malysh*. But let me have this."

My legs spread wider for him and I closed my eyes, exhaling. He pulled my hair off my neck, and I dragged lazy circles around his chest. The heel of his hand cupped my ass as his fingers delved into my tender sex. My hips widened and I exhaled a sigh. Kova breathed and his stomach stroked my clit. I let go and let myself just feel.

"I forgot how small you are on me. I miss it," he said, twirling the ends of my hair.

"I didn't expect you tonight."

"I will not apologize for coming here."

A sad smile tugged at my lips. I was glad he couldn't see it. "I would hope not."

Kova stroked me softly, twirling his fingers into my pussy the way he was twirling my hair. I felt the budding of an orgasm and was immediately humiliated. I didn't want to come like his on him. My thighs squeezed his stomach and he sensed I was close.

"I need you to know something," he said, his voice a touch urgent.

I swallowed, shamelessly rubbing myself on him. My body was pulsing with need. He played my pussy like a violin and made the sweetest sounds as I orgasmed. A long moan left my lips. I was so wet that I felt it trickle down his stomach and along my thigh. Kova noticed and growled in approval.

"I think I have loved you after the first week and I did not know it. I do not regret a single day with you. I only wish I had not been so determined to keep you away. I wish I would have just acted on what I felt for you first so we could have had more time together."

He continued touching me. My breathing was labored and my heart raced. Kova slipped his fingers from my pussy and pressed on the puckered hole, and I stilled.

"Inhale." When I did, he said, "Exhale." He pressed a little deeper. "Relax."

He coaxed me to loosen up. I was weak for him, and my entire body was charged with electricity. My clit tingled and I was suddenly awake with craving.

My mouth fell open and I dug my nails into his chest. "You don't resent me for what happened?"

Tears coated my eyes again. I didn't have to say it for him to know what I was talking about.

"Never," he said, appalled I'd ask such a thing. "If anything, it makes me love you more." He drew his knees up and I felt his cock touch the back of my thigh and drive over my ass cheek. My skin heated. "Your strength is what makes you so damn magnetic. Regardless of what happened that night, I do believe it was how it was supposed to be in the end, as much as it hurts to say it."

I nodded, unable to say the words. I knew what he meant, still it didn't hurt any less.

I started to cry. "I was so worried you'd hate me or find me ugly. I didn't think you wanted me anymore, and then I started to get paranoid—"

"Look at me."

"I didn't give you a choice!" I spoke over him, crying a little more. "I wasn't going to give you a choice."

"What?" he asked, confused.

I was so sorry it broke my heart.

I had to get it out.

I was a horrible human.

Kova sat up and took me with him. "Look at me, Adrianna." His eyes were glowing as he looked at me in awe. I sat in his lap, my body shaking as I cried softly. I tried to look away, but he wouldn't let me. Whatever he was going to say, or whatever he was going to do, he wanted me to trust in him.

"I had made up my mind that I was going to get rid of our baby and then I lost it." I hiccupped. "I didn't even ask you what you wanted. I'm so sorry. God, I'm so sorry."

Kova grabbed my chin and pulled it forward to press a peck to my lips. He pulled back and I drew in a shaky breath. He looked into my eyes, then kissed me the same way again.

"Sometimes you talk too much," he said quietly against my mouth. "You worry too much too."

I inhaled another shaky breath. I frowned. I was so confused.

"I am not mad." He planted another kiss. "I could never resent you." Two kisses. "I understand why," Kova said honestly, and it shattered my heart even more. "The miscarriage is not your fault, and as for the abortion, your decision was the right one. That does not mean I did not want our child, it was just not the right time for us, Adrianna. That is all. Nothing more, nothing less. Please, for me, stop making yourself sick over it. We do not need to keep discussing it."

Tears streamed from the corner of my eyes. I shook my head. "But how come you don't say anything about it? Why don't you even look sad?"

A shadow crossed his eyes. "Because I see how you are dealing with it and I am not adding to your sadness. The truth is, the whole thing"—he swallowed thickly—"fucking kills me, Ria. You have no idea what it does to me and what *we* lost. I am wrecked inside."

Kova took my wrists and guided them over his shoulders. He brought me closer to him then reached between us and palmed his length. His erection moved over my overstimulated clit. Always eager for him, I lifted my hips for Kova to push into me. My lips parted and our eyes met as he pushed all the way in. I sighed. Kova held still and so did I. His nostrils flared and I held my breath. We didn't move.

A moment later, he brushed a lock of hair behind my ear, and said, "If I felt any of those negative ways about you, would I still want to make love to you? Would I sell my gym? I am willing to go against your father for you. Truth is, I would do anything for you, Ria. I would probably kill for you, that is how much I fucking love you." He thrust in and growled. He was so hot inside of me, burning me up. "You always told me actions speak louder than words. Now that I am finally making moves, you question it."

I closed my eyes, feeling guilty.

"No, look at me. You want to know what I feel and how I am dealing, look at me when I tell you."

The demand in his voice caused me to shiver. I moved my hips, needing to feel him. Kova was right. I did ask, and here I was unable to handle it. I met his gaze.

"I cannot even get mad because I created that stress in you. All I can keep doing is trying to prove that you are my one and only forever love. One day I hope you believe me."

A gush of emotion pushed through my lips and I whimpered. "I do believe you. That's the thing, I do believe you. I'm just… I don't know what. Emotional, I guess."

Kova's hips surged forward and my eyes fell heavy from the wonderful blooming heat in my pelvis.

He continued when I couldn't speak. "I love you, and I never stopped loving you. I never will." He rocked harder into me. "Remember that. Remember right now when you question my love for you next time, because I know you will."

I smashed my lips to his and my arms tightened around his neck. Divine fullness filled me, but my heart was still aching. I was so stupid to doubt him. Every time I thought about Kova, my fear was he didn't want me anymore. How many more times did he have to tell me he loved me for me to finally believe it?

"I'm sorry," I cried against his mouth. I said it again as I greedily took his length. "I'm so sorry."

He shook his head, his voice frantic. "Stop. There is nothing to be sorry about."

I was sorry for more than just what happened. Mostly, I was sorry I was leaving him behind.

"I'm sorry," I whispered.

Before I could say it again, Kova spoke a few lines in Russian under his breath, then he kissed me. A sharp pang sliced through my chest at the familiarity of this moment.

Prosti.

All the air left my lungs and I abruptly broke the kiss and we stopped moving.

This was nearly the exact thing as that awful night. Kova came to me and apologized in his native tongue for hours while we made love. The only difference now was we were aware of the outcome, and it was me who was saying sorry.

We really were one in the same.

"*Prosti,*" I said. I licked my lips and looked down.

My voice was quiet, broken. I was truly sorry for my decision even though I knew it was going to wreck us.

He tipped my chin up, and his intense eyes bored into mine.

"*Ya ne mogu predstavit' svoyu zhizn', ne vidya tebya kazhdyy den.'*"

My chin trembled. I waited for him to translate.

"I cannot imagine my life without seeing you every day." Kova's hips pressed forward and my jaw fell open at the delicious pressure between my legs. "I love you, Adrianna."

I inhaled, trying to steady my tears. "Promise me you'll never stop?"

I was such a hypocrite.

Kova sealed his response with a kiss. My hips moved over his in a slow wake, painting every inch of the way he felt pushing inside of me to memory. I had no right to ask him to keep loving me after I left, but I had to do it, and I needed to know he wouldn't forget about me.

Because the truth was, I would never forget about him, and I hoped that would be enough one day.

Wrapping his arm around my lower back, Kova guided us until my back was on the cool mattress. My hips widened and Kova seated deeper in my pussy. My heels drove into the bed and my neck arched, the back of my head pressing into the bed from the blissful pleasure. I let go and sighed, feeling so good.

"Tell me you love me."

Grabbing his face between my hands, I pressed a kiss to his lips. "You had me the first day when I walked into World Cup. I could never not love you, Kova."

His dejected smile crushed my heart. "I am going to make love to you now, *Malysh*, and I am not going to hold back. You are going to see how much I need you. I am not going to stop until your entire body feels how much I love you," he said, sinking deeper.

And that was what he did.

Kova took control of my body for the rest of the night while he made soul-searing love to me. There was no hurry to his kiss. He didn't drive into me like the intoxicating animal he could be. I didn't try to fight him or taunt him just to get a rise out of him.

We were just two lovers immersed in each other with desperate moans and shuddering bodies, wishing time would slow and the sunrise wasn't on the horizon.

chapter 55

I THOUGHT ABOUT KOVA THE ENTIRE TIME THE MOVERS HAD BEEN IN MY condo.

My decision plagued every second of the long day, and it caused an awful headache from the stress. I couldn't stop thinking about the night before and how much my life was going to be so different a week from now. Mostly, I thought about how badly I wished things were different. My head was a mess and I wanted free from my thoughts.

Something he'd said stuck with me. I too couldn't fathom a life with him not around. He'd been the one constant in my world, and I was closer to him than anyone else. Any time I tried to imagine a life without him, this massive gray cement wall appeared before me. It left me feeling uneasy, which made me even more anxious for tomorrow.

I thought maybe Kova would've stayed the whole day too, but when I woke to an empty bed and a little note saying he'd be back to take me to the airport the next day, I was conflicted. I fell asleep with his arms holding me and our legs tangled together between my damp sheets. I was pretty positive we didn't move until he left. Now that he was gone, I was missing him so much and wished he had stayed. However, the other half of me knew it would've just been harder to say goodbye when it came time to leave. A warm ache began between my legs. I could still feel his lips on my back, his nails digging into my ass cheek as he gripped it, the way his thumb stroked the front of my throat as he came inside of me. Chills rolled down my arms and need pulsed through me.

Kova hadn't been joking when he'd said he was going to make me feel his love. I had felt it from the moment I woke up. I'd called Avery a couple of times to vent. I'd decided not to tell her anything about Kova showing up and staying over. It was something I wanted to keep for myself.

I glanced at the time over the stove. Thankfully the movers had been running behind yesterday. It was late by the time they'd finished and I was already exhausted from the night before that I fell asleep shortly after I took a shower. I slept in as much as I could until I got up to pack the last few things in my check-in bag. I had only an hour to spare before Kova arrived.

My knee bounced and I bit my bottom lip until it was raw. I was a mess and paced the floor, looking for last minute things to tidy up. Kova would be here soon and I needed to calm my racing heart and steady my hands.

I told him I'd meet him downstairs, but he said he had something for me and asked if he could come up. There was no way I would tell him no, so now I was waiting—

My heart dropped into my gut when I heard the knock. I wiped my palms down my distressed jeans and walked toward the door. God, I was so nervous that I could feel my heart beating in my throat. Heat broke out over my skin in anticipation. The closer I got, sharp knots twisted in my stomach.

Reaching for the door, I took a deep breath and unbolted the lock to welcome him in.

Kova turned around to face me and I felt a fissure along my ribs.

Oh, God. I couldn't handle it. My heart was on fire, and all these emotions I'd slept on were climbing to the surface again. He looked like shit. There were dark circles under his lackluster eyes like he hadn't slept since he left here.

Before I could think better of it, I closed the distance and stepped into Kova. His arms immediately wound around my body and hugged me to him. My eyes closed feeling his warmth surrounding me. I heard something drop behind me but I didn't bother looking. Not when Kova held me like he needed me.

"Adrianna," he whispered in pure agony.

I pressed my face into the column of his neck and squeezed my eyes shut. Kova tightened his arms and I savored the feeling. I wasn't sure I could do it.

"Tell me I'm making a bad decision," I said, breaking down. "Tell me I'm being stupid."

Kova pulled back and looked into my eyes. He came in and shut the door. The back of his hand brushed over my cheek. My lips trembled. His eyes were glossy and rimmed with a tint of pink. The facial hair helped hide the hollowness of his jaw. Kova was in a much worse state than the other night. I didn't know how I was going to get through another second knowing he wasn't mine anymore, and I wasn't his.

"I think it is a terrible fucking decision. The absolute worst you have ever made." His voice was raw. "But you made the right decision," he whispered, sounding like he was on the verge of cracking.

I released a ragged breath. Kova reached for my side braid and ran his thumb down the fishtail design. I wanted desperately to reach out and touch him again. I ached to, because later today I'd be hundreds of miles away and wouldn't be able to.

"Your hair has gotten so long," he said. I think it was more to himself.

"I'd cut it to my shoulders if it wasn't so thin now."

I was quiet, reflecting. His eyes flashed to mine. Kova liked my hair.

"I used to think my hair gave me headaches." He looked at me in confusion. "It was so heavy when I tied it up in a knot. I thought it was giving me raging headaches from the weight and pull of the rubber band. Now I know it was the lupus because I never wear my hair up anymore for that reason and my head still pounds."

Kova wrapped the braid around his fist and gave it a gentle tug. The corners of my mouth twitched at his playfulness. I lifted my gaze to his and my knees almost buckled.

The distance and raw emotion in his eyes choked me up.

His regret tore at my heart.

His desperation and hunger ran along my skin and sunk into every pore.

Kova was drawn. Lost. I felt him dying inside at the knowledge there was nothing we could do to save us. His defeat stripped me bare. It overrode who he was as a person, and that was upsetting. I didn't want to lose him.

Helplessly, he dropped my braid. "I wanted to give you something before you left."

I wiped my eyes, then dried my palms on my thighs as Kova retrieved the bag he brought in. I'd forgotten about it and realized that was the sound I heard behind me when we hugged.

Kova walked over and placed it on the kitchen counter, then reached inside. Once I got home from the Olympics, I hadn't been able to wear the necklace and bracelet set he'd given me for my birthday since Dad and Sophia were often around. I didn't want them to question me, or worse, take it away. I packed it first and told myself that once I was settled in Oklahoma I would never take it off.

I gasped and covered my mouth when my eyes landed on our spiral bound notebook. A memory flashed through my mind and I stifled a sad chuckle.

"Why did you laugh?"

I looked up at him. "Do you remember when I had this idea and what you said to me?" A crease lined the space between his brows. "You said it was the worst idea and you didn't want to do it."

His eyes flashed and he gave me a lopsided grin. He remembered.

My heart was thumping at the sight of it, wondering who'd had their dirty hands on it and read our personal letters. These words were ours, and ours alone.

It upset me thinking someone read the personal thoughts I fought so hard to get from Kova.

"Where did you find it?" I asked. I hadn't seen it in months, not since Katja stole it and did who knows what with it.

"I got it back from Katja."

My skeptical eyes lifted to his. "What did you have to do to get it?"

He lowered his gaze. "Before I left here the other day, you said something that stuck with me. You said our love makes you sicker."

My jaw trembled and my nostrils flared trying to hold in my emotions. I had regretted saying that immediately after it left my mouth.

"You are right," Kova said quietly, like it was final, and that filled me with dread. "Our love does make you sicker. I hate myself for it because I know I am a huge part in that." He shook his head, struggling to finish. "That was it. It really hit me just how sorry I am for what I put you through when I married her. I broke you."

I moved closer to him, but he stepped back and put his hand up. I frowned.

"You didn't break me. I'm still here."

He lifted his eyes to mine. "I broke you that day, and you were not the same for a long time afterward." My heart ached hearing him confess his most private thoughts. "Regardless, you will never understand how sorry I am for what I did. I thought I lost you for good and made it my mission to fix it. I wish I could void out that part of my life like it never happened." Kova paused, his eyes were glistening. "But then I wonder if we would be where we are now..." His voice trailed off. "So, when I left here yesterday, I picked up a bottle of vodka on my way home and started to pack her things once I got there."

"Kova, you left early in the morning."

He gave me a knowing look. "I was drunk all day." I chuckled sadly under my breath, and he continued. No wonder he looked like shit when I opened the door. "To be completely transparent, I felt bad for her and thought giving her time was fair. I thought I was doing the right thing for both of you. The situation is not so easy to walk away from and start over. Katja and I have a lot of history. I did her wrong, she did me wrong." He paused, then finally handed me our notebook. "There is no reason for her to live with me, even if we are in the process of a divorce, not if it means I am going to lose you forever. You mean too much to me to chance that. I did not mean to upset you with that decision. I was just trying to do right."

My chest was hollow. "Kova—"

"No, let me finish."

I closed my mouth and my shoulders drooped. He was so resolute in us that fresh tears streamed down my cheeks. The dark circles under his eyes now had a cause. He'd been relentless in his pursuit of us. I think I loved him more for that.

"I packed up everything in the bedroom she slept in. I got her a hotel room for two weeks, then I changed my locks and froze her accounts. Katja has plenty of cash and can afford it, or she can make the bastard who got her pregnant pay." Kova glanced away and ran his tongue over his bottom lip. "They were planning to blackmail me and use our affair against me to get what they wanted."

My brows rose as fury flowed through my veins. I was stunned into silence. How heartless of them. I didn't have a leg to stand on, but I was not a vindictive person either.

Kova didn't care about money. He probably would've given her anything she asked for because he was guilty himself and that sickened him. He'd struggled with us until I pushed him to snap. With help from Joy, all Katja focused on was revenge. It was easy when someone was whispering in their ear the whole time.

"I learned their plans shortly after I was released." Kova paused, then said, "I know you are skeptical when it comes to Katja, but I need you to know I am no longer living with her."

My brows lowered. He was right. I did feel a different way when it came to Katja and how he treated her. I wasn't sure I could ever let go of those feelings unless he was completely separated from her and they never spoke again.

"How did you manage to do all of this so quickly? What about World Cup? Please tell me you didn't do anything drastic."

He looked right at me and said, "I told you I was going to accept Danilo's offer. Madeline and Danilo are a good team and kept the gym running smooth."

chapter 56

TEARS WELLED IN MY EYES.

"Why would you do that? That gym means so much to you. I wish you hadn't."

World Cup was his everything. It was his second home. Where he was himself. It made me sick to think he'd sold it for me.

Kova shook his head vehemently, though his inconsolable gaze didn't match the tone in his words.

"Enough. I am not talking about it anymore. It is done and contracts have been signed. The gym is not worth more than you." With a jut of his chin, Kova gestured toward our notebook. "Take that. All the pages are intact."

My thumb dragged down the silver spirals thinking back to the day we started this. I flipped through and the pages fanned out. I caught the faint sent of Kova in them and I drew in a quiet breath. I held the book close to my chest and my eyes closed. There were so many memories in these pages that I wanted to hold on to forever.

"Thank you."

Kova reached into the bag and pulled out something wrapped in black tissue paper with scotch tape all over it like it was a decoration. He flipped it over and there was an envelope attached to it. Taped down, of course. My lips twitched.

"I do not know how to wrap," he said, self-conscious of his wrapping skills.

My brows shot up as Kova handed it to me. "You have a gift for me?"

He gave a blasé shrug. I glanced down and eyed the white envelope. I reached for it, but Kova stopped me.

He massaged the back of his neck. "There is, ah, a letter I wrote for you. I wrote it the other day. Do not open that now"—he pointed to the black tissue paper—"or read the card. Open it when you are settled…in."

He couldn't even finish the words. I choked up inside and looked away, letting out a breath.

"Do you want me to call you after I do?" I asked.

A shadow passed through his eyes that made my stomach flutter nervously. It was short-lived, but I'd caught it, and I didn't like what I saw.

"Just read it first."

I shifted on my feet. "I feel like you don't have anything of mine to hold onto now."

Kova's green eyes glittered under the bill of his hat. He placed his hand over his heart, right where the A was that I'd carved.

"I have what I need…for now."

A blush crept up my cheeks. I averted my gaze, more eager to read his letter.

I was so touched by his thoughtfulness. "This notebook means a lot to me. I looked forward to your letters. It was one of the few ways you'd tell me what you were thinking. I used to reread them at night. Sometimes I would laugh, like when you said you loved cotton candy. Other times I'd cry a little reminiscing, or just feel bad. I hated that this disappeared. I didn't think I'd see it again. Thank you for getting this back. Do you think Katja shared it with anyone?"

"She did not show anyone. Trust me on that."

"Why are you so sure?"

"Because she was hysterical over what I had written for you when I had not once shared myself like that with her. I did not speak to her the way I spoke to you." He paused. "She was humiliated and swore she did not have it in her to show anyone. I believed her."

My heart was racing so damn fast.

Avery was right.

I wanted to cave right now and say fuck the consequences and do anything I could to be with him, but I couldn't do that.

"Do we have time? I have one more thing for you. This one you can open."

I blinked and checked the time over the stove. "Yeah, we have a little more time."

Kova reached into the bag again, this time retrieving a black velvet square box. He studied it for a moment, his thumb stroking over the top.

"I wanted to give you this at the Olympics, but the timing did not feel right."

I flinched. My heart hadn't recovered from that night yet. Kova looked at me like he wanted to say something. Instead, he placed a quick kiss to the top of my head then handed me the box.

My heart was fluttering wondering what else he gave me. I shot him a half smile then lifted the top to reveal a thin chain with the five Olympic gold rings clasped together. My lips parted in awe and I gasped. "Kova," I whispered. Tears welled in my eyes. The charm was positioned off center so the symbol would rest over my left collarbone. The pad of my finger grazed the shiny metal as I stared at the circles.

I tilted my head up and sadness clouded his features. I blinked a few times. "It's so beautiful."

"May I?" he asked. I nodded.

He stepped closer and bent over, squinting his eyes. "I did not want you to mark up your skin. At least, I hope that you do not. I thought this was a better alternative." He released the necklace from its holder then placed the box on the counter next to us.

I smiled to myself remembering how I had once told him I hoped to have a tattoo like his one day. That felt like ages ago.

Kova stepped behind me. I lifted my braid and felt him exhale across the back of my neck. He raised the necklace and laid it over my chest. His fingers shook as he clasped it together.

Kova arranged the necklace then placed his hands on my shoulders. I peered down. My skin was creamier than usual from lack of sun and it caused the gold to stand out. His fingers splayed down the chain and grazed the delicate symbol that lay near the slant on my neck.

"Seeing you up there was the best day of my life," he said.

I swallowed thickly and my stomach clenched. I would forever hold this moment close to me. He had his set of rings, and now I had mine.

Leaning back against his chest, Kova slid his arms around my hips to embrace me. He pulled me to him and his large body engulfed mine. His arms were my security.

"Are we really going to do this?" I asked, my voice shaky.

I scooted closer and turned slightly to the side, resting my head on his bicep that was the perfect height as a pillow. I pressed my face into his arm and inhaled softly. We folded into each other and held on tight. My heart filled with warmth. He smelled like home. Kova leaned down and placed a kiss to my cheek.

Kova had once said there was no Kova without Ria, but the truth was there was no Ria without Kova.

Neither one of us had truly been living until we connected with each other. I'd taught him how to find true happiness, and he'd showed me how strong I could be. He'd prepared me for the battle I would soon face, and I was ready.

"Thank you for the necklace. I like your idea much better."

"I had it custom made. It is engraved underneath."

My eyes widened. I leaned forward to look, but he tugged me back. "Look at it later," he whispered. "Stay with me a little longer."

A soft smile tipped my lips. I nestled into Kova and absorbed his essence when it dawned on me. "What if I hadn't made it to the Olympics?"

"I had something else picked out for making the National team, but once I knew you were chosen for the Olympic team, I rushed the order."

"I love it so much," I said, my voice throaty. "I'll never take it off."

Kova kissed the space under my ear, his nose grazing my cheek. After a few last moments together, his next words twisted my stomach with instant nausea.

"Let us get your luggage."

I tensed, tightening my grip on him. My heart started to pound. His raw voice wreaked havoc on my heart. Tears instantly rose to my eyes and I squeezed them shut. I sniffled and anxiety swelled in my throat.

After a few moments I finally responded, and Kova dropped his arms.

Inhaling a deep breath, I walked to get my belongings. I'd only lived here for a couple of years, yet these walls held enough memories to last a decade. I wished I could take them with me.

I turned off the lights and my knees weakened. This was getting more and more real and I was beginning to question if I could actually go through with it or not. I loved him with all my heart.

Walking back into the living room, I found Kova near the front door. He had my World Cup duffle bag over his shoulder and my large rolling suitcase in one hand. He extended his arm and I faltered in my steps and stopped walking.

I stood across from him and my breathing labored. My chest was spasming in one breath and constricting in the other. Eyes widening, I felt the onset of a panic attack starting. Kova's eyes narrowed and I tensed, feeling the pressure intensify. My fingers flew to my throat and I was instantly scared. I tried to push against it with a slow pull of oxygen and it only backfired. Lips parting, I stared at Kova, trying to swallow and I couldn't.

Kova dropped my bag and stalked over to me. He grabbed my upper arm and yanked me to him. I gasped and my chest expanded right before he gripped the back of my neck and slammed his lips to mine. His hard kiss was intended to snap sense into me, and he instructed me to breathe as he let go of my arm and wrapped his around the small of my back. His fingers loosened on my neck.

I listened, steadying myself.

Kova gave me one more kiss and reached for my hand, tugging me behind him. "I love you. Now let us go."

I locked up my condo for the last time.

Timing, man. It loved to fuck with me.

chapter 57

WALKING DOWN THE HALLWAY, KOVA PRESSED A QUICK KISS TO my shoulder.

I leaned into him and placed my other hand on the fold of his elbow. He kissed the top of my head as we made our way toward the elevator together.

I had a gut feeling he was scared himself despite trying to seem like he had it under control. Kova kept me glued to his side and kept giving me little kisses.

Neither one of us spoke while we walked to his car. Once my luggage had been stored away, Kova opened the passenger door for me. I turned to thank him, but he was purposely looking elsewhere. He blinked, noticing me but still didn't look. I pulled back, feeling the pinch in my heart sharpen until I saw that his eyes were glossy.

I didn't say anything and took my seat.

The drive to the airport was exceptionally quiet. We didn't waste the time talking. We laced our fingers together over his console and I rested my head on his arm as he drove the forty-five minute distance. He kept his gaze on the road the entire time. I couldn't see his eyes behind his sunglasses, but I noticed the harsh lines around his mouth.

Time passed too quickly and we were exiting the highway.

"You can do the drop off so it's easier for you," I suggested.

"I will park."

My stomach cramped. I had a feeling he was going to say that. I wanted him to park, but I also didn't.

It took no time to park and check in my suitcase. Kova took my hand and didn't let go. We walked into the terminal and checked the departing times. Kova looked at his watch then looked over my head. He read the signs, then he took a step and I followed.

It was funny how emotions worked. Kova and I knew there was no point

656 | LUCIA FRANCO

in trying to make light of our situation with feeble talk. There was nothing either of us could say that would bring even an ounce of comfort. The fact was the end result wouldn't change. I was still leaving.

I eyed the escalator knowing Kova couldn't go with me past that point.

The closer we got to it, the warmer my blood heated. My heart viciously attacked my ribs. I watched the moving stairs climb and realized I didn't want to do this.

I was going to be sick.

Kova tugged me toward an empty luggage area. He dropped my duffle bag then turned toward me and cupped my face, encasing us under the lip of his hat. My hands automatically slid under his arms to hug him tight.

My emotions were already elevated and they broke the moment Kova pressed his body to mine. Tears seeped from my eyes as he swept a kiss across my mouth. His lips were damaging, and his fingers wrapped around the sides of my head and gripped me. I drew in air through my nose and fisted his shirt in my hand. He didn't want to say goodbye.

Kova ripped away, his eyes pierced my heart and his voice held me hostage.

"Understand something, Adrianna." A soft whimper escaped my lips. "I will come for you."

I was shattered.

Completely shattered inside.

I never thought we would come to this. Nodding, my jaw trembled in his palms. I wanted to make him promise he would come for me.

Drawing in a breath, my words shook as I cried softly. "I wish things were different and you were coming with me."

He didn't respond. He couldn't. Tears blurred my vision again. I glanced over my shoulder at the escalator. Once I stepped on, there was no turning back. Knowing I was running out of time, I started to panic.

I looked back at him. "You said you sold the gym. Come with me," I whispered.

"No, *Malysh*."

My heart sank. Kova's eyes shifted back and forth over mine. I'd seen him suffer in the past, but nothing compared to how he was now. He was bleeding love and drowning in it…like me.

"You are going alone."

"But you said you sold the gym," I said, a cross between a beg and a whimper.

My eyes filled with fresh tears and his gaze softened. Heat bloomed in my cheeks from the blood pumping through my veins. I was scared to leave him.

Scared to leave us. Scared to go on this journey alone. Scared I'd get too sick to live with him.

"Come with me," I begged. "Please."

Clenching his eyes shut, a low growl pushed through his chest.

"I'm scared I'll never see you again," I said, baring my heart. "And if I do, what if you've moved on?"

Kova slammed his mouth to mine and plunged his tongue between my lips. He let go of my face and hauled me to him. He said I love you without breaking the kiss. His fingers grasped my braid, twisting it as he deepened our love.

My heart dropped.

I knew what this was.

This was a goodbye kiss.

Kova was kissing me goodbye.

Unleashing his emotion, Kova kissed me ruthlessly, passionately, all him. There was no shame in his fiery strokes that stormed my mouth. I fell into him, and released a sigh savoring this moment.

Kova severed the kiss and shoved me away. I stumbled back, stilling in shock. My jaw fell open and I stared at him, unblinking.

All I could hear was the sound of my heart beating in my ears.

No.

"This is not over, Adrianna. It will never be over between us."

I shook my head vehemently and ran to him. Kova caught me, but he didn't let me speak.

"This is only goodbye for now," he said.

A breath hitched in my throat. Kova's lips were on mine again, and I knew in my heart it was the last one.

He broke the kiss again and took a step back.

Tears were flowing from my eyes. I couldn't stop crying.

This was it.

He was leaving, and so was I.

"No." I panicked and ground my teeth together. My feet carried me to him. "I'm not ready to leave yet. I just need a little more time."

Reaching up, Kova brushed a loose lock of hair behind my ear, his knuckles grazing my cheek. He eyed me with empathy. One corner of his mouth quirked up and his eyes glistened with unshed tears. I stepped closer, needing to feel his body pressed to mine one last time.

"My dearest *Malysh*," he said with the utmost affection. "I love you, and I will always love you. Do not ever forget that."

My lungs ached for air. My heart was a burning stone in my gut making my knees weak. Any second, I was going to crumble to the floor.

Kova held me close and our lips met one final heartbreaking time.

We pulled apart. Kova threw his hands in the air and spoke something under his breath that I didn't catch. My eyes caught the subtle shake in his fingers. He placed his fist to his mouth, his eyes pleading for me to go.

My face slowly fell as his response settled over me.

He wanted me to leave. No—he needed me to leave.

"Go, Adrianna. Just remember I am coming for you. And once I have you, I will never let you go again. That is a promise I intend to keep."

I liked his challenge.

Kova gestured with his head to the area behind me. We were standing across the room from the escalator.

"Leave, Adrianna."

chapter 58

I T WAS ON THE TIP OF MY TONGUE TO ASK HIM TO WALK ME TO THE
escalator.

I didn't. After all, I was doing this for me, and that meant I had to
walk away on my own.

Bending down, I picked up my duffle bag and placed it over my shoulder. I
blinked my eyes rapidly trying to stop the tears. His chest rose and fell and his
hands were clenched, hanging at his sides.

My heart, how it ached for him. We were saying goodbye. Did he even realize he was giving me the strength I needed to walk away? He was the push I
needed to keep going, the firm voice and bold eyes encouraging me to be better.

I inhaled a deep breath and turned around. Each step I took, I drew in a
quick breath—faster, harder, tighter. I thought about my decision one last time
and if this was what I wanted. I looked inside myself, really questioning what
I truly wanted.

It was so easy to convince myself that I was making the right decision by
leaving for Oklahoma, but in this moment it was so fucking hard to stay positive. A part of me knew I needed to leave, yet the other part wanted Kova to
take me back home and never let me go.

Swallowing thickly, I gripped the railing and stepped onto the lifting stair.
I turned to look over my shoulder to find the man who held every part of me
in the palm of his hands.

There was an emptiness in my heart the moment our eyes connected. A
real void that only he could fill. Cold, hollow, damp. Soft tears streamed down
my flushed cheeks. I couldn't believe this was really it.

I didn't care if he saw me crying, or anyone else for that matter. Gymnastics
had taught me so much through the years that transformed me into the person I was now.

I learned self-discipline at a young age, and that money couldn't buy everything.

As an early teen, I had discovered that I needed an abundance amount of patience to accomplish a dream.

The deeper I got into the sport, I'd decided how to receive criticism and if I was going to use it in a constructive manner or cause me to crumble.

My goal had drained me, pulled tears from my eyes, and ripped back layers and layers of my skin to prove a point. But it had never made me second-guess myself. I never questioned if I couldn't handle something. It was where I discovered how strong of a person I really was.

There was so much more to gymnastics than how many back flips somebody could do.

I went to Kova for one reason, one goal. I had a dream, and he said I was going to fight for it. He showed me how to thrive and conquer, that giving up wasn't in my vocabulary because you don't just challenge your body with a dream, but you challenge your mind too. He taught me that a little fear was okay, but to always trust in myself. I came to Kova with a dream of going to the Olympics, and he gave it to me. The least I owed him was unveiling my true emotions and not hiding myself from him.

Now our time was over.

Halfway up the stairs, I clung to the railing harder, and Kova pressed a tight fist to his mouth again. I was about to go out into the world on my own, taking what I'd learned from the sport that had captured my heart as a kid. Kova dropped his head for a spilt second then looked back at me. I knew that look in his eyes all too well. He'd reached his point of no return and was already succumbing to the darkness in him that made him who he was. He fought it while I embraced that part of him and drew it out. He'd fight it now too until he couldn't anymore. Kova was an emotive man who deeply ached to express love and feeling with someone who he truly connected with. I was that person.

Our gazes never wavered the higher I went. We were too afraid to look away, not wanting to break the connection.

Stepping blindly onto the platform when I reached the top, I slowly walked in the direction of my gate, still watching him through blurry eyes.

Kova stayed where he was, rooted to the ground and fixated on me. We only saw each other, and all I could hear was the roaring sound of my heartbeat in my ears the further I got away from him.

Kova's lips parted and my heart plummeted as he took one step in front of him only to stop.

This was too much.

My jaw trembled and my teeth clamped down on my lower lip as his head dropped between his shoulders and he faced the floor. He couldn't stomach to see me walk away.

Gripping my duffle bag strap in search of courage, I turned and stared straight ahead, letting the tears fall freely in waves. There was no way to disguise the pain of losing a loved one and I wasn't going to even try. I was going to let myself feel every emotion to remember that this was real and it would never be forgotten. I was leaving someone I loved behind. There was no reason to shut the door on those feelings.

Kova was as devastating as a tornado.

A quiet sob escaped my lips. I puckered my mouth together.

I thought back to the first time I saw him again as a teenager at World Cup, how he stole my attention and took my breath away. We were inevitable then and we didn't even know it.

Kova had supported me and pushed me to be better than the day before. He believed in me and showed me how to succeed with the right skills, not just in the gym but in life. Even on my worst days when I wanted to give up, he encouraged me to do more, try more, knowing if I didn't give it my all, I'd regret it. He was the flame to the fuel in my veins. He saw the drive in me and ignited it.

Blinking my eyes, I felt a fresh need course through my body.

A new goal sprang to life.

It would be the riskiest one yet.

I was my new goal, and my incentive to thrive would be Kova. It was going to hurt so good.

That was how I was going to view us—a risk worth taking while I got better, healthier. Because I would. I refused any other outcome. I wasn't going to let lupus and kidney disease steal me any more than I already had, not when I had a lot of life in me left to live.

I took a seat near my gate away from people and placed my duffle bag on the floor near my feet. I reached inside and pulled out the gift wrapped in black tissue paper with the envelope attached to it.

I carefully tore off the envelope and accidently pulled back some of the tissue paper. The scent of his cologne bled from the paper as I slipped his note out of the envelope and unfolded it.

Sniffling back the last of my tears, I wiped my eyes with the back of my hand.

My Dearest Malysh,

I was scared to want you. I still am.

Damn it. Fresh tears instantly filled my eyes.

Do not feel bad for the decision you have made. Even though it kills me, I do not regret a fucking thing. Every moment with you was worth having all the way until now, even the bad. If that was all the time I was allotted with you, then I will die a happy man. I hope it is not, though. I hope that when your mind wanders to the past, you think of us and the connection we made. I hope our goodbye opens a door for us to spend a lifetime together. This separation is one of many boulders for us to overturn. I want to be the one to help you lift them when times are tough, but I understand why you want to do it alone. After all, your fight is what I love about you.

You were right to leave.

When I came to your hotel room on the night after the meet I had pulled you from, it was then that I started to write about us every single day. What you made me feel, what you were going through, how I saw you through my eyes. Your strengths, my weaknesses. Our ups and downs. How I learned you were sick and keeping it from me. When I realized I loved you, and how I knew you loved me before you said it.

I smiled at that. I'd only allowed myself to love him in the dark until I couldn't hide anymore.

It is all there in my journal. Every thought, every feeling, they are yours.

I gasped, my hand flying to my mouth to cover it. Tears welled in my eyes. Kova gave me his private journal.

Read one page a day, no more.
Our time is not over, Malysh, but it is for now.
Ya lyublyu tebya vsegda I naveki.

X
Kova

I smiled sadly to myself and felt a fresh tear slip down my cheek. That was the first time he'd signed his name.

Taking out my cellphone from my bag, my screen lit up with the picture of us from that night in the hotel room. It felt like ages ago but the feelings came rushing back as if it happened yesterday. I decided to send him the picture.

He'd know why I'd sent it.

I shouldn't have thrown away my burner phone. Oh well. If my dad was monitoring my messages, let him see it. What was the worst that could happen at this point? I was leaving.

Just as I was about to slip my phone back into my bag, it dinged. I slid the screen open with my heart in my throat and grinned at Kova's response.

A black heart emoji.

I rolled my lips between my teeth and tasted my salty tears. It was so Kova, and I loved that.

Something happened when Kova came along. He changed me for the better, he gave me strength and helped me see my worth, even if it was a struggle at times. He also hurt me more times than I wanted to count, but I wasn't going to focus on moments that would only harden my heart.

The way we understood love started with pain. Our love story wasn't an easy one, so our ending wouldn't be either.

There were no hearts and rose petals about it, no white picket fence and butterflies. No children. No happy ending. But it was raw, it was real, and it was ours. It was tragically beautiful. No one could take that from us.

I didn't think either of us realized how deeply intertwined we truly were until we had to go our separate ways.

It was utterly devastating.

chapter 59

One Year Later

"**3** ... 2... 1... HAPPY NEW YEAR!"

The small crowd in the student center went wild. I huddled in the corner, regretting letting my teammates rope me into coming. I still had months before I could join them in the gym and competitions, but the coaches had thought it would be a good idea to come on board now and build the camaraderie. It turned out to be a good thing and had helped to occupy my mind for a while. I didn't have that team bond with them yet since I hardly knew them, but it felt nice to be included. It was a good start.

Avery knew what New Year's Eve meant to me and who I thought about.

I'd flown home for three days to spend the holidays with my family. Avery flew back with me the day after Christmas and has been here ever since to support me. Three days was all I could handle knowing I was in close proximity to him. The temptation was too strong to see him. There wasn't a doubt in my mind I would have borrowed Dad's car to drive south.

"Happy New Year, bestie!" Avery said excitedly, wrapping her arms around my shoulders. I pulled back and forced a smile on my face. "Still thinking about him?" I nodded solemnly, dropping the phony smile.

"Do you think he thinks about me as much as I think about him?" I asked, my voice small. Sometimes I wished I didn't think of him as much as I did.

"I do." She nodded. "He can't not be thinking of you," she said.

"Really?"

"Yes," Avery said, and I actually believed her. "I think it's as hard for him as it is for you."

I hoped so. This was agony.

Not incorporating gymnastics into my daily routine was a tough adjustment. Same with not incorporating him. I knew it would be hard, especially while going through dialysis. Just not this kind of hard. I reminded myself daily that this wasn't forever and that I would go back to the sport that I loved with every fiber in my body soon. I would take what I learned from him and apply it. Fortunately, I had the absolute best friend in the world by my side even if she was living states away. Like Avery had said, "I'm only a phone call away." And she was.

"I'm going to miss you when you leave," I said, pouting. "Who's going to braid my hair and read sex scenes with me out loud?"

We giggled. I'd convinced Avery to read a romance novel a few months ago and the rest was history. She said boys were better in books. I agreed. Even though we both loved the steamy scenes, her way of putting a smile on my face was to narrate a book while I was at dialysis. She had come to three sessions with me and my cheeks bloomed with heat. It was the three best sessions I'd had.

After I'd arrived in Oklahoma a little over a year ago, Dad and Sophia had flown in to help me unpack and get settled. Sophia ended up staying then for close to a month. I'd initially wanted to go at it on my own, but after my first few dialysis treatments, I had to admit it was nice to have her help. Once I'd felt confident I could make it to treatments and care for myself afterward, she returned home to Georgia. We spoke and texted all the time. Truth be told, the month she'd spent here was exactly what we'd needed to work on our bond. I was really happy to have a mom who wanted me. There was a part of me that longed to be able to say my mom was my best friend.

As the New Year's celebrations continued, I wanted to creep toward the exit and drop the empty smile from my face. All day I'd reminisced on the past, and as the day had drawn to an end, my veins had filled with a vibrating need for the one person who wasn't here. I hadn't heard from him since the day I left. He'd said he'd come for me, and while I desperately wanted him to, I was partially relieved he hadn't yet.

Avery left a couple of days later and I already missed her so much. Some days, like today, were lonely. I didn't regret my decision to move here, but it wasn't easy either. Life lessons and growing up and all that jazz.

I retrieved a bottle of water from the refrigerator and took a sip as I sorted through the mail I'd left on the counter earlier. I smiled at the postcard Avery had sent from Florida.

Working on my holiday tan in the sun. How's the snow?

She could be such a brat. Avery wasn't a fan of the cold weather and almost bailed after she arrived here. Apparently Oklahoma had one of those rare cold fronts where it felt like negative three degrees. She said she wasn't built for cold, and I'd have to agree that I wasn't either. However, it was where I felt I needed to be.

I flipped the grocery ads aside and revealed a padded yellow envelope. My brows furrowed wondering who had my address and what I received.

Turning it over, my heart stilled at the familiar writing on the label. Chills raked down my arms. My stomach twisted into knots and I sat on the stool before my legs went out from under me.

It had been sixteen months since I last had any form of contact with him. I'd counted.

I had zero shame.

Quickly, I tore open the package and saw three journals inside. Lips parting on a gasp, I pulled them out along with a letter attached to the top one. Each journal was wrapped in black tissue paper bound with a green sticker that reminded me of his eyes.

My Dearest Malysh,
Enclosed is my soul.
X
Kova

With shaking hands, I lifted the first journal and lost myself in his words. It started from the day I left.

He wrote about his divorce process, my dad dropping the charges against him, selling World Cup... He was raw and honest, and I found myself tearing up every few pages. I missed him every day, but I never realized I missed him this much until I stayed up all night reading the journals. At times the pages were filled with his dark thoughts or ramblings that I couldn't make sense of. I gathered he'd had copious amounts of vodka those days when he penned his feelings. Still, I savored them. They were his thoughts, ones I begged him for when I was in Georgia. I would take what I could get. It was a little view inside his head and I was grateful for it. My heart ached and relief flooded through me. He still loved me. He hadn't come for me yet, but he still loved me. I was somewhat okay knowing that.

The second journal turned slightly personal. I cried a lot.

I do not know who I am without her here. I thought things would smooth over once the divorce proceedings began, but they have not. It has only worsened.

I miss her and I do not know how to handle these thoughts raging through my head without her to talk to me. It is painful. Strange enough, she could look at me and know my head was filled with chaos and iron it out for me. She would push, half the time I hated it, but I always felt better when I spoke to her. If only I realized that then.

I need her more than anything in the world, but I know I cannot have her. It is not right, but fuck, I am dying inside without her. I want to run to her and take her in my arms and never let her go. They say you do not know what you have until it is gone, and now I understand that sentiment more than ever. I never should have let her leave.

What a fucking mess my head is.

I am alone, stuck in this house with the walls closing in on me. I want to burn it to the ground and leave. I should go back to Russia.

I hate Russia. It is too far from her.

I have nowhere to go, and yet all I want to do is runaway and leave.

Everywhere I look, I think of her. I see her. I smell her. I wish I did not. She is hundreds of miles away, yet she feels right here with me.

I lost you her. I feel like I lost you her for good and I do not know how to handle this. I am going out of my mind.

I hate myself for causing her pain. I want to numb myself from feeling. Board up my windows and shut the world out. It is better that way and how I used to live, until her.

Why did she take my black and white world and splash it with color? I wish Frank never called me, and I wish she never stepped foot in my gym. The moment I saw her was a punch to my gut. It is still fresh, like it happened yesterday.

But then I would never have experienced love and laughter. She showed me that. She changed me for the better. I think, anyway. I cannot tell. Did I ever do the same for her?

I hated myself for feeling what I did when I saw her again. She was not a child with pigtails anymore. I was repulsed and sought my therapist immediately. I did everything in my power to keep her at arm's length but the temptation was too much for us to combat. I did not have this reaction to Katja, and I questioned why not so many times until I eventually gave up. I tried with Katja, but my heart was with her. Always with her. After I experienced life with her, there was no going back. I was sold and I desired every second with her.

Some things are not meant to be explained.

She is my other half. That is all, and I will not question it further.

I woke sick to my stomach, reaching for her. It makes no sense since we rarely were able to share a bed, yet it does not matter. I know what I feel and what I want. I need to touch her to know she is real and what we have is real. This gnawing feeling in my stomach that she needs me will not go away. I keep thinking I am going to see her, then I wake up and reality hits me. Does she need me?

Fuck this, I am going.

No, I cannot. I said I would give her time, and that is a promise I planned to keep.

FUCK. I want to fight for her now and show her we need each other. She stood by my side when I needed her the most. I should be by her side as she begins the hardest journey of her life, and I am not. She does not want me there and I have to respect that.

I let her down.

I have to believe the one thing I did right was let her go. I tell myself that often.

But the truth is, she is stronger than me. She said goodbye.

She let me go. For her. If that is not strength, I do not know what is.

I love her more for it.

Frank may have dropped the charges, but that does not change a thing. He and I will never be the same. There is no friendship, no acquaintance. Nothing. We are strangers.

Does it bother me? Yes, it does. Immensely. I want to rectify it, but I know there is not a single thing in the world I can do or say to fix this. I am not looking for friendship or forgiveness. I am not sure what I want from him. He was a good friend, and I ruined the bond between us. That is not who I am. I let him down, another person who trusted me, and lost faith in me.

Was it worth it? Ten times over. I would do it again in a heartbeat for her without remorse. Only this time it would be ten times better. I would love her harder, prove to her she is my world and that we need each other. I would love her first.

Love, what a finicky thing it is. It made me do things I did not know I could to another person. So many regrets, so many highs. I hate myself.

I guess I want to apologize to Frank for hurting him, but I will never apologize for loving her. And if he asked me if I could go back and change history, I would tell him no.

I guess there would be no reason for Frank and I to talk in the end.

The divorce was finalized and I drank myself into a stupor for a solid week, just like the night I married her. I should have found relief I am no longer tied to Katja, but all I felt was loss. Loss over her, not Katja. I should have said no to Katja from the start, but there were too many forces working against us.

I ruined three lives, and I am still without her. I am no one without her. What is life without her?

Katja had a baby boy. I am glad that chapter of my life with her is closed for good.

There is a beast pounding against the walls of my chest desperate to break free. I hear his voice in my head, his negativity is eating away at me. My world is so dark and the vodka does not quell this hunger.

I wish I did not love her as much as I did. I wish I could turn off the feeling. World Cup used to be my safe haven, a place where I could release my stress in the dark and alone. I joined a gym, but a regular gym does nothing for me. Ethan said I should attempt CrossFit, but flipping over a tire does not motivate me. The one thing that has helped has been running as far and as fast as I can until my legs give out.

I am a hostage to my emotions. I fear one day I will not break free from them.

I shut the journal and held it close to my chest, sinking against my head-board of my bed. I closed my eyes and exhaled. There was too much sorrow in his words for my heart to handle another page. I wanted to call him and

670 | LUCIA FRANCO

make sure he was okay, just hear his voice to know and then hang up. But I wouldn't.

The nights were the hardest for me. It was when my mind raced with thoughts and my heart beat a little faster. I wondered if I hurt us both for my decision to leave. I wondered if we could ever come back from this. Sometimes I wished I could fast forward the days and months just to see if it was all worth it in the end. I didn't have this feeling that something wasn't going to happen, I just didn't like the unknown.

chapter 60

Two Years Later

I T WAS A WEEK INTO THE NEW YEAR, AND JUST LIKE THE YEAR BEFORE, a padded envelope arrived. Only, this time it looked bigger. I rushed into my condo and ripped it open. He'd sent four journals this time.

My Dearest Malysh,
I am a man still in love with someone I have no right to love.
X
Kova

I was so engrossed in his writings that I hadn't noticed two hours had passed. I needed to eat something and take my medication before I was due to meet my personal trainer. I'd started competing again months ago, but these days I didn't push myself in the gym like I used to. My body simply couldn't handle it. Instead, I played it smart and when I felt worn out, I stopped and took a break. Thankfully my coaches were understanding and didn't ridicule me otherwise.

Before I left, I decided to read a few more entries. I couldn't not, knowing I had a long night ahead of me. Even though I'd been taking my training slower than I wanted to, it still wore me out. I knew once I got home I would crash and I wouldn't be reading anything else.

However, that all changed when I picked up the third journal. I canceled my training session, knowing I would be in no position to work out. I wasn't prepared for the way his entries switched from him writing about how he felt and his life, to writing directly to me.

I found myself in a sea of emotion and longing. My chest ached and tears gathered in my eyes as I continued reading his entries.

As you know, I sold World Cup. I cannot even walk inside the gym without thinking of you, despite Madeline and Danilo requesting for me to come back. I have not coached since you left. I cannot bring myself to. It reminds me too much of you. Of us. You are everywhere I look inside of that gym. The day you left you took every part of me with you. I am now an empty shell of a man and nothing more.

I rushed the divorce with Katja because I was afraid of losing you rather than leaving her on my own when I wanted to, before it all came to a head. I made rash decisions when it came to us being together, always assuming I was doing the right thing. I acted out of fear instead of consideration. I know now by doing that, I never truly saw you. It kills me that it has taken me this long to finally grasp what you meant when you wanted me to put us first. I thought I was. I only wish I had understood when you were still here with me.

I know now that I am not half the man I thought I was. You trusted me with your heart, your body, and your soul. You showed me unconditional love, and what did I give you? Nothing. I gave you nothing but painful memories and tears that soaked your pillowcase at night. You must know I have a plan to fix all of the damage I have caused you.

Every day I miss your touch. Every minute I miss hearing your voice. Every second I hold out hope for us.

One thing I refused to miss was your return to the sport that brought us together in the first place, so I came and watched you. I purposely hid from you, but I was there in the stands as you lit up the room with your passion for gymnastics. You only competed on bars and floor. O bozhe, what a sight that was to see you again. I watched you. I watched the people watch you with nothing but awe on their faces. I am so proud of the gymnast you have become. You left a mark on your teammates and the spectators that day, the same way you left your mark on me.

It was then that I realized I needed to fix me before I came for you. What I am saying is, I need to find me too in order to be enough for you. I must work on myself to be a better man. I wish I could have you by my side as I figure out who I am, to help me fight this battle raging inside of me to find the truth, but you have already done so much for me, and if you can do it on your own, then I can too. Do you remember when I told you that you inspire me? That has not changed. Your strength gives me strength. I admire the fuck out of you. I was a wreck when you left, but you leaving was the right decision, and the best thing you could have done, not just for yourself, but for me as well. I am glad you left even though every damn second without you makes for a very lonely, miserable world.

I will come for you, but only when I am the man you need, one you can be proud of. One that will never hesitate to put you or our love first. Until them, I will take the time I need to work on myself to be good enough for you, and then, only then, will I come for you. That is a promise I intend to keep. You were once a reflection of me for a short period of time, but now I want to be a reflection of you for the rest of my life. I will come for you, Malysh. And once I have you, I will never let go. I just pray you accept me and have not lost hope in us before then.

I am a man of many flaws and too many sins to atone for. The regret I live with on a daily basis eats away at me. I pray one day you have it in you to forgive me for how badly I have treated you. I will not make excuses for my behavior. I will own them and face them like a man. We had many odds working against us. I just hope I did not chase you away forever. Please, you must know, it was never my intention to cause you pain. I do not want to lose you. You are my other half, and well, I need you in order to be me. I am not whole without you.

You say I left an indentation on your heart. You have done the same with mine.

I see it every day when I look in the mirror.

It is us against the world. I took you for granted, but I promise you I will never do that again. Please just give me a little more time. If you send me away when I come, then I will respect your wishes, but I pray that is not the case.

Until I see you again.

Ya lyublyu tebya vsegda I naveki.

I never contacted him after receiving the journals last year, and still I wouldn't contact him after getting these. The ball was in his court. It was his move to make. He'd said he would come, so I would wait for the day he decided to show up.

I think back to his entry of how he felt the decisions he made in moments of fear were right at the time. His regret suffocated me. They were right for him, and maybe a little for me. He shouldn't have regret because I too had made decisions in the moment thinking they were right. It was a sweet-and-sour taste on my tongue. My decision to leave wasn't one made out of fear for him or us...I had done it for me. Okay, maybe a little for us. It was a moment of clarity I knew we both needed. If I had acted in fear, then I would not be in Oklahoma now.

He said he gave me nothing. But he was wrong. He helped give me my dream...and myself.

chapter 61

Three Years Later

I STARED UP AT THE SCREEN AND AWAITED MY SCORE. MY VEINS FILLED
with electricity and my knees were shaking with adrenaline. My smile was
plastered across my face. I'd been competing for two years now, but this was
my first televised meet since the Olympics, and I was a ball of nerves. I wanted
to prove I still had what it took to be on the team, but it was hard when I knew
all eyes were on the girl battling kidney disease and lupus. The support this
university, my teammates, and my incredible coaches showed me was invaluable.
I competed my heart out. That was my gift to them for what they gave me.

Since officially returning to the sport, my worries were laid to rest once I
had sat down with my coaches and we devised a safe plan for me to compete.
Committing to Oklahoma was the best decision I ever made. I was iffy when
it came to the bigger competitions because I was scared to fail and let my team
down. They all reassured me that if they didn't believe in me they wouldn't let me
risk it. He'd always told me I shined under pressure, but I didn't have him here
with me and I wasn't sure I could pull it off again without his words of encouragement. My new coaches were stellar, I wouldn't complain, but they weren't him.

I glanced toward the crowd. I knew Dad and Sophia were somewhere in
the stands. They'd refused to miss this day and booked their flights the moment
I was given the schedule for the season. A part of me couldn't help but wonder
if he was in the audience too. My heart said he was here.

The crowd cheered, breaking my wayward thoughts. My teammates engulfed me in a hug and tears once again filled my eyes. I was my own worst critic
and their support meant the world to me. These women were the best part about
joining the gymnastics team.

I looked back up at the screen in disbelief. My vision blurred and my jaw trembled. I scored a nearly perfect score. I couldn't believe it. I wondered if I would ever stop getting emotional over gymnastics.

Shortly before I began training again, I started seeing a therapist once a week. I felt it was something I needed to do in order to stay healthy as a whole. I didn't want to kill myself for a medal, and it was so easy for me to. I was older now, still living with life-threatening illnesses. I wanted to prosper and fly, and I wanted to do that by accepting what I was physically capable of and being okay with it. Reaching out for help didn't mean I was weak like I had once thought. If anything, it made me stronger. My score told me I'd made the right choice.

My coaches high-fived me as I dropped down by my duffle bag to remove my grips. My smile faltered a little, my happiness dimming. I was over the moon with my score, but it just wasn't the same without him here.

It was the ninth of January and I was on edge.

His package should have been here Saturday and it wasn't.

I waited in the lobby by the mailboxes, trying not to pounce on the mailman as he slowly stuffed the slots full. Finally, after an eternity, he closed the metal doors and locked up. And I was right there, opening my assigned box before he even walked away. I rifled through my mail where I stood.

No package.

My heart slipped.

My hope died a little.

Another day went by, and another, and another. The week came to an end and still nothing. I tried to go about my life, putting on a smile for everyone around me when I was crumbling inside. A second week had come and gone, and my misery was replaced with anger. On a whim I opened my messaging app and typed in his name.

Me: I'm going to assume my journals were lost in the mail.

I waited for his response. After ten minutes, I texted again.

Me: I know you read my message. It says read.

I sent him a screenshot and circled where it said "Read" beneath my message. Within seconds, the little dots appeared on the screen telling me he was typing. I held my breath, hoping he'd send a response the size of the Bible back.

Coach: I do not want to interfere with your life.

I groaned inwardly. Of course, he'd be short with his words.

Me: I can make my own decisions, thank you very much. Now send me my journals, Kova.
Me: I looked forward to the package. I read the journals all the time.

The little dots didn't even appear. My chest ached when he didn't respond. Suffocation clawed at my throat.

Me: I need them. Please. Give them to me.

Still nothing. His lack of response was like a punch to the gut. How could he ignore me? My heart thumped erratically. I tried not to cry, but it was fruitless. My heart still ached for my other half.

Me: They help me. Please.

Another week passed and no texts, or journals in the mail. I tried not to succumb to the darkness. I'd come too far to go backward now—surgery on my Achilles, dialysis a few times a week, balancing my diseases while killing it in the collegiate world of gymnastics and attending school. By all outward appearances I was at the top of my game, but appearances were deceiving. I was good at faking it too.

I was dying inside. I never stopped loving him, but I guess he stopped loving me. That was a hard pill to swallow. He said he would come, and I told myself that I would wait for him. Exhaling, I righted myself.

A couple of my teammates had talked me into attending a party with them tonight. It wasn't something I did normally. I was young, single, why the fuck not go out and act my age for once. I needed to stop dwelling on the package I hadn't received and let go for once in my life.

After an hour or so, I found myself refilling shot after shot of vodka and fending off horny college guys. I had zero desire in interacting with any of them, even in my inebriated state. There was only one person who stirred my blood, and I was drinking his poison.

He said he'd come for me, but he never did. He lied.

My chest rose and fell rapidly. Tears were threatening to spill. I refused to cry and pulled my phone from my back pocket, squinting at the home screen. I pressed the wrong buttons a few times before I found the message icon. I was sure I'd regret this in the morning, but it wasn't morning yet and the alcohol gave me the liquid courage to text him.

Me: I went to a dumb drat part and I drunk and now I hate you. I seriously hate u.
Me: Why did you have to make me fall in love with u.
Me: Where are the jounrals?
Me: Send me MY journals, Konstantinn. You know they are mine.
Me: They were never yours to begin with.

I woke the next morning to banging in my head and a twisted stomach. Immediately I checked my phone, forcing back the bile rising in the back of my throat.

I waited all night for a text. He never responded. Taking my phone, I threw it across the room and let it hit the wall. I fought back the tears and clenched my shaking fingers into fists.

The hangover was a blessing in disguise. It allowed me to forget the aching in my heart. I knew better than to drink, especially on my medication. But I needed one night to cut loose and forget the pain of loving someone from afar.

The banging returned and I shook my head under my pillow. Big mistake. I groaned through the raging migraine I was dealing with, my stomach churning once again. I shot up and ran for the bathroom, making it to the toilet before I was vomiting clear liquid and the Taco Bell I'd consumed before passing out last night. I was never, ever drinking again. Or eating Taco Bell.

After I expelled every last drop I could in my body, I stood up and gargled with mouthwash, then rinsed my face before walking back to my room to crash. I halted in my steps when the pounding returned, and I realized it was coming from the door. My brows furrowed.

Bleary-eyed, I stumbled to answer it. The sooner I could make the noise stop, the faster I could climb back into bed and pass out. I wanted to go back to sleep and pray this was all a dream.

Reaching for the knob and bolt, I opened the door and sobered right up.

Heart instantly racing, my lips parted in absolute shock. I blinked rapidly.

After three years of no calls, no texts, nothing so much as a picture, just yearly journals filled with his thoughts and desires, except for this year, the stupid Russian who'd claimed my heart years ago stood in front of me.

My lips parted further. Tears immediately welled in my eyes.

"Allo, Malysh."

epilogue

Thirteen Years Later

Kova

"COME, LILI. COME TO DADDY."

I stayed squatted as I waved my fingers, encouraging her to take a step.

Her chunky bowlegs were apprehensive as she attempted to walk to me for the first time. Drool fell from her toothless smile and plopped on the chalky floor next to her purple toenails. Mia, her older sister, had painted them for her when she was sleeping because she does not ever sit still any other time.

I had four daughters, all gorgeous, just like their mother. And all under the age of six.

I was fucked.

Double fucked.

I was cursed, certain I had pissed someone off in another life. I do not even joke anymore that God was testing me. I knew he was.

Lili picked up her stubby leg. Just like the time before, I held my breath and hoped this would be the first step she took. My knees were screaming in rebellion staying in this position so long, but I held still if that meant seeing her walk.

"Da, Da, Da," she babbled.

More slobber fell to the floor. Lili had a slight Russian accent, but my wife insisted it was just baby speak. I firmly believed she was wrong, and I told her that often. It made her heated and she would argue; she was even more beautiful when she was fired up.

Lili mumbled again, the enunciation in the back of her throat. Totally Russian there and not that American baby speak.

"Yes, Lili, *Da, Da, Da*," I said, heavy on the Russian enunciation.

Lili squealed. She lifted her knee and balanced on one leg, her toes curling into the floor for support. My brows rose and I encouraged her again to take another step, holding my breath. I wiggled my fingers and made a funny face trying to make her come to me. All my daughters have taken their first steps inside our gym. I was hoping Lili would too.

Her cherry chocolate hair was tied up in some messy thing I did for her. She tried to pull it out and whined because she could not accomplish it. I gave her a stern look and she dropped her arms with a pout. My wife had been trying to teach me how to do their hair since Mia was born.

No matter how much I tried, I still could not figure out how to do it without ripping hair out.

Looking at me with massive amber eyes, Lili began to lean too far to the side. I reached out quickly and caught her, making a big splash about it so she would try again. I planted a huge, loud kiss to her cheek. Her eyes twinkled and she giggled as I stood her up again. Lili was the first of our daughters to attempt to walk by eight months. Something told me we were in trouble with this one.

"Lili, come Lili. Come to Daddy, *malyshka*."

She shrieked excitedly then took a step. I held my breath as she placed one foot in front of the other and stayed upright. She hesitated, and I gave her a little push, telling her to keep trying. She did it again and I waved my fingers impatiently just as she took two steps and fell into my arms.

I heard a gasp behind me and quickly turned around, blindly standing Lili up.

My wife. I smiled seeing the happiness written across her face

"Is that my girl walking?" my wife cooed.

I glanced back at Lili and let go, watching as she took three steps this time before falling into her mother's arms with a shriek. She scooped up Lili and held her tight to her chest, right above her growing belly. Lili's fat feet dangled on the sides of her waist.

Our gazes met and my stomach tightened. I will never get over the fact that this beautiful woman was now my wife. How I fucking loved her to the ends of the earth.

Her eyes shimmered up at me and her soft smile made my heart pound.

"*Allo, Malysh.* When did you get here?"

This was my favorite time of the day that I looked forward to after we said our morning goodbyes—when Adrianna brought all of our daughters to gymnastics practice. It was one of the very limited things she could do while being on bed rest. While she should not be doing anything at all, I knew I had to give her something, otherwise she would take the directions lightly and overdo it.

4

She could take the girls to and from school, and she liked to bathe and put them to sleep. That was it.

I reached out to palm Adrianna's belly and stepped close to her with Lili sandwiched between us.

"Just now."

She smiled and rose up on her tiptoes to give me a kiss, but Lili gave her a wet one first. There was slobber all over my wife's cheek and she laughed. My lips twitched seeing her happy.

"Why? Did you miss me?" she asked, and she angled her brows.

"You already left me once, just making sure you were not making another run for it. I never know with you."

Her eyes lit up ready to retaliate and she punched my stomach. I grabbed her hand and held it tenderly. I looked down at her with nothing but love. I do not let her live down the fact that she left me.

My palm skimmed along her pelvis to feel her rounded stomach. Her shirt was too short and showing part of her lower belly. I loved that little space of skin on her. For someone so small, she wore pregnancy extremely well. Adrianna claimed to enjoy being pregnant, and since I loved seeing her grow with my child, it was a win for the both of us.

Breaking apart, Lili rested her head on her mother's shoulder and then placed her thumb in her mouth, twirling hair around her finger.

Though each pregnancy Adrianna glowed more than the previous one, it came with a steep price. I did not want her light to burn out and I was terrified it would. Our growing family was a heavy burden on her body, one I did not wish to keep chancing. We were fortunate enough to have made it this far after several specialists had agreed we most likely would not.

When we were told that Lili's pregnancy was the last her body could handle, Adrianna had cried her eyes out for days. We knew this would come one day. She was not ready and had begged me for one more baby, hoping it would be a boy this time. She did not want that choice to be taken from her again.

She wanted one more chance to give me a son on her terms. Our terms.

I felt we were blessed to have our daughters and I had told her it was not necessary, but Adrianna had this incessant need to defy all odds.

We had argued about it at first. A lot.

Adrianna was the love of my life. We had walked through fire and hell to get here. I had told her she could fight me all she wanted but I was not changing my mind. Call me selfish, I *was* selfish. I wanted her to stay healthy to be with our family. I was not going to lose her for good this time, because I knew I would never survive living this life without her again.

Lili had only been born about two months prior before she went on this emotional tirade. Her hormones were making her crazy. Of course, I could not tell her that. However, I had told her she was being irresponsible and that we had four gorgeous children already and was that not enough for her.

She had slapped me.

The woman *loved* to slap me.

She would not talk to me for a full two weeks, though every night she came to me.

I had tried to put my foot down, but she was adamant. My wife had this endless need to push her body to the limit. It drove me absolutely insane, but I loved her so fucking much that I had eventually caved and we tried for one more baby.

Surprisingly, it had not taken long to conceive.

Adrianna loved to remind me it was meant to be and the reason why it had happened so easily.

I wanted to give Adrianna the world, not hold it back from her. I felt like she was taking a huge risk every time we conceived, but it was hard to say no to her when I knew all she wanted was a big family.

Our doctors were confident she could carry to term one last time, but she was still labeled as high-risk.

As I approached the golden age, I had this constant fear inside of me that something was going to happen to her and my kids. It consumed me. They were little spitfires who took after their mother, and they were my world. I was already wrapped around their boney little fingers, which was why I planned to keep them locked up until at least thirty-five. No public schools. No cell phones. No boyfriends. Adrianna laughed every time I brought it up because she thought I was kidding, but I really was not. I could already feel my blood pressure rising just thinking about who I would have to fight off. It almost made me feel bad for being with Adrianna when she was so young.

Almost. Not entirely.

"Where are the rest of the—"

Before I could finish, Mia, Svetlana, and Nastia came barreling into the gym, running straight for me in a race of who could get to me first. Squatting down again, my knees popped and Ria winced at the sound. I opened my arms as Lili squealed behind me at seeing her three sisters.

"Daddy!" I heard about eight times in the span of three seconds right before they plowed into my chest.

I pretended to fall back on the floor, and they giggled in response, falling over me dramatically. I glanced above their little heads at Adrianna. Our eyes met and she smiled down at me. I loved the sound of our girls' high-pitched laughs. It did shit to my heart that I could not explain and made this life that much sweeter. Leaning my head up, I gave them tons of animated kisses and they chuckled even more. I never knew how much I could love like this until my wife gave us children. Now I felt like I was going to erupt from it.

Nastia jumped on me again and I grunted in response. My wife covered her mouth and tried to stifle a laugh. I could see the smile behind her hand. At this rate, I would not be able to give Adrianna any more kids even if I wanted to if they kept kneeing my dick all the time. I wrapped my arms around the three of them and held them until they were giggling from my tickles, begging me to stop.

At first, we had been concerned if Adrianna could get pregnant after many failed attempts. She had said it was karma and a constant reminder of what we had endured as a couple. She was never able to fully let go of losing our first child and had nearly damaged herself emotionally in the process. It had wrecked me to see her so miserable.

All of Adrianna's specialists had gathered in one room to discuss if she could get pregnant at all when we had decided we were ready. She had not had a regular period for years, and the doctors were concerned about the health risks she could possibly undergo being pregnant with stage four kidney disease. The medication she had been taking for years had caused harsh side effects. She was not the same. The medication damaged parts of her body that would never be able to recover.

After a year of trying to conceive and false pregnancy tests and tears I kissed my way through, we had turned to fertility drugs.

It had not been easy for either of us, her more so. Adrianna had been brokenhearted when we filled the prescription for the first time. She had blamed herself for the pregnancy she lost all those years ago, saying it was her fault she was unable to conceive naturally. I had kissed her all damn night and let her cry on me until she fell asleep, and when she woke with fresh tears the next morning, I stayed right where I was and held her until she stopped shaking. It had fucking devastated me to see her like that, but I stayed strong because she needed me. I owed my wife everything for the life she gave me. If she had wanted a baby, then I would move mountains to give her one.

Weeks had gone by and she began to feel inadequate as a woman, that something was missing from her. I had told her she was crazy and to calm down because she was perfect the way she was—biggest mistake I ever made as a husband. The moment I had said to calm down, she exploded.

Apparently, women did not like to hear those two words together.

We had considered adoption from Russia—her idea—but I was not ready to give up on having our own children one day, even if we were only granted one. I had never wanted little hellions until Adrianna had put the idea in my head. Now I cannot imagine my life without them. I wanted a plethora of them.

"Daddy! Throw me in the air," Nastia demanded, her red ringlets falling in front of her eyes.

"Me too, Daddy!" Svetlana, Nastia's twin, screamed like a hyena in my ear.

I winced, going deaf for a split second.

Yes, twins.

Both my wife and I were still perplexed over it. We knew twins were a strong possibility because of Sophia combined with the potency of the fertility drugs, but we did not anticipate them.

"Again, Daddy!" Nastia said, elbowing her sister out of the way.

"How are you feeling?" I asked and stood up. I gave the kids one last toss each in the air. "Girls, go change and warm up." They dashed off. They loved gymnastics.

Adrianna's dreamy smile took my breath away as she peered up at me. I fucking loved this woman. The light was shining through the large window showcasing the dusting of freckles across the bridge of her nose. The older she got, the more pronounced they became. I wrapped my arm around her shoulder and held her close to me.

"Great? Amazing? Wonderful?" She smiled bigger, then yawned. "I slept most of the day. Thanks for taking Lili for me."

"*Malysh*, I am not *taking* Lili for you. She is my daughter too."

She pouted and I had the urge to kiss her lips deep.

"I know. I just feel bad because you have to work."

I shook my head. "You know World Cup is family. We rotated events—I took her to vault, Danilo took her on floor, Madeline had her on bars, then she ended on balance beam with me."

She grinned, and her eyes lit up. It was the little things we found satisfaction in now.

Madeline and Danilo had phoned me one night explaining that they wanted to expand World Cup, and that they wanted me to come back and coach. They had sweetened the proposal by allowing me to buy my way back into the gym. I countered back with adding Adrianna to the offer.

When I had returned to World Cup with my wife, I was placed under scrutiny. They had no idea we were married, let alone together. It did not faze me one bit, and I had answered every question they asked. I was proud of us and refused to hide what I felt for Adrianna ever again. I knew how it looked, we had heard it all, but that was then, and this was now.

Adrianna, on the other hand, did not have the same reaction. She had been uncomfortable, edgy, like everyone looked at her with disapproving eyes.

It was not until she had become pregnant with our first daughter that everyone had a change of heart. The whole gym shifted and we suddenly became one big family. They saw her go through the emotions of longing to have a child and failing, how her chances had been so slim. They saw how she leaned on me, how I cradled her when she was finally pregnant. They saw how strong our love was during one of the hardest times for us, and it had lifted the curtain for them.

"Need any help today?" she asked eagerly.

I knew where she was going with this. "I got it covered."

Her eyes dropped and a laugh rumbled in my chest. "Tell me you love me." I demanded, my eyes penetrating hers.

"Never," she said with a smile on her face. "Come on, Coach, let me help a bit. It's not like I'm asking to make a comeback. Maybe if you let me help, I'll make it worth your while and we can go into your office like old times…"

She loved to be in the gym as much as I did.

"Go put your feet up in my office. Call a friend or buy some shit online. But I do not want to hear that your blood pressure dropped again or see you rushed off to the hospital."

Her eyes flared. "That was one time, three pregnancies ago."

"And I never want to relive that moment."

Her eyes dropped lower now. Just as I was about to add something else, I saw Svetlana, or as Nastia called her, Lana, stop walking and drop her head. I peered around Adrianna and frowned as I watched her stand alone in her metallic pink leotard. She balled her tiny hands in her mouth, her creamy fingers twisting against her teeth. She was our little pixie of a girl with untamable red curls and sabal eyes. Svetlana was noticeably smaller than her twin.

I nodded with my chin and we both looked at her.

"*Svetlana, idi syuda I skazhi mne, chto ne tak.*"

My children understood both Russian and English, at my wife's request.

Her little feet padded across the floor. Svetlana glanced up with tears shimmering in her innocent eyes.

"What's wrong?" my wife asked, handing me Lili before kneeling down.

We had a rule. When one of the girls needed us, we would give them our undivided attention, if we were capable in the moment, of course. Between their close ages and female emotions, we did not want them to feel we favored one over the other.

I also was trying to prevent meltdowns before they happened. That was a lot of female hormones under one roof.

"I do not want to do the bawance beam." Her little voice squeaked.

I had a good chuckle over her lack of contractions. Every once in a while, my kids sounded like me and I found it hysterical. Now I understood why Adrianna made jokes about it.

"It is scary. Can I just do the other ones and not that one today?"

"Are you still thinking about when you slipped off yesterday?" Adrianna responded, and Svetlana nodded, her chin staying tight to her chest.

Reaching for her, my wife picked up Svetlana and cradled her to her hip. She sniffled and placed her thumb in her mouth. Normally I was against Adrianna picking up the children while she was pregnant, unless it was Lili, but I never said anything when it came to Svetlana.

Her muscle tone had been very weak since she was born. She had to be supported for a solid two years by us holding up her and her neck. Adrianna and I had worked diligently with our daughter to build muscle tone through play.

Doctors firmly believed that Svetlana's hypotonia was actually caused by muscular dystrophy.

Svetlana had no idea gymnastics was more about rehabilitation for her than the actual sport. We did not want to push her to do the balance beam. We both had agreed that if our kids did not want to play the sport, then they did not have to, but for Svetlana who actually liked gymnastics, it was part of her therapy. We gave her a nudge on all the events. She needed gymnastics to live.

"I guess I'll be on beam for the next hour," Adrianna said happily. She planted a kiss to my lips then waddled away. It was a struggle for me to let her go, but our daughter needed her, and, well, Adrianna needed this too.

For the next hour I watched while my fearless wife helped coach our daughter. Tonight I would have to make sure I take the girls so she can get a little extra rest. It was rare when she told me she was tired and wanted to relax, but I knew how much the pregnancies drained her. She was my other half—I felt what she did. Adrianna was determined to be there for her kids. I loved her so much for that and did not want to take it away from her, so I had to be creative about making sure she did not overdo it. Like taking parent duties the entire night. Svetlana was still in pull-ups, and Mia was already fighting us about staying up later. Nastia never liked to sleep and half the time she would climb into Mia's bed. Putting them to sleep could be exhausting, especially if you were pregnant.

After Adrianna had undergone the transplant surgery, the last thing we had expected was to conceive again. We had not even given it a thought, truthfully. Mia had been a newborn when Adrianna's kidneys failed and she was rushed into surgery. She had fought hard to be able to be a mother to our daughter while recovering. Adrianna was, to this day, trying to do her best to keep up with our girls despite being placed on bed rest. I could not take that from her.

Juggling World Cup, my children, and a very pregnant wife was a challenge. Danilo and Madeline took my teams while I stayed with my wife twenty-four seven. Luckily, Sophia stepped in and offered to help. The woman was a godsend, a true blessing. She did not have a single mean bone in her body and often reminded me of my late mother, who Svetlana was named after. I would like to think they would have gotten along well.

Lili was now sleeping in her stroller a couple of feet from me while I was coaching the elite girls on beam. I overheard Adrianna walk Svetlana through her fears and encourage her back onto the lower balance beam. She told Svetlana stories of how she used to be scared and said it was okay to feel that way because one day it would go away.

Like mother, like daughter, I thought. They both hated the balance beam.

"*Dade*," she said, standing on the floor beam. "*Ya smotri*."

My lips twitched and I walked over to her. She wanted me to watch her. Svetlana's Russian was mixed with English and typically backwards. We did not have the heart to correct her yet. She was too cute for words when she tried to speak.

Grabbing both of my wife's index fingers for support, Svetlana slowly walked the beam. Her legs shook and her fingers were screaming red from holding onto her mother. I shot a glance over her head to my wife, and our eyes locked. I was not sure if it was possible to fall in love with someone a little more every day, but I did with her. She was a wife, a mother, my other half. My world revolved around her and our children.

Our soft smiles mimicked each other's, but there was a sadness inside of me I was hiding from everyone, including Adrianna. Seeing Svetlana walk the balance beam without tears was a big moment for us.

Svetlana was the runt of the twins. Nastia had crushed her in the womb. We had initially thought she was just a lazy baby with floppy limbs, but when she continued to miss the milestones while her twin surpassed them with flying colors, we took her into the pediatrician to have her examined.

Adrianna was neurotic these days and took the girls in for every little thing.

"Come on, baby girl, you can do it." Adrianna encouraged softly.

I could hear the tears in her voice that she worked hard to hide. She was terrified she was going to pass her illnesses down to her children, and she felt responsible in some way for Svetlana's disease.

We both had deep fears we did not speak of.

That did not mean we were not aware of them. We were. And we addressed them without making it obvious. It was how we worked, otherwise it was too easy for the both of us to slip into darkness and spread ruin. Communication was key, Adrianna had said.

Adrianna's gaze was fixated on Svetlana's feet, watching her step one shaky foot in front of the other. That way if she slipped, my wife would catch her before she had the chance to fall so she did not lose her courage. We planned to incorporate calf raises into her practices to help steady her ankles.

Svetlana glanced up, her dark eyes glimmering. Her cheeks had the cutest dimples when she was really happy, and right now they were all I could see.

My daughter glanced into my eyes and I nearly lost my breath. My children were my life and I felt this need to protect them at all costs. I never knew this kind of love existed.

Letting go, she held her little body as tight as she could, then walked straight to me.

"You did it, my sweet *malyshka*," I said, then scooped her up into my arms. I held her tight, giving her an exaggerated kiss on her cheek. She giggled and kicked her legs excitedly against my stomach. I held her back to support her. "I am so proud of you. Soon you will be doing flips off it."

"Mommy said she was scared."

Her lisp melted my heart.

"She was, but you know what? She had a really good coach who helped her overcome those scary thoughts and showed her that she was strong enough to handle it. Those scary thoughts only stay if you let them."

Her round eyes looked at me. "Wike you, *Dade*."

I grinned, hoping Adrianna heard the accent. "Exactly."

"Mommy said she used to do fwips."

"She did."

Svetlana sucked in a breath like she had a lot to say. Her brows rose and she tapped my shoulder. "Mommy said you can do fwips too. Fwip, *Dade*."

"*Dade* is a little old for that now."

Putting Svetlana down, I told her to rotate to the next event, but she would not budge. She stared up at me with huge eyes that flickered with optimism like her mind was spinning. She reminded me so much of Adrianna.

"I want to do fwip like Mommy," she said, and threw her arms in the air like she was describing an explosion. My lips twitched. Most words that included an L in the spelling, Svetlana said them with a W sound. It was too adorable. "I want to do big fwips wike mommy one day. Big ones, *Dade*." She paused, then said more so to herself, "I wike big ones wike dat." She was watching an elite tumble across the floor, mesmerized by her twisting in the air. Her eyes widened, her voice a collection of bouncy tones and innocent words.

Svetlana wobbled to the side. I reached out instantly to steady her. She fell often and had bruises all over her milky skin. One would think we beat our kids.

I squatted down in front of her and looked at her. "Remember, if you ever feel like you are going to fall, just squeeze your butt and your tummy. It will help."

She blinked at me. "Wike when I try handstands."

It was a simple rule in gymnastics, but it made me so fucking proud that she remembered. "Yes, exactly like that. Now go tell your sisters about the flips you are going to do one day. While you are there, tell Mia to lose the attitude or she is working bars for one week without grips."

Svetlana nodded. "Okay, *Dade*," she said, then turned around and ran in the direction her sisters were in.

Little brat gave her sister a hug and did not tell her shit.

"A really good coach, huh?" my wife said, sidling up next to me when our daughter was out of ear distance.

My brow peaked. "Is it not the truth? Am I not a really good coach?"

"Maybe." I could hear the smile in her voice.

I looked at her. She shrugged one shoulder indifferently and crossed her arms in front of her chest. Her breasts were swollen and full, and exactly where my eyes fell. They had been full like that for years, ever since her body started going through maternity. She was rounder and softer in all the right places, and I could not keep my hands off of her.

Like right now. I wanted to drag her into our office and make her ride me until she could not stand.

I stifled a growl. Maybe I would take her up on her offer from earlier.

"Kova."

My eyes snapped to hers. The sounds that left her lips made me feel weak for her.

"Come. We have a matter to discuss in my office."

After asking Madeline to look after Lili, we walked together, and when we reached the office, I stepped in first and moved to the side. Before she could blink, I was pulling her to me and kicking the door shut so I could press my lips to hers. A soft gasp of surprise feathered her lips and then I was kissing her speechless.

"Wife," I said, growling against her mouth.

Her lips turned up in a smile against mine. "Husband."

It did not get any better than this.

"You know how much I love seeing you nurture our daughters, yes?" She nodded, arching into me. We were looking at each other. Her body was so warm and inviting against mine. With my hand on her stomach, I said, "And you know how I love to see you grow with our child, yes?" She nodded again, her smile growing bigger. She made my fucking heart race when she looked at me like that, like I was her entire world. I craved this look every day the sun rose. "Then you know how much I want to be inside of you, yes?"

She purred like a damn cat and my cock was erect in seconds. My tongue traced her lips and her gasp was hot, immersed in desire. Fisting my shirt, she leaned up on her toes to reach my mouth. My hands smoothed over her belly to the crease at her thighs. I cupped her ass, my fingertips digging into her with need. I swear she wore these little linen shorts to torture me. There was hardly any material, but she insisted they were the only comfortable thing to wear because she was hot all the time. Her little ass was heavier now, and her thighs swept into a tender touch that made me want to dive between them and spend all night there.

My hands swooped to the front of her expanding belly, the pads of my fingers gliding gently over the C-section scar from the birth of our twins. She hated this scar, along with the other one she did not like to talk about. The transplant one. I told her that I loved her even more for them. They were battle scars and she should wear them proudly. She is still working on that.

Her legs spread automatically, and she rolled her hips up toward me. A growl escaped my throat. I loved when she became needy for me. Our bodies were not our own when we were like this. My fingers slipped inside her elastic shorts, making a beeline straight to her clit. She let go of my shirt, breaking the kiss to yank down my shorts. I smiled against her lips, nipping at them. Her sex drive when she was pregnant was worse than mine.

"You do this to me on purpose." Her voice was a breathless whisper.

I played innocent. "All I did was kiss you *allo*."

"Yeah, right. You kissed me like you wanted to fuck me." She bit my chin.

The corners of my mouth curled up and my eyes bore into hers. She made me the happiest man on earth, and not because she was stroking my cock with purpose and focused on a steady execution, but because of the feeling she gave me every time I looked at her.

"*Malysh*, I want to fuck you all the time."

Her wispy giggle made me harder. "Babe, you know I'm always wanting sex now. You can't do that to me," she whined. "Give me five minutes? We have time before the appointment. I need you."

My brow peaked. She rubbed her sweet body all over me. How could I deny her? I never had been able to in the past, and now that we were married, it was even worse.

Plus, she was right. We had time to spare.

Clearly, I did not need much convincing.

Within seconds, I was on the couch positioned against the corner with Adrianna sitting on top of my lap with her back against my chest. Our shorts were gone, her legs were spread and knees bent and pulled up, and I was deep inside her pussy, driving into her wetness. It was easier for her in this position and the one she preferred.

With one foot on the floor and the other propped on the cushion, I rocked into her, building a steaming surge of pleasure between us. I fisted her hair to one side as I struggled to contain the pure warmth of euphoria from being inside of my wife. I exhaled across her neck and she let out a loud and hearty moan like she had been waiting for this moment. It gave my cock a heartbeat of its own and skyrocketed my need for her.

"Do whatever you want to me," she said, already feeling enraptured. Her head fell back onto my shoulder.

I smiled against her neck and nipped her. "I always do, *Malysh*… I always do."

Taking her left hand in mine, I placed it where our bodies were joined and laced our fingers together. Her diamond wedding ring cut into my palm as our fingers glided over the wetness together. Her hips reared back into mine. She had yet to take the ring off, not since the day I pushed it on her finger.

"Go deeper." She moaned, her fingers tickling the space under my dick. I thrust in deep and she took my sack in her hand. I tensed, feeling my balls tighten as she caressed them like silk. "How do you always make it feel so good every time?"

"It is my goal to drive you out of your mind when I am inside of you."

I groaned in her ear at the feel of her soft fingers caressing my skin. Cupping the back of my head, she turned to the side and pulled my lips to hers. My wife was feisty when she felt our bodies fused together.

I could not see past her belly, but I had a vivid imagination. I reached around and my palm ran circles on the inside of her thigh, and she quivered in response. I gave her a good grab and her legs widened willingly. It was one of those things that made her hot for me. She liked the pressure on her leg because it teased her pussy.

Adrianna drew in a slow breath the deeper I went. Her swollen pussy soaked my balls, her pleasure dripping over them. Her sex tightened around my cock and squeezed me so hard I almost shot inside her.

"Feel that?" she asked.

I moaned my response. "Of course, *Malysh*. Any deeper and I will split you in two."

Her hips began moving on their own, her thighs clenching. Her moans fought to break past her teeth biting into her lip. She was needy as hell when she was pregnant.

"No, no, no." I gritted the words out through my teeth, trying to hold her back. Sometimes she made me come before I could stop it. "We still have a minute left."

She whimpered. "I need to—"

"Shhh, I know what you need," I said.

"Oh, Kova."

My name was like a sin on her lips as her pussy leaked all over me. She tugged the hair at my nape, but I made her work for it and yanked away, taking pleasure in the sharp pain she caused. Our bodies moved in harmony. I was sliding into her with ease.

"I'm so glad I married you," she said, and it caused me to loosen my lips and laugh.

"As am I, *Malysh*."

"Maybe I have an addiction problem," she said out of the blue. "Like I'm addicted to sex with you."

I shook my head and grinned. "You know what problem you have? You talk too much during sex. You always have. Shut your mouth and let me have my way with you."

"Yes, sir."

I kissed her neck, then slapped the inside of her thigh, chuckling under my breath. She hissed, her pussy clenching around my cock.

Her hand came up and wrapped around my bicep to hang on. It was how I knew she was close. She needed to hang on to me.

"Straighten your legs," I said, my voice low.

Binding her ankles with mine, I held her legs down and stroked her clit until she was dripping and straining on me to let go. I lifted my hand in the air only for my palm to come down and slap her pussy as I drove in until I was balls deep and she was squirming.

Her pussy tightened around my cock and she began spasming, letting the sexiest purrs escape her throat. The heat of her body liquefied on me and Adrianna was riding the wave. She tried so hard to rock into me. She let out a sigh and my eyes widened. I was lost to the pleasure and slapped my hand over her mouth. The last thing we needed was someone knocking on the door. Her hips pumped back into mine and she was like this tiny little ferocious animal in heat.

Her teeth bit into my fingers, her entire body shook with such extreme pleasure, and it caused me to unload inside of her. My hands trembled from sheer desire as I poured my seed into her. There was something about knowing my cum was inside of her that turned me from animalistic to caveman. Always had since the first time I came inside her pretty pussy. I pinched her nipple and my body folded into hers as she drained my cock.

"I feel like stars are dancing on my skin," she said, her voice in a dreamlike state.

I knew that feeling all too well.

"No, this is just us, Ria. It is what has always been there since day one."

"Do you think it will ever go away?"

"I hope not."

She paused, panting. "Same." She cupped the back of my head and smiled up at me before bringing my lips to hers for one last kiss.

Once we cleaned up and dressed, we were on our way to the gynecologist office to find out the sex of our last baby. Juggling four kids was not easy. We were basically pros at quickies these days and jumped at the opportunity when it arose. It did not help that I had a wife like Adrianna. I wanted to be in her and around her all the fucking time.

The doctor walked in and went over her vitals before she was pushing a wand with a clear lubricant over my wife's belly.

Thank fuck her vitals were good and her blood work came back normal. Normal for her, anyway.

The doctor turned the screen our way and pointed between the legs that were wide open to reveal the gender. "It's right there," she said.

Chills covered my arms. I leaned in and Adrianna rose up on her elbows to peer at the screen. My jaw dropped. I had been so certain God had a vendetta against me, maybe my debt was finally paid.

The doctor printed out a few ultrasound pictures with some comments to explain what we were looking at.

She did not need to explain this one. It was obvious.

I was exuberant on the walk back to the car with a little pep in my step, whereas Adrianna was quiet. I opened the door and helped her sit inside, then I looked at her melancholy eyes. Adrianna leaned into me sadly.

"What is wrong, *Malysh?*" I asked, stroking her hair away from her neck.

She shook her head, unable to answer.

"Is it because the doctor said the baby could be over ten pounds? You are having a C-section again so—"

"It's not that," she said quietly.

I thought for a second when it hit me.

"I thought you wanted a boy."

We were actually having a boy. Finally.

A healthy boy ahead of his due date by a few weeks, actually. He was already so big, bigger than the girls.

She lifted her head and her green eyes shifted back and forth between mine, filling with tears. Her lips turned into a frown and my chest started to feel tight from seeing her like this.

"Adrianna? Sweetheart? What is wrong?"

"I just…" She stammered, her chin wobbling before she burst into tears. I wrapped my arms around her. "I just… It just hurts to name him after my dad when he's no longer here anymore. He wanted a grandson so badly, you know? And now all these feelings are back and I'm just really upset."

Her tears were falling faster now and I had nothing but my shirt to offer her. She couldn't stop crying, so I lifted the hem and gave it to her. She wiped her eyes and then sniffled.

Frank had gone into cardiac arrest three months ago and passed away suddenly. Adrianna thought she was good at hiding her grief, but I saw it every day and mourned her loss with her.

He loved all his granddaughters equally and spoiled the shit out of them, but he wanted a grandson. He wanted to be able to teach him golf and watch sports with him.

It had taken a while, but after Mia was born, Frank finally accepted us. Adrianna had joked that first he did not want us to be together, then he was telling us to have more kids. In the end, he had nothing but love for his daughter, and wanted to see her happy.

"I just can't believe we finally get a boy and he's not here. It's so unfair."

Her voice was so small and she trembled against me. All I could do was hold her closer to me.

"*Malysh*, please do not cry."

Adrianna sniffled and burrowed her head against me. She wrapped her arms around me.

I stroked the back of her head and played with her hair. "It is bittersweet, but that seems to be our theme, yes?"

She nodded quietly.

"You can change the name, you know," I told her gently.

She shook her head and looked up. "No, I don't want to change it. I'm just sad he's not here to see we finally have a boy. He won't get to hold him…" Her watery eyes studied mine. "Unless we should name him after you." She paused, then said, "We should probably do that. How about we make one long name?"

"You allowed me to name the twins after my mother. Whatever you name our son, I will be happy with. I promise."

Her chin quivered and she looked so fucking adorable. I kissed her lips, and she said, "Really? So, if I wanted to name him Konstantin Frank Rossi-Kournakova you would be okay?"

"I think it sounds like a mouthful, but if it is what you want, then yes."

Her lips puckered and I returned the gesture knowing she was purposely baiting me. Her face was pinched, twisting with indecision. She was quiet for a long moment, visibly torn between names. Truly, I did not care. I would be happy either way.

Cupping her face, I smashed a kiss to her lips.

"How about we decide when he is born? That way we can look at him to see which name fits him best," I offered. I did not want her stressing out over this right now. We had time. "Just want to add again that I am okay with whatever you want to do."

She leaned up and pressed a kiss to my lips, then let out a heavy breath, and nodded. Gratitude blanketed her face. "Thank you," she said softly. "I'm ready to go home, hubby. Let us go get our babies."

Later that night when my wife and kids were long asleep, I took out my journal and penned my thoughts for an hour or so.

Only when I filled a journal was Adrianna allowed to read my entries. She loved to see what I was writing, and was always trying to peek over my shoulder. She too now had a journal and traded with me. She only filled one over the years, though, because she was so busy with the kids.

Adrianna shifted in her sleep and whimpered under her breath. She rubbed a spot on her stomach and scissored her legs. I placed my pen down and reached over.

Carefully, I slid a pillow under her growing belly and then one between her knees. Our bed was overflowing with foo-foo pillows she had accumulated over the years.

Picking up my pen, I started writing again.

Countless times I lined the pages with words of how I saw her with our daughters and the way they adored her. It was beautiful and I never wanted to forget the feeling they gave me or the look of utmost love in their eyes. Each daughter had their own journal that Adrianna and I wrote in. It was something we would present to them when they got married one day. Some people had pictures to capture memories, we wrote letters.

Turning to the side, I placed the pen and journal on my nightstand. I shut off the light then scooted underneath the sheet until my wife's head rested on my chest. I pulled her in as close as she could get with her growing belly between us and tangled my legs with hers. I wrapped my arm around her and kissed the top of her head. She sleepily kissed my chest before throwing a heavy leg over mine and sprawling across me, kicking the sheet off her body. She nudged her head into me until she was comfortable. The woman was like an inferno. Her body was scorching hot and twisted in an uncomfortable position. Yet she looked so peaceful, so I did not dare move. One thing I had learned was to never wake a sleeping Ria, even if I was sweating.

I stroked the small of her back and she let out a soft breath. I never held her from behind when she was pregnant. Adrianna said her back got too sweaty for that nowadays. Half the time she only wore a T-shirt—usually one of mine—and a pair of panties to bed because she was too hot for anything else.

I gazed down at my wife under the soft glow of the low light she left on in the hallway for the girls if they needed us at night. She was the most remarkable woman, and for some reason, she had chosen me.

"I love you, *Malysh*," I whispered, and hiked her leg up higher on me. Her legs jerked all night looking for cool spots.

She mumbled under her breath and stretched over me again. "I love you forever."

My lips twitched. She had no idea how off key she sang that response. I was pretty certain she had no idea she had.

I hugged her tight to my chest, feeling a torrent of heavy emotions rush through me. Our anniversary was a few weeks away. I had a feeling she would be more emotional than usual simply due to her pregnancy, and the perfect time for me to convince her to name our son Frank. Frank Konstantin. I knew it was something she wanted. I did too.

Adrianna was the love of my life. Her happiness was a radiance I was drawn to. I planned to give her a life to remember, one where she was smiling and glowing all the time.

Time.

Our love tested time.

What I would not go through to have a thousand lives with her.

Looking back, I had no idea how we made it to this point. We should not have. The foundation of our story began with lies and deceit. Our relationship at the time had been filled with more sorrow than happiness. Yet, here we were, and in love more than ever.

I had joked that God was testing me, but the truth was, he had been watching over me the whole time. He gave me her.

Adrianna rocked into me, a soft whimper falling from her lips. Her hand flew to her stomach and she inhaled, holding still. I brushed her hand away and gently rubbed her stomach until she was breathing normal again.

"Relax for me, *Malysh*," I whispered, then kissed the top of her head.

The End.

About the Author

Lucia Franco resides in sunny South Florida with her husband, two boys, and two adorable dogs who follow her everywhere. She was a competitive athlete for over ten years—a gymnast and cheerleader—which heavily inspired the Off Balance series.

Her novel Hush, Hush was a finalist in the 2019 Stiletto Contest hosted by Contemporary Romance Writers, a chapter of Romance Writers of America. Her novels are being translated into several languages.

When Lucia isn't writing, you can find her relaxing with her toes in the sand at a nearby beach. She runs on caffeine, scorching hot sunshine, and four hours of sleep.

She's written nine books and has many more planned for the years to come.

Find out more at authorluciafranco.com.

Lightning Source UK Ltd.
Milton Keynes UK
UKHW022006010223
416337UK00006B/153